STORIES OF WHITE SANDS

THEM! AGAIN!

PAUL DOLAN

THEM! AGAIN!

STORIES OF WHITE SANDS

ex libris

Paul Dolan

THEM! AGAIN!

DEDICATED TO
the people who made
classic science fiction films.
Where would we be without THEM?

Table of Contents

INTRODUCTION

All of this started in the last century, in the 1950s — that's when science fiction emerged from a fringe diversion into a new genre of mass entertainment. Movies led the way, starting with the 1951 release of *The Thing from Another World*, a film that established the sci-fi form for the following generations.

The Thing was to be a 'scientific reenactment,' a movie purpose-made to inform the masses of a significant occurrence in the Arctic. The authorities initially decided that a motion picture, honestly delivering information to the public, would be the best way to avoid sensational headlines and the expected widespread panic when the news of the crashed extraterrestrial was released.

Initial test screenings of the film proved surprising. Moviegoers mistook the facts for fiction, as entertainment. Despite prefacing the film with clear statements assuring the audience it was all for real, they just wouldn't take visitors from outer space seriously.

At one screening, the survey takers gave up trying to convince anyone and falsely admitted it was staged for their entertainment. The crowd cheered, accepted that explanation without hesitation, and rated the film highly.

After brief reconsideration, a new path was determined. The facts of the Arctic event were to be concealed, and the entire incident was denied. It soon became standard procedure to ridicule and fictionalize any events deemed 'unsuitable for public consumption.'

Science fiction movies became a key part of the deception. Extraterrestrials became little green men from Mars, and everyone laughed. Radioactively triggered mutagenesis was just another silly film at the drive-in. Everything was a big joke, just fiction.

More films followed to fictionalize other real events: *THEM!, The Blob, TIOTBS,* and plenty of others successfully formed your species' response to the unordinary – if it's too new or doesn't fit, it's fiction; if it's from a threatening future or a monstrous past, it's science fiction. And it's so easy to dismiss fictions. That was what the all-powerful Agency counted on to keep their secrets. But sometimes, secrets can get out and start eating people . . .

"And there shall be destruction and darkness come upon creation.
And the Beasts shall reign over the Earth."
Dr. Harold Medford, 1954

CHAPTER ONE

THE DOLL

That little girl, the one they found in the New Mexican desert in 1950 – she was big news for a while, they even made a movie about it – and that was what? Seventy or 80 years ago? Something like that. Well, she's now an old woman alone driving a desert highway far from home, back to the beginning to put an end to things.

She turned off the pavement and stopped at an old pipe gate blocking a pair of dusty ruts that pointed from the highway into the white sands and to the end of the woman's journey.

She went on a trip only once before, when she was very young, and a family vacation took her from the Chicago suburbs to this same New Mexican desert long ago.

The woman put the car in park and clasped her hands at the top of the steering wheel. She looked past the broken gate, down the dirt road, into the scrub brush desert.

"I can't believe it. It's like my dreams," the 80-year-old girl said, dabbing her eyes with a tissue and then covering them to cry. "Like all of my dreams," she sobbed.

She had to return to the desert. This was the birthplace of her nightmares.

She was that little girl found wandering alone in the White Sands of New Mexico, near death from shock and exposure, wearing pajamas and carrying a broken doll. The event made national and international headlines in the early 1950s.

A few days after her rescue, authorities discovered the wreck of her parent's car and trailer more than six miles away. It was another day before they identified her as the sole survivor of a single-car accident that took the lives of her family and orphaned her in the wasteland.

Her mother's sister, Aunt Betty, took her to live outside Chicago, a green world away from this dry sandscape.

They rarely spoke of the accident. Once, later in life, her aunt had an extra glass of wine and told her a few things about the attention the case attracted. All of the news services had carried the story. The phone calls, telegrams, and people at the door went on for months, some even longer.

Everyone wanted to know how the little girl was doing. Had she spoken yet? Did they find her family? Every paper carried her tale; her rescue was dramatized on radio. There were newsreels and, finally, even a movie, spinning her ordeal into one of the new science-fictions. There seemed no end to the unsolicited interest.

But it did end and all at once, too. The big news organizations stopped asking, and in no time, the independents disappeared, too.

There were newspaper clippings in a shoebox. One had a photo and a caption naming the desert area where the girl had been found. She stole it from her aunt's things and kept it safe until the paper crumbled away.

Physically, the girl had mended quickly. She had sustained surprisingly minor injuries in an accident that killed everyone else and, according to the local sheriff's report, 'destroyed the car and trailer to an extraordinary extent.'

But the psychological scars of such a horrific accident were more profound. She was the lone witness to her family's demise, and the trauma had proven too much for her developing mind.

Emotionally and mentally, the child collapsed. She drifted in and out of an unresponsive state, diagnosed as an 'aphasic stupor,' and each episode was lasting longer, necessitating treatments considered extreme, even by the evolving standards of mental health care of the time.

She often tried not to remember her summer of shock therapy.

Grueling though they were, the treatments must have worked; that's how she looked at it. Maybe it took a lifetime, but she came back. She spoke regularly by her teens and, on her thirtieth birthday, was ready to volunteer at the local library twice a week, and in just a few years, they hired her as a full part-timer. It was very good for her. Sometimes, she would go for a week without a nightmare.

Her rehabilitation became a lifelong journey. Setbacks occurred, but here, at the end of her long life, she felt she had done a good job extracting herself from the darkness of the accident.

It would be hard to imagine a worse scenario for a child. As an adult, she understood that the catastrophe had struck at a formative time and had long-term consequences. She did not doubt that those early treatments did more harm and undoubtedly compounded her frailties. And she knew it was all just bad luck, nothing personal, and it was up to her to get over it. She had a lot of pluck.

But why did feeling better have to take so long? The woman had spent her entire life recovering from a single event she could not fully recall.

And that's why she was here. She needed to find her dreamscape, to see that it was real, this constant setting for her nightmares. She hoped traveling to the origin of the tragedy would provide closure at last.

She stared along the rutted road into the lonely desert. There was a measure of relief in simply being there, in knowing this place was as real as her dreams. The only thing missing were the monsters.

Of course, her aunt assured her there were no monsters. She would sit with her during those long nights when they crawled out of her nightmares. Kind Aunt Betty devoted herself to caring for the girl, and they lived a pleasant, quiet life in suburbia until the older woman passed away.

She barely remembered her parents or anything else from the time before her aunt. There were some black and white photographs of her mother but only one of her father in her parent's wedding photo. Her aunt blamed him, saying it wasn't a safe place for a family back then.

3

She would sometimes see her little brother's face when she slept.

She would see him playing in the desert, laughing until he screams and is pulled under blood-soaked sand. The dreams of him would vary in the details but always started the same. The little boy happily played like a lamb in the bright sunshine as the shadows gathered around him. He had such a round and healthy face.

She never knew him, not really. He was so young. Sometimes, his name would escape her. If she could only forget him, never think of him, never see his beautiful face in her dreams again, she would be closer to the peace she sought.

She wiped the tears from her eyes and turned, squinting up and down the highway. There were no cars on the road. She pursed her lips and looked down at an old, broken doll in the passenger seat.

"What do you think?" she asked it, "Is this the place?"

The woman opened the driver's door and got out of the car, putting her hands behind her neck to stretch away the stiffness of driving. She twisted her head from side to side a few times, reached into the car, brought a water bottle out, and took a few sips. She looked in both directions of the highway. There was not a car to be seen. She was alone. A chill passed through her. She was alone in the desert again.

There was no lock on the trail gate, and the sun-bleached wooden sign, presumably prohibiting trespass, had been shot full of holes.

She trotted to the gate in her new sneakers, leaving overlarge footprints in the smooth sand. She pushed the barrier open, then hurried back to the car, sliding behind the wheel and putting it in gear. The vehicle went in, then stopped so she could go back to pull the gate closed behind her trespass.

Back behind the wheel, she looked down at the doll. "After all, how much trouble could a little old lady get into?" She shrugged. The mended piece on the little head had discolored over the years, making the patch obvious.

The old woman had no reason to choose this turn-off from the highway. She often acted on instinct, mostly about little things, and it usually worked out.

She lifted the doll she had carried through the desert many years before and tenderly pushed back the hair to touch the broken head.

Wiping away another tear, she looked out the window. This was the place. Maybe not the place her parents had been, not exactly the same place, but close. She had been here. She had a feeling.

She put her seatbelt on and drove slower than she would have walked. She didn't want to go too far down the dirt road but did want to find the right spot.

A hundred yards from the highway, the trail opened into a flat area behind a rocky ledge. The natural stone wall might provide the privacy she hoped to find from any passerby.

Driving carefully along the tire-track trail, she found her spot. She put the car into park and let it run for the air conditioning. The woman leaned forward and rested her chin on her wrinkled hands over the steering wheel.

Looking across the desert basin to the mountains, she exhaled slowly and closed her eyes. It was so familiar. She had been cast onto this hardscrabble stage so many nights, running from impossibly cruel embodiments that grew from the terrible accident to overrun her dreams.

Her eyes opened to the red sun floating on the sawtooth horizon. The shadows had lengthened during her brief pause. She didn't want to be there in the dark. Lifting her head, she looked at her companion and reached over to pat the worn-out doll. "Time to go. Finally, time to go." She smiled sadly and grasped the door handle.

A large grasshopper startled her when it jumped onto the windshield. The woman recoiled and then tapped the glass beneath it to encourage it to leave. The wipers would make a mess. She tooted the horn a few times, but for all she knew, that might attract more insects. The noise seemed to do the trick, and it flew off. She hated bugs.

The doll went with her as she got out of the car. "Now it's your nightmare," she said as she closed the door. "I don't want you around anymore – you or your broken head."

A few steps from the car, the immensity of the desert stage stopped her. Some rocks were taller than the brush, and everything seemed too big and twice her height.

She cradled the doll to her heart as she walked carefully between the smaller rocks. She felt an urge to reprieve the memento from her plan to bury her past. After all, it had been with her all of these years. But, no, it had to go back to the beginning, like a sacrifice.

She picked her way to a table-sized rock at the base of a tall ledge and held the doll out to look at it one last time. Shaking her head, she said, "I'm sorry, but you have to stay here. I'm the one that made it. I'm the one that survived."

The sun slumped to the horizon and soaked everything red, like her dreams right before they change. She closed her eyes and took a long breath.

There was a smell, a faint odor blooming in her senses, and it took the woman off-balance. She felt like she was falling and steadied herself at the table-rock. She lifted her hand to her spinning head. Her blood chilled. Her hand had the smell. That smell! Her chest heaved, and she was losing her breath. That smell, always in her nightmares, was on her hand. It had come from the rock. The smell was on the rock. It was real. It was here; it crackled through her head like a bolt of electricity, short-circuiting every synapse with panic.

She lurched from the rock and fell to the ground. The doll hit head first, and the mended piece popped out, opening the old wound. She looked at the broken head and screamed, kicking away from it in the sand. She got to her feet and ran toward her car. She fell again, hard against a sharp rock, cutting her hand and abrading her forearm.

She struggled up with a wail. Her breathing was rapid and insufficient. Holding her hands out as if she could grasp the faraway car, she stumbled toward it. Blood dripped generously from her hand, and that terrified her.

She reeled drunkenly over the sand, digging in her windbreaker pocket for the keys. By the time she got them out, she was exhausted and sobbing. She got in and pulled the door shut, looking through her tears to start the car.

Her bloody fingers fumbled, and she dropped the keys to the floor. She hyperventilated and couldn't see them in the shadows. She bent over in the seat, feeling for them.

The car moved, gently bouncing on its springs as if someone pushed down and let it go.

She looked out of the passenger side windows. It was dark outside, but just on that side of the car. She didn't move, and, just for a second, the world held its breath.

The car jolted violently, bouncing hard enough to lift the woman from the seat and slam her down.

The darkness moved, filling the windows as it went. Her eyes widened, her hands covered her face, and she screamed. The car lurched, grinding out screeches so loud she moved her hands to her ears and curled into a tight ball. The car lifted then and was so savagely shaken the old woman was bashed against the steering wheel like a speed bag.

The car was dropped back to the ground, crashing down on its roof.

The woman lay battered and bleeding, staring at the dashboard and seats.

The car rocked again. Then it was flipped over, back on what was left of the tires.

The woman was cruelly tumbled, smashing into the dashboard and thrown into the back seat. She was dazed. Broken glass was everywhere.

She was hurt. Her foot was excruciatingly snared in the steel framework under the seat.

A shadow moved outside, and that smell flooded the car. The car was shaken violently, and she was tossed side to side, painfully tethered by her trapped foot. Blood streamed from her mouth. She prayed to lose consciousness.

Steel screeched as the roof of the car was torn open and bent back. She saw the body of her nightmare rise against the red sky. The impossible monster's head lifted, gnashing huge sickle-shaped black mandibles, snapping as they peeled away the thin steel skin.

The head turned, moving its sensory antennae over the twisted metal and into the car, probing and tasting, touching the seat, then touching her. They paused, but only for a second. The creature pushed its hissing head forward, and emitted slow, loud clicks – the score to all her nightmares. The pincers grabbed the old woman, piercing her torso and connecting through her abdomen. It tugged once and again, violently pulling her from the car, leaving her right foot wedged under the seat.

The monster dropped her flat on the sand, pinning her with a clawed foot and crushing her ribcage. The mutant curled to sting the woman with the thick barb on the end of its abdomen. More than overkill, the venom had the additional effect of a marinade, preserving the contents and preparing the food for later consumption.

The large ant pinched the bundle with its mandibles, folding it into a more manageable shape to carry back to the nest.

Arriving at one of the main trails, the scout met three minor worker ants. They were only five or six feet long, a third of the scout's major worker size. The ants tactically communicated by touching each other with their legs and antennae. The three quickly examined the scout, sensing this nest member was distressed.

Inspecting the big ant for injuries, two of the worker ants reacted to a deep gouge on her right foreleg that scored the tough exoskeleton, a result of ripping sheet metal from the car.

Using their mouthparts, they alternately expressed milky exudations from glands on the other's back and plastered the protective and antibiotic substance onto the wounded area of the larger scout's leg. They finished the dressing by sealing the wound with an elastic cast formed from a waxy discharge.

The third ant groomed the scout using bristled forelegs to brush away dust from breathing areas and cleaned her sensory-stubbled carapace.

The two workers finished with the wound and took charge of the meaty bundle, turning and inspecting it. They uncurled the carcass and snipped it in half using their mandibles. The workers started back to the nest with the repackaged morsels in advance of the impending storm.

Alone again, the huge scout left the path and climbed onto a rocky outcrop. Rearing back on four legs, she used her two front limbs to generate a low rattling call that quickly grew in volume and frequency to a shrill strigulation broadcast over the darkening desert.

It was an overture to war.

CHAPTER TWO

THE AUNT

The young woman waited until the attorney looked up from his handful of paper notes before she asked, "Then that's it, we're all done?"

"That is it," he answered. "Everything is settled, apart from the sale of May's – well, your houses, and that shouldn't take too long. They are very desirable properties. Very. And, if I might add, considering the complexities of the estate – the number of properties and the size of her portfolio, I must say, you made very wise decisions."

She pushed her hair along the side of her face and smiled, handing him the papers she had signed. "I know I made one wise decision, and that was to take your advice, Mr. Matos," she said.

He took the sheaf of paper, leaning forward to peer at her through his thick glasses. "Your great-aunt was very fond of you, Nikki," he said. "She has left you very well provided for and was happy to be able to do that." He smiled at the young woman. "It turned out to be a very large estate. Very."

"I had no idea she was so well-off," Nikki replied. "I have to say, even though it's been a few months since I found out about all of this, I am still in shock."

"Well, my dear," the lawyer said, "May Carrington lived a very long life and was a very intelligent woman, like yourself. Intelligence runs in your family. Remember her brother?" The man looked up, tapping his index finger rhythmically on the desk. "Remember her brother," he repeated. "There was something I was supposed to remember. He was a scientist way back when I was just a boy. He won the Nobel Prize, didn't he?" the sun-dried man mused, thinking back.

"The great Professor Carrington," Nikki said. "The family legend. He did win a Nobel Prize in physics. I never met him, of course. He died years before I was born, but I heard all about him," she said. "He was involved with the atom bomb and other things."

"Many people around here had to do with the bomb and even the other things, but he was at the top," the lawyer said. "I never met him either, but May talked about him." The old man looked into the ceiling fan and stroked his neat white beard. "Oh, that's right," he remembered. "That brings us to the package." He pushed away from his desk and went into an adjoining room, finishing his reminiscence as he shuffled through the doorway. "I take it he became sick for a time before he passed, and May took care of him along with that other woman, his assistant — what was her name?" he wondered aloud.

"Nikki. The same as mine. She was my namesake," the young woman called to the next room, but he didn't hear her.

"Vicki maybe?" he guessed loudly. "Anyway, it was something to do with his work that got him. Probably the radiation or some such thing. Very dangerous, that atomic business. Very."

Nikki heard a metal file cabinet drawer slide open. A groan came from Mr. Matos and then a few from the file cabinet. "That does it," she heard him say, and then, "There it is," followed by a grunt and the sound of the file cabinet drawer again.

The attorney returned carrying a package wrapped in brown paper and tied with string. Nikki thought it looked old enough to be from the pyramids.

"Here it is," Mr. Matos said. He placed the bundle on the desk in front of her.

"She said he went on an expedition to the Arctic, and when he returned, he was never the same," Nikki said, eyeing the bundle. "Auntie May blamed the cold. He died within a few years of his return."

"The cold," Matos repeated, and he smiled. "That's right, that's what she would say," the aged attorney agreed. He went around the desk and sat in his executive chair, looking up at the slow-moving ceiling fan. "That is what she said. He was never the same after coming home." He turned his chair to look out of the large window and into the distant desert. "Very sad. She cared for her brother very much. Very much."

He turned to look at her and rocked his chair slowly. "A fine lady, your aunt, your great-aunt, that is. She really was great," he chuckled softly. "Your Aunt May was a force for good, and she had a big heart. Helped many people over the years – myself included. She was one of my very first clients and stuck with me for over forty years. And I know for a fact she sent a good many referrals." The attorney stared into the past for a few moments before he came back to the present. "That's one more thing from her," he said and nodded at the package. "That's her brother's effects. His journals and whatnot. Three little books, like diaries. Handwritten. Lots of notes with arithmetic and scribbles. A few hundred pages, I suppose, but, as I said, didn't mean much to us, your aunt and myself. We looked through the books a long time ago. She wanted them put away, hidden. May was convinced the government wanted to get them, so she gave them to me for safekeeping many, many years ago, before you were born. Later on, she told me to give you the package after we were done with everything else. So, there it is. Professor Carrington's secret notes."

Nikki studied the bundle. "Secret notes? About what?"

The old attorney turned his chair to face her. He lifted his shoulders and hands, palms up. "I don't really know," he said. "I must admit, I am not the scientific type, and it was so long ago. Whatever was in there meant nothing to us. Maybe that's why she wanted you to have them – after all, you're a scientist."

She laughed. "Not really," she said. "I grow weeds."

"That's scientific. I'm sure you're just like your famous great-uncle," he said to the young woman.

12

"Mmm, just like him, except without the Nobel Prize, career, or achievements," she laughed again, "I grow weeds for the county back home and then come up with ways that stop them from growing. Grow, measure, repeat. Not very exciting, I'm afraid."

"My dear, excitement is very overrated. Very. And it is usually unpleasant. I prefer quietude, myself," the attorney tapped his index finger on the side of his nose.

"You may be right, Mr. Matos, I wouldn't know. I've never had any excitement. This is the furthest I've ever been away from home and the longest I've ever been out on my own," she said with a slight sigh. "But I'm ready, maybe even for a little adventure. Perhaps on my trip home."

The man smiled. "I hope not for your sake, my dear. I wouldn't wish excitement on anyone."

She looked down at the package and pulled it a bit closer by the string.

"How about surprise then?" she asked. "A mysterious package hidden away for years. That's not something you get every day." Nikki picked up the compact parcel, "It's not radioactive, is it?" She turned the bundle over, feeling the items through the paper.

"I hope not. It's been here a long time," he said, wagging his finger at the package. Then he remembered. "Oh, along with the books, there's a box with a few odds and ends in there, too. Some pebbles, a few pieces of metal, a bottle of seeds – specimens, I suppose you'd call them."

She turned the package, examined the brown paper wrapper, and looked quizzically at the attorney. "Why do you think it was so important to Aunt May to leave her brother's notes to me?" she asked him. "Did she leave any instructions about them? I mean, what am I supposed to do with them? Should they be in a museum or something?"

"No, she didn't say anything specific. She only told me to make sure you got the package once we had concluded all other business," the attorney said.

13

His chair squeaked as he leaned forward. "She did mention what she didn't want to happen. May didn't want the authorities to get their hands on them," he said in a low voice.

"Really? I thought her brother worked for the government. He was one of their prize scientists, from what I understand. A big wheel."

"True, true, very true, my dear," the attorney replied. "Their biggest of wheels. A very important man. Very important." He half-turned his chair and looked out the window. "He started it all, he ran it all. After he came back from the North Pole with his discoveries. They got too big, then things changed. That's what May said," his voice trailed off, following his thoughts.

Nikki politely waited for her attorney's return trip.

The old man shook his head slowly, tightening his lips, "No. No good came of that. Wasn't himself anymore. Had some odd notions that consumed him. She was never quite clear on what, but whatever they were, he fell out of favor. All very bad. Bad, bad, bad," he clucked, shaking his head.

She took the package off the desk and held it in one hand as if she were guessing its weight, "Do you think there are any legal restrictions or liabilities connected to these books?" she asked.

"Now you sound just like May. That's the common-sensed Carrington mind." He smiled and turned his chair to look out of the window. "To answer your question, no. Anyone with any interest or memory of these things has been gone for a long time. A very long time."

With the chair sideways to the desk, Mr. Matos could turn his head to look into the desert or at his client. He faced Nikki. "I wouldn't make an issue of the property. Best if you don't publicize that you possess something on which the government may have had a claim." He leaned toward her. "I wouldn't go putting it up on the eBay or anything. Just keep it quiet and keep it in the family. That's what May wanted. Keep it all very quiet," he said.

"I can do that," she answered. "Maybe they will make for an interesting read," she said, picking up her large slouch bag from the floor. She opened it and dropped in the package, rising from her chair.

"Well, it's been quite a tale as far as I'm concerned," Mr. Matos said, coming from behind his desk and extending his hand. "And, I think we have taken care of quite a few things. As I mentioned, my office will keep you apprised of your real estate, and we will handle everything on this end. I imagine you want to get back to your home and your normal life. I'm sure you've had enough of all of this estate business by now. Although it was as straightforward as these things can be, as you were the singular heir."

"You made it seem simple. Thank you, Mr. Matos." The young woman smiled and shook his hand as she shouldered her bag. "As all of this begins to sink in, I guess my life will be changed. It might not be so normal from now on."

"Well, all for the better, though," he said as they walked through his office door. "I would be very interested to hear about your plans for the future. I hope you will drop me a line now and then."

She laughed a little and said, "When I have some plans, I'll let you know. Right now, my only direction is driving up the coast back to Oregon. I thought I would take my time and the scenic route – maybe think about what I want to do."

"That's a very good idea. Very good. Take your time and think it over." He nodded to the receptionist as he spoke. "That's what May left you, you know. She left you the time to do what you want. Take a nice long ride. Are you going Interstate 10?"

"Maybe?" Nikki answered, "I'm going from here to Las Cruces, then to Los Angeles, and then up the coast."

"Well, that means when you leave here, you'll be taking 70 and driving past White Sands. That's a sight to see," he said, walking to the exit. Nikki exchanged goodbyes with the secretary and caught up with the attorney, who was still talking to her.

15

"I hope to hear from you soon, my dear." He took her hand in both of his and shook it gently. "You remind me so much of May, when we first met, that is. It brings me back. But you also make me feel as though a chapter is coming to an end." He looked at her warmly. "However, I suspect another is just beginning for you. I think you have a very interesting story ahead of you. Very." He patted her hand, let go as she turned, and started down the steps. "You're a lucky young lady, my dear," he said after her.

She half-turned, smiled, and waved to the man as she walked to her car.

"Very," she said quietly as she opened the driver's door and got in, swinging her bag onto the passenger seat.

Nikki watched the attorney wave a final time and waved back to him as he went inside. She put the key into the ignition and started the car.

She fished her phone from under the parcel in her bag, turned it on, and tapped the map. "Directions to Los Angeles," she said.

"Los Angeles is 834 miles from your present location by the fastest route. Would you like to leave now?"

"Yes," Nikki answered as she pulled onto the street. The phone directed her turns to the highway, leaving the city.

From Alamogordo, US-70 dove into the Tularosa Basin, which is nearly 7,000 square miles of white sand desert bounded all around by mountains.

After only a minute on the highway, she was behind a line of stopped traffic. A yellow sign to the side warned of road closure if the lights were flashing, and they were. The notice depicted a rocket and the White Sands Missile Range logo. It said to expect a one-hour delay.

"Really? This is my excitement?" she asked aloud. "I just get on the road, and it's closed."

16

Past the line of pickup trucks, she could see police vehicles through the shimmering highway heat. The traffic, what there was of it, was turning around and leaving.

As she crept forward in line, an orange food truck selling tacos caught her eye. Tacos seemed like a better idea than going nowhere for an hour. A tractor-trailer was parked next to the sign, and a big guy was sitting on the hood of a car, eating. Nikki thought he looked like a good judge of tacos, so she pulled onto the dirt and parked near the trucks.

"Road food – that could be adventurous," she thought as she got out of her car. She slung her bag over her shoulder and walked to the brightly painted truck.

The lunch truck man sported a short-brimmed black fedora complementing his 'Taco Doctor' T-shirt. He leaned through the window and smiled at her, "Hola, hola. What can I get you, Miss?" he asked. "Our chicken tacos are the best."

She looked at the menu on the side of the truck, "That sounds good. Two, please," she said, "and a Coke," she added.

"You got it," he said, fading into the sizzle and clatter.

Nikki eyed the large man that she had seen from the road. He was making the last of a short-lived taco disappear. A well-worn cowboy hat topped him off, pushed back to show the front of his bald head.

Nikki looked at him, looking at her. She smiled and asked, "Do you have any idea how much longer the road will be closed?"

"Mmm-mmm," he replied as he finished the last bite. He touched his hand to his brim while delicately wiping his mouth with a paper napkin, "Pardon, ma'am. Yes, ma'am," He finished dabbing, "The way I reckon it, the road should open up after I eat three, maybe four more tacos."

She returned his deadpan stare, let her eyes drop to the sizable stomach hiding his belt, then looked him in the eye and said, "So, about five minutes?"

17

She smiled just a little.

The big man sat stone-faced for another moment, then laughed. "About five minutes? That's pretty funny. You're alright," he said. He started laughing again, harder, then caught his breath and reiterated, "That's funny. You got sauce, you do, little gal."

He wiped his mouth again and nodded toward the food truck. "Like I was saying to my amigo there, I've been driving this road for more than twenty years, and this is the first time I've been held up by one of these missile tests. Never got stuck before – even though they do them a couple of times a month. But they've been doing even more lately."

"A missile test? Really? That's why the road's closed?" Nikki asked.

"That's a fact," the big man said, sliding off the front of the car. He walked to the window of the taco truck, "Hey, compadre, three more beef tacos, por favor." He turned, looked down at her, and laughed again, "Five minutes, that was good. You're alright, little lady."

The man in the truck stuck his head through the window and called out, "Two chicken tacos and a Coke, coming up!"

"That sounds ominous," Nikki said as she collected her food.

The cook leaned through the window as he put the order on the shelf. "Sauce in the bottles," he said as he disappeared into the truck. His arm came out with a cold red can.

Nikki paid the man and put the change in the tip jar. She dashed green sauce onto her tacos, went to her car, sat on the hood, and put the paper-wrapped food and the can next to her.

As she was eating, the big man came over with his food, "Mind if I join you?" he asked.

"No, not at all, pull up a car," Nikki answered, motioning to the empty area on the front of her vehicle.

The man placed his wraps between them and sat on the edge of her car, causing it to sink noticeably. He pushed with his legs to bounce the car up and down, "You know, this little buggy might need some new springs." He smiled and bit into the first wrap.

"I see you have Oregon tags. You heading to or from?" he asked her.

"To, at least, that's the plan," she said between bites. Nikki sized up the large fellow and thought he was a regular guy. She popped the cool can of Coke and took a few sips, "I'm going to go up the coast and see the sights along the way."

"Hmm-hmm," he said, into his second beef wrap, "There's plenty to see between here and there, that's certain." The man nodded and crossed his legs, getting comfortable on the car.

Nikki noticed his over-tooled cowboy boots, complete with cow skulls and desert flowers.

"Mighty long ride, though," he went on. "But it's a good one. I haven't done anything on the coast in quite a spell. Sand, that's all I see. All beach and no ocean." He chewed.

"Mmm, these are delicious," she said, pushing the escaping taco into her mouth.

"That's for sure," the trucker agreed. "Taco Doctor knows what he's doing." The big man made another bite disappear.

"Where are you heading?" she asked.

"I make the same run all the time," he continued. "Oklahoma City to Las Vegas, with points in between." He swallowed. "That's my rig," he said, jabbing his thumb a few times at the green and white tractor-trailer idling next to the food truck.

"Honey's Hauling – like it says on the door," he saluted with his beef wrap to introduce himself with a nod and another mouth-dabbing with a napkin, "I'm Tom Honey, at your service, ma'am. Honey's Hauling – sweetest ride on eighteen wheels." He smiled broadly at her.

19

"Nice to meet you, Tom," Nikki said, extending her hand, "My name's Nikki Carrington."

"Oh, much obliged, Nikki," Tom said. He wiped his hand on his pant leg before quickly shaking hers. "Nice to meet you, too," he said.

"So, they really test rockets out in the desert?" she asked the trucker, taking another sip from the can.

"They sure do, ma'am. Rockets are big goings-on around here," he answered, "Like I said, they close the road at least once a month to shoot them things off." He finished the second wrap. "But I never got stuck before — just luck." He dabbed the napkin to his mouth and tried to stifle a belch, "Pardon, ma'am," he said sheepishly, "What brings you to Atomic City anyway?

"I had family here once, but they're gone now. I'm just driving through, seeing the sights. But I never heard it called Atomic City," she replied.

"That's what the old-timers called Alamogordo, 'cause of all the atom bomb work back in the day." The big man lifted his last taco from the paper on the hood, "These are pretty good, these little sandwiches. And I know a thing or two — Honey's Hauling carries nothing but the best cuts of prime beef to the finest eateries in the Southwest. That's my specialty — nothing but the best rides in that reefer."

Nikki's face squeezed into a quizzical expression, "Reefer?"

"That is what you call a refrigerated trailer, ma'am," the driver said, pointing to his truck. "While we're settin' out here in the desert heat watchin' our woolies wilt, there's prime-cut beef sittin' in there just as cool as can be at thirty-eight degrees Fahrenheit."

Nikki laughed, "Maybe we should be sitting in there," she said.

"Well, now, that sounds like a good idea, doesn't it? But I can tell you something that might make you think otherwise." He nodded portentously. He took another bite and nodded some more while he chewed, then said, "Once, making my run, the cab's air-conditioning conked out, just stopped working. I'm driving and driving, windows wide open; it only got hotter. Must have been a hundred and thirty in the basin." He bit into the taco and continued talking, "Driving and roasting, roasting and driving. I thought I was going to melt away, so I got a bright idea."

The big truck driver was a few bites from the end of his meal. "I got to get some relief, so I pulled over and figure to climb in the back and cool off for a time – and that's just what I did."

"Sounds sensible," Nikki said.

"So, you would think," he nodded and refrained, "so you would think."

"And?" she asked.

"Well, I pull to the side, go round back, and climb in. It feels like heaven. I sit in the box, cooling off, letting that icy air blow. Like I said, I am a man in heaven. I'm in there for a good half-hour, maybe even forty-five minutes, soakin' up cool like a towel at a polar bear plunge. It was just the thing I needed after roasting in that cab – just the ticket." The driver sat back, putting both feet on the ground and then both hands on his knees, "Or so you would think." He paused, waiting for encouragement.

"So, I would think," she agreed. "And then?" she asked, thoroughly enjoying the dinner-theater.

"Well, I figure that's enough. I open the door and climb out – and I swear the last thing I heard was little drops of ice water falling off of me, sizzling on the hot pavement."

"The last thing?" she repeated as she bit into her second chicken wrap.

"Yes, ma'am, the last thing." He took a long drink of his canned lemonade before continuing. "Stepping out of that icy truck into this God-forsaken furnace was just too much for old Tom Honey. Passed out clean as a whistle. Fell flat on my back onto that hot tar and laid there for who knows how long before a trooper stopped and got me up.

Wouldn't you know it? Because of one of those missile tests, traffic had been stopped from both ends. Not only was I laying smack-dab in the middle of the highway and could have been run over, but I might have been blown to smithereens, too!"

"Wow," she said, "I guess that was some shock to your system to make you pass out."

"Well, you guessed right – but the biggest shock was yet to come. That trooper, helping me up, he kept eyeballing me in an odd sort of way till he finally said, 'Tom, you better take a look at yourself in the mirror.'"

"What was it?" Nikki asked.

"Well, I climb onto the step of my cab – still needing a little help from the trooper – and I look into the mirror. You could have knocked me down with a feather, for what I saw," he paused again.

"Tell me, what the heck was it, Tom?" she encouraged.

"Well, ma'am, as far as we could figure – the trooper and me – when I keeled over, my hat come off naturally, and I lay out in that broiling sun getting the granddaddy of all sunburns. So, when I look in the mirror, what do you think I see?"

She could only shrug dramatically and hope for the answer.

"Right up here," he pointed to his forehead, "square in the middle of my head, was a white scorpion. That is, the white shadow of a scorpion. I'm burned to hell – begging your pardon, ma'am – except for my naturally ivory skin shaded by that bug. Clear as day, right dead center on my head."

The trucker nodded gravely, "The way I reckoned it, when I got out of that reefer, all chilled up and passed out. Well, the little guy just climbed up on me to cool his self off and stayed there while I was getting the burn."

Tom looked her straight in the eye, "You can't blame the little guy for that," he said.

22

"Well, Tom," she said, staring right back at him, "all I can say is that is one honey of a story."

His round face broke open in a wide grin, and he raised his hand to rub his chin, "You know what? That is exactly what it is. It is one Honey of a story!" He broke a big laugh, and she could see he loved laughing. "That is just what it is," he said again.

The trucker wiped his eye as his laughter wound down. "Life is strange, little lady, life is strange. Always seemed to me that, just when you figure nothing's going to happen, that's just when it does," Tom Honey said to her and went in to finish the last of his beef flautas.

Pausing mid-chomp, he looked past Nikki down the highway and squinted his eyes, "Looks like the rocket police are about done over there."

Nikki turned to look down the road and could see the police cars leaving, and the traffic had moved on. She ate her wrap, finishing it off with her Coke. "I guess it's time to get back on the road," she said, standing from the hood of the car.

"I reckon so, Nik," the big man said as he stood with her. "I can only say that the weight on my heart from parting is lightened by having met," Tom said, tipping his cowboy hat with a flourish.

"The pleasure has been mine, Mr. Honey," she replied, smiling wide. "I hope our paths might cross again sometime."

They shook hands again, and the trucker walked to his cab, saying, "Who's to say, little lady? Life is strange."

Nikki picked up the wrappers, walked a few steps to the trash can, and put the empty can on the food truck's window ledge. A hand pulled it in. She returned to her car, watching the trucker climb into his shining cab.

As she opened her door to get in, the trucker put down his window and called out, "We'll be on the road together for just a short stretch – my first stop isn't far – the Air Force base."

He tapped his cowboy hat and pointed to her, "You have yourself a good trip, little lady. Vaya con dios!" he called to her and gave a quick double-pull on his airhorn as his truck lurched forward and onto the road.

Nikki gave him a big wave as she got into her car. She pulled out of the dusty lot and onto the highway, following the big rig toward the afternoon sun.

After driving for several minutes behind Honey's reefer, her new friend's truck moved into the right lane under the Holloman Air Force Base sign. The trucker's air horn blew a goodbye as he turned into the entrance. Nikki tooted back and continued along the desert highway.

As she drove deeper into the Tularosa Basin, the buildings along the roadway became fewer. To the right, steel-framed high-tension wires marked her progress along the highway.

She soon saw a sign for the White Sands National Monument. As she passed the entrance, the snowy peaks of the white sand's dunes rose from the desert, paralleling the highway. They were striking, even at a distance, and she wished she had visited.

High above the dunes, another natural wonder caught her attention. A storm was forming over the sands. Twisting clouds boiled into the sky out of nowhere, blotting away the light and chilling the desert.

The gathering clouds were so unusual that Nikki pulled onto the shoulder, stopped the car, and got out to stare across the dunes. She was transfixed by the brewing weather, materializing as she watched, forming as a high-altitude cauldron bubbled over and poured a massive tower of frigid air straight down to smash into the earth.

Nikki was spellbound by the roiling pillar of clouds falling out of the upper atmosphere, crackling with sheets of lightning, and dive-bombing into the desert sands. A violent flash of light and crack of thunder made her realize the enormity of the far-off spectacle, and when that mass hit, it would make a big splash. It was time to leave. She shook off the hypnotics, got her car on the road, and stepped on the gas.

Lightning cracked with intensifying ferocity as the column fell, generating immense static charges. She drove, watching the road ahead and the clouds to the side as the pillar grew. She thought of tornadoes and stray remarks about the violence and changeability of desert weather and didn't want to be in anything so unpredictable. She thought it could be bad.

The threatening storm quickly delivered.

After a particularly scorching stretch, hot even for the New Mexican desert, a huge mass of dry-roasted air rose into the upper atmosphere, where it froze. Cubic miles of the super-cooled air crashed back to the desert floor, smacking into the white sands and splashing the gypsum dust into a violent wave of sand sweeping out from the impact – a sandstorm.

Within a minute, Nikki could see the sand tsunami rising. The storm front was prehistoric in magnitude – a thousand feet tall and sweeping over White Sands at a hundred miles per hour.

Hoping to outrun the wall of dust and sand, she pressed more speed from the accelerator. Ahead, the highway curved away from the storm – at least she would be driving away from it rather than paralleling the incoming wave.

She rounded the bend of the desert highway and stomped the gas to make a run for it. Her small car shot down the road, but the storm was hot on her tail. Her eyes jumped between the straightaway in front and the wall of sand in her rearview.

The wave rose, cresting to fall. She caught something out of the corner of her eye, large like a pickup truck, and instinctively swerved from the dark shape and lost control, skidding over the blowing sand; the world went into a spin of light blobs and dark blurs flying past the windows in high-speed slow-motion.

She gripped the wheel, jammed both feet on the brake pedal, and stiffened for the crash that didn't come. The car did a three-sixty and stopped, rocking from the hurricane winds and pointing the wrong way.

Through the dust, she could see the phantoms of the high-tension poles silhouetted against the relentless sheet lightning through her driver's side window. They were on the passenger side a few seconds ago.

Nikki took a deep breath, let her feet off the brake, and turned the car back on course. She didn't think it would be a good idea to be stopped on a highway in the middle of a blinding sandstorm just in case anyone else was foolish enough to be on the road.

As she turned the car, a shadow ran through the blowing dust, and she hit the brakes. She couldn't tell what it was but instinctively knew it was something.

Whatever it was, it disappeared. She put her foot on the accelerator and drove through the whirlwinds, picking up speed as the storm grew in intensity. And it did. It sizzled outside as the winds sandblasted the car.

The wind howled and pushed the car while it whipped the dust around in clouds thick enough to hide the road. Nikki kept driving. She didn't want to stop because of the storm or maybe because of that dark shape.

A strong gust hit the car, and Nikki gasped at the sheer force of the wind. If this was excitement, Mr. Matos was right; quiet was better. She gripped the wheel, leaning forward as she drove, peering into the churning dust, hoping to see – a light.

Maybe that was a light she saw. She saw something winking in the roiling dust, like a light pole. It was getting harder to see anything. She could barely make out the road but wanted to drive faster.

There was the light again. It flickered a few times through the clouds. Lightning crashed behind the car. The flash cut through the swirling murk, illuminating a building across the divided highway. She stopped the car in the blowing dust, peering through her side window into the tumult.

Another bolt crashed in just the right place to flashbulb the whole scene for her.

Across the median over the highway, there was a building with a few cars and trucks in the lot and a light pole in the middle. Another flash showed her the median. It looked flat enough, so she pushed on the gas and drove off-road, over the grass, the other lanes, and into the parking lot with bolts of lightning lighting her way. It was perfect timing.

The storm's full force hit the second she rolled into the lot. Visibility went from really bad to nothing exists. She was sure she was near the building but couldn't see anything, and the sensory overload was disorienting. The wind roared. Lightning was crashing all around, but now the sand was blowing too thick to see anything.

She was sure the car was pointed at the building. She couldn't see anything through the windshield. Maybe the glass was caked with dust — she turned the wipers on and heard them for a moment, then was pretty sure the wind tore them off. The car was rocking nonstop. She had to get to that building.

Nikki held the wheel straight and crept the car forward, even though she wanted to push down on the gas. Seconds took long ticks, and then there was a bang, and she felt it in the car. Nikki pushed the brake and squinted through the windshield. She must have hit the building.

There was another bang, then a dozen others, and they didn't stop.

Hail hammered the car.

Radial fractures blossomed across the windshield. The sunroof exploded, and then the back windows blew apart. Hand grenade-sized hail pounded the glass out of its frame and shot through the sunroof hole in an unrelenting barrage.

Gale-force sand sprayed in like stinging bees, and Nikki reflexively brought her hands up to cover her face and stamped down on the gas. The car shot forward and hit something. The airbags punched her in the face, and the car rolled back. It had to be the building this time. She turned the keys, pulled them from the ignition, held them for a split second, and then threw them to the floor. The hammer chorus of hail continued, and ice bombs shot through the roof. The wind whirlpooled in the car, alive with the stinging sand. She squeezed her eyes shut, felt in the back seat for the folded blanket, and pulled it over her head.

She huddled under the blanket for a moment, trying to focus on her plan of action, not on the improbability of getting through this OK.

Nikki snatched her bag from the passenger seat, risking the hail coming through the roof. She pulled the bag under the blanket and the strap over her shoulder.

She took a deep breath and lifted the door handle, forcing the door open against the storm. The wind grabbed the door and flung it wide, bending the hinges open to the howling gale.

She pulled the blanket tight over her head and pushed herself into the roaring whirlwinds with immediate regret. The blowing sand hurt, the sound was overwhelming, and the wind pushed her any way it wanted. Within two steps, she lost her bearings, stumbled, and was blown off her feet. It was so dark and painfully disorienting that all she could do was clutch the life-saving blanket to her head with one hand and flail blindly with her other as she crouched and crawled against the chaos.

Nikki fell on the ice chunks, got up, and fell again, pushing herself through the bruising hail. She managed a few more stumbling steps to fall against the side of a wooden platform, being beaten like a thousand drums.

Though her head and shoulders were under the thick blanket, she kept her eyes squeezed tight and felt along the planks to pull herself up, helped by the force of the wind at her back.

The storm was too strong for her and blew her down. She fell forward against the planks of a wooden walkway. She climbed onto the boardwalk, got to her feet to be blown off-balance, and stumbled into the concrete wall of the building.

Flattened against the building by the blowing storm, she felt her way to the right, inching along until her hand found the door just where she hoped it would be.

Her fingers ran over rough wood and metal nail heads and found a large handle. With the wind pressing her against the doorway, she gripped the iron ring and pushed, but it wouldn't open. She let go of the blanket to use both hands, and it flew from her head and disappeared into the storm. The sand stung as she gripped the handle and twisted, pushing against the heavy planks. She tried again, slamming her body against the wood. Again, she tried turning the rough metal handle as she threw her shoulder against the entrance.

The double doors blew wide, and Nikki stumbled inside, twisting, falling on her back, suddenly looking up at the swirling dust from cool terra cotta tiles.

She gasped, out of the hail and the full force of the storm, and caught the blowing doors with her feet to slam them shut.

The wind dropped to a low moan on the other side of the wood. Nikki lay on the floor for a minute, soaking in the still as her breathing calmed. She wiped her face and sat up, sputtering sand. It was quiet and smelled like beer.

Nikki got to her feet, quietly swearing as she patted dust clouds from her clothing and looked around her shelter from the storm. She was in a short hallway, a few steps from the outside to the saloon. She knew that because a sign read 'SALOON' over a set of swinging barroom doors at the end of the hall.

It seemed very quiet in the next room, in the saloon, but it was a bit brighter.

Nikki wiped the sand from her eyes and followed the louvered light into the Bunker.

CHAPTER THREE

THE NEST

As the sun set, the scout that had bagged the old woman climbed onto the rocks and emitted a piercing call. To perform the stridulation, she reared back and rapidly brushed her barbed forelegs over a bristled comb on the underside of her abdomen. The penetrating sound carried far over the desert, not only audible to anything with ears but containing another channel of subsonic chords transmitting commands to the other ants from her nest. The vibratory tones pulsed through the darkening sky to excite the uniquely tuned stubble of receptors that carpeted the carapaces of the giant insects.

Their late afternoon foray had just begun when a shift in the wind coupled with an increase of airborne particles precipitated the scout's call in advance of the sandstorm. The act was reflective of the collective consciousness of the colony. The other giants relayed the rumbling broadcast, echoing the order that all the scouts and tenders return to the nest.

On hearing the call, the giant ants turned from their tasks and followed the chemically marked trails to the nest's recently reopened entrance. The foraging mutations were the major worker caste, easily identifiable by the colossal size of their bodies and the disproportionately oversized heads. Only a few smaller, minor worker castes followed the giants out of the nest to relieve them of their finds and minister to any wounds or grooming needs.

The colony was dead for years, except for the queen, barely existing and diminishing. The monarch's metabolism had slowed to no sign of life, and her egg production had ceased decades before as the population succumbed to environmental factors and the human effort to eradicate them. In their last hours, the expiring workers had sealed the deep chambers, sequestering the queen. Their final attempt was to harvest the fungus and force-feed the nutritious chum to their matriarch even as they starved, stocking the royal's reserves to see her through a long sleep at the root of the subterranean network of caves. They dragged themselves into the dark farming areas to die, leaving the cavernous tunnels empty.

She was one of three queens that were issues of the original outbreak of mutated ants, the second generation of monsters brought about by atomic testing in the Chihuahuan Desert.

The mutant insects quickly manifested after the first atomic bomb test in New Mexico, erupting from the desert in the early 1950s, only a few years after the Trinity blast. Their metamorphosis had been triggered by lingering radiation distorting the basic building blocks of life, causing the ants to grow into giants.

Their structure changed, their biology altered, but their social ability to build a nest into a colony and the colony into a superorganism did not. Ants have survived countless eons. That these deep-digging desert inhabitants mutated into a greater form of themselves was testament to the species as the most successful life form on earth. They may have been mutants but were fundamentally ant – fearless, ferocious, and merciless.

While most heirs to a throne leave to start a nest of their own, nature occasionally encodes a developing queen to return from her mating flight to the nest that bred her, ensuring the colony's continuance and territorial footprint. Even everyday ants find it prudent to have more than one egg layer safeguarding their future, and only a queen can reproduce.

All members of an ant colony are female, except for a few specially developed males whose sole purpose before death is the insemination of a new queen, and these mutants followed that biology.

When the princess emerged from the pupal stage complete with wings, she and her sister queens-to-be left the nest pursued by the similarly winged males the colony produced to court and copulate in flight. Once they had mated, the males fell to earth and died, their life's mission complete. Queens have to mate only once to store the male's seed for their lifetime, producing thousands upon thousands of eggs deep in the new nests they establish.

This queen had been programmed to return home. Once impregnated, the workers read her body chemistry at the entrance, and she was escorted to a new system of chambers in the deepest levels of the nest. She would be separate from the queen mother and have fungal farms and attendants of her own.

But fate had turned against the mutant ants before she could begin egg production.

It wasn't long before the secret of their existence leaked. While few people lived in the desert then, the ants made them fewer. Unlike the subtler effects of atom bomb testing, the disappearance of the local population and the appearance of car-sized insects were difficult news items to downplay, even in the 1950s.

It was decided the mutations must be utterly erased.

A small and secret group of scientific and military personnel were based in the strategically unnoticeable desert town of White Sands. They were tasked with destroying the bugs. In that task, the humans failed, though conflict with the planet's most invasive species cost the ants heavily.

There was never a clash between two more dissimilar opponents. The humans could not comprehend the singular determination of the creatures. Humans plan, strategize, and evaluate possible outcomes. The ants did not plan, they acted. They lived an existence of ant or not ant. They followed no train of thought, only instinct.

Against any conventional opponent, the response of the military would have been overwhelming and final. The tools of war encircled the entrance to the nest. The troops massed, and the artillery softened the area around the giant ant holes to drive the monsters deep into their nest.

But the ants responded to the attack in their own way. At the first concussion from the bombardment above, workers walled off the deep chambers to protect their queen and her troop of attendants. Their goal was the continuation of their line.

Unknown to the aggressors, the ants were already in a weakened state due to the falling desert aquifer lowering moisture in the colony. Survival had become the ants' predominant concern. Normally, every member would fight any invader to the death, but against the thirst of the desert and failing fungal crops, they had no chance of prevailing against the humans. Not until the waters returned. Evolution had prepared the deep desert ants to wait as well as to fight.

For the ants in the nest nearer to the surface, battle was instinctive. Hundreds of the insects awoke from a state of torpor and filed into long caverns just below the surface, alert to the humans' movements above.

Immediately following the artillery barrage, the humans launched a gas attack. Several brave soldiers in protective gear raced to the nest's entrance and dropped hundreds of pounds of cyanide bombs into the opening. The heavier-than-air vapors would diffuse through the chambers and eradicate the monsters. After the poison had time to act, the military planned a foray into the nest to ascertain success. Then, the opening would be filled in, and the evidence of the atomic mishap would be entombed to keep the secret from the world.

That was the plan.

The reality was that cyanide was ineffectual in the network of tunnels. The heavy gas spilled down the vertical shafts, bypassing legions of ants in the side tunnels. The fumes formed poisonous pools in the colony's deep recesses while, just below the surface, hundreds of mutant insects stood unaffected in the dark under the attackers.

The humans waited for the gas to do its work. The ants waited for the humans to move. The humans attacked.

The ants beneath the surface sensed the vibrations as the attackers moved toward the entrance, and they acted. Some excavated away supporting columns along the tunnel's length, while others scraped at the shaft walls and roof.

The ground below the moving armor and human soldiers collapsed beneath them, sending man and machine spilling into the emerging jaws of the monstrous ants. The giant insects clawed their way out of the sliding sands by the hundreds, over the crashing vehicles, plucking the foundering soldiers from the cave-in in their snapping jaws.

The defeat of the humans was swift and total. The losses were kept secret, and only a handful of soldiers escaped grisly death. However, while the human forces lost the battle, the ants had lost the war. Their queen was dead, poisoned in the deep recesses of the nest, and without a leader, without their larvae, their future, they were a lost cause.

But the second queen was a secret from all.

After the botched attack and with a new sense of caution, the military methodically eradicated the remaining insects. They determined the local outbreak was under control and concentrated on locating the two escaped queens.

The first was found in California and quickly dispatched with little loss of life. Only a few civilians were lost, and they were explained away in the hill fires set to consume the monster's remains.

The other escapee wasn't located until sometime later, on the verge of reproducing in a South American jungle close to the equator. This second queen was destroyed, and the jungle quickly consumed the evidence.

Deep reconnaissance was abandoned at the original nest site due to the health consequences of a cyanide-soaked environment. The decision-makers were forced to satisfy themselves by burning the ant carcasses, filling in the entrance to the nest, and monitoring the area for signs of activity. They established a reporting station on-site, set seismic sensors, and posted round-the-clock guards that kept watch for years to follow.

34

One decade passed into another. No ants were reported, and no disturbances were recorded. The mission faded into forgotten secrecy. By the time the program came to an official close, the desert observers had thought the stories of giant insects were just that. As they understood, their assignment was to monitor seismic fault activity that may have been caused by the bomb tests years before. There was no activity; the guards were finally relieved, and the Agency removed the outposts. Solar-powered sensors took over monitoring. Years of uneventful logs were erased, and the events of a lifetime before were forgotten.

Over time, the watchfulness was put to rest, along with almost everybody involved.

From the first appearance of the monsters in the early 1950s, the Agency directors were unanimous in agreement that the creatures, while remarkable in their mutation, were rightly eradicated. Giant insects that had been spawned by residual radiation, that threatened to overrun the planet, that had murdered dozens of civilians, and slaughtered an undisclosed number of military personnel were not a plus to the advancement of atomic energy and nuclear weapons, essential to the continued successes of the Cold War. The ants had to be eradicated.

In addition to killing the bugs, the Agency was anxious to control public opinion concerning the giant ants and some other realities deemed too disconcerting for the populous.

In the pursuit of shaping common perceptions, the powerful extended their reach into popular media to influence the masses through entertaining books and movies with the new 'science fictions' conditioning the public to accept new technologies and realities ushering in the atomic age.

It seemed as though the Agency had everything under control.

But the dawn of the nuclear age was full of surprises – modern times compound change. The embryonic technologies of the early twentieth century had been distorted through war. Once quaint flying machines evolved into flying fortresses, steamships grew into modern war fleets, patrolling the seas and brimming with death. The business of technology seemed to be destruction, which was not the brand that atomic power wanted to carry; it was to be the savior of the future. Peace was on the horizon, and it was to be a peace powered by the atom. Mutant insects had no place in that future, and these ants, dead or alive, would be the fly in the ointment.

Federal and state authorities were enlisted to sanitize published accounts by reissuing doctored newspapers and sequestering uncooperative individuals. Fortunately, at least concerning the effort to keep it quiet, the ants' aggressive efficiency had left few civilian witnesses. Most survivors were military personnel, and that provided a great deal of leverage in assuring cooperation. Civilians with any knowledge of the mutations soon learned to keep it to themselves. There were one or two eyewitnesses who persisted with stories of monstrous desert insects, but it didn't take too many retellings before they found themselves isolated with no one to listen to their outlandish tales.

For decades, the solitary monarch slept in an extended period of dormancy induced by an unusually dry time in southern New Mexico. It was so dry that the deep water had receded from the nest, no longer providing the moisture the giant ant colony required. Before the drought, the tunnels contacted the water table, increasing the nest's humidification. Humidity was especially crucial to the growth of the colony's fungal crops. When the dry time came, it was catastrophic, as it would be for any society dependent on farming, and these ants were farmers, cultivating the spores in vast growing chambers.

It was to feed the fungus that the insects foraged. The giant ants, just like their small counterparts, hunted and harvested any organic matter, plant, or animal, which would be processed to feed the crops.

A symbiotic relationship existed between the ants and the fungus; neither would survive without the other. The fungus could not grow in the desert but flourished in the dark caverns tended by the ants. The farming insects, in turn, harvested the fungus as their only nutrition, perpetuating a cycle that evolved over millions of years.

Through countless generations, ants have changed little. They labored in the desert, raising the fungus on a processed stew of insects, carrion, or any plant matter that could be found. They were relegated to be minute scavengers, depending on meager finds overlooked by the other scroungers trying to survive the harsh environment. For millennia multiplied into epochs, they were mere ants; their savagery and conquest were kept in check by their small size.

The rhythms of nature continued, and the water table rose again in time. On the surface, the effects of the rehydration were noticeable in the resurgence of the deep-rooted yucca plants. Below, the seepage humidified the nest and signaled the queen's reawakening.

Forces, natural and calculated, conspired to reanimate the wasting incarnation of the mutants, and against the odds, the queen was sparked to life and began egg production.

Most theorized the giant ants were a consequence of the A-bomb tests and attributed the queen's prolonged slumber to the same cause. Whatever the reason, the result was she survived the drought. Like other insects, her torpor was induced by external factors, lasting more than seventy years.

The queen stirred in the utter darkness. Chemical changes caused her protective casing to molt, and as she reawakened, the final reserves of nutrition within her emaciated frame were released. Respiration increased, and eggs formed. Her survival depended on the production of serving ants.

Over several weeks, a small clutch of eggs disgorged, which the queen gathered with her long-unused legs. She pulled them beneath her to slowly turn and lubricate them with chemical indicators she produced, directing their transformation into the minor workers that would attend to her needs.

The eggs formed into larvae in the blackness, twisting as they developed into her attendants, growing to maturity inside their translucent cocoons. They emerged fully developed and ready to serve their queen.

The workers left the queen's chamber carrying chewed and digesting pupal parts in their social stomach, a secondary organ used to transport and share the nutritious chum they produce.

The spores had also lain in the dark chambers for years, awaiting food and water.

The workers found their way to the lowest tunnels, where the rising water table seeped in and formed running streams. Vast antechambers opened from the tunnels to a network of farming halls where the mummified carcasses of the giant ants from years before had been eaten away by the fungus. They were spiked with brittle spore sacs laden with the waiting seed of new crops.

The ants toiled to prepare beds for growth, regurgitating the stew they had formed in their gut to fertilize the soil. They instinctually removed the dry sacs and broke them open over the plots to spread spore clouds onto the wet mass. Farming in the inky darkness had begun again, and they would need more food for the growing crops of fungus.

As the days and weeks passed in the deep tunnels, the queen was supplied with the nutritious remains of the long-dead workers and two weaklings from the new ants. It was enough to support egg production and develop new ants, larger than the servants. These eggs were coded to produce major workers – the foraging scouts and soldiers of the colony. Metamorphizing from egg to larvae and then the cocoon stage, they soon hatched, breaking out of their pupate covering, emerging as did the minor workers, fully formed but three times their size.

The smaller workers groomed the new scouts, contaminating the giants with the communicative chemical signals that encoded their mission and set them to work, breaking through the walls built to safeguard the queen by their predecessors. They instinctively found their way through the tunnels, always traveling upward, leaving the minor workers to repair the reopened tunnels as the big ants headed for the surface.

The huge ants unblocked the entrance to the nest filled in by the humans many years before. They cleared the passage, reinforced it with a discharge expressed during excavation, and mixed it with sand to form concrete-like walls.

After days and nights of labor, they climbed out of the reconstructed shafts, into the desert, and into the world again. Their mission was to gather food to feed the fungi to grow the colony.

Two giant ants busied themselves, spreading the earth pushed out of the hole to form a cone-shaped mound surrounding the entrance. The third ant left them to the labor and ventured into the surrounding desert, circling the nest entrance at varying distances and chemically familiarizing the paths to be used. She returned as the earth-forming completed, and the three swept their sensing antennae over each other, instantly sharing their experiences.

The chemistry of life is evident in the ant as no other species. In their lightless world, chemical signals carry complex information immediately read by nestmates and spread at synoptic speed. Waxy exudations deposited in the tunnels provide clear guidance to members of the colony, marking trails, routing workers, and designating areas of action.

Information, alarm, and intent travel electrically fast within the nest and can be initiated by any member of the superorganism. Each ant is a chemical factory that can mix complex messages to spread through the nest, detectable in parts per billion and particularly suited to communication in the dark confines of their underground world.

To the ant collective, everything that could be consumed should be consumed, including injured or aged colony members. In times of deficiency, workers and soldiers alike determined extraneous were dismembered without struggle and reduced to the nutritious chum that fed the essential fungus plots in the farming chambers. When processed by the smaller workers, virtually any organic material could support their farms; the fungi could grow on anything – animal or vegetable, and because the fungi were not particular, neither were the ants.

To avoid the heat of the day, the ants foraged at night, consuming the only material available – desert vegetation. The giants grazed, storing the mastication in their surplus stomach, further digesting and preparing it for transfer to the smaller workers who would carry it to the nest's farm chambers.

Within a few weeks, plants in the surrounding area had been cleared in an ever-widening radius, contributing substantial biomass to the colony's development.

The fungal farms were in full production and grew rapidly. The infusion of nourishment accelerated the large ball-shaped fruiting masses sprouting on stalks. As they ripened, the spheres became bioluminescent, emitting a soft glow to counter the ant's inky world of absolute darkness. The delicacy of the light tracing the thinner and thicker parts of the glowing molds may have been lost on the ants, but they could sense the light.

Though there was no need for vision in their underworld, the ants possessed rudimentary optical organs, the classic large and faceted insect eyes, sufficient only to distinguish contrasts of dark and light, though particularly attuned to the emissions of the fungi's wavelength.

The small workers harvested the orbs as the fungal fruit brightened, sucking the glowing goo into their stomachs to be prepared for sharing. In the time it took to travel to the queen's chamber, the stew was ready. The insect mouthparts coupled with the monarch's maw to disgorge the gruel gulp after restorative gulp.

The smaller workers scrupulously attended to the queen's hygiene and sustenance, feeding her continuous egg production. As the eggs slid out of her distended reproductive organs, they were collected and taken to the egg chambers by the workers. While tending the clutches, they coated the cases with a protective antibacterial mucous that also delivered enzymes to encourage or delay developmental stages based on environmental factors, food supply, and the security of the nest.

The eggs were monitored to ensure proper development as a minor worker or major warrior.

The oversized head of the giant scout ants had savagely serrated mandibles used to grab, crush, and tear, working in concert with grasping forelegs and the poisonous sting at the end of her body. The ant could curl her body by pinning an adversary with her front legs or clenching it in her jaws, bringing the stinger forward beneath her to administer a lethal injection or paralyzing cocktail to an unfortunate victim.

The giant ants were omnivorous, though the only meat added to their fungal feed were the few snakes and a dead coyote they happened upon in their ever-widening forays from the nest entrance. As the slow-growing desert vegetation disappeared into the nest, the number of colony members increased, minor and major, as did the distance and duration of their forays. They widened their searches and began earlier in the day, before nightfall when the sun was still low.

Now better fed and well hydrated, the scouts ranged further, designating trails to patches of vegetation to be harvested and widening their territorial perimeter, marked by oily deposits released from the glands beneath their abdomen.

One afternoon's patrol led a lone scout to the warm trail of US-70, the highway that crossed the desert basin. As the monster's feet contacted the macadam, she felt the amplified vibrations of distant activity rapidly coming closer. The scout quickly moved from the road to lie flat in the scrub beneath the tall utility poles carrying high-tension wires. Remaining motionless for hours, she monitored passing cars and trucks, assessing their movement and frequency. As the vehicles sped past, fanned behind them was an invisible plume of waste gases tinged with the signature of life, of meat, unmistakable to the scout. Chemical receptors lining her antennae fired in a new sequence, determining this as a higher source of nutrition than the usual scrub plants. This would be marked as a high-value game trail for harvesting.

The vibrations were a clear sign of large prey moving at high speeds. Responding to these factors would necessitate a collective strategy. The trail was not heavily trafficked but could be a rich source of new food – food that came to them. She would communicate her finds when she returned to the colony.

The huge scout was about to leave when she felt an approaching vibration, moving slower than the others. She sensed it leave the asphalt trail, move over the sand, and stop. She remained prone, absorbing every minute resonance, and felt the footfalls of a much lighter body.

The scout rose and stalked the disturbance, waving her antennae, collecting the molecular signals of warm and salty meat. She innately coordinated the changing intensities of odor and wind, correlated with regular vibrations of movement to forecast her quarry's location.

New combinations of receptors excited in the beast, signaling larger value prey. While intent on her target, the scout mindfully traveled parallel to the highway, though there was no activity coming from there to distract her. Focused on the vibration and scent signatures, she knew contact was imminent and that the object of her attention was just beyond the rocky rise. She stopped, lifting one antenna as the other lowered to provide counterpoint locations. The odors were faint as the wind was not ideal, but the vibrational activity filled the gap.

The vibrations ceased momentarily, then picked up again and increased in frequency. The prey was running, not away from the scout but towards her. Her antennae detected a familiar odor from her quarry, the same scent of the vehicles that traveled past in her hours of reconnoitering.

The ant was between a car parked in the desert and the highway. The prey ran toward it and moved irregularly, with uneven steps indicating distress, inviting the monster to attack.

As she mounted the rocks, the desert breeze brought a sudden increase in the prey scent. The wash of aroma carried the new odor of fresh blood, of a wounded animal, firing the huge scout into action to scramble down the rocks and charge across the sand to the woman's car.

Her antennae swept over the inedible exoskeleton, and with little effort, the monster overturned the automobile. The huge ant's mandibles found purchase on the door frame and turned the car over again to peel back the thin metal roof and examine the interior, poking her feelers into the car and contacting the injured woman.

The ant realized her prize and pulled the doomed old lady onto the sand, crushing and mangling her, stinging her repeatedly with her thick, venomous barb.

A form much like their own, the hard shell of the automobile contained a soft and nutritious center. The connection between car and carcass was made and would soon be shared with the community.

Carrying the package in her jaws, the large scout made her way along the trails to the nest. She was intercepted by minor workers and relieved of her trophy. They excitedly communicated the find to each other as they ministered to her laceration from the car's jagged metal.

As the sun fell and the winds rose, the scout climbed onto the rocks to broadcast the call to return to the nest. While they had just begun their afternoon foray, the impending storm and the new food source in abundance were more important. The information would be disseminated through the colony; the collective would attack.

From atop the rocky ledge, the scout's primitive eyes sensed the lights of another vehicle moving on the highway, passing only a quick run from her perch. She remained still on the rock, only turning her head to perceive a few low glows dotting the desert landscape. The distant buildings lit up early because of the dark clouds moving in and obscuring the sun.

The red sky behind the western mountains rimming the desert basin dimmed as the massive sandstorm rolled off White Sands. Night's fast fall caused the scout to linger, observing the number and location of the stationary lights. To the ant, they looked like the luminescent fungi ripe for harvest. To the ant, it was the distant glow of food.

CHAPTER FOUR

THE HIGHWAY

The driver and his truck waited out the sandstorm inside a large building at Holloman Air Force Base. The haboob moved in fast and was fiercer than anything he had seen in all his years driving the Southwest.

But Tom Honey also saw his usual good luck was at work. As he pulled into the warehouse to offload his delivery, the dark wall on the horizon was moving toward the base. By the time the last of the prime cuts were off his truck and the paperwork was finished, it was plain he should stay put. The trucker joined the loading crew in the huge doorway as they watched the mountain of sand rolling across the desert, coming straight at them.

Flashes rippled through the cloud wall as the dust thrown up from the desert churned, generating colossal static charges and dazzling the dark clouds with huge flashes of lightning. The front grew in height as the miles-wide column of air from the upper atmosphere smashed into the White Sands basin, and the concussion kicked out a shock wave of sand at express train speed.

The group's comments in the warehouse doorway mostly consisted of one-word exclamations alluding to the imminent arrival of the stormfront and the sand wall's growing size. It grew so fast and large that it occluded the late sun and tinted the afternoon light with a sickly green as the low rays were filtered through the dust.

The mountainous tumult advanced, and the cloud wall grew opaque, cutting off the sun's light and plunging the world into the dark of an eclipse. Outdoor lights automatically snapped on as the winds of displaced air began blowing through the airbase.

"Seems a might unhospitable out there," Tom Honey said to the manager of the crew standing next to him. "If it's all the same to you, I aim to sit out this duster in here." Neither of the men looked away from the clouds. "And, as long as I'm not going anywhere, it just might be time to close up these doors," he added as the lightning flashed across his face.

The base siren wound up from a low-volume start to a loud and steady wail, perfectly accompanying the approaching score of thunder and wind. The foreman tore his gaze away from the mountain of sand coming at them and calmly made a few suggestions to his workers.

The group sprang into action. A couple of them ran outside and pulled vehicles inside while the wall-sized doors were already in motion, rolling closed. A few more workers hot-footed it across the warehouse to shut the large doors on the other side of the building, checking windows in the steel walls along the way.

Tom Honey walked across the concrete floor, headed for his truck as the Air Force busied themselves preparing for the storm. He thought of the young woman he met at the food truck and calculated that she would not beat the storm out of the valley. She'd be on the road and most likely get caught in the thick of it. He further figured she was a bright kid and would just sit it out, no harm done.

The storm clouds towered impossibly high as the cataclysm pushed forward. It rolled into its own shadow and crested, balancing an unsustainable mass until the wave fell, toppling forward to engulf the airbase, the highway, and the desert basin in its explosive energies.

The steel building flexed as the first of the real wind hit. It echoed inside the giant structure as the sheet metal was pushed and squeezed from the outside. The sand came next, sizzling against the metal skin like a high-pressure steam hose. The warehouse groaned under the nonstop spray, threatening to blow apart in the hurricane-strength winds.

A boom reverberated through the tin can of a building. It was so loud everyone involuntarily crouched and covered their heads. Tom Honey fell back, leaning against the cab of his reefer, ready to get under it. He looked up at the dim ceiling behind the hanging lights, expecting it to fly off.

There was another bang, just as loud. Then another and another until the drum was pounded with such force and fury that everyone ran for cover. They slid under tables and crawled into crannies as the incessant pummeling continued at explosive levels. The trucker dropped to his knees and bellied under his Peterbilt, watching two workers running with their mouths wide open. He was sure they were screaming, but the only noise that got past the hands over his ears were the hundred-decibel hammers on the roof.

The lights went out, and the strobe of lightning flashes arcing through the windows broke the pitch-black into separate acts. Tom Honey watched from under his truck and saw panicked workers freeze-framed every few steps by lightning in their frightened dash for refuge.

Everyone covered their heads even though they were already hiding under shelves, tables, or trucks – anything to protect them when the roof came down. The steel building was pounding, the hammering intensified, built to a crescendo – then relented, and the din wound down as the storm passed.

Tom pulled his hands from his ears and propped himself on his forearms.

It was after-hanging quiet until someone in the warehouse called out in the dark, "What the hell was that?"

Another voice answered, "Are we still here?"

Someone else chimed in, then another and another voice, mixing with the buzzing light fixtures as the noise of the storm died away. The big bulbs flickered back to life. There was a small chorus of cheers as the people began to come out from their hiding places.

The trucker maneuvered into the open space of the warehouse and got to his feet, taking his cowboy hat with him and putting it back where it belonged. Tom Honey's boots clacked on the cement floor as he took a few bowlegged steps to survey his surroundings.

The building had held up. The sandstorm had blown by, and the doors to the warehouse were slowly rolling open.

He walked to the entrance, collecting a few people as he went. The small group stood on the threshold of the giant door, looking at the nearby structures and out into the airfield. The tarmacs were covered in chunks of ice, smoking on the hot concrete. Grapefruit-sized hail filled the field to the horizon from their doorway. Melting ice balls slid off the buildings.

The sky was clearing. Looking to the south, they could see the sandstorm rolling away and disappearing into the far-off desert, pulling the dark clouds along.

The group took a few steps outside. The base siren began to sound again, and many people turned back to the warehouse.

"No, it's alright. That's the all-clear," the officer called to them as he lowered his handheld radio. He turned to Tom Honey and shook his head in disbelief. "From what they just told me, we only got the tip. That was just some of the storm. Most of it was west of us. At least there's not much out there."

The trucker thought of the young woman out in the middle of that not much.

The siren faded, and it was so quiet they could hear the ice hissing on the hot airfield. The officer bent down and picked up a chunk of hail. He lifted it to show the trucker. "This is incredible," the airman said. "It's a miracle we didn't get clobbered."

Tom Honey toed a couple of chunks on the pavement, "I think you did," he said.

"What do you mean?" the warehouse boss asked.

Tom Honey nodded at the nearest building to the warehouse. In front of it was a line of six transport trucks that didn't make it under a roof before the hail hit. All of the windows were smashed, and the canvas tents were shredded. They looked like they had been through an eggbeater. A small civilian car was parked at the far end of the truck line. The windows and sunroof had been blown out, and the lighter gauge sheet metal of the body had been pounded apart and even ripped in a few places.

The car made Tom Honey think of the girl again. There would have been no sitting tight and riding this out in a car – not if she ran into the same blow with the same ice bombs. But that's one thing he knew about desert weather – it could be one way, one place, and completely different a half-mile away. That's what he hoped. Maybe wherever she ended up, she just got a dusting. That's what he wanted to think.

Holloman began shaking off the storm. Civilians and military personnel cautiously left the protection of their shelters across the base and throughout the surrounding town, picking their way outside through the ice and broken glass to survey the damage. Battered vehicles began to move. An ambulance without a windshield or top lights came around the corner and drove by the doorway, plowing through the ice chunks. The warehouse workers hustled off to join in the recovery.

Tom Honey walked alone into the warehouse as the military machine busily regrouped. He stepped onto his cab, climbed behind the wheel, and fired her up. Leaning through the open window, he gave a couple of workers hurrying by a quick salute and rolled his rig out the door, cracking over the melting rocks of ice and toward the gates exiting the base.

It took extra time to move through the base town because of emergency vehicles and disabled cars. He navigated his way out, but the slow-going allowed his thoughts to divert more and more to that young woman caught in the storm. The frustrating pace made him want to step on the gas, but he kept his head. The only thing that would slow him up more would be running into one of the fire and rescue trucks flying around.

49

Finally, he reached the last exit. The big rig stopped at the guardhouse, and he put his window down. The sentry slid the empty metal frame to the side and looked up at the driver. Most of the glass from the booth was on the ground. A couple of pieces fell out as he pushed the partition open.

Tom Honey leaned out and looked at the battered military car next to the post, hammered and smashed like every other vehicle caught outside. He looked down from his undamaged cab at the booth, wrecked by the storm. The air cop had dried blood on the side of his face and a good amount on his shirt.

"That storm must have given you a hell of a ride in this little box," the trucker said to the guard.

"That was one for the books," the sentry replied. "Fact is, I got out of this fish tank. I wouldn't have lasted another thirty seconds once those rocks hit. I had to get under that car."

Tom Honey looked at the distance between the guard post and the car and thought of the young man making a run for it through the blasting sand and pounding ice. He moved his eyes back to the shattered framework of what was the glass booth and looked down, noticing the sentry's bruised and most likely broken left hand.

The guard leaned out of the booth and looked up at the trucker. "Today's the day I fell in love with my hard hat," he said, tapping his helmet with his good hand and painfully smiling with a split lip.

The trucker looked down at the guard and said, "Well, you've had a day." He shook his head and laughed, "Keep up the good work, son," and laughed again, touching the brim of his hat as he put his rig in gear and drove through as the gate opened.

As the big truck pulled into the westbound lane, Tom Honey noticed the ice blocks diminishing in size, maybe from melting but maybe because they just weren't that big when they came down in this direction. He picked up speed. There weren't any other vehicles, and the hail on the highway had shrunk down to golf balls.

50

He kept his eyes peeled for Nikki's car and paid attention to any marks going off-road, slowing a few times to give something a double look just to be sure it wasn't her gone over the side.

He kept the speed down, though his foot wanted to push the pedal, but he couldn't risk missing something and leaving the young woman stranded. She may need help. He drove the empty road, looking for any tracks or glints that might be a car. It was getting pretty close to dark.

He had driven about two miles when he saw an abandoned car on the shoulder with driver and passenger doors wide open. It wasn't her car. He stopped his rig and leaned across the front seat to look out the window. Nobody was around, the car was covered with dust, and the windows were broken. The trucker blew his air horn and watched for any movement around the vehicle or in the scrub leading to White Sands, but there was none.

Someone must have picked them up; there were tire tracks in the layer of fine sand blanketing the highway, but these were being smoothed over by the last breezes of the storm.

He took his foot off the brake and drove down the double-lane divided highway.

In a few minutes, he passed the first sign for the White Sands Visitor Center. The next sign pointed to the turn-in for the national monument, and as he drove past, Tom Honey craned his neck to see there were cars in the lot, but the buildings were dark. He figured they had lost power. He also calculated the girl would have been past the visitor center before the storm hit. He drove.

Within the next half mile, he saw another deserted car and stopped his truck. This one had no driver's door and was flipped onto the passenger side in the middle of the highway. The roof was peeled back and opened like a sardine can. Debris from the car was scattered around the wreck.

He squinted at the pop-top car but couldn't come up with any accident that would cause that sort of damage.

From his high perch in his truck's cab, Tom Honey could see a trail of disturbed sand from the demolished car to the shoulder of the road and into the scrub.

That didn't make sense. Nothing would come out of the desert to the car, and nobody from a wreck like that would be in any shape to go into the desert. A tornado was the only thing he could think of that would be strong enough to cause such destruction, but this looked like something happened after the storm – the way the sand was tracked up.

The trucker took his phone from his shirt pocket, and the screen illuminated to show no signal. He put it in the holder on the dashboard and stared through the windshield at the highway, the wreck, and the trail to the dunes rising from the scrub at the side of the road. Mostly, he kept looking at the tracks.

The sun was going down.

Tom Honey hooked his big fingers around the horn cord. He paused, then took his hand away. He didn't blow the airhorn this time; instead, he moved his foot from the brake, shifted gears, and slowly rolled onward. He gradually gained speed as he approached the first bend in the road. The sheriff's station would be coming up. He'd go there.

Tom Honey knew every mile of this stretch. It was the only way west of Alamogordo, and he must have done that a thousand times over the years. He figured he had been on this road so many times that he'd seen almost everything there was to see. But he had never seen the sheriff's station dark before.

He slowed to a stop.

He thought to walk across the median to tell them about the girl and get the general lowdown on the storm. A little turnaround road crossed over the highway divider for access to the station, but, like most turnarounds, it would be too tight a squeeze for his eighteen-wheeler, so he'd walk.

He looked across at the police complex. It was dark. He put down his window, peered through the deepening desert night, and could make out the building shapes on the small hill and the parking lot in front. He squinted into the gloom but didn't see one glimmer of light, not even a flashlight, coming from the offices or in the back by the inspection stations. He listened, pointing his ear at the station. The night was after-storm still, but the only sound he heard was the synchronized hum of his engine purring like a happy cat, wanting to go.

He looked up and down the highway, then back at the station. It sure was dark – no lights anywhere. He squinted across the median, trying to make out what was moving. There was something in the shadows going through the lot. Big – the size of a car or a van, but no lights, and he couldn't hear an engine.

"What do you think about that, Honey?" he whispered, leaning out the window and squinting across the road. The trucker thought about leaving the truck and going over to the buildings to maybe see what was going on over there. The dark shape disappeared into the darker shadows.

He pulled his head in and put his hand on the door handle as he caught a note on the night air over the low bass of his motor. He put his head back out the window and took his hat off, cocking his head from side to side to listen. A long, low buzz came from the desert, far off. It came and went, and he leaned out a little more, trying to catch it.

The trill was deep, but the way the note rose and fell on the breeze, it sounded far away. Tom listened, thinking it sounded like a cross between a cricket and a bee., but if it were that far away, it would have to be a pretty big bee.

He sat back in the cab, stared at the shadowy buildings, and decided not to get out to see what was happening. The big man felt sort of small, alone in the desert night and, all of a sudden, not that curious.

His window went up; he put the truck in gear and started down the road. There were one or two more bends up ahead and, beyond that, a straight run through the desert to the mountain pass and Las Cruces. He wouldn't mind getting out of here and felt a little better about the girl.

He saw no sign of her car, and it looked like the storm and the hail wasn't as bad down here as it was at the airbase. She probably just drove straight through and maybe didn't even know about the sandstorm. He wanted to believe that.

His spirits picked up with his speed and the distance from the station. He puckered up to start whistling when a formation of lights flying through the dark sky caught his eye and stopped his tune. The lights were heading across the desert in the direction of the airbase, so that wasn't unusual – it was just that there were so many of them. And it wasn't a formation; it was more of a crowd. He whistled after all, long and low as plane after plane headed east.

He watched the air parade a second too long, but his luck jumped in again. His sixth sense stamped his foot down hard on the brake, turning his attention ahead. The truck squealed to a stop, grabbing the pavement through the loose sand and avoiding a collision with the wrecks in the road by only a few feet.

He gripped the steering wheel tight with both hands and leaned forward, mouth open and eyes wide. At least a dozen vehicles were strewn over the highway in his headlights. Some were upside-down, some cut open like the other one he saw; a couple were still steaming fresh.

But there were no people to be seen. Not a soul.

Cars and pieces of cars were all around.

A minivan was on the side of the road in two halves, not neatly cut but torn with jagged flaps of metal hanging in the air. There were no skid marks. The sand was disturbed by the wreck, but it looked like drag marks. Not tires. It had been dragged onto the sand. Distinct tracks led from the van, over the dunes, and into the White Sands. They weren't tire tracks.

He swallowed and looked at his phone on the dash. There was still no signal. He wanted to turn around or go ahead. Whatever happened was all wrong, and he had the feeling that it wasn't over yet. But he sat there, foot on the brake, hand on the knob, looking at the automotive carcasses strewn across the road.

One of the wrecks closest to his truck was overturned in the scrubby median. He could see shredded tires in the air in the spill of his headlights. They weren't blown. They were torn off, chopped up, gone. As he stared dumbly, registering the improbability of four blown tires, the wreckage suddenly burst into flame with a small bang. A high-pressure jet of white smoke hissed out of the side of the car, and then black smoke billowed from the upside-down engine.

The fireworks snapped the trucker out of his trance. He took his foot from the brake and pushed gradually on the gas, inching the semi forward. Tom Honey slowly guided his truck through the debris field, rolling between the large pieces and over the smaller ones.

The truck moved through the wreckage. Tom Honey could feel the tires bump and drop as they rolled over the junk on the road. He could tell which tire was up and which was taking the bounce, even if it was one of the inners on the trailer. He had spent more time in the cab than out of it over his years of driving, knew every inch of his rig, and felt everything it felt.

He was almost clear of the wreckage when there was a jolt from the back end of the trailer, but it wasn't a tire bounce. He slowed even more and squinted into both rear views. He saw nothing but the wrecks he left behind in the red glow of his taillights.

There was another jolt, a heavy one, and the trailer was overloaded. Something had climbed aboard. Instinctively, he moved his foot from the accelerator to the brake, but he hesitated and put it on the gas. Whatever was on his truck, he wanted to get away from it.

The rig lurched as the weight moved. He shifted, pushing faster. He clipped the remnants of a car and picked up speed, leaving the wreck spinning in the road. He felt the load in his trailer shifting, and any trucker would've stopped to check, but that was the last thing Tom

Honey was about to do. He just knew his best bet was to keep moving, and at that moment, he did not want to know what was on the trailer.

The trucker picked up speed as he left the wrecks behind. But no people, no emergency vehicles, not even bodies, just ruined cars and smoke in his high beams. None of it looked like Nikki's car, which was a relief because he was pretty sure if he saw her car out there, he'd stop to find her, and he really didn't want to stop.

A rhythmic drumbeat came from his trailer, coinciding with feeling the load shift again. The box he hauled became front-heavy. Tom felt the weight on his couple, but that's where he would want the load, so he stepped on the gas. He flipped the switches on his header, lit every light he had, and pulled on the air horn, highballing through the night like a lit rocket blasting down the highway. The high-tension poles along the road flew by faster and faster.

The tractor trailer was moving dangerously fast. The rig was flying on a thin rug of white sand from the storm, and that's as dangerous as ice. He could feel the tires skittering over those tiny ball bearings as his truck shot down the highway.

There was a left bend in the road coming up, but he wouldn't slow down – he couldn't. The faster he moved, the more distance he felt between himself and what was in his trailer. He didn't know what it was, but he knew it had wrecked those cars. He knew it came from the desert, and he figured that's where the people ended up, and he didn't want to join them.

As his speed increased, the noise from the trailer stopped. The curve in the road was coming up fast, and Tom Honey was peering ahead into his headlights, watching the sanded highway and readying to make his approach at a reckless speed.

His high beams suddenly outlined half a car dead ahead, and he nearly lost control, veering to the outside and bouncing on the narrow shoulder. He could feel the trailer jump into the air; a couple of the tires lost contact for a split second and squealed as they crashed down to the road, grinding through the sand and into the asphalt.

He kept the rig moving and on the road. He could feel a twisting realignment of his load – something reacted to this crazy ride, and if it didn't like that little bounce, it would hate the next part.

The left was ahead. Tom Honey gripped the wheel like a brand-new driver. As he entered the arc, he felt the truck sailing to the right, drifting at high speed to the outside of the highway.

As his load of steel and meat hit the apex of the curve, he pressed down on the gas and shifted. The sudden increase in acceleration tailed the trailer's last tires off the road and onto the shoulder. It moved the traction in the skid back to the heavier cab and gave it the muscle to pull, keeping the truck and trailer on the tar as he shot into the straightaway.

The turn broke out of the surrounding dunes and onto an expansive runway view of the broad plain of the desert. It was washed in a bright, rising moon, silhouetting tall steel utility towers on his right spaced only about two seconds apart.

The landscape seemed dangerous in the cold lunar light, all soft grays like some sort of black-and-white science fiction movie where things sneak around and people disappear. He thought about the freak storm and the wrecks on the road and decided to highball it. He was going for broke.

Tom Honey had seen enough of those movies to know that something new and unexpected would show up, and that would be bad, or, in real life, his luck would run out, and he would hit one of the wrecks that peppered the highway, and that could be even worse. Then he'd find out what was on his trailer and what ripped the cars in half. He kept blowing his air horn.

He was moving like a bat out of hell. Out of the corner of his eye, he saw the long moon shadow of his rig flying over the scrub and sand. He kept his foot on the gas, and that shadow stuck right along with him, both of them shooting down the dusty highway.

Tom kept looking down at his shadow. The starboard moon perfectly projected his cab and trailer onto the rushing sand. For a few seconds of looking back and forth between the road ahead and the shadow to the side, the trucker tried to figure out just what the large shapes on the top of his trailer could be. His first thought from his first look was that they couldn't be there. His second thought was they shouldn't be, and his third was that they were on the top of his trailer and they were big. They were the shifting weight. They were what caused the carnage, and they were holding onto the high-speed trailer so they wouldn't get blown off.

He pushed down on the gas and kept that horn howling, but this couldn't go on much longer. The road was straight from here to the mountain highway, about twenty miles ahead. But, if he shot into the pass at this speed, he'd wreck for sure.

The bright moon was behind the electric towers, keeping the shadow of his truck on the scrub and sand dividing the highway to his left. Across the median were two eastbound highway lanes as empty as his west.

Almost empty. Another ripped-up car on the road nearly got him. As he sped by, his front bumper hit one of the chunks, knocking it out of the lane and off the road as he rushed past.

The way he reckoned it, if he made the San Augustin pass at this speed, he had about fifteen minutes to live. He looked out his window at the monstrous shadows riding right behind him, waiting for him to stop.

He wanted a different end to his day.

As he shot down the highway, his lights flashed over the remnants of an old sign with only a few ghosted letters left on it. He remembered the new sign inviting folks to 'The Bunker – The Only Watering Hole in the Basin.'

He knew the old bar was still there and still open. At least it was on his last run and the thousand before. It would be coming up fast. Tom

Honey knew that just before the bar, he'd pass a single-mast radio tower used by the missile command. That would be his marker. That's where he could try for the lot. And no slowing down for the turn. Otherwise, he might meet whatever was on the roof of the trailer.

The miles went too fast. He eyed the moon flying through the high-tension wires and wondered how real this was. Maybe he was still lying in the road serving baked brain topped with a scorpion, and this was all a fever dream.

As the road bent a few degrees, the moon moved, and the shadow of his truck fell behind. He couldn't keep tabs on whatever was up top. He adjusted the outside rearview up. Whatever it was up there was holding on tight. He pushed down on the gas.

Down the long straightaway, maybe two miles – about a minute and change – the light at the top of the radio tower blinked red against the night sky. His appointment with the Bunker was coming up. He pushed down on the gas, pulled his seatbelt tight, and reached for the horn to let her wail some more.

Tom Honey flew on the sand-covered road past the tower and saw the lone light pole of the Bunker just ahead without a light. The moon lit the parking lot entrance across the median on the other side of one of those crossover paths, coming up fast. He tied the horn cord down to keep it blaring and grabbed the wheel with both hands.

Tom timed it just right. He jammed the brakes and cut the wheel sharply to the left. His cab leaned way over. The tires screamed as they bounced violently off the highway and into the median. He heard the kingpin snap and the trailer tear loose. The cab went airborne, jumping over the divider and crashing onto the other side of the highway. Honey held tight to the wheel and got smacked by the exploding airbags as the cab bounded off of the asphalt and hurtled past the 'Parking for Bunker Patrons Only' sign, clipping a utility truck that sent him spinning the rest of the way across the lot to smash into the rocks. The big cab lifted against the granite ledge when it impacted, then fell onto its passenger side, 500 horses still whining.

The cab dropped like a rock, hanging the big, semi-conscious man from his seatbelt.

Through a crazed windshield and fluttering eyes, he saw an upended parking lot and part of a building. Darkness slowly filled his vision, accompanied by the hiss of his dying engine.

"Don't let me burn," he mumbled as his consciousness faded. Blood dripped from his nose onto the broken passenger window.

It was dark and heading for dead quiet as the engine seized and wound down. The shredded tires had flapped to a stop and smoked curled in the moonlight.

Snug in its cradle, Honey's phone illuminated and emitted a tinny but upbeat 'ta-da' sound. It had finally gotten a signal.

CHAPTER FIVE

THE BUNKER

The *Land of Enchantment* license plate rattled as the sheriff's Bronco pulled into the parking lot. It stopped in front of the wooden sidewalk, next to the hitching rail with 'PARKING FOR HORSES ONLY' hand-painted along its length.

The lawman sat in his truck, looking through the passenger window over the lot and across the highway into the desert at the wall of clouds blanketing the setting sun. The wind was coming up, whipping little red dust devils to dance in the lot around the lone lamppost. The light atop the pole buzzed and flickered to life as the sky dimmed. The sheriff pulled the handset off the dash and pushed the transmit button.

"Car five-ten to base. Show me ten-fifty-one at the Bunker." He released the button and looked around the lot. He knew the two pickup trucks parked at the end of the building but not the two cars sitting under the light in the middle of the lot.

A smoke-roughened voice crackled back. "For your information, Cal, we have one car; you're not in it, and it doesn't have a number. And a ten-fifty-one is to report a drunk and disorderly, but I'll take that to mean you have plans for the evening. And for the last time, we don't use ten codes anymore. Go ahead." The radio clicked clear over to him.

He smiled. "I'm going inside to confab with Walt, and I'll sit out the storm there. Better put me out of touch for a while. Call the Bunker if you need me," the sheriff replied.

"Will do, Cal. Don't you two get into any trouble," Bernice said. "Oh, wait a minute. Luis will be heading your way," she added. "He checked in a few minutes ago from a call on a wreck down at two-thirteen. He's arrived on scene. Said it's a single-car, upside-down and torn up, is what he said."

The sheriff watched the churning clouds as they grew to cover the sky.

"Alright," he answered. "Sounds like another mess. I don't know what's going on this week, Bern. I'll talk to Luis when he gets here. He's probably forty-five minutes out by the sound of it." He let the transmit button pop up for a couple of seconds, then pressed it again. "If he calls in, patch him through to Walt's phone."

"Will do, Sheriff," Bernice came back. "I'll let him know where you're at."

"Ten-four base, over and out," he replied and tossed the handset onto the front seat, took his Cattleman, and smiled quickly as he got out of the truck. The lawman put the cowboy hat on and walked around the tether. He stepped onto the wooden walk and crossed the boards to the weathered fortress-style door. It was festooned with square head nails hammered into the planks. He reached for the wrought ring handle to open the door when a sound from the desert made him turn back to the clouds.

A strange, pulsing noise carried on the wind rose in pitch and speed, then fell away, leaving him listening to the empty breeze. The desert makes weird sounds.

"Dust storm," he said like a curse and turned back to the entrance.

The sheriff pushed the heavy door open and smelled beer on the cool air coming out as he went in. He walked the short tile floor hall to look over the top of the saloon doors.

His eyes moved beneath the brim of his beaver as he scanned the barroom.

Walt was working his crossword in his spot behind the bar. Three locals were warming their usual stools at the other end under the TV bull-riding competitions. In the foreground, an older man and woman looked uncomfortably out of place at one of the usually unoccupied tables. A woman sat alone at the next table with half a glass of beer, talking with the couple.

The sheriff pushed the doors wide and walked into the barroom as a sheriff should.

The man at the table nodded to the lawman as he entered, and his companion gave him a surprised smile. The sheriff checked the woman next to them in the shadow of the hanging lamp. She looked briefly at the sheriff but did not interrupt her conversation with the couple.

The lawman hitched a thumb in his gun belt, walked across the room to the rail, and put his cowboy boot on it as he leaned to the old barkeep.

"Hey, Walt," he said. He took his weathered white beaver off by the brim, slapped it on his leg to knock it clean, and then put it on the bar. "Looks like something's stirring up that sand. One hell of a blow coming."

Walt looked up from the nearly complete crossword puzzle on a stool behind the bar. "Why Cal. You're a surprise," he said. "What's that you were saying?"

The sheriff narrowed his eyes and moved them from Walt to the large mirror behind the bar. Reflected between the bottles, he saw the middle-aged woman at the table had turned in her chair to watch them while she chatted with the older couple.

He looked back at Walt. "I said there's a duster on the way. And it looks like it's big enough to bury this place." The sheriff pointed to the bottle on the shelf behind his old friend.

"Shifting sands, Cal. Bury us all sooner or later." Walt brought a pair of small glasses up from under the bar and put them down. He reached back to the shelf without looking and brought forth a fifth of Rocking Chair whiskey. He pulled the cork, poured a couple of fingers into both glasses and then put the bottle back on the shelf.

"What took you so long, anyway?" he said as he pushed the glass across the bar top to the sheriff. "Held me up. You know I don't like drinking alone."

"I know, Walt. Don't worry. I won't let you down." The peace officer lifted his glass to the barman, then took a sip, closing one eye and cocking his head as he swished and swallowed. He exhaled. "That's the stuff," he said to Walt. "How much of this you got left, anyway?" he asked the old man.

Walt swirled his glass and took another gulp, tightening his lips, and then blew through them. "Enough left for me, probably not enough for you," he answered breathlessly, taking another swallow.

The sheriff smiled at him and moved his eyes back to the new faces in the mirror on the wall. He turned to the room and leaned back with both elbows on the bar. He looked the trio over and raised his glass to them. "How y'all folks doing tonight?" he asked, draining the remaining whiskey. He put the glass down hard on the bar with a satisfied exhalation and nodded at the newcomers.

In a soft voice, the woman with the man replied, "Good evening," and smiled nervously, looking away. The man with her lifted his glass to the sheriff and nodded to him. The woman who was by herself gave him a suggestive glance or one of disdain – he wasn't sure, but either way, it was a dirty look.

"Guess we're going to be in here for the duration of the storm," the sheriff told them. "You were all lucky to make it here before it got up to speed. Looks like it's going to be a big one. It will be pretty dangerous out there tonight."

The man at the table turned to face the lawman. He was old, had a neatly trimmed, nearly white beard, and wore wire glasses. "Luck was all it was," he said. "We saw those clouds coming up at the same time we saw the Bunker. We're not from this area and wouldn't have known where to go – so here's to luck," he raised his glass.

"Don't do that, Russell," his companion scolded. "It's bad luck to toast with water."

"Oh, right you are, my dear," he replied, lowering his glass of seltzer.

"Ain't so," Walt called over to them. "Nothing better when you're in the desert. Water is the best kind of luck out here. Toast anything with water."

"In any event, we are certainly glad to be inside," the bearded man continued, "Luck to us all," he concluded. "By the way, I'm Russ Yates, and this is my wife, Emma. From Phoenix by way of El Paso just today."

"All you folks together?" the sheriff asked the small group.

The middle-aged woman leaned into the shadow and out of the overhanging light. "I'm on my own, Captain. I just happened to be following these folks on the highway and saw them pull in. Seemed like a good idea."

The sheriff smiled in a friendly fashion at her shadow. The low howl of the rising wind made its way through the heavy front doors. "It was a good idea," he said to the woman. "And it's 'Sheriff,' not captain," he added.

"Sheriff, it is, Sheriff," she said. She picked up a short beer from the table and lifted it into the shadow to take a drink. She put the glass back on the table and said, "My name's Sylvia, by the way. Syl for short."

"Sheriff Jeffries, ma'am," he said to her with a slight nod.

"Keep that outside light on – you might get a full house. Be a beacon to the lost," the sheriff said in a lower voice as he turned his attention back to the barkeep. "That storm's going to be in full swing in no time, but there could be a few cars on the road." He pushed the empty glass across the smooth wood to the barkeep. "They'll be looking for a place to hole up. Could be a busy night."

"You don't plan on going out, do you?" Walt asked. He got off the stool and supported himself on the bar to walk over to the taps and pull a short beer for each of them, "Stranded motorist, damsel in distress. Just don't know what you'll find in a duster," Walt said. The barman put a beer in front of the sheriff and climbed back onto his stool with his glass. "Could be all sorts of trouble out there."

"That's alright. I'm not looking for trouble. There's already been enough this week," the sheriff said. He lowered his voice and spoke confidentially, "There've been five missing persons. Two fans of the desert are overdue from their hike, then that old fellow, Wills – he's missing along with his dogs. Just came from out there. No sign of him."

Walt raised his eyebrows and wanted the rest. "You're two shy," he said.

"The others were passing through. One of them, going to Phoenix, filled up in Alamogordo, and the other was a weekend biker doing the open-road thing." The sheriff took a drink of the cool beer. "Both disappeared between Alley and The Crosses."

The phone rang as Cal lifted the cold beer and took another swallow. Walt answered, "Bunker." He raised his eyebrows as he passed the old phone to the Sheriff. "Guess who?" he said.

The sheriff took the receiver and said, "Caught me again, Bernice."

He listened. "Yeah." He listened some more, "Right." The sheriff looked at Walt and raised his brow. "Alright. Will do, Bern." He handed the receiver back to Walt. The barkeep twisted to hang up the receiver and turned back to the sheriff.

"Bernice said the storm's there," he said. "Starting to hit the station now. She said they're getting beat to hell with hail. All they can do is stay put until it's over. Heading our way. Be here in a couple of minutes." The wind whistled a little louder through the front doors.

"Sounds like it's stirring up out there," Walt said.

The lawman stared at the barkeep for a moment. "You sure can be selective about what you hear," he said with a shake of his head. "Anyway, if you don't draw that full house soon, maybe all you're going to get is three of a kind," he nodded at the tables. "Nobody's moving in this once it gets started," he said to Walt. "Rosales is supposed to be heading this way. There's a good chance he's going to run straight into it. Storm's going west, and he's heading east."

"Has he checked in with Bern?" Walt asked the lawman.

"Before. She can't raise him now, radio or cell. The storm," the sheriff answered. "Guess he'll find out about it on his own."

"Ahh, don't worry about him. Luis can take care of himself. He'll get here OK. He knows where to go," Walt said, shifting on his stool and lifting his beer. "Like I always say: The Bunker's the only place to be at the end of the world."

The two men turned to the threesome at the end of the bar as one called down, "Hey Sheriff, have you seen what's on the TV? It's all about the big storm. They even cut into the rodeo," said the middle barfly. He pointed to the wall-mounted small-screen television.

"Turn up the sound, Walt," the sheriff told the old man. "Let's hear what they have to say." He climbed onto his barstool across from Walt and leaned back to look down the bar at the weather map on the television screen.

Walt picked up the remote and fiddled with the buttons. The volume came up so everyone could hear the meteorologist intoning the dire possibilities and emphasizing the approaching sandstorm's magnitude. "…visible from space with winds reported at hurricane-force …"

One of the three guys at the end let out a whistle. "Sounds like the big one! We're all gonna be in sand up to our neck. I guess we better stay here all night. I'll watch the beer." The three fellas at the end laughed loudly.

Walt was leaning forward on his stool to see the screen. The sheriff called down the bar, "Guys, we want to hear this."

The TV weatherperson went on, "…as this unusual windstorm blows through White Sands, it looks like it's picking up a tremendous amount of dust and is forecast to move down, blanketing the Tularosa Basin southwest of Alamogordo, which, fortunately, is sparsely populated."

"That's us – sparsely populated," Walt said. "Guess all we account for is…" he was interrupted by the trio at the end.

"Three more beers, barkeep – and make it quick." Another one of the fellows yelled a little too loudly to Walt.

The sheriff turned his head to the three. "Guys," he said firmly.

They quieted. "Sorry, Walt. Three more beers, please," the middle guy said more to the sheriff than to the old barkeep.

Walt hopped from his stool and manned the taps, setting up three full-sized mugs and sliding them down the bar one at a time to the trio. He looked at his friend, the sheriff, and said, "They're just feelin' comfortable, Cal. Don't get peevish. Besides, without them, it'd be up to you and me to drink all this beer."

"You're the boss, Walt," the sheriff said to the barkeep as he climbed onto his stool.

The television weather expert summed up, "…so it could be worse; at least it isn't tracking toward any population centers. But anyone in the path of this should stay inside until it is over. We'll keep you up-to-date with any developments, so stay tuned to…."

Walt lifted the remote and turned down the volume as the forecast ended and the bull riding came back on.

"Stay inside – that's good advice for all," Walt said. He called over to the people at the tables, "You folks need anything else? It might be a long haul. May as well keep your whistles wet."

Russ stood and walked over to the sheriff and Walt.

"Well, yes, I guess we are going to be in here for a bit," he said, smiling at the sheriff and then looking to Walt. "Maybe another club soda for me and a wine spritzer for my wife. And, if you have any snacks –

pretzels or breadsticks, anything like that. We didn't expect to have to stop anywhere. As I said, we were driving from El Paso; the next stop was Santa Fe. Straight through, we thought it would be a five-hour drive, but it looks like it may take longer."

"Well, sir," Walt said to him, "we don't have wine anythings. Warm and cold beer, water, whiskey, and assorted hard liquors, Cuervo, and ginger ale – that's about it. There are peanuts and pretzels. I'll put together some sandwiches later on if it comes to that." Walt was off the stool again, filled a glass with soda water from the hose, dropped a swizzle stick in it, and took a can of ginger ale from under the bar with a glassful of ice. He lined the glasses and popped the can open on the bar in front of the man.

The sheriff looked the newcomer over and decided he was a retired teacher, and a look at his wife solidified his opinion. He gave the man a polite nod and pushed the bowl of pretzels closer to him.

"Thank you, Sheriff. Nice to know that Western hospitality is still the Code of the West." The teacher said in a friendly fashion. He took the ginger ale and glass of ice to his wife and came back to the bar.

"Now, did you mention the Code? There's more to it than hospitality," Walt said, "though that's a big part. And you're all welcome in the Bunker as long as you're thirsty, hungry, or need a place to lay your head."

"Oh, do you have rooms to let, too?" the man asked.

"No, but plenty of folks have slept on the bar when the need moves them," Walt replied. "Plus, there's a pass-out couch over on that side of the room if you just want to stretch for a spell," he added, pointing with his thumb to a far wall of the barroom.

"Well, not yet," the teacher laughed. "We noticed there's no cell signal in here. Can I presume that is because of the unusual nature of this interesting structure? It's built like a fortress – no windows, all concrete. Most likely constructed in the 1950s? Perhaps the early Sixties?" he said, looking around the barroom and up at the ceiling shadows.

"Of course, it wasn't built to be a bar — a tavern, that is," his eyes left the supporting columns, and he smiled again at Walt. "I'd say it was a military structure — yes," he continued, "Definitely a military structure. Most likely a hardened communications center." He looked at the large black and yellow sign over the door to the back. "Height of the Cold War, yes? Certainly, they don't build them like this anymore." He turned back to Walt. "It is quite a gem you have here," he said to the barman, climbing onto the barstool beside the sheriff.

"Please excuse my going on. I used to teach architecture before retiring. Went from California to Arizona," he said to the two men. The sheriff smiled.

"California? Arizona?" Walt said and shook his head. He leaned forward, took the glass of soda water from the bar, and dumped it in the sink. "How about a beer, professor?"

"Well," he paused, and his eyes went to his wife talking to the other woman, "Yes, I would like a beer — I would like one quite a bit, thank you."

"Uh-huh," the barkeep said as he squirted the brew into the empty glass. "Here you go," he said, setting it on the bar. "I'm Walt," he said to the professor. "And like he said, this here's Sheriff Jeffries. He's the law around these parts." The proprietor stepped back to his stool and climbed aboard.

The sheriff smiled at his friend cowpokin it up and said, "Name's Cal," as he lifted his boot to the brass rail and his glass of beer to meeting the professor again.

The retired man responded in kind, raising his foam-topped glass to each before taking a three-swallow quaff. He smacked his lips and smiled contentedly, which deepened the lines around his eyes worn by too many years of contentment. "That is very tasty, I must say."

"Well, don't say it too loud," Walt cautioned him as he threw a stage glance at the man's wife.

The man smiled, drained the short beer, and put the empty glass on the bar. "Quite tasty," he pronounced.

"As I was saying, gentlemen, I notice buildings. Noticing buildings has been my business for over 45 years. And this one is quite noticeable." He hiccupped.

Walt filled his empty glass with suds again, replacing it in front of the retiree. "Take two; they're small," he told the man.

"Oh, I probably shouldn't," he replied. But he did, lifting the head to his face. "Now, where was I?" he resumed. "Oh, yes. Oddly enough, I think this was a communications center because there's no cell signal here. While thick concrete will inhibit signals, it doesn't usually eradicate them – quite an interesting structure. Are you familiar with any of its history?" he asked as he lifted his beer.

The sheriff sighed and said to the professor, "Russ, get ready for tonight's ten-cent tour."

And Walt began.

"Well, professor, you are right about that. No radio waves, signals, not sound nor fury will pass these walls. For this here structure is the one and only Bunker. Built by the United States government in 1952 as a secret and remote command and control post for the White Sands proving grounds. Impervious to anything but a direct hit of an A-bomb. Safe from fallout, the red menace, and most of the local vermin." He bent his head toward the three fellows at the end of the bar. "Most," he said again. "The walls are ten feet thick, steel-reinforced concrete with lead lining, and it is also one big Faraday cage. It has power generation, air and water filtration, and enough fuel for a year. And all this was made back when they built things to last."

The proprietor took a breath, and the teacher took the opportunity to interject, "An absolutely magnificent building. It is a moment frozen in time. And underscored by the fact that there's not a clock to be seen in here," the professor said.

The sheriff smiled at Walt, leaned to the professor, and said, "You got right to the sweet spot of the Bunker, Russ. Not a clock to be seen."

The old teacher smiled at the lawman, "Well, I admire the décor, too — atomic age. This collection of science-fiction movie posters and civil defense memorabilia is astounding." He said, sweeping his half-a-glass around the barroom and ending on the black and yellow air raid shelter insignia over the concrete arch to the back room. "I take it there's a substantial subsystem to this structure – a basement or two?"

Walt narrowed his eyes and pursed his thin lips. "What, are you writing a book?" he asked. "Most folks would have taken that for just another sign," the barkeep said to the teacher. "Looks like you know what you're talking about."

"Military construction projects were always a special area of interest to me. I assumed that that sign was originally intended to direct people to the deeper shelters and living quarters," the professor said with a broad smile.

"You're right about that, Russ," Walt told him. "Makes me think you knew all about this place before you got here."

The suspicious undertone eluded the retired teacher. "No, no. I didn't know anything about this structure, but I'll tell you that I would have made a special trip if I knew it was here. What a wonderful example of mid-twentieth century Cold War it is," he said as he turned his stool to all points of the barroom. "Just spectacular," he said as he came back around to the bartender. "I have to ask – is there a chance I could see more of the building?"

"Well," Walt said and smiled slowly. He looked at the old fellow and then past him to his wife, chatting with the other woman at the table. "I guess you're on the up-and-up. I suppose that might be OK," he turned to the lawman. What do you think, Sheriff?"

The sheriff pulled the bowl of pretzels from the professor and picked one out. "Russ is alright with me," he said.

The professor beamed. "Thank you very much, gentlemen." He pushed the beer glass back and slid off his barstool.

"Whoa there, Russ," Walt said, waving him back in place. "Not so fast. We got the whole night ahead of us — at least some of it. Besides, this will be at least a four or five-beer tour, and you're still on your second."

The former teacher laughed and returned to his stool, "If you insist, Walt. I will comply to the best of my ability." Russ lifted the half-full and drank it down, putting the short glass back on the bar top. He ate a few pretzels while Walt replenished the brews for the three men.

"I notice you sent large beer mugs down the bar to the gentlemen at the other end. Up here, you seem to use small drinking glasses for the beer. May I ask why?" the retired man asked. "By the way, not that I am complaining, not at all." He smiled happily at the barkeep and lifted his refilled glass.

"Well, a matter of preference, that's all," Walt answered. "Smaller glasses keep it fresher. Beer's no good that's lost its zest." He reached over and patted the taps. "Besides, the well's right here."

"I think I agree with you, Walt," the professor responded after savoring another sip. "Very, very tasty," he said as he continued surveying the interior of the barroom. "Just a remarkable structure," he said, "I doubt if there's another like it." He stroked his cropped beard in a habit of thoughtfulness. "Just how was it that this building ended up a tavern?" he asked Walt.

"Well, it was easier than you might think," Walt replied. "And all thanks to your government." The old barkeep settled into his high-backed stool, stretching his stiff leg to rest on a lower shelf.

"In a nutshell, they build it to last a hundred years and lose interest in it in twenty. As you may remember, the atom bomb lost its luster by the Seventies. They couldn't get shod of their silos and shelters fast enough. As far as the Bunker goes, they just couldn't figure out how to demolish it."

Walt took a swallow of his beer to keep the professor and sheriff company. He smacked his lips and lifted the glass again.

"Now me, being a young entrepreneur at the time, could not resist such an opportunity." The barman motioned to the room with his free hand, the other held his glass. "I got familiar with these parts, passing through, doing some work around here when I saw this place. It was abandoned – closed up with 'No Trespassing' and 'Keep Out' signs, but it beckoned me, you know? Guess I found my white whale in the middle of the desert. The Bunker."

"Anyway, I staked my claim and, with a little finagling with the military and who-have-you, it was mine – lock, stock, and barrel. Seemed like the best idea in the world to put a watering hole in the middle of the desert – especially with all the thirsty military folks around." He lifted his beer and finished it, smacking the glass on the bar. "And I got it for a song. Take some comfort in the fact that the government benefits the people occasionally, even if it's by their wastefulness."

"Well, I can certainly see the attraction, Walt," the professor said. "It's your castle in the sand, and what man does not want to be the king in his own castle?"

His wife chimed in right on cue from over at the tables. "Russel, did you get any snacks?" she called sweetly to him.

The professor smiled at the two men and pushed his empty beer glass across the bar to Walt. "Excuse me, gentlemen," he said as he got up. "I may not have gotten a castle but ended up with the damsel in distress," he whispered as he picked up the pretzel bowl and stepped off the barstool. "Or, I should say, the fair maiden," he added, turning to take the bowl of pretzels to the table.

The sheriff smiled as the professor walked away. "Some colts are happier in the corral," he said to the barkeep.

"Well, he ain't no colt, but I'd say he knows what's what," the barkeep said. "Might be something to be said for taking the bit for some comfort."

"Trying to tell me something, Walt?" The sheriff pushed his empty glass across the polished bar and aligned it with the professor's. "You're not thinking of settling down, are you?"

The old barkeep pulled his wrinkled face into a frown and pointed it at the lawman. "You're just about the funniest cop I ever met," he said to him. He pushed the empty glass back to the sheriff, then leaned back in his stool. "Get your own," he said, picking up his crossword puzzle.

The sheriff leaned over to fill his glass from the center spigot. Just as he finished the head, the noise of the front doors opening and the howl of the wind coming inside made him look into the mirror. The saloon doors were swinging back and forth.

The lawman turned with his beer as one of the slatted swinging doors was pushed open by a bright yellow hardhat in the hand of a large man as he stepped into the bar, followed by a younger, thinner version of himself.

"How's it going, folks?" the utility worker said to the room as he dropped his goggles and helmet on the nearest empty table. He looked from face to face. "We were hoping to hide out in here until this blows by." The younger lineman followed suit, putting his gear on the table.

"Make yourselves at home, boys. Belly up, we're glad to have you," Walt called over to them as he put his puzzle down. He got up from his stool and hop-stepped to man the taps. "Beers for you two?" the barman asked.

"Sounds good," the big man said. The pair made their way to the barstools, nodding to the folks at the tables as they passed. "Great, thanks," the older lineman said to the barkeep. "It's pretty dry outside," he added as he lifted his beer to Walt.

"What's it doing now?" the sheriff asked the pair. He was back on his stool and spun to face the newcomers.

"Blowing like Hell itself. Hot, dusty, and dark. Going to be a mess to clean up, but there'll be lots of OT on the lines," the senior man answered. "I'd say the main act is just getting warmed up. The wind must have doubled the time it took to cross the lot. We got here just in the nick. That storm's been on our tail for the last five miles." The big utility worker ran his hand over his jaw, then wiped each of his eyes and picked up his beer. He prompted the young man to follow suit. "Take a swallow, Brandon. Wash some of that dust down." His junior partner lifted his mug and took a drink.

"Anyhow, we saw a couple of boxes blow along the way here – surprised you still have power," the senior man continued. "My name's Mike, by the way," he tipped his glass at Walt and the sheriff, "and this is Brandon, another line monkey that keeps the juice flowing," he said, clapping the young man's shoulder. "Guess the local power's holding up. That's a surprise. Must have been what, four transformers we saw blow on the way here?" he asked the young man.

"Yeah – and don't forget what that crew by Holloman said," his young partner added. "They said there was huge hail. That was before the radio stopped working. They said it was as big as softballs. If that hits, and with all that lightning and wind out there, it's going to be light's out all over the place."

"Well, then, lucky for us. We've got the only electricians for fifty miles," Walt laughed. "We're going to have to take good care of you fellows."

The young lineman took a good gulp of beer and licked his lips. "You sure knew the right place to head to, Mike." He looked at his partner, then the barkeep. "That's what he said when we saw those clouds coming in – 'time to get to the Bunker, he said – and we tore up the road, too. Must have gone a hundred and twenty to keep in front of that storm." The young man smiled, then looked at the sheriff's badge. He straightened his smile and said, "Well, we probably didn't go all that fast."

The sheriff lifted his beer into the air without looking at the workers. "Here's to desperate times," he said and took a drink.

The young lineman's partner laughed quietly as he drank his suds.

"Headed straight here, is that right?" Walt asked. "Don't recall ever seeing either of you guys before," he told the linemen.

"Never been here," Mike said. "Always noticed the place, though. Seemed like the best bet the way the storm was moving in."

Walt got on his stool and leaned back, overtly studying the two. "That's the motto: the best place to be at the end of the world," the bartender said. He stretched to pick up his glass. "Hail, you said? I hate hail."

The sheriff slid the TV remote to Walt. The barkeep picked it up, squinted at the buttons, and leaned forward to point it at the set on the wall at the far end of the bar. The picture changed from the rodeo channel static to one of the parking lot's security cameras.

"Whew – would you look at that?" the barman said.

Everyone in the bar looked up at the screen; the new fellows leaned back to get their best view. The sheriff's Bronco parked in the front was centered in the grainy image, showing now and then through the dense gusts of sand. Walt turned his head to the lawman and said, "What's the matter with you, Cal? Can't you read? It says, 'Parking For Horses Only' right on the rail."

"Sheriff's emergency," the lawman replied. "I was ten-fifty-one."

Walt considered that for a moment, then relented. "Well, in that case," he said. "Anyway, take a look out there. The best I can make out is the storm's here. Between what it looks and sounds like, I'd say we're in it."

The wind howled and pounded the front doors. Walt looked at the big lineman and said, "That's some wind outside. That's a fact." He listened and shook his head. "According to that weather fella, the storm's coming down from the north," the bartender said. "That will drive the Downwinders nuts. That's about all they need."

The young utility worker looked at the others and asked, "Who are the Downwinders?"

The senior lineman put his mug down, elbows on the bar, and answered. "The Downwinders are people that live out in the desert, mostly south of, downwind of White Sands, like around here. There's a lot of radiation from atom bomb tests left over in the desert." He lifted his mug and took a drink of his beer before he went on. "Did you know there were over two hundred atom bombs blown up in New Mexico alone?" He shook his head and took another sip.

"No way," his junior associate exclaimed. "Two hundred nukes right out there in the desert? Really?" The young man shook his head. "That's insane," he said.

"It's true what he said," Walt interjected. "And that's just New Mexico. Hundreds and hundreds of A-bombs went off in this country – all for testing. We were in an atomic war, and no one knew it."

"I had no clue," Brandon confirmed.

"Anyway," Mike continued, "when the wind kicks up, it blows that radioactive dust all around. Usually south, straight to the folks down there. They're downwind. Get it? Downwinders?"

"I get it," Brandon answered. "They are downwind – and that's bad."

"Lots of people have gotten sick. Lots," Mike went on. "I think they get a bad wrap, and the whole thing is underplayed – that's what I'm saying. My aunt was a Downwinder. She was a good woman, but she got sick. Radiation is bad stuff. I don't know why we live around here."

"Might be that not everyone believes it, that's why," Walt said.

"A lot do," the lineman said, turning back to the barman. "My uncle believes it."

One of the bigmouths from the end of the bar called down, "Not everyone lives in a lead-lined bunker, Walt."

The sheriff looked at the three guys, and they went back to talking to each other. Billy could never keep his mouth shut.

The wind wailed, trying to get in, rattling the heavy wooden doors.

Walt was fiddling with the remote, switching between exterior security camera views, each showing darkness. "Well, maybe it will move out as fast as it moved in. Bet it's gone in two more beers."

"I'll drink to that," said the sheriff.

The young man spun slowly on his barstool, taking in the room. He said to his partner, "Hey Mike, check that classic sci-fi on the walls? This stuff is vintage. Where did you get all of this?" he asked, peering through the dim bar light at the assortment of posters.

"You collect things over time." Walt smiled as he pulled two more beers from the tap. "Been here so long, it accumulates." The old man scratched his stubbled chin and looked around the dim barroom.

"A fellow used to come in – he was married to a woman who worked at the movie theater in Las Cruces, way back when. That's where most of the movie posters came from," the barman remembered. "He had them at his house. He became a regular after his wife passed. Started bringing all of this in. Wanted to make it a home-away-from-home."

Walt put the mugs in front of the utility workers. "As a matter of fact," the barman pointed to an old poster on the wall, "that one you're looking at was one of the first he brought in, as I recall."

The guys at the bar looked over to the dingy sheet, smoke-cured over time and showing angry-looking giant ants, one with a woman in its jaws, invading a burning city. The title below the illustration read "*La Humanidad en Peligro*" in large red letters.

"What does that mean?" Brandon asked.

The sheriff slowly swirled his half glass of beer and said, "Look out, everyone!" He took a few swallows, finished his beer, and put his glass down.

"Close enough," Walt agreed.

"So that was a Mexican movie?" Brandon asked.

"No," Walt replied. "That was one of the first Hollywood sci-fi movies. A big hit. That poster was made for the dubbed version they sent south of the border. The original version is hanging up somewhere over there." The barman pointed to the posters on the far wall.

"Yeah, I see them. Next to the giant robot poster, in the middle," Brandon said, identifying the wrong group of movie sheets.

"No, no," Walt corrected him. "Not them," he said, dismissing the young man's pointing hand. The bartender pointed further along the wall. "THEM!" he pronounced.

"Never heard of it," the young man said. "When did that come out?"

"A long, long time ago. Back in the 1950s," Walt answered.

"Wow, no wonder I never heard of it," the young man said.

The bartender smiled at him, leaned back in his seat, and folded his arms. "That's not why," he said.

Walt went on, "But, anyway, one thing begets another. The first poster goes up because that fella brings it in. Like I said, he was a regular here for a while. Then he brings in some others, and it sort of catches on. Pretty soon, other folks are bringing in the strangest things as if I wanted them. That was back when this place was more popular." He pointed above the mirror behind the bar. "How about that? Three-horned cow skull; you don't see that every day."

"Anyhow, like I said, after a while, it all accumulates. I think everyone for fifty miles around emptied their attics into this place." Walt laughed and looked around his barroom. "Hardly a bare spot on the walls now." He turned back to the two workers. "There sure were a lot of oddballs in these parts. Especially then," he laughed again, "and especially around here. This is one weird place, you know."

"Strange thoughts go with living out here," the senior line worker said, looking up at the old man.

80

"The desert is a place of mirages, that's for sure," the barkeep said. He studied the big man for a moment. "But it's also a place of strange truths, especially this place," he said to him.

The lineman shrugged and lifted his mug. "I suppose one place is as strange as the next," he said to the bartender.

"You're right, especially around here," Walt replied. "Ever look at a map and connect the dots?" He leaned to the utility workers and lowered his voice, "White Sands, Los Alamos, Area 49, Trinity, Sandia – not to mention Radium Springs and Roswell. And definitely don't mention military bases not on the map."

The young utility worker paused mid-pretzel, "You think there's a connection between all of those places?" he asked.

"All of those places?" Walt scoffed. "You know what they are? They are warehouses storing the truth; they are laboratories experimenting with our beliefs; they are factories manufacturing our future."

The wind rattled the front doors and moaned when they wouldn't open.

The sheriff pushed his empty glass across the wood to the fill'er up side of the bar.

"I love it when he talks like this," the lawman said. Walt turned his head to look at his friend and smiled. He took his glass, held it under the tap, and limped over to put the refill in front of the lawman.

The young utility worker continued a slow rotation, surveying the surroundings from his stool. He stopped, then spun himself back to face the bar and Walt.

"So, there's a conspiracy." The young man said.

The old man half-agreed. "I suppose. But that's a small word for it."

Walt let the storm talk for a minute, then shook his head.

Brandon smiled at his partner and shrugged. "What about that one?" he said, pointing his almost empty mug at a poster. It featured a screaming woman threatened by a monstrous space alien under the title *The Thing From Another World*. "Didn't they remake that?" he asked no one. "It's very retro, like a museum. Altogether awesome," the young man pronounced.

"Look at that one with the robot." The young utility worker said, pointing to a poster on a support column. "That one is awesome too. I don't know what it's about, but it's awesome. If I had these, I'd wallpaper my house with them."

"Looks like that's what our host did, Brandon," the older lineman said.

"Nope, even better than that," Walt replied. "Other people did this. I might have given them a thumbtack or two, but I didn't pay a thin dime for any of this. Folks just kept bringing it in. Most I did was not stop them," the barkeep said with a grin.

"Seriously?" Brandon said. "Do you have any idea what all of this stuff is worth?"

"No, do you?" Walt growled back at him.

"No. Not exactly. But a lot, I bet," the young man replied, finishing his beer. "I just meant it's all very cool," he added.

"I guess it is at that," Walt said, taking a long pull of beer and taking a new look at his familiar surroundings.

Brandon pointed to a poster of *Tobor the Great* wrapped around two sides of a concrete column and large enough to disappear into the shadows of the ceiling.

"That one is great," he said. "It says so."

"It's awesome," the older lineman said into his beer.

Walt laughed and said, "That's Tobor. Robot spelled backward. It wasn't that bright. Your phone's got way more smarts than him. But even that pile of junk was part of the real web."

The old man motioned for their empty beer mugs and hopped off his stool to the taps. Mike pushed them across the bar to Walt. He half-filled one and slid it back to Brandon.

"What real web?" the young man asked, looking into his beer.

"The web of lies," Walt replied, filling Mike's mug to the top and pushing it over.

"Uh-huh. The what?" the younger lineman asked.

"Nothing," Walt replied, pulling a small towel from under the bar.

Pointing over his shoulder with his thumb, the twenty-something smiled. "OK. What's with *The Thing*? That is cool – I mean, the artwork. Looks like some fun sci-fi," he said.

"There's nothing fun about that one, son," Walt said, pushing the refill to him. "That's not science fiction. That is science faction."

The sheriff looked at his old friend over the rim of his glass and shook his head.

"Faction?" the young man said. "What do you mean? Like it's supposed to be true?"

"I mean, there are more things that come down from the heavens and up from hell than you know about – and they don't want you to know about."

The young man lifted his new beer, took a drink, then asked, "Who don't?" He took another sip and waited for Walt to answer.

The barkeep eyed both utility workers and wiped the bar. After a few swipes, he leaned forward over the bar top.

"Let 'em have it, Walt," the lawman said without looking up from his beer.

The small group listened quietly. The moan of the wind was low and twisted into a voice asking somebody to open the door.

The old man nodded slowly, staring intently at the two men. He wiped the bar top some more and looked around the room. "Who doesn't want you to know the truth?" he asked in a whisper. "Why the people that control the world. That's who."

The big utility worker smiled broadly, looking into his glass of beer. "I'm not following," he said.

Walt sighed and ran his fingers through his white hair. "They control information: the educational system, the news, media, everything. They control what we think, what we believe, and what we know to be true. Everything. They control the world." He gave a lazy wave to the movie posters everywhere in the bar room.

Mike shook his head. "I don't know. That's kind of hard to believe," he said politely.

"Believe what you want," Walt answered, waving at the poster collection. "That is the fatal flaw of humanity. We can all believe what we want." Now Walt laughed.

"They turn fact into fiction. We've been told all of this isn't true. They have manipulated everything, so even the idea of real mutations or alien visitors is only for the fringe. Everyone knows it's all just made-up science fiction."

"Science faction," the young man corrected. "So, you think there's a plot, a plan, or whatever to keep the truth covered up by making it all unbelievable?" Brandon thought for a moment, then said, "Why not? That sounds as good as any of the others. But it's a conspiracy, even if you want to call it something different."

"There it is," the sheriff said, and he put his empty glass down. "What's in a name?"

"Well, whatever you want to call it, it's worked," Walt said. "What you believe now was cooked up by the government and the real powers behind them. They are people interested in particular outcomes." Walt wiped the bar some more. "But of course, the ones that started it are gone now. Most of them, anyway. Still, they'd be tickled pink to see how deep their plan took root – everyone's been bamboozled into believing just what they wanted them to believe from way back." He limped back and climbed onto his chair.

"Oh, black helicopters, mind control, caught in the matrix, like that," the young guy said dismissively, putting his mug down on the bar. "Like I said, the big con-spiracy, emphasis on 'con'."

Walt leaned in his seat and looked at the young man. He laughed, threw the towel over his shoulder, brought a fresh bowl of pretzels from under the bar and slid it to the two utility workers. "You're talking about now," he said to them. "I'm talking about back then. I'm telling you about what started all of this," he whirled a finger through the air.

"You know, it's not the same people running things now. You have to remember, I'm talking about a time gone by. Must have been what – seventy, eighty years ago?" The old man ate a few pretzels and leaned back again to get comfortable. "But what these behind-the-scenes types started still goes on: half-truths, outright lies, misinformation. That's the world now."

"So, how is that new?" the senior lineman asked. "I'd say it's always been that way. As long as people have been around, the ones that put themselves in charge do whatever they want and say whatever they will." He picked three pretzels from the bowl and popped them into his mouth in quick succession.

"Not exactly what I'm talking about," Walt said. "Of course, it's not new for the ones in power to lie. Look at how religion has been manipulated throughout history. For thousands of years, religions, even about forgiving and the Golden Rule, were used to start wars. Not because of the religion but because of the people that ran them. Power-hungry people."

The barman stretched his bum leg and shook his head. "There is something fundamentally wrong with anyone that wants to be in charge.

They always think too much of themselves and too little of everyone else."

"What was new were the methods of control through the airwaves, movies, and mass entertainment. It was new because of the sheer numbers influenced. Millions of people believe what they see, what they're shown."

"Maybe the amount of people is more impressive," Mike said as he put his beer on the bar. "But just because people started going to the movies every Saturday night instead of church every Sunday morning doesn't make this anything that hasn't been going on since the Stone Age," he said to the barkeep. "The message's the same – believe what we say – only how it's delivered has changed."

Walt shook his head. "Like I said, that was only part of what changed. The other part was what they were hiding," he said. "Things had changed, the world had changed, and they were sure of what to do with it." He paused, then added, "And if there's one thing that scares me, it's people who are absolutely sure they are right." Walt nodded knowingly and let the barroom go quiet, except for the groan of the storm. Looking past the linemen, he saw the people at the tables were listening to their conversation.

"Now, don't overlook the fact that these were people used to making decisions," the bartender continued, "These were the people that made this country and the modern world. Remember, we started with the horse and buggy and ended up putting a man on the moon in the span of fifty years. That's impressive. People were different."

"Oh, hooray, the great generation," Brandon said. "No other generations measure up." The young man rolled his eyes dramatically. "You know, that's all you get from old ... I mean, guys from your side. But we have our problems, too, you know."

"Oh sure, you're right. You'll get no argument from me." Walt smiled. "Most of your problems come from having too much time on your hands. But I'll tell you what; there's nothing like building a country, fighting Nazis, and keeping a couple of hundred million people safe from the Red Menace to keep you busy for a few years."

"Yeah, and now it's all falling apart," the older lineman said, taking a few more pretzels.

"Thanks for making my point. But priorities are different now. Everyone's concerned with what other people say about them." Walt shook his head, "I can't see giving a kick in the dirt about what other folks think."

"Is that right?" the sheriff chuckled.

The barman looked at the sheriff, gave a quick laugh, and went on, "The public needed to be protected, at least in the mind of the authorities, shielded from some harsh realities, especially the new realities of the time. And it wasn't really to protect people, but the society, the status quo. I guess they treated the public like children. There were things you couldn't tell them. They'd get too scared. They had to be protected."

The older lineman motioned to the walls, the civil defense signs, and the atomic bomb pictures hanging up. "Like that? That was pretty scary for people."

"Sure," Walt said, pointing to the black-and-white photo of the atomic mushroom thumbtacked behind the bar. 'Trinity - 1945' was neatly hand-lettered on the lower right. "They couldn't keep a lid on everything. It wasn't all under control, but it generally worked out. We're here, right? Stack the wins against the losses, and they come out on top. You can't argue that."

The lineman shrugged and drank some beer.

"Besides," Walt continued, "they kept the worst of it from us."

He paused, took a long breath, and leaned a thin arm in a worn flannel sleeve on the bar, "Take that movie poster you pointed out before, young fellow. You said it was 'unbelievable.' It is unbelievable – they wanted it that way. Want to know what is believable about it? I'll tell you

87

– and I can tell you because you hear plenty of things over fifty years, especially when you're the only watering hole around all of these secret government bases. There are plenty of secret doings around here, too, all those places I mentioned before and a couple of others I haven't. Heck, it's just a little too strange that on one square of the map, the first atomic bomb went off, a UFO crashed, there are more secret bases than you can shake a stick at, and twice as many coverups than even the conspiracy nuts know about."

Walt hunched over his elbows on the bar, "And I can tell you something about a good many of these 'science fiction stories,'" his eyes went around the barroom, "there's as more truth in some of them than there is fiction."

"And I'm not the only one that knows it, isn't that right, Cal?" Walt looked at the sheriff.

"Don't ask me. I'm busy drinking on duty," the lawman answered without looking at any of them.

Walt snorted at his friend and went on without him. "Matter-of-fact, more than one of those fellas would come in. Ones that worked on the bases back in the heyday. More than a few settled around here when they retired. Like they could never leave this desert behind. One in particular. He was the guy I told you about that got all of this started, all these movie posters."

"He was old when he started coming in just after I got the place. He had been a metalworker over at Holloman. He was in the original crew on Trinity, then Roswell. He worked on the whole shmear from the get-go," Walt went on, "and he could never get over some of the things he knew. No sir, big secrets become big burdens, he'd say."

The barkeep took a refresher from his beer glass and looked thoughtfully upward, "That's right; he started bringing in these posters." The old-timer stroked his chin, "Granville was his name. He brought that *Thing* sheet in and hung it up one night, a while after we became chummy. I didn't care what he hung up. He'd bring in another and another from time to time, and that's what caused other people to start adding all sorts of things to this grand collection." He spun his hand in the air, made a crazy face, and motioned to the walls and curios.

"Then, old Granville asked me if I wanted to hear the truth about the science fiction. And now, I guess I'm going to tell you what he told me …."

The storyteller leaned on one elbow toward the linemen and said, "He knew the truth behind these FBI productions from the 1950s. He told me how the feds ran the show, worked with Hollywood, and put out these fake films and books, even comic books. All of them were made to hide the real goings-on and keep the truth away from the public."

Walt lowered his voice so everyone in the bar could barely hear him, "Old Granville knew the facts behind these phonied-up shows, this one, that one, that one over there, and all the others," he said, pointing to one movie poster or another as he spoke.

"And, as he got to the end of his days, the secrets were too much for him to keep in," Walt continued, "That one you asked about, *The Thing*, Granville told me that it was the granddaddy of them all, the first science fiction propaganda movie they made. Originally, the films were a way to break the truth to the public. That was the plan. That's what he told me. But the Hollywood people and powers that be saw it was better to sell it as entertainment, to make fun of the whole thing and keep a lid on the truth. So that's the business they got into, discrediting real reports of what was happening, of what was going on, whether it was here or at the North Pole."

Walt furrowed his well-worn brow at the group and lowered his voice to a whisper, "And, it worked. Worked like a charm. Mention anything now about a UFO, and you're a lunatic. Worked like a charm," he repeated with a knowing nod.

They were silent. The sheriff quietly finished his suds and abruptly put his glass down too hard on the bar, making the pair of linemen jump. He smiled.

"So, you're saying the government was involved in making these old sci-fi movies, and they made them to hide the truth," Mike said over his beer, "and to make anyone interested seem like a looney."

"Yessir, that is it in a nutshell. And it all started right here. If it doesn't seem odd to you that the start of the atom bomb, the time of the flying saucer, and the age of the cover-up all kicked off from here, maybe it should. Granville knew plenty and told me plenty," the barkeep said. Walt looked from side to side, leaned in, and lowered his voice. "So, about that *Thing* poster, he told me …"

The secret was cut short by the loud bang of the front door flying open and the roaring wind. The inside saloon swingers flapped on their hinges. Everyone jumped and turned to the doors, holding their breath. Then the outer doors slammed, shutting out the howl of the wind.

It got quiet as everything settled down, and they all watched the doors. A young woman's voice came from the hallway, quietly cursing, spitting, and sputtering. Then footsteps came to the swinging doors. Small, dusty hands wrapped around the top of the doors and pushed them slowly open. A gray-haired, gray-faced woman in gray stepped through the doors and into the barroom. She looked at the silent faces.

She was covered in dust from head to toe. The wind groaned against the front doors.

"Hello," she said, slowly looking across the room, ending on Walt and the sheriff. "I wanted to get out of the storm."

Walt was about to answer when she continued, "It is unbelievable out there," the newcomer went on, "I couldn't see a thing. My car was pulverized by that hail. It broke the windshield, the sunroof. I barely made it in. I couldn't see a thing. I just ran. I got lost right outside in the parking lot," she took a breath and paused, then said, "Is it OK I'm in here? I mean, you're not some human sacrifice cult or anything, are you?" she asked the group.

They stared at her.

She stared back, then murmured, "I'd like it a lot better if somebody said something." She paused to take a breath.

"We were just waiting for a chance," the sheriff told the monochrome woman.

"Don't mind him," Walt said. "You just come on in and sit yourself down. Join the group. You're safe in here. You're in the Bunker, and that's the safest place there is."

The professor stood politely from his chair. "Yes, yes. Please come in and join us," he gestured across the room. "We are all taking refuge from the storm. I'm Russ, and this is my wife Em," he said, holding a hand on her shoulder, "and, in that chair, is Syl, also a refugee from the weather. Over by the bar, our host is Walt, and next to him is the sheriff. I'll let the other gentlemen introduce themselves so I don't get their names wrong."

His wife and the other woman added their welcomes, and the others greeted the new arrival.

"Thank you," she said to the group, dropping her bag next to the linemen's gear on the table nearest the swinging doors. "My name's Nikki." The lamplight filtered through the small clouds of desert dust falling from her, "Sorry about all this – I'm all dust."

"No problem, dearie," Walt said with a wink to the sheriff. "You can leave your clothes over there."

She stared across the room at the old barman, then laughed. "Any port in a storm, I guess."

"Don't mind them, hon," Syl called over to her, "They're harmless."

"Thanks," Walt objected. "But she's right, Nikki. Just funnin'. You come on in and make yourself at home."

"Thank you," she said, wiping the grit from her eyes. "It's crazy out there. I'm lucky to make it in."

"Honey, did you say that it was hailing? Did it really damage your car?" Syl asked her.

Gray Nikki answered, "Yes, it was awful. Broke all the windows. I ran with a blanket over my head. Lucky there was enough of it to protect me."

"Oh no," the professor's wife said, "What about our cars? Should we check?"

"Nothing you can do about it now," Walt said, "You'll have to wait for the storm to pass – shouldn't be too much longer."

Nikki walked to the bar. She pushed her hair back, streaking the grime on her cheeks, and looked at the palms of her hands; then, she looked at the mirror behind the bar.

"Holy mackerel! Look at me – I'm covered. I look like a ghost." She pushed at her hair again and tilted her head, looking at her reflection. "I have to clean up. Where's the restroom?" she asked, walking back over her dust trail to retrieve her bag.

"The ladies' head is to your left, madame." Walt pointed to a door with a retro cowgirl silhouette burned into a wood placard hanging unevenly from a single nail on the door.

"Delightful," the woman said. She shouldered her pack and smiled at the sheriff as she walked past him to the door.

"De-lightful," the barkeep said, looking after her and giving the sheriff another wink. "She seems like someone worth knowing."

"I don't know how you could tell," the lawman replied. "Anyway, I like women a little cleaner than that," he said as she went through the door.

"That's your problem, partner. Anyway, she's going to clean up just fine, you'll see. In the meantime," he went to the taps, bringing back three more cold ones and putting two in front of the sheriff.

"One at a time's good for me," the sheriff said.

"One of them ain't yours. One of them's hers, and one's mine. Now, use your head and move your ass over a seat and make room for the lady."

The sheriff smiled and said, "You're the boss." He shook his head as he moved his new beer, hat, and himself, one seat to the right and two stools from the linemen.

"So, what were you saying about that poster?" Brandon asked Walt as the barman reached the shelf for the bottle of Rocking Chair. He poured two fingers, put the bottle back on the shelf, and pushed the glass to the empty stool.

"Not yours either," Walt said, looking at the sheriff.

"That's right," the bartender continued, looking at the utility worker, "I was telling you what that fella Granville told me about all these old movies. That's why he collected these posters. He'd go and see these movies. In fact, he went so much he ended up marrying the sister of the guy that owned the movie house – did I tell you that? Anyway, he knew the real story behind those flicks. Knew the people involved in making them, too, the government people, you'd say."

The sheriff sat at the bar and watched his beer go down as his friend talked.

"Quite a thing, hearing people laugh and have fun, all the while knowing what was really going on. There was plenty of science behind these fictions," Walt continued, "I guess that's what got to him the most, realizing what he knew to be true, most thought to be only made-up stories. And they were fed fiction by their government over and over. But like I said, it worked."

Brandon pushed his empty beer mug forward. As Walt began to climb off his stool to refill, the young man held his hand over his glass. "You mean you believe in flying saucers and all these other stories? I mean, no offense, but they're pretty crazy."

"Agreed," Walt said, sitting back. "But I've been around a bit and met a lot of people. I've listened to some of them, too, ones that have been involved with secrets and always surprised me how close-mouthed they can be, even after drinking. But two things make a person open up," he said, leaning back.

"What's that?" the young man asked.

"Old age and a conscience," Walt replied. "Though a couple of drinks can help."

"Probably helps if you want to see a few monsters out in the desert, too," the older lineman said.

"Well, Granville took a belt now and then, but not much," Walt laughed. "And the fact is, he told me some pretty credible tales of monsters in the desert. Not very far from here, either. Even had some photos he sneaked."

"If that's the case," the big lineman answered, "why would you stick around? Monsters!" he snorted. "Why wouldn't you leave?"

"Leave?" Walt straightened up, feigning surprise. "That's why I stayed."

The cowgirl hinges squeaked, and the gray woman who went in came out dusted off. She walked to the empty barstool next to the sheriff, eyeing the glass of beer.

"Is this for me? I hope so." She said, dropping her sack on the floor by the stool.

"Just for you, sweetheart," Walt said. "And this, too." He leaned forward and pushed the whiskey toward her. "Private stock. Take a few sips; best thing for jangled-up nerves."

"I've never been in anything like that before," she said, lifting the whiskey, "It sounded like a million rocks hitting the car. That ice hurt, too – and that wind! I have a couple of bruises, but I was so lucky to find this place and get inside. Just luck – I couldn't see a thing."

"Well, you're safe as can be in here, hon. Get some of that in you. That'll warm you up." Walt smiled kindly at her, "And you're in the seat of honor too, right here by me."

She sipped the liquor and blew air through her pursed lips. "Oh, that is terrible," she gasped in surprise. "I thought the tall, hard-drinking sheriff was the guest of honor." She smiled as she hopped up on the stool and looked at the empty glass collection on the bar. "I don't want to dethrone him."

"Naw," the bartender said, "He's just a regular."

"And you're wrong on another count," the sheriff said as he turned to look at the woman. He stopped mid-sentence when he saw her all dusted off.

"You were right, Walt. She cleaned up right nice," Cal said, increasing his drawl and looking her up and down, head to toe.

The woman's smile widened, "Wow. You guys really are old-school." She laughed. "Gotta love it, I guess. Anyway, you're too old to change now." She looked at the sheriff. "Well, you won't let the little lady drink alone, are you?" She lifted the whiskey and asked, "and what was the other thing, sheriff? You said I was wrong on another count. What's that?"

The lawman smiled at her and replied, "You said I was hard-drinking." He raised his short beer to her, "Nothing hard about it, ma'am," he said as he finished his glass.

"Right you are," she said, draining her whiskey in one gulp. "I needed that. Whew!" she exhaled the fumes. "Wow!" she gasped, "Why does anyone drink this?" Her voice was different.

"Might want to go easy on that," Walt told her. "That was a double shot."

"A what?" she asked, reaching for the cool beer chaser.

"Never mind," Walt said, raising his brow.

The woman smiled, and her eyes passed by the sheriff, taking in her surroundings. "This place just might be heaven," she said, sipping the suds with a little laugh, "Except for this beer – it's pretty bad, Walt. Do you mind if I call you Walt, Walt? Like I said, my name's Nikki."

She extended her hand over the bar, and the barkeep took it briefly, saying, "Well, pleased to meet you, Nikki, much obliged."

"Me too, Walt," she said. "You're a good egg. I haven't made my mind up about this guy yet." She tilted her head to the sheriff.

"Aw, he'll grow on you. He can't help it. Doesn't say much, but he's a good fellow in a clutch."

The sheriff was looking at her in the mirror, and she met his eyes in the reflection. "Thanks – I'll consider myself warned," she said to them both.

"Sounded like you were in the middle of a conversation when I came out. What were you talking about?" She took her eyes off the sheriff and looked at Walt.

He motioned with a nod to the utility workers next to the sheriff. "Those two fellows were asking about all the junk that got stuck on the walls over the years."

Nikki leaned forward and waved down the bar to the linemen. "I noticed. It is quite a collection, Walt," she said, slowly swiveling on the stool to take in the exhibits. "Looks like you're a real fan of the Atomic Age."

"Not really," he said.

"Science fiction movies, then?" she ventured.

"Not so much," Walt replied with a head shake, "at least not the fiction part."

"The old west, the desert?"

"One's cliché, the other's too dry, too hot, too cold, and too damn dusty," the bartender answered.

"You're a man of contradictions," she laughed as her seat came around again to face Walt.

"You don't like the desert, you don't like the west, not a fan of the atom or science fiction movies, and yet, here you are in the middle of the Chihuahuan Desert where they test rockets, surrounded by cow skulls, brandin' irons, civil defense signs, atom bomb photos, and monster movie posters from a hundred years ago." She accented her remarks with an index finger from the beer glass, pointing to the items on the walls without looking as she named them.

She turned to the sheriff, put her empty glass down a little too hard, and brought her elbow to the bar, propping her chin on her hand. "I don't rightly know if I believe this hombre. What about you, Sheriff?"

The sheriff noticed she swayed slightly on the stool as she smiled at him. "I think the little lady needs a refill, barkeep," he said to Walt.

"I think she needs a sandwich," Walt replied.

Nikki turned her head on her hand back to Walt, "You are right; hardly had a bite all day," she said, then paused. "All I've had is a couple of little tacos. I'm so hungry, I could eat a house. You are absolutely right about that, but living in the desert is wrong if you don't want to. I don't get that. Do you tall, dark, and sheriff?" She batted her big eyes at the space between the two men.

The two friends looked at each other and then back at the young woman.

"Maybe you're right," the sheriff said, sliding her glasses to Walt, "No refills."

Walt called down toward the three fellows at the other end of the bar, "Carlos – want to go on the clock? Let's rustle up some grub for everyone. It's employees drink free night."

"I'll do it, boss." One of the guys replied, but it wasn't Carlos.

"No. Not you, Billy. Remember what happened last time you went into the kitchen? Let Carlos do it," Walt said. "Besides, when he drinks free, you all do, anyway."

Carlos laughed and left his perch to go into the employees-only door into the kitchen, saying, "You bet, Walt, sounds good. I'll see what we got back there."

Walt nodded and wagged his thumb toward the other people in the bar. "Make a big platter up, OK?"

Carlos called back from the kitchen as the door swung back and forth, "You got it – platter up."

The barman was at the taps and filled three mugs, lining them up on the bar. He told the utility workers, "Clear the lane, fellows – outgoing."

The pair lifted their arms and beers off the bar.

" Billy – catch," Walt called down to the regulars and expertly propelled the full mugs of suds the length of the bar into Billy's waiting hand.

Nikki's head was propped on her hand, her elbow on the bar, "Wow," she said, watching the beers slide the length of the bar, one after another.

"All in the wrist, Nik. But you got to have the knack," he said to her and followed the glasses with, "Don't forget to leave one for Carlos," to the two at the far end.

Walt put another round of drinks on the bar for the tables and called over to them, "Hey folks, here you go. Keep your whistles wet. There'll be some grub out here in a couple of minutes."

The professor got up from his seat to go to the bar. He reached over the empty stools between the sheriff and linemen to collect the drinks. As he ferried them back to the tables, he stopped at the sound of the front door opening.

Everyone in the barroom turned to the door except the sheriff. He moved his eyes to the mirror to watch his deputy push the saloon doors open and walk in with a bum leg and an egg on his forehead. He stopped a step in, looking with surprise at the people at the tables.

The sheriff said into the mirror, "Luis, what happened to you?"

His reflection walked across the barroom, favoring his right leg, nodding to the professor and his missus, and smiling at Syl.

"Me, not too much. The car plenty," he said as he got onto the stool next to the sheriff. He felt the knot on his head. "It was that damn hail. The car's beat to hell. All the glass is knocked out, roof lights, too. I'd say it's a total."

"So, what happened to you? Did you get out in the storm?" Walt asked, pushing a glass of beer to the deputy.

"No, stayed in the car. I got whacked right through the windshield. All I could do is sit it out," the deputy said, putting his hat on the bar next to the sheriff's Cattleman and lifting the beer. "I was about half a mile down the road, but this thing came on so fast I had to pull over. Man-o-man, was it wild! I have never seen anything like this. That hail demolished everything."

The professor spoke up. "The cars in the parking lot, too?" he asked.

The deputy turned his head to the man and nodded, "Everything out there has been pounded. Still drivable, maybe. That includes your truck, Cal. I saw it outside and thought you'd be here. Couldn't get a hold of Bernice once it started."

The sheriff looked at Luis' forehead, "You should put some ice on that."

"More ice," the deputy laughed, leaned on the bar, and said to Walt, "Two bags, por favor. One's for my knee." He looked past Cal to the young woman resting her head on her folded arms. For a moment, it seemed he recognized her. "She in custody?" he joked.

The sheriff gave him the required smile and nodded for him to proceed with his story.

He turned back to his boss and said, "I was taking a look at a TA off-road. Up a trail all by itself. Damndest thing, Cal. The car was peeled open like a tin can." The deputy leaned in and lowered his voice so only the sheriff and Walt could hear him. "Lots of blood in the car, but no body. And something else …," he whispered.

The sheriff waited, raising an eyebrow to his deputy.

"A foot," Luis replied. "Stuck in the car. A damned foot in a sneaker. I screamed like a kid when I saw it. I was glad that storm came up and chased me out of there after I found that thing," he said under his breath to his boss.

The sheriff nodded. "That would do it," he agreed. "We'll go down there after this blows over," Cal said.

Rosales leaned back on his stool to continue the conversation in a normal tone. "The storm ran out pretty fast, though. Just blew over all of a sudden, then I headed here." He looked back to the barroom.

The professor's wife asked, "So the storm's over? Can we go outside? Maybe we should take a look at the damage."

"I don't know, ma'am," the deputy said, turning to face the tables. "I can't say it's over, could start up again. Still seems dicey out there."

Nikki had propped her head on both hands, elbows on the bar. She rubbed her eyes and yawned her vacant smile away, "What? The storm's over?"

Walt pushed a bowl of pretzels toward her, "You sure get a lot of mileage out of one drink, hon."

"It was a double, remember? Shouldn't have drunk that so fast," she yawned again. "I could use a nap. It was kind of a big day for me, even before I got lost in the parking lot. You might have an overnight guest unless the sheriff's going to arrest me for public intoxication and put me in the hoosegow," she said, looking up at the lawman.

"I don't know what he's going to do, but I'm pretty sure you've got him thinking," Walt said. "Personally, I've about had enough of you two."

The professor returned to the bar and put an empty snack bowl down, "Do you think it's safe to get back on the road, Sheriff? Or at least to go outside, to use our phones?"

"We're going to have a look first," The sheriff said to the professor. He took his cowboy hat off the bar and added, "Power lines, things like that. Sit tight for a few minutes."

He looked at Nikki and smiled. "How about you? The fresh air might straighten you up," he said. "Maybe I won't have to take you in after all."

She slid off her stool and lifted both hands, wrists together, ready for the handcuffs. "Take me away, sheriff," she said. Nikki looked up and then raised herself on tiptoes. "Wow, you're one tall tumbleweed, pardner."

"About time for you two to take it outside," Walt sighed as he put his puzzle book down and picked up the remote. "Go on, get going. People here are wondering about their cars." He flipped through security camera views of the parking lot. "Doesn't look too bad out there from what I can see. The camera's clouded up, though. Give it a brush when you go out there, would you, Cal? After all, you're so tall," he called in a high voice after his friend as they walked to the swinging doors.

Nikki looked back at the old barkeep and laughed, then looked up at the lawman. "Cal?" she asked, "What's that short for? Caleb? Calvin, maybe? No, you're not a Caleb. Maybe it's a nickname. Don't tell me – I'll get it – give me a chance."

"Take all the chances you want," the sheriff said, opening one of the swinging doors for her with one hand and putting the other on her back to usher her into the short hall to the outside doors.

"I know. I've got it. Caligula. Cal's short for Caligula. That must be it," Nikki said at the end of the hallway as she grasped the handle to push the door open.

"You sure have plenty to say, don't you?" the sheriff said.

Nikki turned and leaned back against the wooden doors, looking up at the lawman.

The sheriff moved close to the young woman and smiled. He looked at her a little extra and leaned a little closer. "And you're pretty as a desert flower when you're saying it," he said quiet-like.

"Shucks, sheriff," she looked straight into his eyes, "You say the sweetest things," she murmured as she reached up and fingered one of the buttons on his shirt. Her lips parted slightly, and she spoke softly, "Now I know what Cal's short for," she said sweetly.

The sheriff put his arm against the door next to her and spoke softly. "You do?" he asked. "Now, just what do you think it means?" he asked as his eyes wandered across her face.

"Cal-culating." Nikki laughed mischievously and twisted the handle behind her, pushing the front doors open and letting the sheriff stumble forward.

"Let's see what's happening in the real world," she said over her shoulder as she stepped across the walkway.

The early evening sky had cleared, and the moon was climbing above the sheriff's beat-up Bronco parked parallel to the hitching rail. The air was cool, and the stars were popping out over the desert.

Cal followed her across the planks. His boot heels knocked the wood and crunched the icy leftovers as he walked to the end of the tether. They stood on the edge of the boardwalk, taking in the parking lot and the desert vista. The melting hail turned into a low smoke swirling slowly like a dry ice fog, animating the otherwise still and colorless scene.

"Strange looking," Nikki said, as much to herself as to Cal. She moved her gaze across the lot from car to car to trucks and then to the silver vapor trail of the smoky highway. "It looks like a scene from one of Walt's old black-and-white movies. Like science fiction with that steam." She stepped off the walk and stirred the ground fog into small eddies.

The sheriff scanned the highway from west to east. "Nothing moving out there," he said. "I was expecting a car or two now that the storm's passed." He watched a series of low flashes brighten the eastern horizon. Nikki followed his stare and saw the lights.

"What's that?" she asked. "What's over there?"

"I'd say that's around the airbase," he replied, peering more intently.

"You can just about make out some thunder to go with the lightning if you listen," Nikki said quietly.

"That's not lightning," the sheriff said. "Sky's clear. Should be lightninged out by now," he added.

They watched for another minute, waiting for the next flash. The sheriff stepped off the walkway into the lot and turned his attention to his truck.

"This is a mess," he said. Cal walked over to his Bronco and knocked away the broken glass from the rear gate. He looked through the truck and saw the smashed windshield up front. The side windows didn't fare any better.

Nikki was leaning on the corner of his truck.

The sheriff ran his hand over the edge of the roof, feeling the palm-sized dents. "Hard to believe ice could do this much damage," he said. "I don't guess this old truck could be in any worse shape." He stepped toward her to go around to the passenger side of his truck.

Nikki moved and blocked his path. "Well now, Sheriff Cal, you never know what's going to happen in a storm like that," she said.

He looked at her, wrinkled his brow, and straightened his hat. "No," he said slowly, "I guess you don't."

"I mean, a storm like that could cause anything to happen. After all, people can't see where they're going. It's all sand and hail, lightning and wind. Nobody knows what might happen." She let a guilty laugh out and stepped back.

"Uh-huh. I reckon that's so," the sheriff said, taking a step forward and looking at the young woman quizzically. He turned his head to the left and saw the side of his truck was smashed in. A small car was a few feet from his Bronco, also beat to hell from the storm. The front of the car looked like a perfect match to the concavity in the side of his truck.

The sheriff looked down at Nikki and firmly grasped her forearm.

"I take it that is your car that hit my police vehicle," he said to her, looking back at his mangled truck.

"I reckon it was," she said, shaking with repressed laughter. "I knew I hit something, but, honestly, I didn't know what." Some of the laughs leaked out. "If I knew it was the sheriff's car, I would have tried to hide the evidence," she said, straightening up.

The sheriff looked at her and shook his head slowly.

"Guess we were just meant to run into each other," Nikki laughed again. She wiped her eyes. She pulled her arm away and patted him. "Oh, c'mon," she said to the sullen-acting sheriff. "Your car was all beat up anyway. I just put it out of its misery." She laughed even more. "And think of how I feel. I'm the one that forgot to get the rental insurance." Now she just burst out laughing, trying to catch her breath, and wiping tears from her eyes.

Niki wound down and caught her breath and Cal's smile. She looked at him and shrugged her shoulders.

His smile grew a bit, and he shook his head again. "Before I forget, I'd better check in with the base." He walked to the passenger door window

104

and knocked out the cubes of remaining glass. He leaned in, pulled out the handset, and pushed the transmit button. "Sheriff to HQ," he said. "Go ahead." He released the button and waited, looking over at Nikki doodling in the dust on his truck.

After a moment, he lifted the transmitter and pressed the button. "Sheriff to base. I'm waiting on you." He stared past Nikki and saw more low flashes in the distant eastern sky. She thought he was looking at her.

"Base, go ahead. Hey, Bernice, where are you?" he lowered his arm to rest on the window frame while waiting for a response.

He clicked transmit a few times. Nothing was coming in. He tossed the handset onto the seat of his truck. "Just dead air," he said. A serious expression went across his face. "Hail or lighting, maybe. Knocked out the tower." He straightened up and turned to the parking lot. "Let's see what's left of things out here," he said. "Check your phone. See if you have a signal. Folks inside will want to know."

Nikki took her phone out of her back pocket and watched the screen as it glowed on. "I'm not surprised – no signal," she said, turning it off and sliding it back into her pocket.

"Do you have anyone to check in with?" the sheriff asked out of the blue.

"Not really. No," Nikki answered. She smiled.

They walked to the lamppost in the middle of the lot, crunching pieces of ice. One of the cars under the light belonged to the professor and his wife, and the other to Syl. As they approached, the sheriff noted the Arizona plate and that the other was a New Mexican rental. The windows in both cars were broken, and the vehicles were beaten beyond redemption.

Pushing his hat back, the sheriff looked up at the lamppost. The hammered metal shroud was swinging quietly on electrical wires connecting to the base of a large broken bulb.

"Walt's not going to like that," the sheriff said. He looked down at the pieces of the heavy glass globe on the ground. "But I guess that's about all the damage the Bunker took. Except for the wrecks in the lot." He looked at the two pickup trucks and the large utility truck parked next to each other.

"The pickups belong to the fellows at the end of the bar. They're Walt's regulars," the sheriff said to her. "Even from here, I can see their trucks are totaled, too. That'll be bad news for those fellows. Carlos will have insurance, but not the other two." He bent over and picked up a small melting hailstone. "Amazing the damage this did. This might have been as big as a fist when it hit," he said, flipping it back into the dust.

"Bigger," Nikki said. "No kidding, I was lucky to get inside when I did. You should see my bruises."

He smiled. "Well, first, I have to take a look down the highway," he said, motioning across the parking lot. They walked to the road, kicking eddies out of the low fog as they went.

"Remember, I said let's go out in the real world?" As they walked out of the lot and onto the divided highway, Nikki whispered, "This isn't it." She looked across to the desert. The smoke slithered down the road in ragged patches. "This is the surreal world," she said. "This is science fiction."

Nikki and Cal stood on US-70 and looked east, in the direction of the airbase and the city of Alamogordo. They scanned the horizon to the west. Nothing moved under the desert moon.

But there was a sound.

The sheriff took his hat off and cocked his ear east. There was a buzz in the night.

"What is it?" Nikki asked, looking at him. "Do you hear something?"

"Listen …" the sheriff answered in a low voice. "There's something … listen. There it is. There's something in the air."

He paused, pushing his ear against the night, straining for the sound.

"Yes," she barely whispered, "I hear something."

A far-off note grew from imperceptibility to a hearing test – a tone, the hum of a bee fifty feet away, flying toward them. Nikki touched Cal's arm and pointed east to a glow in the sky of far-away lights moving their way.

They watched as the shimmer over the highway grew, and the sound rose as the lights came closer.

Listening for a few long moments, Nikki and Cal looked at each other, and at the same time, she said, "Horn," he said, "Truck."

"Truck horn," she concluded in a whisper.

They watched the long stretch of road that ran to a bend in the highway. The lights of the horn-blowing truck appeared in the distance as it rounded the curve, highballing with all the lights lit and running at top speed.

"He must be loco," the sheriff grumbled.

In another two seconds, the lights of the far-off truck were much closer, and they could see it was running recklessly, weaving back and forth on the road at breakneck speed.

"What the hell is he doing? He's never going to hold the road," the sheriff put his hat back on.

"Do you have to go after him?" Nikki asked as she watched the fast-approaching lights.

"Got nothing to chase him in." He shook his head. "There's no windshield in my truck. Besides, he's going to pass us in a minute," the sheriff said.

It wasn't that long a wait. The truck horn's blaring bass had all of the volume of a diesel train, and the driver was leaning on it nonstop. The engine screamed as the big rig Dopplered into full view about a mile down the straightaway, pushing and pulling dust clouds of lights and sound. The truck was swerving and bouncing in the westbound lanes, pulling a forty-foot trailer swinging side to side behind the nearly out-of-control cab.

The blare pushed so hard it made Nikki unconsciously step back from the edge of the roadway, even though the truck was on the other side, separated by the divide of gravel and weeds.

She had just exhaled, "Oh my God ..." when the semi highballed glaring lights and blaring horn onto the stretch of highway across from them. They expected it to rush by, like an express going through a local station. But this time, the cannonball was stopping.

As the truck shot out of the night, the airbrakes hissed explosively and locked the big rig into a screaming skid. The tires jammed, trying to grab asphalt, skidding over the sand and ice cubes.

The truck abruptly veered left into the median — too abruptly to keep the reefer. The rig jackknifed and tore its hookup. The cab snapped free and bounced on the short car path that crossed the median, going airborne and then smashing into the gravel bank, rebounding to careen forward, bouncing over the eastbound lanes, flying into the parking lot, and twisting sideways in the air as it came in for a landing.

At the same time, the sheriff rushed Nikki, knocking her on her back and sending them both sledding into the ditch that ran along the road.

As they slid down the gravel, the cab sailed over them to crash into the ground, blowing a couple of tires and grinding across the asphalt on its side, pulling a fantail of showering sparks. It clipped the utility truck on the way, ricocheted into an accelerated spin to the far edge of the lot, and plowed into the large rock outcrop, stopping dead and laying on its side. The wheels spun down, lights flickered, then went out, and a high-pitched whine accompanied the death rattle of the engine.

When the cab jumped the divider, the kingpin tore apart and dropped the front end of the ant-heavy trailer to plow into the tar and snap to a stop, catapulting the box, cargo, and the two warrior ants across hundreds of yards of the moonlit highway.

One of the ants was killed outright. One of them was not, tumbling into the White Sands by the side of the road.

Down in the ditch, the sheriff pushed himself off Nikki and lifted her head. She was struggling to breathe. He slid his arm under her shoulders and lifted her. "You're OK, just got the wind knocked out of you. You'll be alright in a minute," he said.

She caught a breath, then a deeper one. "OK. OK," she gasped, "getting it back." She sucked in air and tried to sit up, but he held her. "OK. Whew," she said a few times. "What hit me? You or the truck?"

"That's it, you're alright," Cal said, squeezing her shoulders. "You're OK. You did good," he smiled.

"All part ...," she caught her breath, "... part of my plan ... stand there and wait for the truck to hit me or you to tackle me." She saw the relief on his face and managed a smile. "Wow," she said, "that was close."

"Close enough," he replied. He got his feet and helped her up, "C'mon, up you go. Let's make sure everything's still connected."

"Oh, I'm all here, I think," she said as she stood. The sheriff steadied her momentarily and took a few steps to pick up his hat. He knocked the dust off against his leg.

They looked back into the lot. The cab was lying on its side. The only sound coming from the wreck was the sizzle of the dying engine and the hiss of the steam venting from the front.

"Guess we oughta go and see if that fellow made it," the sheriff said as he put his hat on. "At least that damn horn's stopped."

"What was that?" Walt asked. He stopped in his well-worn path to the taps and listened. "Sounded like something outside," he said to the senior lineman. The barkeep took his beer mug and held it under the spigot. "Turn that thing off, would you?" he said to Billy, leaning over the jukebox. "TV's off, so you got to go for the damn music. Seems like you can't stand peace and quiet," the old barman said under his breath as he filled a mug. "What are you blasting that thing for anyway? Can't hear yourself think in here," he yelled over the Western music.

"Thought I heard something, too," Mike said. "I don't know, maybe." He shrugged and lifted his beer.

Walt looked over to Luis, sitting on the sheriff's stool, holding the small ice bag to the knot on his head. It seemed like no one else heard anything.

"Yeah, guess it was nothing," Walt said to the lineman. He turned to the other utility worker and asked, "Hey, Generation X, did you hear anything outside a minute ago?"

"What?" Brandon mumbled. Both elbows were on the bar, and his head was in his hands. He opened his eyes and focused them on the old man. "Me? No. I didn't hear anything."

Walt nodded and looked across the room at the saloon doors and eyed Syl on the way. She was talking with the professor and his wife under the low umbrella of light, and this time, she wasn't watching him.

The barman stood staring and listening, but not to whatever Mike was saying. In the middle of his sentence, the barkeep looked at the guys at the end of the planks. "Slide that TV remote this way," he called to them.

Ray slid the controller the length of the bar into Walt's hand. The barkeep leaned forward with the remote and switched the TV to camera one outside the door. It showed a smudged view of the sheriff's Bronco parked alongside the hitching rail.

He switched to camera two on the west end of the building, pointing into the lot. A night-vision image of cars in the parking lot came on the screen. Walt leaned forward to look down the bar at the monitor.

"Can you guys see anything on there?" he asked the regulars. They looked up at the TV and shook their collective heads.

"Camera three," Walt said and switched to the eye on the other corner of the building, closest to the highway.

"There they are," Billy pointed up at the set. "They're out by the road. Looking friendly, too," he laughed.

Everyone in the barroom looked up at the TV watching a small couple walking across the screen, close together.

"Well, lookit that," Billy laughed again, "looks like Sheriff Cal's got himself a girl in tow. Got his arm around her, walking in the moonlight."

Everyone smiled.

"All right, all right," Walt said. "Guess nothing is going on out there."

"Don't know if I'd say that, Walt," the big lineman said. A few people in the bar laughed good-naturedly.

Walt pointed the remote down the bar. "Well, nothing we have to worry about, anyway," he said.

"Don't think I'd say that either," Deputy Rosales replied. There were a few more laughs.

Walt pushed the remote back down the bar to the guys at the end. "That's the trouble with this place," he told the two utility workers. "Quiet as the tomb in here. Can't hear a damn thing."

CHAPTER SIX

THE OUTSIDE

Nikki groaned as they climbed out of the ditch. "I think that was Tom Honey's truck. It went by kind of fast, but I'm pretty sure," she said.

"I think you're right," Cal replied. He was surprised. "Do you know Tom Honey?" he asked.

"Of course, we had lunch today," she answered, limping up the slope after the sheriff.

Cal looked back and noticed her hopping along. He stopped and caught her as she lost her balance coming out of the ditch. "I guess you're not alright. You should have said something. C'mon." He put his arm around her and supported her across the lot to the pair of cars under the lamppost. "Sit down," he said by the first car. "You must have sprained something."

She groaned dramatically. "Sprained something? I was rolled over by a ten-foot tumbleweed." She winced when she sat against the hood of the car. "But never mind me, you've got to see about Tom," she said.

He was already heading to the truck. "On the way," he said over his shoulder.

Nikki leaned back on the car, stretching her arms behind her. Her leg was starting to throb as she watched the sheriff trot across the lot to the cab, following the trail of skid marks. She'd take a minute to get herself together and then join him to help with Tom Honey. Nikki tried bending her leg. Her knee hurt plenty.

She sat on the car and rubbed her leg. The truck had scraped deep ruts in the lot. Nikki turned her head to the spot where the sheriff knocked her out of the way of the flying Peterbilt and peered across the divided highway to the scene of the crash.

Her eyes followed the path of wreckage to the largest scraps of trailer. She strained to see and leaned forward as if that would bring the pieces nearer and clearer. Nikki felt another reminder from her leg.

It was moon-bright, and her eyes narrowed to study the scene, then widened in surprise. She shook her head to clear the apparition from her sight. Cal must have hit her harder than she thought.

Something moved in the debris. Something big. Something alive.

It was dark and bigger than a car. She thought it moved, and it did not move like a car. Then it moved for sure, and she jumped. It was not a car. It was very big.

Nikki leaned forward, and her mouth opened as she watched the black shadow creep through the debris, taking shape with every step until it climbed onto the largest piece of trailer and was starkly silhouetted against the bright night sand.

It was a gigantic ant.

Its round head rotated, switching long antennae through the air and reflecting moonlight in the glinting, tire-sized eyes. It moved about on six powerful legs, capable of maneuvering the enormous body with surprising speed and agility.

Nikki's eyes widened. Her heart pounded like a drum, and then everything went dead silent. She just watched the giant ant show.

It did move like a bug, stepping through the debris in sudden starts and precise stops rendered in the stilted animation of an insect. Absolutely still or altogether moving, the big bug efficiently examined the debris, including a few large pieces of its nestmate.

Nikki watched as the impossible ant collected objects into a pile, tending to them, often brushing the pieces with its antennae. Then the huge

113

insect stepped onto the heap and arched into the air, holding its forelegs high.

Nikki stared at the shape and considered an alternative explanation. She was injured, perhaps in the storm, and was unconscious, lost in this bizarre fantasy.

That was a calming thought. If injured, she'd be in a warm and safe hospital until she wakes up. While not as exciting, she thought that would be preferable to a world with a twenty-foot bug nosing around.

That could have made sense, except for reality. She closed her eyes and inhaled slowly and deeply, then opened her eyes to the desert. All was still. The giant ant wasn't moving anymore. There was no giant ant. It was just a big piece of junk in the road. Whatever it was, it was still there, but now she knew it was only a coincidence of shapes and shook her head. "The tricks your eyes can play," she thought aloud.

That junk really looked like a big ant, but it wasn't moving and lots of things can look like lots of things, especially after that storm she went through. Who could blame her for seeing things? She stared. That thing really looked like a giant ant. She squinted at the statue of the monster sculpted by the crash and shook her head.

She turned herself and her thoughts across the lot to Tom Honey and the sheriff and hopped on her good leg in their direction.

She had gone three hops when the trill stopped her. Of course, it came from the highway and naturally sounded very insect-like, a cricket chirp sort of sound. Nikki's eyes closed, and she shook her head. She didn't know why she was turning around; she didn't want to look, but she did. She turned around and opened her eyes.

The humongous ant was stretched into the air, pawing the moon with its front legs and snapping her monstrous mandibles. The soldier ant's respiratory orifices vibrated to produce the rolling trill, a quiet prelude to her major vocalization.

While the ant was arched, bent back into a semi-circle, its two front legs fanned a seam of folded keratinous material under her abdomen, causing the organ to generate a call, a piercing stridulation at an unbearable volume.

The sound was loud enough to be a weapon. Nikki dropped to her knees, clamping her hands to her ears. Nikki could feel the high-pitched oscillation vibrating her insides. She bent over, crouching from the acoustic shock of the 200-decibel siren of the enormous insect. Wave after wave from the sound cannon pushed her lower to the ground. She covered her ears and protected her head with her forearms, balling herself into a smaller target on her knees, curling to duck and cover. The sound stuck a knife into every receptor in her body as she flexed her muscles, hardening herself against the sonic assault.

It stopped abruptly. The only noise was the ringing in her ears.

Nikki uncurled and looked at the highway. Her knee hurt, but that didn't matter. The ant was moving again.

Adrenaline fountained through her body. Her focus sharpened, zeroing in on the massive bug as it clambered from the pile and crawled through the wreckage. Her pain moved down the list.

The giant ant was searching. It lowered its big bug head with super-sized pipe cleaner-like feelers, switching the air and ground, backtracking the debris trail.

The creature paused on the highway, where the cab veered into the median. It rotated its giant head slowly as the antennae sampled the air. It seemed to stare across the road, peering into the lot and at Nikki. She shrank and wanted to run.

The warrior ant followed its antennae. It wasn't wandering; it was tracking, creeping into the median, and crawling over the gravel crossway, following the truck marks.

Nikki gasped.

The ant crossed the highway divider, climbed onto the eastbound highway lanes, and stopped in front of the entrance to the Bunker.

It reared, a Rorschach cutout rising against the desert moon, with a barrel-big head and cruel curved jaws hanging open as the antennae swept the night air.

The bug was huge and very real. In an instant, Nikki knew this was not a dream or a trick of her mind. She could never conjure up anything so horrible.

The bug moved in fits, waving its feelers and then scuttling forward to stop and wave them again, sampling the strength of the trail to stay on course.

Nikki stepped back without breathing or taking her eyes from the monster. She was instantly grabbed from behind and would have screamed, but her mouth was covered.

"Not a sound," he whispered in her ear.

She nodded. The sheriff removed his hand to take her arm, pulled her from the trail, and hopped her behind the dented cars beneath the lamppost. Nikki looked at him, then at the long black gun in his left hand.

"Stopped at my truck on the way," he said.

Her stare stuck on the rifle. She felt an icy chill sweep across her body. "This is real," she stated.

"Looks that way," the sheriff replied.

She looked again at the weapon. She knew that was the only thing between them and that monster. That made it very real.

Nikki turned her gaze back to the super-reality, drawing closer. "So, what's going on? I mean, what is this?" she asked in a hurried whisper. "Is that a giant ant? Am I out of my mind?" She took a deep breath. "This is impossible, you know. It's unreal!"

Cal watched the bug and agreed. "It is a hell of a thing," he said.

"Oh my God," she said. "You'll have to bear with me," Nikki watched the giant mutant pick its way along the debris trail. "But I think I'm going to say, 'Oh my God' a lot."

"Seems sensible," the lawman replied. He reached into his jacket, pulled out a magazine, and snapped it into the gun as he watched the insect enter the parking lot.

"Do you think that will stop it?" she asked him. "That thing is pretty big."

"This is a pretty big gun," he replied.

"OK. Why don't you just shoot it from here?" she asked.

"Not the way it works," the sheriff answered. "Makes a better impression if you get personal," he added.

"What about Tom Honey?" she asked.

"Didn't see him," the sheriff answered. "He's in there – one way or another, but that cab's a mess. Wasn't there a minute when I heard that thing sound off?"

"Do you think he's alive?" Nikki looked back to the cloud of steam rising from the cab lying on its side.

"Can't say," Cal said as he knelt behind the front of the car. "We'll get back to him after we're done with this."

"Done with this? Oh my God. What are you going to do?" She took a deep breath.

The giant insect swept the entrance to the lot, casting its feelers back and forth, spending extra time at the spot where they hit the ground. It dipped its massive head into the ditch where they fell, then raised it, waving the antennae in the air, and quickly returned to the trail.

They watched from behind the cars, several yards from the path. Nikki stuck her head over the roof, peeking at the monster. The sheriff crouched at the front of the car and held his long gun with both hands.

"You should go inside," he said to her. "And you have to go before that gets any closer." He looked at her and nodded to the Bunker. "Go now."

"It might hear me," she whispered as the ant moved along the trail of tire pieces, sweeping the path for scent. The sheriff looked over the hood at the giant bug.

"When it gets to where we were standing, it will either stick to the truck trail or get more interested in ours. If it picks us, it's coming our way.

"I can't even run. My leg," she said, watching over the top of the car.

"Not a time for can't," the sheriff said. "It's a time for got-to."

She thought of the ant finding them and swallowed. "OK, let's go."

"Ladies first," he said, quietly laying the shotgun across the front of the car. "I'll give you a head start and be right behind you. Get moving," he said as he stood. He took her arm and a few steps to encourage her toward the bar.

"Tell Walt and Luis, the deputy, tell them not to come outside. I'll be there in a minute," he said as he returned to the car. Watching the bug, he picked up the 12 gauge. "Keep low and be quiet. Now go," he said with finality.

Nikki frowned but turned to limp across the lot, picking up speed as she went. Only a little ice was left, but every crunch made her cringe.

The ant was on the trail, sniffing and stepping, waving its antenna low to the ground, then running a few steps forward. Whatever it was doing worked because that bug was tracking like a bloodhound. In a few more yards, the creature would be at the point where they left the truck trail.

The lawman took cover behind the car, watching over the roof as the behemoth hunted.

When it reached the fork in the trail, the bug paused and drummed the dirt with its forward legs, trying to make up its mind about which way to go.

The sheriff looked over his shoulder. Nikki was back at his Bronco.

She leaned against the truck, watching the giant ant and the sheriff. The big moon was hanging over the lamppost, and she could see Cal against the car, holding the long gun. The ant was past the vehicles, waving those feelers around where the trail split. It went a few yards following the truck, then turned back. It decided to go after the people instead.

The huge bug covered the distance to the cars quickly, and there was just enough time for Nikki to gulp and Cal to pump the shotgun. He crouched with his back to the car and shotgun ready.

The giant swabbed the car with its feelers, then turned its head like a curious puppy, sensing the sheriff. Like all warm-blooded animals, he constantly shed an organic plume of a complexity known most intimately by the cold-blooded creatures that hunt them. The man's markers swirled in the air, dispersed in the breeze, his personal vapor trail leading the ant right to him.

The giant stepped onto the car, crumpling the hood and blowing a tire. The lawman hunkered down and pushed the safety off on his shotgun.

Moonlight flashed across the facets of the monster's large eyes and glinted on its gaping obsidian mandibles. They snapped shut, and the sheriff cringed.

He watched the ant feelers swaying over him, darker against a dark sky. They were as thick as his arm and could bend at any point, and they were writhing to find their prey.

The antennae swept left and right and quickly centered on the sheriff, pointing to their target like a thirsty dowser finding a bucket of beer.

The ant head slid into his view as the bug moved forward. The serrated jaws chomped together as the head rotated downward to the sheriff, dropping its hairy feelers on either side of his head, tasting the air, licking the car, looking for him.

The sheriff held his breath and raised his weapon slowly, pointing it at the monster's head.

The antennae to his left came close. If he hadn't ducked, it would have found him.

The ant rattled and leaned forward, working its dripping jaws and bouncing the car as she moved.

The sheriff swung the shotgun up to fire point-blank into the monster's face. The 12 gauge cannon blasted a steel slug deep into its head, and the monster recoiled, slipping from the car. The creature lifted its two front legs to examine the wound and walked backward a short distance on the other four.

The sheriff moved quickly around the vehicle, keeping the gun up to advance on the creature. He pumped and fired again into the beast's head.

This blast really made the ant mad. It dropped its forelegs and leaned forward, shaking its head like a wet dog but at a blurring, buzzing insect speed, then it crouched and sprang. The monster's furious scramble clipped the sheriff with a leg as he dove clear, sending him through the air and his 12 gauge skittering over the gravel.

The enraged ant drove its front legs under the first car and lifted, throwing the automobile into the air. Cal kept moving, rolling out from under as the vehicle smashed back to the ground.

The mutant ant rushed the other car, flipping it, then springing onto the turned-up underbelly. The lawman shook the pavement from his face to see the enormous bug atop the car, curling its body and thrusting the barbed end of its abdomen, stinging the metal chassis.

The monster pushed off, backed away, and then charged, striking the car with its full mass, lifting it, and smashing it into the lamppost.

Its adversary pinned, the creature raised its right foreleg high and stabbed down, piledriving its limb through the top of the car, then ripping the roof wide open, folding the sheet metal back with its four-foot jaws.

The attack ceased, and the ant swabbed what was left of the car with its antennae.

Satisfied there was nothing else to kill, the monster turned its face to the moon and examined the gunshot wounds in its head with its forelegs.

The creature was engrossed in its self-assessment and far enough away that the lawman thought it was a good time to leave. Cal pushed himself up while keeping one eye on the giant insect and the other out for his shotgun. He hid behind the upside-down car and watched the bug for a moment before taking a few steps to the Bunker.

The bug didn't notice him. He calculated the intervening space between the bar and the wounded insect in motivated human and injured insect steps. As long as the bug kept licking its wounds, he should be OK.

The sheriff took another step from the cover of the upturned car.

The ant stopped its rhythmic grooming, hanging its huge head motionless under the moon. The sheriff froze.

He felt a slight cooling on the back of his sweaty neck. "Damnation," he whispered. The evening breeze blew over him and straight to the ant.

The colossal head pivoted in the air, and the antennae swayed back and forth. They spread wide and stopped, narrowing their focus and pointing at the sheriff.

There was no cover for thirty yards. He knew he wouldn't make it ten before the bug was on top of him.

The giant ant turned to him, moving like a machine, arranging its legs, and facing the lawman.

There was no place to go. The sheriff turned and squared off. He unsnapped the leather retention strap over his .45 and let his gun hand hang. His other hand took a full moon clip out of his jacket and squeezed it tightly in his fist.

The monster coiled to strike. The black scimitar jaws clacked together. Liquid oozing from the bullet wounds dripped into the sand.

Cal licked his lips and moved his right hand four inches from his holster. He narrowed his eyes and waited for the bug to make its move.

It did.

The massive ant charged the lawman, powering forward on synchronized legs working like an array of pistons. The monster covered half the distance between them in a sudden spurt before the sheriff drew.

His .45 cleared leather and fired fast. The first three rounds hit the ant dead-on, perforating a line between the creature's giant eyes. Stunned by the hot lead, the monster veered to the left, stepped back, and stopped. Cal moved forward and put the other three into the beast's head. He popped open the cylinder of his Redhawk and smacked the rod to eject the hot shells. He pushed the moon clip in, snapping the fast-load home just as the ant got up the steam to come at him again.

In two steps, it got six more rounds in the head. The behemoth reacted, rearing into the air and clawing the sky with its forelegs. It rattled like paper in a fan. A big fan.

The giant ant moved unsteadily forward. Its left legs collapsed. It lay on the ground and heaved, bleeding from the wounds.

Cal was out of clips and reloaded his gun with the singles from his belt. He spun his pistol back into its holster and stepped back, eyeing the bug as he went. The antennae twitched, and the sheriff reflexively froze. The huge head moved weakly to the side, then lifted. The bug's front legs pushed its head and thorax from the ground.

It struggled to get itself up and succeeded.

The sheriff cursed under his breath and backed up a few steps as the giant ant got on its feet.

The monstrous ant leaned forward to walk at him, but its legs failed, and it fell, bullet-riddled and face-first into the dust of the lot. Now, it was just a heap of dead weight.

Cal watched; the bug didn't move, not even a tick. He exhaled.

The sheriff turned to Nikki at the back of his truck, standing with one hand covering her mouth. Behind her, the doors to the bar opened, and his deputy walked onto the wooden walkway with the two utility workers following him. A few of the other people looked out from the doorway. Cal waved them back as he walked toward the group.

"Don't come out," he called. "Don't come out until we know what's going on here."

He retrieved his Mossberg from the dirt, checked the gun, and clicked the safety on as he walked to the bar.

"Luis, get everyone inside," he said in his loud sheriff's voice. As he closed the distance, he looked back at the bug a few times. It looked like it was staying dead.

Nikki waited by the corner of his truck. She seemed tense, so Cal played it casual. "The harder they fall," he said as he walked up, smiling at her.

"You take this sheriff thing mighty serious," she said. Her arm went around his, and she leaned against him as they walked around the tether to the bar.

He sized up the deputy and the others clustered at the Bunker entrance and felt he should say something about the gigantic dead ant in the parking lot. "Get inside," he told them.

"What's going on, Cal?" Luis called back. "What the hell is that thing? Walt turned on the security camera, and we couldn't believe what was happening."

"Understandable," Cal answered.

At the front of the group, the deputy peered past the sheriff into the lot. "Is that ... is that a ... what is that?" He looked down at the sheriff from the wooden walkway.

Cal shrugged. "Whatever it is, I hope it's dead." He turned and looked back at the large insect. "Ask Walt. He's been talking about those things for some time." He turned to help Nikki onto the walk.

Just before he let her go, he felt Nikki tense. She stared across the lot with wide eyes. Cal followed her eyes past the dead bug and the wrecked cars, over the median, past the wreckage, and into the white sand desert underneath the moonful night.

Things were moving.

Dark shapes crossed the sands, heading straight at them. Cal looked at her and repeated quietly, "Go inside."

He looked up at his deputy. "Deputy Rosales, get these people inside, everyone, and on the double."

Luis looked down at the sheriff, surprised at the change in his tone. The sheriff repeated his order by raising his eyebrows at the deputy.

Rosales turned and barked at the crowd, "Inside everyone. C'mon, let's go." He waved them back, fanning them into the doorway.

The sheriff boosted Nikki onto the boardwalk, "You too, I'll be right along," he said after her.

She turned and looked down at him from the wooden walkway. "That's what you said last time. Where are you going?"

"I forgot something," he replied.

"Oh, of course," Nikki brought her hand to her forehead. "Poor Tom Honey."

"No. My hat," he answered as he turned. "Left my hat out there in the lot."

"You have got to be joking," she said to him as the deputy took her arm and urged her to the doorway.

"Some things you don't joke about," he called over his shoulder as he trotted into the lot. "A hat's one of them. And I'll look in on Tom Honey, too."

Rosales shouted after him, "Cal – you want me with you?"

Halfway to the big dead bug, the sheriff stopped and yelled back, "Not with that leg, Luis. I'll let you know if I need any help with Tom."

Cal jogged past the dead creature and, by the overturned car that had come close to squashing him like a bug, spotted his hat lying upside down in the dirt. He picked it up, swatted it across his leg to knock the dust off, and looked across the highway as he put it on his head.

The ants were still pretty far off. Cal cupped his hands like binoculars and took a good look. He shook his head and hot-footed it over to Tom Honey with both hands on the shotgun and both eyes on the action in the desert.

Cal ran across the lot to the upturned cab and was completely winded, bracing himself against the chassis of the Peterbilt as he caught his breath.

The sheriff pushed himself off the cab and stood straight up. "I hate running," he wheezed. He tapped the undercarriage with the butt of his 12 gauge.

"Tom! Tom Honey! You in there?" the sheriff called out as he looked across to the desert. The dark shapes were closer and more discernable. He squinted. There were twelve, probably answering the call from the one he shot. They might spend a few minutes on the debris before they made the way across into the lot, but that was a big bet, especially if he was wrong.

The sheriff took a deep breath and tapped the truck's underside two more times with his rifle stock. "Tom! Let me know you're there!"

"Tom!" he called as he walked around the front of the cab to the shattered windshield. The truck wasn't flat on the ground but was hung up on a large rock at the edge of the parking lot, propping the cab off the ground.

He tried to see inside, but the low light and fractured glass made it impossible to see anything.

He kicked at the bottom of the big windshield again, but the thick laminated safety glass only flexed.

"Damn it." Cal looked up at the truck lying on its side. "These things are hard enough to get into when they're right-ways up," he muttered. He figured the truck's other side would offer him more ways to climb up to the driver's door and turned to go back.

It was as if he had mainlined ice water. A giant ant was standing there, ten feet away, and it was big, monster-big.

The insect didn't move. Cal didn't move. He knew that wouldn't last, but he had nowhere to go. He was stuck in the corner of the hood and the windshield. The rock ledge that held up the cab blocked one way; the ant blocked the other.

The sheriff's right index finger slid to the shotgun safety and clicked it off.

He could get two, maybe three slugs into the ant before it got hold of him. If the first few shots disoriented the bug like the other one, he might be able to get around the truck. It was a mighty slight might.

He slid his foot to the left, scraping the gravel. The ant reacted, shifting its two front legs like a cat anticipating the pounce. Its antennae moved against the night sky, divining his position. Cal swallowed and leveled

126

the gun at the bug. The bug snapped its pincers three times, not too hard and slowly.

The jaws sprang open, and the creature charged the lawman in a blur of bug legs and snapping jaws. The monster rose as it attacked, running on four hind legs and spreading the front ones wide to snare its prey.

Backed against the truck, the sheriff brought the Mossberg up, pumping en route and rapid-firing four times on arrival. Adrenaline works – he blasted round after round into the creature.

The monster shrank from the scorching steel slugs smashing through its outer shell and burning deep into its vitals. It fell back, swinging its huge head from side to side and snapping its shearing jaws. Within a fast count of three, the ant shook off the slugs and attacked with brutal force, charging straight for the lawman.

Cal had already moved.

The sheriff threw his shotgun under the cab and dove after it. The giant ant collided with the truck as his boots disappeared under the 30,000-pound Peterbilt. The impact of the huge bug smashing into the cab lifted the diesel from the rock, almost righting it before it crashed back onto the ledge. The sheriff saw a sliver of the sky for a second, cringing as the wreck slammed back onto the shelf, inches from flattening him.

The mutant ant was mad as a hornet, and the truck shuddered from the bug's assaults. Cal crawled with his shotgun for the other side of the cab. As he wormed his way under the rig, he could see an illuminated screen of a phone through the passenger door window floating in the dark, but no Tom Honey. The sheriff continued elbowing his way forward, cradling the long gun in his arms.

At the other end of the cramped crawlway, Cal stuck his head out to see if anything was waiting for him. As he got out and on his feet, he saw the giant insects climbing out of the desert and onto the roadway.

He ran around the truck and got behind a tire. Breathing hard, he wiped the grime from his face and realized he was hatless. "Where the double damn is that damned hat?!" he exclaimed, kicking the truck in a burning ire.

The 15-ton truck rocked violently. Cal stepped back, and it shook again as the ant tore at the front end. Cal figured things wouldn't get any quieter here, and if Tom Honey were still in there in one piece, he might appreciate a diversion.

He counted shells. Three for the first bug and four for the next equals two to go. At least they were steel slugs. "Car-stoppers," Luis called them.

He edged along the overturned cab, relying on the noise the ant was making to cover his approach. It went quiet, and Cal stood still, listening, straining to hear where the bug was, when the giant stepped off the truck and planted itself right in front of him.

The sheriff let out a quick rodeo yell and pumped that nasty black gun. The spent shell flew out, a new live round clicked into the chamber, and he fired it into the creature's leg.

The steel slug nearly severed the segmented limb. The monster retracted the injured leg, and Cal stepped back from the truck to see what it was doing. An ant droned from the desert, and Cal turned to the sound and saw the wounded ant climbing over the rocky ledge behind the truck. The bug was sneaking up on him.

The sheriff ran.

The gigantic insect took off after the lawman, fueled by the finality of its mortal wound, the insect was unstoppable. Racing after its attacker's vibrations and scent, the insect dragged its useless appendage along until the few ropy connections broke and fell off. If the missing leg slowed the creature, it was not by much.

Cal made great time across the lot for a guy that hated running, and he ran like hell, making for the front door of the Bunker. But the five-legged bug was the favorite.

Nikki and the deputy were at the back of the sheriff's truck, taken off-guard by the impromptu footrace.

"Run! Run!" Nikki screamed so hard she bent over with the effort. She started forward, but the deputy held her back.

The sheriff was closing the gap to the front door fast, swinging his shotgun like a runner's baton in a sprint for his life.

He heard Nikki's voice shrill with fear. "Run! It's right behind you! Run!" she screamed.

He ran, and he ran with everything he had, moving too hard and too fast to look back. He knew the bug was closing and would have him in another second, but he pushed, hoping a final burst would get him close enough to his truck to get something between him and the monster.

Luis got in front of Nikki, forcefully pushing her back. "Get inside!" He shouted and jumped on the boards right after her. He grabbed her by the upper arm and threw her into the entryway. He turned, straight-arming his Glock, and began firing into the ant. The rounds cracked past the sheriff's head as he ran for the door.

The odds felt like they were moving and maybe in his favor. Get past the truck, over the boardwalk, and he might make it inside.

It was all slow-motion as the muzzle of the deputy's pistol sparked and sent streamers through the air inches from his head. It looked like Luis was firing straight at him, but a bullet held no fear, and he ran straight for his deputy's gun.

He charged past the back of his Bronco with the 12 gauge in his left hand, and Rosales contorted his face, dropping his gun hand as he scrambled back, violently pushing Nikki through the doors and into the alcove again.

The sheriff vaulted the hitching post, holding the long gun high for balance. He landed on the boards, sliding over them as the monstrous ant barreled in at full speed, hitting the back of the Bronco, spinning it aside, and crashing through the tethering beam. The monster's jaws were wide as it caught up with the sheriff a step before the doors and snapped its toothed jaws around his chest. The giant bulldozed onward, pushing Cal's body ahead, bowling the deputy down the hallway into Nikki.

Luis and the woman flew down the hall, smashing through the swinging doors and into the tables and chairs in the barroom.

The behemoth wedged into the doorway, its head thrust into the hall with the sheriff trapped and twisting in the enraged beast's jagged mandibles.

The ant, struggling to extricate her head from the doorway, tried to lift the sheriff and bring a leg forward to pin her struggling prey.

He had held tight to the shotgun, but his left arm was in the vise and barely able to move. The unescapable squeeze tightened; he was going to burst; his bones were near to snapping. Luis sprawled on the floor, tried to get himself up, and fell dazed. He managed to lift his pistol, trying to get a clear shot past the blood running into his eyes and the captive sheriff.

The ant's immense head lifted to position the sheriff for the coup de grace when a hammer hit the bug.

Concussion shocked the Bunker. Felt as much as heard; it set anyone on their feet back a step and made the bottles and glasses jump throughout the bar.

Suddenly, the sheriff was free, on the floor at the far end of the hallway, gasping for breath and still holding his Mossberg. His chest heaved as he brought the barrel to bear on what was left of the ant.

Cal gulped in air as the scene came into focus. The ant was clearly out of commission, based on the fact that only part of the ant - a large portion of the head - was on the floor, and the rest of the monster seemed to have disappeared.

The sheriff dropped the shotgun and ran his left hand along his ribs and torn, bloodied shirt. At that moment, he didn't know if he was alive, going to die, or was already dead. The pain made him think he was alive.

Where the front doors had been, there was a wall. That didn't make sense. The sheriff laid back on the floor and turned his head to look under the swinging remnants of the barroom doors and into the bar. Inside, he saw his deputy looking back. Past him, Nikki was mixed in with overturned chairs. She waved to him.

Cal looked up, and Walt's face looked down at him from the saloon doors.

"Hey, Walt," he gasped. "What are you up to there?" He coughed. He felt the way the bug looked.

The old barkeep leaned against the doorway and looked down, then laughed.

The sheriff looked back at Nikki and the chairs. Her mouth was open a bit. She must have been thrown straight through the swingers. She looked back at the lawman, didn't close her mouth, and shook her head.

The sheriff was getting his wind back, "You OK?" he rasped at her.

She looked at him, "I guess." Her voice sounded soft in the thick silence. "I'm glad the big ant didn't eat you."

It hurt when the sheriff laughed.

He looked to Luis, who tried to get up, wavered, and slid down the wall to sit. "How about you, deputy? You alive?"

"Yeah, boss," he answered. He let the gun slide out of his hand onto the floor, "I guess I am."

The sheriff looked back at the ant head at the base of the new concrete wall.

Nikki's voice came from the furniture pile, "What the hell happened?" she asked, pushing a chair away.

"Dynamite," Luis rasped.

The sheriff pushed up against the wall and tried to stand. He stayed seated for another minute, tried again, and got to his feet. He looked back at the severed ant head and the ponderous stone slab where the front door should be.

Leaning against the wall, he checked his shotgun's safety and removed the magazine and unfired cartridge. He used the Mossberg business end down to help himself to hop into the barroom.

Cal limped to what was left of the swinging doors, pushed them open, and gave Walt a quizzical look. The old man was standing in the corner by the door, smiling.

The sheriff walked to Nikki and helped her to untangle herself from the chairs. As she stood, she looked the sheriff over, sat him in the chair, and put his shotgun against the wall.

Cal looked at Walt, "The lady wants to know what happened. Me too." He coughed some more.

The barman patted the concrete wall and looked into the short hall at the bug's remains. He made his way over to the sheriff, picked up a chair, and lowered himself into the seat with a groan.

"Blast door." Walt said, "When we saw what was happening on the TV and got a gander at the size of this thing, I knew it would have to come down. Nothing else would stop them. Just glad you all made it back in time," he said with a wink.

The sheriff said, "Blast door?"

"They don't make 'em like this no more," the old man laughed. "Guess I never told you about it, Cal. I figured it would do this bug just right. Push the big red button and an eight-ton door drops in less than a second. It's on air shocks but packs a heck of a wallop. That's the way they built things in the atomic era. Looks like it took that bug's head clean off." The old man looked at the insect head, "Well, maybe not so clean. Anyway, glad it worked."

"You're glad?" The sheriff coughed and then held his side. "I have to say, Walt, that was one hell of a bang."

The sheriff looked around the bar, then at himself. Both were a mess. He figured he had a cracked rib the way every breath felt. There was a good cut on his right forearm, and his head buzzed like a sidewinder in a hot pail.

The regulars usually planted at the end of the bar were ducked down behind it, looking over at the barkeep and company.

Syl was standing by the two linemen at the bar. The older couple were by their table, but Emma was sitting on the floor. Her husband, staring dumbfounded, hadn't noticed yet.

"You folks alright?" the sheriff asked toward them. The architectural professor said nothing, then quickly shook his head, "Yes, I, yes, we're OK." He saw his wife and helped her back to her chair. She was hyperventilating.

Suddenly, the kitchen door pushed open, and bright light streamed out, framing Carlos carrying a tray of food. "Time to eat," he said as he entered the barroom.

No one said anything.

"What was that big noise I heard before? Sounds like you got boiler problems, Walt." He looked at the silent group. "What'd I miss?" he asked. He gave his huddled friends a puzzled look and put the tray on the bar. Carlos looked around the room at everyone staring at the doorway.

He joined them, turning to look at the doors. "What's up?" He turned his head to look at his friends and again at the doorway, "What's going on? I heard a big noise."

His two friends on the floor got to their feet, and Billy said, "I don't know, man. It all just happened like out of nowhere."

A soft voice came through the buzz in the sheriff's ear, "We're going to have to clean that up," Nikki said, gently lifting the sheriff's torn shirt sleeve to look at his wounds, "How about you, Walt? Are you OK?"

"Fantastic, hon," the old man replied. "Just fantastic."

She walked over to the swinging doors and helped the deputy get to his feet. As they walked to the table and chairs, she said to him, "That doesn't look too bad. We'll get you fixed up."

"I'm alright," he said to her as she put him on a chair by the sheriff and Walt.

"I'll be back in a few minutes," she said, walking by the men to the bar. "I bet all you guys need is a beer. Stay where you are."

As she passed Cal, she said, "You forgot your hat, sheriff."

He grimaced and thought about getting up but decided to stay in his chair for another minute or two. Things were still circling his head to accompany the buzzing. He was looking under the swinging doors at the hunk of ant.

The barflies came over and made their way to the broken swinging doors, pushing them open and looking into the hall.

"I never seen anything like that. Not ever. What do you make of it, Walt? You've been around here longer than anyone. Did you ever see the like?" one of them called back to the barkeep.

"Maybe," the old man said from his chair. "Maybe I have."

"You've seen this before?" Billy asked Walt.

One of the other fellows chimed in without looking away from the dead insect, "No way. Nobody's seen this before. We would have heard about things this big."

134

"That's what you think," Walt replied. "There are lots of secrets in the desert," he continued, "that's why we're in the Bunker."

Nikki returned to the table, carrying a tray with a pitcher of water and three glasses of beer. She had a couple of towels over her shoulder.

"Yeah, I've seen them before," the old man said, lifting one of the beers, "just didn't think I was ever going to see them again."

CHAPTER SEVEN

THE TRUCK

The patrons of the Bunker made their way across the barroom to look at the ant head. They peered around the door into the small hallway to see what was left of the insect that crashed into the safest place in the world.

The sheriff stayed in his chair and pressed a wet towel to his throbbing head. Nikki was cleaning the blood from his arm, and Walt drank a beer. The deputy sat silently, watching the people gawk at the giant head and holding his hand to his own.

The group moved through the doors in short steps, closer and closer to eyeball the monstrous details of the insect face, the long antennae, and the savage mandibles that had been a quick second away from crushing the sheriff. Black jelly pooled around the bristly bug chunk, and an ammonia smell filled the hallway, but still, they got closer.

The professor was nearest to the specimen. He leaned over and extended a finger to touch the monster's jaws. His wife stood back by the door with her hand over her mouth.

"No, no, don't," she said in a trembling voice. "Don't touch it, Russell. It's horrible."

"I just want a closer look," he replied without taking his eyes off the face of the ant. Few of them could.

"It's fantastic," the professor said, "Absolutely fantastic. Defies logic. Completely impossible." He ran his fingertips along the hard, round outside of the ant's crushing jaws, then fingered the serrations of the inner arc.

"Oh, good God, Russell," his wife said, looking away, "leave it alone. It's filthy. You'll get a disease."

136

The older lineman piped up, "Or contaminated. It could be radioactive. Isn't that where these things come from?" he asked.

At that, the professor lifted his hand, and the group shuffled back a step or two.

Walt heard the utility man's remark and answered, "Radiation made them, you can bet. I doubt if it's hot, though. I do have a Geiger counter around here somewhere. But we oughta get that out of here and mop it up in there."

"Don't open the door," Syl said to the barman, "There could be more of them out there."

"There are more," the sheriff said from under the towel. He sat up and took the cloth from his face to look at Walt, "But you can open the door again, right?"

"Sure," the old man replied. "There's a chain drive. Might be messy out there, judging by the size of the bug that had a hold of you."

The lawman grimaced, "Even so, Walt, we can't stay in here forever."

"Well, how about waiting a little while longer?" Nikki said as she took the wet towel off his arm. "Your bleeding stopped – more or less, but I think you need to go to the hospital."

The sheriff examined his wound, "Umm. Looks like it could use a couple of stitches. You got a sewing kit handy, Walt?"

Nikki looked at him and raised her hands. "OK, that's where I'm out," she said, getting up from her chair. "I can't sew people."

"I can," Syl volunteered. She left the others and walked out of the swinging doors to the sheriff, "I'm a nurse," she said.

"Do tell," Walt said without surprise. The barman turned in his chair to yell, "Hey Carlos, there's a medkit in the gray locker. Would you get it for our nurse here?"

Carlos heard him, stopped staring at the ant, and came out of the hallway. "Sure thing, Walt," he answered vacantly. "Sure thing," he repeated, then went to the back room to find the kit.

The visiting nurse was the first of the crowd to shake off the shock. She examined each of the injured matter-of-factly, starting with the sheriff. Syl glanced at his wounds and smiled, pushing the towel back to his head. "I guess you'll make it," she said.

She turned to the deputy and inspected the gash on his head, "Just a little band-aid or two for you, and you'll be fine. She looked into his eyes and moved his head from side to side. "You'll be fine," she said again.

"Thanks," he said to the nurse, "what's your name, anyway? Mine's Luis."

"You can call me Ms. Sylvia," the nurse said with a smile.

The deputy asked, "You from around here or just passing through, Syl?" The sheriff eyed his deputy from under the towel.

"Little of both," she replied. "I get around."

"Well, glad you were here today, Syl," Luis said as she felt the eggs on his head. "That's for sure," he said.

Nikki returned with more water and more towels. She wet a couple and gave one to the nurse, who wiped her hands on it and then began cleaning coagulated blood from the deputy's forehead.

The sheriff watched the nurse as Nikki handed out fresh wet towels. Walt wiped his face and began the difficult process of getting out of his chair.

"Where are you going?" Nikki asked him.

"Another round of anesthesia for the patients and encouragement for the caregivers," he answered.

"You can stay there, Walt," she smiled and kept him in his seat with a hand on his shoulder. She turned to the bar, but Cal took her arm.

"You're OK?" he asked her. "You made quite an entrance through those doors."

"Only hurts when I laugh," she said as she limped away.

Carlos returned from the storeroom with the medical kit. He put the army surplus bag on the table in front of the nurse. Sylvia opened the sack and put items on the table. "This will work. Everything we need to get you guys patched up," she said.

Carlos swung his leg over a chair and sat, looking at the lineup of curved needles, disinfectant, and bandages laid out on a white cloth. He looked at the lawman's bloodied arm and his open wound.

"Think I'll go look at the bug," Carlos said. With another glance at the needles, he left the table and went through the hanging doors.

Nikki came back from the bar and took a seat at the table.

"What about you, hon? Are you OK?" the nurse asked the young woman.

"Oh, I'm alright, thanks, Syl," she looked at the nurse. "Just bruised my pride, I guess," she laughed. "Felt like I was only in the way out there."

"You did great," the sheriff said, looking at her seriously. "Lot of people would have frozen."

"I was too scared to freeze. I just wanted to run. I was so afraid," she looked away.

"Sensible," the sheriff replied. "Stood your ground," he added. Nikki pushed her hair away from her eyes and smiled at him.

"Well, I declare," Walt piped up, "I just don't know when I've heard our constable go on so." He laughed. "Do you ever remember him being so talkative, Deputy Luis?"

Luis gave a big smile, glancing at the sheriff, then winced, trying to pull away as the nurse cleaned his forehead and applied antiseptic. She didn't let him get away until she had stretched three small butterfly closures over his wound. "There you go, Deputy, you look like a man with a past," she said, patting his shoulder. "Any other complaints?"

"No, ma'am," he said courteously, "thank you very much."

"Alright, time for the serious case," Syl looked at the sheriff. "Your turn," she said to him.

Sheriff Jeffries extended his arm on the table, wound up.

"This is a military medkit you got here, Walt," the nurse said. "It's got just about everything – except painkiller," she said, looking at the sheriff. "This is going to smart a bit."

"Guess we better get on with it then," the lawman replied.

"Might help if you hold on to the edge of the table," Syl said to him.

"But keep the other hand free," Walt said to him, then looked at Nikki, "Maybe you could get the sheriff that Rocking Chair from behind the bar?"

"Rocking chair?" she repeated with a note of confusion.

The barkeep looked up at her and smiled. "Made of glass, hon," Walt said and made a tippling gesture.

"Oh, right. I get it," Nikki said. She looked at the surgical items on the cloth and went to get the bottle.

Syl put on disposable gloves from the kit and swabbed the sheriff's wounded arm with a liberal amount of Betadine.

Nikki returned with a large tray of beers, the bottle of whiskey, and five empty glasses. "I thought we could all use some anesthesia," she said.

"Good idea," the nurse said, threading the curved needle. "You should take a belt, sheriff."

Nikki poured him three fingers, and he downed it without hesitation, then took a swallow of beer.

Walt said. "Never needed bottled courage just for a little needle and thread." He nudged the whisky bottle to Cal.

The sheriff smiled. He lifted his beer with one hand and made a fist with the other as Syl pushed the suture needle through the meat of his arm.

Walt and Luis watched. Nikki looked up into the darkness past the hanging lightbulb, away from the operating table.

The sheriff gripped the edge of the table to keep his arm still while it was fixed. Nikki put her hands over his and could feel it flexing against the pain. Cal looked at her and smiled.

There was a painful groan, but it came from Walt, who had become too engrossed. The old barkeep looked away and cleared his throat to cover.

"You all right there, Walt?" the sheriff asked. His friend replied with a grunt.

The nurse popped the needle through his skin, again and then again, using the forceps, drawing the thread after the point and expertly tightening the crescent-shaped gash together. "How's it going, sheriff?" she asked without looking from her task.

"No problems," he answered, lifting his beer to her, steady as could be. "You do nice work, Syl."

"Just about there, maybe two more," she said, crossing the thread over to pull down some loose flesh.

Walt was back to watching his friend's new seam develop and asked him, "How many of those ants did you see out there? On the camera, guess I made out about two."

"There were more than that," the sheriff answered.

"That's what I figured," Walt said. "Ants usually got a nest somewhere."

Nikki kept squeezing Cal's hand and asked the barkeep. "That thing is really an ant?"

"Yep," Walt said, "Mighty big one."

"Hard to believe, isn't it?" the nurse asked as she tied off the suture. She patted the sheriff's hand, "You're all done, big boy. That should hold you together for now."

"Finally," Nikki said. Cal felt her grip relax and smiled at her. He noticed the rest of the world disappeared. They both smiled, and she held his hand. He was sunk.

"I said you're all done, Sheriff," Sylvia repeated.

"Guess so," the lawman said, lost in thought. He bent his arms, the one with the new threads, then the one with the glass.

He came back to the present and said to the nurse, "Couldn't have done better myself. You in the military?"

"No," the woman replied. "Been in the ER a lot. You pick things up," she said, wiping her gloved hands on a towel.

The deputy continued about the bugs. "Good call on the monsters, Walt. They're just like the things you've talked about, like those movie posters. Matter of fact, there's one about giant ants in here, isn't there?" he asked.

"Two. One in Spanish, one in English," the old man said. "The movie was a big hit when it came out. That's what that old fella Granville told me. I was telling our guests about him before." He smiled at the nurse as she snapped her gloves off.

"That ant movie was one of the first ones in the cover-ups. The A-bomb was blamed for the giant ants, but other stories were coming out," Walt said.

Nikki looked at the old barman. "These giant ants were here before?" she asked him.

The old man nodded. "Granville told me the original nest was just a few miles from here. Told me that's why this building was built. Giant ant-

142

proof. It was the headquarters for the monitoring station. They kept a little observation post closer to the nest, but this is where the scientists worked. Ant-proof," the barman repeated. "Course, they said it was built for the A-bomb, for the Cold War. But it was really about the ants."

"According to Granville?" the nurse asked.

"From before your time. Don't worry, he's long gone, along with most of his secrets, I guess," Walt replied.

"How could they keep them a secret?" Nikki asked, "It's too crazy."

"Did you see what you saw out there?" Walt asked her.

"I guess I did," she looked down at the sheriff's new seam and looked away quickly.

"Did you ever hear of giant ants before?" Walt asked her.

"No."

"Then I guess it was a secret," the old man concluded.

Nikki's looked at the sheriff. "This is unreal," she said. "What are we going to do?"

"I vote for sitting tight for now," the visiting nurse answered as she packed up her needles and thread. "One of them was enough," she added.

"And I saw more of them out there," Nikki said quietly to the sheriff. She handed him a fresh wet towel and one to the deputy. Luis wadded his up and held it to his forehead. The cool felt good.

"I wouldn't worry too much," Cal said to her. "They're just ants. Big or not, they're bugs."

The ant oglers were coming back into the barroom, filing through the broken saloon doors.

"What's next, Sheriff Cal?" Billy asked, "What's the plan?"

Walt answered, "Maybe you could give him a couple of minutes, young fellow. The Sheriff's just got done with a medical procedure." The old man turned in his seat to face the group. "And by the way, he was about snipped in half a few minutes ago."

"We'll figure it out," the sheriff said to the patrons as they passed. "Important thing is, we're safe in here for the time being."

"The only place to be at the end of the world," Walt said to the quartet at his table. His deep crow's feet spread across his face as he grinned.

Nikki stopped attending to the sheriff and said, "From what I saw out there, that may be a real possibility."

"What's that?" Walt asked.

"The end of the world," she answered.

Walt's smile disappeared, but his wrinkles stayed.

The sheriff lifted his beer and winced with the effort.

"Might be a good idea if we see what else that thing did to you," Syl said, pointing to the torn shirt beneath his jacket. "Stand up, and let's have a look."

The pain flashed across his face as he stood. "It does feel a might strained," he said.

"Let's see," Syl said as she pulled the jacket off him and lifted his shirt. The side of his chest was scraped red and purple, and it was swollen along a line of deeply discolored dashes, the toothmarks of the insect jaws.

"Look at that," the nurse said, "cut along the dotted line. Close call, Sheriff. Can you lift your arm up?" she asked him, reaching for the bottle of antiseptic.

"I could, but I'd just as soon not,' he answered.

144

"Well, give it your best, big boy." Syl spread the iodine over the abraded areas and then broke open a large bandage pack. "I'm going to wrap you up tight with this. It will help with the pain," she said. "Lift your arms and turn a bit."

He pivoted and faced the table. Nikki was looking at him as the bandage wrapped around his chest. She put her chin on her hand and fluttered her eyelashes at the lawman. It hurt when he laughed.

Syl finished tying him off and said, "There you go, Sheriff. Good as new."

"Thanks again," he said. "That feels a lot better." He sat back in his chair, lifted his beer for a few swallows, buttoned his shirt over the bandages, and looked across the table.

Nikki shook her head and sipped. "It feels like one minute this is real, and then the next, it's nail-your-shoes-to-the-floor crazy." She took another sip, then another.

"You know what I mean?" She looked at the sheriff, "I mean, did you see them riding on that truck?" she asked him, then paused mid-sentence, "They ..." Her eyes widened, "Oh my God – Tom Honey's truck. What happened to him?"

"I couldn't see him in the cab one way or another," the sheriff answered. "I don't know what's happened to him."

"I recognized the truck. I just met him today, or a hundred years ago," her hand came to her mouth, and she leaned toward the lawman, "Do you think he could still be ..."

"No way to know. Odds ain't great," the sheriff said, looking at her and then to Walt, who was shaking his head.

"Well, that's something," Walt said to her. "You know the White Scorpion? Thought you didn't come from around here."

"I met him just today," she said. "The White Scorpion? You mean that crazy sunburn story was true?"

"Well," the old man began, "that's one part of the story about how he got that name. The other part is how once he …"

"That was some wreck," the sheriff interrupted, looking at Walt. "Those things are on the hunt out there. Still, no way to know. Not unless we go out there. And I think we ought to."

He grimaced and sat straight, looking at Walt, "You said you could lift that door, right?"

"Yeah, we can lift it," the old man said. "Just thought you might want to wait a while."

"I do. Don't think Tom does," the sheriff said. "Besides," he said as he smiled across the table at Nikki, "I left my hat outside."

The deputy shook his head. "Wondered when you were going to get to that," he said.

Nikki said to Walt, "So you guys know Mr. Honey?"

"Course we know Honey, honey," the old man laughed a little, "You're the one from somewhere else, remember? Tom's been driving this road for years. Matter of fact, he probably has more cards on the bulletin board than anyone."

"Really?" she said. "Where's the bulletin board?"

Walt jabbed his thumb a few times at the swinging doors, "On the wall in the hall, right in front of our visitor."

"Great," she said. Nikki left the towels on the table, disappeared into the hallway, and quickly picked her way past the debris to the wall. She looked down at the bug remnants and shuddered. She scanned the board, removed a card, went to her bag at the bar, and returned to the table. "Let's call him," she said, turning on her phone.

"You know, I did see a cell phone in his truck as I went by," the sheriff said.

146

"Use the line behind the bar, Nik," Walt told her. "Cellular phones don't work here,"

"Cellular phones," she laughed. "You two are adorable," she said as she hurried to the bar and dialed the number on the card.

Tom Honey was wedged against the center console and snugly secured by his seatbelt. He was still out when his phone began playing "Reveille." His eyes opened, and he blinked. He didn't know where he was, but he heard the bugle call.

He stared blankly at the illuminated animation of an incoming call in the dark, upside-down cab. The phone played another round. He stretched out his hand and pulled it from the cradle, puzzled for a moment, then answered the call. "Honey's Hauling, sweetest ride on eighteen wheels," he said dreamily.

"You're kidding," Nikki's voice came through the phone, "Is that you, Mr. Honey? Tom, are you alright? I thought you were in the truck outside that crashed."

Resting his arm on the console and holding the phone a few inches from his face, Tom closed his eyes and slowly exhaled. He was confused, things hurt, and gravity was going the wrong way. He shook his head and rubbed his eyes.

Her voice came through again, "Tom, Tom – are you outside the Bunker? Answer me."

"Yes, ma'am." Everything was becoming sharper and clearer. He opened his eyes wide. "Yes, ma'am, that's me. Guess I wrecked, I guess." He wiped sweat and blood from his face and looked at the phone again. The faraway pain was getting closer, running to his head along his jangled limbs.

He focused his eyes on his surroundings and tried to shake off his stupor, suddenly blurting out, "What? What the – where?" He rubbed his face again and looked at his phone, "Who's this? What's going on?"

"Tom, it's me – Nikki. We met at the taco truck today, remember? Are you OK? We saw you crash." She put her hand over the mouthpiece and called over to the sheriff, "I got Tom Honey on the phone. He's alive. I don't know if he's hurt or not. He's sort of out of it."

The sheriff pushed himself out of the chair, picked up his glass, and walked across the room to the bar. "Let me talk to him," he said to Nikki as he climbed onto his barstool and put his beer down.

She handed him the receiver. "Tom. Tom Honey, you there?" he listened and looked at Nikki.

Honey's groggy voice came over the phone, "Who's this? Who's there?" he asked.

"Tom, this Cal Jeffries, Sheriff Jeffries. We saw you wreck outside. What kind of shape are you in?

The sheriff pointed toward his half-empty glass, and Nikki reached for it to refill, but he waved her off and pointed again to the TV remote control behind the bar. She picked it up and handed it to him.

"Uh-huh, I can tell you more about it when we get there," he said into the phone. "No. You'd better sit tight and wait for us. We're going to come and get you." He looked at Nikki. "And keep quiet, too. Those things that got your truck are still out there." He pushed buttons on the remote and cycled through the security cameras in the parking lot. The screen divided into four pictures showing the dark lot. The moon was shedding enough light to suggest the parked cars. The sheriff watched the screen intently.

"No, Tom. We were outside, saw you crash." He paused, listening to the truck driver on the other end of the connection. "Nah, that was a smart move. You're still ticking, right?" He paused again and looked at Nikki with a smile that didn't fit the conversation, gesturing Tom was talking too much.

"Giant ants, Tom," the sheriff said into the phone.

"Giant ants," he repeated after a pause.

"OK, not too long," he said. "We're coming for you. Make sure you stay quiet. Seems like those things …" the sheriff heard a clicking sound and nothing. The line had suddenly gone dead.

He handed the phone back to Nikki. "What's the matter?" she asked. She put the receiver to her ear and then looked at the sheriff. Her eyes widened slightly. She hung the phone up on the wall.

"That's not good," she said.

Walt and the deputy made their way to the bar. Luis sat next to the sheriff, reloaded his gun, laid his mags on the bar, and began his weapon check. Walt leaned on the corner of the bar next to the sheriff.

"Hard to say, but I think I've seen some more of those things moving in the dark out there," the sheriff said to them. "I told Tom Honey we'd be coming out to get him." He looked from the TV to his deputy and then to the old man. "We're going to need some more firepower, Walt."

The barkeep nodded and pushed off from the bar, shuffling past Nikki and taking her in tow by the wrist. "Lend a hand, will you, hon?" he asked, leading her into the back room.

"Just the two of us outside, Luis," the sheriff said quietly. "Panicky gun will kill you just as dead as a bug." He nodded toward the people at the table. "And it's not their job, so we don't ask."

"I'm with you, boss," Rosales replied as he lined up his magazines and checked his pistol. "But we're going to need bigger guns."

"Walt's getting them," the sheriff replied.

As Walt and Nikki went through the padded lounge door into the back room, the old man flipped on a few more lights and gave her the Cook's tour. "Guess it'd be a good idea if you knew where things were around here," he said. "There's the kitchen, pantry, walk-in refrigerator, and freezer," Walt waved his hand to the doors on the right of the big room.

Nikki looked at the large pots and pans hanging overhead, dull from disuse. A small coffee pot sat at the front of a commercial twelve-burner cooktop.

"Plenty of canned food in the pantry over there. Frozen food is on the right." He sauntered ahead toward a gray steel door, "And this way to the nether world," he said over his shoulder. "The belly of the Bunker."

Walt flipped a switch and opened the door to a steel staircase leading to a large basement. It was like a warehouse with fenced cubicles stacked with wooden crates and boxes. Along the walls were more steel doors bordered by rivets.

As they clanged down the staircase, Walt pointed across the room to the doors. "The first one leads down to the next basement, housewares, linen, and sundries." He laughed. "Really, it's the power plant and fuel reserve, spare parts, and fix-it shop. The door to the right goes to the living quarters, cafeteria, dorm, and rec room. That's where we're heading."

They got to the bottom of the staircase. "All this," he said as he waved at the warehouse of caged items, "is mostly junk I brought in over the years," he said. "We're going this way," Walt ushered her to the door on the right and opened it.

They went in, and he flicked a switch to light up what looked like a doctor's waiting room. There were three dozen padded chairs informally grouped around coffee tables, all used to sitting in the dark. He motioned to a door across the room. "After you," he said.

They went into another hallway and passed by a couple of doors to one at the end. Walt unlocked the door, stepped in, and turned on the lights.

"Oh. This looks a little right-wing," Nikki said as walls of guns lit up.

"Might come in handy," Walt said as he took down an assault rifle. He laid it on the table and got two more from the wall, placing them side by side. He opened a locker and squinted as he selected ammunition boxes.

"Maybe you'd like to pick out something for yourself? There's a pretty little pocket-sized number over there. A .32," he said and pointed to a chrome pistol. "Although, I suppose you might want something with a bit more bang for the bugs."

"No, no, thanks. I'd probably shoot myself," Nikki said. "But I must say, I feel better knowing we have these." She looked at the wall. "Still, Walt, it all looks a little nuts," she said. "Were you expecting a war?"

He laughed. "That's you kids these days. Be crazy not to have them if you ask me," he said. "Just help me tote this pile upstairs. I think this will be just the thing, these three," he said, patting the rifles, "and these boxes."

Nikki took hold of one of the metal ammo cans by the pop-up handle, "Wow, these are heavy," she said.

"That's why I brought you along, hon. Women's lib," Walt chuckled.

"You're a hoot, Walt," she said, taking one of the boxes in each hand. "I'll make a couple of trips," she told him as she limped through the door and down the hall.

Walt followed empty-handed. "Alright, I'm going to rummage around down here and get a few odds and ends together," he said. Nikki carried the two boxes to the stairs.

"Just make a pile, Walt. I'll be right back," she called back as she climbed the steel staircase. Her leg still hurt.

Tom Honey was coming out of it. The phone call woke him up, and so did the pain. He unhooked his seatbelt, squirmed from under the steering wheel, and lowered himself into the sideways truck.

Everything hurt, but it all seemed to work.

Tom got himself situated, sitting on the side of the seat with his boots on the passenger door window. He took a breath and looked up to the stars over the driver's door, then tried to see past the spray of silver cracks filling the windshield.

Tom didn't feel like there was a hurry, so he sat back, staring vacantly into the dim outside. He looked at his phone and turned it on again. It had no power and shut off.

His mind went over the wild ride, the crash, the things on his truck. The sheriff said there were giant ants out there.

He had known the sheriff for a lot of years, and he could be a serious man. Not exactly sociable, and those loners can be a might fanciful at times. But giant ants coming from the sheriff – that was unexpected.

Everything was quiet in the cab. He leaned back against the upholstered door to the sleeper compartment, sitting on the sideways seat.

A large shadow passed across the windshield.

Tom straightened. He seemed to have some adrenaline left after all. He watched, narrowing his eyes, and settled back into the cushioned wall. His thoughts went to those abandoned cars ripped apart on the highway – all those fresh wrecks without a person, living or dead.

"Giant ants," he said softly and closed his eyes.

A gentle tapping opened his eyes. The sheriff said they were coming to get him. It came from the driver's door over his head.

Tom looked up through the window. The sky was full of moonlight, and only the brightest stars were out. Someone pounded the side of the truck. He opened his mouth to shout a response when the cab got shoved around. Kind of easy at first, then harder.

Tom's cowboy boots pushed against the dashboard, pressing him deeper into the cushioned wall.

The fifteen-ton cab suddenly bounced. Tom stretched his arms out to steady himself and gasped as the vehicle heaved. It lifted a few inches and then dropped hard.

There was silence, then another tapping. The rhythm moved across the sheet metal, tracing a path, feeling its way over the cab.

Tom Honey was frozen right down to his surprised expression. A black shape rippled past the distorted glass of the windshield. Tapping and rubbing noises came from other directions as it sought a way into his cab.

The sounds stopped, and silence lingered. He waited in the dark.

Giant ants. That is what the sheriff said. If that was true, it was them that attacked those cars and left wrecks spread across the highway without bodies. Tom thought of regular ants cleaning up dead animals, carrying everything away except the bones. But bones wouldn't be a problem for giant ants.

The silence seemed deeper in the dark, and Tom Honey felt like he was all on his own, waiting for that next jolt.

A shadow passed, and the truck lurched. Tom slipped off his perch to hide between the seat and the dash. The heavy cab rocked violently. He held on, eyes wide and mouth open as blackness eclipsed the heavens, covering the stars.

Tom's heart pounded as he twisted in the awkward confines of the tumbled-over truck. He stretched his hand into the gloom and slapped at the dashboard to pop open the glove compartment.

It wasn't hard to find his Dezzy. The fifty-caliber handgun was massive. It was loaded as always and fit his big hand fast and easy. His chest heaved with adrenaline-soaked breaths as he double-handed the gun, pointing it straight up.

The cab groaned as it was lifted and then dropped. The cab moved again, rocking in place, scraping against the rocks. The driver's door window exploded, raining cubes of glass on Tom, then the door was ripped away, and a foul odor flooded the cab. Honey pulled the trigger, firing at the blackness filling the hole.

The Desert Eagle let go three rounds. The truck rocked, then was still, and Tom could again see the starry sky through the empty door frame as the smoke cleared. Whatever was up there must have caught all three slugs.

He didn't want to be in his truck, but he didn't want to be outside, either. If something was waiting out there in the dark, it was probably mad. This could turn out to be one of the worst nights he ever had at the Bunker.

Tom wedged the cannon into the dash while he got himself on his feet. He tried to listen and smacked his head a few times with the heel of his hand to knock the ringing of the shots away, all the while paying extra attention to the hole over his head. He kept thinking of those cars with no people.

Giant ants, the sheriff said. Giant enough to rip truck doors off and cut cars in half.

Tom finally got on his feet and the right way round. He found his cowboy hat hung up in the steering wheel, put it back where it belonged, and pulled his pistol from the dash. He held it up with one hand, like he was in a duel, and slowly raised himself to poke his gun and head out of the cab. He did a quick look around and ducked back inside.

He took a few breaths, then raised up for another look. There was a bright moon, and he could see cars in the lot, torn up like the ones he saw on the highway.

Nothing was moving except Tom. He pulled and pushed himself up and out of the cab to sit on the panel behind the door hole. His boots swung in the empty tractor as he twisted to get a gander at what was around. The Bunker was way across the lot, but even at a distance, it seemed real inviting.

He scanned the lot again and then the highway. Nothing was moving. The sheriff said to wait, but he wanted to get into the bar. He calmed himself to think rationally, considering that he now believed the sheriff's report of giant ants. It was pretty convincing when that bug ripped the door from his truck.

Tom Honey accepted that something phenomenal was occurring, and he could, as a logical person, take all of these factors into account and make reasoned decisions.

Or he could jump off the truck and run like hell to the Bunker.

He slid over to the side of the truck to look before he leaped, which was good because the more he looked, the more the shadows shaped up to be a giant dead ant. Tom sucked air through his clenched teeth and pushed back from the edge to the other side of the truck. He looked over the side, then dropped down to the ground.

He tiptoed to the front of the truck, straining for sight or sound in the gloom. There were no giant ants to be seen, and it was dead quiet. He peered around the corner at the big ant, just to make sure it was still there. An enormous lifeless eye sparkled as the moonlight reflected in the facets. There was no mistake; it was a giant ant.

Between the aroma and the close-up look, Tom Honey was now a true believer in anything. He leaned forward and took another peep at the freak show. His face pinched up, and he shuddered. He had enough and turned to skedaddle.

Tom was a few furtive steps into the lot when a buzzing bug call stopped him. It was a distance off in the desert night. A moment later, there was a shrill answer from a different direction and then another from the other way. Tom acted like he was in a jailbreak. The noise to his right drove him left, then the one on his left … forward or back, he panicked. He turned to each call, pointing his big pistol. There were more calls, more giant ants shrieking from the desert.

Then, a new sound joined the fracas. A mechanical noise came from the building.

Light leaked out as the door began to rise, accompanied by the sound of a chain drive. Before it was another inch higher, Tom was hightailing it across the lot. Halfway across, he could see the silhouettes of two armed men crouched against the light with long guns.

He yelled out as he jogged through the lot, "It's me! It's Tom Honey! Don't shoot! It's Tom Honey! I'm no ant!"

Tom was not exactly built for running and for sure wasn't made for running and yelling at the same time, and, after his ordeal and all, he was slowing his jog. About fifty yards from the doorway, he had to stop. He leaned forward, bending over to prop both his hands on his knees and catch his breath.

As the door ground its way up, the lawmen scrambled into the lot and headed straight for Tom, one of them limping behind the other.

The trucker looked up as the sheriff hurried past the winded driver, calling out as he ran by, "Tom Honey – glad to see you!"

Cal passed the newly deceased ant by Tom Honey's truck on the way to his hat. The sheriff picked it up and carefully flicked away some debris before slapping the dust off on his leg. He snugged it on as he turned and trotted by the big bug dripping head goo into the moonlight. "Good shooting, Tom!" the sheriff uttered as the equilateral triangle of bullet holes in the monster's head caught the light and reflected uncanny placement.

He beat it across the lot, catching up with the driver and deputy, almost to the door.

"Glad to see you made it, Tom. Let's get you inside," the sheriff said, coming up to the driver's side and taking him by the upper arm, hurrying and helping him to the building. The deputy let go of the driver, dropped behind to limp after them, and scanned the lot as they made their way inside.

"Could you fellows pick up the pace?" Deputy Rosales called to them. "I get the feeling we are not the only ones out here."

As they got to the door, Walt and Nikki were waiting just outside. The others were standing behind the swinging doors as the trio entered.

"Mr. Honey," Nikki said to the driver, "I'm so glad you're safe." She took charge of his arm and walked with him through the doors. His face and the front of his shirt were covered in his dried blood. The crowd made way for them as they entered. Concerned about Tom's bloodied countenance, she looked around for Syl and waved her over from the bar.

Tom sat heavily in the chair, put his pistol on the table, took his hat off, and covered the gun. "Thought I was ant food for sure," he said, putting his head in his hands and taking a deep breath. Nikki gently patted his back and walked to the bar, saying, "I'll get you something to drink."

Walt walked by, clapping Honey on the shoulder as he passed on the way to the door controls. "Glad to see you, Tom. Heard you ran into one of our new mascots out there."

"Did you see that thing?" Tom asked, shaking his head. "That beats all get-out."

"You were lucky," the sheriff said, "that was a little one."

Tom Honey looked at the sheriff. He wasn't kidding.

The lawman nodded and took a seat at the table, pushing his reclaimed hat back on his head. The deputy sat on the edge of the neighboring table, just outside the overhanging light.

The driver wiped his face and looked at Sheriff Jeffries, "Giant ants, huh?" he shook his head, "Didn't know what to make of it when you told me that, Cal. But I'm favoring believing you."

"Pretty wild, eh, Tom?" the deputy said.

"I reckon. But someone here's been hinting at these things for a long time," Tom answered.

Walt came over to the table, pulling his leg along, "That's me you're talking about. I heard. Just not one to say I told you so." He clapped Tom Honey on the shoulder again and said, "I knew no stinking ants would get the White Scorpion." He laughed and clapped the driver's shoulder again and then again.

Nikki came back to the table with a large glass of cold water for the driver and put it in front of him.

"Thank you, ma'am, I'm parched," he said, taking a long drink, emptying half of the glass, and smacking his lips. "That hit the spot, for sure." The driver took a kerchief from his back pocket, wet it, and began wiping his face of dried blood and dust.

Nikki was about to sit down and said, "Oh, I forgot the towels. Wait a minute, Mr. Honey."

He looked up at the young woman, stopped mid-swipe, and dropped his jaw. "It's you!" he shouted in delight. "I'll be fiddled!" he exclaimed, jumping from his chair and burying her in a bear hug. He broke the embrace to hold her at arm's length and said, "I have to admit, I was a bit worried about you out there." He squeezed her again. "I am glad to see you, Nik!"

"And I'm glad to see you – especially after that wreck. I'm so happy you're OK!" she said with a wide smile and went in for another squeeze. "But I have to say, it looks like you didn't exactly come out untouched." She gently lifted the big man's chin to the dim light of the barroom. "Ouch," she said.

"Aw, it's nothing," he laughed and winced. "You should see the other guy." He laughed and smarted as he returned to his chair and sat across the table from Walt.

"We can get you fixed up, Tom," Walt said as Syl walked to the table. "Could you take a look at Tom here? He's had a night."

Walt turned to the big driver and said, "The Bunker's got medical staff now. We like to keep up with the times." He laughed, reached across the table, and patted Tom's hand. "A real live nurse. She'll give you the once-over and patch up what's needed. This is Syl."

Syl dropped the kit of medical supplies on the table. "Hi," she said to him. "Tom, right?" she asked, pushing his kerchiefed hand from his head and looking at his nose and face. She took a wet towel and finished cleaning his face. He yelped when she dabbed his nose.

"That looks broken," she said to the driver. "That is unless it was always that ugly. Can you breathe through it alright?"

"It's a little hard to get air through it. Kind of hurts, too," he replied with a boxer's last-round smile.

"Not surprised," she said, holding his head in both hands and moving it back and forth in the barroom light. "Pretty swollen. Looks like you caught an airbag or the steering wheel. The good news is it doesn't look too broken," the nurse told him. "Here, blow your nose like a good boy," she handed him the wet towel. "Might be a little bloody and sting a bit."

She turned to Walt and asked, "Some ice?"

Walt started to stand, but Nikki pushed him back in his seat as she walked by, saying, "I'll get it. I know where everything is now. Need anything else, Syl?" she asked over her shoulder as she returned to the bar.

"No, just the ice – oh, well, maybe another towel, too," she answered. Syl turned to her patient and said, "We'll get something cold on that,

159

and it will feel a lot better." She ran her fingers over both sides of his nose, gently feeling the placement and asking, "Does this hurt? How about this?"

"Just a little," Tom answered, "Not too bad, kind of sore, just a ..."

The sheriff squinted up at the dark ceiling away from the driver.

There was a sudden, grinding crack as Syl pushed straight down on his nose, and Tom yowled loud enough to make everyone in the bar jump.

"There you go, Tom. All set," she said to him with a satisfied laugh, "How about that? Did that hurt?"

The shocked and pained expression began to clear from his face, and he answered, "Well, yes, ma'am – it did hurt. Hurt considerable. That kind of surprised me."

"That was the idea," Syl said as Nikki returned, and she took the ice and towel from her. "Can you breathe better now?"

Tom tried an experimental inhalation through his nose. "Well, I'll be darned," he said. He took another, "It is altogether better. I'll be darned."

"No charge," the nurse said, "Compliments of the Bunker."

She wet the towel, rolled up some ice cubes, and handed the cloth to the driver. "Here, keep this on. It'll help," she said to him.

"Thank you, ma'am,' Tom said. He gave her the thumbs up. "You do have a knack for setting a fellow straight."

"That's my job,' she said, rearranging the medical supplies and stowing them in the bag.

The sheriff leaned back in his chair outside the ring of lamplight and pulled his brim low, peering from under his hat across the table at the nurse.

CHAPTER EIGHT

THE SWARM

Environmental circumstances had changed to favor the giant ants, and the nest deep below the desert thrived. Water had returned, and there was enough food to encourage a growing population.

In the deepest chambers, the queen was surrounded by attendants that fed her and nurtured her eggs throughout their metamorphosis to more workers, more soldiers, and even more queens. The old monarch had already produced several eggs chemically destined to hatch egg-layers, the future queens that would leave the nest and establish new colonies.

The accelerated development of these eggs soon produced writhing larvae in abundance, all protected by the nursery workers, but also measured for conformance to immutable standards.

One pupa in the clutch had not developed properly. The rhythms of her undulations were discordant, and chemical challenges produced unexpected responses. When the dissimilarity was detected, the embryonic queen was pulled apart and consumed by her caregivers. She became part of the digested mash deposited in the farming chambers, food for the glowing fungi that fed the nest.

Other queens would emerge, each matched to a pair of suitors, the only males in the colony. Their life's mission was to compete with the other male to inseminate their princess in a courtship flight. Successful or not, the males return to earth to die while the impregnated females land and establish new nests, fertilized for a lifetime of reproduction.

Wriggling from their pupal sheath, the new kings and queens hatched and made their way through the long tunnels to the surface. They climbed out of the nest and into the desert dawn, where they completed their metamorphosis with the help of their attendants. Workers groomed the royals as they circled the anthill, vibrating their bodies and unfurling their membranous wings to stiffen in the warming rays of the rising sun.

The cone of the anthill was alive with the giant insects; a dozen new queens and their suitors were crowded by their attendants. The giants' vibrations combined into an intense resonant buzz that echoed to the mountain walls of the vast desert basin.

In seeming chaos, the ants carried out their tasks; workers groomed, inspected, and stimulated their royal charges. The collective trill grew until the attendants unanimously scurried into the nest, filing down the hole and leaving a dozen queens-to-be and their eager followers above ground.

In the red light of the early morning, the first queen lifted off. As she took to the air, the buzz of her expansive wings rose to a stone-splitting vibrato. Her pair of princes ran in circles, panicked by her abrupt absence, and rose on their backmost legs, pulsing their wings faster and faster until they were a blur of power that pulled the creatures from the sand in pursuit of the once-in-a-lifetime chance to mate.

One after another, the future queens and rivaling suitors flew into the air with the sound, backwash, and velocities of a squad of Harrier jets. They hovered, zoomed up and out of sight, and were lost in the vast cloudless altitudes, heading to points plotted by their inborn compasses.

A dozen giant queens, soon to seed hundreds of thousands of offspring, singular in their genetics and unified in their imperative of conquest, were loose on the world. Within a few hours, they would seek safe shelter, living on their reserves while they populated their nests.

Now, there was no movement around the nest; all of the colony members were inside, where they would wait out the heat of the day. The soldiers and workers lined the tunnels with long lines of resting insects, motionless and waiting in the darkness until night signaled them to resume their instinctual expansion by extending their marauding raids.

"Did you notice there were no dead ants outside?" Walt asked the sheriff.

"I've been watching the monitors and saw them come up and take the dead ones away," the lawman said to the barkeep without looking up from his sandwich.

"Is that a fact?" Walt asked. "You'd think you might mention that, considering you guys were going out there."

The sheriff took another bite and chewed a bit. "We were going out anyway," he replied.

"To get your hat," Walt said.

"Got it." The sheriff smiled at the Cattleman on the bar next to him. "What about bedding down tonight, Walt? Need to make some arrangements for these folks."

"There's enough room downstairs. Shoot, more than enough in the dorm. The last time anybody stayed in there was your fortieth. Remember that bash?"

"No," the sheriff replied.

The barkeep laughed. "I'll get the fellows to help me set up, plus I want to secure a few things. There's a couple of secrets I think we should keep to ourselves for now. Like the gun room," he said, leaning over the bar to the sheriff. "They seem like decent enough folks, but you never know what a fix like this can bring out in people."

"Agreed." The sheriff finished his sandwich and washed it down with the last of his beer. "We'll keep it all on the Q.T. for now."

Walt nodded and shuffled behind the bar to Carlos, Billy, and Ray. Nikki joined the sheriff, and they watched the three guys follow Walt into the back.

The sheriff turned to the small crowd at the tables. "We're setting up accommodations for the night," he announced to the group. "There's pretty good quarters downstairs; rooms, bunks, showers. You'll all be comfortable and safe."

The professor's wife asked, "Sheriff, do you think we can go out to our cars to get our things?"

Everyone stared at her for a moment, then the sheriff replied, "No, ma'am, I wouldn't advise that."

"But my husband has medication he takes every evening, and I would like my suitcase," she rejoined.

"Yes, ma'am. That will have to wait until morning. We're not going to open the doors tonight," the sheriff said to her in a pleasant voice.

"But it would only take a minute or two. Don't you think it would be safe enough to …" she continued to insist until Deputy Rosales interrupted her.

"Lady, I don't think you want the doors open. Take a look," he said, motioning to the television.

Everyone turned their heads to the screen. Mike and the professor got up and moved closer to the video. The others followed along, clustering under the set. The deputy sat on a barstool in the middle of the group, holding the remote control as they watched in silence.

The security camera showed a night vision image of two huge ants immediately outside the door, inspecting the ant head. One busied itself, examining the door, running its long antennae across the slab's surface and the sidewalk in front. The other hoisted the large chunk of her nestmate in her jaws and walked off-screen.

"Waste not, want not," the professor said quietly, watching the show. "I think we can do without tonight, dear," he said to his wife. She nodded quietly.

"They've been pretty busy out there," the sheriff added. "They'll calm down in the daylight. There's nothing to do tonight but get some rest."

Walt and the fellows came back into the bar through the swinging kitchen door.

Billy stopped and looked at the group. "What'd we miss?" he asked.

"Nothing much," replied one of the linemen, "We were just watching TV."

The only ant on the screen moved out of view. Walt took the remote from the deputy and pointed it at the set. The screen changed, showing a wide shot. Other ants were moving, probing the wrecks.

The moon illuminated the scene.

"Look there," Tom Honey said, pointing. "That's my truck. Something's going on there."

Deputy Rosales half stood on the rungs of his stool and leaned closer to the screen, "Yep, that would be where your truck is, Tom. There are a couple of them back there. They sure are big."

"Must be after that one I left there. I'm pretty sure he was dead," the driver said.

"She," the professor said. "They're all females if I remember my biology. And I don't think they are there to help her. Just help themselves." He added again, "Waste not, want not."

"You mean they are going to eat it?" Nurse Syl asked from outside of the group.

"They eat everything," the lanky teacher replied. "They would have to eat everything – anything. You can't afford to be picky if you scavenge in the desert. And, based on the size and number we can see, they've been quite broad-minded as far as what's on the menu." He climbed onto a barstool and pulled a bowl of pretzels closer, "After all, I doubt if we have seen every one of these monsters. There's a high likelihood that there are many more of them. And, like all insects, they are occupied by only one purpose." He popped a pretzel in his mouth and crunched.

Everyone stared at nothing after the professor's noisy punctuation to his remark. After a moment, he crunched another pretzel and broke the silence.

Walt followed up, saying, "Alright. I guess we're all set downstairs. There's plenty of room for everyone. Three bunkrooms, two for the boys and one for the girls, or however you want to arrange things – blankets and cots for all. If anyone wants to turn in now, these fellows know where everything is," he gestured to Billy, Carlos, and Ray. "They can show you where the showers are, towels, whatever you need."

"That's not the worst thing I've heard today," said Tom Honey. "I think I'd feel better being deep down in this fort of yours, Walt."

The professor chimed in, "You shouldn't forget, Mr. Honey, the ants are at home 'deep down.' You could say the deeper we go, the more on their level we are." He felt his wife's hand on his shoulder. "Of course," he added, "the walls of this structure are quite substantial. I have no doubt they are just as thick below ground as above." The professor reached up and patted his wife's hand on his shoulder. "Maybe it would be a good idea to get some rest. Let's turn in early. What do you say, dear?"

"Yes, I think so," she said quietly to her husband. "That is a good idea," she managed a faint smile. "Tomorrow's another day, after all."

As the professor stepped off the stool, Walt interjected, "You know, there is an extra room down there with two cots, if you want. You could bunk in there."

The professor's wife replied to the barkeep, "Oh, that's very nice of you, thank you very much," she put her arm through her husband's. "I'd much rather be together," she said, looking up at her tall husband.

"Sure thing, ma'am," Walt said. "Could one of you guys show them where everything is and get them set up in one of those spares?"

"You bet, Walt," Billy said. "C'mon down," he smiled at the elderly couple. "You'll be snug as a bug in a … oh, well, not as a bug. Sorry," he corrected himself.

The couple and the barfly started toward the kitchen door and headed to the back room with a few others joining the retirement party. The truck driver left the bar, saying, "I'm done in. If you point me to a bunk, I will trouble you no more tonight."

The older lineman followed, "Count me in. I could use some shuteye." He turned to Walt, "Anything to read down there? Reading puts me to sleep."

"There's a shelf of books and some old magazines. Also, a TV with a VCR and a good-sized pile of movies, if you want," Walt said.

The young lineman perked up at this. "TV sounds good," he said. "I'm going, too."

The retirees left the barroom and went through the serving door to go downstairs. The remaining people sat without talking for some time. Walt turned off the television and put out some more beer for those that wanted them.

Sylvia asked for a soft drink. "I guess we're all trying to process this," the nurse said to the abbreviated group. "Really doesn't make sense," she said, but they remained quiet.

Nikki looked over to the nurse. "I don't see how it can," she finally said. "Today seems unconnected to every other day. It's weird. It's not like it was anymore, and it's like it won't go back to the way it's supposed to be."

The nurse lifted her ginger ale, "Here's to reality," she said and took a sip. She toasted again, saying, "I mean, here's to a new reality." She took another drink.

The sheriff came out of his brooding silence. "Luis," he said to his deputy, "You look like you had a long day. Maybe you should turn in, too. Some rest would do you good."

The deputy pushed his glass across the width of the bar and exhaled loudly. "I think you're right there, boss. I'm done." He pushed off from the bar, "I'm heading down. Which way do I go?"

Carlos spoke up, "Follow us, deputy. We're turning in, too." The two remaining regulars got off their stools and led the deputy through the door.

"Maybe you should, too," the sheriff said to Nikki. "It's probably later than you think, and you've had one hell of a day."

She smiled in response and said, "Honestly, I'm exhausted. But I don't know if I could sleep."

From his seat behind the bar, Walt said to the sheriff, "Well, you seem to be awful concerned about everybody's bedtime but mine. Imagine that. Not one thought for an old, tired man that saved the sheriff's hide. Well, I'm turning in, too, except I stay up here. Too many stairs." He wagged his thumb at the door across the barroom, "That's my digs. Usually, I sit on the deck outside before turning in, but I think I'll skip that tonight."

The barman slipped off his stool and made his way to the door to his room, saying, "I've had enough of today, plenty of it. Let's hope things look rosier tomorrow. Help yourself to anything you want," he said, closing the door behind him. "Sleep tight," he called back.

The nurse finished her soda and asked the sheriff, "So, where do I go?"

The sheriff pointed to the kitchen door and said, "Through there, go to your left. The big gray door opens to the basement staircase. Once you're down there, you'll hear the others."

"Then I'm off," Syl said. "Guess I'll see you two in the morning. Goodnight." She left the bar and went through the door, leaving it swinging.

The sheriff looked at Nikki and asked her, "Want to go for a moonlight stroll?" He smiled.

"Very funny," she smiled back at him.

"Don't worry," he said, lifting his beer. "Things will look worse tomorrow."

The night took a long time to tick by, and it felt like nobody slept. By the time morning got there, they were already up and anxious to see what was outside. Congregated in the barroom, the group spoke in short sentences about the plan: maybe do this or maybe do that. The fact that no giant insects were on any cameras bolstered their desire to open the door and see the outside for themselves.

Walt said to the sheriff, "The TV hasn't said anything about this, just the usual junk on the news, no mention of atomic monsters. I guess it's just us that's been infested. I keep switching back to see if anything shows up, but it makes me think they're already covering this up."

The sheriff looked up at the television, "It won't be covered up again, Walt. There are too many ways to get the word out these days. Help will be here soon, you can bet on it." He put on his cowboy hat.

According to their plan, the sheriff and the deputy went through the busted-up swinging doors, and Walt was at the control box. The old man pushed the button, and they crouched with their assault rifles behind the slab.

As the door opened, the desert dawn came into view, and in the light of a new day, things did look worse.

The monster ants had been active during the night. They had destroyed the vehicles in the lot. Some had been turned over; some were sheared into pieces by the giant jaws. Tires were torn off, the trunks and car roofs were ripped open, and the contents were spread over the parking area. There wasn't a usable vehicle in the lot. But at least it wasn't dark.

Nothing moved across the parched landscape. The ant tracks covered the lot, and paths led to and from Tom Honey's overturned cab and the front door of the Bunker. Half of the sheriff's Bronco was wheels up in the dirt, and the other half was across the lot.

The sheriff and deputy split up and headed past the broken posts of the tether rail. Each took a position in the lot to reconnoiter their surroundings.

Nothing moved.

Tom Honey stepped onto the wooden sidewalk with the glinting Desert Eagle, and the others filled the doorway behind him. The sheriff held his hand up, motioning for them to stay put. He looked over to the deputy and nodded him forward to the next wreck. Rosales trotted over and assumed a supporting position, covering the sheriff and sweeping the area.

Cal squinted from the rising sun to scan the horizon of highway and desert scrub.

Still, nothing moved.

The lawman crossed the lot, picking his way through the wreckage to the road. A thin coating of sand from the storm covered the pavement and lot, and it was all tracked up by the ants. The monster trails disappeared into the desert.

There were no tire tracks to be seen in either direction. No vehicle had tried the road during the night. The ants were the only sign of life.

The people had collected outside. Some fiddled with their phones. The deputy kept his eyes open for monsters.

Nikki walked to the highway beside the sheriff and stared into the desert. "How's the arm?" she asked. They hadn't talked much that morning.

"Not bad," he answered. His sore side had made him forget about the gash in his arm.

"The nurse fixed you up pretty good, I guess. We can check it later," Nikki said.

He didn't answer but smiled at her.

"See anything out here?" she asked.

"Kind of what I haven't seen that bothers me," he answered.

"What's that?"

"Look at the road," he said. "See all the marks in the dust from the bugs?"

"Uh-huh."

"See what you don't see?" he asked her.

She stared for a moment and looked short and long down the highway. "There's no other tracks,' she said. "There's been no cars all night."

The sheriff nodded grimly. "That's about the size of it," he said. "Makes me think we weren't the main event. Like the professor said – there's probably more of them."

There was a sudden rush of wings behind a pile of torn metal and tires as two ravens broke into the air. The sheriff wheeled and pointed his rifle in their direction, lowering it when he saw the birds. He straightened up. "Let's go back and see if anybody's been able to get any news," he said to her.

The people were picking through the wreckage in the lot, retrieving whatever belongings they could find, shaking off dust and broken glass. The deputy was by his squad car, now a convertible, holding the radio handset. He looked at the two, shook his head, and threw the mic back into the junk pile.

As the sheriff and Nikki got closer, the deputy took his hat off and leaned against the remains of his car. "We have to come up with a plan, boss," Rosales said.

"Already got one," the sheriff said. "I plan on getting something to eat." He looked along the roofline of the Bunker. "Get these folks inside. If one of those bugs shows up while they're out here, it won't go well."

The sheriff stepped past the small crowd onto the boardwalk. He got their attention with an upraised hand. "Let's go inside and talk over what we want to do. We can get something to eat and take it from there," he said to the group.

Walt was standing in the doorway behind him and chimed in, "Good idea. We can get a pretty decent breakfast going. Everything's on the house, folks, c'mon in. You can't beat a free feed."

The older lineman looked over at his utility truck, which had been pushed onto its side, "Not like there's much choice. Not unless we want to hoof it." He looked at the cherry picker that had been ripped from his truck. The boom was several feet away, bent over most of a car. "I'd like to find out what's happening in the rest of the world. This is getting kind of hard to swallow."

"Even for me," his young partner said. "And I'm a fan. This is a zombie apocalypse, except with ants." He laughed nervously. "Really, I'm freaking out." He added in a lower voice.

The people clustered around, listening to the sheriff but not moving. "Look, I don't know if there is any good explanation for all of this. There's no cell signal, the sheriff's radio is off the air, and there's nothing on TV about this, but you can't shut down a highway and expect no one to notice. There's a pretty big military base right on this

172

road, they'll notice. The best thing to do is to wait for help, and the best place to wait is inside."

Tom Honey leaned against the broken hitching rail post. "Nothing on the highway, Sheriff?" he asked.

Sheriff Jeffries looked at him and said, "That's a fact, Tom. Doesn't look like anyone's been on the road all night. East or west. That means nothing from Las Cruces, nothing from Alamogordo. No tracks in the dust. No tire tracks, that is," he added.

The professor said, "That's disturbing news. You don't think those creatures can control such a large area, do you, sheriff?"

"I don't know any more than the rest of you," the sheriff answered. "Except maybe it would be better if we went inside."

Dawn had broken, and the desert brightened.

They stood quietly, staring across the highway, until the trucker chimed in. "Sure, sure. Anyway, with what I saw on the road yesterday, all those cars without a soul around, well, just because of that, there's going to be cops, the Army, National Guard. They'll be here. Anyone that can do anything will be on the job, you can bet," he said and looked at the lawman. "You know what I mean, Sheriff."

Cal smiled at the big trucker and said, "I know. But I'm going to say it again. Let's go inside. For all we know, one of those things could come around the building at any time, and we don't want to be out here if that happens."

That got a rise from the group. Faces turned in all directions, looking for anything coming around any corner.

Nurse Syl was the first one to move. She started for the door, stepping onto the boardwalk, saying, "That's enough for me. I'm all for going inside."

She stopped when the professor said aloud to himself, "Or whatever might come with them."

Syl looked at the elder educator. "What? What do you mean by that?"

"Oh, just thinking out loud," he said, stroking his beard. "Doesn't matter. Idle speculation."

"What is?" the young lineman asked. "What are you talking about, professor?"

"Well, you see, I was just thinking, speaking academically, that is," the professor answered, straightening himself. "I was wondering if there might be anything else accompanying these mutations. That is, life doesn't evolve in a vacuum. And this is a very definite evolution. Insects are part of an ecosystem, with their flora and fauna, parasites – even ants. It would be odd if these monsters could develop independently of their dependents, so to say." He cleared his throat then continued, "I, for one, would not be surprised if these beasts were accompanied by ..." he stopped, looking at the faces of the small crowd, then putting an arm around his wife. She buried her face in his shoulder.

"You mean there might be other freaks of nature around here?" the young man asked.

"Just speculation, as I said," the professor quickly concluded, comforting his wife. "Just thinking out loud. Probably nothing to it." He leaned his head into his wife's hair and held her.

The small crowd stood silently, looking away from each other, concentrating on their own thoughts.

The sheriff exhaled slowly, thinking about what to say to the group, when a faint buzz drifted across the road from the desert. Their faces turned upward to the sky. That's where the noise came from.

They listened over the highway as another and another buzz came from the dunes – more insects adding their voice to the chorus, building the distant drone to a resonance that vibrated the sands of the desert.

The volume rose, filling the air and riveting the small audience watching the skies. Nikki spotted them first. She pointed, squinting into the sunrise, and said cautiously, "Look. Look at that. What is that?"

They shaded their eyes, straining to watch the insect fly into the red skies of the morning sun. It hovered as two more quickly followed, and the three sped off. Then another flew into the cloudless morning, also followed by two companions. Then, three more. The line continued, riding the buzzing crescendo into the sky, turning and wheeling away in different directions. At last, the final trio of insects disappeared as faraway specs.

The desert was quiet again.

"It was them," Rosales said, staring after the insects.

The faces of the group pointed up, searching the morning sky, everyone except for the truck driver. He sat on the edge of the wooden walk, looking across to the desert. "So, now they're flying?" he asked in a hoarse voice.

CHAPTER NINE

THE SCOUT

They were back inside, in the safety of the Bunker with the protective door closed.

"I didn't know they could fly," the young lineman said to the group in general and no one in particular. "I don't get how something that big could get off the ground."

"Well, we all saw it," said the trucker.

"Anyway, Bran, if you're going to buy into giant ants that rip cars apart," the older lineman opined, bending his head to Tom Honey, sitting across the table, "then what's the big deal about them flying?"

Brandon was sipping his orange juice and stopped, holding a pose momentarily while he thought. "You're right," he conceded. "This is the ant-alypse and anything can happen. Totally makes sense. We are living in science fiction," Brandon said.

The professor spoke up, "Not all of the ants fly, you know. I believe the ones we saw are newly hatched queens leaving the nest to start their own colonies. That is if these monsters follow the behaviors of the everyday ant." He leaned back in the low chair and locked his fingers behind his head.

"You mean, these things are spreading? There are going to be more of them? More nests?" one of the barflies asked.

"Undoubtedly," the professor replied, "that is the objective of life, is it not?" He leaned his chair back on two legs and rocked it slowly. "Interesting interaction, the lower life form with less complex motivations versus human beings, considered, at least by themselves, to be the most advanced form of life, but beset by every type of motivation: greed, love, lust, envy, and the list goes on." An old accent

176

popped out as the teacher, lost in thought, stroked at his well-groomed beard.

After a moment away, he came back to the present and let his chair down. He leaned forward into the light, putting an elbow on the table. "Ants, on the other hand, need no diagnosis as to motive. They eat and reproduce. They consume everything to spread their progeny. As I recall, they've been around since the dinosaurs, so they have survived far longer than humans ever will. A simple, successful strategy." The professor chopped the table with the edge of his hand on each of his last three words.

He leaned back to conclude for his rapt assembly, "The lowly ant. So simple compared to humankind, yet our aims are the same – two very distinct approaches to the same goal. Theirs is very simple. And ours, tangled in layers of foolish complexities." He illustrated the tangle by twirling his fingers in the air. "The advantage goes to the ant. And, they have another – they cooperate after all."

"So, the lofty goal of life is just to keep going?" Nikki asked, in idle contradiction.

"Perhaps ultimately," the professor answered. "But we should allow intention to count." He laughed and added, "Even if the outcome is the same. For instance, we imagine a planet dominated by humans but filled with other forms of life as well." He shrugged and clasped his hands behind his head. "How true that would be, who knows?"

The professor returned to the table and leaned into the circle of light. "Not the ants," he said as if he were telling them all in confidence.

"Their goal is to be the dominant species, to the exclusion, more correctly, to the oblivion of all other types of life. A planet of nothing but ants, always at war, feeding on their own kind," the educator answered, absently tracing his finger on the tabletop as if puzzling a problem. "Ironic, isn't it? Perhaps poetic."

"I might see the irony," Nikki said, "but where's the poetry?"

"Well, maybe not poetry, more of a dirge." He stopped doodling and looked up at the people around his table. "Because they may very well succeed," he concluded.

The people silently sat in the professor's circle until his wife spoke. "I don't know if I can believe any of this. After all, how could such things exist – and what proof do you have? I mean, common sense says they can't exist. They can't be." She looked around at the group. None met her watering eyes. "They can't. Can they?" She broke down and cried, leaning against her husband. He brought his arm around her as she sobbed into his shoulder, murmuring, "Maybe I've lost my mind, and this is all a crazy hallucination."

She repeated a few times quietly, "This can't be happening."

Walt and the two lawmen were at the bar with cups of coffee, talking quietly about the road and the options.

"The thing that concerns me is what you said about the highway, Cal," Walt said. "No cars went by all night? That is not a good sign." He shook his head. "How many of those bugs do you think there are? Enough to have taken over?"

Deputy Rosales looked at Walt and said to the old man, "You saw them flying off into the air, Walt. Must have been fifty of them, big as busses."

"Not fifty, not even half. Not the ones that count," the sheriff said, looking at Rosales. "And they weren't that big."

"Well, boss," the deputy replied, "they were pretty damn big for ants."

The sheriff looked up at the TV and switched camera views around the lot. "I'll give you that. They are damn big ants."

"Well, don't you think it's about time to call somebody?" Rosales said.

"It is," the sheriff answered, "maybe even past time. The problem is no phone, no radio, and no one's getting a signal. Makes it sort of hard to call anyone."

Walt drank some of his coffee during the pause, "Sounds like someone's got to do some reconnoitering," he said, looking over his cup at the sheriff.

"That's what I was thinking," the lawman said. He switched back to the early morning TV news. "Guess I'm going for a walk."

The old barkeep nodded slowly, "Figured you would be."

"I'll take two ARs and what ammo I can carry," the sheriff said.

"I'm going with you, right?" Rosales asked.

"I'd feel a lot better if you were, but no, Luis. That leg leaves you here. One of us has to stay anyway," Cal said to him. The deputy knew him well enough to leave it at that. The sheriff changed the TV back to the parking lot cams, switching through the views.

"I have a set of walkies, a couple of other things I got together last night that could be of use," Walt said. "There's a pile downstairs."

"Good. Sounds like a plan," he said. "Let's get this show on the road."

Walt called to Carlos, and the two of them went into the back to fetch the equipment for the sheriff's trip. The sheriff and deputy went to the hallway, taking Nikki in tow. They went to the control box for the front door.

The sheriff opened the panel and pointed to the buttons. "Be a good idea if you knew how this worked." She smiled at him, and he started to get distracted, smiling back.

"Maybe I can get some pointers, too," Luis said, reminding them he was there, too.

Cal blinked and returned to the control panel, directing Nikki's attention to the five round buttons, each with a metal guard over them. "Now, whatever you do, do not push the big red button that says 'drop' on it," the sheriff instructed her. "Just the green 'up' button or the yellow 'down' button. They will raise or lower the door slowly. The red 'drop' button drops it fast," he said to her in an extra calm and clear way, as if he were talking to a child with a stick of dynamite. "OK?" the sheriff concluded.

"I think I get it," she said, looking up and batting her eyelashes. "If I get scared or excited or start thinking about nail polish, push the red button that says 'drop' on it. But only if you're under the big rock." She smiled, fluttered her lashes again, and then cooed, "OK?"

He smiled. "Yeah, OK. You got it, alright." The sheriff turned and walked to the deputy by the slab door. He took his hat off and hung it from the cow skull's horn on the wall.

"Now, sheriff?" Nikki called from the swinging doors.

He shook his head, smiling.

Carlos came in with two ammo boxes and a rucksack, "Walt's bringing up the rest; said for me to hurry these up to you."

"Thanks, Carlos," the sheriff said, taking one of the cans. Kneeling by the outside door, he opened the ammo box and transferred magazines to the canvas backpack. "Fourteen mags," he said.

"You have to take water, too," Deputy Rosales said.

"I'd rather need water than bullets," he told the deputy.

The sheriff stood and put on a windbreaker for the pockets. He pulled the pack on and adjusted the belts.

Walt came into the hallway with another sack and took a few water bottles out, putting them into the sheriff's pack, "Five bottles. Good for most of the day if it doesn't get too hot. Figure you're heading to your station. That's only about two hours from here afoot."

The old man took compact binoculars and a small radio out of the sack and handed them to the lawman. "The next best thing to being there. Stick these in your pocket."

The sheriff straightened up, adjusted the pack, and slung the two rifles. His hand went to his gun belt, running his fingers over the full run of bullets on his waist. He looked back to the swinging doors.

"I'm ready to go," the sheriff said, turning to the outside door and reaching for his hat.

"Not quite," Nikki said. She was next to him and holding his hat. "Be careful. Come back." She reached up, put her hands with his hat behind his neck, and kissed him quickly. "I've never been this forward, but these are crazy times," she said.

His face felt warm. She turned back to the doorway, he caught her arm, turned her around, and pulled her tight, kissing her on the mouth strong enough for both of them to forget where they were. He held her by her arms, pushed her back, and let her go. "I'll see you later," he said.

Nikki shook her head slowly; her eyes were watery, and her breathing was noticeable. "I...I don't know what to say about all of this..."

"You don't know what to say?" Walt injected from behind the couple. "I am absolutely speechless."

Cal looked at his old friend and smiled. Nikki laughed and handed Cal his hat. "Be safe out there," she said.

The sheriff winked at her and said, "Back to your post."

Nikki went to the control box. The sheriff nodded to her, and the door started up. The lawmen crouched, peering into the outside. It looked clear, with no bugs in the lot.

Nikki's voice came from behind them, "Be careful, Cal."

The sheriff and deputy went under the door and came out in the early morning sun. They walked the wooden planks in front of the Bunker, eyeballing the lot with their rifles.

Most of the deputy's car was at the end of the building. The broken emergency lights hung from the roof by a wire.

"Don't forget about your handset," the deputy said to him. "We tested it last night. Keep me posted." Rosales eyed the desert past the sheriff. "Careful out there, Cal," he said.

"Watch yourself in there, too," the sheriff replied. "Keep one eye on those folks and the other on your back. You never know what people will do in a bad situation." The sheriff flicked his fingers off the brim of his hat toward the deputy. "Remember, the only one you know in there is Walt," he said as he stepped off the boardwalk.

"Will do," the deputy replied. He reached down and shook the sheriff's hand. "If you get a chance, bring back a pizza." He flashed a faint smile at the big man.

"Stay loose, Luis," the sheriff replied. "Keep an eye on Nikki. Keep her safe," he added as he walked away.

He crossed the lot to the highway and walked toward the morning sun and the smoke columns blooming along the horizon. If they were smoke signals, they didn't spell out anything good. He guessed the nearest was at the Air Force base, maybe 12 miles ahead. Hard to say, as the base covered a few miles on its own.

He crossed the scrub divider and continued walking east on the westbound side, keeping an eye on tall patches of weeds and drainage ditches along the way, anywhere an ant might lurk.

Cal kept a steady walking pace until he stopped at the motorcycle skid marks – a black rubber line smeared across the road to the weedy ditch. The sheriff walked to the edge and saw glints of chrome in the wide swath of overgrowth.

Past the ditch, a dotted line of footprints went into the weeds, running into the desert, ending at a dark area in the sand. Even from a distance, Cal could see the tracks were made by the running boots of the motorcyclist. Last night, the bike crashed, the biker ran out of the weeds, onto the flat sand, and intersected with the giant ant that made the giant ant trail. That left a disturbance in the sand that attracted flies.

The ant tracks from the blood puddle led across a quarter mile of flat sand to the base of a tall dune, then up and over the top.

Cal looked both ways down the highway, then to the sun. He wanted to make his sheriff's station before it got too late. But he also wanted to know what these ants got up to. He wanted a look over that dune.

He crossed into the ditch and made his way through the brambles to the motorcycle. There was a red skull emblazoned on the fuel tank. The engine was cool, and the key was in the ignition.

He wiped his brow, put his hat back on, climbed out of the ditch, and followed the tracks. They ran across the sand to the puddle of blood. As Cal approached the syrupy spot, he saw a black motorcycle helmet atop the snow-white sand. A fiery skull was intricately painted on the back of the helmet. Letters curled in the flaming artwork spelled 'Bite Me.'

He stared. The helmet was upright as if someone had placed it carefully. It faced away from him. The visor was pulled back.

The sheriff didn't like it.

He lowered his gun and touched the muzzle to the helmet. It rolled easily onto its side because it was top-heavy. The biker's head was inside, looking out. His dead face rocked with the helmet, looking up with dry eyes as a swollen, sand-coated tongue swung in rhythmic counterpoint.

Judging by his expression, the motorcyclist seemed horrified at his situation. Cal inhaled and tightened his lips, then carefully put a boot on the helmet to steady it and pushed the visor closed with the barrel of his rifle.

He lifted the gun and looked across a quarter-mile of nothing at the base of the dune. He'd be in a bad spot if an ant popped up. He was far from the road, on foot without any cover, and there was no way he could outrun them.

But he wanted a look over that mountain.

The sheriff crossed the flat quickly. He stopped at the base of his climb, pulled out his water bottle, and drank, wondering what he would do if those giants suddenly topped the dune and headed his way. Probably wouldn't do too much, he thought. He swallowed another mouthful of water.

He knew from the parking lot that they could be shot dead, and he was packing a fairly good punch with the ARs. He would have taken his Mossberg, but there were not enough slugs.

He put the water bottle back in his pack and started his climb, paralleling the trail in case the ants came back using the same path to the road. He kept about thirty yards between him and the tracks going up.

It was tough going through the sand. He thought about leaving his backpack and picking it up on the way down but couldn't risk losing the water and ammo, so he toughed it out.

It was midmorning and getting hot. He stopped about halfway up and rested on his knees, looking across the snow-white face of the dune at the line of ant tracks he was dogging.

Cal sat in the bright gypsum, squinting up the hill with his first gun across his legs. He pulled out the half-full water bottle, drained it in a few gulps, and stuck the empty back in the pack. He looked down at the road, watching a little dust devil dance down the highway.

The sun was getting higher. He got up and started slogging again, pushing against the damn sand to the top of the dune.

Cal was counting on the idea that the ants were less active in the heat of the day. Probably weren't many about, and he figured he could do his entire recon without running into a single one of them.

A staccato trill rolling over the dune stopped him in his tracks. The same song came from the bug that tried to eat him last night. The sheriff had a bad association with that tune.

He crouched with his rifle pointed at the top of the dune. The music stopped, and he strained to hear any new sound. He narrowed his eyes and scanned the ridge. Nothing. He breathed again and pushed off, doubling his effort to the top. As he reached the crest, he slowly raised his head to look down at the ant colony on the other side.

An involuntary oath came out as he stared over the summit. There were six distinct cones with holes centered in them, like typical ant hills, except these were large enough to swallow a car. From his vantage point, he could see well-worn trails that ran from the mounds into the surrounding wasteland, snaking over the dunes and into the desert. They went in all directions, though most ran parallel to the highway, heading east and west for as far as he could see, running behind the cover of the dunes.

He pushed the stock of his rifle into the gypsum, standing the gun in the sand, and pulled the mini binoculars from his jacket pocket to get a close-up of the ant holes. There was no movement.

The sheriff calculated the mounds to average thirty feet tall and the diameter of the openings around ten feet or more. He felt like he was looking through the wrong end of the binoculars as he scrutinized each hole, watching the surreal diorama for signs of life.

Then he saw it. One of those huge bugs emerged from the furthest hole in the group, lifting itself from the darkness into the searing desert sun. It paused on the brink, rotating its huge head slowly, letting the antenna drink in the local news. The way the wind was blowing, Cal didn't think he'd be part of it but shrank behind the crest of the dune to peer at the distant beast.

185

It might have been a type smaller than the ones at the Bunker, but it was still big. For its size, the ant easily exited the shaft, scuttled down the cone, and ran over the white sand without any trouble. It was pretty nimble, the way it made its way over the loose powder. He was glad it was heading away and thought it was time for him to do the same.

Propped on his elbows, he stuffed the glasses back into his jacket and got to his knees, picking up his rifle. He turned and sat on the sand, keeping the top of his hat below the top of the dune.

He had seen what he came to see and rose, looking down at the highway. He gasped. Two giant ants were creeping along the road.

He shook his head, pulled the glasses out, and cursed again. He watched the pair of mutant insects catch his trail. They stopped, and each cast their long feelers over the roadway. Their antennae touched, and then the monsters were on his scent, following him to the edge of the road and into the ditch. One of the ants lifted the wrecked motorcycle, carried it back to the highway, and dropped it on the asphalt. A moment later, the clatter reached him.

He repeated his curse a little louder as he watched the movie unfold through the field glasses. The ants were curious, and they were onto something. They were sniffing him out. He could see them putting his trail together.

"Damnation," the sheriff muttered beneath the binoculars.

From his perch at the top of the dune, he watched the two monsters cross the flat sand, following their feelers and his footprints as if they could see. The ants stopped at the base of the slope. Lifting their antennae to sample the air made it seem like they were looking up at the sheriff. He unconsciously shrank into the sand, still peering through the glasses, transfixed.

"That's that," he said.

He couldn't outrun them, and he couldn't elude them. He watched them move across the sand and follow his trail. They were fast, better than bloodhounds. Even if he could make it off the dune, they'd track him.

A breeze came over the dune and cooled the back of his sweaty neck. He cursed. Upwind, just where all good game should be.

The sheriff could almost see the air carrying his scent down the dune right into their faces. He could tell when it hit their noses or feelers or whatever they had to smell out their game because they got a snootful of sweating sheriff.

The ants stopped sweeping his tracks in the sand. One of them raised on her rear legs, swiveling her giant head in the scented breeze. It lowered, and the ants communicated, brushing their antennae together and touching each other to exchange chemical messages.

In unison, both began climbing the white hill, coming straight for the sheriff. They no longer needed to sniff his trail from the sand; he was on the wind, and they knew exactly where he was.

He edged back to the top and glanced over to ensure that while his attention was focused on the front, he'd get no surprises from that side.

The sheriff looked past his boots to see them eagerly charging up the dune.

He would start blasting when they got close. He hoped the ARs would make short work of them, but he didn't know if the commotion would rouse the nest.

The giants made steady progress up the slope, right into his trap. The sheriff liked that this was his trap, not that he was the bait, and he had the high ground. He stood and smacked the magazine and clicked the safety off.

Cal dropped his backpack onto the sand and put his loaded rifle on top of it. He pulled a magazine from his jacket and snapped it into the other weapon, pulling the charging handle back to put a round in the chamber. He laid the rifle next to the other on top of the bag.

The lawman got comfortable on the sand and lifted one of the guns. He pushed his heels into the gypsum and propped his arms on his knees. He took a bead on the lead ant, closing the distance at a good pace.

The dune had a fairly good grade, but the first bug was really moving and was about two ant lengths ahead of the other. She was big and coming on strong.

When the colossal ant had scrambled to a 100-yard downslope, he fired deliberately. Each pull of his finger put a round into the monster's head. Then he picked up the pace, firing rapidly, emptying half of the ammo into the charging beast.

The huge insect covered more ground, then slowed and staggered off course. It stopped, took a few faltering steps, fell on its side, and began sliding and rolling down the steep incline. The other ant following the first was now exposed and charged past her dying sister without slowing. He gave her the other twelve rounds, but she kept coming.

The bullets had no apparent effect. He put the gun on the bag and snatched up the other loaded weapon. He pushed the safety and pulled the trigger.

Click. Nothing. The rifle didn't fire.

The sheriff cursed loudly as the ant closed the distance. He tested the safety with his thumb and released the magazine; it slid from the gun into his hand as it should, and he reinserted, hitting it home with the heel of his hand. He racked the slide to clear the rifle. He smacked the side of the gun; everything was in firing order. He pulled the trigger, and nothing, another click with no bullet.

The ant was moving fast at thirty yards and closing the gap. The sheriff released the magazine, let it slide out, pushed it back in, and smacked it home. The creature shaved another ten yards off the run. The sheriff brought the gun up and clicked. Nothing.

The ant doubled in size as it got closer.

Cal threw the malfunctioning weapon into the sand and snatched the other rifle from his bag. He dropped the empty mag with his left hand, grabbing another from the pack with his right. He snapped it in. The huge insect was close enough that the sheriff could see every detail of the bug's face and snapping jaws in the bright sunlight.

He pulled the bolt back, pushed his heels deeper into the sand, and braced for the impact. The mutant was an ant length away and reared on its back legs, throwing sand all around. Her scissoring jaws gnashed as the monster rose, twisting for the attack and curling her stinger forward.

The lawman was on his back and had his weapon up, pulling the trigger again and again. This time, each pull blasted a steel-jacketed round into the nightmare.

He emptied the full clip into the monster and dropped it stone dead. The ant fell forward, her mandibles plowed into the chalky sand inches from the sheriff's boots.

Cal lay in the sand, his chest heaving like he'd been running. He held the gun up with both hands and released the empty magazine. Reaching into his bag, he pulled another one out without taking his eyes off the bug. He slapped the new mag in and pulled the bolt.

The sheriff pushed up in the white sand to put a few more inches between himself and the giant jaws. He figured the noise of another few shots wouldn't matter and sat up to put half a dozen more rounds in the bug's brain or into the general area where he thought it should be. Leaning back on his elbows, he stared at the motionless carcass, then dropped back, flat on the sand, and closed his eyes on the blue morning sky, patting the hot gun across his chest.

Sheriff Jeffries opened his eyes after only a moment away from reality. He was lying on the white sands of the Chihuahuan Desert. All he saw was a bright morning sky. He exhaled forcibly and sat up, looking at the body of the massive ant at his feet. It wasn't a dream; it wasn't some late-night movie with too much whiskey. It was an impossibility at his feet.

The breeze rolled over the top of the dune and cooled his back. That was good. He had seen the giant ants' reaction when they caught his scent on the air. As soon as they got wind of him, they charged. He didn't want his scent going the other way, down to the colony. Two of these giants were enough, especially with one gun.

That thought got him to his knees. He picked up the malfunctioned rifle, released the magazine, and cleared the chamber. He collected the spent magazines and pushed them into the bag.

The sheriff got to his feet and shouldered the backpack, looking over the crest at the holes.

He scanned the ant village with the binoculars and saw no movement, nothing but the six enormous cone-shaped mounds, each with a cavernous entrance in the center. From his position high on the dune, the excavations looked like a collection of volcanoes rooted in the valley.

Turning his head, he looked west and saw bits of the highway's long ribbon. Guessing the Bunker's location, he figured this was where they saw the ants take off early that morning.

Satisfied it was quiet at the nest, and there were no giant surprises sneaking up, the sheriff turned to make his way down the dune and back to the road. He took a few steps through the shifting powder and stopped next to the giant's body, studying it in the full light of the sun.

Bullet holes in the front of its head leaked thick amber syrup into the sugary sand. The sheriff prodded the bug with his rifle. Satisfied again that it was dead, he examined the monster, struck by the physical complexities of the enormous creature.

He shook his head in awe, then fired three more rounds into its head. "Try to eat me, will you?" he snarled, then kicked the mutant.

The smell from the insect remains reminded the sheriff of the deep ammoniac odors of cattle urine mixed with dirt, then of the night before when the ant tried to bite him in half. The first smell made him a little homesick; the second made him mad.

He kicked the carcass again.

The head was massive, strongly constructed, and ended in a savage pair of jaws with large toothy serrations to grip and tear. He put his hand on his holstered .45 and toed the mandibles. The length of the insect was about fifteen feet. The head was wide, maybe seven feet, proportionately too large for the body. Three of the six legs were curled under the body. The other legs dangled, hanging limply in the air. The stubbled shafts of the appendages were jointed and ended in two-pronged claws for grabbing and climbing.

The ant was armored in a black shell – extremely hard but not bulletproof. This one took two dozen rounds from a shooter in a superior position in broad daylight. And there were only two ants. Fighting them in the dark would be a losing proposition.

As he walked by the critter, staring at the nightmarish body, the sheriff bumped into a claw hanging from one of the uplifted legs. He stepped back and peered at the pincer, barbed and big enough to fit around his throat. Cal rubbed his neck.

The sheriff was as familiar as most with the shape of a typical ant, and this giant seemed to follow the basic design. The close-up view of the insect's anatomy made him wonder if these details were on the regular-sized versions or if they were exclusive features of these freaks, resulting from their genetic mutation.

He figured everything on the ant's body served a purpose, but it boiled down to the fact that they were armored, fast, and deadly in any number of ways.

As predators, the ants impressed the sheriff. They had found his trail and attacked without hesitation. They had no problem scenting him off the wind and worked together. The fact he was alive, and they weren't, was a testimony to his assault rifle, not to him. Man, beast, or monster, nothing survives a dozen rounds to the head.

And despite being kind of beat up, its head was fascinating. The eyes were as large as truck tires, bulging and covered with hundreds of facets, like a fly's eye. The long L-shaped antennae attached to the face with ball sockets, allowing a complete range of motion, and were covered in fine and coarse hairs along their length.

Most of the ant's jaws were buried, as it had crashed face-first into the sand when he gunned it down, but the parts above grade showed savage tearing teeth rimming the sickle-like mouthpart's inner arc. The sheriff felt his bruised ribs thinking of the near miss he had with the bug bite at the bar and tried to shrug the thought away. His ribs still hurt like hell.

He shook his head again, pulled his hat on tight, and started down the dune, walking along the huge ant that terminated in a foot-long stinger. A day ago, he couldn't have guessed if an ant had a stinger. Now he knew for sure. It was a poisonous-looking barb, black and shining sleek, the perfect end to these deadly nightmares.

He stopped a few feet past the bug and pulled the glasses from his pocket. He wanted a better look at the next dead ant further down the dune. He wanted to be sure it was still good and dead. The sheriff watched for a moment through the binoculars and saw no movement. The ant that had tumbled halfway down the slope lay in the sand, legs up to the sun. It looked about as dead as he had hoped, but even so, as he made his way down the dune, the sheriff cut to his left and gave the ant carcass a wide berth.

Going down the sand was a lot easier than climbing up. The sun was just past noon by the time he reached the bottom. He crossed the flat desert floor to one of the high-tension poles next to the highway. Unslinging the backpack, he knelt in the sand to go through his kit. Three bottles of water, eleven full magazines, and one in the good gun. He reached over and took the malfunctioning assault rifle and examined it, turning it in his hands, looking for any clue to the problem. He checked the chamber, pulled the takedown pin out, and broke open the weapon to remove the bolt carrier. He checked inside the assembly. There was no firing pin.

He remembered Luis said they had checked everything.

The sheriff stared at the useless assault rifle for a moment, then put it down in the sand at the base of the pole. He took the other gun and checked it thoroughly. It was all good. The lawman stood in the sand, drank half a water bottle, screwed the cap back on, and stuck it back in the pack.

He threw the empty magazines next to the useless rifle and pulled the small radio out of his jacket pocket. He flipped the power switch on and saw the little green light glow to life. He pushed the transmit button and said, "Calling the Bunker, come in, Bunker." The sheriff released the talk button and pressed it a few more times, on and off. There was no sound, not even the static he should be hearing. Cal changed the frequency selector a few times and tried it again – still nothing.

The lawman held the radio in his hand, stared for a moment, then threw it next to the useless AR. He tightened the straps on the backpack, picked up the loaded rifle, walked to the roadway, and looked in both directions.

He could return to the Bunker, which was his closest option, or go on to the highway checkpoint, which was another hour of walking in the other direction. The facility also housed the sheriff's office, border patrol, and state police. His dispatch, Bernice, hadn't been on the radio when she should, and he wanted to know why.

Wherever he was going, the sheriff just wanted to be sure he wasn't on foot when the sun went down. He didn't have enough ammo for that.

According to his calculations, if he got to the station and it was bad news, he could make it back to the bar before dark if he double-timed it. And the way he figured it, he was on the road to find out something, not to go back empty.

The sheriff walked across the highway divider to the eastbound lane to put more space between him and the ants and White Sands. He hadn't much to do with the dunes over the years, what with them being a national park, but at this point, he'd developed a positive aversion to the place.

The sun was well past noon and hotter than he wanted. But the highway was all his. There was no sound, near or far, and he walked through the silent heat, always watching the landscape. The ants were smart to stay inside because it was set to broil. He was thirsty but decided to ration his water for the walk as he still had about three or more hours round trip back to the bar.

The sheriff stopped in the road and took his hat off to wipe the sweat. He stuck it back on and unbuttoned his shirt as he started walking, licking his dry lips.

It wouldn't be too much longer before he got to the station. He assumed the ants had hit them; otherwise, he would have seen patrol cars on the road. Nothing was moving on the road except him, and a new smoke column joined the others on the horizon. It had been a bad night for a lot of folks.

The sheriff slowly rounded a curve in the highway and saw an overturned car. As he approached, one look told him there was nothing of use. The vehicle had burned and was a charred framework of gray metal and burnt seat springs. Small wisps of smoke curled from the wreck. It might have been one of the columns of smoke he saw earlier. He noted tire tracks leading from the highway divider to the car. He stopped, surmising the vehicle was traveling in the lane opposite, and tried to make it to this side before being caught. The driver saw the ants coming and tried to get away but didn't.

The lawman kept walking, carrying his AR at the ready.

At the end of another mile, the graveyard of dead cars Tom Honey had told him about came into view. This was the place where the ants got aboard his rig. As the trucker had described, cars were torn open, tossed around, and burned up. The sheriff could see some of the vehicles were abandoned. Their doors were flung open and left wide as the people ran for their lives. It had been a slaughter.

And, as Tom said, there wasn't a trace of a person, living or dead.

He crossed through the weeds to the wreckage.

Picking his way through the debris, he kept his eyes on both sides of the road, scanning for movement. Nothing moved. He walked slowly through the car parts, checking if any vehicles were operational. They were not.

He tread quietly. Ant tracks led off the road, under the power lines, and into the desert. The way he read it, the monster ants were the first on the highway once the sandstorm let up. When traffic started moving again, they were waiting.

He wondered if it was the predator instinct to ambush the cars around a curve. Selecting a spot like that would mean they scouted and planned, and that would mean a whole different type of monster.

After they got the first one or two vehicles, the road would be blocked. Maybe the first few hits cost an ant or two, but after that, the wrecks themselves stopped anything from getting by and set them up for the kill.

The lawman leaned against the leftovers of a minivan and pulled out a bottle of water from his pack. He swallowed and looked at the overturned cars and crushed SUVs, evidence of the cold intelligence of the ants at work, letting their prey come to them. They staked out the trail.

He took another long draw on his water bottle as he contemplated. The same thought that struck Tom Honey, that he repeated more than a few times to the lawman, got to the sheriff. There were no bodies. No body parts. Neither people nor ants. They cleaned the scene when they finished. The tracks from the wrecks went up and over the dunes. Once over the hill, they'd get on the trail back to the nest, running parallel to the highway, hidden behind the dunes.

The sheriff had underestimated these mutations. They weren't bugs. They weren't mindless scavengers grabbing at whatever came by. They planned their predation and attacked with discipline. They were far more dangerous than he thought, something the professor in the bar had hinted at.

Surrounded by the remains of their attack, he knew it was only luck that he and his little group survived. They would have been carried off to the desert if they had been caught anywhere other than the reinforced building.

He thought of Nikki and how close she came to adding her car to this pile. She must have missed this bloodbath by minutes. On the other side, Tom Honey came through when the ants were cleaning up. He could have run into dozens of monsters if he had come through a few minutes earlier.

The sheriff drained the bottle and threw it onto the road. As he stood and snugged his pack on the hood of a wreck, Cal noticed a pickup nosed off the road. The driver's door was closed, and the window was up. The truck seemed untouched at first glance.

Cal walked over and opened the door, and looked through the cab. The passenger door was gone, ripped from the frame. The inside looked OK. There was a soccer ball key ring hanging from the column.

He opened the door, leaned into the truck, and turned the ignition. It started. The gauge read half. The lawman unslung his bag, took off his jacket, and threw them onto the passenger seat with his rifle. He got in and tossed the coffee container with lipstick on it out of the missing door.

Finding the truck seemed like good luck, and good luck made him antsy.

He put the pickup in gear, cut the wheel, and got back on the road, heading down the wrong side of the highway again. Now, he was moving. Within a few minutes, the debris field was more than a mile behind, and he could see the checkpoint station coming up ahead across the divider.

He stopped on the road across from the facilities. The ants had been there, and the compound had been destroyed. The face of the building had been torn away, exposing the offices inside through the jagged openings.

The sheriff drove across the weedy divider and into the lot in front of the demolished building. He rolled around back, looking for any signs of life. He put the window down and blew the horn a few times, listening between blasts. Nothing responded. Nothing moved.

On the far side of the complex, away from the road, large window walls were designed to afford law enforcement unobstructed views of the vehicles pulled in for inspection. The ballistic panels were smashed, and fractured glass shards hung from the twisted metal frames. Hundreds of bullet holes riddled the walls that were still standing.

At the end of the inspection plaza, three police cruisers had been piled together, one upside down, all ripped open. The white hood of the official car on top of the pile was smeared with congealed blood.

At the end of the long inspection shed was a semi with the cab door torn off and the driver's seat hanging through the opening. The trailer was splayed open as if a knife had been run down the side, pouring cardboard boxes onto the ground.

A tour bus was angled across the drive past the tractor trailer, blocking the exit. It looked undamaged. Cal drove over the curb to the other side of the big vehicle, but there was no other side. It was ripped open like a snack pack and picked clean of the passengers that belonged to the luggage spilled from the bus.

Exiting the checkpoint, he had to drive around the fallen communications tower. That explained why no one was getting a cell signal, and it wouldn't be back soon.

The sheriff left the facility, slowly driving over sheets of paper. Hundreds, thousands of them animated the parking lot, disturbed as he rolled past the crushed and broken office furniture and file cabinets. A dozen dismembered cars were strewn across the lot, torn open like the foil in a candy box.

Cal stopped at one of the wrecks. It was ripped apart and turned on its side in its run for the highway. Pieces were spread over a short path to the main carcass of an old model Bronco. The roof was torn off, the backend crushed, and the driver's side pulled open and painted with a large bloody Rorschach. He stared at the words 'No Más' hand-painted over the tag. A few years ago, it was his truck. He had sold it to Bernice for next to nothing.

He pressed down on the gas and rode over the bumpy median to get back on the wrong side of the highway, heading to the nearest column of smoke.

CHAPTER TEN

THE NEWS

Deputy Rosales watched the sheriff disappear down the highway, then hung his rifle over his shoulder and went back to the Bunker, weaving his way through the car parts in the lot.

Carlos and his buds were sitting on the edge of the wooden boardwalk. Billy was smoking a cigarette and drinking a beer, and Ray was drinking a beer.

As he walked up, Rosales looked at the three amigos, shook his head, and said, "Sort of early for the chelas, don't you think?" They laughed as he walked by them and into the bar. The deputy looked up at the massive concrete door and stepped faster. He took his cowboy hat off as he entered the passage and went through the broken bar doors into the barroom.

The professor sat at a table with his wife, Syl, and Tom Honey. Walt was behind the bar at his usual spot. Nikki came from the kitchen carrying a tray of food. She put it on the table in front of the utility workers and joined them. Looking up at the deputy, she said to him, "Hey, Luis – grab a seat. We're still eating. Have something."

Rosales dropped his hat on the back of a spare chair and sat at the table with the group. The truck driver asked him if he had seen anything outside.

"No, it's all quiet," the deputy answered, reaching for the toast.

The nurse turned in her chair to face the deputy. "You've missed the next chapter on the end of the humans," she said. "The professor was just telling us more about how great ants are compared to people."

"Oh, I hope it didn't seem that way, Syl," the professor said. "Just a few observations I thought might be interesting."

"Is that so, Professor?" the deputy asked, mustering interest.

"He's like that," his wife interjected. The woman looked worn. Rosales glanced at her and smiled as he buttered his toast.

"I wish you would call me Russ," he said to the deputy. "I don't profess anymore," he smiled. "Well, not professionally. And I think you met my wife, Emma," he said, patting her forearm.

"Ma'am." The deputy nodded to the couple.

"Good manners at the end of the world," Syl said, giving the deputy a sly smile. "I don't think you're always so well-behaved." The nurse stirred her coffee. "Are we supposed to stay in all day? Not that I want to go outside just this second, but I was wondering."

"Staying in is probably the best idea," the deputy responded. "Best if we follow orders." He took another piece of toast from the pile and popped open a jelly pack. "I wouldn't want to be outside." He stopped smearing the grape goo and looked at Nikki, "Don't worry about Cal. He's smart. He'll be alright." The deputy took a bite. "I shouldn't have said it that way. Just don't worry about him."

Nikki looked over her coffee cup, "I won't if you won't. We'll both not worry about him, OK?"

The deputy nodded. "Anyway, we should just stay in here," Rosales said, looking at the nurse.

"Kind of hard to stretch your legs inside," Syl said.

The group sat at the tables, eating their continental breakfast à la Walt, and stuck to small talk. They steered away from the subject of bugs or their immediate future for the time being. The professor stayed safe by talking about the solid construction of the Bunker and a few of the hidden features it might contain.

"As Walt said, they do not build them like this anymore. A building like this would be tens of millions of dollars today and ten times that if the government built it," the retiree said. "But I don't understand how it can operate as a club, a bar. It only has one point of egress," he said, motioning to the front door. "Quite against the fire code, of course. And yet, there's his state liquor license over the bar. Perplexing," he added.

Syl interrupted, "Whatever it is, we're here, and I like it. And it's a good thing it only has one door if you ask me. All the better to keep them out," she concluded.

"Well, as long as we've decided to stay in for the day, it might be a good idea to close up," the professor said. "If one of those creatures returns, I think it would serve us much better if she were to find the door shut."

"Good point," the deputy replied. He got up, took his hat off the chair, and went through the hallway and under the blast door. "You guys have to come back in," he said to the three fellows on the walk. "We're going to close this place up in case one of those bugs shows up."

The three buddies looked at each other and lost no time getting back into the bar. "You don't have to say that twice, Luis," Billy said, finishing his beer as he walked inside. "I want to be on the right side of that door."

"Then get inside," the deputy replied. The lawman stood on the dusty wood walk with his thumbs hooked in his gun belt as he looked past the high-tension poles across the highway and into the desert beyond. He went into the bar, moving quickly under the overhead door. He stopped at the control box, pushed the yellow down button, and the door began to lower.

Rosales walked into the barroom. The barflies were taking their usual spots under the television. Behind them, the linemen went through the kitchen doors into the back room.

Walt caught the deputy's attention and motioned him over. Rosales picked up his coffee mug and another triangle of toast on his way to the end of the bar. He put his coffee down, finishing his toast as he climbed onto the barstool. He dropped his hat onto the bar and asked, "What're you doing, Walt?"

"Thinking," the old man said. "Thinking that we might have some time to kill in here, but maybe we shouldn't waste it. Maybe help will be here soon, maybe it won't." He nodded his head toward the swinging kitchen door. "I asked those two power guys to take a look at the generator and make sure it's all in running order. As a matter of fact, I'm surprised we still have electricity. But if it goes out, we can make our own. There's plenty of diesel in the tanks."

"Sounds good," the deputy answered. "Guess all we can do is sit tight."

"For now," Walt said. "When are we going to check in with Cal?"

"He said to give him a few hours. We can call him after noon," the deputy said over his coffee. He looked up at the clock. "Another couple of hours, anyway," he added. "He's been gone a while, so he should be getting places." He looked at the radio and wanted to change the subject.

"Well, not too late," Walt said. "Remember, we have to go outside to use the walkie-talkies."

"Uh-huh," the deputy replied. "What about food? There's a pretty good crowd here to feed, Walt."

The old man leaned back on his stool. "Well prepared," he said. "The good stuff will last for about a week – if it comes to that." Walt waved toward the kitchen. "After that, we have the long-term stores, freeze-dried, MREs – plenty of that stuff. We're good for a while. You know I have a big deep freeze back there, right?"

"I heard. Cal told me that's where you keep the bodies," the deputy said.

The barkeep smiled, and the deputy turned as Nikki came over to them.

"When are you going to radio Cal?" she asked, looking at the handset on the bar. "Maybe we should see how he's doing."

202

Walt looked at the deputy and said, "Well, the sheriff said to give him a couple of hours out there. We'll give him some more time before we start bugging him."

"Don't say bugging," she said, making a face.

The deputy shook his head, and Walt laughed a little, "Well, what I can say is…."

Carlos called down from the end of the bar, "Hey, Walt, check this out. Look what's on TV. They're talking about the big bugs."

Walt and the others looked at the screen on the wall. The news was on, and Walt stretched from his stool to pick up the remote and turn the sound up.

"…from more than one source. Photos have been popping up, showing the large insects, but, like so many things today, these must be taken with a grain of salt," the newscaster was saying, "because that is one big bug in the picture and, yes, that is a pickup truck next to it, to give you an idea of size."

The professor led the way from the table to the bar with the others behind him. They gathered at the television end of the bar. Walt, Nikki, and the deputy made their way to join them.

The anchor shook her head, saying, "Just a little hard to believe, but that's some good photo editing. I think someone has a lot of free time in Oklahoma today." The TV face smiled, "And now, onto some news that's not so creepy-looking…."

Walt lowered the volume. "Sounds like the story's getting out. I guess that was one of those flying bugs we saw this morning. Wonder what did it in?"

Standing at the bar, the professor spoke up, "One of the males, perhaps. Once they mate, they die."

Nikki said, "Too bad you don't get the internet. At least we could find out what's on the web about all this."

"The worldwide web of lies is where I drew the line. I don't want it. The TV's bad enough," the barkeep said.

"Oh, brother," Brandon moaned.

Walt threw his bar towel at the young utility worker. "w-w-w shut the hell up dot com," the old barman said.

"Did they say where in Oklahoma?" the nurse asked.

"Nope, didn't hear where. Oklahoma's Oklahoma," Walt said. "We'll see if any more news comes out or if it all gets shut down."

Syl climbed onto a barstool and looked at the old man. "That's a big cat to let out of the bag."

Walt stared at the TV as he turned the volume down. "Bigger one to put back."

The barman slid the remote down to the three fellows at the end of the bar. "Sing out if there's anything else," he said to them, limping back to his perch. Nikki and Luis went with him while the others settled in to watch TV.

"See what happens. There will be a cover-up," he said quietly.

"I don't know," Nikki said to him. "There were a lot of them flying away, and if they are trying to make nests, nobody can cover that up. It's just too big; they're too big," she insisted.

"She's right," the deputy said. "Maybe you should have gotten the internet, Walt. You'd see how easy it is to put something out there and how hard it is to get it back."

"Maybe," Walt replied. "But covering up isn't just suppressing information. A lot of times, it's broadcasting competing information, fake stories to obscure the real ones."

"Wow, Walt," Nikki said, "for somebody that doesn't have an email address, it sounds like you know a lot about it."

"Started before the web, hon. Before TV, before radio. Controlling information has always been the number one mission," he said. "An effective message isn't made for the medium. It's made to appeal to the worst in human nature."

She nodded, digesting what the old man said.

He looked at the deputy, "Do you think the authorities can cover this up? You've seen it in action, haven't you, deputy? You were in the service, been in law enforcement for more than a few years. You've seen it happen, haven't you?"

"Sure," he said, looking at both of them, "I've seen it. If somebody upstairs doesn't like something that happened, in no time at all, it didn't happen," he agreed. "But sometimes, there should be cover-ups."

Walt leaned on the bar and shook his head. "Might surprise you, but I think you're right, Luis. There are some things people are better off not knowing. Not sure if this is one of those things, but I'm with you in spirit."

The linemen came back from the basements and joined them at the bar. Mike asked if they were interrupting.

"No, no," Walt said, "we're just flapping. Go ahead, what have you got?"

"We took a look down there, and I'd say we're in good shape," Mike said. "It's a great set-up. Maybe it's on the old side, but it's ready to go. No worries about keeping the juice on, no matter what happens outside."

"That's good news," Walt replied. "And a damn good thing you fellows are here, too. I have to admit, I don't know if I'd remember how to turn that thing on if I had to."

"Nothing to it," Mike said. "It's set to kick in if the power cuts. We tested it, too. Ran like a top. And I bet you didn't even hear it running up here. This place is built like a fort."

"Good thing," the deputy said.

The lineman looked at Rosales and nodded grimly in agreement with the deputy.

Brandon produced a spray can of Raid Ant and Roach Killer and waved it in the air. "Look what I found down there," he said. "A secret weapon. All we need for those bugs – one squirt, and they're done for." He brandished the aerosol while mimicking a spraying sound. "Says so on the can."

He flipped the can in the air, caught it, blew over the top as if it were a gun, and mock-holstered it. "Deadeye," he said.

"Well, you better hold onto that, Deadeye," Walt said to the young man. "You might need it."

The group at Walt's end turned when they heard the sound come up on the television. Carlos called down, "The bugs are on TV again."

Nikki leaned back on her stool to look, and the two linemen walked down to the TV end to join the other group.

It got louder as Carlos pointed the remote at the set, "…that makes three reports in total. Oklahoma was the first. We have photos from Louisiana, around Shreveport, and south of the border near Monterrey, Mexico. This suspected hoax has taken on an international flavor. We're going to have pictures for you in just a moment."

They all watched in silence. The newswoman came back. "Here are the images we promised, and I must add, they certainly look realistic. Alright, here they are. First, you see the photos from a golf course in Stillwater, Oklahoma. The report is that this is a real giant ant – an insect estimated to be fifteen to twenty feet in length." The anchor looked off-camera for direction, then proceeded with the report, "As you can see in the still image, many people, including law enforcement, are on the scene. The supposed insect appears to be deceased, and this was the first of these reports to come across our news desk."

Nikki took her coffee and joined the group, standing behind the professor and his wife. Everyone was watching TV.

The screen showed the picture they had seen earlier: a pickup truck stopped behind the enormous carcass of a winged ant lying on the grass with a crowd of golfers and a pair of state troopers up front. A crawler ran across the bottom of the screen, reading 'Giant insects found in multiple locations. Sophisticated hoax or new phenomena?'

The news voice continued, "Hard to believe, but another report has surfaced from Shreveport, Louisiana, from the residential community at Cross Lake. Again, that's in Shreveport, and this time we have video, and here it is." The anchor sat silently with a serious expression before the video came on, then said, "OK, here's the video."

Walt and Luis joined the group. Everyone in the bar was under the television, looking up.

The TV showed a suburban street jammed with emergency vehicles and thronged with people: first responders, media, kids on bikes, and neighbors, all looking in the same direction as the camera approached the front of the crowd.

The ant had fallen from the sky into the kitchen, crashing through the roof and shearing away the exterior wall. It lay legs in the air, nestled in a cradle of broken lumber and kitchen appliances.

The video framed the bug, and the amateur videographer's narration began: "This just happened like maybe twenty minutes ago. This is my neighbor's house. She's OK. She's walking around here in shock. She was inside, and this thing crash-bombed her kitchen. I was in my house next door and almost got knocked off the couch. This is unbelievable. This thing looks for real, I mean, take a close look." The video zoomed into the bug's face, detailing its large multifaceted eyes, limp antennae, and relatively small mouthparts. The view pulled back to show the entirety of the body. A membranous wing lay across the ant in the rubble.

An unkempt woman in a bright housedress crowded into the scene waving a smoldering cigarette. "Oh Bobby, isn't this an awful..." the audio was bleeped, "...thing? It smells like..." bleeped again, "too. I was in the bathroom and, all of a sudden..." a particularly long bleeping sequence ensued, punctuated by, "the next thing I knew, I was on my..." and, "the whole house just..." then, "sounded like a..." quick bleep and finished with, "went off."

The woman exhausted a stream of smoke, holding her extra-long cigarette with her best manners, and added, "I've never been so . . ." bleep, bleep, bleep, then "And now, my house is . . ." bleeped, she concluded.

The video ran out, and the shot returned to the anchorwoman, "An incredibly honest story," she said and continued. "And there is yet another report from Mexico, Monterrey, Mexico, to be precise. Let's take a look at the third report of these huge insects, this one from in the Guadalupe area."

A map of Mexico successively zoomed from the country to Monterrey on the east coast, then to a close-up of the metropolitan region encompassing the City of Guadalupe.

The newswoman's voice accompanied the video, "I've already watched this, and I have to say it is like nothing I've ever seen before. If this is a hoax, well, it's a very good one, and I'll add, I still hope it is just that, a hoax."

The video began moving through a crush of onlookers packed into a narrow street lined with colorfully painted rowhouses. The camera made its way to the front of the crowd and stopped several yards from the huge insect, then moved in, panning the length of the bug, the cameraperson approaching closer than any others.

"This isn't a secret anymore, Walt," Nikki said over the bar. "Look at how many people there are."

The audio was low, but the sound was unnecessary to convey the fear running through the crowd.

"Yeah, man – there must be two hundred people around that thing. Where is this, down in Mexico, right?" Tom Honey said to no one in particular.

"Monterrey," Syl said. "Over the border."

The crowd in Guadalupe ringed the mutant insect, leaving a wide moat. A few people with cameras ventured closer to the beast. One young man suddenly darted from the crowd, ran to one of the monster's wings, touched it, and ran back to the ring of people. Another ran out to do the same, then another.

Then the ant lifted its big head.

The crowd reacted as one, recoiling, running, stumbling back, and falling over themselves as the monstrous ant tried to stand. It turned its head and swept its sensory antennae through the air.

The cameraperson fell backward, showing the tops of the rowhouses and the sky, then running with the crowd. People's screams and shouts of alarm could be heard as they stampeded to safety, even in the faint audio. Some fell and regained their feet, scrambling to escape, dragging down the others who had helped them run from the monster.

The ant turned to the camera and rotated his head, bringing a front leg up to clean its antenna. It walked several yards toward the lens, and stopped to continue to preen, pulling its front leg through its small mandibles.

Bursts of automatic weapons fire crackled. The camera came back on the ant just in time to catch it taking a step and collapsing in the street. More gunshots could be heard, but the video didn't show who was doing the shooting.

The video ended. "That would be hard to fake," the newswoman said. "I don't know what to add to this, but we will keep you updated with any developments. Please stay tuned." The news station began showing commercials.

"Change the station, would you, Carlos?" the deputy said.

Carlos had been frozen with the remote pointing at the TV from the beginning of the video. He snapped back to life, clicking through the stations. The next channel showed the picture of the Oklahoma ant and a breaking news logo with the headline 'Giant Insects Found in Midwest.' The news then cut to a split-screen of a national news host and a hastily acquired expert commentator introduced by the anchor as one of the nation's leading scientists.

"That guy," the professor groaned. "I can't take him."

"Do you know him, Doc?" the trucker asked.

"Only from television. He does pop science," the professor answered.

The news anchor began with some incredulity, "Can this be true, Doctor? Can a bug get this big? I mean, they do look like ants, but can ants be that large?"

"Well, first of all, let's be clear. There are bugs, and there are insects..." the visiting scientist began.

"Change the channel," Walt and the young lineman said simultaneously.

Carlos clicked through more stations, stopping on the Shreveport video running a crawler, "20 Foot Insects Crash To Earth – No Hoax Says Law Enforcement." The news anchor narrated: "...Louisiana and Mexico. And now we hear of another location," the camera switched to share the Shreveport video side by side with the anchorman. He had his finger to his ear, listening to off-camera direction, and looked genuinely concerned. "Yes, OK," he said. "Another insect has been found. It has crashed out of the sky onto the interstate about ten miles south of Little Rock on the I-530. It is reported that this giant creature fell onto the highway and caused a very serious, multi-vehicle accident, possible fatalities, again about ten miles south of Little Rock."

The newsman was earnest. "This is not a hoax. People are reported injured, and people are reported dead. As impossible as it sounds, the injuries and fatalities result from collisions with a giant insect that came out of the sky. Our affiliates in the area are rushing to the scene. We will have more after this break. Stay with us for all the news." The screen went to a pharmaceutical commercial about bladder control.

The small group was quiet for a few moments until the professor spoke up. "Well, that advertisement is apropos," he said. "When it's discovered these are only the males from the mating flight and there are queens out to establish new nests, there may be a rash of wet pants."

"Wow, this is really out there now," Nikki said.

Rosales looked away from the screen and lifted his mug, "Doesn't mean our problems are over."

"At least we're safe in here," the professor's wife murmured. "Thank goodness for the Bunker."

Walt looked at the professor, suddenly laughed, and said, "A rash of wet pants, that's good, Doc, that is good. But what's going on? What's on the news? Are these the ants we saw flying away this morning? They chase each other around, mate, then these, the males, they come crashing down?"

The teacher nodded, "That's it in a nutshell, Walt."

"Well, wasn't that all pretty quick? I mean, we saw them take off a few hours ago, and now they're dead and on TV from hundreds of miles away," the lineman asked, talking over the TV rehash.

"I suppose," the professor said, "but after all, there are other factors. There were quite a few insects. I believe we saw about a dozen or so queens, each followed by a pair of males. For all we know, this may not have been the first flight. There may have been other queens leaving the nest prior to what we witnessed."

"Yeah, I didn't think of that," the lineman conceded.

"And even so," the professor continued, "reporting is ubiquitous now. And the news is disseminated almost instantaneously, especially when it is this sensational."

"Think I'd come up with a different description. A trip to Hawaii would be sensational," Tom Honey interjected. "This is bull."

The professor nodded. "I stand corrected with that more accurate description. In any event, news spreads fast."

"I heard that," the deputy said.

"But were these the creatures we saw fly off this morning?" The professor continued, "I'm no engineer, but the flight capabilities of these enormous creatures must be spectacular. They could probably cover those few hundred miles in no time."

"Plus, males don't take that long to mate," Syl added.

A little laugh went through the group.

"Again, I stand corrected," he smiled at her and sat back on the stool. The teacher concluded his lecture and turned back to the TV and the Monterrey video.

Most of the group watched the news repeat for the next hour or so, some going downstairs to wash up or just walk around. Walt and Carlos took the professor and his wife on a tour of the building's backroom and basements.

Nikki sat at the end of the bar next to the deputy. She stood up on the barstool rungs and reached over, retrieving the radio handset. "Think we should call Cal yet?" she asked the deputy.

"Yeah, guess we could. It's about time. Let's wait for Walt to come back, though," he answered. "He'll want to hear what the sheriff's found out. Guess we all would."

"How long has Cal been gone? About five hours, right?" she asked, swiveling the stool to lean back on her elbows.

212

"About that," Deputy Rosales replied. "Could have made it to Holloman by now."

"The military base?" she asked, turning her head to the deputy.

"Air Force." The deputy leaned back with his coffee mug. "It's a pretty good hike from here."

"Is there anything between here and there?" Nikki asked.

"Well, our office at the checkpoint. Isn't as far.' He looked back at his cup.

"What is that – like a police station?"

"Yeah, more or less," Rosales said. "Cops and border patrol. Usually a number of people around there."

"But then he should have been back with them by now if everything was OK there, right?" Nikki asked in a lowered voice.

The deputy didn't say anything but gave an ambiguous nod. "I don't know. Maybe," he said.

Nikki turned on her stool and propped her arms on the bar, resting her chin on her hands. She turned to look at the group at the end. "Tom was right. This is not sensational."

She looked up at the television as the channels were changing. The nurse had picked up the remote. It looked like almost all of the stations had preempted programming for special news reports about the enormous insects.

"Whoa. This is really all over the place now," the trucker said. "Hey, look, stop there, looks like they got a helicopter over that highway in Little Rock. Would you look at that crash?" he exclaimed.

They watched the aerial view move along the highway and hover over the center of the disaster. The large ant's body was broken into pieces, mingled with the smashed box truck and several passenger cars that had collided with it. Emergency vehicles and an army of first responders overflowed the scene, and traffic was backed up for miles.

"Man-o-man, what a thing," Honey added. "What an awful thing," he said, shaking his head and staring at the screen.

Billy piped up, "Look at the size of that bug. You can see the wings on the highway. Holy jeez. That bug must have crashed right into those people."

"What a mess," Syl said from the end of the group. "These bugs are getting out of hand," she added as she sipped her coffee.

Walt came in from the kitchen and walked the length of the bar to his usual seat.

As he went by Syl, she asked, "What'd you do with Professor Sunshine and the missus?"

The old barkeep smiled and said over his shoulder, "Carlos is still showing them around downstairs. They're getting the twenty-five-cent tour."

"You're not letting your secrets out, are you?" The nurse asked as she poured more coffee from the glass pot on the bar.

The senior lineman sighed heavily and got off his stool, pulling his partner along, "Let's go downstairs and look over that jenny again. I feel like doing something instead of just sitting around."

"We do?" his younger half asked.

"We do. C'mon," the senior man said, leading the way to the kitchen door. "And bring that with you," he pointed to the young man's tool belt hanging over one of the chairs.

The two utility workers went through the door to the back.

The trucker got up and stretched, "Me too. I've had enough of this bad news. TV news is just the same thing over and over anyway. And I feel a might peckish," Tom Honey said. "Hey, Walt, is it OK with you if I go in the back and root through your fridge?" he called down the bar to the old man.

Walt stared at his crossword book, "Sure thing, Tom. Help yourself." He looked up as the large truck driver walked toward the door. "Just leave something for the rest of us. And don't touch that chocolate cake in the cooler. Anita brought that over special for me yesterday." The old man put his crossword book down on the bar and took his puzzle glasses off, saying, "Gee, Anita. I wonder how she's making out? I didn't even think...." He stared off into the barroom.

The deputy got off his stool and walked into the kitchen after the trucker, "I'm with you, Tom. Let's go get that cake," he said in a loud voice over his shoulder to Walt.

The bartender called after them, "You guys leave that cake alone. I'm warning you." He smiled as they went through the kitchen door and left it swinging. His face went gloomy again.

Nikki walked to his end and climbed up on the first stool. She noticed the old man's troubled expression. "Quite a crowd of people here, safe and sound, thanks to you and your crazy building." Leaning closer, she said to Walt, "I can't tell you how lucky I feel that I got here last night. Was it just last night? In that storm, too. And then to find some real people here, like you, Walt." Even in the low light of the barroom, her eyes glistened. She blinked and rubbed them. "Thank you, Walt."

He looked at her and slowly shook his head. "Dammit," he said, looking at the nurse a few stools away. With a wry smile, he said, "Dammit," again.

Syl walked down to them, keeping her hand on her coffee mug as she pushed it along the bar. "Mind if I join you two?" she asked with a thin smile as she got onto the stool next to Nikki. "What are you guys talking about, anyway? You seem thick as thieves down here," Syl made herself smile some more.

"Oh, nothing really," Nikki replied. "I was just telling Walt how lucky it was for me, he was here, that this place was here. It's a fortress, a lifesaver."

"Really," Syl said, drinking her coffee and still smiling. "Imagine all this here. What are the odds?"

Walt answered, "I'm pretty sure they're the same they always been. Six to one, half-dozen to the other." He looked straight at the nurse. "Besides, I believe in luck."

"Me, too," Syl replied. She took a drink of her coffee. "Problem is, it always runs out, sooner or later." The nurse leaned closer to Nikki and asked, "So what's your story, hon? This guy is too tight-lipped to converse with socially."

Nikki replied, "No story really. Just passing by when that storm made me come in here. Dumb luck. Guess I believe in luck, too," she said, smiling at Walt.

"Hmm. That was lucky, hon. There's nothing better than luck. But I don't believe in it. It seemed like it was just in the nick of time, too. But what brings you around these parts?" the nurse asked, friendly as warm pie.

"Oh, I just had a few things to do over in Alamogordo," Nikki felt Walt watching her as she answered the woman, "The thing was, a relative of mine passed away, and I was here clearing up her estate."

"I am sorry, honey," Syl reached out and patted Nikki's hand on the bar. As pleasant as Syl seemed, Nikki wanted to pull her hand away. But she didn't want to be rude, so she didn't flinch.

Syl held her mug with both hands as she sipped. "I'm sorry to hear that. That's too bad. Was it somebody close?" she asked.

"Well, yes. My aunt – really my great-aunt," the young woman said. "She was a terrific person. Lived a long time around here."

"Oh, really?" the nurse continued with Nikki while she looked at Walt, "I take it you're not going to do that, hon," Syl said as she lowered her coffee. "Live a long time, around here, I mean," she smiled at Walt.

"No, I'm pretty far away from home. I just started the trip home when I got caught in that crazy storm," she answered.

Syl raised her eyebrows to Nikki, prompting her for more.

The young woman complied, "I'm from Oregon. Haven't been here very long, in New Mexico, I mean."

The nurse nodded, motioning for more with her mug.

"I've visited a few times, visited my aunt, but not for a while," Nikki added.

"Well, we all lose touch, you know," the nurse patted her hand again. Nikki reflexively pulled it back an inch this time. The nurse smiled a little more.

"Nikki's your name, isn't it, honey?" she asked. "That's sort of an unusual name." The nurse picked her mug up, took another sip, and said, "I like unusual names. Now let me guess, what's your last name, by the way? I bet it's an old English name."

Nikki looked at the nurse and furrowed her brow, "I think it is. It's Carrington. What made you guess that?"

"Oh, like I said, I just like names, like to guess about them," she drank more coffee.

"Want to guess mine?" Walt asked.

Syl said, "Hmm," into her coffee. "I don't think so. We can just stick with Walt."

"Carrington," Syl said to Nikki. "That's a good name. It seems I've heard that name before. You say your aunt lived around here for some time?" she asked.

"Well, my Aunt May was in her nineties," Nikki said. "I think she lived here all her life. At least most of it. I know she came here to take care of her brother. He was a scientist – a famous one, too. He worked at...."

"May Carrington..." Walt interrupted. "Now, where have I heard that name?"

Syl brought her mug to her lips and looked over the top at the barman, narrowing her eyes just a little.

"Might have met her once or twice," the barkeep said, studying the nurse.

Nikki looked at him with some surprise, "Really? You knew Aunt May? That's amazing," she said. "But I could see the two of you being friends," she added.

"I wouldn't say friends, nodding acquaintances, more like. And, I wouldn't say amazing either," the bartender added. "Both around here long enough. Bound to run into each other sooner or later. I didn't really know her. I think I met her first, oh, twenty or more years ago – probably more." He smiled at the young woman and put his hand on hers, pulling it toward him across the bar and away from Syl. "She was a great lady, your Aunt May. Sorry to hear of her passing."

"Thank you, Walt, that's nice of you to say," Nikki said softly.

"I guess that's enough climbing through the family tree," the nurse said. She got off her stool and started back to the television end of the bar. "Better be careful, Walt. Might start shaking the nuts out of yours next," she laughed.

Nikki looked at Walt quizzically. The old man smiled at her, and she shrugged.

Billy called from the far end, "Hey Walt, how about a beer?"

The barkeep looked down the bar to Billy's eager face. "Bar doesn't open till two," he said. "Maybe three, if I feel like it." He balled up his bar towel and threw it the length of the bar at Billy.

218

"OK, OK," Billy said and caught the towel, "No need to be ornery about it, Walt. Just asking. Always work up a thirst doing nothing," he said.

"Well, you must be about the thirstiest human there is. Try doing something," Walt shot back at him. "Go in the back and get Luis. He's probably eating my cake. Tell him it's time we call the sheriff and see what's going on out there."

CHAPTER ELEVEN

THE BASE

I f he hadn't found the abandoned pickup and was walking, the sheriff would have turned back to the Bunker by now. He had to be inside by sunset, but the truck made the miles to the Air Force base only a few extra minutes.

He took off from the sheriff's station, leaving the demolished facility behind, bouncing over the dirt and brush dividing the highway, and got on the westbound side, heading east to the columns of smoke.

The road took him past more wrecked vehicles surrounded by ant tracks and dark patches. As he sped down the straightaway, he saw the White Sands tourist trap coming up and let up on the gas, slowing down to surveil the scene as he approached the exit.

The complex had several buildings, and the sheriff figured to do a drive-through to see if anyone was around.

He turned into the visitor's parking in front of the adobe-styled welcome center and saw what he had expected. Ruined cars evidenced an overwhelming attack by the giant ants. At the far end of the parking area, vehicles were turned over and torn open by the monsters. It seemed like when they were done, they piled the empties together.

As before, there were no remains, human or ant. The sheriff drove around the dark spots as much as he could. He blasted the horn and leaned out the driver's window, listening for an answer, looking for any sign of life. There was none.

He left the lot, turning into the narrow drive that led to the big attraction, the dunes. Behind the visitor center were smashed utility sheds and vehicles. Around the corner, behind a building, a camper was on its side and ripped open.

The sheriff stopped his truck and got out. He stood by the door and blew the horn, listening for any response, but there was none. The only thing to do was leave.

Cal got in and turned the truck to the highway. He slowed as he rode past the squat concrete park police headquarters. There was no front to the building. Blocks of the toppled wall formed a jagged ramp to the interior through a hole large enough for a giant ant.

He peered into the cavity. Like his headquarters on the highway, everything in the building had been demolished. Offices were torn open, desks and cabinets were bulldozed into piles, and paper was everywhere.

He let off the brake, drove the narrow exit to the highway, and turned east into the westbound lane. Columns of smoke rose across the horizon. He hoped there would be people putting fires out at the Air Force base.

The sheriff picked up speed and covered the few miles to Holloman in no time. There hadn't been any wrecks on the road, and everything looked normal, except there was no sign of life anywhere.

Ahead was the western gate to the base. Cal slowed to drive over the curb and enter the exit.

He knew a little about the base. It was big, he knew that much, almost a hundred square miles. And there were lots of people. Around twenty thousand people were on the base, military and their families. It was nearly as big as Alamogordo. The town had schools, churches, restaurants, and bars. It was a regular place.

As he pulled through the decorative brick walls flanking the gate, the sheriff knew everything was wrong. There were no guards.

There was a security vehicle next to the inspection area. Smashed windows and hammered metal were the signs of the ferocious hailstorm, but not ant damage.

As he drove into the base town, the extent of storm damage became apparent.

The hail had hit hard. Every structure was damaged, every window was broken, parked cars had been battered, and everything was shredded, leaving debris everywhere. But there were no signs of cleanup like everyone was already gone when the storm hit. It was a ghost town.

Over the rooflines, columns of smoke loomed, sprouting from the airfields behind the town. Cal wheeled out, sticking to the main drag and looking for a way to the airstrip.

A couple of blocks down, he found an entrance to the airfield. He turned and slowed at the end of the street; the gate was wide open. He stopped, blowing the horn three times, and listened to nothing.

The sheriff drove through the gate and onto the vast concrete plain of airfields. The desert had been smoothed, sealed, and dotted with buildings to the horizon. Across the great flatness, from the base of a towering pillar of smoke, a speck of a helicopter lifted into the air, banked, and sped off into the east.

"Don't be the last one," the sheriff said as he stepped on the gas and shot over the tarmac, heading for the smoke. As he approached the burning building, an armored vehicle topped with a gun turret came out of nowhere and pulled ahead, steering the same course.

If they saw him, they didn't care because they kept going. If they didn't see him, they would soon enough because he was catching up.

The big khaki truck crossed the open airstrip to another building that wasn't on fire. The military vehicle stopped, and the driver and passenger doors immediately opened. Two men in fatigues got out and waited for the sheriff. One raised his hand, signaling the lawman to stop.

Cal looked up from his driver's door window at the young soldier. The other stayed back with his hand on his holstered sidearm.

"How are you today, sir?" the young soldier asked, looking at the sheriff and into the cab at the assault rifle and noting the missing passenger door. Then he saw the badge on the sheriff's shirt. "You a cop?" he asked.

"Sheriff," the sheriff replied.

"Alright, Sheriff," the soldier replied. "What can we do for you?"

"You could clue me in as to what's going on here, who's in charge, and what the plan is," the lawman answered.

"A man with questions," the young soldier replied.

The other soldier nodded and said, "Yes, sir," into the transmitter on his shoulder. Above the doorway was a camera dome. "You can go in," he called over.

His companion opened the truck door, stepping back as the sheriff got out.

"You don't mind if I take this along, do you, Corporal?" Sheriff Jeffries asked as he pulled his assault rifle out of the cab. "I just feel better with it." He looked into the young man's eyes. He was tired, too.

"Not a problem, Sheriff," the corporal responded. "After you, sir," he motioned to the building. The other soldier held the door open.

The three filed through the small door into the dim heat of an empty hangar. Empty except for a cluster of desks in the middle of the abandoned building, an illuminated island of computer monitors showing terrain maps, aerial photos, and screens of churning data.

A lone man wearing a headset sat amid the monitors.

As the peace officer crossed the hangar floor to meet him, the colonel turned his chair and looked from the monitor to Cal's badge and then to his face. The army officer was older than the sheriff, and his drawn expression added a few extra years.

"Sheriff Jeffries," the officer said. He extended his hand to the lawman. "I'm Colonel Smith."

"Colonel," the sheriff shook his hand. "Guess I fit the description," he said.

"Close enough," the military man replied, leaning back in his chair. "We'll go on the assumption that it's you."

The sheriff nodded. "Maybe not the same fellow I was yesterday."

"None of us are," the colonel said.

Cal looked over the knot of desks crowded with displays. "Looks like a war room, Colonel." He turned back to the officer. "So, how goes the war?" he asked.

"Depends," the army officer answered. "Last night it went bad. Today, so far, so good." The colonel grimaced as he shifted in his chair. "I'll bet you have more questions, Sheriff. Why don't you go first, then I'll ask mine."

Sheriff Jeffries put his rifle on the desk and took his hat off, dropping it on the gun. He pushed his hand back through his hair. "Well, my first question is, where is everybody? I drove through the front gate and the town, and no one was around. What happened last night?" He hesitated, then said, "I don't know if I want the answer."

Colonel Smith flickered a tight smile, "We did good, considering. They surprised us, but we did pretty damn good. Air Force is something to see when they're on the move." The officer leaned back. "The entire base was evacuated, Sheriff," he nodded and smiled broadly. "We did not lose one civilian. Every one of them was taken to safety, the young, old, and in-between."

"That's good news," the sheriff said. "Must have been some operation. What were there, more than twenty thousand people here?"

"You're close with that number, but that was before. Most of the non-essentials have been quietly moved over the last few weeks. But, close to

224

six thousand souls bugged out, excuse my choice of words, in just under five hours. Most by air." The officer leaned his head back and looked into the shadows of the high ceiling. Then he turned to face the sheriff and continued, "All unscheduled flights, too. I never saw so many birds in a night-op. Choppers, transports, they even moved the secret machines out of here. Air Force does one hell of a job."

"That's good news. I'm glad to hear it. Must have been some operation," the sheriff repeated.

"Considering a swarm of monster ants was attacking us at the time, I guess it was." The colonel looked up into the dark again, then shifted his eyes to the lawman, waiting for his response.

The sheriff picked up his hat and sat on the desk beside his assault rifle, holding his Cattleman by the brim. He studied the army man for a moment. "They are pretty big. For ants, that is," he said.

The colonel laughed abruptly, then pushed himself up from his chair. Cal saw the officer's right thigh was wrapped in bloody bandages. "We're going back to the scene of the crime. Take a ride. We'll talk on the way," he said to the sheriff.

Sheriff Jeffries followed the limping officer to the truck. One of the young soldiers held the door open for the colonel, and the other did the same for the sheriff. While the colonel was climbing in, the sheriff went to the other side.

"This is one heck of a rig," the sheriff said as he got into the truck. It was crammed with instrumentation and as solid as a slab of steel. He got buckled up, stood his gun between his legs, and hung his hat over the barrel.

"Good trucks," the colonel answered, "but they're out-of-date now. M-ATV, military all-terrain. MRAP: Mine-Resistant, something, something," Colonel Smith replied. "Over fifteen tons, some have remote control weapons systems up top; chain guns, thirty mil-cannons, anti-tank missiles. Some doggone firepower in these buggies." The colonel grimaced as he hauled his bandaged leg in behind him. "Last night, we had three of these trucks. Today, this is the only one left. Not the fancy one, either. All it's got is a measly fifty-cal up there," he jerked his thumb to the round turret above them. "But it does the job on those bugs."

The colonel leaned forward to the corporal behind the wheel. "Oz, let's get moving," he ordered, slapping the back of the driver's seat. The young man put the truck in gear and started across the airfield.

The colonel leaned back and looked at the sheriff as the truck rolled over the strip, "Where were you last night, Sheriff? If you were within twenty miles of this base, you must have been under cover or damn lucky."

"Both," the sheriff said, looking through the thick ballistic glass at the empty airfield going by. "I stayed at a friend's place. I have to get back there, too. It's already late," he said to the window framing the darkening sky in the east.

"I won't keep you too long. I just want to hear what you know. I haven't been off the base in three days. I feel I'm missing a few pieces; maybe you got one of them."

The sheriff turned to the officer, "I don't know what I can tell you. You must know a lot more with your drones and all. You have to know more about the comings and goings of these things than I do."

"I'm not sure, Sheriff – plenty of moving parts. Which direction are you coming from anyway?" the colonel asked.

"Started out this morning west of here. Walking," he answered. "Picked up an abandoned truck along the way."

"You were lucky to find anything in working order. They seem to have a thing for vehicles," the colonel said. "And they don't overlook too many of them. Maybe they think they're like other bugs." The military man adjusted the red and white wrappings on his leg. "I'm going to guess you had your own run-ins with them yourself." He looked at the bandage on the lawman's arm.

"I imagine anyone still around today had a run-in with them. From what I've seen, it looks like they were just about everywhere last night," the sheriff said.

"You can say that again," the army officer replied, looking at the buildings and airstrip moving past his window. "That's for sure," he said quietly to himself. He turned to the sheriff and asked, "So, what else did you see on your hike here?"

The sheriff looked out the window past the reflection of the colonel in the glass. "Started out from my friend's place. That's the Bunker, the only watering hole in the neighborhood." He smiled into the window.

"I've heard of it," the colonel replied.

Cal turned back to the officer. "You know quite a bit about the goings-on in the middle of nowhere, Colonel Smith."

The army man shrugged slightly, "It's the information age, Sheriff. I'm just a product of my time. But keep going. Tell me about your bug collecting."

The sheriff exhaled. "Started last night. That's when they first showed up. We had a run-in with one of them. I holed up in the Bunker for the night. This morning, like I said, I followed a trail up into the dunes. Saw the nests. Ran into a couple of them. I won. I left on foot and found a truck after a few miles. After that, I checked the BP station, that's where my office is, was, but I guess you know that. They were hit, out of commission. Stopped at White Sands center on the way, that was in the same shape. Here I am."

The Army officer nodded as the sheriff spoke and, when he stopped, said, "Man of few words."

"Not big on adjectives," the lawman answered. He pursed his lips, then asked, "You don't happen to know anything about survivors from my station, do you?"

"Afraid not," Smith answered. "Plenty of bad news for the locals, but there's always some good, too. Here's hoping," he added. Colonel Smith held his index finger to his earpiece and leaned forward to answer the driver, "No, back to ground zero."

"Yes sir, Colonel," the soldier in the front replied, loud enough for the sheriff to hear. The MRAP took a wide turn to the left.

Smith turned back to the sheriff, "We know where the nest is, of course. Known for a while. What we didn't know is that the ants would mount such a widespread surprise attack." He shook his head at the lawman, "I kid you not, these bugs are natural campaigners. They came at us just after dark. We had seen increased activity. Turns out they're hard to track at night for all of our tech. Body temperature is the best guess. Their skeleton's on the outside, you know, it's like armor, but it's pretty good at reflecting temperature, too. Anyway, they don't pick up too great on night vision."

"You've known about these things for weeks?" the sheriff asked.

"Even longer," the colonel nodded. "At the start, the bugs were few in number and stayed local. We kept forward observation on them, and they looked like they were sticking to themselves. The decision was made to eliminate them, and we were getting ops underway. That's why I'm here. Then it all hit the fan. Late yesterday, the forward post stopped reporting. Ants' activity pattern changed. More of them outside of the usual areas. People watching decided something was brewing, and they were right." The colonel shook his head, "I'll tell you, Sheriff, no one expected this to boil over so fast. They walloped us, but good. Those things must have come in at thirty miles an hour. Two waves."

"The bugs had a plan of attack?" The sheriff watched the officer's face.

The colonel laughed grimly, "Sure seemed like it. First of all, they circled the base to the far side. A couple of them came in and drew us out. I hate thinking they did that on purpose, but I do." Colonel Smith looked at the sheriff. "Like I said, two waves, lots of bugs." He straightened his injured leg.

"How many?" Jeffries asked.

"Plenty. Take a look outside." The colonel motioned through the truck window.

The sheriff looked through the thick glass as the truck drove between two of a group of three huge buildings onto the vast tarmac. They rounded the corner and stopped in front of a jet hangar.

The sheriff gave a low whistle as he looked out of the vehicle.

The front of the hangar was demolished. The mammoth doors had been pushed in and lay crumpled, half in and half out of the building. Across the pile of twisted metal, the carcass of a huge ant was sprawled, legs stiff in the air.

The two guards jumped to the ground, weapons at the ready. The driver opened the colonel's door, and the other young soldier opened the sheriff's door as Cal unbuckled.

The sheriff put his Cattleman on and climbed out with his rifle, looking along the broad expanse of runway peppered with dead ants and demolished vehicles.

There were four wrecks of military flatbed trucks. One was upside-down. Two had been ripped apart, and their pieces were all over the place. The fourth was only missing the driver's door. Smashed cargo was everywhere – leftover confetti from the ants' war party.

Two insect bodies were inside the building, past the pile of doors. Both carcasses pointed to the back of the hangar, dropped in their tracks, charging through the breached door.

The colonel limped over, carrying a bottle of water to stand by the sheriff. "A lot of it went on here," he said, shading his eyes. "All out there in the open," he added, pointing down the runway.

He was lost in thought for a moment before recalling the events. "Down there," he said. "That's where it started. It was already dark; we were back in our hangar." He took a drink of water. "Funny thing is, we were strategizing when they got here. They acted while we were talking."

The colonel poured water on his hand and wiped his face and the back of his neck. "Guess the bugs are more doers than they are planners. Anyway, they made the first move, and that's what counted."

Colonel Smith dragged his bum leg to the front of the truck, leaning on the hood for support. The sheriff went with him to hear more of the attack.

"Over there," the officer continued, pointing to the first building, "We were loading trucks. A couple of transports were lined up, people getting the show on the road. Everyone was in bugout mode." He leaned against the brush bumper, grimaced, drank, and spit.

"We know the nest is a couple of miles in that direction," the colonel said, waving past the expanse of concrete to the desert. "But they came in from over there," he said, pointing in the opposite direction. "So those sneaky bugs went all the way around there," he swept his arm across the broad area between the opposing points. "They avoided the perimeter fence all the way to come in behind us." The colonel looked at the sheriff, "How do you like that?" He took another drink from the water bottle, "Think they had a plan?"

"Sounds like they did at that," the sheriff looked over the far-off flat.

"Damn right. I think it's built-in with them." He drank again. "I think we've met something better at war than us," the colonel said. "Waging war might be in our nature, Sheriff, but it's deeper down with these things. It's instinct. Like eating or breathing. They are born to conquer or die trying."

The colonel leaned back against the front of the truck and swirled the water in the plastic bottle.

"Anyway, from what I know, about a dozen of these buggers came charging in between these three buildings. Two columns came out on the attack." Smith took another drink, swished, and spit again. "Now, I don't want to think the bugs coming over open ground used these buildings as cover because if that were true, that would be scary." He turned his head to the sheriff, "And I'd just as soon think of them as plain old unthinking monster ants."

The sheriff lifted his assault rifle, laid it on the truck's hood, and took his hat off to wipe his brow. "What happened to the perimeter? The outer fence has got to be a couple of miles from here. Didn't they trip something when they came through? It must be alarmed," he asked.

Colonel Smith gave a short laugh, "They sure did. The fact is, they set off too much. About a mile of the fence went down at once. It was so big that security thought it was a glitch." The colonel shook his head. "No fault. They were on the ball. They sent two crews to check it out."

Smith called over to soldier number one, the big corporal. "Hey, Oz, were those peeps checking the fence ever accounted for?"

"No, sir," the soldier replied, "the only things accounted for were their vehicles, and they were not in good shape."

The colonel shook his head, then turned back to the sheriff. He pointed to the battered buildings. "It just so happens there was a couple, well, more than a couple, about ten Air Force Security personnel stopped in front of hangar number one there." He indicated the first building in the group of three. "That was bad news for the bugs." He bent over to pull at the bandage on his leg. Looking at the hangars, he said, "That small group of glorified cops, no offense meant, Sheriff, I just mean they are not the trained killing machines my guys are. Well, anyway, they held those bugs and kept them from getting to the people loading up on the runways. They saved a lot of folks," he said, looking over to the hangar and the bug bodies.

Smith swallowed more water and continued, "You know, every once in a while, you need to hear about the higher human spirit." He wiped his neck again. "Those men and women stood their ground, got the word out, and stopped those nightmares." The colonel nodded, staring through the rippling heat rising over the field. He laughed and shook his head. "Any sensible person would have run for their lives."

"Should I ask you how they made out?"

The colonel raised his brow and looked away from the lawman, "No," he said. The army man grinned, radiating wrinkles from his eyes and running deep lines across his forehead. The sheriff had seen that expression plenty of times when people put the squeeze on their emotions.

The lawman turned his head to look out over the concrete plain. "How many ants?" he asked after a minute.

The colonel turned back and looked past the sheriff, motioning at the alleys between the hangars, "Best guess, forty to fifty. They came in, split on either side of that middle building. They ran in and hit those deuces being loaded by about half a dozen guys. Look at them. How many tons? I don't know. They just tossed them around like toys," the colonel said, tilting his head at the transports. "Those people didn't stand a chance, even though the Air Police were just over there." The colonel pointed to the right, in front of the third hangar. "But by the time they covered the distance, everyone in the loading crew was done for, probably before they knew what hit them. After all, not too many folks had the inside scoop."

The sheriff listened to Colonel Smith, looking over the scene of the attack and imagining the sudden onslaught of the giant ants coming out of the dark. The trucks were grouped in front of the middle building; a half-a-dozen workers are carrying crates out of the hangar, using the now overturned forklift. The ants rushed in, attacking, knocking the trucks onto their sides, climbing over them, and going for the workers. Long red streaks and pools of thick blood marked the spots where they met their ends in ant jaws that could shear steel.

"That security team got lights on them and got us on the radio. We were out the door in thirty seconds. On the scene in under three minutes," the colonel continued. "Long minutes. Our MRAPs tore in here just to see those two mothers in the hangar finishing off the last of the AP. We couldn't do anything for them except kill the bugs that killed them."

The sheriff followed the colonel's gaze to the two young soldiers standing by the pile of hangar doors where the bug bodies lay. "That young man, Ozzie, the one that drove us, he was out of the truck before it stopped moving. Killed both of those bugs himself. He ran up guns blazing while it was busy doing in some poor son of a mother. That young man put a dozen rounds into that bug from a few feet away. Right on top of it. Solid brass. Then he gave the other bug the same," the colonel added. "That boy is a natural defender of his species. He is a bug-killing machine." The officer paused, looking over the airfield. "I'm afraid he might have his work cut out for him."

"You think there's many more of them? In that nest, I mean," the sheriff asked.

"Enough," Smith replied. "Between our observation post and satellite imaging, we've got five birds watching White Sands round the clock now. They've shown us numbers up to three hundred or so. That was last night," he looked at the sheriff and narrowed his eyes. "That's intel that came in today, by the way. Like they say, a dollar short. Anyway, before that, we've never seen more than a dozen at a time," shaking his head, he said, "Those bugs are just full of surprises."

"Three hundred," the sheriff repeated. "That's hard to take in." He shook his head and pulled his hat back on. "The world's changed since yesterday," he said.

"Since this morning, man," the colonel said.

They looked at the remains of the trucks and bugs for a long minute when the sheriff prompted the officer, "How'd it go, once your team got on-scene? Looks like you had a pretty close scrape yourself," he said to Smith.

"Yeah. Well, if you think losing one soldier to them is a failure like I do, then we got our ticket punched." The colonel drank from his water bottle, "But like I said, those bugs are full of surprises. We tear in, and there they are, crawling over the trucks, broken down the doors, and chewing up whoever was in there. Hell was poppin'."

Smith pointed down the field littered with truck and ant parts, "One of our other MRAPs plows into two of the bugs. Pisses them off. Gunner pops out of the top, swinging the chain gun on one, the one coming straight at him. Splits its head wide open while the other bug runs around back of him."

"I just happened to catch it," he lowered his voice and leaned to the sheriff, "Truth be told, when we stopped, I fell out of the truck." He shook his head at the lawman, "Sucks getting old, doesn't it?"

The sheriff raised his eyebrows, then frowned at being included.

The army man pointed to the runway and went on, "Anyway, I hit the ground and got the wind knocked out of me. While I'm lying there trying to get it back, I see the truck quick turn to face the other bug, and it backs into the dead one. It got hung up in the mess, spinning its tires in the goo, trying to get off. The other one of them charges, climbing up on the back of the truck. The gunner spins around. I don't know how he even knew it was there."

"But my guy won the draw. Turned just in time and cut loose. What a sight that was. That big thing was all legs on top of the truck, towering over that soldier, ten feet at least, but, like I said, my guy won and turned that thing into a thousand pounds of bug slaw." The army officer pointed at a dark, wet-looking mound far enough away that it didn't stink too bad. "That's all that's left of him."

"Her." The sheriff corrected the colonel. "All of these ants are female. That's the way ant nests are, so I've heard."

The colonel rubbed the back of his neck and turned to the sheriff. "Is that so?" he snorted at the lawman, "Ha. Well, why the hell not? Know your enemy, right? Amazonian ants, here's to them." He took another drink from the water bottle and spat on the tarmac. "Damn bugs," he said.

234

The colonel pointed to a different pile of ant. "And that is what's left of the bugs they rammed coming in. Look closer. You can see the truck in there." The heavy-duty, sand-colored vehicle was on its side on the runway. "That got knocked over by the second wave. Before you could spit, more bugs hit, moving fast. I mean, they were really moving. Swarmed that truck. One of them gets up on it and pulls the gunner out, most of him anyway. Three of the ants knocked that big truck over. I told you those trucks are over fifteen tons, right?" He looked at the sheriff. "Pretty heavy."

Colonel Smith drained his water bottle and limped a few steps past the sheriff to the open door of their transport. He threw the empty inside and turned back to the lawman.

"That was a surprise," he went on. "They worked together, too, the bugs. Anyway, the truck got knocked over. It was quiet for a second, then the rear door dropped, and the driver came sliding out on his back with two ARs, ventilating those bastards." The colonel mimed two guns with his hands pointing upwards.

"Bear in mind all of this takes place in less than a minute. We were preoccupied with the second line coming out from over there," Smith gestured to the other alley. "A stream of them came pouring out pretty fast. They cut us off from truck number one. I'm on my back, looking up, and I see one of those mothers climbing over our truck. I thought it looked right at me, but I guess it didn't. Anyway, it climbed down, stepped on my leg, and ran after some of the guys over that way." He waved one arm to the right without looking. "That was my moment of valor against the enemy," he had to add.

"Anyway, most of the scrap is happening on the other side of my vehicle. I look over and see that driver backing up, shooting at that bug on top of his truck." The colonel looked at the wreck. His voice was hoarse for all of the water: "He was laying a lot of rounds into that freak, that kid, that is, that young man, is a good soldier." The colonel's face pulled tight like there was a taste in his mouth. "Anyway, the bug didn't charge him. You know what it did? It twisted round, twisted itself up, and sprayed some sort of sticky crap all over him. Some kind of acid. He is more than twenty feet away, and this spray shoots all over him. All over his head, his arms, his chest."

The sheriff watched the colonel's face as he told the story, watching the man's eyes move from spot to spot on the airfield, reliving the night before.

"Even from over here, I could see it was thick. He let go of his weapon, but that was caught in the crap, too. The gun didn't even fall. It was stuck in the goo." The colonel's eyes were fixed on a spot in front of the wrecked sand-colored MRAP. The back door still hung open on the overturned vehicle.

"He was trying to raise his arms, get his hands to his face. Normal reaction, I guess, when you feel like you're melting. But he couldn't. That stuff was so thick. He ran. He could run, his legs didn't get any of it. He could scream, too. Anyway, I guess he couldn't see, and he ran right into one of those trucks, that one there," the colonel moved his eyes to the transport truck without a door.

"When he hit it, he just stuck there. Stuck against the truck," the colonel stared at the wreck. "He died in a while, I guess. So, another surprise from them. The bugs spray acid." He turned to look at the sheriff and added, "Hell of a way to find out."

"Sure is." The sheriff looked over the field with the officer. "Sounds like it was pretty grim here last night." He put a foot up on a broken axle with a torn tire and leaned forward, looking across the runway to hangars and the spaces between them, the alleys the ants came from the night before. "But you won the battle, Colonel. I know you did because anytime these things have a chance, they take everything away, including their casualties."

"Well, we did the cleanup this time," the colonel said. He narrowed his eyes and looked over at the wrecked trucks. "The only way we could get that soldier out, the one that got the acid, was to take the door off the truck." His shoulders heaved as he controlled himself.

The lawman studied the carcasses of the ants across the tarmac. "This is the first time I've seen any of their dead left behind. What made them break off the attack?" the sheriff asked.

"Firepower, I suppose," the military man answered thoughtfully. "We took out a dozen or so of them."

"You said there were forty or fifty of them altogether, right?" the sheriff said over his shoulder to the colonel.

The officer didn't reply but watched the lawman.

The sheriff continued, taking his foot off the truck part and turning to face the colonel, "You'd expect bugs just to attack. It sounds like these withdrew. Unacceptable losses."

The officer nodded slowly at the lawman for a short moment. "Half of the battle is what you do — the other half is guessing what the other guy's going to do," he said. "You're an interesting fellow, Sheriff."

"I don't know, Colonel. I'm feeling pretty dull compared to these bugs," the lawman answered.

"You don't guess they're going to want to negotiate, do you?" the colonel laughed grimly.

"Why would they?" the sheriff said. "But I'll guess they'll be back."

The army man nodded. "We're sort of counting on it. And, this time, we're going to be the ones that act."

"I take it you're waiting for a few more assets to join the party," the sheriff said, looking across the empty field.

"Just look up," the colonel said. "We're waiting for a team of real hard cases to drop in. Right now, they're flying circles, keeping an eye on everything." He pointed upward with his index finger and spun it.

"Hard cases, huh?" the sheriff replied. "Hope there are a lot of them."

"There are," the colonel answered. "And they have a plan."

Sheriff Jeffries nodded, looking over the airstrip, his thumbs hooked in his gun belt. He half-turned to the officer and said, "You know, Colonel, it seems like every time fellows like those come up with a plan, it's to blow the hell out of everything." His head turned to the military man. "Not that I'm altogether against that idea; I just wonder, how can you be sure it works?"

Cal took his hat off, pushed his hair back, knocked the Cattleman against his leg, and put it back on his head. "You know this isn't the first time for these bugs? They've been here before, and the military got rid of them before." The lawman turned to face the colonel. "But here they are again."

"You are pretty well-informed too, Sheriff," the colonel responded.

"I keep my ear to the ground," the sheriff said.

Colonel Smith pursed his lips and nodded. "Well, I guess if you know what happened before, I can't blame you for wondering," he said. "But there's a bigger plan now, a lot bigger. It's got to be bigger now that these things have gotten out across the country."

"What do you mean?" the sheriff asked. "What do you mean 'across the country'?"

"That's right, you haven't been sitting in front of the TV this morning like I have," the colonel answered. "Last I saw, it was Oklahoma, down in Mexico, and Louisiana, I think. That's right, Shreveport. Flying giant ants came out of the sky. It's all over the news."

The sheriff nodded, "Might fit with what I heard. One of the people back in the Bunker knew something about ants. Professor of some sort. He said that the males follow the females out of the nest, they mate in flight, and the males die afterward. Fits with what we saw this morning."

The colonel waved to the soldiers standing in the hangar entrance, calling them back. "And what was it you saw?" he asked the sheriff.

"Saw them taking off from the nest," the lawman replied. "About two dozen. According to the professor, they were new queens. Each of them followed by two males eager to do the deed and die."

"That must be what we heard this morning. Didn't see anything. Like I said, the forward post went out," the colonel said. "This professor add anything else?" he asked.

The sheriff absently watched the two soldiers as they neared, "He did. He said the new queens would establish nests after they mate. Painted a pretty gloomy picture, too." The sheriff put his cowboy hat back on. "And to be clear, the gloom was for us, not them."

The young soldiers walked up to the colonel, waiting for orders.

"Let's mount up and get us back to the hub," the commander told his men. The driver, Ozzie, went with the colonel to the opposite side of the armored vehicle. The other soldier opened the sheriff's door.

The sheriff climbed in and shut the door as the colonel got into his seat. When the last door shut, Ozzie wheeled out, turning the truck in a wide arc to their headquarters.

The sheriff took his cattleman off and hung it over his rifle barrel. He watched the officer pulling at the bandages on his leg to straighten them out.

The colonel looked up from his leg and met the sheriff's gaze. He raised his eyebrows and wrinkled his forehead. "We'll pick up a few things and get you back to your truck. Thought you'd be going on to the Bunker."

"I will," the sheriff replied. "Mighty kind of you, Smith. I appreciate the help. The Bunker's a pretty tight place, but they may need a hand," the lawman said.

The colonel leaned back, "Could be," he said. "There are plenty of moving parts to this play, and you don't know the whole cast yet. But I am going to shed a little light your way."

He leaned back in his seat. His lips tightened as he shifted his leg. "There aren't too many people I trust," he started, "two of them are in the front of this truck, Ozzie and Reese." The sheriff saw the driver's eyes glance back and then look at his companion with a smile when the colonel referred to them.

"And you, Sheriff Jeffries, might get added to that illustrious shortlist," he said to the lawman. "I'm a pretty good judge of character, I guess, and I'm a big believer in fate. You're here. We met, all meant to be. Fate is really how wars are won."

"Anyway, that's my dish of destiny." The colonel tapped the side of his nose with a knowing expression, the way the sheriff had seen Walt do too many times. It made Cal want to trust the colonel, too.

"So here it is," the army officer went on, "I told you we've been watching these bugs for some time while everyone was planning what to do. Well, there were plenty of opinions, and it wasn't just the military, and it wasn't just the eggheads. The fact is the ones that usually make the final decision are the ones you'll never know about. They are the ones that run the spooks, the spies, the double-dealers. And they're running this."

"And what's their plan?" the sheriff asked.

The colonel reached into a cooler between the two men, pulled out a water bottle, handed it to the sheriff, then two more, and passed them to his soldiers. He took one for himself and twisted off the top, taking a drink. The sheriff followed suit.

"Well, the short answer would be they are planning something stupid and underhanded, but it gets a little longer if you want to understand it," the colonel answered.

The sheriff took another drink.

"First off," the colonel said, "They want to keep this under wraps."

"I don't see how. You said it's all out, even on TV," the lawman responded, anticipating more to come. "If ants are dropping out of the air around the country, they can't keep it under wraps."

"No. No, they can't," the officer said. "So they'll accept deniability. They don't want it known that the bugs originated here. Natural for them to lie."

They pulled up to the door. The two soldiers hopped out and opened the back of the truck.

His leg had stiffened enough that Ozzie had to help his colonel, who cursed along the way. He swore through the doorway and across the hangar as he limped to his chair. He lowered himself into it and drank some more water.

The lawman followed, took his hat off, and sat on the edge of the desk next to the colonel. "As I said, Colonel, I appreciate the help but don't get the reference to the spies."

The officer looked intently at the lawman and said in a low voice, "Deniability means no witnesses."

"No witnesses?" the sheriff repeated. "Listen, Colonel, I may be slow on the uptake, but what are they going to do about all of the people in Shreveport and those other places?"

"Probably nothing," the colonel answered. "At least not to all of them. They'll take care of the noisy ones. But it's your friends in the Bunker I'm concerned about right now."

"The people at the Bunker?" the sheriff repeated.

"You know, Sheriff, you might just be a touch slow, at that," the colonel said. "Yeah, the people at the Bunker. They saw the bugs take off, right? That means that giant mutant monster insects originated here in White Sands. The next thing to be asked is 'Who's behind it?' and they don't like those questions."

"But how would they even know those folks saw the bugs take off?" the sheriff asked.

The army officer smiled at the sheriff. "Well, right off the bat, you told me – and I'm going to say you're fairly tight-lipped. Just goes to show you how easy news travels. People talk. People love to talk. And now, they put everything online. They post videos. Love doing that, too. There's just a couple of ways secrets travel," the colonel said. "Those people will blab on themselves."

The sheriff rubbed his chin. "I suppose you're right about that," he agreed. "But, since the start of this thing, there's been no cell signal back there. They took photos, but we could just collect their phones. Nobody will listen to them." He leaned toward the colonel. "Besides, based on the number of bugs that took off, this will be one big mess. A couple more folks talking about it won't matter. This is never going to be covered up."

The colonel shook his head. He gripped both arms of the chair and leaned back as he raised his good leg to put it on the edge of the desk. He rocked slowly, staring at the lawman.

"That's not how it will be handled, Sheriff," he said after a moment. "There are people that will take matters into their own hands. People that are closer than you think."

CHAPTER TWELVE

THE LOT

E veryone in the Bunker was at the TV end of the bar, looking up at the set. Walt moved his stool to join them, and he never sat at that end. The last time there was something big enough on TV to make him watch for any amount of time, he was young enough to stand.

But the ants were pretty big, and they were getting a lot of coverage.

Special news had broken into every program. No matter which stations they switched to, the talking heads, no longer skeptical, reported the events in their most solemn manner. The networks were so serious that many ran with limited commercial interruption.

Billy was controlling the remote and would switch to a new channel whenever an ad interrupted the coverage. The small group of patrons was generally quiet as they watched the breaking news, sometimes remarking when a discovery was announced or a new video was shown.

"…which brings us to a total of eleven of the giant insects found dead or dying and three, even larger insects, very much alive, although two of them have been killed. This is Randall Sanders reporting from Covington, outside Memphis, Tennessee. Back to you, Bethany."

The in-studio anchor replaced the remote reporter on the screen, "Thank you, Randall, for that on-the-scene coverage of the alarming developments from a peaceful rural area of Tennessee. There is such beautiful scenery there, but the countryside and farms are now marred by the horrific attack of a giant insect and the terrible battle that ensued before it was killed. As Randall reported, authorities and witnesses have confirmed multiple casualties, as many as eighteen people dead and many injured in the intense fight with the creature. We're going to have more about this very bizarre series of events. Can this really be an invasion of giant insects?" The news anchor smiled and shrugged. "We'll be right back after this short break."

Tom Honey spoke over the commercial as it began, "Just to get this straight, Professor," he said, turning to the elder teacher beside him. "The bug they just showed – that was one of those queens that flew off this morning looking to make a nest of her own?"

"That would be my surmise, yes," the professor replied. "From what the reporter related, the insect landed at the farm and entered the barn. I would imagine she would look for immediate cover to establish her nest. The dead or weakened ones that have been found are the males."

Tom nodded, looking up at another pharmaceutical commercial on the screen as the professor continued.

"Yes, yes, these are the same insects we saw," the professor went on. "They covered a great distance since this morning, true. But there's no other sensible supposition. In all probability, there is a single nest in the desert across the highway, which is the source of these mutations."

His eyes moved to his wife, who was staring vacantly into space. "And I'm certain that, as these creatures come to ground, they will be discovered and eradicated, and this event will not be repeated." He reached out and put a comforting hand on her arm. "But it was something to see," he went on. "A very singular event, seeing them take to the sky. That was something. Something in all likelihood no other people were fortunate enough to witness." The professor concluded, "It will be some story to tell."

Walt was watching the group instead of the television as the professor spoke.

"Looks like there's going to be plenty of folks with giant ant stories if the television's any measure," Tom Honey said. "Why, these bugs are crashing down everywhere and causing all kinds of calamity. They're all over."

The professor nodded at the trucker, "That's true, Tom, that's very true. But we are the ones that saw it begin. We know the genesis of these mutations. And according to our esteemed host, this is not the first appearance of these bugs."

The professor looked to the barkeep for corroboration and almost got it. "I suppose," Walt replied. His eyes went to the nurse's hands on the bar. The rest of her was obscured as she was sitting on the other side of the trucker.

"Well, this time, and as you said before, it is a fairly large cat to put back in the bag." The academic smiled at the barkeep. "This time, the whole truth may come out."

"Maybe," Walt said, returning his attention to the professor.

"Well, I know one thing," the truck driver said. "This puts all my other yarns in the back seat. When this is over, I don't suppose I'll ever have to buy myself a beer again."

Billy and Ray sat up straighter, hearing the trucker conjecture about the possibilities of future royalties.

"Hey, Walt, that's a good idea. Is the bar open yet?" Billy asked. "I haven't had a beer since this morning."

The deputy got off his stool with a quiet groan, twisting the kinks from his neck. "I'm going to raid your refrigerator again, Walt," he said, walking to the kitchen door.

"Help yourself, Luis," the old man replied, studying each person at the bar.

Nikki's gaze was fixed on the television, her head propped on one hand while she slowly spun a coaster with the fingers of the other. Her bag was on the wear-polished bar in front of her.

Tom Honey followed the deputy into the kitchen, hopping off his barstool and revealing the nurse behind him. Syl sat with her arms folded on the bar. Walt's eyes moved to her and hers to him.

"What about you, Walt? Think it will make a good story?" she asked the barman.

"If it gets out, I suppose it will," Walt said.

"I suppose you're right – if it gets out," she replied quietly.

The old man leaned forward to look at the three at the end. "I guess it's time to open up. Wouldn't want you fellows to die of thirst," he said.

Walt started the trip to his regular spot at the head of the bar, pulling his stool along. He stopped at the taps and drew three. "Clear the decks," he said loud enough to startle the professor. Nikki sat up and pulled her bag off the bar. The professor put his arm around his wife's shoulders as the mugs slid down the alley to Billy, who collected them for his buddies.

"Anyone else?" Walt asked. "The sun is officially past the yardarm."

Nikki leaned over the bar and smiled down the alley at the old man, "Not for me, but don't let that stop you," she said to Walt.

"Nope. Think I'm going to wait for my drinking buddy. He should be back soon," Walt said.

Nikki smiled a little more. "I hope so. He's been gone a while," she said. "I thought he'd be back by now."

"Too bad about the radios. Guess they were used up. But don't you worry about Cal, hon," Walt said to her, "He'll be alright." He cocked his head and gave her a wink. "He usually uses his head."

"I hope so, and that's good to hear," she said to the bartender as she slid off the barstool. "He's been gone so long." She pulled the strap of her bag over her shoulder. "Anyway, I'm going downstairs and stretch out for a while, maybe catch up on some reading," she said, walking away from the bar. "I've seen enough TV."

"Good idea, sweetheart. Take a load off for a while and relax," Walt said after her.

She walked the length of the bar to the kitchen door with her cloth bag slung over her shoulder. As she pushed the butler's door in, she looked at Walt and smiled. He saw her and smiled as she went through.

"Nice girl," Syl said to Walt, a few stools from the old man.

He turned back to the nurse. "Come on up to my end. You want a beer?" he asked her.

"No, I'll take another ginger ale," she answered.

The old barkeep reached under the bar and came up with a can and a glass, filling it with ice along the way. He opened the can and pushed them across the bar top to the nurse.

"Anything you can't pull out from under there?" she quipped as she poured the soft drink. "I remember a surprise or two."

"I'm more comfortable up here where I can get to things," he said to Syl as she paralleled him along the bar. She stepped on the brass rail and climbed onto a stool across from the old man.

"You just met her, right?" Syl asked him.

"Who? The girl?" He looked at the nurse. "Never saw her before."

"Seemed to take a shine to her, Walt. I'm jealous," Syl replied, swirling her soft drink. She looked over the rim as she took a sip. "Men never change, no matter how old they get. Always swayed by a pretty face." She smiled insincerely.

"Naw," the old man responded. "I think it's the honesty. I think what you see is what you get with her. An uncommon trait in humans. Makes her likable." He leaned back on his high stool.

"I don't like her," Syl replied and refilled her glass from the can of ginger ale. "Or any of them, not really. I think they all talk too much."

The deputy and the truck driver came through the kitchen door. The trucker carried a large plate stacked with sandwiches, and the deputy balanced a pile of dishes, condiment bottles, and a large piece of cheese.

247

"I have to say, Walt, you have a well-stocked kitchen back there," the deputy called down, "Thought it was time to get lunch going."

"That's a good idea," Walt replied. "Everybody ought to have something to eat. Not much else to do in here, anyway."

"You're not kidding," Syl said as she took another drink. "I'm starting to get cabin fever. Maybe we could open up, go outside, and stretch our legs before dark."

Walt looked at the woman and narrowed his eyes. "Thought you were the one that didn't want to open the door," he said in a monotone.

She shrugged and replied, "There's still an hour or two of daylight left, right? We'll be alright sticking close to the door. I just feel cooped up." She looked down at the rest of the group and raised her voice, "What do you think? Anyone else want to go outside and see some sunshine?"

Billy watched the plate of sandwiches walk by him. "That sounds good. I want to go outside. It doesn't seem normal to be shut in all day and not see the sun," he said as he hopped off his stool to follow the food.

The deputy carried the tray to the table and said over his shoulder to the barfly, "That's right, Billy. Not normal for you to be shut in a bar all day and all night." He laughed. "Who're you kidding, anyway? This is heaven on earth. You locked in the Bunker? You dream about this."

Billy laughed alcoholically and agreed, "You're right. You're right. I could stay in here forever!"

"Not happening," Walt called down, picking up his crossword puzzle book.

The deputy and truck driver put the plates and everything on the nearest tables. The group got off their stools and went to the food. As he left the bar, beer in hand, Billy slid the remote down to the trucker.

"Ain't you going to eat nothing, Walt?" the barfly asked him.

"Yeah, I guess. Get me a sandwich, would you, Billy? Fact, bring a couple up here for our ministering angel, too," the old man replied as the group moved to the table.

"You want anything on them?" Billy asked him.

The old man looked back at him, "No, thanks, chef. Just bring a couple of damned sandwiches over here."

"Alright, alright. Just asking, man." Billy whined.

Tom Honey turned the sound up as the news came back from the commercial, and it looked like a new story was on screen. As the sound rose, the group at the table turned to the newscast. Billy walked a plate of sandwiches to Walt and Syl and returned to his seat.

"… a horrific scene is unfolding in metropolitan Dallas. This video is live, a very active story." The anchor was on a split screen with the new footage as it came in.

The Texas reporter narrated. "Moments ago, the huge insect landed on the roof of one of the tallest buildings in Dallas. People from a neighboring high-rise are shooting this video. Oh no, look at this: the creature seems to be purposefully ripping the panels and breaking the glass to get into the building. It is hard to imagine the destruction." The anchorman didn't fully close his mouth as he shook his head in disbelief. "Oh no, oh no. Look, the pieces of the building are falling. Fifty stories to the street. Just a horrible, horrible scene." The video panned up and down, showing a cascade of debris tumbling and spinning from the top of the building. The onlookers below fanned from the skyscraper's base, running for their lives.

The small group in the bar watched the television, holding their sandwiches and drinks. Tom Honey forgot he had the TV remote as he watched and listened.

"Look, look!" the news continued, "This monster, whatever it is, is crawling through the opening it tore into the top of the building. The wreckage is falling, possibly injuring many, many people and pedestrians below." The newsman's eyes followed a monitor off-screen. "There, now it's completely disappeared into the building." He put his fingers up to his earpiece, listening as he continued to talk. "As reported, this is a live story, happening now as we bring it to you," he said, then paused briefly, hand still at the earpiece. "This is a busy workplace. A building full of people, many of whom will, without doubt, encounter that monster ant or insect or whatever it is."

He looked down at the small prompter built into his anchor desk, then back into the camera. "And now, we have an affiliate on the scene. Yes. It's the traffic copter getting exclusive shots from the air showing the awful destruction at the top of the skyscraper in the middle of Dallas. We're switching to Traffic-Copter-One."

The television went to a full screen of the video with the anchorman's voice on top.

The newsman narrated the scene as the airborne camera hovered above the damage, trying to keep pace with zooming shots and close-ups of the jagged breach on the roof. At times, the helicopter got dangerously close to the building, close enough to show its reflection in the windows flexing from the rotor wash.

"I wish we could get audio from the chopper," the newsman said, "but we're having technical difficulties with that right now. We're working on it and will get it fixed to bring you their own words describing this horrible occurrence in downtown Dallas. Our affiliate in the traffic copter is bringing you exclusive coverage of this disaster."

Suddenly, the live video from the helicopter was jarred. The camera tilted rapidly upward, panning the side of the building at high speed. The rotorcraft's reflection could be seen for an instant as the camera swept past the glass façade. The skyscraper diminished in size as the helicopter pulled back, the camera riding along a dizzying swirl of the Dallas skyline.

The anchor recovered his narration with a more urgent inflection. "We don't know what's happened to our eye in the sky. It looks like, wait a minute now, yes, yes, that looks better. It looks as though they are recovering from some sort of emergency. Some sort of very dangerous, wait now. What's that? Look over there. There, at the side of the building. Oh no, is that...."

The helicopter was now further from the skyscraper and had regained stability. The camera moved along the building's side, reorientating itself, and then locked on several top floors, zooming in and out a few times until the view focused in on the fortieth story, a hundred feet below the hole torn in the roof.

One of the large windows was missing. Twisted metal dangled in mid-air from the empty frame. The camera zoomed into the interior of the destruction as paper swirled and broken lights inside sparked and strobed.

"We didn't see what happened, but it appears that a window has been broken out high up on the building, and this has got to be related to the attack of the giant...." The newscaster's voice cut off mid-sentence.

Several other glass panels in line with the missing window bulged and erupted in an explosion of glass, debris, and human beings as the queen ant bulldozed her new home clear of obstacles and inhabitants. Partitions, office furniture, and people were catapulted through the glass to become a horrific avalanche of death, pouring forty floors to the pavement.

Three people remained in the scene, pushed to the edge of the precipice, falling over each other but stopping short of plunging out the broken windows after their fellow workers.

The camera silently watched them help one another back from the edge. A middle-aged man was seriously injured. His white shirt bloomed red. A younger man and woman dragged him a few feet from the edge, pulling him over the green carpet.

The wounded man lay on his back. The woman was on her knees, beginning to stand, and the young man was on his feet. The camera lingered on their moment of survival.

The anchor said nothing as the seconds stretched over the desperate performance.

The grainy, long-distance shot from the helicopter's camera showed three people starkly displayed against the carpet. The young man looked back into the office and began a crouch, then retreated toward the gaping hole in the building. The woman ran to the side as the giant ant's head came into view and caught her in its jaws. The huge ant stepped on the middle-aged man, and even in the telephoto shot, he was clearly killed instantly.

The woman was still alive, struggling in the ant's mouth, as the monster pivoted to corner the young man. With a quick step, it scooped him into the wide mandibles, effortlessly shoveling them both to the brink of the blown-out windows. It dropped the couple over the edge. Without pause, the giant ant turned and picked up the middle-aged man's body in its pincers and turned to dangle the limp body over the precipice for a moment before dropping him.

The giant insect posed at the edge of its new world, looking over the urban sprawl and slowly turning its bug head as the sun set over the city.

The video was abruptly cut, and the newsman returned alone on the screen. He looked at the camera briefly, then said, "That was being shown live. I'm sorry. That should not have been broadcast. I'm very sorry for those poor people. We're just going to take a minute and regroup. Please bear with us while we go to station identification. That was just awful, ladies and gentlemen. Horrible. We are deeply sorry about that and pray for those poor people."

The television showed an animated network logo changing colors on the screen.

The people in the group turned from the television one at a time. Everyone was silent until Billy said, "Man-o-man, that was unbelievable." He waited but elicited no response.

"Just about the worst thing I've ever seen," Billy said. "That was just terrible, right? Freaking awful." He shook his unshaven face at the rest of the patrons around him. "Just terrible," he repeated, nodding to the group.

Tom Honey quietly put the clicker down. "I wished I hadn't seen that," he said, leaving the bar to sit at a table. He pushed a plate of food a few inches away.

Brandon, the young lineman, kept watching television while most turned away even though it was only the station's logo. "I guess it's extra bad when you know what they're really doing; I mean, it's different when you see it for real," he said.

"And how many of those things took off this morning? Twenty or something?" Billy asked. "I don't know if they know it out there, but there's plenty more coming. We're going to see plenty more of this," he said.

The nurse had leaned toward the television and squinted her eyes to watch. As it concluded, she sat back and looked at Walt. She got off her stool, walked to the table, and made a ham and cheese sandwich.

Everyone was quiet as she returned to her stool. She chewed slowly while looking at the group, then spoke up. "What do you think, professor? Now that the word's out, what do you think the outlook is for the big bugs – or maybe us people?" She took another bite of her ham and cheese.

The professor's wife was leaning over the arm of her chair against her husband with her head on his shoulder. He turned halfway to the nurse and said quietly, "Well, as the young man said, we saw quite a few of these creatures fly off this morning. And there will likely be more unfortunate encounters like the one we just saw."

The academic shook his head and patted his wife's forearm. "But I'm sure the authorities will be able to deal with these monsters in short order. Remember the preceding report? The local people killed the creature when it was discovered. As large and as savage as they may be, a single ant is no match for humanity. I'm sure this will be taken care of soon, and this will all be over." He squeezed his wife's arm.

The nurse stopped chewing and asked him, "You said they're out there to make new nests, right? How long do you think that takes?"

"Before they produce new offspring? Before they multiply, you mean?" the professor asked, his voice a little more engaged. "Oh, a few months, I would think. Of course," he continued, removing his hand from his wife's arm to gesture, "we are dealing with radical mutations. The fact they are so large may presuppose many aberrations in their typical life cycle. For all we know, normal reproduction has been completely altered. They could reproduce at an accelerated rate, corresponding to their phenomenal growth." He leaned forward to look at the nurse, causing his wife to lift her head from his arm and sit unsupported by her husband.

Syl smiled at the educator and replied, "So I guess the trick is finding all of these mothers-to-be, sooner better than later. Before they start a nursery."

The senior lineman said, "They were plenty this morning. If you're going by the news and based on what we saw, they got, what, two or three of the queen ants?"

"Well, as familiar as I am with Formicidae, it's difficult to say from the view on television," the professor answered.

Walt looked at Syl. She smiled, shook her head, took another bite of her sandwich, and chewed.

The professor continued, "It seems likely the incident we just saw, the terrible incident," he corrected himself, "that was, in all probability, a queen."

"I'm counting that one and the one in Tennessee, the one the locals killed in the barn, and that one in Mexico, right?" the lineman said.

"Difficult to conclude," the professor looked up and rubbed his chin. "The one in the barn seemed to be exhibiting nest-building behavior, finding shelter. But for all we know, it could have been the death throes of a suitor simply blundering into a barn. Plus, we never really saw that ant, and as the barn was burning, I suppose it would take a forensic investigation to determine the ant's gender. Now, the one in Mexico was undoubtedly male. Seemed to have relatively small mouthparts. It's hard to tell over the TV. Difficult to come to any sound conclusion through any television news reporting."

"Well, one conclusion is for sure: there's plenty more to go. That was a real airshow this morning," Mike replied.

The educator nodded. "And, like so many problems, the unknown quanta are often the decisive factor. It's not the ants they find that will be the danger. It's the ants they do not find. If any of these insects escape notice for whatever time they need to establish a nest, the results could be disastrous. Just imagine if every time a nest is established, a percentage of queens escape, reproducing successfully. Those percentages will catch up with humanity fairly soon."

"They have to know how many of them took off this morning," Brandon chimed in. "They would have shown up on radar all over the place, things that big. Everyone's probably out looking for them now."

"I suppose that's true," the professor responded. "These days, not too much goes unnoticed. But…" he hesitated.

The group waited for the professor to finish his thoughts. Syl stopped chewing and asked, "But what, Prof?"

"Well, I mean no offense, of course, as I do not know what it is each of you may be involved with by way of profession or affiliation…" he said.

"Yes?" the nurse prompted. "I'm sure we can take it, especially under the circumstances."

The scholar replied quickly, "It always seems as though, speaking of the collective, when people want to accomplish something, they don't. They more often get in each other's way, it seems." He shrugged his shoulders. "I guess I don't have too much faith in collective enterprise," he concluded. "No offense meant."

Walt snorted from behind the bar without looking up from his crossword puzzle.

"Really?" the nurse said. "That's it?"

"Well," the professor continued, "I just wanted you to know that I was not impugning the deputy's or the sheriff's efforts. I certainly don't mean to say…"

Walt laughed again, glancing at the deputy.

Rosales laughed, too. "Hey, Professor, listen. I'm a vet, did two tours, been in the Sheriff's Department for a couple of years, and work with local, state, and the feds all the time. And, with all that experience, I can tell you for a fact that you are right. People are the problem."

"I have to say, Prof, that's something," Syl said. "You must come from a pretty cozy place if you think it's a big insult to tell someone there's a chance they might screw up." She laughed. "You know, that's what most people do most of the time. They screw up." She laughed.

"Well, that's kind of scary, what with you being a nurse," the junior lineman said.

She stopped laughing and shrugged, reaching for another ham and cheese half from her plate. "Everybody does," she said. "What are you going to do? As the professor might say, it's just the human condition." She munched on her new sandwich.

"I might," he responded. "But I just wanted to be clear. I didn't want to offend anyone."

Walt piped up, "No offense taken, Doc." He put his puzzle down and leaned toward the group. "Besides, it'd take more than that to wrinkle up ol' Luis here. He gets the job done. He's a fellow you can count on more than most."

The deputy looked over at the old man from the table and laughed. "Oh-oh," he said. "I don't like where this is heading. Anytime Walt butters you up, you end up on the grill."

The barkeep cocked his head at the deputy and winked with a smile. "You are right about that, Luis. First, I get you comfortable and relaxed, then move in for the kill." Walt laughed, shaking his head back and forth, and laughed again. He suddenly stopped laughing and said, "It's the same way in your business, isn't it, Syl? Get the patient relaxed, unsuspecting, and then," the old man snapped his fingers in the air. "Same way you set Tom's broken nose. The art of surprise."

Tom Honey piped up, "That was some surprise, I have to say."

Sylvia stopped chewing but didn't turn to the bartender. "Yeah, I guess you could say that. That's the way I was taught. That's the way to do it." She pushed the last bite of her sandwich into her mouth and turned on her stool to look at Walt. "But it sounds mean the way you put it, Walt," she said in a sugary tone. "But you know it's the best way to get the job done."

"And, that job – that's everything, ain't it, Nursie?" Walt asked.

She dabbed her mouth with a paper napkin, balled it up, and swished it into a small wastebasket crammed with Walt's old crosswords behind the bar. "I guess it's got to be," she replied and slipped off the barstool.

"After all, what else have you got?" she said over her shoulder to the old man. She walked to the group at the other end of the bar.

"What do you say? How about if we all get some fresh air?" she said to the deputy and the group. She turned to the rest and smiled, cajoling them to the door. "C'mon, it'll be good to get some air and stretch your legs. Let's take a little walk outside," she motioned to the door with an inviting smile.

The professor's wife asked if it would be safe.

"Of course, hon," she said softly to the woman. "Your husband will be right there, and the deputy, Mr. Honey – all of us will be together, and we won't go far from the door – just outside. It will be the best thing for you."

The nurse leaned over the frightened woman, putting her arms around her shoulders. She stood her up and guided her toward the door with the professor following.

Deputy Rosales went along and took his assault rifle off the table on the way. "Not a bad idea," he said. "I'll take a look outside."

"Check the cameras first," Walt said.

Carlos picked up the remote control, and they looked for monsters in the empty lot.

"Doesn't look like anything's going on out there," the senior lineman said. "Looks pretty quiet."

Tom Honey nodded, "I could use a long look at that desert – that is if nothing is moving in it. Always found the desert quieting. At least until lately," he added.

The deputy drew the bolt back on his rifle and said, "I'm for that. So, let's get a look, Tom. Bring your Eagle."

"You got it," the driver said, "As a matter of fact, I don't think I'm putting this pistol down for some time to come." He bent his arm and held the big gun straight up as if preparing for a duel as he walked to the doorway.

Deputy Rosales pushed the button to open the blast door. It rose slowly, grinding upwards in recessed tracks. Tom looked under the door as it went up. The two linemen joined him at the threshold. Each of them was armed with assault rifles from Walt's collection of weapons, piled on the table by the door.

The younger lineman stuffed two magazines into his back pockets and examined his gun.

"Ever fire a gun?" his older partner asked him.

"Xbox," he replied with a grin.

"X-what?" the older man asked.

The door opened, and the deputy walked to the front of the group and stepped out onto the walkway, moving his eyes over the debris-strewn parking lot and the desert beyond.

"Looks quiet," he said.

Tom Honey stepped out onto the boards, stuck the big pistol into his ample belt, and rested his hands on his hips to survey the dusty lot and the emptiness beyond.

"Maybe too quiet," he said and spit into the dust.

The deputy stepped off the boardwalk into the lot and scanned the surroundings. He walked a few paces into the lot and stared at the torn and twisted car carcasses. "I'm going to take a look around back just to be sure everything's alright," he said to Tom and Mike. "Let them come out, but stay by the door. I'll be back in a few minutes. Just going to walk the perimeter."

They watched the deputy disappear around the corner with his rifle pointing the way.

"Maybe we should have gone with him. Think he should have gone on his own?" Tom asked the lineman.

"I think he should have looked before we let everyone out here," he replied. "There could be a whole nest of those bugs back there for all we know."

"That's a good point," the driver said. "Maybe you should have mentioned that."

"The deputy's in charge," the lineman answered. "Guess he knows what's up."

"Well, if he doesn't, we'll be hearing some shooting any minute now," Tom Honey said. He turned to watch the people trickling out of the bar onto the plank walk and into the lot.

259

The three barflies came out one after another, each carrying a beer. Two of them sat on the edge of the sidewalk. Carlos carried a rifle and stepped by them off the walk and into the lot. He lifted one of his cowboy boots onto the walkway and stood, beer in one hand, gun in the other.

Brandon came out, carrying an assault rifle, to join Mike.

"No sign of the bugs, huh, boss?" Brandon asked.

The older man looked away from the horizon to his partner and rifle.

"Hey, watch where you're pointing that thing, Bran," he said to the young lineman, pushing the muzzle of the assault rifle away from his belt buckle.

"Sorry, Mike," Brandon said, lifting his weapon.

The senior lineman shook his head and gripped the gun, forcing the young man to point it straight into the air. "You have to watch where it's pointed. Keep it up or down, but you got to always know what it's aiming at," he said to him.

"Alright. Sorry, Mike," the young man said.

The three friends quietly talked as they nursed their beers, watching the desert across the road. Carlos looked up to see Syl standing just inside the doorway. In the shadow, the low sun colored the nurse's face a devilish red as she looked over the group.

The professor and his wife slowly walked by the nurse. Syl smiled at them as they passed and said, "It will be good to be outside and stretch your legs. And don't worry about a thing, hon. The menfolk will keep their eye on everything. Any time, you can come right back inside."

The professor held his wife's hand as they took a few steps along the wooden sidewalk, looking over the wreckage across the lot. In response to the scene of the ant's destruction, the woman shrank to her husband. He put his arm around her and held her closer as they looked across the lot into the desert.

Carlos tipped his mug and poured half his beer down his throat, watching the couple over the rim. He looked sideways into the door, but the nurse had disappeared. He went to the edge of the walk and sat next to his friends. They had their backs to the doorway.

CHAPTER THIRTEEN

THE BOOKS

Nikki pushed the kitchen door open and walked into the empty barroom. Surprised by the unoccupied chairs, she turned to Walt, sitting by himself, perched on his stool, and studying his puzzle. She started down to him.

"Didn't know I was gone that long," she said, carrying her bag along the bar in one hand. "Where'd everyone go?" she asked.

He looked up and smiled, setting off another set of wrinkles.

"So, that was you sneaking around back there," he said to the young woman.

"Yep," Nikki replied as she climbed onto the stool across from him. She smiled back and replied, "Sneaky me." She looked around the vacant bar. "So, where'd everybody go?"

Walt nodded to what was left of the saloon doors and said, "They went that-a-way. Wanted to sit outside for a while."

"Not you?" She put her sack on the bar and leaned toward the old man.

"Naw. Just as glad they went, though. There's been a lot more people around than I'm used to," he said, laying his crossword on the bar top. "I'm used to peace and quiet."

She reached for her sack on the bar. "Oh, I'll go out. Everyone needs some time for themselves," she said and started off the stool.

"No, no. Not you," he said. "You stay put. You're just fine where you are."

Nikki smiled, stayed in her seat, folded her arms on the bar, and looked at him quizzically.

He sat back on his stool. "You've got something to say," he said. "Say it."

"Really, Walt?" She lifted her eyebrows. "The day before yesterday, my big decision was what shoes I should wear. The next day, there are sandstorms, hail, giant ants, and a fortress in the middle of the desert. It's a lot," she said all at once.

He folded his arms. "And?" he asked. "You came to some conclusions? Like I said, if you got something to say, say it."

"Conclusions? You've got to be kidding," she said, laughing. "I'm more bewildered than ever."

Walt stared at her and nodded very slowly. "Bewildered," he repeated and stared at her for a moment. "Son of a gun, that's it." He brought his crossword puzzle closer. "People doing this puzzle," he read. He looked over at her and smiled. "Ten letters, first one's a 'b,' the fourth one's an 'i.'" He laughed. "I thought it was 'behindbars,'" Walt said with a big smile as he picked up his pen and wrote in the answer.

He folded the puzzle and put it under the bar. "Next one's on the house, hon." He smiled with satisfaction.

She looked at the old-timer fondly, smiling warmly. Her expression changed to perplexed as her new thoughts came back. "But really, Walt. It's all kind of hard to believe, isn't it? All of this science fiction?" she asked him. "I mean, hard to believe it can really happen, giant bugs, monsters, space invaders."

He watched her closely and sat back on his stool as she spoke. "Space invaders? Have the flying saucers shown up, too?" he asked with a smile.

Nikki shrugged and laughed, "I don't think so. Well, maybe. It's all pretty crazy," she replied, motioning with her right hand around the barroom at the movie posters on the walls. "Have you seen all of these? The space movies, the giant bug movies?" she asked Walt.

"Yeah, I suppose so. At one time or another," he answered.

She spun her stool from one classic piece of sci-fi to another, completing a full rotation to face Walt. "A lot of crazy-looking movies," she said.

"That's for sure," he said, narrowing his eyes. "Anyway, I'm back to 'if you got something to say, just say it,' sweetheart."

She laughed and reached for the pretzel bowl. "There's the Walt I know and love. No dancing around, just lay it on the line." She popped a pretzel into her mouth.

"It works. Try it sometime," he answered. His smile was fading.

After tasting the first one, she dropped the second pretzel back into the bowl. "Alright, alright, Walt. I will. Gee – just give me a minute to warm up. I'm not used to being crazy. You'll have to let me ease into it, will you?" Nikki shook her head and took a breath.

Walt said, "So, something crazy? I wouldn't worry about it. That measure has changed lately. Go as nuts as you want."

"Thanks, I will. The worst part is, I'm starting to believe it," she said, exhaling her calming breath.

"If you don't like the taste of what you've got to say, spit it out," the old man said.

"OK," Nikki said as she took another deep one. "The only other thing I have to say before I do is that I am always the practical one. The one with the common sense," she said. "I don't believe in things, you know?"

"Alright, already," Walt said. "Let the record stipulate that the young lady is not usually nuts. Now, will you get to the point?"

Nikki put her palms flat on the bar and pursed her lips. "Ready," she said. "OK. I've been doing some reading. I have these books from my aunt's estate, my great aunt, really, and they were from her brother...."

"Your great-uncle, Professor Arthur Carrington," Walt interrupted.

"Yes, that's right," she said without breaking cadence but wrinkling her brow. "Well, he was a scientist that worked for the government back in the day, even before these movies were made," she circled the room with an index finger. "Back with the atom bombs," she raised her eyebrows and leaned closer. "Back when everyone was seeing UFOs, like when Area 51 started up."

She nodded knowingly. Walt thought she wanted him to nod in agreement, so he did. They both nodded to the same beat. The bartender held his hand up. "Stop that," he said. "What are you saying?"

"My uncle, great-uncle, he was a superbrain involved in a lot," she emphasized the quantities, "a lot of crazy things. All these UFO references, genetics, extraterrestrials, the ants, he kept notes, he wrote everything in these journals," she explained hastily, then tugged her hobo sack closer, and said, "And I mean 'these journals,'" she added, reaching in her bag to pull out three small, leather-bound books. "Here they are." She put the books on the bar in front of Walt. His eyes fell on them, and his eyebrows went up. The old man reached over, hesitated, then laid his fingers on the cover of the top volume.

"What's in them?" he asked without looking up from the books.

"I just opened one of them and started reading. Holy mackerel, Walt. There's a lot. A real lot," she answered in a low voice so only Walt would hear, though they were the only ones in the bar.

"You know he won the Nobel Prize?" she asked in a whisper. Walt nodded without looking up from the books. "Well, he was either in on just about everything, or he was a complete lunatic. He wrote about a government base in Alaska when a UFO, a real live flying saucer, crashed. They found aliens and a spaceship. Bad things happened. It was an alien invasion. He said they were here to use the human population as a food source. They called it the Thing. That operation led to the base at Roswell, the development of White Sands, new technologies, and even to these movies, the disinformation."

Walt looked up from the books. "You don't say," he said.

265

She turned on the stool and pointed to a movie poster on a column. "Especially that one," she said. "He specifically mentioned that movie. He said it started as a documentary. It was a way to break the news to the world that spacemen were real."

Nikki stared at the screaming woman depicted in the green poster of *The Thing.* She was quiet for a moment, then turned back to Walt.

"My uncle said that because the invasion was stopped and the way people reacted to the story, the decision was made to treat it all as fiction, science fiction. Admit nothing and ruin and ridicule anyone that tried to tell the truth." She looked at Walt very seriously. "This is what you've been saying all along, isn't it, Walt? You knew all about this, didn't you?"

The barman looked away from her earnest expression and down at the three books. "Not all," he answered. "There are plenty of questions hanging around."

Nikki nodded. "You know, he was even involved with the first outbreak of these giant ants. Because he was a big shot with the military and government, he pretty much ran the atomic tests. And he was running things when the first giant ants showed up. He wrote all about it in the journals, how they decided to use the same methods to cover it up as they did with the UFOs. Make movies and sugarcoat the whole thing." Nikki pointed to a nearby poster. "Like that one," she said of the *THEM!* sheet, showing a monstrous ant with a young woman in its jaws.

"By the way, have you noticed the common denominator of these posters?" Nikki asked, looking over her shoulder at Walt. "The monster's always after someone that looks like me." She fake shuddered and struck an overly dramatic pose of a terrified movie poster heroine. "This isn't a movie, is it?" she asked.

"You never know, Nik," the barman predicted. "With all the crazy things that happen around here, it would have to be a series." Walt looked around at the time-faded posters and back to the small books on the bar; he moved his fingertips across them. "People have been looking for these for a long time," he said. "Not very nice people."

"Really? You knew about these books?" Nikki asked.

"Put them back in your bag," he said to her. He drummed his fingers on the small diaries, then pushed them at Nikki. "These are very dangerous. Put them away."

Nikki gave him a puzzled look that changed to a smile. She put her hand on top of his. "You're the best, Walt." She squeezed his hand. "You've known me for only a few hours, and you're already looking out for me." She squeezed again. "Thank you," she said softly.

Walt's mouth opened a little, and he pulled his hand back. "Oh, don't, I mean, nothing, never mind," he said. "Anyway, you just put those away until we figure out what to do,' the old man motioned to the journals.

"You know, Walt," the young woman said in a hushed voice. "If I had read them a week ago, I would have thought insanity ran in my family, all of his talk about spaceships and mutant insects. But, today, everything's different."

"That's for dang sure," Walt agreed.

Nikki picked up the small books and put two in her bag. "I knew these were important, something more than crazy scribblings from seventy years ago."

She thumbed through the remaining book and said, "They ruined Uncle Arthur's life. He died early. He might have killed himself, or maybe they did it. That's what Aunt May thought." She stopped talking to open the book and read silently for a moment, then thumbed a few leaves through the diary.

"But, like I said, I've got more than just these books; ahh, here it is," she said as she opened the book wide and looked at Walt.

"He was writing about the spaceman, the Thing. You know he was a consultant on the movie and made them use his real name in the story?

267

A little weird." She ran her finger lightly back and forth and down the page over the fountain pen cursive. "And did I mention I was named after his assistant? It's all in here."

Her finger stopped. "Here it is," she said again and began reading: "The Thing's hand contained seedpods which could be dislodged with some effort with a sharp tool. The seedpods were surprisingly easy to germinate, using any organic matter as a medium. Contact with any consumable substance at once stimulated activity. Growth was startlingly rapid. The implication was clear. The Thing's hands carried an invasion. These seeds were to breed an army on our own Earth. Our visitors have delivered an invasion."

Nikki laid the book flat on the bar and looked up at Walt.

"More scribbles," he said.

"More proof," she said. "Besides the books, there was also a little jar that had...."

Walt looked to the doorway and put his hand on hers.

Nikki stopped talking to see Syl walking quietly through the door into the dim barroom.

Walt sat straight on his stool, bringing his pen back to his folded crossword.

She walked across the room to sit next to Nikki. "Aren't you going to stretch your legs, hon?" the nurse asked her. "You won't get another chance until tomorrow to go outside. It's getting pretty late."

The young woman smiled at the nurse, "I don't know. Maybe. I was downstairs for a while. I even fell asleep. Guess I'd just as soon sit here and talk to Walt."

The nurse smiled. "What's that you're reading? It must be pretty good to keep you in here," Syl said as she reached over to take the book from the young woman.

268

Nikki covered her great uncle's journal, putting her hands over it and blocking the nurse. "Nothing, really. Just a family diary."

"Uh-huh," the nurse pulled her hand back and stared at the book. "Anything interesting?" she asked as her eyes moved up to watch Nikki's.

The younger woman closed the little book, lifted it off the bar, and pushed it into her bag. "Not really. Doesn't even make sense. Just ramblings, I guess," she replied, lowering her eyes as she closed the journal. "Personal family stuff," she added.

"Well, if you've finished reading, how about taking that walk outside? Everyone else is out there," Syl said. "Come on," she persisted with a broad smile. "Your books are safe in here. Walt will keep an eye on them. We'll go outside." The nurse motioned to the door and slid off the stool. Nikki gave a slight shrug and stepped down, turning to cross the room in front of Syl.

Walt tightened his lips in thought and dropped his puzzle on the bar next to Nikki's bag. He watched the women walk to the outer door.

The young woman went through the broken swinging doors and into the short hallway to the outer doors, wide open and framing the red sun lowering over the desert.

Nikki stopped a few steps from the threshold and turned to Syl. "Them?" she asked the nurse.

The two faced each other an arm's length apart. "What?" the nurse asked.

"You said 'them.' You said that Walt could watch 'them' – my books. How did you know there was more than one book? The others were in my bag."

Syl glared at her. "Just go outside," she said in a low voice. "You might have a chance out there."

"A chance?" Nikki repeated. "A chance for what?" she asked.

269

"To live," the nurse replied.

Nikki stared, and her lips parted slightly as if to say something. Then she gasped. Her eyes had gone from the woman's expressionless face to the pistol in her hand.

"I don't understand. Why are you doing this?" Nikki asked.

"Nothing personal, hon," the nurse answered, "Think of me as an enthusiastic book collector." She waved the handgun toward the doorway full of red sky.

Nikki turned to look through the door at the people in the lot. The three saloon regulars sat with their backs to the door on the edge of the wooden boardwalk. They were the closest to the entrance. The deputy and truck driver were walking back from the highway past the trio. The young woman turned to the nurse.

"None of your boyfriends are here to help you, honey. Not your fat truck driver or your macho sheriff. You're all on your own, so make up your mind. You can go outside with or without a hole in you," the nurse said menacingly. "But you are going outside."

Nikki took a slow breath and looked straight into Syl's eyes. "I read them, you know. I've read the books."

The nurse raised her brow. "And?" she asked.

The young woman continued, "I probably know more about the whole thing than you do. My great-uncle, the ants. Even the other thing. The Thing in the Arctic."

"Well, after you go outside, I'll read the books, then I'll know, too," Syl smiled. "Get moving." She waved the gun to the doorway again.

Nikki turned toward the door, "OK. OK. Just don't shoot me, OK?" Her voice quivered, "I'll go. The books are in my bag inside."

"I know where they are," the nurse said.

"All the books I got from my great-uncle are in the bag," Nikki said. "All three of them. Everything's there. The whole story's in there," she whispered nervously as she took small, slow steps to the door.

"Good, just keep going, honey. Don't worry. I'm not going to hurt you," the nurse said quietly. "Just go outside, and you'll be alright. I just want everyone out of the way for a while."

"I promise, everything's in the bag," Nikki said and stopped, facing the doorway with her back to Syl. She took a deep breath and added, "Everything except the seeds." She squeezed her eyes shut and waited for the nurse's reaction.

"What?" Syl said. "Stop. Look at me!"

Nikki turned to face the woman and the gun. She tried to control her breathing to push back her fear. "You know about the seeds," she said to the nurse and the chrome pistol pointing at her heart. "I hid the bottle with the seeds. I read about them in his journals. They were in a glass bottle. It was too dangerous to carry them around in my bag, so once I read about them and what they were, I put them someplace safe." She swallowed, watching Syl's expression.

The nurse stared at her for a long moment, then smiled with one corner of her mouth.

"Nice. Good for you, hon." The nurse nodded approvingly and thought. She waved the pistol the other way, back into the bar. "Get inside."

Nikki walked to the barroom, and Syl jammed her pistol into her back and pushed her along.

As she went through the swinging doors, Syl pushed the large red button on the door control without breaking stride as she passed. The outer blast door crashed down, sealing them in the Bunker and sealing the people outside to their dark fate as the sun fell.

The door slammed into the frame, and shock waves pulsed through the building. Nikki backed against the wall and looked from Syl to Walt. He was sitting in his spot behind the bar with a crossword puzzle on the bar.

She looked at the nurse, "You're leaving them out there? You're leaving them out there with those monsters?"

Nikki called to the barman, "Walt, what's going on? Do you know what she did? Everybody's outside – on their own. Aren't you going to do anything?"

The old man looked up without expression from his puzzle.

"Walt? How can you…." Nikki's voice trailed off.

Syl laughed. "These moments are too few and too far between. I love it when it dawns on the civilian that everyone's a bad guy but them." She laughed again. "Ahh, that's good," she wiped her eyes. "Harsh life lesson. You can't trust anyone, hon," the nurse casually motioned with her gun to the table nearest Walt's end of the bar. "Sit," she ordered.

Nikki walked across the room and sat. The nurse followed and sat across from her, her back to Walt.

"Where's the bottle?" she asked the young woman.

Nikki looked past her at the old barman. "Walt, you know those ants are going to kill everyone outside. People you've known for a long time, the deputy and Tom Honey and that old couple. Are you going to let that happen?" Nikki asked him, "How can you?

The nurse answered, "How can he? He has to, that's how. They are all witnesses to the origin of this mess. Everybody saw them take off this morning, and they have already killed God knows how many people. What difference will a few more make? Besides, the powerful have ordained it, isn't that right, boss?" she asked the bartender over her shoulder.

"You mean the government?" Nikki said. "You both work for the government? Even you, Walt? I thought you were the anti-everything guy. This whole line of yours is a crock?" Her voice rose. "I can't believe

272

you work for the CIA or whatever, that you're just some government thug."

"She keeps blaming the government. Isn't that cute, Walt?" Syl snickered. "The government's nothing, honey. They work for us. We make the government. We make all the governments. And we don't want to be associated with giant bugs that eat people. Bad branding."

"And what about Cal, Walt?" Nikki said to the old man, ignoring the nurse. "Are you going to let him die, too? I don't know if you care about the others, but no matter what you pretend, I know he's your friend."

Walt didn't answer, and it was quiet for a few moments. The nurse looked over her shoulder in the old man's direction and kept a smile on her face. Nikki shook her head when Walt didn't respond. He just kept to his puzzle.

"I can't believe you," Nikki said to him.

"That's it, honey. Now you're getting it. You can't believe anybody," the nurse laughed at her again, "Not even the lovable old barkeep." She lifted her right pant leg, revealing her ankle leather. She twirled her little pistol on her trigger finger before palming it back to the holster.

Nikki watched her put the pistol away, and Syl smiled at her. "I don't need a gun for you. I'm a trained killer." She leaned toward the young woman and drew her finger across her own throat while making an unpleasant sound effect.

Nikki tried not to make eye contact.

"And besides, I've got my old boss watching my back," Syl added. She tilted her head in Walt's direction.

"The lovable old barkeep," Walt said. He lifted his double-barreled, sawed-off shotgun from under the bar and pointed it at the back of the nurse's head. The hammers clicked when he pulled them back.

Syl watched Nikki's eyes open wide.

"Sounds like you've made a decision, Walt," the nurse said over her shoulder to the old man.

"Get out of the way, Nikki. Get away from her," he said. "And you, don't move," he said to the nurse.

Nikki started to stand, but Syl said, "Don't. I'm getting up. I want this over with." She stood and turned toward the bar.

"Your call," Walt said to her. The shotgun moved with her. "Breathe wrong, and I'll cut you in two."

Syl smiled and shook her head. "That is one corny line. You are obviously too old for this, Walt. And the same old shotgun from under the bar? What was that? Thirty years ago? C'mon."

"It'll work again," he said.

Her smile widened. "Will it?"

The nurse lifted her arm, pointed the pistol she hadn't put back in the holster at Walt, and fired once, hitting him in the right side of his chest. Simultaneously, he pulled the triggers on the old shotgun. They clicked, but his gun didn't fire.

Walt stood on the rungs of his stool before falling backward into the shelves and liquor bottles. Everything went down in a shower of broken glass and high-test, crashing to the floor with Walt in his spot behind the bar.

After the noise, his bottle of Rocking Chair whiskey rolled off the shelf and fell on top of him, then to the floor, but it didn't break.

The nurse walked to the end of the bar and looked through the open bartender's gate at the old man's feet. The shards of glass sounded like a windchime as he moved in the debris.

"Walt, Walt, Walt," she clucked. "Firing pin, yesterday. You were always telling me to check my gear. And now look at you," she chastised, shaking her head. "For the sake of a nail."

Without looking at her, Syl motioned with her pistol for Nikki to sit down.

"All-talk Walt. And you're such a creature of habit, too. That gets me more than anything,"

"Like this," she reached up, grabbed the wooden bar gate, and slammed it down. "I bet that hasn't been closed in twenty years," she sighed. "You're really kind of lazy. I'll never understand how you went so far." She looked under the closed gate at his legs moving in the broken glass. The old man groaned, and his eyes opened and closed a few times. "That wasn't nice, Walter, trying to shoot me like that," she said and stepped to the front of the bar.

"But still, it's such a rush when a gun is pointed at you, and someone that wants to kill you pulls the trigger." Syl leaned over to look down at him. "Especially when it doesn't go as they planned, you know Walt?" She stood on the brass rail, stretching over the bar top, and shook her head at the bloody man. "Well, maybe not this time."

Syl peered down, then squinted. "Ouch. That doesn't look good." She shook her head again as the bright red blood spread across his shirt. "That is bad, old-timer." She casually pointed her gun over the bar and down at Walt. "If you want, I could finish you off, no prob." She gave him an extra big smile. "What do you say, boss? Tough it out, or draw the curtain?"

The old barkeep groaned and tried to focus his eyes on her. He coughed and blew blood out of his mouth. "No wonder you never had any friends, Syl," he sputtered.

Syl's lips tightened, and her eyes flashed. "Double ouch on me," she said. "But, if you notice, you're the one dying alone. So, just for that, I'll leave you to it, call it professional discourtesy. Hard feelings, I hope," she said. Syl stopped mid-turn and reached out to pick up the remote control. She held it up, pointed it at the television, and clicked. The news came on the screen, and the reporter was giving the latest update about the giant ants.

The nurse turned to Nikki and waggled the gun in her direction. "I'll be right with you, sweetie. You just sit tight."

She leaned over the bar again and looked down at the old man. "I thought you might like something to watch while you die," she hissed softly. "Everything you talked about is coming true, but you're not going to be here to see what happens."

Syl turned to the young woman sitting open-mouthed and rigid in her chair.

"C'mon, hon," the nurse said to Nikki. "Let's get that bottle and wrap up your little part in this drama." Syl motioned for the young woman to stand. "Let's go. Where'd you stash the seeds?"

Nikki's wide eyes followed the gun as Syl waved it around.

"Honey! Up! Let's go," the nurse said in an irritated voice. She stared at the petrified young woman for a moment and, with an exasperated exhalation, pointed her pistol and shot. A round smashed into the tabletop a few inches from Nikki's hand. She jumped to her feet, staring in shock at the bullet hole.

"That got you moving," Syl laughed. "Now, do what I tell you." The nurse straightened her arm and pointed the pistol at Nikki's face. "I'll be the first to admit that once I start killing, it can be hard to stop. That might be a character flaw," she shrugged. "But that's just me. Now, for the last time, where's the bottle? Where are the damn seeds?" She thrust the gun in Nikki's face and shook it, white-knuckling the weapon.

Nikki breathlessly answered and pointed to the kitchen door, "The bottle's in there. It's in the freezer."

Syl looked across the bar at the door to the backroom. "OK. Go. Show me where," she said.

Nikki stepped from the table to the bar and reached for her bag. Syl knocked her hand away, cruelly hitting the young woman's arm with her pistol.

"Don't worry about that, you won't need it," she sneered. The nurse motioned with the gun. "Move," she said.

Nikki walked to the kitchen with Syl right behind, her pistol raised. As she pushed the door back, the old man called from behind the bar, "Syl, for once, don't. Don't hurt her, Syl." He sounded like he was gargling.

"OK. You're the boss, Walt," the nurse answered sweetly. Syl lifted the pistol above her head and fired carelessly, shooting down at the bar in Walt's direction twice. She didn't care if she hit him or not.

Syl grabbed Nikki by the hair and pushed her so aggressively into the kitchen that the young woman fell on the floor, leaving the door swinging back and forth. The nurse stood in the doorway, grinning at her victim prostrate in the stainless-steel butcher shop.

"Hey, Walt!" Syl called into the barroom. "You better hurry up and die because if you don't, you'll hear me get to work on her. I might even drag you in to watch." Syl laughed and walked to Nikki, standing over her. She grabbed her throat, cruelly choking her, clamping her thumb and index finger under her jawline and squeezing until murder filled her. The hands-on killing made Syl feel predator vitality.

She still needed the young woman, at least for a toy. Syl hissed and lifted Nikki with the hand around her throat and planted her on her feet, easing her grip so the young woman could breathe but holding her up until she regained consciousness.

Nikki's eyes fluttered open, and Syl let her go. The young woman faltered but remained standing as she came to.

"Let's go," Syl growled and muscled her past the stainless-steel counters and pots and pans to two thick doors, one the freezer and one the refrigerator.

"Where'd you put it, hon?" Syl asked her, poking the short barrel of the pistol into her ribs. "And don't stall."

"It's in there," Nikki pointed to the door with frost patterns on the window.

"Open it up," the nurse said, throwing her against the door.

Nikki pulled the handle and dragged the heavy door open, stepping back for Syl to enter.

"After you, hon," she said, pushing Nikki ahead with the gun into the walk-in freezer. Syl flicked the light switch, and the metal ceiling lamps buzzed, brightly illuminating the frozen room. It wasn't overstocked. A few grocery store boxes and a dozen ice cream containers were stacked on a wheeled wire rack.

Syl said to her, "No BS, hon," she pushed her forward again. "Remember, I'm amped up with the domination thing now, so it's best to do exactly what I tell you to do."

The young woman said nothing, just pointed weakly at the motor unit high on the rear wall of the freezer.

"Up there, huh?" Syl said, smiling at Nikki. She motioned upward with the gun to the dual fans spinning in the box. "You get it," she ordered. "And don't get any cuter than you already are. It would be fatal," she added.

"I'm afraid," she said to the nurse. "You're not going to hurt me, are you? Walt said…"

"I know what he said. Don't be such a wimp. Just get up there and get the seeds," Syl snapped.

"OK," Nikki said meekly. She walked to the back of the unit, lifted a stepstool leaning against the wall, and opened it. She looked at the nurse, her eyes wide. "Please, don't hurt me," she said to Syl.

"Don't be silly, hon," Syl answered extra-sweetly. "I'm going to hurt you so bad you will beg to die. Now do what you're told." Her tone changed as she spoke, becoming a wicked snarl. "Where is it, anyway?" she asked gruffly. "In the fan?"

278

Nikki's voice trembled as she answered. "No, up on top," she said, pointing to the metal blower box.

The nurse looked at her and frowned, poking the pistol upward. "Well, get it, honey." Her breath created a cloud in the freezer air.

Nikki climbed onto the first step and then the second and stretched to feel along the top of the freezing metal box.

"There's a recess up here," she said, running her hand along the hanging metal assembly.

"Skip the travelogue and get the goods," Syl snarled.

The young woman lowered her hand, holding a small glass bottle with a metal top. It looked like a saltshaker.

She held the glass container out to show Syl, and it glinted under the bright utility lights. Her hand trembled. The nurse smiled.

"Give me," she said to the young woman and stepped forward to take the bottle.

Nikki was breathing audibly, puffing out fog, and her hand shook doubly from cold and fear. As Syl reached up and her fingers opened to take the vial, it slipped from the young woman's grasp and fell to the cement floor, breaking with only a slight sound. The handwritten label kept the halved glass together; it cracked open like an egg to spill four dark seedpods onto the floor.

Syl's face flushed with anger, and she lifted the pistol to the girl's face. "You stupid, clumsy...." She looked down and shook her head. "You idiot," the nurse said as she knelt, putting her pistol on the cement and picking up one of the seeds. "Do you know how many people have been looking for these? And, for decades. What do you do? Drop them. Idiot."

She held the pod between her thumb and index finger, examining it in the bright light, bringing it close to her face, bathing it in her steamy exhalations.

"So, this is what everyone's been trying to find all these years. A little bean," she whispered, then laughed. She opened her left hand and dropped the bean onto the flat of her palm, bringing her face close to inspect the kernel.

"It is strange looking," she said, peering at the shiny husk. "It looks like…" she suddenly started and pulled her head away from her hand.

"Wow, that is doubly weird," Syl said. "It felt like it moved. Ha. In the bottle all this time, and it moved. I think it did. Like a jumping bean." She studied the seed, moving her hand from side to side under the bright freezer lights.

Nikki stepped down to the floor quietly, watching the nurse, relying on history, and trusting in the potential of the beans.

"It is definitely moving. Not a lot, but it is. Find something to put the seeds in," Syl said without looking away from the pod. She pushed it around with her finger. "Life from outer space," she whispered to herself, puffing small clouds with each word.

"Tear some foil from one of those packages on the shelf," Syl said distractedly. "We should probably keep them from the air." She stared at the seedpod, now almost ignoring the young woman. "Get some for each seed. I want them separate. There will be more than one interested party for these."

"OK," Nikki said softly. She thought about making a try for the door.

Nikki took a careful step by the nurse as she gazed at the seed in her hand.

Syl felt the pod subtly move. Exhaling, her fog enveloped the bean.

Nikki stood behind Syl and looked over the nurse's shoulder at the small black pod in the middle of her hand and the chrome gun on the floor.

They stood still. The only thing that moved was the bean. It clicked and shifted slightly.

Syl whispered to herself, "It's vibrating. I can feel it. It's amazing."

Suddenly, the seed pod split, leaking goo onto her hand.

"What the…" the nurse turned her hand to let the liquid run off, but it absorbed through her skin instead. Syl shook her right hand violently as if it were on fire.

The nurse screamed, "Oh, my God!" She frantically rubbed her hand on her pants to wipe away the vanished liquid. She scratched at her palm with her other hand and looked at Nikki with wild fear.

Syl jumped to her feet, grabbed the waist of Nikki's jeans, and threw her to the back of the freezer. The young woman crashed into a wire cart, knocking ice cream containers and frozen dinners off the shelf as she fell on the floor.

Syl picked up her pistol with her left and pointed it at Nikki, stepping back as she held her other hand up.

"What did you do to me?" the nurse screamed. "What's going to happen to me? Tell me! You read the books!" She gasped at her. "That's right. You read the books. You did this on purpose! You knew!" she screamed.

Syl suddenly jolted and stepped back from Nikki. She brought her palm around to stare, wild-eyed, at the inflamed, red ring raised in the center of her hand. "Oh, my God! What is this?" she screamed. She shot at Nikki but missed as she lost motor control.

Nikki held her hand up as a shield against the flailing gun and screamed, "It will be alright. There's a way to fix it. We can fix it," she lied at the top of her voice.

Syl weakened and stumbled backward, flat against the freezer door.

Her gun was up, swinging in the air and not aiming. The nurse slid down the wooden door to a sitting position, staring blankly at her infected hand, holding the pistol in the other.

The nurse looked up at Nikki. "You knew…" she whispered. Her eyes couldn't focus, and she was sweating in the icebox.

Nikki slowly sat up against the back wall of the freezer. Both sitting on the floor, the women faced each other across the floor with the glass and seeds between them.

CHAPTER FOURTEEN

THE ATTACK

The deputy and truck driver were at the highway across the parking lot from the Bunker. Rosales looked over the dusty, chewed-up world in both directions, and Tom Honey dwelled on what was left of his truck, spread around the local area.

"Not one piece of meat," the trucker said. "I was hauling more than a ton of beef, and now there's not a speck of it to be seen." He shook his head and took his cowboy hat off to wipe his brow. "Those bugs don't miss a morsel."

The deputy didn't reply but stared down the road the sheriff had taken earlier that day. He hoped to see him walking back, but nothing was moving.

"Getting pretty late," Rosales said. He looked across the desert at the sun dropping to the distant mountains.

Tom put his hat back on and said, "Ah, he'll be back in no time at all, Luis. Or maybe he's at Holloman. Might be holed up there for the night."

"Maybe," the deputy said. "Hope so. Don't know what went wrong with the radio." Rosales shook his head and turned back to the Bunker. "All I know is it's getting late," he said. "Guess we oughta get everyone back inside."

The deputy did a head count as they walked to the building. He could see the three bar buddies sitting on the walk in front of the doorway. The professor and his missus were not far from the entrance, and the linemen were in the lot talking.

"I don't see Syl or Nikki. Did they come outside?" the deputy asked as they walked between car-halves.

283

"Don't rightly know," Tom responded as he ambled along. "You'd think so, at least the nurse. She was awful keen on getting everybody outside to stretch themselves." The large man turned his head, surveying the landscape. "But no, I don't see her. Come to think of it, I don't remember seeing her outside. Not Nikki, neither."

The two were halfway across the lot when the only door into the Bunker came crashing down. They felt it slam shut through their boots.

Rosales and Tom Honey stopped in their tracks. The people closest to the building recoiled from the noise, startled by the sudden impact of the concrete and steel blast door as it shut them out.

The three barflies were on their feet. Billy jumped at the door and pounded on it. His fists made small sounds against the thick cement slab, slapping through the sudden silence of the lot.

The professor and his wife were frail silhouettes of fear in red against the sun-soaked wall.

Rosales was dumbstruck. He stopped open-mouthed. The consequences of being sealed outside as night approached with no shelter, few guns, and little ammunition played out in his mind. The ants would come back after sunset. None of the vehicles were operational, and there was no place to hide.

He started for the doorway at a fast walk, which turned into a trot and then an all-out run, leaving the rotund trucker to catch up.

The deputy jumped onto the wooden walk and ran past the two utility workers to the door.

"What happened? Why did she close it?" he asked no one in particular as the isolated gathered before the door. A few reached out and touched the slab in disbelief.

Tom Honey did his best to run across the lot and was breathing and wheezing when he joined the group, trying to catch his breath. "Must be something wrong." He gulped air. "They're probably trying to get it open right now."

"Yes, that must be it," the professor agreed. "A malfunction of some sort. I believe there's a manual mechanism to pump the door up or down. Whoever's inside will be able to operate it."

Carlos looked at the anxious faces turned to the huge door. "Who is inside, anyway?" he asked.

Mike answered, "Looks like it'd be the nurse, the girl, and Walt."

"It's going to open," Brandon repeated as he ran his hands over the smooth cement. "It's got to," he whispered to himself.

Billy heard him and said, "It better open. I can't be out here at night. No way." He turned and looked at the sun as it touched the faraway mountains. "In another couple of minutes, it's going to be dark. Dark, man."

"Oh no, oh no," the professor's wife began crying. She became too weak to stand and sobbed deeply. She faltered and swayed. The professor had his arm around her. He cradled the woman, and they sat on the wooden planks, their backs to the wall.

Rosales shook his head at the immobile slab, cursing under his breath. He cursed again and unshouldered his assault rifle. He had one full magazine. The deputy looked from person to person, assessing available weapons. Tom Honey had his Desert Eagle, probably a few rounds, but not many. Both of the utility workers were carrying ARs with a couple of mags. Carlos had taken an assault rifle, too. Ray and Billy had no weapons, nor did the husband and wife.

As a group, they were unprepared for more than one stand. Maybe they could deal with two or even three ants if they were lucky. Rosales looked at the impenetrable stone door, shut and silent. He didn't feel lucky.

"What are we going to do here, Luis?" Billy asked. "I mean, we're pretty far up the creek on this one, man." Fear formed his face.

"I don't know. We have to hope that door opens," the deputy replied as he looked across the lot. "But I know one thing, we've got nowhere else to go, so we're here for better or worse."

"I vote worse," Billy said.

"Well, it's not a democracy, especially if you don't have a gun," Rosales told him. "We're just going to have to hunker down and hope for the best."

"That would be a good start, deputy," the professor said quietly. "The ants respond to scent. It might help if we all sat down rather than standing. It may cut down on our profile in the breeze," he added. "Also, we should sit quietly. They are sensitive to vibration, as well." He stroked his wife's hair. "We'll be fine," he said softly.

"That sounds like some good advice, Professor. Good idea, yeah. Everybody sit down and be quiet," the deputy whispered loudly to the group. They seated themselves along the edge of the wooden walkway and stared across the highway as the sun touched the mountaintops.

After a few minutes, the junior lineman broke the silence. "You know there's probably gas in some of those wrecks," he said, pointing to the auto parts in the lot. "If we could siphon it off, we could make gas bombs. You know, like Molotov cocktails."

His senior partner turned his head to look at the young man. "Brandon," he smiled. "Brandon," he repeated. "That is a great idea."

"It ain't bad, at that," the trucker said. "All we have to do is get a couple of jars or bottles, and we'll be in business."

Billy stood up, looked at the highway, and quickly crouched to whisper to the group. "Walt has a ton of empties round back under the lean-to," he said. "There's a mountain of bottles back there. Mostly that Rocking Horse stuff he drinks."

"Alright, let's get this going," the deputy said. "Why don't you guys collect bottles?" he suggested, motioning to Billy and Ray. "We'll check out the wrecks and see what we can find." He looked at the professor as he said to everyone else, "And everybody be quiet as you can."

The overturned wreckage made it easy to get to the fuel tanks. One of the linemen got a spike from their wrecked truck to pierce the tanks, and they had a bucket to catch the gasoline.

Mike held the bucket as Brandon punctured an overturned gas tank at its lowest point. The gasoline arced out into the pail.

"You might have saved the whole show. Great job, Brandon," Mike said.

They brought the first bucket of gas to the bomb-making spot on the walkway to fill bottles and stuff wicks. The Molotovs quickly lined up.

"An excellent defense, gentlemen," the professor said from his place against the wall. "That puts us in a much better position. And, if I may add, very well done, young man," he said, calling over to Brandon. "An excellent idea. If there's one thing that keeps a beast at bay, it is fire," the professor said as he softly patted his wife's hand. He smiled again at the young lineman.

They got more fire. They started a line of blazes in front of the walkway, fed with dry boards from behind the Bunker. Some boards served as torches, half-stuck into the flames to be used to ignite the bomb wicks when the need arose.

The group settled into watching the fires and waiting for the door to open. Thin smoke from the parched firewood hung in the air while Billy nervously tended the blazes, hurrying back and forth to nudge the brands and search the darkness beyond the firelight.

"Wow, I didn't realize the sun was down. Look," Billy pointed, "the moon's already coming up," he said as he trotted back to his place between his friends on the edge of the walk. "Nothing's going on out there," he concluded.

"And that's the way we want it," the deputy said absently; his attention was on the fire, watching it pop and hiss.

"I wonder what's going on in there," Tom Honey said from the end of the walkway. "Doesn't make any sense that they couldn't get the door open by now."

"That's what I was thinking, too," Carlos added. "Walt would get that door working, and if he couldn't, he would dynamite it. I don't get it. Something must have happened to him." He looked at the door.

The deputy threw a broken board into the fire.

"That door was made to stay closed," the professor said quietly from behind them. "If the opening mechanism has a problem, a bulldozer could not open it." He was sitting with his wife, who appeared to be sleeping, leaning against him. He had his arm around her.

"Nothing I'd like better than for that door to open and get inside with a cold beer," Billy agreed. He looked over his shoulder at the solid slab door and then back into the flames.

The staccato siren of a giant ant blared from the night fallen over the desert. It was dark, and the monsters were out.

The professor's wife soundlessly stiffened and covered her face with both hands. She gulped for air, choking with terror. Her husband held her in his arms.

There was another screeching call from the desert. Closer. Then another across the road.

"Oh, God!" She hyperventilated. "It's them. THEM! THEM AGAIN!" she screamed. "They're here!" The old woman cried and struggled to her feet. She pulled away from her husband and ran to the giant slab that barred their way to safety, slapping against it wildly with her bare hands.

"Please, please, open, please let us in!" she wailed. Her husband was behind her as she collapsed before the monolith, sliding down the concrete to the wooden deck. He knelt and cradled her.

288

Those with guns were pointing them into the darkness of the parking lot, waiting for something, hoping for nothing.

The night darkened around the fires.

The professor sat with his wife against the wall next to the doorway. The others formed a picket line without speaking, standing along the front of the wooden walkway. They stared into the dark, watching moving shadows past their small fires.

The minutes ticked by like a time bomb.

Everyone jumped as a piece of wood in the fire exploded and shot sparks into the night. Billy laughed nervously. "Oh, man, that freaked me out, man. I almost…" he left off and stood, took a few steps toward the fire, and peered over the flames, trying to define the shadows. Then he realized the shadow was peering back at him.

The giant scout's feelers switched, sampling the air. It turned from the firelight and walked to the utility truck, brushing the wreck with its feelers, then climbed on top of the vehicle. The monster arched into the air and blasted out an earsplitting call that ended abruptly.

The ant dismounted the overturned truck and disappeared around the corner of the building.

"What the hell was that?" Billy croaked. "Is that it? Where'd he go?"

"I think he went to get some friends," the deputy said quietly. He looked at the line of men, pointing their guns into the darkness past the flames and breathing hard.

"Your idea, why don't you get a couple of those bottles?" Mike said in a hoarse whisper to the younger lineman. "You can baptize those bugs when they come back."

Brandon nodded and went to the walkway to collect the cocktails. He took a firebrand from the flames and wedged it between the boards in the walk to hold the torch. Tom Honey did the same thing down at his end of the line. Carlos followed suit at his.

The deputy clicked the safety off his AR. Another click from one of the guns answered. "Everyone watch where you're pointing those cannons," Rosales said. "Keep them on the bugs."

Tom Honey hopped up on the walk and got a few more bottles from the stash to add to his private collection. He stepped heavily off the wood and into the dust of the lot, holding a bottle in each hand.

Everyone, ready or not, faced the darkness.

"They're out there," someone whispered.

There were noises in the lot. Things moved in the dark.

"We don't want to start it, just finish it," the deputy warned them.

There was a scraping noise beyond the light. A soft chatter answered a low clicking.

"I don't know, Deputy. I think I'd like to see what's out there," Carlos said from down the line.

Rosales saw him light the wick on a gas bomb and stretch back for a long, high throw. He let it loose, and they all watched the flaming tail arc through the darkness to explode in a fireball, illuminating the dark lot and three giant ants crawling through the junk, heading for them.

"Here they come!" shouted Rosales.

The ants moved quickly out of the dark and charged the group. Three large scout ants came in fast, scuttling over and around the wreckage.

"Let them have it!" the deputy roared as he opened up with his assault rifle on the ant heading straight at him.

Tom Honey had two bottles alight, one in each hand. He threw both of them at the monster charging in on his right. The bombs burst, the first missing its mark, but the second landed under the mutant bug, throwing flaming liquid onto the beast. It instantly recoiled, rearing on its back legs, emitting a high-pitched distress call.

Brandon finished Tom's monster ant by throwing another Molotov. The bomb blew up right on target, enveloping the already burning insect entirely in flames. It stood on its rear legs, teetered, and fell backward from the group. The flailing legs stilled and curled inward from the heat.

Mike paired his gun with the deputy, pumping lead as fast as they could into the charging insect, but the bullets didn't have the stopping power of the firebombs. The stampeding ant's momentum carried it through the hail of bullets to crash into the deputy, jaws open. It scooped Luis into its grinders and snapped them shut, crushing his chest and instantly killing him. The bullet-riddled bug smashed into the front wall of the Bunker with the deputy and dropped into a heap. Mike jumped onto the walk next to the bug, firing point-blank into its head, opening a gaping wound in the hard shell. The monster was dead. The lineman threw aside his rifle to extricate the lawman, buried under the massive head and a thicket of crumpled legs.

Once he got a look at Rosales, he realized there was no hope for the lawman. He pushed himself out of the mash of dead ant, dripping and foul. The deputy was dead.

At the other end of the walk, the three bar mates pelted the attacking scout with two, then three, then four flaming shots. The insect lay in a burning heap twenty feet before them. Billy was on all fours in the dust, gasping for air, and Ray was standing with an unlit bottle in one hand and a short torch in the other. Carlos looked around and pointed his rifle into the parking lot, made brighter by the burning ants.

Tom Honey pulled the big Desert Eagle from his belt, staggered back to the walkway, and sat heavily on edge, breathing hard. He looked at the burning bugs and then turned his head to the carcass against the building, not realizing the deputy was dead, crushed under the beast.

Mike was sitting on the edge of the boardwalk next to the trucker. Tom Honey had his pistol on his lap and had almost caught his breath. "Looks like we won this round," he gasped.

The lineman stared vacantly at the ground.

"At least we're still here," the trucker puffed. His eyes moved to the huge carcass of the scout pushed up against the Bunker.

The lineman just kept staring. "Rosales is dead," he said after a moment.

Tom Honey's face contorted. "What?" He stood, turning to the heap of dead bug. "What?" he repeated. "I didn't know."

Mike released the magazine from his AR and turned it to the firelight to look inside. He cursed and dropped the empty to the dust. Leaning the gun against the wooden walk, he closed his eyes.

The trucker climbed up and took a few steps to the front of the dead ant. Tom leaned over, bracing himself against the wall. He could see the crumpled body of Deputy Rosales. The dead man's eyes were closed, and his mouth hung open. He was covered with blood, and his head was turned at an unnatural angle, too far back.

Tom Honey stopped breathing when he saw the lifeless countenance of the deputy. With a groan, the trucker pushed himself from the wall and returned to the edge of the walk, stepping through the twisted bug parts.

He sat next to Mike. "That's rough," he said to the lineman. "Luis was a good guy."

The utility worker half-turned his head to the trucker and replied, "He stood his ground right in front of them. Last thing he did was push me out of the way. If he didn't, I'd be in there with him."

Tom Honey nodded silently.

The three bar mates joined the young lineman standing by the dead ant. They talked in low whispers about the deputy and took no notice of the professor and his wife huddled against the wall several feet from the monster.

The old professor disengaged himself from his wife and gently leaned her against the wall. She wouldn't stay in a seated position. He tried twice, laid her down, touched her face, and removed his jacket to cover her.

The small group of men standing nearby became quiet as they watched him. The professor gently arranged his jacket to cover her face. He struggled to stand from his kneeling position. Carlos quickly stepped over to the old man and helped him to his feet. He walked him to the group, his arm around the old teacher's shoulders.

He looked at them with wet eyes. "She died," he choked and broke into tears. "She grabbed me so tightly. She died so terribly afraid," he sobbed and slumped over. Carlos took him across the planks and helped him to sit on the edge of the walk. He sat next to the old man, holding the assault rifle and keeping a comforting arm around the professor. The old man hid his face in his hands and cried.

Tom and Mike looked from their place on the boardwalk and got the gist. The trucker looked past the ant to the slab blocking their way into the safety of the Bunker.

Brandon walked over to stand beside his partner. Mike looked up at the young man. "You did real good, Brandon," he said, nodding approvingly.

"That's too bad about the deputy. And, now, that lady," the young man said, lowering his voice. "How do you think we'll do the next time, Mike?"

The lineman looked at his partner earnestly and said, "Depends on two things: how many gas bombs we've got and how many of those bugs are coming. We're about done with the guns. They're better than nothing, but my bet's on the fire."

"We still have a pile of those left," Brandon replied, motioning toward the groups of Molotovs waiting along the walkway. He looked at the smooth face of the blast door. "I sure wish they'd get that door open, though."

"Well, hope for one and plan for the other," Mike told him. The young man shifted his rifle to his other arm and followed Mike's gaze into nothing.

The two regulars sat at a respectful distance from Carlos and the professor. The old man's sobs had stopped. No one had anything to say. All were exhausted and sat staring into the dark or the small campfires. The bug fires were burning out, making the air smell awful.

Tom Honey got up to drop some more wood into the fire. He returned to his spot on the walkway as the flames danced higher. An insect call screeched from the desert.

"At least that sounded far away," somebody said.

"Doesn't matter. They know we're here now," someone else replied.

The fire was low, dying down. A series of rapid clicks came from the night across the highway.

"Great," Mike said, and spit cotton.

Carlos stood and helped the professor up. "Come and sit by the door," he said quietly to the old man. "You can be by your wife and be ready to take her inside when the door opens." He smiled kindly at the bearded man as he helped him to his feet and onto the walkway.

"Come on. You can sit over here," he said, leading the broken man to the wall of the building and helping him to sit with the cement at his back. He grasped the professor's shoulder and then turned to collect more gas bombs to get ready for the next attack.

The old man held his arm. "Thank you. You're very kind," he said to Carlos and smiled weakly.

Carlos patted his hand and then went down the walk to set up his bottles. His two friends went with him. Each carried several cocktails in their arms.

Mike stood. "Get ready, guys," he warned. "Let's have a pile of those bug bombs behind us, ready to go. We don't know how many of them will be coming this time."

Another shrill call, closer, came out of the dark. Mike turned to his young partner and said, "Why don't you do the honors this time? Chuck one out there, as far as you can, and light it up. Let's see what's going on."

Brandon lit one of the cocktails and took a running start to throw the bottle as far as he could. The flame traced a long path through the night and fireballed right next to a pair of giant scouts, moving silently through the lot.

"There they are!" Tom Honey yelled. He pushed his large pistol through his belt as he readied to light a bottle in each hand. A pile of gasoline-filled glass was on the walkway right behind the trucker.

At the other end of the line, Ray lit one of the firebombs and ran to the firewall to throw. His bottle flew far and came down a direct hit on one of the ants in the dark. The flaming liquid ran over the monster's middle and wrapped fiery veins around its legs.

Enraged, the creature charged, fanning the flames. Ray executed an impressive leap for his life, springing out of the path of the flaming insect as it rushed in. Carlos and Billy launched another volley of firebombs, engulfing the beast in flames.

The monster veered off and ran into the overturned utility truck, collapsed, and rolled over to burn with its legs in the air.

The fires in the parking lot revealed there were more giant ants.

"There must be twenty of them!" Billy shouted as he backed up to the building.

Mike yelled out, "They're on the way! Get a perimeter fire going, ring us in!" He lit a bottle and threw it into the edge of the darkness surrounding them. It exploded, illuminating the ants approaching beyond the blaze.

Carlos did likewise. Then Ray and Billy threw bottles, connecting the burning fires into a wall to keep the monsters at bay. Brandon threw two bombs, completing the burning semi-circle, encompassing the survivors in front of the Bunker.

Mike yelled out, "How many bottles we got?"

"Maybe two dozen down here," Carlos called back.

"Same here," Tom Honey yelled, picking another from the pile.

"Look out – there! One's coming through," Billy shouted, pointing to a gap as one of the fires began to burn down. "Throw one over there!"

Brandon pitched a perfect bottle to fire up the fence, and an ant scuttled back from the heat.

"Great, kid," Tom Honey yelled over to him. "Great arm!"

"Yeah," Brandon called back. "Great while they last. But, at this rate, we're out pretty soon," he said in a lower voice to Mike.

"We're going to have to let them come in and burn them up. Holding them back is going to get us nowhere and cost too much gas," he said grimly to the young man.

Carlos came down the line to Mike and the other two. "Hey," he said to them. "We are going to run out of gas soon. We have to get smarter about this, you know?" He took a deep breath and continued, "Why don't we let the fire in the center burn out? Give them a gate to come through and cook 'em. Maybe the other ones will get the message."

"Sounds like a plan," Mike looked at his junior partner and the trucker. They nodded. Tom went to the bottle collection on the walkway and returned with a couple of fresh ones.

Carlos said, "Give 'em hell." He trotted down the line to his guys.

As the fires burned down, Ray threw another bomb to refuel the side and keep it burning. Tom Honey did the same a minute later for his side of the blaze, but they let the center of the wall burn out.

296

Within a few minutes, a large insect head materialized from the darkness. The bordering fires reflected thousands of times in the lenses covering the two-foot eyes. The head pushed into the gap between the blazes and turned, sweeping the air with its antennae and sensing a breach wide enough to enter. The monstrous scout lunged with surprising suddenness, propelling itself through the gateway and directly at Carlos and his companions. The colossal bug's speed caught them all off guard.

Armed with a firebomb, lit and ready to go, Carlos threw a fastball into the advancing insect's face. The bottle struck the bug's head but glanced off and skittered along its body to break on the ground behind it.

Mike and Brandon ran forward from their side of the line, and each launched a cocktail at the big bug. Both hit on target and exploded into flames, drenching the monster in liquid fire. The gas dripped burning from the bug, leaving a flaming trail as the beast charged.

Blinded by the fire, the flaming beast swerved off course and ran onto the walk, slamming into the building, and the cache of gasoline bombs in front of the professor huddled with his dead wife.

The explosions were instant. Several bottles broke simultaneously, and their eruption was immediately followed by the remaining bottles exploding, shooting streams of flaming gasoline in all directions.

As the firebug came careening in, everyone was in motion. All instinctively put ground between themselves and the giant ant, getting as far away from the imminent explosion as they could.

When the burning monster smashed into the cache of fuel and ignited an inferno, its momentum and the force of the explosion propelled it upward. The flaming giant scaled the wall straight up to die, then toppled sideways and crashed into the wooden walkway in front of the Bunker. Half on, half off the walk, the monster roasted on the planks.

The center of the walkway was engulfed in the blaze, and dozens of fires were scattered in front of the building. Carlos rolled in the sand to extinguish his right leg, spattered with burning fuel.

Billy and Ray were well clear of the blast. Ray was laying in the dust, but Billy was up, running back and forth in a panic.

The linemen and Tom Honey were on the ground. As Mike rolled over to get back on his feet, he saw the professor struggling out of the searing furnace. He was engulfed in flames, walking mechanically, moving like a marionette. His arms were stretched out, grasping at the flames. His fiery rags fell off; he dripped fire. He clawed at his face and became incandescent, returning to the flames and stepping in. He fell forward, disappearing into the fire.

Mike got to his feet and looked at the men near him. Tom Honey was on all fours. Brandon was standing, staring at the professor's final act, and holding the neck of a broken bottle in his hand. His jacket was drenched in gas.

Mike yelled at his young partner. "Get away from the fire! Go back there!" He flagged him away, gesturing to a section of the wall spared from the flaming debris of the insect's impact. "Get back there!" he yelled as he waved him off.

The young man took a step away from the fire in front of him and unknowingly toward the torch he'd stuck in the planks of the walkway.

Tom Honey jumped to his feet, ran up behind Brandon, and pushed him from the danger.

"Get that coat off, son! It's soaked with gas!" the trucker yelled. He rushed over and pulled at the jacket, stripping it from the dazed young man. "You were lucky you didn't go up."

Brandon looked at the trucker with a steady expression of fear, rerunning a movie in his head. He didn't blink. "Did you see him? That professor? He was all fire like he was made of fire. He was walking in it. He just walked around in it," Brandon said in a monotone. "Then he went back in like he belonged in there. Like he wanted it that way."

"Well, he didn't," the trucker said, squinting at the young man backlit by the boardwalk conflagration. The young man was trembling.

He led Brandon to the furthest end of the boardwalk. "You'll be alright, kid," he said to him. "You can sit down here; you'll be alright now."

"I'm thirsty," the young man said to him in a hoarse whisper. "I wish I had something to drink."

"Me too, Brandon," Tom put his hand on the boy's shoulder and sat him on the end of the boardwalk.

The trembling young man looked up at Tom Honey. "He was all fire," he said in disbelief.

The fires growled in front of them, consuming the planks and the massive ant. The cooking insect jetted steam and hissed stink.

The driver patted the young man's shoulder. "You sit here for a little bit. I'll be back soon, Brandon." He went over to the three friends and the senior lineman as they collected a sensible distance from the conflagration. A board or a piece of the ant exploded in the blaze and threw burning coals into the lot, causing the men to duck for cover.

They raised their heads tentatively and stepped a few paces from the fire, watching the walkway burning or looking behind them into the darkness beyond the glow.

"No way we can put this out," Carlos said. The flames jumped into the night sky and licked the windowless building, greedily consuming the thick wooden planks.

"It might keep them back for a while, anyway," the senior lineman said, nodding toward the dark lot and the fading line of fire. "We have to keep that going, too. We've got sixteen bottles left," he said. "All at that end in one pile. That's not enough to keep the fires going for the night. Maybe another two hours, tops."

He looked over the low wall of fire into the lot and saw a giant ant moving through the gloom.

CHAPTER FIFTEEN

THE PAN

Corporal Oz relayed the message to his commander, "Colonel, the team is coming down in ten minutes."

"Alright, Oz, let's get out there. Be sure we have a full raft of fifty-cal," Smith called after the soldier.

"Yes, sir!" the soldier sang out as he went through the door.

The colonel adjusted the bandage on his leg, pulling it tighter and grunting. The officer sat back in his chair. He looked like a man who needed sleep but knew he wouldn't get any.

He stretched across his desk and reached into a cardboard box beside his computer monitor. He handed the lawman a round badge with a clip on one side and an LED on the other, the size of a large coin.

The sheriff turned it in his fingers, then raised his eyes to the colonel.

"Wear it in your shirt pocket like this," the army officer said. He reached up and twisted his breast pocket inside-out to reveal an identical blank screen LED clipped inside.

"What is it?" the sheriff asked, looking again at the box behind the monitor. There was a skull and crossbones crudely sketched on the box. He looked back at the colonel and raised his eyebrows for an answer. "Radiation detector?" he suggested.

"Sort of," the colonel smiled. "More like a weather report. It'll tell you when to get inside."

The lawman slung his AR and clipped the disc inside his shirt pocket under his badge as he said to the officer, "All right, it's the weather report, but I'd just as soon you plain tell me what it is."

The army man laughed as they started across the hangar to the door. "Sorry, Sheriff, I don't mean to be evasive, just having a little fun. That little gizmo you just put in your pocket is two things: one, it's a secret device you are not supposed to have, so don't let anyone see it. And two, it's...."

The door flew wide, and Reese stepped in. "Colonel, we have an ETA for pickup," the soldier said, holding the hatch open.

"Alright, good," the colonel replied to the young man, then turned to the sheriff and laughed. "The perfectly timed interruption. That's how you know you're playing in the big picture," the colonel said as he stepped through the doorway and stumbled at the threshold. The soldier caught him, and the older man cursed from the pain and his failure but couldn't refuse the young man's helping hand.

"All right, all right," the colonel said as he got past the door. "Just get me into this buggy, and I'll be fine."

"Yes, sir," the soldier replied, supporting his limping officer to the MRAP. The colonel allowed the young man to help him to the truck. He held his hand up so Reese wouldn't close the door.

The colonel looked at Cal. "Want to meet the saviors of the world?" Colonel Smith asked.

"Course you can suit yourself, Sheriff, but I'd say take the look ahead. See what's coming your way," he advised.

The sheriff nodded, considering. "Guess I want to see what you've got up your sleeve, at that," the lawman said. The colonel cocked his head at the other side of the truck as a reply and spun his fingers in the air, signaling Reese to close his door.

Reese closed it and went around the truck with the sheriff. The soldier waited for the sheriff to climb aboard, slammed the hatch after him, and joined the corporal in the front of the vehicle. Oz rolled out, and they drove for a few minutes, heading away from the debris of the previous night's battle to the open plain of the airstrip.

When they stopped, the buildings were specs, far across the tarmac.

The soldiers hustled out, opened the doors for the officers, and went to the front of the truck. Both watched the sky with binoculars.

"So where were we, Sheriff?" the officer asked. "Oh, that's right, besides that little button I gave you for good behavior, I guess I was going to tell you about what's coming down from above," the army officer replied. "Give me a hand getting out, would you, Sheriff? This leg is locked up pretty good."

Cal got out and went around the truck. He held the colonel's arm and helped him out. "Looks like it's still bleeding, too," he said. The military man grunted and leaned against the truck. "Should probably sew that up," the sheriff added.

The colonel grimaced. "I can make more blood," the army man said. "Can't make more time."

At the front of the truck, Oz pointed upward, and the colonel squinted into the sky. "Do you see them, sir? Coming in at your 10," the corporal called.

The colonel searched the sky. "I see them. There they are," the colonel called back. The officer pointed for the sheriff's benefit. "See those birds? Those shiny specs are five C-17s packed full of death."

"The hard cases," the sheriff replied. "The ones here to blow the hell out of everything."

"And how," the Colonel responded as he watched the planes grow against the falling night.

The Globemasters got lower and larger as they approached. They formed a wide V over the immense field, with the point plane touching down two miles away, the others following suit.

The aircraft decelerated over the miles and taxied up to the red smoke marker. The engines screamed as the leviathans maneuvered into a half-circle of building-sized airships. The tails pointed to the center of the

302

circle, and as each flying freighter locked itself into position, the turbines wound down, and the tail sections lifted to disgorge their cargo.

Two columns of troops ran down the ramp out of the center aircraft, continued a hundred yards across the cement, then broke into three lines, loose formation.

Six tactical vehicles rolled out of each of the flanking jets. They were smaller than the colonel's ride, but the guns on top were bigger, and the turrets more substantial. One of the armored trucks was topped with a bristling array of small missiles.

"JLTVs," the colonel said to the sheriff. "They'll do a lot better in the sand than this old thing," he shouted over the roar of the jets, slapping the side of his MRAP for emphasis.

The new vehicles wheeled into lines next to the ranks. The soldiers hustled to their trucks and wasted no time getting aboard.

As loud as it was, a deep bassline was added to the high whines of the aircraft as an Abrams battle tank rumbled down the ramps of the last two jets. Their turrets swung to life, lifting the big guns to point the way as they bucked onto the airfield. Their menacing cannons swung forward as the armored war machines clattered over the concrete to take positions in the line of trucks, one of the tanks snout and the other tail.

"They carry something like fifty shells." The colonel cupped his hands around his mouth and leaned toward the sheriff through the noise of the jets. He gave the sheriff a thumbs up. "Our monsters can kill every one of those monsters for two miles around," he shouted with renewed vigor.

The ramps to the enormous transport jets withdrew, and the doors closed. The aircraft began to roll and turn. Within a few minutes, they were roaring down the airfield and climbing back into the sky, their delivery mission accomplished.

The colonel leaned against his truck and rubbed an ear. He turned to the sheriff. "How about that noise?" he asked in a loud voice. "What do you think? Impressive, eh?" he asked the lawman.

The sheriff watched the first truck in line wheel out in their direction. "Plenty of bang, that's for sure," he replied, looking at the colonel. "But, after you mentioned seeing a few hundred bugs, I thought there'd be ten times that firepower."

The colonel hopped forward. Over his shoulder, he said to the sheriff, "There will be." He turned to the lone truck from the convoy, slowing as it approached. Reese and Oz came from the front of their MRAP and flanked the officers. The new vehicle pulled alongside. It was lower than the colonel's truck. The sheriff looked over the JLTV, ending on the long double-barreled machine gun on the roof.

The rear door opened, and the sound of multiple communication channels streamed out of the truck. A fit-looking, middle-aged man in fatigues hopped out and looked at the four men, twice at the lawman. "Colonel Smith." He shook hands with the army officer. "Understand you had a night of it," he said.

"We kept busy, Drake," the colonel replied. "But it's your show from here on." He looked past the man in fatigues at the tanks and column of armored vehicles. "Looks like you're ready to make a statement."

"We are, Colonel. Been waiting for it," Drake answered and looked the officer up and down. "Thought you fellows could use a rest," he added, gesturing to the colonel's bandaged leg. "Maybe a little R&R."

"Ain't fun getting old," the colonel answered. "Can't say I wish I was going with you, though."

Drake smiled in response. "Evac will be here pretty soon. They'll get you out. Everyone's gone that's going, Colonel?" he asked, turning to the sheriff. There were no markings or insignia on Drake's fatigues. He wore a .45 low on his leg.

"We four are the only ones left. Everyone's gone, for sure." The army officer nodded to the lawman. "This is Sheriff Jeffries, a sole survivor of a party of his own last night. Sheriff, Drake, here is the chief dragon slayer."

"How about you? Has he given you a title?" Drake asked as they shook hands.

"I told you, Drake. Survivor. He's the sole survivor," the colonel answered. "And he's sticking with us," he added.

"That's the plan, Sheriff Jeffries?" Drake asked the lawman. "Sticking with them?"

"That's the plan," the sheriff lied.

Drake said, "Glad to hear it." The sheriff got the feeling that was a bigger lie than his. He smiled back.

Another man in an anonymous uniform leaned from the shadows of the truck and said to Drake, "En route, on time." The man pulled his head back into the dark interior.

Drake nodded and said, "Got to go." He looked at his armor idling on the runway, then squinted over the vast flatness. "That's us, right, Colonel?" He pointed to the nighttime in the east. "That's where we get to the gully?"

The colonel looked across the field with him. "Yep. That's the way. Look for a mile or so of knocked-down fence. Once you're in the sand, you'll see their trail. Can't miss it, just head west."

Drake turned to the open door of his truck and climbed in. "Catch up with you later, Colonel," he called over his shoulder. He got into his seat, leaning out of the shadows to add, "Don't forget to keep your eye on the time."

"Good luck, Drake," the colonel said as the man quickly waved and closed the door. The sand-colored truck returned to the front of the column.

The tank in front pulled out and started the parade. The tactical vehicles followed, chased by the other tank at the end. The caravan rolled across the concrete plain to the dark horizon.

The colonel exhaled. "I thought they'd never leave," he said and faltered in his step. Oz caught him and helped him into his seat in the truck.

His large corporal said quietly to the officer, "Time for us to go, Colonel." It was a statement, not a question. The colonel closed his eyes and nodded. He adjusted his leg, and the pain showed. He opened his eyes and looked out of the truck at the lawman.

"C'mon, Cal. I just got my orders – time to go. Act three is coming up. Get in," the officer said to the sheriff.

The sheriff got in, and the colonel said, "Back to the Emerald City, Corporal Oz." The corporal wheeled out and drove back the way they came.

Cal watched as the dark closed over the square miles of flat concrete. "Drake said evac would be here soon, didn't he?" the sheriff asked. Oz looked at him in the mirror.

The colonel turned his head to the sheriff. "That's the plan," he said. "Air support will catch up with that column when they're on target. Whirlybird's going to come and get us." He shook his head to clear it. "Guess I'm done here. I'd offer you a ride out with us, but I know you're not interested."

"Thanks anyway, but I got a date," the sheriff replied. "Tell me, Colonel. What's this boiling down to?" He took his hat off and hung it on the barrel of his assault rifle that he held upright, butt on the floor. "I feel I ought to know."

The colonel pulled himself up and swiveled his seat to face the lawman. "OK, Sheriff. Here's most of it. Drake and those fellows are riding over to the ant nest. And they're going to go into it." The officer watched for the sheriff's reaction.

The sheriff looked at his hat and gave it a spin. "I saw those nests this morning. I'd have to say that seems like a bad idea."

"I do not envy them their mission," the colonel said gravely. "But it was decided that was the only way to accomplish the objective." The colonel raised his hand in anticipation of the sheriff's next question. "He's got a special delivery for those bugs."

Cal barely nodded. He leaned back and watched his hat swinging on the gun as the MRAP tore across the field.

The army officer waited for the sheriff.

The sheriff asked, "Will the Bunker survive?"

The officer's head was nodding in rhythm with the moving truck. Responding to the sheriff's question, he nodded purposefully. "Yes," he said. "According to a recent eval," Smith said, "the calculations indicate full survivability." He pulled a water bottle from the cooler by his seat, unscrewed the top, and took a long drink. "To be square with you, Sheriff, I could say we might try to get your friends out. But then they become a known quantity," the colonel tapered off, and he shrugged.

"Frying pan or fire," the sheriff said and waited for him to finish. The colonel took another swig.

"Honestly, if I were your friends back there, I'd take my chances in the bar," he concluded.

The sheriff nodded and looked out at the night. "I guess they already are," he said.

The colonel fished a water from the cooler and handed it to Cal.

The sheriff took the bottle and drank. He didn't realize how parched he was until the cold water soaked into his tongue. Cal licked his lips. "So, when is the big event?" he asked the commanding officer.

"Up to Drake," the officer answered. "But, once they set the ticker, you know, arm the nuclear device, that watch in your pocket will start a count down. That's the clock to keep your eye on," he added.

The truck pulled up in front of their temporary headquarters, and the soldiers hustled out and opened the back doors. The sheriff put his hat on and started to get out, then turned to the colonel. "Why don't they just drop it from the air?" the sheriff asked.

"Be easier," the colonel agreed. "However, the bomb has to go underground, into the nest." The army officer shook his head. "And those poor sons of mothers have to get it down there. I guess that's how it's got to be. You know somebody estimated that ant nest, the tunnels, could be more than three thousand feet deep and run for over a hundred miles? There is no ordinance for that. Hope is that the concussion of a deep detonation does the job, so down it goes. Who knows?"

As the army officer spoke to the large corporal, the sheriff climbed out of the truck.

Oz followed Reese into the hangar. The sheriff walked around the truck and was about to say his so-longs to the colonel when a helicopter flying low and fast came out of nowhere and roared over them.

A hot wind ripped across the runway after the chopper, blasting sand in every direction.

The colonel took a drink and leaned out of the truck to spit. "Every one of those chopper pilots is a hot dog," he said.

The helicopter banked hard and came back fast to rise steeply and stop in the air, appearing to drop, then hover about a hundred yards out and up, outlined by its lights, hanging in the night. After a pause, the gunship lowered to the runway. More lights came on, and the engine throttled back as they waited for their passengers.

"That's my ride," the colonel said to him. He stuck his hand out to the lawman. "One piece of advice: when you are back safe and sound in your Bunker, trust no one."

Sheriff Jeffries took the officer's hand and shook it. "Never do." He studied the colonel and released his hand, looking down at his blood-soaked bandages. "You take care of yourself, Smith."

The colonel replied with a casual two-fingered salute and a confident smile as the lawman turned away from the armored vehicle. The army officer called after him as he walked to his pickup. "And, like Drake said, keep your eye on the clock."

The sheriff glanced down at his shirt pocket as he pushed his rifle onto the seat. Cal pulled the soccer ball key ring from his pocket, got in, and started the truck. He put on the headlights, stepped on the gas, and raced across the airfield to the gate. It should only take him twenty minutes to get to the Bunker if it was smooth sailing and like the colonel said, nothing ate him along the way.

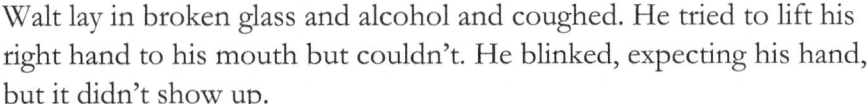

Walt lay in broken glass and alcohol and coughed. He tried to lift his right hand to his mouth but couldn't. He blinked, expecting his hand, but it didn't show up.

A disembodied voice talked about giant insects.

He coughed again and tasted iron. His other hand appeared, and he wiped his mouth and then looked at his bright red fingers drip. "That's that," he tried to say but coughed the words out. His chest felt full, and he would drown if he didn't sit up.

Walt moved and heard broken glass and felt bees stinging, but he got himself sitting up, propped against the cabinets under the bar. He pulled his shirt open, losing three buttons and revealing an active hole in his chest. When he coughed, the hole bubbled, and if it wasn't bubbling, blood leaked out.

Walt put his head back and stared upward. The stock of his sawed-off shotgun came into focus, sticking over the edge of the bar. He shook his head. "She was right," he laughed, coughed, and laughed. "I am too old."

In the broken glass was an unbroken bottle, and Walt stretched to snag it by the neck. He dragged it through the glass and stuck it between his legs so he could pull the cork.

It popped. Walt lifted the bottle to his mouth and took a long couple of swigs. The familiar warmth ran down his throat and met up with the glow of massive blood loss. He didn't cough.

Walt stood the whiskey bottle in the puddle of his blood and stuck the cork back in the hole.

"Alright," he wheezed. "One more thing to do."

The old man's right arm wouldn't work at all. He grabbed his barstool to help him stand. He tried but couldn't and fell flat. He cursed loudly and pushed the stool away.

Walt knew this was going to be the hard way. He was on his side, lying on the floor with his back against the cabinets. He rolled onto his stomach and started on his path, crawling through the glass. The jagged fragments hurt and made him wish he had downed more whiskey, but the bottle was behind him, and like he always said, 'There's no going back.'"

The barman made his way under the gate and across the floor to the first table before the blackness caught up to him. He passed out at the end of a red slug trail smeared over the floor, sparkling with broken glass.

If there were a clock in the Bunker, it would have ticked away a few more minutes before Walt rasped and rattled, then coughed himself to consciousness, opening his eyes wide and suddenly bringing the floor of the barroom into view. He sputtered and waited for the surroundings to become familiar. He was breathing like a runner.

The memories came back, flashing by, bringing up to speed on who he was, the bar, getting shot, a life of deception affiliating with dubious individuals. It got him to the present.

He coughed more blood and pushed up with his forearm. Pain racked his right side from his head to his hip. The cold clamps turned into hot vises and made him groan. He stared across the floor to the far wall of the room and started crawling again.

The old man wormed a few more feet across the floor. His breaths slowed. He cursed and coughed, then dragged himself a few more feet. "Long trip, long trip," he panted. Walt pushed again, then stopped and put his face down. "Oh man," he said into the floor, "I'm shot."

Walt laughed with blood in his mouth and lifted his head, pushing for the wall.

He crawled, painting the planks with his ebbing life, dipping in and out of consciousness. Almost at the wall, almost there. He could reach out and touch the base.

He pushed closer until he was there. His breathing was drawing down, becoming shallow, but his determination was final. There was just one more thing he had to do. He crawled along the wall, making his way to the broken doors.

Walt coughed more blood, spraying the base of the wall as he dragged himself into the corner under the door controls.

He pushed himself up with his left arm to sit and leaned back against the wall. The fading man turned his head upward to the button box. He exhaled dejectedly and closed his eyes. "Just get to your feet, even your knees. Reach the button," was his last thought as unconsciousness rose around him. Blood ran from his mouth and was lost in his red shirt.

Walt watched himself standing behind the bar a long time ago. He looked up as the swinging saloon doors pushed open and a young woman walked halfway across his barroom and stopped, smiling at younger Walt.

"Howdy, partner," she said across the empty room.

The barman leaned forward onto the bar and put his crossword puzzle down. He spoke to the young boy perched on the barstool without looking away from the newcomer. "You've had enough pop for now. Time to vamoose." The bartender took the half-empty glass from the boy. "Off you go. You can finish your chores tomorrow."

The youngster shrugged and dropped off the stool, saying, "OK, Walt. See you later." He turned and waved to the woman as he ran out.

"Nice kid," she said to the barman.

Walt took the towel from his shoulder and ran it over the bar top. "I told them no," he said to the woman. She pulled a chair back and sat at a wooden table under a hanging lamp.

"And no means no." She drummed the fingers on the table and looked absently around the dimly lit room. "I don't get all of these movie posters. Why don't you just hang a couple of pictures? Maybe with a western theme." She took out a cigarette and lit up.

He threw the towel over his shoulder as a distraction while bringing a glass from under the bar way too fast. She flinched. "Want a drink?" he asked.

"Funny. Make it two. We're going to have company," she answered. The outside door opened. "Now, this will be funny," she said, taking her eyes off the swinging doors and watching Walt.

A large man pushed the saloon doors open, carrying the limp body of the child who had run out of the bar. He walked to the young woman and rolled the boy onto the table.

"Oh, Martin," she clucked facetiously. "What have you done now?"

The heavily muscled man smiled at Walt. He walked to the bar and stared into the barkeep's face. "The kid was leaving. I told him not to leave, but he wouldn't listen. I don't like it when people try to leave. And, when they don't listen, then it gets bad." He didn't blink.

Walt broke the staring contest and looked around the man at the young woman seated by the child on the table. She smiled and blew smoke into the hanging light. A soft moan came from the boy.

The large man grinned menacingly at Walt. "I only choked him to be quiet. Then he got blood on me," he said to the barman. "And anyway, he saw me." He stared at the barkeep. "Now, you saw me. Give me that towel," he ordered.

Walt felt the calm and inhaled. He took the towel from his shoulder, put it on the bar, and slid it to him, watching the Goliath's eyes follow the rag.

His other hand swung the sawed-off shotgun from under the bar, ending the arc of its travel when the barrel touched the center of the big man's chest, and Walt pulled the trigger. The explosion killed the man instantly, dead before his carcass crashed to the planks. Walt shifted the double barrel to the young woman. She froze, reaching for her ankle.

"Don't," Walt said. "One left, and I haven't decided."

The shotgun smoke drifted through the light.

"Sit down," he said to her. She didn't move fast enough.

"He's going to need a big hole. Room for two," Walt pointed out.

"I'm good here," the woman answered. "I'm OK with this. He wasn't legit, just an independent. Kind of weird, too." She took a cigarette from the pack on the table with Walt's OK and reached over the boy for the cobalt blue Bunker ashtray. She put it on the kid's chest to be more convenient and lit up.

Walt kept the gun on her. "First of all, why don't you toss that cap pistol over?" he suggested, and she complied, pulling her .32 with thumb and index and throwing it over her companion's body to Walt.

He nodded. "And take your jacket off," he said to her. "You have some digging to do, Sylvia," He motioned with the muzzle.

"Uh-oh. Now it's Sylvia. I must be in big trouble." She stood from her chair and ground her cigarette in the ashtray on the child's chest.

The boy moaned again as he regained consciousness. Walt walked to the table, bringing ice in a towel and pocketing her pistol on the way. The barman shook his head, took the ashtray off the boy, and helped him sit on the table. He examined the gash on his chin and wiped the dried blood away. The barkeep patted the youngster's shoulder, put the cold towel in the boy's hand, and brought it to his jaw.

Walt checked the cut again. "You're alright," he said to him. "You'll get a good-looking scar." He pushed the towel back. "It will make you look interesting," he said, winking at the boy.

The child smiled, looked blankly at the woman sitting next to him, then at the barkeep, and smiled again. He stopped smiling when he saw the man on the floor behind Walt. The barkeep realized what he was looking at and moved to block the boy's vision. "Sit there until you feel good enough to go home. We have a few things to do. I'll be gone for a while, so you're the boss, Carlos," he said to the boy and mussed his hair as he turned away to put the woman to work.

The boy never spilled to anyone about the assault by the large man at Walt's or what happened in the bar. He told his mother he fell off his motorbike. She took it away from him, but he kept quiet to keep trouble from his friend.

Syl was sitting on the floor in the freezer with her back to the door. The woman did not move. Across from her, Nikki sat still, trying to process what had happened to the nurse after she picked up the seed. The space seed changed into a liquid in the nurse's hand. The goo disappeared, absorbed through her skin.

It had invaded the unfortunate Syl within moments of physical contact. She looked dead and didn't seem to breathe. She just lay there, sprawled at the base of the freezer door, motionless other than an occasional twitch.

Nikki didn't want to go near her. She had purposely dropped the glass vial, hoping Syl would act impulsively and pick it up. She seemed like that type of person. Of course, she wasn't a nurse but an imposter who meant to kill her.

"I might be able to help you, Syl," she said loudly. "Let me go and get the books. They can help." Nikki cautiously stood, watching the nurse. She was surprised that Syl's eyes followed her as she rose. The infected nurse lifted her pistol, pointing it unsteadily in Nikki's direction. The nurse smiled with a cadaverously open mouth. The gun swayed widely, and Nikki slowly slid back to the floor to stare at the dying nurse.

It was fortunate Nikki had read her uncle's journals. His notes told of years of discovery and deception and the campaign of misinformation he had masterminded for the powers that be, as Syl described her employers.

Those small, handwritten books detailed how they changed the world, beginning with the alien spacecraft crashing in the Arctic, her great-uncle's expedition of discovery, and the aftermath.

The volumes were titled by date. Nikki opened the first book and an ancient newspaper clipping fell out of the pages. She unfolded the brittle newsprint, and it broke into three pieces.

315

The long column of text was an article commemorating Professor Carrington on the first anniversary of his death. It extolled his many achievements over a range of advanced disciplines, delivering breakthroughs in genetics, optics, and astrophysics, and fistfuls of other lifetime achievements.

Nikki was surprised. She had no idea of the scope of the man's work. As it turned out, Professor Carrington not only developed the United States' atomic program in the 1930s but received three Nobel Prizes and shared or was cited in eleven others.

None of that brainpower explained his publicity photo at the top of the article. It was so phony looking that it was hard to believe people went for this stuff. The professor was wearing a yacht captain's hat, smoking a pipe, and looking out from the helm of a sailboat. The caption to the old picture read, 'He Charted Our Course Ahead – Mankind's Scientist.'

Her great-uncle was apparently more popular during his life than after. Today, in the history of science, Professor Carrington is little more than a talented footnote.

However, in his day, when a UFO was reported down in Alaska, he was unanimously approved by the world scientific community to oversee the joint military and scientific expedition.

It was true. There was a ship. It had crash-landed in the sub-zero winter of the Alaskan Arctic. Wreckage was recovered. There were occupants. Their remains were recovered. There was more; there were world-changing consequences, and it was all chronicled in his diaries.

The wreckage and remains were ultimately transported to the Air Force base at Roswell, New Mexico. At first, her uncle was a proponent of secrecy at any cost, and his journals matter-of-factly condoned the ruination of any opposition. Blackmail, extortion, and even murder were perpetrated to silence the loose-lipped. His clinical outlook on the necessity of these measures would have been more disturbing if it wasn't for their context.

New technologies were taken from the aliens, from the 'Things,' as the great man referred to them. His writings pointed out that, while humankind was beginning to perceive the possibilities of a technological future, they were far from any real breakthroughs, and progress was gruelingly slow.

He posited that the arrival of the craft and our ability to learn from their advanced sciences were purposeful. This insight into the future had arrived at exactly the right time and precisely the right place.

The craft had impacted the most remote area controlled by the United States. Carrington's expedition was backed by the military and he would have complete authority at the scene.

As for the timing, the professor asserted that had these advances been delivered earlier in human history, they would have been lost, never utilized, or worse, unleashed prematurely. Had the spaceship arrived later, it would have been too late for a world in the death grip of a Cold War and losing control of its self-destructive impulses.

Passages in her uncle's journals alluded to the remarkable coincidence of the event. Though she had only skimmed through the first section of the first volume, Nikki saw through his own words that his belief grew from coincidence to luck and then to transcendent destiny. With even a superficial reading, she could see that the magnitude of the occurrence quickly overcame the man and interfered with objectivity and reason.

Nikki was alone on her bunk when she opened the package. She pulled the cord off and unwrapped the brown paper covering a cardboard box, throwing the wrappings on the floor and keeping the bed clear so she could spread everything out for a good look.

She bent back the cardboard flaps and saw Professor Carrington's journals. She held one of the small books in front of her and studied it. In the corner of the top volume, the years '1948-1950' were written on the leather. Nikki placed the three books on the blanket, pulled out a small old box, put it on the bed in front of her, and lifted the lid. It was filled. There were a few small stones, three keys on a metal ring, two vintage matchbooks, and a few other items that fell down her interest meter as she studied the thing that looked like a salt shaker.

First of all, it wasn't a salt shaker; it looked like one – a thick glass container with a screw-on metal top, but no holes. A rectangle of paper was affixed with brittle yellow tape bearing the message 'DO NOT TOUCH SEEDS!' in her great-uncle's peculiarly tight handwriting. The sentence was below a carefully drawn skull and crossbones.

When she examined the bottle and saw the labeling, Nikki took it seriously. She had yet to read his notes, but knowing he was involved in atomic research, she feared these might be some sort of radioactive pellets. She wasn't even sure they were seeds. That's why she hid them in the freezer, not just to hide them, but to put them a distance from her and the others and keep them on ice. Then she began thumbing through his journals to see if she could find any mention of them or an explanation of the warning taped to the vial.

She did. Skimming through the cursive, Nikki noticed occasional diagrams or simple sketches illustrating her uncle's writings. There weren't many, but a series of drawings caught her attention. They depicted several views detailing the seedpods and the accompanying text was also illuminating.

Her uncle, Professor Carrington, had written in detail of the recovery of several seeds from the forward appendages of a dead extraterrestrial. The aliens were described as more plant than animal in their basic physiognomy by a consensus of the first examining team on the scene.

While they agreed on several broad points, the preliminary discovery of hundreds of thousands of seeds carried by the ETs led to speculation about the purpose of their visit. The military and many of the scientific team felt it was an invasion, that the aliens had arrived prepared to reproduce in large numbers to conquer our world.

Up to this point in his writings, Professor Carrington had remained unbiased. Feeling there was insufficient information for a hypothesis, he wanted to experiment. He wondered what fruit the seeds would bear.

The professor soon found out.

An alien spaceship had crashed in the Far North of Alaska. Newly established Cold War surveillance stations detected the event, and the U.S. government mounted a large and top-secret response.

Within a few weeks, heavy equipment, scientific apparatus, and personnel were working at a pair of new bases secretly built in the frozen desolation. Outpost One was still under construction when Carrington's expedition arrived, and it served as a base of operations to investigate the crash site, 70 some miles away. Outpost Two was the crash site. Several buildings were erected to protect and conceal the wreckage, and plans were underway to greatly expand the facilities.

The downed alien ship was enormous, and it brimmed with sciences unknown on Earth. Hundreds of experiments were on display on their science deck, and any of them could have fueled multiple technological revolutions worldwide.

As one of the surviving members of Carrington's expedition stated, "In a single afternoon, a dozen new sciences were born."

While the crash caused significant damage to the alien ship, most of the vessel remained intact. It could have been survivable, but evidence pointed to an incident at the ship's power plant, which may have caused the crash and killed all of the Things.

Every alien on the ship was dead at first.

On the first visit to the crash site, a young scientist, referred to as 'B' in the text, recovered an extraterrestrial limb and brought it back to Outpost One. That night, severe weather prohibited travel and interfered with outside communications for days. Revisiting the crash site during the storm was impractical, and the group's attention focused on the representative arm of the aliens.

The examination would begin after a night's rest as it had been an arduous day for the scientists.

Despite keeping the specimen on ice overnight, the arm had degraded, withered to a dry husk, and unrecognizable as the original.

A handful of scientists clustered around the failing remains of the arm, gloomily aware that the same process of decay was destroying the collection of alien cadavers at the crash site.

They examined what was left of the limb, noting the advanced and continuing decomposition. The arm had degraded uniformly to a fibrous material, easily reduced to powder by the slightest touch. Within an hour, nothing remained of the appendage other than a pile of black dust and a cluster of seed pods.

A singular structure survived the disintegrating arm. A leathery cord, attached with numerous bundles of small, elongated spheres was discovered and immediately termed 'seeds.'

The dissected part looked so much like a typical plant pod with seeds that the conclusion was obvious. Even Professor Carrington agreed with the description.

With renewed hope, the group rallied. Even though the original visitors may have been lost, there was a chance that they might be able to grow their own.

The next step was further analysis of the kernels.

B easily detached a dozen seeds from their stalks with forceps and placed them in a dish for the scientists to observe. He lifted one into the light, turning the small bean for all to admire. "Meet our future spaceman," he said, then added, "I hope we can sprout this little devil."

With that, B dropped the seed onto his rubber glove, showing off the tiny treasure as he rolled it to and fro in his palm.

The learned faces tightly grouped in the light, quietly marveling at the limitless potential held in the young man's hand when it suddenly disappeared. Receptors in the little bean sensed the organic latex and liquified, soaking through the impermeable glove.

To those observing, it appeared as if the seed had melted and then evaporated, but it had passed through the organic rubber and soaked into B's skin. The scientist turned his hand under the light as the puzzled group searched the table for the little bean, thinking he had dropped it.

B absently rubbed his itchy palm as he looked, then groaned. "Aww, what is…." He rubbed his hand and shouted in pain, tearing the glove off. He held up his hand, bright red with a clearly defined swollen ring throbbing in the middle of his palm. His howl curdled their blood.

"Cut it off!" he screamed. "Now! Now! I can feel it moving!" The stricken scientist grabbed the largest scalpel from the tray and slammed his infected arm onto the table, raising the blade in his other hand before the recoiling group of scientists. Before they could stop him, he stabbed and pulled the surgical blade through his elbow joint, severing his forearm in one stroke. He was an anatomist, after all.

B dropped the instrument and held his half an arm up, spurting blood onto the scientists. He didn't look good, even for a guy that just cut his own arm off. He looked like he was going south.

The young scientist opened his mouth, about to say something or scream, but he just fell backward, leaving his arm at the edge of the table. He seemed dead.

His infected arm lay there, flexing its swollen fingers. The movement unbalanced the severed limb, falling from the table's edge onto the original owner's body, slapping him in the face.

The small group of scientists reassembled, peering over the examination table at the unfortunate B on the floor. They moved cautiously, one leaning closer, removing his glasses and wiping the poor man's blood from his face. He turned to his colleagues and convulsed. He fell forward onto the table, turned onto his back, and ripped his shirt open, screaming at the lesions swimming subcutaneously and diving into his organs.

Another member of the group splattered with blood was stricken and dropped to the floor.

And then another.

Though the team was made of scientists, disciplined and governed by logic, they panicked and ran for the door, jamming the entryway as one after another fell, screaming as the alien consumed them from within.

Two of the eleven scientists made it out of the exam room.

Scientific and military personnel quickly instituted isolation procedures. It was decided to leave the bodies undisturbed for the time being to avoid further contamination.

At this point, her great-uncle's writing was replaced by another hand. The larger, flowing script was preceded with the reference initials 'AC:nn.' Nikki realized her namesake, her great-uncle's assistant, must have taken these notes.

His assistant was more than that. She was part of the great professor's inner circle and a member of the family. Aunt May told Nikki that she had worked with him from the 1930s until his decline and death after more than 25 years.

Nikki smiled and lightly touched the woman's writing that had played such a large role in their family history. She thought their handwriting was somewhat similar.

Nikki imagined his assistant documenting the events with the great scientist. After all, she was one of a handful of people in the world who knew what was happening at the isolated Arctic outpost.

As she was reading, Nikki recalled Aunt May had told her the woman had died in an airplane accident in the 1950s, soon after her great-uncle's death. Many people involved with Professor Carrington met untimely ends. Aunt May believed without a doubt that her brother was poisoned because he was a threat to the secrecy that his own Agency demanded. They had the reach to silence anyone, including world-famous scientists and their confidants, including their founder.

The notetaker's script continued the observations of Professor Carrington; it began: "4:17 PM, Approx. 6 hours from exposure. Note: Access to the subjects is restricted to viewing via the observation window to the examination area by order of Maj. P."

"Weeping eruptions have formed over the bodies, giving the appearance of a pox. The fluid expressed has covered the subjects in a uniform coating, congealing with remarkable rapidity into a protective cocoon, which Professor Carrington hypothesizes will realize metamorphosis. No interference is planned to provide an unmolested conclusion. Sign out 5:30 PM."

The next paragraph began with the words "nn notes: 8:40 PM. AC is still resting. On my own in the observation room, watching the cocoons. Maj. P. arrives to see his orders executed / destruction of the bodies / he told us about earlier in the evening. (He is watching me write this now). Soldiers wearing gas masks and protective clothing are removing them to be burned outside. They use large tarpaulins and poles to carry the bodies."

"11:32 PM. AC notes: Only two of the chrysalids remain. The military men have incinerated the others despite objections."

"11:48 PM. The soldiers have returned for the next specimen and are preparing it to move. They have maintained adequate . . ." The handwriting stopped, and the remainder of the page was blank. The narrative renewed on the next page.

"10 AM. Last night, humanity came perilously close to losing their world to alien invasion. Soldiers were moving one of the chrysalids when the other opened and our butterfly emerged."

"Bipedal but not bibrachial, the Thing had two legs and six arms," Professor Carrington continued in his notes. "To be more descriptive, this newly created organism had an array of arms, resembling cephalopod limbs, three on either side of the torso and each terminating in an articulating tentacular club of twelve digits, quite like human fingers in structure, but longer and undoubtedly stronger."

Professor Carrington introduced the next section of neatly margined handwriting with an underlined sentence centered over the text; "Our first encounter with the Thing."

"Carrington, Carr, Nicholson. Observation room. As we monitored the progress of disposal detail removing one of two remaining cocoons, the other hatched."

"Our attention, and even the lighting in the examination room, was fixed on the work. We did not notice the metamorph standing in the shadows until it made a large movement, lifting its six tentacles as the newly emerged entity stretched itself taller, gaining a half meter over the original host. It was the height of the room."

Thin lines of ink drew a box to bring attention to the line, "The following events transpired in less than one minute."

"The Thing and the soldiers sensed each other simultaneously. The men had no opportunity to respond to the attack. The thing crossed the room (10m.) in two leaps. Whipping its tentacles perpetrated great violence, and the five men were immediately dispatched."

"Dr. Carr, my assistant, N., and I were behind the glass of the observation window, too stunned by the sudden events to react. The Thing lifted the still unhatched chrysalid and put it on the exam table.

With two of its writhing arms, it held down the ends of the long cocoon. A third arm took the scalpel B had left on the table, made a long incision, then pushed another hand into the wound, ripped tissue from inside the chrysalis, and threw it to the floor."

"The Thing, having successfully resolved the future challenge of a genetic competitor, turned its attention to us. It walked purposefully to our observation window."

Carrington noted that his fellow observers were 'apprehensive.'

"It looked at us," Carrington wrote, "with large eyes pushing forward on the sides of its head. Between them, in the forehead, three vertical slits that moved like fish gills. The bottom of the face ended in folds of flesh. The creature was immense and had to bend to look through the glass. Its head turned, and the eyes moved. You could tell where they were looking, and the Thing looked at each of us in turn."

"The tentacle arms were relaxed and swayed loosely at its sides. The folded flesh around its chin was a mouth, and it opened. The being spoke in five short bursts with a blowing, deep amphoric voice, evidencing large round teeth, especially at the end of its remarks."

"It turned and walked from the window. The Thing went to the doorway and examined the bodies of the soldiers. It was very physical, utilizing many of its arms, lifting and turning the corpses in the course of its inspection. It selected two of the most intact bodies, opened the door, and walked through, carrying them with little effort."

Nikki noticed the following line looked as though it had been added later. "Before leaving, I collected several seeds in a glass bottle." She thought it sounded like a confession.

Professor Carrington's notes continued.

"The xenotype has proven difficult. Within a few hours of the Thing's escape into the camp, the majority of the humans were no longer human. Based on the number of survivors, Major Polk has sabotaged all but one transport plane. Within minutes, our group will attempt to board. It's our only hope," the handwriting concluded.

The first words on the next page read, "We escaped. Seventeen souls out of over one hundred. We lived, and they did not." After the last line was a small pen and ink drawing of a mushroom cloud.

Nikki turned to the next pages and saw they began at a new time and with a different pen. She put the book on the bed and lifted the glass vial, watching the small shapes inside tumble as she turned it in the light. Nikki got a chill and put the little bottle carefully on the table by her bed. She couldn't take her eyes from the perilous portent taped to it.

She picked up the book and started to read again, but her eyes kept going back to the jar on the table. What if the description of events from her great-uncle was true? Those seeds would be the most dangerous things in the world. Whatever happened up in the Arctic, it seems like we won. Seems unbelievable. But more and more, it all seems to be true.

That's when Nikki decided she didn't want the seeds near her. She got up from her bunk, took the vial from the bedstand, and went to find a safer hiding place.

When she returned, Nikki laid back in her bunk and read deeper into the book and further into the ramifications of the discoveries. The professor and original Nikki (as she thought of the woman) would speculate on the new technologies' long-term effects.

Both writers agreed on the need for absolute secrecy.

Her great-uncle returned to Roswell and orchestrated cover-ups and the ruination of anyone reporting flying saucers or "giant insects." Those words caught her eye.

The authorities asked Professor Carrington for guidance in a movie project that would tell the story of the downed UFO clearly and honestly to inform the public.

The secret was considered uncontainable, and they wanted to get ahead of it. They believed the populous would accept developments as dispensed if they came from trusted sources, such as popular entertainment.

Part of the studio process was 'pre-release testing,' which screened the film to small audiences and gauged their reaction. The results surprised everyone involved in the production of the movie.

Audiences tested rejected the possibility that the spaceship could be real and weren't interested unless the movie was presented with more action. They also wanted romance added to the story.

At Professor Carrington's suggestion, Hollywood moviemakers gave the public what they wanted. A new film genre was created that entertained and, most importantly, declared that the unknown or unexplainable was just fiction. As the popular reaction was studied, production values descended to broad lampoons of extraterrestrials and overlarge insects. The effort to misdirect the world was a resounding success.

Nikki read page after page of his revelatory confessions, detecting a change in the great professor's opinion of his deeds. At one point, he asks in a bolder hand, "Was it mine to decide how this new knowledge was to be used?" A large question mark filled several lines of the page below his interrogatory; beneath that, his answer was written in his tidy script. "No. By my hubris, I have given this power to the worst of our world. I have handed them the capability to obliterate everything. I have abused this precious authority."

She didn't like being alone, so she took her bag and the three small diaries upstairs to join Walt in the barroom. She thought she would share what she had learned from her great-uncle's journals. He already seemed to know quite a bit about the decades before and the conspiracies that had precipitated their current situation. Walt might have some good advice.

The pistol swayed weakly, and Syl let her gun hand drop back into her lap.

She hissed, and her chest heaved as she tried to replace the expelled air. She convulsed, her jaw opened and closed like a fish on the wrong side of the surface. The doomed woman's muscles were spasming, pointing the pistol one way then another.

Across the freezer, Nikki curled into a ball, trying to be small.

A low sound came from Syl. There were no words, but the misery was unmistakable. A wet spot spread across her shirt. It grew and got wetter. Clear gel oozed from the site, spreading and crystallizing across her body. She made quick gargling noises as the cocoon crept over her torso.

Nikki couldn't watch.

The gun fired. It was still in her hand, by her side, and it just went off, shooting a hole through Syl's foot and hitting the wall next to Nikki.

The young woman jumped with terror at the shot, pushing against the wall and screaming.

It jarred Syl into action, too. With extraordinary willpower, she bent her arm, lifting the pistol. She hung her head over the barrel and pulled the trigger.

The bullet made a small hole in her cheek and blew the back of her head wide open. She rebounded from the freezer door, paused, then fell to the side onto the concrete.

Nikki recoiled from the shot, covering her face. She opened her eyes and saw Syl's body through her fingers, slumped in front of the door. Three seeds lay on the cement between her and the dead nurse.

Her eyes went back and forth from the body to the seeds. She remembered the description in her great-uncle's journals about what would happen to the body in the next few hours. She thought of Syl shooting Walt, leaving him to die, and about the people Syl had doomed outside.

Nikki's mouth was open, and she was breathing fast. She had never killed anybody before.

She thought of the infected bodily fluids Syl had just atomized into their confined space, closed her mouth, and tried not to breathe.

That got her up, disregarding her cold-stiffened body and the bruising she'd undergone.

In two steps, she was standing over the deadly pods. She went to the shelf for a square of aluminum foil. Nikki knelt and carefully collected the seed pods, scooping them into the foil without letting her fingers come close. She folded the aluminum and carried the envelope in two fingers as if it were holding a spider.

Syl had a gruesome head wound. She looked like she had laid her head on a pink pillow. Nikki gasped and turned away, feeling sick. She put the foil envelope on the cart beside her, removed her jacket, and dropped it to cover the nurse's face and upper body. Nikki saw the woman's arm, red and swollen with stretched, shiny flesh. She still gripped the gun in her other hand.

Nikki pulled on the heavy freezer door, but Syl was in the way, and she wasn't budging. When the nurse blew her brains out, the whole mess froze her to the floor.

She took a deep breath, looked away, and grabbed the corpse by a foot. She held the foot at arm's length, imagining it bursting open and spraying alien pods all over her. She pulled on the woman's limb again, and Syl's final thoughts let go, and she slid out of the way.

Nikki let the foot drop, pulled the door open, and stepped into the warm air of the kitchen. She gently placed the foil pack on a nearby table and closed the freezer door, pushing the handle down to secure it. She stood on her toes to look through the small window into the freezer. The lights were still on. Syl's body was next to the door, but she could only see her legs.

She carefully held the foil pouch and turned from the freezer, running across the kitchen and into the barroom to help Walt and open the outside door to let everyone inside.

Tom Honey sat on the planks, swabbed in the orange light of the fires that protected the small group of men from the giant ants stalking the parking lot. He looked along the walkway to the bonfire crackling in front of the Bunker's closed doorway, burning the boards and the carcass of the giant ant that had charged through their perimeter and killed Deputy Rosales. The smell and sounds of the sizzling bug made the big trucker queasy. Honey stared into the pyre as it consumed the deputy's body alongside the monster that killed him. He shook his head and turned, walking to the boundary line of fires.

The truck driver squinted over the ring of flames. The bugs were out there beyond the fire. It was difficult to see into the dark parking lot, but he was dang sure there was more than one of the monsters moving beyond the flickering firewall.

The other guys were pacing in the narrow alley between the fires. Mike's grimy face strobed in the flames. "Not much more to go," the lineman said, nodding at the cache of gas bombs against the building.

"Not enough, that's for sure," the trucker replied without looking at the pile.

Mike agreed without thinking about it too much. He had been staring at his young assistant sitting against the wall.

"Kid took that last dust-up pretty bad," Honey told the lineman. "That was too much for him to see, that old man on fire like that."

"It was," Mike said. "Guess I'll go and get him on his feet. Can't let him give up." He turned to walk to the young man.

"That's not an option," the trucker said. "No one's taking prisoners."

Tom Honey walked to the three fellows standing dead center in front of the Bunker. They stood with their backs to the building, watching the lot. Tending the firewall, Ray threw another of the gasoline bottles into the faltering perimeter of flames.

The trucker joined the trio as the fireball exploded. Beyond the blast, they could see the dark shape of a giant ant in the flare of the fireball. The ants stayed out of range.

Behind the men, the plank fire crackled around the ant's charring carcass; the fluids that leaked out of the huge insect slowed the flames from consuming the boardwalk too quickly.

The remains of the 1000-pound ant shifted and sent sprays of sparks and steam shooting and hissing into the smoke-soaked air, making the men jump. It smelled like a burning tire. The fire licked the impenetrable blast door.

"Grilled ant," the truck driver said. "That's the way I like them. Well-done."

Carlos nodded at him. "We found about eight more bottles down here that didn't get blown up," he said and gestured with the muzzle of his AR to a small pile of Molotovs lined up at the front of the boardwalk, well away from the fire.

Tom Honey looked at the collection and replied, "That's good. There's about a dozen and half down the other end, I reckon."

"Hey guys, take a look at this," Billy whispered loudly to the trucker and Carlos.

Billy and Ray were backing away from the lot. Past the firewall, the head of a giant ant was silhouetted against the night sky as the moon lifted over the far-off mountains. The bug was standing on one of the wrecks in the lot, surveying the surroundings and objective.

The large obsidian head swiveled slowly, moving the antennae in response to scent and vibration.

"Now that is one big son-of-a-gun bug, that is," Tom Honey said.

Billy turned and trotted over to the stash of gas bombs. "I think I could get it," he said, grabbing one of the bottles.

"No," Carlos said to stop him. "That's a longer throw than you think. We can't afford the gas, anyway." He looked at his friend, "I think we're going to need every drop." Billy put the bottle back in the short line.

"That's the truth," Tom Honey said. "But I don't like the way that big mutt's looking at us." He walked a few steps toward the firewall and moved his head side to side to see what he could of the bug. The trucker had his left hand on his hip and his right arm hanging by his side, weighted by the hefty handgun glinting gold in the firelight.

"I don't know what this ol' boy's up to, but I'm going to give him something to think about," the trucker said over his shoulder. He lifted the heavy gun, clicking off the safety with one hand and then using both to bring it to a shooting stance. He couldn't see the ant clearly, but he could see the shadow against the moonlight. As he steadied the heavy pistol, the giant ant's head suddenly disappeared.

Tom was surprised and lowered the gun. "Will you look at that?" he said. "Darn if that bug just didn't run off. Do you think these things can see us after all?" The man turned back to the group.

There was a sudden, stridulating scream and three ants crashed through the flames. They came in fast, jaws snapping. The fire exploded as the ants barreled in, throwing burning wood and showering sparks, disorienting the first creature, which stumbled face-first and then trampled by the two charging after the lead ant as they made for the men in front of the boardwalk.

Tom Honey was sent sprawling as the two ants rushed by him. He dropped his handgun into the dust and fell to the ground. The trampled ant was getting up and lifted its two front legs to rejoin the attack. Its long sensory appendages swept the air, and she turned her head to the truck driver. The firelight illuminated the insect and Tom Honey kicking in the dust, pushing away from the creature as it stepped toward him.

The big ant cocked its head and snapped its shining mandibles, advancing on the truck driver as he wriggled in the dust, struggling to gain traction.

The next step of the mutant brought its clawed front foot down between the trucker's legs. He stared up as the head hung over him, the jaws snapped open wide, and the antennae swept the air to zero in on its prey.

A scream began to rise around the ice in his chest, and he splayed himself flat, slapping his hands back into the dust. His right hand fell neatly on his Desert Eagle, cocked and waiting.

The huge gun lifted of its own accord as the head of the big ant turned, following its feelers, bringing jaws to the victim.

As the drooling mandibles lowered, the .50 caliber cannon exploded, sending three rounds through the insect's gigantic head. The thumb-sized, high-velocity shells rocketed through the head, blowing baseball-sized holes out of the top of the exoskeleton as they exited.

The bug's legs buckled, and the ant fell. The head dropped dead to a jolting stop on its open mandibles, jammed into the ground and bridging Tom Honey's body. Fluid poured from the massive wounds in a steady stream between the trucker's legs. He pushed his way out from under the bug, holding his hand cannon in a death grip.

The truck driver was out from under but still on the ground and turned his head to see that the other two monsters had reached their mark. One of them had Billy in its jaws. The horrible, fire-framed profile of the ant arched its back and raised her monstrous head with the screaming man flailing against the hard shell in slow motion.

Honey scrambled to his feet as the other ant attacked Carlos and Ray. The trucker whirled, winded, and off-balance, to see Mike running from the far end of the boardwalk and skidding through the dust to collide with the giant bug battling the two men. The ant spun, knocking Ray to the ground and throwing Carlos against the burning walkway, showering sparks as he crashed into the blaze.

Billy's shrill screams cut through the chaos as Carlos, on the ground with flames growing from his clothing, brought his rifle up and fired, emptying his gun into the ant's head.

Mike recovered his stance, swung his rifle around to the back of the bug's head, and let loose, pumping several steel jackets into its exo-skull. The bug reared back, turning with so much force it hit the lineman and threw him a dozen feet through the dirt.

Carlos put out his shirt, added a mag, and ducked past the spinning insect on his way to help Billy. He aimed and rapid-fired, six rounds hitting the monster in the side. It took no notice of the bullets but wheeled and raised her head higher, holding Billy in the smoke. He screamed vowels. The ant shook its head back and forth like a dog with a rabbit.

Mike came around the back of the ant and lifted his rifle to fire. The giant bug arched back, lifting Billy high above the ground.

A geyser of blood shot from Billy's mouth as the insect's jaws snapped tight, crushing his chest. His hands clutched at the steel-hard mandibles, scissoring through his torso. His body went limp in the behemoth's maw.

As the big bug finished shearing, Billy's lower half dropped to the ground. His legs stood on their own for a moment. Carlos and Mike fired until the beast fell dead.

Carlos dropped to a knee, breathing hard, and gasped to Ray. "Ant's coming in. Throw two more." He pointed at the giant insect heads, testing the flames. "Keep that fire going," he gasped.

Ray's terrified expression was stuck on his face as he hustled to the bottles and picked two. He lit their wicks and threw the gas bombs where they were needed to fire up the wall.

Mike was bent over, catching his breath as the trucker joined him and fell onto the boardwalk. Laying on the planks, he looked down at the far end and could see the form of Brandon, shrunken against the wall of the Bunker.

Carlos and Ray walked past the fires to the men on the edge of the walk. They sat next to them, breathing heavily.

"Another like that, and we're done," Tom Honey said. He lay back on the planks to watch the sparks fly into the night sky.

"We have to close this up," Carlos said, sweeping his hand across the firewall. "We have to keep a tighter circle so we don't use that much gas," he said as he got his breath back.

"OK," Mike said. He laughed, and his voice cracked. "Guess you plan on getting through this." He dry-spit and wiped his face with the back of his sleeve. "I'd sure trade one of those gas bottles for a bottle of cold beer," he said and tried to spit again.

A distant trill rose from the dark beyond the fire. The insect call bounced off the concrete façade of the Bunker. The group stared into the night, waiting for the siren to end. As the screech wound down, a section of the walk collapsed into the fire. A crack and bloom of sparks made them look at the pile of ant that killed Billy. The fire grew, chewing its way down the walk.

Tom Honey sat up and laid his Eagle across his lap, looking into the lot. "This is getting a might gloomy," he said, staring past the fire.

Mike stepped onto the walk to see about his young partner, Brandon. The hollow knocks of his hard-heeled boots on the dry wood followed him along the planks.

The oversized head of a gargantuan scout rose against the smears of the moonlit sky and turned slowly toward their fires. Her antennae swayed silently in the dark, collecting the heavy scent of animal protein, dead and alive, burned and bloody. She correlated the odors with their signature vibrations and footsteps.

One trigger after another tripped, and she released chemical messages, filling the air and marking the area for harvesting. The huge scout lifted, arching her back and generating a night-tearing screech to summon the other ants to join in the next attack.

CHAPTER SIXTEEN

THE SANDS

When the monsters erupted from the desert, Drake was one of a handful of people first notified of the incident. He wasn't in the military. Neither was anyone else in his group. They weren't in the government, they were not officials, and not one was known to the public. They were strictly behind the scenes.

A pilot from Holloman Air Force Base spotted a giant ant on patrol in the desert. The helicopter buzzed the enormous insect and got video before the aberration scurried into a huge hole. The chopper hightailed it back to base to report the sighting.

The pilot didn't know what to make of the creature but knew it was real. He went straight from touchdown to his base commander, prudently deciding to keep the discovery off the airwaves.

The colonel commanding the Air Force base wasn't skeptical. He had been acquainted with the history of the area. He watched the video and immediately escalated the event, calling a brigadier general.

That call and all other communications, even secured military transmissions, were filtered through White Sands for analysis to discern subject matter, priorities, and topics of interest to the Agency.

A constant monitor alerted to the conversation in progress between the base commander and his central command, prioritizing the event. The real telephone operator had asked the colonel to hold while they located the general. The Agency eavesdropper broke into the call, representing itself as a new operator. "Colonel? I'm sorry, but the general is unavailable at the moment," it said. "Could he return your call in a few minutes?"

The base commander replied, "Sure. Tell him it's urgent."

337

"Yes, sir," the new call coordinator responded. "Will do."

While this conversation was underway, another Agency monitor canceled the call with the general's office on behalf of the base commander, explaining that everything had been taken care of and there was no need for a callback. Henry listened to the exchange and was surprised at how willingly the human liaison acceded without any real security measures.

He shook his head as he watched new instances attaching to this event on a 3D scatter plot, slowly turning on his desk display. Each new node was generated in response to the task requirements of the developing strategy to control the mutant outbreak.

Henry watched the graphic twist on the screen as new points outlined in red continued to appear. He knew this was already on track to be the biggest project he'd ever seen.

The colonel commanding the Air Force base wasn't skeptical. He had been acquainted with the history of the area. He watched the video and immediately escalated the event, calling a brigadier general.

That call and all other communications, even secured military transmissions, were filtered through White Sands for analysis to discern subject matter, priorities, and topics of interest to the Agency.

A constant monitor alerted to the conversation in progress between the base commander and his central command, prioritizing the event. The real telephone operator had asked the colonel to hold while they located the general. The Agency eavesdropper broke into the call, representing itself as a new operator. "Colonel? I'm sorry, but the general is unavailable at the moment," it said. "Could he return your call in a few minutes?"

The base commander replied, "Sure. Tell him it's urgent."

"Yes, sir," the new call coordinator responded. "Will do."

While this conversation was underway, another Agency monitor canceled the call with the general's office on behalf of the base commander, explaining that everything had been taken care of and there was no need for a callback. Henry listened to the exchange and was surprised at how willingly the human liaison acceded without any real security measures.

He shook his head as he watched new instances attaching to this event on a 3D scatter plot, slowly turning on his desk display. Each new node was generated in response to the task requirements of the developing strategy to control the mutant outbreak.

Henry watched the graphic twist on the screen as new points outlined in red continued to appear. He knew this was already on track to be the biggest project he'd ever seen.

A review of records found no incidence of familiarity between the Air Force base commander and this general. One of the monitor instances posed as the brigadier to return the colonel's call on his secure line and listen to his rundown of the situation.

"Not entirely surprised by this, Colonel," the nonexistent general replied. "The fact is, we've had rumblings and already have a plan underway. You will stand by for further instruction – and let me give you a heads-up – this will be big, so be prepared. I will also stress that immediacy is paramount," the artificial officer ordered. "And by the way," it added, "you know it goes without saying, not a word. And I want you to destroy that chopper video. Clear? This is top secret."

The voice generation paused, then added in a response patterned to the colonel. "One other thing. There's more than your country relying on you – the whole world will need you in on this to get the job done. This is bigger than any of us, Frank."

Henry leaned back in his chair with his feet up on his desk. He smiled at the sincerity of the imitation voice, the exhausted tone of a commander at the end of his options but resolute, and with a grim determination that can only result in final victory. It was wonderfully convincing.

"Yes, sir," the base commander responded, complete in his transformation to the savior of humanity.

Henry disconnected the voice-modulating headset and drummed his fingers on the arm of his chair as he watched the expanding plot turning on his screen. He guessed it already had the tactical team in motion.

At that moment of Henry's speculation, the recon video was being scrutinized by Drake.

Within thirty minutes, the airbase commander received formal orders through channels to immediately place the pilot and his crew in isolation.

Within the hour, it had been decided to eradicate the ants and pursue deniability, and Drake was on his way to White Sands to see that it happened.

Round-the-clock drone reconnaissance of the desert began on the day of discovery. Before dawn the next morning, a satellite was locked into a synchronous orbit over the desert basin. The following day before noon, monitoring teams installed a wide network of sensors in the sands to track the creatures' movements.

Drake and three Agency reps landed in a Gulfstream at Holloman, taxiing close to a waiting car on the tarmac. Four passengers in civilian clothing deplaned, got into the black sedan, and drove across the runway to the airfield exit. Drake spoke to the commander on his phone, and the gates opened to let them pass unchallenged. The car left the base without stopping and turned onto the highway, heading to the small settlement of White Sands about forty miles west of Holloman, on the far side of the Tularosa Basin.

On the ride to the nondescript headquarters in the missile range town, Drake said little. He stared at the white desert streaming past the window as they sped down the highway, occasionally passing a car or pickup. His reps spoke now and then. The woman driving mentioned she hadn't been there for years. The big guy in the passenger seat didn't look at Drake when she said that.

And she didn't turn her head as they raced past the Bunker.

The car pulled onto the turnoff that ran south from the highway to the little town. They sped down the middle of the access road and flew by a sign telling them to be prepared to stop for Air Force Security Forces.

Two SUVs came out of nowhere to intercept their car about a mile past that warning, one in front and one behind, forcing their speeding vehicle to a stop.

Drake turned his head to look at the truck behind them as the doors opened and said, "At least they're on the job." He pulled a deck of identification cards from his shirt pocket and picked one.

"Air cops," Drake's driver said.

"Be polite," Drake replied to the woman behind the steering wheel as their windows went down.

A large Security Forces airman walked cautiously to the vehicle, looking in the windows as he approached the car.

He draped his left arm over the roof of the four-door and leaned to look inside. His eyes went from face to face. If there were any trouble, he'd shoot the man in the passenger seat right off. He looked like trouble.

"Y'all driving a tetch on the speedy side," he drawled into the car.

"Uh-huh," the woman behind the wheel said. "I guess we were at that. It's these open roads and all this room. They just make you want to get up and go." She smiled.

"That's a fact," the missile policeman replied. "The wide open can have that effect on some folk." His hand was still on his sidearm, and two of his fellow officers had taken positions with their rifles casually leveled at the occupants.

"Now, before y'all tell me just where you're heading, what your business is, and your most secret and personal beliefs, I wonder if you could oblige me with some form of identification?" the sergeant inquired with

341

a voice that didn't do justice to his physique. "And with pictures, if you please," he added, looking at Drake.

Drake exhaled quietly, looked back at the Mississippian's long face, and held his ID between two fingers at the window.

As the sergeant reached for the card, the lead SUV driver leaned out of the window and called back, "Sarge, CC's on. These folks get a pass. They said to answer your phone."

The sergeant stared at his driver, and the phone in his pocket rang. He pulled it out, looked at the display, and brought it to his ear. "Sergeant Simmons," he said tentatively. He listened. "Yes, sir. Understood, sir," was all he said. He put the phone in his pocket and waved the ID back.

"No need for that, sir," he said to Drake. "The only thing I am to ask you, sir, is if you are desirous of an escort."

"Not necessary, Sergeant," Drake responded. "We know where we're going, thank you." He nodded once to dismiss the man, and the windows went up as the car kicked a dust cloud back, pulling onto the roadway and exceeding the speed limit to town.

A car with Air Force tags was not unusual in White Sands, but a speeding car was. It was a very law-abiding place, so they slowed, pulling behind a school bus as they entered the town.

"A school bus?" the young man in the back beside Drake asked, "There's a school here? That's a nice touch. Very authentic. It makes it all seem very...." He stopped talking when he saw the driver looking at him in her rearview. Her eyes moved across the mirror to Drake.

"I'm surprised, that's all," the young man said to excuse his unnecessary observation.

Drake eyed the recruit, turned to the window, and smiled as the street went by.

"I've never been here before," the young man added.

"Or since," the muscular man in the passenger seat said over his shoulder. He glanced back at Drake and raised his eyebrows.

They took a left, drove along a black iron fence to the middle of the block, and turned into an open gate that closed after they passed. The large door in the center of the building opened next, and they drove into the warehouse under a sign that described the facility as 'WEC Remediation Center.'

The large door rolled down behind them, and the black sedan stopped in an empty warehouse. The occupants got out and crossed the painted concrete to a small door in the far wall.

The driver led the group to the door as it buzzed. She pulled it open and pushed it back for the person behind her as she went through. They filed into a carpeted hallway and passed two men in white shirts in a windowed reception area without exchanging a word.

The woman driver led them down the hall and opened the doorway to a conference room. A bald corporate type wheeled a TV out of the corner and indicated the chairs around the table.

They took seats at the television end of the table and waited for him to start.

"Well, I guess we're all here," the man began. "This is your complete team, Mr. Drake?"

Drake nodded. "Yes. Please proceed," he said.

"Very well. All right. OK," the man said to himself as he opened a thick folder on the table and handed a sheaf of papers to the woman. He looked at her and said, "It is very nice to see you again, Sylvia. If you would be so kind as to pass these down to Mr. Drake." She pushed the papers down the table to her boss.

"Nice to see you again, Henry. You're looking so much better," she smiled at the pale man.

"Oh yes, much better now, thank you," he said, selecting a few pages and passing out more pieces of paper.

The man cleared his throat. "Let's begin. As you know, the ants are back," Henry said, looking and nodding to each person at the table. "I believe you have been briefed," he said, then turned to the others. "This is a recurrence of phenomena that manifested shortly after the first atomic bomb test, tests conducted in White Sands about seventy years ago."

Drake interrupted the man. "Before the history, can we touch on current events? Are there any?" he asked.

"Hmm, well, yes," Henry replied. "There have been a few, twenty-three to be precise, missing person reports, and…" the man thumbed through his papers and pulled one to the top. "Yes, twenty-three missing person reports. Locals, a few hikers, and motorists. Reports of serious vandalism, obviously the ants. We'll solve most of the cases and take care of any persistent complainers."

Drake nodded. "And going downhill fast. That's our future, so back to the past." He motioned for Henry to continue. "Go on, Hank. An understanding of previous events can only help."

Henry nodded and moved back to the previous page. "Yes, that's true. Here we are, all right. The first outbreak of the mutations was not very well contained. In fact, the failures led to the establishment of many of the protocols we currently follow."

Henry evened the edges of his papers on the table, picked up the remote, and pointed it at the TV.

The screen showed several black-and-white photos of giant dead ants, many with soldiers or police standing by, and grainy old crime scene photos of desert buildings destroyed and vintage cars torn apart.

He continued. "That first outbreak left twenty-one people dead and twice as many, forty-two, missing and presumed. That does not include the casualties of the military assault on the nest, which did not go as

344

expected," Henry said. "Regarding the low number of civilian casualties, the area was lightly populated in those days – far fewer people than today. The sparse population was undoubtedly the most significant factor for the acceptably low casualty rate. And frankly, many of the people were social outcasts and not missed, you know, old prospectors in the desert."

"You're all heart, Henry," Syl said.

Henry flickered an uncomfortable and uncertain smile. "Yes, well, all right." He started again. "In any event, the mutations left dozens of witnesses alive, and it was a mess," he summarized. "We cannot have that again. And consider the fact that anyone encountering an ant can instantly disseminate convincing evidence of their existence, and we cannot allow that to happen."

"Can't allow what, Henry?" Syl asked. "Witnesses?"

"That's your business." He swallowed and clicked the remote. "All I am saying is that the internet is the plague of our times. I would be hard-pressed to conjure up anything more ruinous to secrecy. Although we have made many advances in controls, it is difficult."

The compilation of monster videos ended with a still image of the carcass of a massive ant with three men standing in front of it. Two were in military garb, and one was dressed like a hunter from a 1955 *Field & Stream*. They were all holding long guns.

"As a point of interest," Henry said as he brought their attention back to the screen, "the civilian in the photo is none other than Professor Carrington, our founder." He looked down at his papers as he spoke. "Professor Carrington also brought into being that first generation of monster ants, one of his many astounding accomplishments."

Drake smiled. "Astounding is an understatement. That reminds me, have there been any leads about the books?" He looked over the table at Syl. "I know you were hot on the trail a few years ago. Anything come of it?"

"No," she said disagreeably, reminded of her failure.

The corner of Drake's mouth went up. "Well, don't let it bug you. There's a lot of hands on deck now. Someone might end up finding the grail, after all."

"Listen," Syl leaned over the table at Drake, "I spent plenty of time cozying up to that sister of his, but I swear she was on to me from the start. And that doesn't just happen. That old lady strung me along. When she was in the hospital, we went through every inch of her houses. She hid those journals and the beans. She knew what she had, and somebody helped her." The woman sat back in her chair and shook her head. "Someone tipped her. I know that for a fact, and I know who."

"May Carrington had many friends," Henry said.

Syl looked at the executive with malice. "Well, she's dead now," she said. "Did you know that?" She smiled. "Her niece has been around with the old dame's lawyer. She's getting everything," Syl smiled again. "And I'm banking that means everything. I'll find out. I have my eyes on her."

Drake tapped the conference table two times with his index finger. "All good, but that comes after mission one, and that's the containment of them," he said, pointing to the old photo of the giant dead ant on the screen.

Syl sat back in her seat and listened without expression as Drake continued.

"A Colonel Smith and about a hundred special ops are taking over Holloman." Drake looked down the table to the strong-jawed man sitting across from Syl. "Max, you know the colonel, don't you?"

"Yep. Worked with him once back in the day," he replied. "He's good, an honest-to-God soldier," he added.

"Not too honest, I hope," Drake said, looking through his papers. "We'll be seeing him tomorrow when he arrives. You can do the introductions. We're also going to start evacuating the NEPs from the base as of tomorrow."

Henry raised his eyebrows in surprise. "Evacuating? Tomorrow? NEPs? Oh, I don't see how. There are more non-essentials there than enlisted," he exclaimed. "Don't you think that's a bit premature, Mr. Drake?" he added in a higher tone. "Evacuation will surely attract attention."

"Maybe it will," Drake answered. He finished leafing through the pages and dropped them on the table. He smiled at the functionary and folded his hands over the papers. "But nothing attracts attention like dead people, Henry. And I want as many currently alive people out of the way as possible. Besides, the military is always shuffling people around. And we are considering certain strategic solutions that necessitate evacuation."

"But there are thousands of people there, tens of thousands. It's the largest population in the Sands," Henry said excitedly. "What difference will moving a few hundred or even a few thousand out make? The cost, the coordination," he stammered, "it would be overwhelming."

Drake laughed. "Only overwhelming for you, Henry, and only because you're in charge. I want half the population out in a week. The rest will go the following week, and you must make it happen."

The three other people around the table stared at Henry. He sat still while Drake flipped through his phone.

"OK," Drake continued, "next is my data. We have orbital, drones flying, and wide net sensors. Even a couple of humans in the mix keeping tabs on them." The boss turned to the youngest member of the group. "How long before you have the feeds coordinated?" he asked the recruit.

"We'll be set up late tonight," he answered.

"Good answer, Link. I'm sure in his spare moments, Henry can delegate any assistance you need." The bald man simply nodded in response.

Drake looked at the newly partnered pair. "Why don't you two get the ball rolling, starting with what we need online?" He smiled at Henry. "Cheer up, Hank. Won't be so bad; at least it will be better than being eaten by a giant ant." Drake moved his eyes to the door, nodded, and the two men got up from the table and left the room.

He turned to the woman across from him. "I take it you have plans to contribute to this operation. I know you have contacts here." He smiled at her and played dumb. "Didn't your old boss retire around here? He'd probably be a good one to check. One of those old Cold War types, wasn't he? They never retire. Sort of a legend, too. When was the last time you saw him?" Drake looked amused.

"It's been a while," Syl answered in a low whisper. "Unresolved issues," she added.

"Really?" Drake grinned. "Must have been something. After all, you've been in the area on and off over the last few years and never looked him up?" He shook his head. "I think friends should always stay in touch." Drake considered annoying her equivalent to sharpening a knife.

Syl was unamused.

"Well, whatever," he said to her. "One thing I know is you will do what you will do. So, whatever you do, stay in the framework. Remember the objective, please."

"Always," she said.

"And who knows? Maybe the scope of this operation is big enough to bring you two together again," Drake said consolingly.

"Maybe," Syl replied.

"OK. Again, remember the framework," Drake said. He added an emphatic expression. "And that is, ants bad, people good, that's the framework of the mission." He smiled and shook his head. "People good," he repeated clearly. "We're on the same side."

"I got it." She stood up from the table, nodded, and smiled at Drake's soldier across the table as she turned to the door.

"And let me know what you're up to once in a while," Drake said as she exited the room.

"You got it, Sir Francis," her voice came from the hallway.

"And say hello to Walt," Drake said under his breath, then shook his head.

He looked at Max and sighed. "I'm going to get some sleep. We'll restart tomorrow morning." He rolled his report and tapped the end of the paper tube two times on the tabletop as they stood.

Drake looked at the monitor and studied the old image, noting the civilian hunter pictured posed in front of a dead monster. "You know they made them on purpose, Max?" he asked his associate.

"Not surprising," Max replied. He twisted his neck, popping out the kinks from the cramped seat on the jet and the night before.

"And we get to solve their problem, as usual," Drake added.

Max snorted and let the boss go through the door first. "Same old story, same old solution," he said after him. He lifted his hand, made a pistol with his fingers, and picked off a couple of bugs as he followed Drake into the hallway. "Nothing to it," he told himself.

Syl went looking for Henry, passing several closed doors on either side of the narrow corridor to one marked 'Area 48.' She pushed it open and stepped into a large room with dozens of desks, each occupied by a person staring into a monitor.

The person at the desk nearest the doorway looked in her direction for a split second, then back at his screen. Syl walked to the young, round man and stood at his desk. He didn't look up. She leaned over him, watching the monitor as he typed. He hunched away from her, and she leaned closer.

"Hey, neckbeard, wanna come back to earth for a minute? Where's Henry?" she hissed.

The data analyst looked hurt and pointed to the back of the long room and three closed doors. "Henry's in the one on the right," he answered, lowering his arm and looking up at Syl. "But I think he's busy right now."

"He is, and that's why he's got an office and you don't." The woman smiled and walked to the end of the room. She pushed Henry's door open and stepped inside. Henry and the recruit, Link, looked up from their computers.

"Henry, I need an office and access. Have to look up a few things," Syl said to him.

"Oh, OK Sylvia. I'll be right with you." His keyboard clicked out a string of characters.

Sylvia sniffed. "But I want you to do it now. You know, so I don't have to wait."

Henry stood, typing as he rose. "Oh, OK, all right. Nobody's using the conference room next door," he said as he finished with the keyboard and looked across at her. "Do you have your own device?" he asked.

"What? No," she answered, annoyed by the question and everything else. "Get me a computer and get me on."

"OK." Henry scurried from behind his desk. "I'll be right back," he said as he passed Link by, "Just as soon as I get Sylvia situated."

Link remained engrossed in his monitor and hummed in accordance as Henry passed. "It's OK. I think I got those connections working now," he said a moment after they had left the room.

Syl followed Henry out of his office and into the neighboring conference room. "I'll be just a minute. I'll get you a laptop," he said, leaving her at the table.

She sat on the edge of the table, took her phone out, and opened the contacts to the Ds. Selecting a listing, she made a call. A man answered, "Hey Syl, is that really you? What's going on? Where are you?" the voice asked.

"Close," she responded. "Let's have dinner. We'll hop over to the crosses and get some tacos."

"Mexican?" he asked. "It's all I eat. How about Asian?"

"No," she said. "I'm tired of that."

"Guess you've been away," the man said. "OK, whatever you say, of course. I won't be able to get there for about an hour. I'm still on..."

"That works out. I have things to do," she said, interrupting.

"Sounds good," he replied. "See you there, Syl. I'll be…." She smiled and hung up.

The door opened, and Henry came in with a laptop. "Here you go, Sylvia," he said as he set the computer on the conference table and placed the mouse on the left. "I know how much you dislike the pointer-pads."

"Thank you, Henry," Syl said as the machine came to life. "You did very well. Now just log me in, and you can leave."

"You're all set up, and you're quite welcome," he said. Sylvia watched as he backed out of the room, dipping his head like he was about to bow. She liked that.

351

He closed the door, and she turned to the computer screen. After a few clicks, she was searching through the personnel files to look up a few old friends.

The database included every resident of White Sands, military, agency, and civilian. Her clearance allowed complete access to all of the locals' records. Access to Agency staff was limited to operatives at her rank and below.

She reviewed local law enforcement and the new remediation reps that had arrived or were on their way. She flagged the files to synch with her phone so she would have the info at dinner.

Before signing out, she opened Walt's file. It showed the same twenty-year-old picture, and 'Retired: No Further Service' was in a red box in the upper right of his screen.

"Inaccurate," she said to his picture.

Syl closed the lid and got up from the table. She tucked her phone into the back pocket of her jeans, left the room, and went down the hallway. She wiggled her fingers in a wave as she passed the guards behind the glass and entered the warehouse.

The overhead door opened, Syl shot out of the building in reverse, did a 180 in the lot, and sped onto the quiet street, backtracking their route to the main highway. She turned west and stepped on the gas, heading to Las Cruces and her dinner date.

Hundreds of Agency representatives live throughout White Sands. To them, "The Sands" means the entire desert basin. It is their home base, their special jurisdiction, and the Agency controls the nearly 7000 square mile area without interference or consequence.

Many reps, maybe even most by now, are born to the job. Being with the Agency is a family tradition, and many have filled their tree with members, following generations of service, some back to the beginning, back to the original eight people who started the whole thing.

In the twentieth century, in the 1940s, Professor Carrington returned from the Arctic with the remains of his expedition and the salvage of an alien spaceship. He demonstrated a few of his discoveries and was immediately given absolute authority to develop the facilities and workforce to house, protect, and exploit the extraterrestrial technologies.

A clandestine enterprise grew unchecked in the seclusion of the desert. It was formed to administer the developments that would change the world.

Over the following years, the military and industry eagerly awaited each breakthrough as the professor's growing organization meted them out. The advances were so extraordinary that his directives for their iterative introduction into the supply chain and public consciousness were carefully followed to advance the world in tolerable steps and maximize profit.

Through his programs regulating the release of extraterrestrial science, Carrington's Agency gained more power, more followers, and less recognition, as he wanted. The scholar had no use for applause.

When the telegram informing him of another Nobel Prize for his works in physics was delivered, he glanced at it and said, "No reply," to the messenger, shut the door, and used the back of the cable to finish working through a calculation. He didn't give the accolade another thought until a colleague telephoned him from the East Coast to convince the professor that the award would be a boon to his research and open doors throughout the world.

"Even I do not have two," the Princeton caller said, "And that headline would be worth something. Notoriety is the work you do for money."

"That's not the type of work I want to do, Al," Carrington replied. "Anyway, I thought you might be calling to tell me something new with your, what was it? Unification thing? What did you title that paper?" The professor tried to remember.

Al laughed. "Work, work, work," he scolded in a thick accent. "Poor Arthur. As a great scientist, you should be aware there is more to life than work. It is a big world out there, my friend. You should have some fun."

"Oh, I keep myself entertained, Albert," Carrington replied to the speakerphone. He absently finished his sandwich and the small drawing of the skull and bones on the warning label. He put the pen down and stoppered the ink bottle. "And I don't think I could enjoy it any more than I do," he added as he taped the paper strip to the vial of seeds.

The professor promised to consider accepting the prize and told the caller to keep in touch. He wasn't rude, but he was engaged with a problem at the time, and that Jersey academic tended to go on with no real point.

Professor Carrington's assistant also wanted him to reconsider. A second Nobel would be historical, take only a few days, and the effects would last a lifetime. She seemed motivated, so he told her to make the arrangements.

The opportunity to expound the accomplishments of the fledgling White Sands team to the international scientific community at the prize ceremonies proved crucial to the development of the Agency. The organization grew, attracting more talent in more disciplines from around the world, and the Nobels rolled in.

As the Agency grew, Professor Carrington did not want to be involved in administration; he wanted to be left alone to do research. Control of the organization was in the hands of the only person with the capability and trust, the original Nikki.

While he continued experimenting, she corresponded in his name with world leaders and intellectual luminaries.

The professor had gathered a following of specialists in many disciplines and influential positions that appreciated his singular insights into the nature of existence and the mechanics of reality. The regard of the scientific community for Professor Carrington was unequaled. When the urgent call came for an intellectual leader to head an expedition of the utmost scientific importance to the northernmost regions of Alaska, his name was unanimously proposed.

As the Cold War got off to a start, the secret organization that was the forerunner to NORAD established early warning radar outposts in North America's Arctic regions, including along the northern coastline of Alaska. Within weeks of bringing the stations online, stations in Alaska reported tracking the path and probable crash of an impossibly large and incredibly fast object. The trajectory they had recorded was inconsistent with a falling object such as a meteor. It was under power and indicated attempts had been made to correct course and gain altitude before impact.

On the day of the report, unsettling images from photographic reconnaissance were delivered to Professor Carrington and the Pentagon. The pictures showed a debris field and the wreckage of what was unmistakably a ship of extraterrestrial origin. Carrington's mission was organized, outfitted, and on its way within the week.

The plan was to establish a base of operations at the radar station closest to the crash, almost one hundred miles from the site. A ski plane would ferry the team as close as possible, and then they would cover the remainder of the distance to the site on foot for the initial survey.

The clock was ticking on their expedition as the dangerous weather of the Far North winter was brewing stronger every day. A pair of Lockheed Constellations took off on a long flight to Dutch Harbor in the Aleutians, their first stop on their way to Anchorage. After that hop, the transport aircraft proceeded to Fairbanks and continued on the last leg to the isolated radar station in the trackless wilderness even further north.

Carrington kept to himself on the flights, absorbed in contemplating the myriad consequences of the obvious hypothesis. All of the information, the reports, and those stunning photographs led inevitably to a singularly unacceptable yet inescapable conclusion: they were on their way to a downed spacecraft from another world.

The Connies stayed their course, dragging the scientists and soldiers through the interminable hours of flight, refueling layovers, and over thousands of frozen miles to a rough touchdown on an ice field at a northern observation radar post.

The planes bounced and slid to a stop, then taxied to the small buildings, blowing a blizzard of ground snow into the blindingly bright blue sky as they pivoted on the pack. They lined up with the other transports and lowered their engines to a background rumble as the ground crew blocked the tires and hooked cables to the aircraft, anchoring them against the fierce winds.

After the cramped and cold trip, the expedition members crept out of the transports, stamping and flapping life into their extremities as they hustled through the frigid air to quarters built only two days before.

As he hurried with the others to the Quonset hut, Professor Carrington stepped out of line, pausing to watch the coordinated chaos of the busy outpost.

Clouds of vapor shot into the air, carrying the orders of the construction manager. A Snowcat chugged through the frigid morning, dragging a skid of timber with workers riding on top. Everywhere he looked in this snowy desert, the scientist saw energy shaped into action, and he knew, he could sense, the larger purpose forming, reflected in this microcosm of his mission. He knew that through his actions in this place, the future of the world would be forged.

The scientists selected for the first visit to the crash site were tired from their long trip but eager to be underway. They would leave in the morning after a night's rest. The soldier in charge of the expedition met with them after dinner.

A leathery Army officer with a savage scar from forehead to jaw began the talk. He sat on the edge of a long table at the front of the dimly lit dining area and addressed the small group of lead scientists.

"I'm Major Polk," was his first announcement. "Apparently, I'm going to take you fellows for a sleigh ride tomorrow." He lit a cigarette from a pack in his shirt pocket. The glow from his Ronson flickered across his scar.

He snapped the lighter closed and looked back at the group as he exhaled a satisfying cloud of tobacco smoke. "Any of you men ever been in the weather before?" The major studied the blank expressions. "By weather," he went on, "I mean any outdoor conditions that can kill you." He took another drag and blew it out. "Because this weather surely can. It will kill you in five minutes if you don't pay attention."

Polk looked for an answer from the quiet group. "I'll take that as a no," he finally said. "Well, don't let that worry you too much. That's what we do: get you there and back in one piece." He took the cigarette from his lips and picked a piece of loose tobacco off his tongue. He looked the group over, from face to face, taking another drag.

"The way we planned it, there'll be a short flight to the general area, and then we're hoofing it to the target." Major Polk took another draw on his smoke and then pointed to the sergeant seated nearby. "Sergeant Cady here and my men have plenty of experience in the snow and handling dogs if we need them," he said as he turned to his NCO. "What did we say, Sergeant? Maybe an hour over the pack?"

"Yes, sir," Cady replied. "That's how we have it figured."

"All right, men," the major said to the scientists. "If you have any questions, we'll try to answer them. Just remember to dress in the gear provided, all of it. Get a good night's sleep tonight, and tomorrow morning, eat the biggest breakfast of your life. That will help to keep you warm. And above all, do exactly what we tell you while we're out there. Your lives depend on it. All of our lives do, and we won't risk

them trying to save some fool that fell down a hole he shouldn't have."
He tried smiling again and was more successful. "So, watch your step."

The major stubbed his cigarette out on the table and field-stripped it,
then dropped the remnants on the floor and rubbed them away with his
boot. He arched his eyebrows at the small group. "So, any questions?"
he asked.

Professor Carrington didn't look at the others but answered quietly, "I
don't think so, Major Polk. I am confident we can rely completely on
you and your men."

The major studied the professor. "Carrington. You're in charge of this
whole shebang, right?" he asked. "We didn't get a chance to introduce
ourselves." The officer nodded thoughtfully, still watching the pale
professor. "Well, if you don't have any questions, Professor, I can come
up with one: What the hell are we doing here?"

The professor smiled. "I don't know if I can say, not really," he
answered.

"You can, if you want to, Professor," the major put his foot up on a
chair and leaned forward. "As a matter of fact, I was told you could do
anything." The scarred man took another cigarette from his pocket and
put it between his thin lips. He flipped the top back on his lighter and
looked at the scientist. "You know, Carrington, there are a couple of
guys going to be putting their lives on the line for you tomorrow," he
said as he struck the lighter to a flame. "And I think we have a right to
know what we're getting into up here." The major lit his Lucky and
snapped the lighter closed.

The professor stared at the officer for a long moment, amused at the
thought that he hadn't been addressed by his last name since his
adolescent years in college.

He stood from his chair, watching the major. Both were tired from the
long days behind them.

"Major Polk," the scientist addressed to the army officer, "I think that's a reasonable assumption. However, I am concerned my answer will interfere with one of your directives." The professor collected the books and file folders from the chair next to him.

"How's that?" Polk asked.

"If I tell you why we're here and what our mission is, I'm fairly certain nobody will get a good night's sleep, as you suggested," he said and smiled at the officer.

"All right," the major answered, "I'll bite. What've you got?"

The professor cradled his pile of books and paper in his left arm and straightened his eyeglasses. He broadened his smile. "I just now realize this will be the first I am saying it aloud, and I am sure to be the first sane man ever to utter these words." Carrington cleared his throat. "We're going to find a flying saucer, Major. A spaceship. Perhaps a visitor from outer space," he announced. He paused and looked around the room. "Someone had to say it, I suppose," he said to himself.

One of his fellow scientists let out an involuntary gasp. The expeditionary group was well aware of the mission. As yet, there were no secrets from the members of the group. But, to hear the world's leading scientist say those words without equivocation or couched in hypothesis was electric.

The two soldiers were also surprised.

Carrington turned, stepped past the chairs, and walked toward the door.

"Wait a minute, Professor," the major called after him. "You're not kidding, are you?"

"Take it all in, Major," the professor answered over his shoulder. "You don't think the efforts of the hundreds of people involved in this expedition, the expense, and the urgency of our departure is for a downed aircraft, do you?" He pulled a photo from his bundle, waving it as he walked. "There is genuine evidence for this conclusion." He barely contained his delight.

Professor Carrington opened the door and turned to the room before stepping through. "Good evening, gentlemen," he said softly. "I hope you all sleep well." He left the dining room smiling to himself.

The morning came too quickly for rest and too slowly to appease their eagerness. The team dressed in heavy gear and ate as instructed while listening to the aircraft engine's rumble, waiting for them in the zero-degree dawn.

They filed onto the plane and found seats on the benches along the walls, cinching their safety belts as the engine roared louder and louder. Dr. Blaine leaned to the soldier beside him and shouted over the motor, "This is extremely exciting! It should be a real adventure!" He nodded with exaggerated emphasis over the din. The doctor cupped his hand by his mouth and shouted even louder to make himself heard, "I feel like I'm on a real expedition," he laughed and patted his chest. "They even gave me my own dog tags." He slapped his chest again. "Pretty swell," he yelled into the man's ear.

The soldier gave the doctor a big smile. "We all got them," he shouted back to the young doctor. He pointed to his midsection. "In case they can't identify our bodies," he shouted over the engine noise. The man laughed and thumped Dr. Blaine good-naturedly on his chest and laughed some more. The doctor's enthusiastic expression melted away as the plane accelerated to takeoff.

An hour later, the cargo transport took a long schuss to a stop on a vast snowfield in the early morning shadows of an immense wall of ice cliffs. The aircraft's gangway dropped open, and Major Polk, his sergeant, and his soldiers jumped onto the packed snow and lined up. The scientific group followed with Professor Carrington in the lead. The scientists milled about and did not form a line.

The expedition stood before a mile of ice stretching to impossibly high cliffs holding up the sky.

"Now I know how an ant feels," the major said, walking next to the professor with Sergeant Cady in tow. "We landed closer than we thought we could. Glad we didn't bring any dogs; we won't need them, and if you ever flew with them, you'd be glad we didn't bring them, too. We'll be on-site in no time."

The soldiers went off to get the show on the road, and the sergeant barked out a few encouraging suggestions to motivate them.

"Everyone helps the other guy pack up," Sergeant Cady bellowed. "Then we're going to make three nice, straight lines, each line alternate dogface and double-dome, if both parties will excuse the expressions. Twenty feet apart, rope up, and thataway." The sergeant pointed over the ice dunes to the cliffs.

Professor Carrington snugged his ushanka hat and gazed over the frozen plain to the sunlit crest of the towering bluffs. The bleached landscape looked as though he were back in New Mexico. There was no sign of the spacecraft. The photographs showed the wreckage crashed into the base of the escarpment.

The line formed with Polk and Carrington at the front. As the last men fell in, the Major gave the nod to his sergeant.

Seargent Cady took a deep breath of the frigid air and shouted, "All right, let's start walking. That's how we get there. And keep your distance; don't let that rope drag. Now, mush!"

With that, the teams began tramping over the uneven snowpack to the distant cliffs. The hikers wore cleats and carried wooden-shafted ice axes, using the long handles to steady themselves and the blades to chop footholds in the glaze.

The jagged expanse was an inlet of the Arctic Ocean, flash-frozen in a storm. Reconnaissance photos showed the wreckage pushed against the base of the rock face, like a ship that had foundered and smashed against a rocky coastline. Ahead, the frozen sea rose and obscured their view.

The troops climbed the icy incline, picking their way around massive ice blocks sculpted by the wind to point the way to the cliffs.

There was no wind. The early morning azure rose to black, shimmering with energized curtains of emerald green racing across space in all directions. Some of the lights arced, dissipating into blue ripples behind the clifftops. Up here, everything was the northern sky.

They reached the summit of the incline and lined the top of their new vantage point, looking across the frozen bay to the base of the cliffs. Professor Carrington stood in the front rank. "Look," he said, pointing across the ocean of ice. "There. See there," he continued, speaking softly, absorbing the scene. "Note the break in the ridge." The professor pointed to the rim of the next ascent and the irregular gap in the edge. It seemed a sizable breach, even at a distance.

"At that point, the alien ship first contacted the Earth," the professor intoned. "When we climb that peak, we shall be walking into history."

They went down the frozen dune and then trudged and chopped their way up the next embankment. Large broken ice blocks littered their climb to the top. The wind-cut ridge had a wide notch broken out of it, and fragments spilled down the face, thrown back from the collision.

The debris provided steps and handholds, helping them surmount the slick ice in their eager climb to the top.

The line of men snaked up the ice and helped each other over the top.

There were no jagged edges up there; it was all melted together like a wound seared smooth with a red-hot iron.

Professor Carrington stood on the edge as the expedition crowded behind him, one after another, standing silently except for their labored breathing as they gazed across the broad stage before them and into the story it told.

A wide plain lay before them, running to the roots of the icebound escarpment. A dotted line of shining ponds skipped across the ice, tracing the path of the ship from the initial strike to its end on the rocks.

Some soldiers and scientists may have uttered an oath at first, but all fell silent and stared across the ice at the spaceship.

As the path progressed, the wreckage increased, marking the trail to the gigantic hull of a crashed spaceship. It looked as if a municipal water tank had fallen and rolled across the snow to smash into the base of the cliffs, then broke open like an egg.

It was unlike anything they had seen; it was alien to their world.

Sergeant Cady broke the stunned silence of the group with a softly uttered expletive.

"Perhaps not the sentiment to be recorded in the history of this momentous occasion, Sergeant," Professor Carrington murmured in reply, "but I do agree with you in your amazement."

"It is momentous," a voice from the stand of men echoed. "Astounding," said another, "truly astounding."

Major Polk pulled his scarf down, exposing his pink scar. "That thing's the size of a battleship," he gasped.

Much of the bright metal fuselage looked intact, stabbed into the base of the cliffs. All sizes of debris peppered the way to the ship. Some pieces were melted into the ice and frozen fast.

Professor Carrington took a few steps to the edge of the broken crest and looked down the gentle slope to the flat expanse. His eyes followed the long ruts carved by the crashing ship as it smashed and bounded over the ice. "I wonder what went wrong for them after so long a journey," he mused. He pointed with the handle of his ice ax along the marks. "A mechanical failure, a miscalculation." He shook his head. "All that way to end like this," he said sadly. "What a catastrophe."

"Maybe. Maybe not," Polk said. "Who knows why they were here? Maybe a catastrophe for us. The Lord works in mysterious ways, Professor."

"Major, let's at least give these new visitors the benefit of the doubt. I want to think that explorers demonstrating such advanced technologies have also evolved ethically," the professor rejoined.

"Tell it to the Aztecs," the major replied.

There were nine ant holes into the nest. The 'six-pack' was a grouping of a half-dozen holes, which was the hub of activity. Three other entrances had been detected apart from the six, and monitoring determined the monsters seldom used them.

One was not only differentiated by distance and traffic but it was constructed differently. Unlike the other holes, this passage was not surrounded by a cone of excavated earth. Instead, it was cut at a slowly sloping angle that could be navigated by the team, at least for the first few hundred yards, which was as far as remotely piloted robots could go before transmission degraded.

This isolated entrance became the focus of Agency plans to penetrate the nest.

There was much discussion about the data and images collected. While the central cluster's entrances showed growing activity, days would pass without activity at the remote hole. Ants would march by the opening at night, traveling extra miles through the desert, ignoring the portal. Only occasionally would a single creature be observed entering or leaving these trailside tunnels. The underused entrance seemed like an easy way into the nest.

Dr. Dhawan, a renowned entomologist, was called to the White Sands complex to brief the decision-making panel, interrupting months of quiet study in a Central American rainforest, an expedition supported by the Agency, as was his entire career.

Uncountable careers were owed to the Agency. The organization fostered success in both private industry and public service. Over decades, representatives from the Sands had left the small desert colony to infiltrate businesses, universities, militaries, and governments worldwide. Wherever they raised families, they continued the tradition of allegiance to the cause.

The doctor had received no indication of his impending departure when a helicopter landed in the jungle village. He looked up from his new specimens under the magnifier with surprise as two board members from his university awkwardly got themselves out of the chopper and scrambled out of the blowing wash with his travel orders. One of them stayed behind to oversee the orderly suspension of his work, and the other member accompanied the doctor on the chopper to a waiting private jet.

The bug doctor arrived in White Sands a few days before meeting with the panel to allow him time to get up to speed. He had access to historical records and visited the nest site in a ride-along with the hunting squads.

After a few days of study and the promise of more field observation, the scientist was asked to present his findings to the executive panel. He was escorted to a small meeting room by Henry and introduced to two people seated at the conference table. "Doctor Dhawan, this is Mrs. Messenger and Mr. Drake."

The academic reached across the table to shake hands. Dr. Dhawan looked with surprise at the very small and old woman as she leaned out of the shadow of the wingback chair, lightly grasped his fingers with her frail hand, and gave them a wobble. She let go, and he moved next to shake Drake's hand quickly.

The doctor sat across the table and looked around the room as Henry took the next chair.

"Just us," creaked the old woman.

"Excuse me?" he said politely as he stared at the woman and narrowed his eyes, then they widened in recognition. "You're the lady from the store. I was there the first day I got in. You were working there." He turned to Henry. "I stopped for some snacks," he said to the man.

"Yes, Doctor Dhawan, you are quite fond of sweets. Three Milky Ways and two bags of peanut butter cups," she said, creasing her face in every direction by smiling.

"I like to have some chocolate when I work. I wish I had gotten more." He smiled at the little old lady and then remembered where he was. "But you work in a grocery store?" the doctor asked.

"I prefer 'superette,'" she replied. "It's on the sign, you know."

"And you work here?" the dark-haired doctor persisted.

"I wouldn't say Mrs. Messenger works there, Doctor," Henry offered.

"Well, Henry, I would disagree. I do my fair share." She wrinkled again to include a laugh. "In the Sands, Doctor, people wear many hats, selling soda pop and candy as well as protecting humanity from monstrous mutants, all jobs that need doing," she chided the scientist. She held a pair of eyeglasses over the papers on the table and studied the print through the extra-large lenses, moving them along the lines. "You are from the Basin, I see." She looked up at him.

"Yes, ma'am. Born at the base, raised Agency," Dhawan replied proudly.

"Very commendable," the little woman said. "And to be held in such high regard in your chosen field. Entomology, is it?" She nodded and looked back at the papers as she scanned them through her spectacles. "Whatever put you on that course?" she asked.

"Well, to tell you the truth, ma'am, an old movie I saw as a child. It had giant ants in it and took place right in our backyard, which made it all very real to me," the doctor replied. He smiled and shook his head. "Little did I know it was," he added.

"In many ways, those movies were the beginning of our broader mission. One that continues today and one in which you have a key role," she replied.

"I'd do anything for the Agency," he responded.

She smiled, nodding slowly. "Such a fine young man," she said approvingly and sank into the shadow of her executive chair. "Perhaps we could start the show. I hope you have had sufficient time to reach some preliminary conclusions," she said.

"Yes, of course," Dr. Dhawan began, pushing the glasses up the bridge of his nose and clearing his throat.

"To start with, these mutations' appearance and general behavior seem in keeping with the normal ants with which we are all familiar. However, I suspect there have been some underlying changes in addition to their size, which may be of some importance. The first one I will mention is, and I am fairly certain of this, their developmental cycle has changed, sped up." The doctor paused.

"That's an alarming conclusion," Drake said. "How could you come to that? We only have a week's worth of data."

"No, no. We have more data than that," the doctor contradicted. "By comparing satellite imagery of the nest area from before the dedicated surveillance, I have mapped the disappearance of vegetation over many months in a widening orbit from the nest," he said as he opened his laptop. Henry leaned over and ran his fingers over the keyboard to cast the doctor's presentation onto the big screen.

A series of high-altitude images progressed, showing an evolution of dotted rings emanating from the entrances to the giant ant nest and growing. "And here," the doctor said as he stopped the animation, "here you can see the development of two new entrances to the colony." He moved the cursor to circle a cluster of dots in the photo. "Right there," he said. "And based on the duration of these developments, it seems, well to put it succinctly, it seems they go from egg-to-ant in record time."

"Wow," Henry said in the silent room. "How many do you think there are?" he asked.

Doctor Dhawan shook his head as he replied, "Very hard to say." He pursed his lips in thought. "You know that most of the population stays in the nest most of the time?" He thought as he spoke. "And there has been data of more foragers and patrol ants since my arrival only, what? Three days ago?"

"Four," Mrs. Messenger corrected.

"Four then," the doctor agreed. "And, based on the analysis of the colony's impact to this point, population increases come in compounded waves. The more ants there are to forage and support the nest, the more are reproduced."

"So, how many are there now?" Henry asked again.

The doctor looked at the bald man and then from Drake to Mrs. Messenger. "My best estimate is lots," he said. "And a lot more on the way."

The members of the decision-making panel exchanged glances and then brought their focus back to the doctor. "Please continue, Doctor Dhawan," Mrs. Messenger said, rolling her spindly fingers in the air.

The entomologist resumed. "I started my analysis of the situation by identifying the originating species of indigenous ant, at least what I thought was the most likely candidate. That way, the traits of the normal insects could serve as a basis to contrast and compare the behaviors and inclinations of their genetic beneficiaries, maybe even a little predictive analysis." He teased, looking to the three in turn, evidently expecting a more enthusiastic reception of his offer of prognostication.

Dr. Dhawan brought up a butcher's diagram of an ant showing labeled body segments and appendages. "Regarding the basic physiognomy of the insects, there are differences, such as an overdevelopment of the sensory receptors and a remarkable ribbed reinforcement to the exoskeleton. But other than these superficial distinctions, the proportions are the same as are the basic societal structure and behaviors, social order, activity cycles, foraging trails, and so on."

The old woman closed her eyes and listened to the doctor's remarks on ant society's hierarchical structure, subsistence strategies, and reproductive methods. The woman disconcerted the speaker, and he lowered his voice not to wake her and directed his remarks to Drake and Henry, who did their best to be interested in ant life.

"Getting back to the nest, what do you make of the isolated entrance?" Drake asked.

"Again," the doctor replied, "not unusual. The main purpose is ventilation. It is connected to the nest, yes, but primarily unused as far as access. The tunnel is used as an air conditioner shaft," he said quietly, looking at the still Mrs. Messenger, her eyes closed.

Dr. Dhawan clicked to a slide on the screen with an illustration depicting the structural features of a typical ant nest.

He pointed to a long tunnel in the drawing leading to the surface with arrows going in and out of the entrance. "As you can see by this diagram," he whispered, "ant nests, though they may seem simple at first glance, just a bunch of connected holes, but they are quite deliberately engineered, including for ventilation. After all, these little marvels have been constructing tunnels for a few hundred million years."

Dhawan looked from the two men across the table to the frail woman lost in the high-backed executive chair with her head bowed. He thought she was asleep.

He started when the woman spoke. "Tell me, Doctor," she asked from the shadows, "how confident are you of the correspondence of innate behaviors from these giants to your everyday ants? Could not the

369

mutagenesis exhibit divergent, even contradictory, processes from what you might expect?" Mrs. Messenger's eyes popped open, and she leaned forward to the table. She propped her head with a veiny hand, wrapping the side of her spotted face with long fingers as she looked to the scientist for an answer.

"Of course, you're quite right. There's always that chance. We are dealing with a complete unknown, and our inferences are drawn from only the most applicable context." The scholastic presenter motioned to the detailed cutaway of the ant colony and continued, "As I said, we have based this illustration on the local species from which I suspect these larger ants descended."

"Ascended," the woman across the table corrected. "If I have ever seen ascension, it is the genetic journey these creatures have taken." She smiled, still holding her head. "But you believe in your very smart head and entire heart that your hypotheses concerning the fundamental structuring of the tunnels and the society that inhabits them are generally correct?" Her bony fingers pressed into the side of her face.

"Yes, ma'am," he answered. "I do. And, without actually going into the nest, I can confidently say that you will find no better conjecture," the doctor added.

She put her hand down on the table and laid it over the other. "And is that conjecture as well?" she asked them.

"What is that, ma'am?" Dr. Dhawan asked.

She smiled and looked at the other members of the group at the table. "Are you conjecturing about going into the nest? If you are, that convinces me you are quite good at conjecture, indeed."

He opened his mouth and observed a moment of silence. "You want me to go into the nest?" he asked.

The elderly woman smiled and replied, "Yes, of course, young man. You are an insect expert, after all." Her hands went to the edge of the table, and she pushed herself deep into the shadow of the executive chair.

370

"But not just you. You'll be going with a few others. Some very determined people, I might add," she chuckled. "Isn't that so, Mr. Drake?" she asked, motioning at the man.

Drake nodded, tapped the tabletop twice with his index finger, and pointed at the scientist. "We're going soon, too," he said. "And want you to come along. We need someone who knows what we might expect down there. And this is a once-in-a-lifetime chance for an ant guy because we're going to wipe them out."

The doctor nodded. "As a scientist, I must say it's a shame. Such marvelous examples of life's adaptation and resiliency. But I see the practical side. There's no room for socially advanced twenty-foot predators in our world. They are extremely dangerous," he said.

The woman's hand came out of the shadow of her high-backed chair. "That's how you view them, Doctor? As dangerous predators?" she asked.

"Oh yes," he replied without hesitation. "The most dangerous that ever lived. You might think of the tyrannosaur as a fearsome apex predator – but imagine a hundred of them, a thousand, working in unison like these giants directed by group intelligence." Dr. Dhawan clicked through his presentation to show a frenzied attack of soldier ants swarming through a Brazilian forest and overwhelming and dismembering a tarantula, much larger than the individual ants.

They watched the large spider disappear on the screen, defenseless against the swarm.

"Ugh. Never thought I'd feel sorry for a spider," Henry said as the drama concluded.

"It's their innate cooperation that makes them so successful," Dhawan whispered as he watched the video. "It's what fascinates me. The impossibility of it," he said as he looked back to Drake and the shadowy old woman. "They have no real intelligence, not as we understand it. And yet, their communication and organizational abilities are uncanny. I have seen behaviors that defy reason." He shook his head. "It's only

371

their size that's kept them in their place, you know." He looked back to the video with the last frame of the army ants frozen on the screen. "Until now, anyway," he added.

The doctor leaned over the table and said, "I am fascinated by bugs. They are intricate and amazing. But I'm not some crazy egghead like in the movies. No, these mutations are so dangerous that they must be destroyed. They pose a genuine threat to us, to humans. As the dominant species of life on the Earth, we will probably be extinct…" The doctor couldn't control his emotions and buried his face in his hands.

Puzzled by the scientist's reaction, Drake asked him, "Extinct? Are you kidding, Doc? How long?"

Dr. Dhawan pulled his hands down, trying to wipe the smile from his face. "Sorry, sorry," he said, composing himself. He laughed suddenly, abruptly. "OK," he said as he regained his composure. "Ah, I'm all right now. It's just that this is a little surreal. It's just like that movie."

"Anyway, I don't know about extinct," he went on, "but I'd say an awful lot of people could get hurt. And, who knows?" he shrugged, "Maybe the whole planet could turn into one big ant nest if we don't stop them." He smiled again. "I mean THEM," he corrected himself with emphasis.

Drake lifted the water pitcher and half-filled his glass. "So, I guess you're elected, Doc," he said as he poured.

Mrs. Messenger came out of her shadow and leaned her arms on the tabletop. "And, if we can, Doctor, we'll see if we can get you a complete specimen of one of the ants for study," she offered. "I'm sure you would enjoy that."

"I certainly would," he said eagerly.

"Naturally, he would have to be dead," the old lady conditioned. The woman lifted a large purse from the floor onto her lap and began rummaging through it.

372

The doctor smiled, then said, "She. She would be dead. Just about all ants are female."

"Is that so?" the old woman responded. "Well, gender makes little difference if you are dead." She stopped churning the contents of her bag and said, "I have something else for you, young man." She pulled a bag of peanut butter cups out and pushed them across the conference table to the doctor. "To help you think," she said.

───────────── ◆ ─────────────

Syl liked driving fast.

She cruised out of White Sands and hit the highway hard, heading west. The desert flew by, and she was over the mountains in no time, running down the asphalt to the café in Las Cruces. The car windows were down, and the hot, dry air blasted in and didn't cool a thing. She liked that, too; the hotter, the better. She was just in that mood.

Syl passed anyone on the road and didn't slow down in the city. She whipped around a few corners and made a couple with a kid jump out of the crosswalk. Their faces went by in a blur of shock and outrage that made her smile.

As she blew a stop sign and slid around the corner, Syl stepped on the gas instead of slowing. She shot past the café and pulled the handbrake to skid into the parking spot behind a police cruiser against the curb.

She left the windows down and went inside. It was cool. She looked at the people, separated at their tables and eating. She saw the cop that belonged to the car outside and walked past the hostess. He looked up from his menu as she approached the deputy sheriff's table.

"Syl," he said with a smile. He motioned to the seat across his table, and she sat down.

"You're early and started without me," she said to him. "You know I don't like that."

Deputy Rosales smiled. "Guess we're not wasting any time," he answered.

The waitress came over to them with another menu and a greeting. "We have a few specials today. There are…"

"No need," Syl interrupted, watching the deputy. "Give me the double-barreled burritos. One red, one green."

"We usually don't mix the sauces," the waitress said.

Syl still didn't look at her. "It's an unusual day," she said.

The deputy looked down at the menu. "I didn't decide yet…" he said distractedly.

"Then why don't you have the same," Syl said pointedly, then looked up at the server. "Make it four barrels. His all red," she smiled venomously. "And don't forget, mine is one red and one green."

Rosales folded his menu and handed it to the young woman as she wrote the order on her pad. Syl called after her, "And a couple of Cokes, too, hon."

She looked at Rosales, put her phone on the table, and swiped it on.

"So, Luis, have you been behaving yourself?" Syl asked the lawman.

"Yes, ma'am," the deputy answered in a mischievous tone. "Nothing too felonious." He paused. "I mean, these were on the house, but that's the curse of the badge." He smiled as he took another chip from the complimentary basket.

The waitress passed by, putting their drinks on the table.

"Of course, there's always room for improvement," he added.

"Don't get ahead of yourself, Deputy," Syl admonished. "I have a purpose in seeing you." She picked up her fork and tapped the tines lightly on the table, then pushed her phone to him with it.

"Take a look at these pics," she said, moving her eyes to the screen. "See these two?"

The lawman looked at the picture of an elderly couple in a candid shot. "Uh-huh," he answered. "What about them?"

"They'll be here in a few days. They're with us," the middle-aged woman stated authoritatively.

"Those two? Really?" the deputy snorted.

"Keep your eye on them. He talks too much," Syl said.

The deputy tried to stop enjoying himself.

"I knew this wasn't just a friendly meal. There's always a point, isn't there?" he asked. He unwrapped a straw, slid it into his glass, and sipped the sweet soda while reaching for another chip from the basket.

Syl smiled at the deputy and turned the fork to bring the points down on his hand. She pressed just hard enough. "Sometimes, there's even more than one point," she cooed.

Rosales stared into her eyes as she pressed the prongs harder, then a bit harder, into the top of his hand. A wince flashed over his face. Syl moved the fork and turned her phone over as the waitress approached with their plates.

The food went on the table, and the waitress asked if they needed anything else. Syl shooed her away and picked up her knife and the fork again. She started with the green-sauced burrito.

The deputy lifted his utensils and dug into his plate, looking at the four deep indentations on the top of his left hand. He took a big forkful of his red and spicy food. He would have ordered the green. They both knew that.

They ate in silence for a few minutes before Rosales motioned to the phone with a forkful of the burrito. "What are those two here for?" he asked.

"The usual," Syl replied. "To report and do what they're told to do. He's a specialist, too. Bugs."

"Bugs?" the deputy puzzled.

Syl shrugged in response. "Bugs. What do you want from me?" She turned her phone up again, swiped to a different photo, and showed it to the deputy. "How about her? Seen her around?"

The deputy leaned over for a closer look at the telephoto shot. "No," he shook his head, still looking. "Nope. Would have remembered."

"I know that," Syl said.

"But not my type," he said as he stared at the image.

"You're right," Syl replied. "She's not. But if you see her, let me know. I want to keep tabs on her."

"What's her name?" the deputy asked.

"Nikki Carrington," Syl answered. "I'll send her details. I want to know where she is in the next twenty-four. Shouldn't be too hard," she stared at the younger man. "I'll even send you the notes on the old couple, too. Remember them?"

"Yes, ma'am," he replied with a smug smile.

Syl reached over and tapped the deputy's badge with her fork. "You know, you wear it well," she told him. "You're a natural cop."

"It's taken a while, but you get used to things," the sheriff's deputy replied.

"A job done well is its own reward," she said.

They watched each other eat.

Syl quit halfway through the second barrel. "That's enough," she said. "Let's go."

376

She palmed the fork, dropped a pair of twenties on the table, and they left the café.

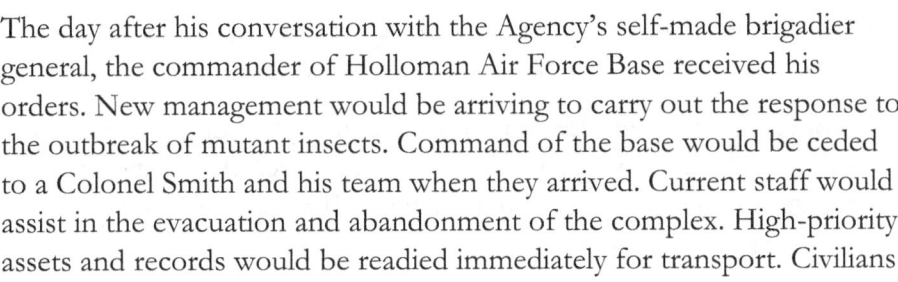

The day after his conversation with the Agency's self-made brigadier general, the commander of Holloman Air Force Base received his orders. New management would be arriving to carry out the response to the outbreak of mutant insects. Command of the base would be ceded to a Colonel Smith and his team when they arrived. Current staff would assist in the evacuation and abandonment of the complex. High-priority assets and records would be readied immediately for transport. Civilians and non-active duty personnel would be the first to be moved out.

The immensity of the directives shocked the commander. Succinct and sweeping, the orders came through proper channels and were effective immediately.

The colonel began preparations as more orders flowed in, itemizing hardware and aircraft to be moved to points around the country. Travel orders and assignments followed lists of people and personnel. The commander had never been so impressed by his military's swift and organized response and detailed knowledge of the base assets.

Of course, it wasn't the military running the show. Henry and his team were working overtime, managing chains of command while utilizing the covert nature of troop and asset deployment to keep a lid on everything. Henry got to say 'top-secret' a lot.

The military was a machine that the Agency revved up and drove wherever they wanted it to go. As more orders churned, the operation took on a life of its own. Within a few days, it was common knowledge in the legitimate ranks that the desert base was being closed due to the sudden depletion of potable water, with rumors of contamination.

In one of his last official acts as base commander, the colonel announced that tests had shown that only a few days of water left in their deep well system and trucked-in water would be inadequate to supply the complex.

The nearby reservoir was surreptitiously drained, and water trucks delivered emergency rations to further substantiate the claims of drought. Maintenance crews restricted water flow and turned off filtration to discolor the water to the entire community. The secretive teams were rewarded with immediate dispersal to distant reassignments.

"We hope," the commander announced, "that engineering may provide a solution, and we will reopen the base in the future." The water crisis was the deception the colonel broadcast; that the base might be reopened was the lie that was told to him.

Outside the base, Drake activated Agency representatives in control points of everyday life. They reduced the movement of the local population and increased monitoring of their communications. Emails, posts, telephone calls, even paper postcards and letters were examined for any mention of unusual happenings.

Traffic across the desert was purposefully slowed and diverted. From the San Augustine Pass in the mountains to the city of Alamogordo across the Tularosa Basin, travel along the connecting US 70 steadily dwindled.

Missile testing alerts and highway closures were increased to make driving inconvenient. When that wasn't happening, there was road work at both ends of the 50-mile stretch of interstate. Phone service on public bands weakened and suffered interruptions. Internet access degraded. Tech support told customers it was everything from system upgrades to sunspot activity.

Directives and alerts came down to Park Police and the sheriff's department through channels. Camping permits in the White Sands Monument were canceled due to an uptick in background radiation, and the visitor center limited their hours. The local cops were instructed to discourage hikers and sightseers in the desert, warning them of a rise in drug smuggling and attendant violence.

As the number of outsiders crossing or visiting the basin dropped, Drake's teams increased their activities. Covert reconnaissance missions located the entrances to the nest and surveilled the giant creatures' movements day and night. Data analysis predicted mutant population growth, forecast the paths of their expansion, and anticipated possibilities of interspecies overlap, or as it came to be termed, 'bug bites being' scenarios.

Drake decided on a temporary abatement plan to keep the insects' irruption in check in response to information modeling. Hunting squads were formed, tasked with the termination of giant ants, one at a time. The plan was to kill the mutations near the entrances to the nest.

It had been noted that the monsters followed no dietary restrictions, and if one of their own were injured, they would be consumed as any other grocery. Gunning down a few of the creatures for recycling shortened their nightly food-seeking forays and kept the bugs busy.

Nighttime drone surveillance was initiated to support tactical hunting trucks locating roaming ants and providing targeting information. That was when it was first discovered the giant insects did not image very well in the night vision bands. The arthropod's exoskeletons were particularly efficient at maintaining ambient environmental temperatures and absorbing the infrared range the systems used to distinguish objects in the dark. More than once, imaging indicated a monster that turned out to be a ghost, a thermal imprint of an ant resting on the sand.

The initial false-negative occurred on the first mission. The remote drone operator transmitted the position of an ant and gave the go command to Hunter One. The vehicle closed on the location, with the three-person crew buttoned up. They were instructed to attack using their top-mounted, remotely operated weapons system. The gunner watched the screen and got optics on the coordinates, but no target was evident.

Requesting and receiving confirmation of the position, the weapons technician scanned the surrounding area. All was quiet. The drone operator, miles away in the White Sands complex, suggested there may be a system malfunction as he was showing two targets a hundred yards in front of the gun truck and closing. The gunner could not confirm.

"Ah, all right, Hunter One. Due to malfunction, suggest you withdraw until we can get a clear reading on your battlespace," the remote operator advised.

The armored vehicle driver looked back at the gunner while he replied to the drone pilot, "Good idea, remote. We're backing off." The front spotlights glared over the white sand. He stepped on the gas. As the JLTV lurched forward, he told the gunner, "Once we get ourselves turned around, you take a peek outside. We're going back and light up anything that moves." The young man at the weapons console gave him the thumbs up, pulled his helmet on, and unbuckled his seatbelt.

The giant ant hit the truck hard enough to spin it almost ninety degrees in its tire tracks. The driver instinctually jammed the brake. Before he finished blurting out, "What the…" the ant hit again and flipped the 10-ton vehicle onto its roof.

The driver and passenger hung upside-down from their seats. The unbelted gun tech fell to the roof of the truck and, trying to break his fall, broke his wrist. He yelled, cursed, and kept cursing until the next crash sent the heavy truck spinning like a plate on a stick. It was hit again and knocked onto its side.

The driver released his belt, and he fell out of his seat and onto his passenger. They pushed themselves apart, and he climbed sideways to the back. The injured gunner was crammed into the back of the truck, wedged between seats. The driver crawled crabwise into the turret tunnel and unlatched, dropping the outside hatch. Pulling himself through to the gun mount, about the only thing he could see was a brilliant ellipse of white sand illuminated by their spotlight. As he stretched his arms to grab something to pull himself out, six huge bug legs drummed past the tunnel-visioned view he had of the outside through the open turret. They scuttled by quickly, throwing sand behind them. He whispered the name of his god under his breath and shrank back a few inches into the steel shaft.

The truck was hit again and then lay quiet. The driver crawled to the fifty-cal, pulled himself into firing position behind the big gun, and pushed the pedals to move the turret. It moved grudgingly but enough to point at the bug.

The huge insect stood in the light, positioning its head and wiping the air with its feelers.

The attitude of the heavy gun made adjustments difficult, but it was pointed in the bug's general direction. The driver's gloves wrapped around the trigger levers. He took a breath and squeezed. A dozen of the big steel-jacketed rounds ripped. A couple of them hit the giant ant, tearing through the legs on its left. The monster, unbalanced and unsupported, fell to its side.

The driver watched the creature try to stand. It got itself up on the stumps. The ant soldier's big head rotated and locked on the truck. The human soldier stopped breathing and sunk behind his gun as the monster screeched, charging into the white-hot spotlight, running on a tilt, dragging the shot-up side of its body through the sand, leaking gallons of bug blood. The screaming rage of the fierce assault shocked the gunner into action. He inhaled sharply and reflexively squeezed the long triggers of the .50-caliber machine gun again.

The burst blew more meat from the same side as before, in chunks the size of Sunday hams. The bug faltered and dropped, motionless except for the liquid gushing from its wounds, drizzling the sugary sand. He pushed against the heavy machine gun and the foot pedals to lift the barrel, but the weapon couldn't move any further, making the bug just out of his field of fire.

The ant got up and dragged itself to the overturned vehicle. It stamped a remaining foreleg onto the front of the truck, bouncing all twenty-thousand pounds like it was on a spring. It pulled itself up and got the other leg on the truck. The gun could not point in that direction. The driver cursed and fired into the sand, kicking up white geysers of gypsum.

The mangled creature tried to pull itself up onto the overturned truck.

The vehicle's side door flung open, and the guy riding shotgun popped out, Kalashnikov first, facing rear and oblivious to the wounded insect rising behind him.

"Look out!" the driver bellowed, "Right behind you! Look out!"

The man twisted and looked up at the head of the giant insect only a few feet over him. The soldier screamed, shooting the ant in the face as he fell into the truck and pulled the hatch down just as the coiled creature struck. Its jaws rang against the armor as it slammed shut.

Rebounding from the steel, the insect realized its wounds. The assault rifle had stitched large, wet holes across the monster's face. The giant ant pushed off the truck, staggered back, and vibrated its head furiously as if to shake off the rounds.

The driver pulled himself closer to the edge of the turret wall and peered at the ant. The huge insect shook its head again, opened its mandibles wide, and snapped them closed. A plate of the exoskeleton from the lower portion of the monster's face broke off along the perforation provided by the Kalashnikov. Everything poured out. If that bug had any thoughts for tomorrow, they were running into the sand.

The colossal bug's head drooped as the monster collapsed from its wounds and fell onto the sand.

A ticking sound began, and the rate increased to a buzz. It wasn't very loud, but there was a hum. The driver could feel it in his chest as much as he could hear it. The sound stopped and then repeated. The monster stilled, and its remaining legs curled inward.

The driver was pretty sure it was dead. He remembered to breathe and felt oxygen fill his lungs, just so he could hold his breath again.

Another ant crested the dune behind the dead bug and scrambled down the sand and through the lights of the upturned vehicle. It headed directly to its fallen nest mate. The new arrival examined the motionless ant, stroking it with its antennae, manipulating the carcass, pushing it, and touching its broken face.

The ant started a louder call that made the driver duck behind the steel, peering through a turret port at the ant as it raised the volume. Lifting his head, the driver spotted lights coming out of the desert only a second before their companion hunter unit roared into view.

Hunter Two wasn't relying on night vision. They came in with everything lit and a gunner in the tower. As they flew past the ant, they filled it with hot lead. They circled the flipped truck, doubled back on the ant-salad they left in the sand, and put a few more pounds of steel into it as they pulled up. The side doors of the truck opened, and two crewmen jumped out and ran to Hunter One.

The driver in the sideways turret called out to them as they came over, "Over here!" He dragged himself out of the tunnel onto the sand and got to his feet. "Perfect timing," he said to the new arrivals.

The side door of Hunter One popped open again, and the rifleman came out, AK leading the way. He hoisted himself onto the side of the JLTV and looked all around, sticking on the pile of ants for a moment. He laid his rifle down and went into the truck to help his injured teammate.

The lights were on the giant dead ants. The driver of Hunter One took a water bottle offered by one of the rescuers and walked to the ant pile, his hand resting on his holstered sidearm. He looked back at his overturned truck as they pulled the gunner out. He took a drink and said, "Some picnic."

From the top of the ice dune, Professor Carrington stared across the frozen plain. The wreck of the spacecraft lay at the base of the cliffs. The other expedition members crowded behind the scientist along the edge of the jagged breach in the peak.

He leaned down and rapped the descent with the handle of his ice ax. "The snow melted from the heat of the spaceship and refroze as it flowed," he said. He hit the ice again. "A frozen stream of glaze ice," he added. "We will have to be careful climbing down."

"The proverbial slippery slope," Major Polk interjected. "I'm first on the rope," the Army officer said. "You can start by lowering me down."

The major stepped off the edge, gripping the stiff sisal rope anchored by the men at the top, and stomped his crampons into the ice. He slipped a few times down the thirty-foot frozen waterfall, but it wasn't bad. At the bottom, he let go of the rope, and the next man started down.

Professor Carrington was the next man and eager to climb down the long lead. The other teams began lowering their members across the drop. Three lines of tethered men made their way down the treacherous grade to the icy plain, regrouping at the bottom to follow the ship's melt trail across the snowpack.

The major pointed to the wreck at the base of the cliffs. "Plenty of rock is showing between here and there, so my best guess is there are fewer snow holes. We'll take off the ropes from here," he said. "But watch where you're walking."

They crossed the plain to the ship's broken hull, walking between the debris melted into the trail.

Major Polk and Professor Carrington stopped at a large silver cylinder, half in the ice, scorched and dented. The Army officer reached out to touch the alien characters emblazoned on the surface, running his gloved fingers over the writing. "Amazing," he said.

"Yes," Professor Carrington replied quietly. He turned his head and watched the men moving slowly among the pieces of the ship. "Doctor

Carr," he called out when he had spotted the man he had in mind. "Doctor Carr, have you been taking readings?" he shouted.

"Yes, I have, Professor," the parka-clad man called back. He held a lunchbox-sized instrument up to read the dials. "No appreciable radiation detected," he called back to the professor.

The major pulled his hand back from the polished surface and looked up. "You needn't stop, Major. It seems safe enough," the professor smiled at him. "At least from radiation," he added.

A shout came from a different direction. "Professor Carrington!" rang through the brittle air. The call repeated, and they could see a man ahead. He had climbed onto an icy ledge and waved his arms. "Professor! Professor!" he called again, beckoning the scientist. Carrington said to the major on their way, "That's Doctor Blain who called. He's an anatomist."

The major felt an extra chill run through his parka.

A circle of scientists and soldiers had formed around Dr. Blain. Professor Carrington and the major walked up, and the audience stepped aside to make way for them.

Dr. Blaine was kneeling on the snowpack next to a naked body, badly damaged, clearly dead.

The doctor looked up at Carrington. "He's human," he said to the professor.

"Human?" Major Polk said in surprise.

"He?" Cady observed.

Professor Carrington narrowed his eyes to study the crumpled body. It was opened from the breastbone to its nether regions, and much of the insides were missing. "Are you certain it's human?" he asked the doctor.

"Well, aside from a striking resemblance to plate 62 of McClellan's Anatomy," Blaine answered, "there's this." He forced the dead man's

385

frozen arm over to show the underside. The group leaned in to see a mermaid tattoo on the forearm. She had a banner wrapped around her for modesty bearing the words 'Lust at Sea.'"

"Quite unexpected," the professor said contemplatively.

"I'll say," Major Polk exclaimed. "All this about spacemen, and what do we find? Some flash-frozen fillet of swab jockey laying here in his altogether!"

Sergeant Cady pushed past the major and took a closer look. "That's funny. I think I know this guy," he said, bringing his glove thoughtfully to his chin. Everyone looked at the sergeant. "As a matter of fact, I'm pretty sure he owes me some money." He nodded his hooded head. "Do anything to get out of paying."

"Not funny, Cady," his major said, grinning behind his muffler. "But really," Polk said to the professor, "what's he doing here?"

"This might be a clue as to how he got here," Dr. Blaine said, displaying the red bands on the cadaver's wrist. He added, "Note these ligature marks. They're on both arms and the ankles." He let go of the dead man and stood up. "One more thing is obvious," he said.

"Oh yeah?" the major replied. "And just what would that be?"

"The opening of the abdominal cavity," Blaine answered, "is not the result of a crash. It's surgical."

"I knew you were going to say something I did not want to hear," Major Polk replied. He leaned on his ice ax and stared across the plain at the looming hull of the spaceship. "All right, let's break it up," he told the group. "And cover up that poor son-of-a-mother so we can get back to our jobs."

The major caught Carrington's sleeve as he turned to leave. "Feeling like one of those new world natives yet, Professor?" he asked.

Just a matter of days from the initial sighting of the mutated giants in the desert, and here he was, rolling through the night in the command vehicle of an armored column, heading for the entrance to the nest to destroy the colony.

Drake absently pressed his fingers against the headset covering his ear as he swayed in the seat with the truck's movement. The interior lights dimly illuminated the personnel, weapons, and communications equipment, submerging everything in a low green glow to preserve their night vision. He listened to the talk between the lead and follow battle tanks and the armored trucks between them as he watched a real-time satellite feed of their progress on the monitor. Their vehicle was the second blurry phosphor moving in a line over a gray backdrop with topographic enhancements.

The column spaced out as they traveled to the nest entrance, with one tank leading the line and another at the end. Six heavily armed and armored vehicles carried tactical and scientific personnel, following the ant's sugar-white trail to the nest. The lead tank moved with its hatch popped and the commander riding high, swinging a thousand-watt nightlight over the desert. The trucks ran their spots over the sands, illuminating everything for a mile around with blazing blue-white beams.

Halfway to their target, the lead tank's light fell on two scout ants moving down the dune toward the column. The 70-ton M1 stopped so fast that the command JLTV following veered out of the tread tracks to avoid a collision. The battle tank turret rotated its 120mm tank gun to the insects. The tank captain locked his light on the bugs while communicating with his crew and the vehicle behind them. A light from one of the trucks hit the bugs; other beams scanned the surrounding dunes.

As the ants closed the distance, the decision was made to try the remotely operated, top-mounted .50 caliber machine gun against the creatures as a test of the onboard targeting system. The commander acknowledged, pulled his light off them, and shut it down. He slid back into the turret and pulled the hatch closed. The other top gunners and lookouts did the same, buttoning up to protect themselves and relying on their electronic targeting systems. Their external lights went out.

Inside the leading tank, the gunner switched to the thermal targeting system to fix the insects.

Drake's voice came through the headset to the tank commander and gunner. "What have you got?" he asked them.

The gunner replied, "Kind of murky, hard to see them. Cycling through targeting options and enhancements." The triggerman was quiet for a moment while he worked, then continued. "All right, that's probably going to be about as good as we get. You see what I'm seeing?" he asked.

Drake responded as he peered at the monitor showing what the tank saw. "Affirm, Lion One. Doesn't look like proximity is helping our image. Is it enough to target?"

"No, sir," answered the voice over the radio. "Not authoritatively. And we couldn't rely on this in a mixed field."

Drake drummed his fingertips on the arm of his chair in front of the electronics. He leaned closer to the monitor and pushed the microphone closer to his mouth. "All right, Lion One. Back outside and take them with the fifty manually. Lion Two, you're outside, too. Rest of the column, stay shut, lights low, and be ready to move." Drake sat back in his chair and watched the screen.

The man in the passenger seat held a Zastava assault rifle on his lap and sat silently, staring out of the window and tumbling a large caliber bullet between the fingers of his right hand. The young man nearest Drake typed and watched his monitor. The driver stared through the windshield at the back end of the tank, waiting for it to move.

The Abrams hatch opened, and the tank commander climbed into the light shining from below. He got comfortable and turned the machine gun in the ants' direction.

"Enough of this e-lectronic targeting horse manure," the tankman said to himself. He flipped a toggle, and the targeting spotlight lit up. "Lights and lead," he whispered as he illuminated the monster ants. They were moving quickly, making a beeline for his column.

The creatures stopped when the light hit them, about a hundred yards from the machine gun. The tank captain spoke into his comm set. "Engaging," he said softly as his hands wrapped around the spade grips and tightened around the squeeze triggers.

A hundred hammers a second of the heavy machine gun split the night air and sent spent brass jangling across the tank's steel skin as the rounds ripped the monsters apart, dropping them into the moonlit sand.

"Easy peasy, lemon squeezy," the man in the turret said under his breath. He had expected more from giant ants.

Cap moved his light, scouring the dunes. Lion Two was doing the same at the other end of the column.

Lion One's light went full circle and came back to the hunks of dead insect. "Clear to go," the tank commander relayed to Drake and the column. His turret rotated forward. "Move out," he said into his mouthpiece.

The M1 rolled through the sand, following the well-defined ant trail to the ventilation shaft. They picked up speed and followed a path parallel to the highway between two tall dunes; the one on their left shielded the roadway, and on the right, a tall dune stood before the vast desert that stretched across the desert basin to the far mountains.

The heavy vehicles churned up chalk clouds so dense that the mechanized column spread further apart for better visibility. Only the tanks used their searchlights. The windows and cameras were coated, and the convoy reduced speed to kick up less dust.

389

"Everyone's riding blind," the young man next to Drake said to him. "The only working tech is the windshield wipers," he added.

Drake nodded and asked how far it was to the entrance.

Link glanced at his computer screen and replied, "Mile point two. In position in four and a half minutes."

Drake nodded and spoke into his microphone. "We'll be on target in less than five. Lion One, you're first. Keep us covered while we catch up," Drake said.

"Roger that," the lead tank commander replied. He wiped the chalk from his goggles and played the searchlight across the trail and the tall dune walls. He looked back and saw the command vehicle's running lights faintly in the thick dust clouds.

The driver's voice came through the tank commander's headset. "Just about there, Cap," he said. "Can you see anything ahead?"

Cap swept the dunes. "As a matter of fact, I do," he responded. The light found the entrance to the nest; a gaping mouth opened in the face of the dune.

"Right on the money, slow to stop, and put the brights on," he told his crew. "Bring us up a little further, Junior, and run us right," he directed from the turret. "A little more," he coaxed the driver. The massive tank pivoted agilely in the sand and rolled forward. "Stop! You got it, right on our mark."

The tank commander swiveled his spotlight over the slopes to be sure there weren't any bugs crawling up behind them.

Drake's command truck arrived and continued formation several yards from the tank. Now, two spotlights were probing the empty sands and the cavernous mouth of the nest.

The tank captain parked his light on the opening. "Column, this is Lion One. We are in place. Look for our lights and assume your position on arrival. It's pretty dusty up here, and so far, we're alone, so take it easy."

390

Cap swiveled the turret to bring the main gun to bear on the opening. It was large enough to drive a tank through.

The JLTVs pulled into formation and positioned themselves around the nest entrance, pointing at the hole. The dust followed the vehicles, swirling into their lights and enveloping the invaders assembling around the mutant's back door.

As Drake climbed out of his seat, he tapped his tech officer on the shoulder. "Link, once we take delivery, get the drone in there so we can see what's going on," he said to the young man at the keyboard. "We'll set the drop."

"Yes, sir," the young man barely replied, absorbed in his screen.

Drake pushed the hatch open and dropped onto the sand, followed by his large assistant. They walked to the front of the truck and looked into the ant hole along the beams of the light. The last truck in the convoy pulled into place, taking its position in the ring around the ant hole.

They walked toward the nest opening and stopped halfway. The big man adjusted the ammo sack hanging from his right side and then the one on his left.

Drake faced the ant colony entrance and looked at his large ex-sergeant out of the corner of his eye. "Got enough ammunition, Max?" he asked.

"No," Max grunted as he shifted the weight of the bulky bags and checked his Zastava again.

From far off in the desert, a call of a scouting ant carried over the night air. Max stopped checking his weapon, looked up, and repeated, "No."

The second Abrams clattered into position at the end of the line. The tank pivoted in the sand, turning in place to face the entrance, and moved forward into position, completing the arc of lights and weaponry.

Drake and Max were inside the ring, closer to the hole. "Throw out the marker," Drake said.

Max walked several yards away, struck up a couple of flares, and dropped them on the sand.

"All right, we're all here," Drake said into his mic, broadcasting to all the trucks in the convoy. "Only waiting for the guest of honor. Link, tell them to bring it in. The marker is on the ground."

"Roger that," Link replied. A few seconds later, he came back. "Air One acknowledged. Flares fixed. Coming in."

Max hustled back from the red fire and growing column of flare smoke.

The beat of the rotorcraft rose in volume as it arrived, hovering hidden high above and bringing a dark windstorm of dust and smoke, blowing like hell and screaming like a tornado, but they still couldn't see the chopper.

A shaft of white light shot down from the maelstrom. Sheets of dust roared through the beam, and the flare smoke was pushed back to the ground. Max pointed into the chaos, then lowered his arm to protect himself against the sand blown by the wash. The two men turned away from the swirling dust as the chopper hovered over the target flares.

A bright yellow cylinder descended in the shaft of light, so bright it seemed to radiate. The heavy drum, lowered by cable from the helicopter, thudded into the sand a few feet from the flares. "Whoa," Max shouted over the noise of the rotors. "You'd think they'd be more careful with that."

Drake laughed in the swirling winds, cupped his headset to listen, and shouted a reply into the microphone. The cable disconnected and retracted, and the light from above snapped off. The sound and fury of the phantom helicopter dissipated, and the two men lowered their arms and stood with the new arrival as the storm abated.

Drake and Max trotted over to the bright yellow oil drum lying in the sand. There was a panel with a keyhole in the middle, steel handles through hoops on both ends, and the trefoil symbol denoting a radiological hazard emblazoned on both ends and repeated around the center.

Max looked admiringly and shifted his heavy rifle to his other hand. He reached out to touch one of the symbols on the drum with his fingertips. "Wow," he said. "I never had one of these before."

Drake looked at the rapt man, shook his head, and spoke into his radio. "Everyone going in, fall out. We're all here now, so let's get this show on the road." Truck doors opened, and the soldiers climbed out, bristling with weapons.

Drake turned to Max and nudged him. "Take an end," he said. "Let's see how heavy this thing is."

They reached down to the handles and lifted the cylinder like a stretcher. "Not too bad," Max said, testing its weight with a few pumps.

"Let's see what you think when we're dodging monster ants and lugging this down a bug hole," Drake answered as they put it down in the sand.

Max nodded at the troops and said, "That's why we brought those big guys."

The company formed up at the flares, clustering around the two men and the yellow barrel. Drake turned to the group and spoke. "All right, you all know what we're here to do. The plan's simple: we go in, come out, and leave this behind." He patted the can twice.

Drake looked across the faces of the small group. He pointed to the trucks arrayed around the entrance to the ant colony. "The agents up here are doing two things for us; they're keeping our exit secure and helping us talk to each other underground. We're using a TTE communication system; these trucks have the antennas and amplifiers to make it work. They can relay our message throughout the nest system. Because they're mobile, communications can follow us down there and make sure we keep in contact." Drake paused and added earnestly, "You know how important I feel meaningful communication is to any successful operation."

One of the ranks called out, "I got a question!"

"Who cares?" Drake snapped back. The troops laughed.

"You've all been on bug patrol in the past week or two," he continued, "so you know what we're up against. What we don't know is how many of them are down there. You've all been over this already, and I know you're itching to go, so just remember, soldiers look out for our civilians; they're unarmed. Doctor Dhawan is our ant expert. He's up front with me." Drake waved the doctor out of the group; he stepped forward, eyes on the bright yellow cask.

Drake next indicated a conspicuously out-of-place man and woman standing next to each other in a crowd bristling with weapons. He patted the steel drum and said, "Mr. Ames and Ms. Medina are with us to fine-tune this hardware once we have it in place. They may end up directing the fireworks tonight, so keep them safe." The two smiled nervously as a few of the militia craned their necks to get a look at them.

Nearby, a woman and two men dressed in blue fatigues and gray helmets stood together. Drake addressed the group. "You may have noticed Oberst Nygard and two operatives from her special tactics group. They are from Norway and add real talent to our force," he said and gave the thumbs-up to the trio. They looked over the force in return and exchanged a few tentative nods.

Drake looked back at the troop. "That's about it. We could get underway or waste our time here if anyone has a question."

One of the soldiers up front spoke up and asked, "Still no fire, no grenades, right?"

Drake smiled at the woman with a bandana who asked the question as she snapped a jungle clip into her AR. He shook his head, "Not for everyone. And flamethrowers are not a good fit in a tunnel. As far as explosives, Burner over there is carrying a few firecrackers if we need them." He pointed to a tall, unfriendly-looking fellow toward the back. "He'll take care of whatever needs blowing up," Drake added. "And, for anything that gets overlooked, we have this." He patted the yellow drum again.

A sudden buzzing caused the group to turn. A few brought their weapons up. The buzz rose in volume when a quadcopter shot out of a truck and flew over the crowd. It rose to take a deep dive and swooped into the ant hole.

All the faces tracked the drone into the nest entrance; then most looked back to Drake as he continued. "That's our tunnel recon drone," Drake said, "it's going to take a look inside. Back to weapons, you may have noticed on the way here that concentrated firepower does the trick. Big bullets work on the ants. That's why Mr. Grunewald has us packing the LMGs along," he nodded to Max.

"SAWs," Max corrected.

Drake listened to his headset. "All right," he said to the group, "the drone shows clear. Time to go. Lift team, grab the keg." Two really big guys lessened the crowd when they stepped forward, shouldered their weapons, and lifted the pole handles stuck through rings welded to the drum.

"Let's get going," Drake announced. He started toward the opening and put his hand on Dr. Dhawan's shoulder to move him along. Max was right behind him with his M90 pointing the way. The pair of tackles carrying the steel kettle followed, and two dozen or so others fell in behind. Everyone was quiet as they pushed against the sugary sand to the rim of the opening.

At the edge, Drake pulled a flashlight from his belt and beamed it into the blackness. His light played across the excavated floors and walls and got lost in the dark deeper down. The slope of the tunnel looked easy enough to walk, and the ridges that provided footholds for the mutants worked for the humans, too.

The lights from the armor converged on the crowd standing on the brink. Drake looked past the group to the circling vehicles. He touched his shoulder mounted radio and said, "We're going in now. Expect communications fade in about ten minutes. And be ready for evac when we return."

"Lion One, Roger. Good luck, Drake. We'll be waiting for you. Good luck to you all," the tank commander signed off.

Drake took a deep breath. Humid air floated from the hole, pulling dank organic odors from the nest. He nodded imperceptibly and stepped over the edge onto the incline and into the ant colony.

Sergeant Cady took a rolled blanket from the pack of one of his soldiers and unfurled it over the mariner's frozen corpse, tucking the edges under the stiff body to keep it in place.

As the sergeant finished covering the corpse, he looked up at the major. "Seems like a long way to go for this guy to get carved up," Cady said.

The major's snorkel hood nodded.

The sergeant looked down at the blanket. "I hope we run into one or two of those spacemen," he said. "I'd like to give them an anatomy lesson."

Polk lifted his gloved hand to point to the main wreckage. "Let's go, Cady," he said. "Right now, we still have humans to worry about." The two rejoined the trek across the uneven ice to the ship, wrecked on the rocky shore of the frozen sea.

The major stopped and pulled his hood back and his scarf off his face, relying on his knitted cap and exertion to keep his head warm so he could light a cigarette. Clouds of steam and smoke hung in the still air behind them as they made their way to the wreck.

"I don't like the cold anymore," Polk said as they drew closer. The officer stopped, squinting over the frozen field, and blew smoke at the ship. "That is some sight, is it not, Sergeant Cady?" the major asked.

The sergeant stopped and moved his attention from picking his path through the debris to look at the big picture. "It is large, but I could have done without it," he replied.

The bright metal hull was enormous, even on the immense stage of the Arctic.

The craft was fish-shaped, pinched at the front and back, wider in the middle. There were large windows for the pilots in the tapered nose. Heading aft, the fuselage widened into a broader profile to provide maximum payload area.

More than anything else, the ship resembled the silvered dirigibles from decades before.

The spacecraft was broken at the last third of the long hull. It had split open, exposing a cross-section of six twisted decks, baring jagged edges and bent beams to the Earth's Arctic sun.

The expedition members gathered at the breach in the ship. Carrington stood at the front of the group, staring up at the mangled tiers of new technologies hanging over his head. He leaned on his ice ax and breathed heavily from the arduous hike across the wide plain in the thin, frigid air.

Soldiers had broken off under Sergeant Cady's direction and gotten to work in a clear area a few dozen yards away. An improvised table was set up, and a radio squawked as a pair of operators worked the set.

Major Polk watched the sky to the east, and a plane appeared, flying low out of the bright morning sky. It banked to track parallel to the bluffs and head for their position.

Faces turned upward to watch the plane as it swept in, bomb doors open. Three large containers fell out on the first pass and hit the frozen ground hard, tumbling end over end into the debris field as the B-17 roared only a few hundred feet over them. The sergeant pointed, and soldiers ran over the ice and rocks to the drop and began pulling the tightly wrapped bales open.

The bomber circled to come back over the site. It came in higher on this pass, and two long tubes dropped out, instantly sprouting white parachutes to slow their fall. Even with the chutes, they fell fast and hit forcibly, hard enough that one stuck upright in the ice and the other hit rock, ricocheting dangerously, causing a couple of the GIs to jump for cover. It torpedoed a bus-sized piece of the spaceship in the debris field and smashed to a stop.

The sergeant bounded over to his men, got them back on their feet, and signaled OK to the major, who signed off with the bomber, giving them a wave as they turned and disappeared into the blue skies. Polk left the radio, walked over to Carrington, and stood beside him. They both looked up into the alien craft's open decks.

"It's a lot bigger in person," he said to the professor.

Carrington turned to face Major Polk. He exhaled steam into the biting air. "It is, Major," he said. "It's overwhelming."

The major nodded, leaning back to look up at the ship.

"I have to say, Professor, I thought you'd be halfway through this thing already," Polk said, eyeing the scientist. "You haven't even set foot inside yet."

"As I said, Major, it's somewhat overwhelming," the professor replied. "One must consider...."

"Oh, I'm with you," the officer interjected, looking down. He toed a twisted piece of metal frozen in the ice. "Hell, the way you people work, this little scrap could keep you busy for years." The major popped the fragment free with the steel tip of his ice ax and kicked it a few feet away. "I don't know how you're going to handle all of this," the officer wondered, waving the axe over the expansive view of the spaceship.

A shrill whistle turned them to watch the soldiers unrolling long pieces of printed material pulled from the airdropped bales and staking them to the ice. Two men stood reviewing large sheets of paper, and next to them, Sergeant Cady was barking out orders.

The professor asked what was happening. "Camouflage, Professor," the major responded. "We're covering up the scene of the crime. Some to obscure, some to mislead. By the end of the day, this will look like one of our transports crashed. At least to the Reds." He looked up and pointed his thumb skyward. "They're always looking over our shoulder."

"Very prudent," the professor approved. "It is paramount this event remains secret."

The officer raised his eyebrows. "You surprise me, Carrington. I had you for one of those 'this knowledge must be shared with all humanity' guys."

"Humanity, Major, is far from ready for this," the professor said, looking up at the hulking wreck. "It is nothing less than providential that this has happened in such an isolated area under our complete control. This was fate."

Polk half-turned his head to look at the scientist out of the corner of his eye.

"I trust you will be covering and disguising the main part of the wreckage as well," the professor said. He stared into the torn hull in front of them. "And keeping everyone involved on ice, as it were," Carrington added, turning to the major. "No one can leave or communicate anything about this expedition or our findings for any reason. And that applies to the personnel at our base camp, as well. It should be made clear to all that any infraction will be swiftly met with the harshest possible consequences. The absolute harshest consequences."

Major Polk nodded. The professor surprised him.

Others from the expedition's academic contingent began gravitating to the professor and the entrance torn in the ship. Several of them congregated behind the bearded intellectual. He did not acknowledge them but stared intently into the shadowed interior. Carrington blew a cloud of steam into the cold air at regular intervals, and then they stopped. He stepped forward, walking over the rubble of churned earth and ice up the small hill to the side of the ship, stopping at the threshold. Disregarding the numbing cold, he removed a glove and touched the mangled metal opening. He ran his bare hand along the scalloped edge.

Professor Carrington paused with his hand connected to the craft. He nodded quietly and said over his shoulder to the group, "Gentlemen, let us begin our investigations." The professor walked through the breach and into the ship.

He stepped from the ice and soil onto the smooth surface of the spaceship's inner deck. The area he had entered was large and became larger as his eyes adjusted from the blinding white snow to the first deck's half-light.

There was no evidence of active power, neither light nor sound. It was still.

Carrington's heart pounded, and he didn't breathe. The enormity of the event intensified his senses and degraded his thought process. His impressions and inferences fueled a cascade of implications and consequences. The scientist's body stood, but his mind fell into darkness.

The professor released the handle of his ice ax, and it fell to the floor without a sound. The only thing he could hear was a steady tone in the note of G. He swayed in place, ready to fall, and reached his hand into the empty air, reflexively to steady himself and stay upright. His left foot stepped back for balance, and a hand gripped him from behind, clamping around his shoulder, and then another grabbed the top of his arm.

The sudden contact snapped the professor back to his surroundings, and familiar voices called his name. He felt his weakness replaced by deep breaths and a better connection to the local reality.

"Professor! Professor Carrington!" the man holding his arm repeated quietly but urgently. "Arthur, you should sit down," another voice said.

He turned his head from side to side to look at the faces of his colleagues as they came into focus. They led him to the wide ramp of the elevated walkway to the next level and sat him on the edge of the incline. They opened his parka at the neck. It was much warmer in the ship.

One of his fellow explorers pulled a flat metal flask from his coat pocket and held it for him. "I think you could use a bracer, my friend," Dr. Carr said, "Doctor's orders." The others nearby encouraged him. The professor sipped the warming whiskey and held the flask out.

"One more, Arthur, for good measure," Carr said, pushing the bottle back to Carrington. "And then I think we could all use the same." The professor took another swallow, then handed it back.

Dr. Carr put a comforting hand on Professor Carrington's shoulder. "As difficult as it may be, Arthur, we must be measured in our approach to this project," he said to the scholar.

The others concurred quietly, passing the spirits as they turned their heads to wonder at their surroundings. The ship had come to rest at an angle, and the interior's uneven attitude emphasized the surreal setting.

Hundreds of cubes pyramided from floor to ceiling at the far end of the chamber where the crash had collected them. Near the breach in the hull through which they entered, a warehouse-sized door was framed in the bulkhead, though no trace of the door was discernable on the exterior. At the center of the deck was a waist-high wall forming a ring ten meters in diameter. A construct of dozens of thick black tubes projected upward from within the circle and then bent at the ceiling high above, running off in all directions.

One of the men walked up the gangway a few feet. He stood behind Professor Carrington and reached up to grasp the railing that sided the ramp to the walkway.

The bar was even with his shoulder as his gloved hand wrapped around the cold alien metal. "If this is a handrail, our visitors seem to be on the rather large size," he said to the group. Everyone looked at the rail and the rest of the deck area, especially into the shadows. Dr. Carr took another swallow from the flask before he pushed it back into his parka.

Professor Carrington stood and took his ice ax from the group. "Thank you all," he said. "I feel much better now." He started up the ramp, smiling at Dr. Carr and patting him on the shoulder as he passed. "The answers await," Carrington said, walking up the incline to the next deck. "Perhaps we will come across the occupants and will no longer have to rely on our conjectures."

Halfway along the acclivity to the walkway above, Major Polk's voice echoed across the chamber. "Professor Carrington!" the major called out. "Hold on a second!" The contingent of armed men cautiously entered the ship and crossed the deck to where the scientists stood with Sergeant Cady and four other soldiers, backlit by the bright snow outside.

Major Polk looked up at Carrington and said, "It would be a good idea to take an escort along. And, until we have this area secured, I'm asking all of you not to go off on your own, not until we know the lay of the land here. This is for your own good, that's all," the officer said, anticipating objections.

Dr. Carr was the first. "Major, we're quite a sensible group, and to be constrained at such an exciting discovery, well, I don't know if that's a very practical approach," he said.

"Practical or not, Doctor, I'm going to insist that no one goes exploring this, this…" the major motioned with his right hand in the air.

"Spaceship," Professor Carrington suggested.

"Spaceship," the major agreed. "Nobody is to go off on his own through this spaceship without one of my men along." The major pushed his hood back and pulled his scarf down. He looked up and around, taking in the shadows and size of the first deck. "Make that two of my men," he corrected. "Everyone stays close," he said, removing his gloves and unzipping his parka. Polk reached in to pull out his pack of smokes. He put a cigarette in his mouth and lit up. "I appreciate your cooperation," he said with the exhaled smoke.

"But, Major Polk," one of the scientists contended, "if we simply want to look through the ship, are we supposed to arrange for...." A sudden metallic clang rang from the deep shadows.

The group jumped as one, startled by the sharp sound in the vast echo chamber. The scientist who was voicing his protest ducked down at the clattering noise.

They peered at the round fountain of tubes to see what was on the other side of the cylinders. The sharp metal ring was struck again, followed by Sergeant Cady walking from behind the obscuring structure, idly swinging his ice ax like a walking stick.

He looked innocently at the group of scholars and said, "Oh, sorry. I was just wondering what this thing was made of." He rapped the head of his ax against the short wall surrounding the pipes growing from the center to produce another ringing report.

The major coolly blew another cloud into the chilly air. He looked back at Carrington halfway along the ramp. The professor met his eye and nodded perceptibly.

"The major is quite right," Carrington said. "We are investigating the unknown, and if safety precautions are not observed, our efforts may be diminished."

"I'm glad you agree, Professor," the major replied, then addressed the scientists. "Gentlemen, I want you to understand what's on the line." Blue tobacco smoke uncoiled over his head and hung in the cold light filtering past the fissure in the hull.

"This might be the biggest thing in history. A lot of you have said as much, and maybe it is." Major Polk took a long drag on his smoke, then squeezed the burning ember from the cigarette with his fingers, dropping it to the ground to grind away with the toe of his boot.

"But as big as it is, there is only one rule. This is a top secret project, and the absolute rule is you must keep it secret." He rolled the cigarette butt between his fingers, sprinkling the remaining tobacco to the floor.

He wadded the smoke-stained paper into a tiny ball, pinching it in his thumb and index finger. "And if you leak secret information, I will shoot you." He flicked the paper into the shadows.

A couple of the scientists smiled, almost laughing at the perceived exaggeration. They looked at the others, not laughing.

"I am not joking, gentlemen, and I do not know how to put it any plainer. If you leak anything about what we're doing here, I will shoot you dead," Polk pronounced gravely. No one laughed this time.

Many in the group looked up the gangway to Professor Carrington. He said nothing. There were a few murmurs, but no real objections were voiced.

The major assumed command. "Thank you, gentlemen. Believe me, I understand how important this is, and we're all on the same side here. It's your safety and the security of our mission that are my primary concerns," he said. "I trust I do not have to remind you of the unfortunate fellow we found outside."

"Now, if you would like to continue up there," he said, pointing to the next level, "these men will be happy to escort you." Four of his soldiers walked by the major onto the ramp with their rifles up, weaving their way through the eggheads to the front of the line.

The army officer called after them, "Professor Carrington, please choose the route and take charge of this contingent." Sergeant Cady walked over to stand by the major and watched the men winding up the ramp to the next level. Two more soldiers came through the ruptured hull and

404

were directed by Cady to take up the rear of the ascent. They ran up the ramp and fell in, their weapons at the ready.

Flashlights strobed the cavern walls as the group cautiously entered the inclined passageway into the nest. No one spoke over the slow drum of their muffled footfalls on the compacted sand.

A hum grew to a whine from the subterranean blackness before they had gone fifty yards. Drake stopped the squad, snapping the order into his microphone and their earpieces as he held a hand up. The troop stopped and just breathed and listened. They pointed their gun lights ahead. A buzz came from the darkness, and a ball of lights appeared down the shaft, quickly growing into the drone flying straight at them on its way out, rushing over their heads to the exit.

A few ducked as they watched it zoom past, fly up the shaft, and out of the tunnel. "Looked scared," a voice from the group said. "That thing was going like a bot out of hell." There were a few laughs.

Drake nodded as he listened to his headset, then turned to the group and said, "Recon saw nothing down there, at least as far as it could go." He signaled them to move on, and Max spread the word to get them going again.

The passage went steadily down. Dr. Dhawan pointed out the tunnel was remarkable in its consistency of construction. Regularly spaced ribs ran across the floor and up the walls to facilitate the creature's footing. The tunnel maintained the same diameter over its length. The shaft was twice the height of the tallest soldier in the group, and the width allowed them to walk three at arm's length as they infiltrated the nest.

"Remarkably uniform," Dr. Dhawan whispered as he dragged his fingertips over the smooth white wall. "Miles and miles of this processed material, that's a new development. Some sort of cemented sand mixture." He stopped to examine the substance with his light, but the soldier behind kept him moving.

405

"Don't hold up the line, Doc," she said, swinging her machine gun to the right and clapping him on the shoulder to urge him forward. Dhawan turned from the wall and smiled sheepishly at the muscular woman as he got back in step.

Drake was at the head of the line, and Max walked to his right. Dr. Dhawan stepped it up to join them in the front rank and interposed himself.

A few steps behind them, the woman carrying the LMG followed in line with two other grunts. After them came the big guys hauling the yellow can with the two techs, Ames and Medina, in tow. The rest of the parade comprised paramilitary hires shouldering climbing gear and heavy weapons.

Drake looked past the doctor to Max and said, "Mapping shows a tunnel connects about three hundred yards from here." He motioned forward with his light. "We'll take that down," he said.

Max acknowledged, replying, "Mapping is going to run out soon. Time to put some eyes in front of us." As they walked down the tunnel, he played his gun light from wall to wall in the ink ahead. "They could find that hole for us, too," he added.

Drake nodded.

"Angel, Santa, take point, a hundred yards ahead," Max growled over his shoulder.

A pair from the ranks double-timed it past the front row to hustle down the tunnel. As they passed Max, one of them said, "Remember, man, it's dark down there. Don't start shooting until I stop screaming."

"You'll stop," Max said as the man jogged past. "Remember, you're looking for a hole down there, so don't fall in," he shouted after the pair as they trotted by. "And radio check once you're in position."

The advance team's lights jumped back and forth as they ran into the darkness, followed by their footsteps bouncing down the burrow.

Their lights stopped moving. Then, one of the points signaled in a slow arc, and Angel's voice came over the headset, "In position, do you copy?" Max acknowledged and told them to proceed.

Drake watched the lights ahead getting smaller and said, "Move out," quietly into his mic. They moved on, following the scouts.

Slow minutes were counted in steps as they dogged the lights down the steady descent. The lights stopped moving ahead, and the troop closed the distance.

Everyone with their earpiece in heard the scouts report they had found the next tunnel entrance. "Roger," Drake replied. "Wait for us."

As they got closer, their lights collected on the two men. They held their hands in front of their faces, and Santa waved his arm. He called out in annoyance, "All right, all right – cut your brights!" Some spotlights lowered, others went up along the top of the tunnel, and some went into the dark hole behind them as the group bunched together.

"That's the hole?" Drake called out as the troop approached.

"Must be it," Angel answered.

"It's more like a side door," Santa added.

The lead men ran their beams around the rim of the entrance to the next tunnel. "Looks like it's steeper, about the same size as this one," Angel said.

Drake walked through the doorway, beaming his light into the deep shaft. "It is steeper. That's just what we want, get us deep that much faster," he said. Max and the doctor stepped into the side tunnel and combined their lights on the incline. "Looks like it bends down there," Dr. Dhawan said as he peered into the ant hole.

"Let's go," Drake said as he started down. "And you two," he indicated the scouts, "You did such a good job, you can do it again. Back in front," he said to them. The pair looked at each other and then turned to double-time it down the new shaft.

The rest filed into the tunnel, everyone playing follow the leader.

The woman in the second rank carrying the light machine gun walked closer to Dr. Dhawan. She tapped him on the shoulder and said, "You know, Doc, I was expecting more vertical climbing. But so far, not so bad. But you know what I mean. When you think of an ant nest, you think of holes that go straight down into the dirt, but these seem more on the level."

The doctor nodded as he marched. "That's true, Miss or Ms...." he looked back at the woman.

"Call me Vic," she said.

He looked at the savage weapon she cradled in her bare, tattooed arms and smiled politely. "That's true, Vic. But it makes sense that these ants changed the way they dig their nests due to their size. They can't climb up and run around like the little ants we see in the garden. They are much bigger, aren't they?" he explained. "When creatures change how they look, they can also change how they do things. That makes sense, right?"

Looking at the doctor, she nodded and reached up to put her hand on his shoulder as he walked. She leaned in and said quietly, "Listen good, bug boy. Talk to me like that again, and I'll accidentally air-condition your sorry self and leave you here for your bugs to chew on. Understand?"

The doctor opened his mouth to say something, but she put her finger to her lips, and he didn't. She patted his shoulder and fell back to her row, pushing him forward.

Drake watched the scout lights swaying far ahead. They disappeared. Max said that maybe they turned a corner. Nothing came from them over the comm, and there was no shooting, so the troop continued.

They reached the bend in the road. They could see the lights down the tube as they rounded the curve. The scouts signaled the group forward over the comm. "We're waiting for you here. Got something new. Can't go on."

Drake frowned and said into his microphone, "All right. Hold position. We'll be there in a few minutes." They picked up the pace to join their scouts.

"What do you have now?" Drake called out as they neared.

"Take a look." Angel played his light over the cave floor in front of them. "We almost walked into it," he said.

As the others joined, more beams followed, then spread out to illuminate a wide band of a greasy-looking slime across the floor, up the walls, and over the tunnel roof. It was a thick deposit, an inch or so in depth. The thick liquid dripped in slow motion here and there in long, viscous strands from above. The stream of goo on the floor was ten feet wide.

Drake stood closest to the muculent ring. "You guys didn't touch it?" he asked.

"No, sir," the taller scout replied. "Came close, but Angel spotted it. Doesn't look like the type of thing you'd want to touch." The lights penetrated the cloudy gunk banding the shaft and barring their way.

Max found a good-sized rock and pried it out of the cavern wall with his knife. He tossed it into the slime. It didn't splash, it just stuck. "Looks gooey," he said. "And too wide to jump."

"I don't think you'd want to fall short either," Dr. Dhawan said as he leaned over the mass, looking closely with his flashlight. He straightened up, reached into his safari pocket, and pulled out an energy bar. The scientist peeled back the wrapper, broke off a chunk, and said, "This should be interesting, if I am not mistaken."

The bug doctor reached over the goo and dropped the chunk of food into the glop at the focus of his light. Wisps of steam puffed out, and foam developed wherever protein snack met slime.

"It's quite corrosive," the doctor said. "A very efficient barrier." He squatted in front of the caustic carpet and studied the foaming treat. "It may be more than that, too," he added.

"Such as?" Drake asked.

"Well, the by-products of the reaction may serve an additional purpose," he said as he twirled his fingers, tracing the steamy wisps rising into the beams of the flashlights. "They may send a chemical message, an alarm, serving as a signal of a trespasser, though chances are the interloper would be in an unfortunate state. But this chemical reaction could alert the nest. Hopefully, not in amounts as minuscule as this," he added.

"Bugs do things like that?" Max asked.

"Naturally. Bugs do many amazing things," Dr. Dhawan replied, looking up from the disappearing morsel. He looked back at the bubbling chew and pointed at it. "To them, Mr. Grunewald, this is you."

Drake rubbed his chin and looked across the acid moat. "We better do something amazing, too. We have to get past this crud." He looked back at the troop and the two bruisers carrying the drum. They had set it down, and one was sitting on it.

"We have shovels, right, Max?" Drake asked.

"You don't go into a hole without a shovel," Max answered. "Yep, we have a couple of trenchers."

Drake ran his light over the slime and said, "Get them digging. We'll bury a path across this crap with a foot of sand."

Max nodded and impolitely suggested that some of the individuals in the group should hasten to engage themselves with the task at hand and sling the results of their endeavors onto and over the gelatinous barrier. The sand started flying, and they began to cover the goo in no time.

Max watched them dig and throw for a few minutes. He handed his rifle to Drake, asking him to hang on to it for a minute, then walked over to where he had extracted the rock. He unsheathed his large knife and stabbed the tunnel, sawing the blade to cut a long piece out of the wall. After he had scribed the shape of a broad, uneven plank, he could pull it free.

The congealed sand was as hard and heavy as concrete. It broke into two pieces when Max staggered back under its weight and dropped it. He picked up one of the pieces, hefted it to the growing dirt path, and laid it down on the edge of the muck.

"Look what I got," he said to Drake and the doctor. He held out a pizza-sized chunk of the ant plaster for their examination.

"It's hard enough, but you can cut through it. I noticed it when I pulled that rock from the wall," he said as he placed the sample on the edge of the goo puddle and took his weapon back from Drake. The big soldier stood on the stone, testing its reliability.

The doctor put his light on the chunk and held it close to his glasses. "Sand mixed with some exudation of the insects to solidify the walls of the tunnels. It's…"

"I know, it's remarkable, right Doc?" Drake interjected. "Well, it is because it's just what we need right now." He turned to his centurion and said, "Get some more of this cement cut up and pave our way over that stuff."

"Underway," the big man replied. He buttonholed a few volunteers from the crowd to start slicing the concretion into steppingstones, using their knives and trenchers to build a path across the digestive ooze.

Drake watched the progress and posted lookouts while the work was being done.

The bridgebuilders progressed, carefully placing the stony steps to avoid splashing the acid. The doctor also warned them to be careful of the hanging droplets as any contact with the substance would have dire effects.

The span was complete. The soldiers stepped from stone to stone over the hazardous paste. Most of them were over. The first of the two big guys carrying the heavy yellow drum stepped off the paver onto the far shore. His partner on the other end of the drum had one more step to go.

The antcrete steppingstone rocked beneath Marco's weight. He twisted and lost his balance, torquing the round metal pipe handles, trying to stay upright. He teetered on the unsteady stone, and Max jumped forward to grab the barrel, boosting its forward momentum. The handler lost his grip, and the drum fell to the dry ground, pushing Libby into the sand face first.

Marco was completely off balance and headed for the acid. Max pulled him back from the muck and into his bear hug, continuing the embrace over the yellow barrel and knocking Libby down again just as he was getting back on his feet. Everyone got bowled over, but no one got digested.

Lights and hands were all over, helping the big guys up, righting the heavy drum, and checking them and the barrel for contamination.

Max picked up his Zastava, dusted himself off, and scowled at the man he saved. "Try staying on your feet, will you, Marco? You clumsy oaf, you almost took a header into that goo and the package with you."

The big man looked back at the goo and wiped the sweat and sand from his face. "I know. I'm sorry, Max." He looked at the muck again, then back to Max. "Thanks a lot, Sarge."

Max shook his head at the man. "Just stay on your feet and watch where you're going. You're ugly enough without sticking your face in that stuff," he said, pushing him back toward the drum. "Hey, Libby, here's your better half," Max said to the other can jockey. "You two get back on the handles and back in step. There's a bunch of bugs waiting for delivery." The ex-sergeant looked at the acid bath and turned away.

The two drum bearers hoisted their load litter style and fell into line behind the others traveling the decline. The remaining troops followed, filing across the steppingstone bridge.

Drake sent the scouts ahead again. The group waited as the pair ran down the tunnel, jostling their lights over the cave walls. About a hundred yards in, they stopped. The scout's voice came through the headsets, "We're in position, move on."

"Roger," Drake replied. Max got to his place by the boss. The two walked a few dozen yards, leading the squad and following the scouts. The incline was steeper, and the air was thicker. The whole place smelled like wet charcoal. The team stayed tight, bristling with gun barrels and beams of light. The two big guys carried the yellow drum in the middle of the parade.

They marched for a few minutes when the radio hissed Angel's voice. "Something else now, debris in the cave. You'll see it. It's bad. We'll wait for you here."

Drake responded, "Got you, Angel. What is it?"

There was a pause, and then the terse reply, "Hard to say. You'll see." The headset crackled.

The column continued to the scouts ahead. Drake and Max were in front as their lights found the two soldiers standing next to a dark mass stacked against the cave's white wall. Max pointed his rifle forward as they slowed in their approach, running his light over the pile.

Dr. Dhawan came up behind them as they stopped a few feet from the waist-high heap.

"What is it?" the entomologist asked quietly, leaning in to get a better look.

"We thought it was bug eggs or something when we first saw it," Angel offered.

"OK, we'll take it from here. You guys get moving. We'll be right behind you," Drake said to the pair. Angel and Santa acknowledged and took off down the tunnel.

Drake squinted and brought his flashlight closer to study the shapeless stack, predominately gray with splotches of bright colors.

"It appears to be some sort of macerated material, like wasp paper," Dhawan said, reaching out to touch it.

Drake grabbed the doctor's wrist. "It's not paper," Drake said. "Look closer. It's clothing. People's clothing." Max stared into the pile as the troops came up behind them. Their lights silently ran over the bales of the indigestible apparel of the giant ants' unfortunate victims.

"I'd say we have more than a few missing persons here," Drake said. His light stopped at the top of the grisly mound, illuminating a small sneaker poking out of the hamper.

"Ants keep a clean house," Dr. Dhawan said in a hoarse whisper. "They remove anything they don't...that they can't..." his voice trailed off. He didn't finish his sentence. Someone in the group cursed, summing it up for the rest.

Even Max stood transfixed. Most of the group looked on with him. A few looked away.

Drake said, "Keep it moving." He turned and walked down the tunnel.

Max looked at Drake's light ahead in the darkness and turned back to the squad. "You heard him! We knew what we had to do. Now we know why. You two, pick up that barrel, and everyone else, get moving!" he snarled in his hardest voice and followed Drake into the tunnel.

Professor Carrington and the other scientists followed the soldiers up the incline, climbing the metal mesh ramp to the next level.

The group congregated at the sliding doors, noting the portal was ajar but jammed from the crash. The opening was barely wide enough for the professor's fingers as he tried to open the doors, but they held fast.

"Excuse me, docs," one of the soldiers said as he elbowed past the scientists. The young man shouldered his weapon and wedged his ice ax into the opening. He pulled against the handle, and the door let go, springing wide. They stepped back as warm air flowed out of the dark doorway.

"I don't suppose anyone has a flashlight," Professor Carrington wondered. Nobody did.

"This is rather embarrassing," Dr. Carr chuckled. "The most important expedition in history and a lack of illumination stymies us."

The other scientists laughed. Someone offered a pipe lighter. Professor Carrington stepped over the threshold into the darkness. The soldier reached after him but pulled his hand back, startled when the lights came on.

Light spread from the professor's position through the entire deck, illuminating aisles of large windows and entry doors into hundreds of isolation and examination cells. Most were complete with specimens in various stages of inquiry. Each isolation unit lit up in succession, down the corridors, around the corners, and across the huge scientific arena.

This was more than a laboratory; it was collection and experimentation on an industrial level. Unit after unit was partitioned by white walls and glass-fronted entryways displaying anatomized specimens. The life sciences seemed to be the predominant pursuit of the visitors.

The professor stood before the first cubicle. Half of a zebra was neatly suspended in midair, split from tail to snout, and divided lengthwise along its spinal column to display a perfectly sliced cross-section of internal organs, somehow fixed in place.

415

The other half of the equid floated next to the anatomy lesson, showing the animal intact with its stark striped pattern and bristling mane. The zebra looked alive.

The scientists were crowding through the doorway. Carrington looked down the lane of brightly lit cells. He walked astonished and absorbed to the next enclosure displaying a domestic horse in progressive transections, sliced like a cucumber and then almost reassembled, each segment disjointed by a few millimeters. He stopped and turned to the unit opposite, which held an African animal he believed to be a wildebeest, halved lengthwise like the zebra, and suspended without visible support.

He looked from side to side as he walked the network of examination chambers. The exclamations of the scientists filing through the door turned his head back to the group. Their reactions reflected his wonder. They opened their parkas to the warm air and widened their eyes to the displays, clustering at the first few compartments, pointing, exclaiming, and discussing. Carrington spotted Dr. Carr with his radiation detector. Their eyes met, and the young scientist shook his head in disbelief as expedition members crowded around the exhibit and involved him in their discussion.

Professor Carrington turned and walked alone past the units, one with a cow, the next with a few pigs, then goats and sheep in the next, all in some surgically precise butcher shop setting, displaying every cut of the animal. The professor paused at a unit showcasing a large animal he guessed was once a water buffalo, now posed standing sans skin as a monument to musculature.

The next few units on both sides of the aisle were empty of specimens, and he thought it might be an end to the exhibits. These vacant cubicles were dimmed, but the light just ahead at the corner was brighter. It held specimens displayed like the others, but they were the only insects in the exhibit. Ants.

Professor Carrington stood still before the glass, moving his eyes along the small black dots in an array of transparent boxes lining the wall, stacked vertically and aligned horizontally, one after another, and, as he followed the line, the boxes became larger, as did the insects inside the boxes. The first few specimens were normal in size, progressing to quite large but within an acceptable range of natural phenomena; the ones after that column began to strain credulity, and the professor wondered if they might be lifelike models. But he suspected they were not. By the end of the row, the insects had grown to the size of a dog. A small dog, perhaps, but an exceedingly large ant. In a clear display box were a set of mandibles the size of his hands.

As he stared through the window at the giant ants, Carrington became aware of another reflection in the glass next to his own. He turned to see one of the British contingent standing silently, also transported by the sight of the strange insects.

"Most appealing, aren't they, Francis?" Carrington asked the young microbiologist.

The Brit nodded. "They're marvelous," he whispered as if to himself. "These beings control the very building blocks of life. Their science is far beyond ours," he concluded.

"Well," Professor Carrington said to him, "it's our science now. Claimed by the right of salvage." He watched as the young man peered, leaning toward the ants on the other side of the glass.

"I don't think it would be a good idea to go into the chambers until we can do so safely," Carrington said to the rapt man. "But, when the time comes, I would like you to head the research in this area. I think you're just the person for the job."

The biologist turned to the professor and nodded. "It's exactly what I want to do," he said.

"Good, good," Carrington smiled. "Genetics is not my field, but from this example alone, one can only wonder at the possibilities."

The professor looked back to the entrance and saw the other members of his party making their way along the aisle. The extraordinary exhibits and enthusiastic discussions slowed their progress.

Carrington wanted to be alone for a time.

He left the thin, mop-headed man staring at the ants and walked down the aisle. Turning the corner, he strode briskly past more surgical examinations. One of the displays contained hundreds of rats, neatly arrayed in clear rat-sized boxes, stacked to create a wall of dead rodents.

He counted nine examination units on each side of the aisle to the intersection. To the crossway, he estimated three times that amount in each direction and as many before him. The facility was massive.

Carrington turned right at the next aisle, and after passing a few more goats and pigs on parade, he got to the monkey house. There were several enclosures of smaller primates and then, next to them, two more with baboons in various stages of dissection. The professor stared into the chamber of large monkeys. He dwelled on one specimen in particular. It was not as artfully exhibited as the others. Its arms and legs restrained it to a clear table, angled like an easel. The animal's head was thrown back, and its large canines bared. The front of the baboon had been cut open and organs removed. It reminded him of the tattooed man they had found outside.

The professor moved on, losing himself in thought. There was a connecting thread to these specimens and a purpose behind their collection. It was something other than science. He walked past another intersecting aisle and to the next, turning left.

One step around the corner, and he stopped. The lights weren't on in the units before him, and cold air blew out of the dark. He took a few tentative steps, each bringing him further into the shadow.

He could see a faint glow ahead. As he walked closer, the source of the light became evident. The bottom of the compartment had been ripped away in the crash, and the light was coming from outside, filtering up through a dangerous rupture in the deck only a few feet before him.

He carefully slid his feet along the floor, feeling his way in the near darkness past unlit examination cubicles. He steadied himself against the glass walls, tapping with his ax handle along the ruptured floor.

Stepping carefully to the edge, Carrington squinted into the light from the jagged metal shaft. He looked up and saw the breach continued to the deck above. Whatever discoveries were past this rift in the corridor would have to wait.

He shook his head and turned to retrace his steps but stopped, looking up at the black shapes silhouetted against the backlight of the labs. The breath squeezed out of him in a gasp as the subjects came into focus. Though dissected, disjointed, and dismembered, the dark forms suspended in the air were unmistakably human.

He slowly comprehended the array of specimens. There were dissection specimens of torsos and limbs, bones and muscles, organs and systems of the human body. There were many parts of many people.

Despite the uncompromising resolve of his intellect, fear rushed from his body and filled his mind. His usually overlooked adrenaline got its chance. He inhaled sharply, his eyes widened, and he pushed back from the ghastly shadow show, catching the heel of his boot on a curl of bent metal at the brink of the fissure. He stumbled and fell to the side, hitting the floor on his back and staring at the gruesome shapes. Hyperventilating, his vision fixed on the most prominent specimen behind the glass, the black silhouette of a crucified man without a cross, hanging in the air, waiting to finish falling.

The professor lay on the floor in the dark. One leg hung over the jagged edge of the drop, his chest heaved, and he struggled to regain his breath.

Carrington pushed himself up and staggered by the dark exhibits back to the lighted area in the maze of cubicles. Ahead, he saw a few members of the expedition coming in his direction. Two military men were walking behind them. He straightened and regained his composure.

Dr. Carr hastened to meet his friend as the professor exited the shadows. "Arthur, there you are. We were wondering where you had gotten to," he said as he approached Carrington. "Astounding, is it not?"

Carrington knew the display in the dark would affect some of the men, especially the less mentally disciplined, and that their reactions could have detrimental results. There were a handful of scientists he hoped could maintain a clinical outlook about these discoveries, but there were others that should not be informed.

He looked past his friend at the soldiers walking toward them. "Indeed, it is astounding," he replied to the doctor. "Quite a collection of specimens." He put his hand on Carr's arm and turned him toward the guards coming their way, changing the doctor's line of sight from the shadowy area of the human exhibit.

Dr. Carr noticed his absently delivered responses. "Are you all right, Arthur?" He peered closely at the professor. "You look upset. Did something happen?"

"Yes," the professor answered, looking past the doctor at the approaching guards. He looked back at his colleague and smiled. "I went into the section down there, in the dark. Foolish of me, perhaps," he said.

"What happened?" Dr. Carr asked. "I know you're not afraid of the dark."

"The deck is breached down there," he replied. "I almost fell through." Professor Carrington steadied himself with his friend's arm. "I suppose I am afraid of gravity."

"You're all right, my friend?" Dr. Carr persisted.

"Yes, quite all right. Just a close call," Carrington said with irritation, then smiled. He looked at his friend and said, "I'm sorry, Jakub. I am just annoyed at my foolishness." He grasped the doctor's shoulder and patted it as he found his footing.

The guards walked up. "Gentlemen," the professor addressed the escorts. "As you know, by Major Polk's instructions, I am to determine our course through the ship." He studied the pair, waiting for an indication of agreement.

"We were looking for you, Professor," one of them said.

"Well, as I was relating to Doctor Carr, I foolishly went into that area," he pointed into the shadows down the lane. "As you can see, there are no lights down there, and I am afraid the ship's structure is seriously damaged. Quite hazardous and unstable." He waited for a response, then continued. "Until it can be marked, cordoned off, you should post a sentry here and let no one pass." The soldiers stared at the professor and did not reply.

"I'm certain Major Polk will agree with this. We don't want any accidents," Carrington concluded.

The nearest gunman shrugged and said, "Sure, Professor. Whatever you say." The talking sentry shifted his rifle and then slung it over his shoulder. "Just don't go getting lost again, OK, Doc?" he added.

Carrington nodded, and one of the military men stayed put, looking into the monkey cubicles while the other walked behind Carrington and Carr as they returned to the group.

Dr. Carr glanced over his shoulder at the trailing guard, then asked Carrington in a low voice, "What was that about, Arthur?"

Carrington looked at the group ahead and caught the eye of two other colleagues. He waved them over, then turned to Carr to answer.

"It is my opinion that this look into our visitors' scientific curiosities is not suitable for everyone, not even some of the members of our expedition. It is up to us to determine who has access to the discoveries," Professor Carrington said as the two others joined them. The guard ambled past the four, heading to the intersection of the aisles.

"Doctor Blaine, Professor Carlysle," Carrington nodded to the others as they walked up. "I was just suggesting to Doctor Carr that we take a measured approach in disclosing our discoveries."

The three men looked at each other, then to Carrington. "That's not quite what you were saying, Arthur," Dr. Carr said softly with a smile. "According to you, the exhibits were not suitable for everyone, and while I will agree that this is a bit grisly," Carr replied as he motioned to the glass-encased specimens. "I think we all see it in the context of science. After all, would we not do, have we not done many times, as a matter of course, the very same things? Collect, examine, and exhibit?"

Carrington let him finish and smiled in return, saying, "And, I was about to tell Doctor Carr something interesting, perhaps disturbing, about the area behind us, back there in the dark." The men looked into the shadows. "And," he continued, "I don't believe it is something we should share with the entire expedition, at least not now."

Blaine looked down the alleyway into the dark, past Carrington. "What's back there?" the young anatomist asked.

Carrington drew them close. "That could be the area where the unfortunate man we found outside came from." He watched their faces for reaction as he spoke. "And there are others, I'm afraid. Many others."

Dr. Carr's eyes went to the shadows, and he asked quietly, "There are people in there, Arthur?"

"Yes," Carrington replied.

Carr nodded, slowly forming his next question. "And they are like these animals? They are cut apart?" he asked, moving his eyes from one compartment to the next.

Carrington nodded. "Yes," he answered.

Dr. Carr visibly shuddered. Blaine and Carlysle remained implacable.

Carr made the sign of the cross and exclaimed under his breath. "This must change things."

"Must it?" Carrington asked. "What's done is done, but you made my point. It is horrible, yes. But we cannot let emotion dictate our response. Think for a moment of the immensity and meaning of these discoveries. And, as you said, Jakub, 'Have we not done the same thing?' You know our history, and we have done the same and worse."

"Perhaps, Arthur," Carr answered hesitantly. "Human history is no measure of morality," he added.

Carrington sighed patiently at his friend. "Well, in any event, you must agree that further investigation is necessary before we tell the others," he said, leaning closer for emphasis. "Reason, above all," he summarized.

Dr. Carr nodded.

Blaine agreed.

Professor Carlysle took his pipe from his mouth and casually repacked it, pushing his thumb into the bowl and then thoughtfully imbibing the cold briar.

"There may be another indication here," Carlysle said as he motioned with his pipe from case to case, indicating the scope of the facilities. "This seems to be a very comprehensive collection, and there is much more to see, no doubt," he said in upper-class English. "But I must say, as I have been standing here, one thought has come to me."

"What is that, Professor?" Carrington asked.

"Well, zebra, rats, pigs. No reptiles, no sea creatures," Professor Carlysle said. "And, in fact," he continued, "the most represented animals, and I say this with regard to the fact we may as yet find more specimens, but it has struck me that all of these animals, and now humans, we have seen, share two principal characteristics."

Carrington raised his eyebrows.

"The one exception, perhaps you noticed the ants back there, other than that, in all of the other compartments I've seen have only exhibited mammalian specimens," Carlysle continued, "and they are the most numerous mammals of a certain size. By that, I mean they represent the most populous types of large mammals on Earth. But not all types; there are no lions, giraffes, aardvarks, or rhinoceros. They are, humans included, social animals. Exclusively herd animals," he concluded.

The others silently pondered Professor Carlysle's observations until Dr. Blair said, "You mean livestock."

Professor Carlysle eyed the young doctor, rummaged through a parka pocket to fetch his pipe lighter, and got a flame to his tobacco. He gave it a few puffs and looked through the dense cloud of apple and brandy-scented smoke. He nodded and replied, "Quite."

Their presumption of the visitors' noble scientific motivation was wavering.

"It's early for such suppositions," Professor Carrington said.

"Perhaps," Dr. Carr responded, "But I cannot understand how an advanced species does not realize that human beings are sentient. If they do, their disregard for this fact is not only frightening, it is foreboding."

"But right now, we do not know," Professor Carrington countered. "However, if we conclude that this ship journeyed to our planet for purposes other than peaceful study, my position is further substantiated. This is not information that should be hastily imparted."

Dr. Carr nodded. "I am beginning to agree with you, Arthur," he said. "As this turning point in humankind's history reveals itself, I begin to understand the need and your conviction that this knowledge must be controlled. In fact," he added, "the analysis and adoption of these technologies may be our only salvation." The other scientists concurred.

"Gentlemen," Professor Carrington pronounced, "I believe it is our responsibility, more, it is our destiny, to oversee the future of this project, to determine its course, and to guide the beliefs of those involved, especially those in charge. We four are the nucleus. We will grow and recruit a force dedicated to this mission. To these ends, we must resolve to apply ourselves to understanding not only the aliens and their technologies but the reaction of our contemporaries to our discoveries."

He looked at each of the men, ending on his longtime friend. He said, "Then we agree, Jakub. I have no hesitation in saying that the very existence of the human race depends on what we do from this point forward," he concluded. The small circle stood silent, apart from the guards and other academicians.

Professor Carlysle lit his pipe again, knocked the bowl with his gold lighter, and then reignited the shag. 'Well, it sounds like we have our future cut out for us," he said as he puffed. He took a long draw through the stem, held the briar in his hand, and studied it thoughtfully for a moment. "Maybe we could get on with the rest of the tour before resigning ourselves to our cloisters." He smiled at the others. "I am rather curious, you know," he added as he tapped his pipe out on the blade of Dr. Blair's ice axe.

As the group started down the aisle to the intersection, Professor Carrington looked back at the watch posted on the walkway in front of the shadows and called back, "Remember, no one is to pass. It's too dangerous back there!" The sentry waved in acknowledgment, and the four men continued to the crossway.

Major Polk rounded the corner. "Ah, Carrington, there you are," he called out, waiting for the professor to cover the distance between them. "We found something up on the next deck. C'mon." The major turned quickly and talked over his shoulder as he hastened down the aisle with Carrington and the others hurriedly following. "You're going to love this, Professor," Polk said as they went through the doorway and onto the ramp going up. "We found a couple of the spacemen. They're up here," the officer whispered as they went along the platform to the door behind the two armed guards and onto the next level.

There was a wall of polished black brick just inside the door. It was set back from the entrance, leaving an open area to walk to either end of the barrier. Past the wall, the smooth gray floor spread unobstructed over the enormity of the deck and ran into shadow around the perimeter and into three hulking machines on the other side.

As the small group approached the machinery, the monolithic forms of the installation became clearer. They were black and heavy looking, without detail and blockish by design, rising in height twice their width. Like the apparatus on the first deck, each machine was connected to the ceiling and each other by convolutions of black tubes.

As they approached the mechanisms, it was apparent the one in the middle had suffered a catastrophic failure. The black tubes were broken at their connections, and the body of the large middle unit was upended in the back, torn from its mounting, and the floor was uneven and infused with bubbles. The machine had failed and overheated, boiling the floor. It solidified as it cooled, hardening like lava.

Polk turned as he walked over the slag. "You think this is something," he said, "look up there."

He gestured to the roof over the ruined machinery. A circular, smooth-edged shaft cut through the decks and the hull above. The scientists looked up through the tunnel to the blue sky. Around the hole, stalactites grown from molten metal hung down.

"It's been melted straight through," Dr. Carr said. He looked up at the dripping edges of the opening and then to Carrington. "What kind of power could do this? Straight up, at least forty meters through the ship. And at least a meter in diameter." He pointed at the hardened mounds of metal, drizzled like wax from a candle.

Carlysle frowned and puffed on his pipe. "One point, gentlemen, if you will forgive my interruption. There is one point I cannot puzzle away," the Britisher began, taking the briar from his mouth and pointing from floor to ceiling. "There simply isn't enough dross," he said, all upper crust and correct.

Even the American anatomist got it. "Hey, yeah. Look at that," he said in support of Carlysle's conjecture.

"Quite so," Carlysle acknowledged, nodding at the Yank. "There should be considerably more debris in evidence." He relit his pipe.

"Vaporized?" Professor Carrington suggested.

Dr. Carr whistled. "Enormous. The power," he whispered.

"The power," Dr. Carrington echoed.

The professor looked upward with the others, studying the long shaft punched through the decks above. "I think that group from Stanford will be interested in this. I believe they are still on the deck below. We should bring them up."

"We can get to them later," Polk offered. He had been listening to the scientists conjecturing about the hole drilled through the ship and said, "My guess is these three things are the power plant. It looks like the middle unit blew a gasket and got plenty hot." He shook his head. "Then, whatever leaked out of it shot straight up. Maybe it caused the crash, I don't know. I can't even imagine anything that could cut through all that metal. Must have been like a blowtorch in an igloo," he said. "Anyway, you saw the melted floor over there. With that thing shooting off, this deck got pretty warm. It must have turned the whole place into an oven, as you'll see at our next stop on the tour. You might even forget about the engine room here."

The officer walked the scientists across the deck to another black brick wall, just like the one by the entrance, except this one had Sgt. Cady leaning against the end blocks, parka open and his thumbs hooked behind his belt.

"Sorry to leave you alone with them for so long, Sergeant," Polk said to the noncom.

"I've had worse company," Cady replied, moving aside to let his commander and the scientists pass.

"Hold onto your breakfast," the major said as he turned the corner. "This isn't pretty." The scientists looked at one another as they followed him behind the wall.

Like the other side, a large door was in the wall behind the partition. Unlike the other side, there was a charred heap of alien remains in front of this door. It wasn't easy to calculate how many extraterrestrials were in the pile. They were big creatures, a foot taller than an average human and broadly muscled. But these examples were badly burned.

Major Polk ran his flashlight over the tangle of constricted limbs, reaching toward the door. "One thing's obvious," he said in a monotone. "They die a lot like we do. I've seen this before. They wanted out and were climbing over each other for the way." The officer moved his light to scratch marks on the door.

The scientists stood in the dim area behind the wall by the waist-high stack of bodies, their attention guided by the major's light. His beam went from the door back to the mound, illuminating the uncoiled appendages stretching to the doorway from the pile of burnt remains.

The end of the limbs branched into stubby tendrils. What was most likely a roasted foot poked out, cramped, and contracted. A round head protruded from the side of the heap. It was lifeless, scorched, maybe deformed from the heat, but it had a face.

The light lingered on the alien physiognomy. "That is some kisser," the sergeant murmured.

Though the sear may have ruined the finer points of its features, the face was wide and evidently binocular. A large round eye was high on each side of the head. The front of the face was devoted to three horizontal slits at the top surrounded by bunched flesh that hung over a larger orifice below contorted into a pumpkin's grin, baring a circular arrangement of flat teeth. The grimace may have been the result of the heat.

"My guess is twelve. What do you think, Professor?" the major asked, moving his light to the standing group of scientists.

428

Carrington looked up at the light. "What?" he replied as if he had been woken.

"I figure there's twelve of these…these things…in the pile. What's your guess?" the major repeated.

"Oh. I don't know. I don't know," the professor responded. He stared, and the major brought the light back to the heap.

"Well, I guess it doesn't matter right now," the office said. "We'll sort them out in due time."

"Yes, we will sort them out," Professor Carrington said, slowly coming out of it. He turned from the bodies to the officer. "In the meantime, have you informed anyone else about these remains, Major Polk?"

"No, Professor," the officer answered, surprised at the professor's authoritative tone. "I went straight to the top with this one." He lifted the light slightly to let the spill illuminate Carrington's face.

"Excellent. Thank you, Major," the professor replied. He looked over the beam to the silhouettes of the two Army men. "At this time, I think it's best we keep this collection to ourselves. Perhaps we could restrict this deck due to, say, radioactive contamination?" Dr. Carr nodded.

"Whatever you want, Professor," Polk answered. "We'll take care of it." The officer looked at Cady, then to the mesmerized scientists, and motioned upward with his flashlight. "There are three other decks above us. The sergeant and I have been up there already, at least as far as we could get. There's a lot of damage from the crash. The top two decks are inaccessible, and the one above looks empty."

"I wonder what's on the other side of that door," Carlysle murmured.

"We're not going to find out today," Major Polk replied. "We have to head back to the base soon. We're not equipped to spend the night here. This was only a quick recon, remember?" he reminded them.

"Yes," Carrington agreed. "There is much to consider. The major is quite correct, gentlemen. There will be ample time for our investigations.

429

We would do well to begin formulating our plans." All the time he spoke, he stared at the alien pile.

"That is sensible," Dr. Carr agreed. "We will be back many times. For some of us, this will become a second home."

"Well, I don't want to return empty-handed," Dr. Blaine interjected. "I want to bring back at least one specimen for analysis," he said as he knelt by the pile of alien bodies. "I'll have to find a container for..."

"You can't bring one of these back," the major interrupted. "Get a load of the size of these things."

"Oh, I don't need a whole one," the anatomist said as he reached out and gently manipulated one of the extraterrestrial's tentacular limbs, stiffened by the heat that had killed the aliens. "Just a piece will do for now. Just an arm or a leg," he said, distractedly turning the appendage, flexing it, and looking closely at the folds.

The major held his light over the crouched doctor, shining it on the tangle of charred corpses.

"Could I borrow that?" Dr. Blaine asked the officer.

Polk handed his flashlight to the doctor and took out a pack of Luckies. He pulled out a cigarette and lit it. "I guess one little piece can't hurt. Better than bringing a whole one of these beauties back," he said as he exhaled.

Blaine brought the light to the specimen he was examining, peering closely at the stubby terminations as he carefully squeezed the limb along its length. Dr. Carr was looking over his shoulder as he worked.

"I don't think you could dissuade him in any event, Major Polk," Professor Carrington said. "Doctor Blaine is determined and eager to examine this new life form."

The major took another drag. "Uh-huh," he replied. "Well, if he wants to take a piece of this pot roast back with him, that's up to you fellows."

Dr. Carlysle was holding the light for the young anatomist. Blaine laughed at the officer's remark and said, "I don't think these things are the roast." He said as he fished a pocketknife from his parka. "They seem more like the vegetables," he said, opening the blade.

"Ah, yes." Dr. Carr leaned down to look more closely at the corpses. "You think they are not animal in nature?" he asked.

"Of course, I'm not certain at this point," Blaine responded, puncturing the arm 25 centimeters from the wrist. "But there are distinctly plant-like aspects to the tissue." His knife sliced smoothly through the arm. Dr. Blaine lifted the amputated limb, peered closely at the end, and held it up. "Like this," he said, looking back at the small group, "no bones."

"That's about enough for me," Sergeant Cady exclaimed from the shadows. "These space people, whatever they are, these things that made all of this, did all of this, cut up all these animals, that poor sailor, all of this was done by plants?"

"It could be," Dr. Blaine said as he stood. "Take a look." He smiled and offered the arm to Sgt. Cady, hand first, like it wanted to shake. The sergeant passed.

"A bunch of carrots came from outer space," Cady muttered. Everyone laughed.

"I wouldn't exactly call them carrots," Dr. Blaine replied to the sergeant.

"And certainly not to their face," Dr. Carr added, and they all laughed except the major. He looked at his wristwatch.

"Let's have this party on the plane flying back to the base," Polk said to his charges. "Don't forget, we have to hike back." Polk shook his head. "So whatever you want to take back, pack it up. We have to get going. It's getting late." The major knocked the ember from his cigarette, peeled the butt, and spread the contents on the floor. "And I want to know about any other souvenirs. I don't want anything dangerous on that plane with us."

431

Carrington nodded as he stared at the charnel mound. "Prudent, Major. Caution is our byword. In any event, I'm certain Doctor Blaine's examination will keep us engrossed in an evening of quiet study."

The sergeant turned from the pile of dead spacemen and said, "I don't know, I just can't get past the thought that those things are vegetables."

"Perhaps it is difficult to reconcile the visitors' obvious accomplishments with the use of a commonly pejorative term," Professor Carrington opined.

"Maybe," Polk placated the professor. "But no matter how you slice it," he went on, "animal, vegetable, or mineral, these are some scary-looking things."

"Listen!" Drake held up his hand.

The detachment stopped, and the noise of their movement subsided. Another call came out of the darkness in front of them. No one breathed until the stridulation stopped, and the echoes faded.

Dr. Dhawan squeezed his eyes closed. "That's them," he whispered in the dark.

"No kidding," Max replied, staring along the flashlight beams into the pitch black.

Drake turned back to his squad and raised his voice. "Let's step it up. The sooner we get down there, the sooner it's mission accomplished." His light led down the sloping passage into the darkness, and two dozen beams followed the leader as the invaders descended into the nest.

After a thousand yards of walking on eggs and waiting for them to crack, Drake held his hand up to stop the troop at the brink of a huge opening going straight down. The shaft was dead center in the tunnel, with ledges on either side providing footholds for the ants to bypass the opening.

Drake peered into the hole. "Rope," he said into his comm set. Two soldiers edged through the ranks, each with bundles of climbing ropes over their shoulders. Drake pointed, and they quickly got to work, twisting long anchors into the rim of the drop, rigging the rope, and throwing lines over.

Max walked to the rim and pointed his rifle down, shining the light into the hole. One of the ropers came up behind him and ran a rope through his harness.

"Make sure it's leading back, Tran. I'm going in face-first," the ex-sergeant said as the climbing specialist patted Max on the back.

"No sweat, Max. You're ready to go," Tran replied.

The big man held his assault rifle in his right and the rope in his left, twisting it tight. He lowered himself over the edge, then rappeled facing down, walking the wall.

Drake's voice crackled in the climber's ear. "What do you have, Max?" he asked.

"Easy drop. Not vertical, maybe sixty degrees," he answered. His light showed more of the same going down. "About a hundred feet to the – wait a minute," he squinted ahead into the light from the barrel of his Zastava. "I think it's bottoming out. Hold on." He lowered his large frame a few more yards into the shaft. The going became easier as the angle became less acute.

The tunnel floor leveled to a navigable slope, and the harness loosened as the pull lessened. He stood, twisting his head from side to side to get the kinks out of his neck. "I'm getting too old for this," he said to himself. The air stank and was more humid than the shaft above. He strained his eyes to follow his light into the dark tunnel. The beam slid over the sugary walls and then, at its limit, fell away. Max leaned forward to study the dark and smell the air.

He took a few steps, and the rope tugged him back. Drake's voice was in his ear again. "What's going on down there, Max?" he asked.

"Hold on a second," the lone man answered. He reached back and unhooked, dropping the rope to the ground. Max listened, then cautiously walked into the tunnel, stopping to listen again as he scanned the darkness with his light. He spoke into his mic, "So far, I'd say the tunnel's a good path. Gets us another hundred feet downtown and then levels out to an incline like the one you're on, still going down." He swept the beam methodically left and right, straining to hear any sound. His light found the end of the tunnel.

Max traced the perimeter with his light as he walked to the threshold. He couldn't see anything for sure, but he got the impression this tunnel led into a very large area.

"I think it opens up ahead," he said into his comm set as he walked to the entrance. "Like it goes into a big cave."

Max moved his light around, but it didn't land on anything. It was a huge cavern full of darkness. The only thing he could see for sure was the top of a broad ramp leading down. Max decided to go in.

The soldier followed the illuminating barrel of his assault rifle down into the subterranean stadium, and it was enormous. His light barely reached the lowest parts of the domed ceiling. At the bottom of the grade, he stepped onto a level floor. The faint echoes of his footfalls gave a sense of space in the darkness. It was a natural amphitheater.

Max shook his head and exclaimed impolitely under his breath at the sheer height and breadth of the cavernous excavation. His expletive whispered back and forth in the dark, and his laugh mixed with his oath. The soldier lowered his light to the path before him, touched his comm button, and held it, signaling for a response.

Static came back, interrupted by a few word fragments. Drake's voice phased in and out. Max could pick out the phrases 'can't read' and what sounded like 'coming down' or 'coming around.'

He turned to the ramp but hesitated. Before he went back, he should find out if this place was one way in or had another way out. Or just what this place was.

Max picked a direction and followed his light into the dark. After a dozen yards, his light suggested some shapes, something in the ink ahead. He slowed and squinted at the forms, large and dark. He crept, trying to be quiet, and then he realized that his was the only light in a world of darkness, so he'd be pretty easy to find.

Creeping forward, he slowly played the beam over the round, dark shapes.

One more step and the visual connected with the mental. Giant ants. The shapes were giant ants, the wall was a wall of giant ants, everything was...there were hundreds of them, and they all seemed to be asleep.

Max opened his mouth to swear, then shut it. Quietly. He pointed the light at the floor and backed away, stepping softly. His finger played along the smooth concavity of the trigger.

The large man carefully turned and retraced his path to the ramp, taking each exaggerated step like a cartoon character trying to be extra quiet. He was just beginning to breathe normally again when he saw flashlight beams swinging back and forth over the top of the ramp. Then he heard the soldiers, walking and talking, echoing through the chamber. Max quickened his pace up the incline and was nearing the top when one of them put his light down the ramp, lit him up, and shouted, "Max!"

The soldier's brash voice skipped across the huge cavern, and a hundred voices called the big ex-sergeant from every direction.

"Shut up!" Max hissed at the soldiers as he ran up the remainder of the ramp. "Quiet! Put your lights down!" he snapped as he got closer. "This whole place is full of THEM!"

The soldiers reacted and fell back to the entrance to the huge chamber and were in firing positions as Max hurried over the top and ran into the tunnel, breathing hard. He turned and tentatively pointed his light down the ramp, probing the darkness for any sign of moving bugs.

Without looking at the soldiers, Max said, "As soon as I heard someone making too much noise, I knew it was you, Angel. Do you ever keep your mouth shut?"

"Sorry, Sarge," Angel replied from somewhere in the darkness. "We were looking for you and…"

"See what I mean? Just be quiet," Max growled. "And stop calling me 'Sarge.'"

"Yes, sir, just force of habit," Angel said.

Max shook his head. "Who else is here? That you over there praying, Santa?" he asked as he turned his light on a kneeling figure by the wall.

"Yep," came the terse reply as the mercenary held his hand against the light. "Me."

"And Tran," the shadow on the wall added in a whisper.

"OK, the rope guy," Max said. "And who's that? Vic? Got that SAW with you, I hope."

"Yes, sir," she replied, patting the side of her machine gun. "Just the two of us."

"Good enough." He liked her; he had seen her in action.

Max exhaled slowly. "Guess they didn't wake up," he said. He looked back into the tunnel and saw more lights coming their way. "What the? That looks like the whole party," he exclaimed.

"I was going to tell you," Angel said, "the tunnel up top is a dead end. It goes nowhere, so Drake packed us all down the drop. Said it was the only way to go, Sarge."

Max nodded and stood from the wall, watching the bristling beams approach. He wagged the muzzle of his rifle slowly back and forth to signal them. "I told you, don't call me 'Sarge,'" Max said absently as he watched the lights advance.

"Sorry, Big Max," Angel replied.

Max took a few steps back to the top of the ramp. He switched off his light and stared into the dark. "Go back to 'Sarge,'" he said.

Drake was at the front of the main body as they joined up at the entrance to the amphitheater. Max turned to meet them and watched the two big guys plant the yellow drum on the cave floor, each sitting with their backs against the cave wall. The ordnance experts examined the canister while Max brought Drake and Dr. Dhawan up to speed about what awaited them below.

Dr. Dhawan replied that it was common behavior for members of the colony to lie dormant. "Ants are the very model of efficiency," he said. "Most of a nest is typically in a state of torpor. They will not wake until needed."

Drake looked into the darkness, and though he couldn't see anything in the space, it felt big. "And just what will wake them up?" he asked.

Dhawan shook his head. "Not known, not really," he answered. "A chemical trigger from the nest would rouse them. They could be on some internal schedule. We don't understand the mechanisms."

"I'd guess the dinner bell would do the trick," Max said. "Anyway, it's another thirty meters down, then it levels out. There's a central path through the chamber, but I didn't make it across because of the bugs, so I don't even know if this will take us anywhere," he said, obviously disapproving of the route.

Drake listened, then said, "We have no choice. The shaft above was a dead end. Stands to reason this one has to have an outlet somewhere. What do you think, Doc?" he asked the entomologist.

"That does seem logical. I'm certain there's an outlet at the far end," the doctor agreed. "If our mapping and our assumptions are correct," he added.

"Ifs," Max shook his head. "What about those sleeping beauties down there?" Max asked him. "What if we ring that bell and wake them up?"

The doctor smiled. "Well, based on your estimate of their numbers, we should anticipate a very poor outcome for ourselves."

Max looked from the doctor to Drake's deadpan expression. The large man laughed abruptly. "Well, OK," he said, "just as long as we know what's eating each other." He laughed again. "So, let's go."

Max walked back to the troop and got them on their feet. He instructed them in a low voice as they walked toward the chamber entrance. "Keep quiet. No talking. One light on, next two lights off. Those with lights, keep them on the path and keep them low."

At the brink, Max looked at Drake and nodded. "We'll use lights to signal when we can. Comm's been in and out," he said to Drake. He pointed to the four soldiers of the advance squad. "You're elected." He motioned into the chamber. "Let's go."

Angel started to reply but stopped as Max's eyes flashed. "Quiet," the big man said as he walked over the edge, leading the others down the ramp.

They moved silently, illuminating the compacted sand trail before their feet as they crossed the immense chamber.

Max stopped walking, and so did his soldiers.

He turned to the dots of light at the entrance above the ramp. He listened and could hear, very faintly, very far off, the trilling call of a giant ant deep in the nest. He stood silently, expecting a sudden eruption of answering calls from the hundreds of ants surrounding them.

Max waited a full minute, visualizing a second hand sweeping the face of a stopwatch. At the minute mark, he lifted his weapon and signaled to the soldiers far behind them with the gun light. He saw a luminous dot moving side to side in reply. Specks of light traced the path of the troops coming down the ramp.

"Keep moving," he said quietly to his group as he turned and walked on.

They kept close and quickly covered the packed sand path under Max's light. He'd look back to mark the progress of the pinpoints. The trail ran level and straight, bisecting the chamber and the sleeping swarm of giant ants.

An exit was going down on the other side; a large shaft dropped from the floor. Warm air welled from the hole, stinking of bugs and carrying the echoes of faraway monster calls buzzing like a night thick with flies.

"OK," Max's voice whispered, "Let's go." His light came back on and pointed into the hole. "Tran, put a rope down there. We'll leave it for the troop." He touched his comm set and spoke softly. "Exit from the chamber takes us down another level. We're leaving you a line." He listened, and there was a brief burst of static, then the word 'Roger' chopped in half. Max tapped his headset, but it didn't fix anything.

Tran finished twisting the climbing anchor into the earth. He threaded a rope and tied it off as Max shined his gun light down the hole.

"Looks like no one's home," he said.

Vic elbowed Angel and Santa aside to be first down the drop. She shouldered her machine gun, pulled her gloves snug, and hooked the line onto her climbing harness. "I'll flash you when I'm down." She winked and went over the side.

She descended quickly, and her light came on. The beam moved from side to side and then pointed at them, flashing on and off.

Angel went next, followed by Santa. Tran looked at Max and shrugged, then took the line and lowered himself down the drop. Max followed, taking the rope and turning to rappel. The large man groaned, "I hate climbing," under his breath.

The slope was steep and got steeper as he went. The ridges molded into the floor of the shaft were pronounced and helped the climb.

Max dropped quickly to the bottom and unhooked the rope, letting it swing back against the slope. He was winded. "Must be some pretty energetic monster ants with all of this up and down," he said, panting as he pulled a water bottle from his jacket.

He drained the plastic bottle and dropped the empty on the cave floor. He lifted his finger to his headset and spoke. "Drake, you read me?" The big man walked on, waiting for a reply. He tried again, but there was no response except static in his earpiece.

Vic was walking next to him. She motioned to her headset and said, "I'm not getting anything. No voice, no tones, nothing." The others tried their comms and agreed. The signal had been lost.

The troops walked through the tunnel to another shaft opening in the middle of their path. "Hold up," Max said quietly as he stepped to the edge. Clicks and hums drifted on the humid updraft.

"Put another rope down there," Max said, nodding to the rim of the entrance.

"We're not going in, are we?" Angel asked.

Max smiled at the foot soldier. "Of course, Angel. The sooner we find the way, the sooner we finish the mission."

Tran had screwed in the earth anchor and was securing a line. He threw it over the brink and shined his light down the rope. "Doesn't look too bad," he said over his shoulder. "Think I can see the bottom," he added as he leaned over the rim.

"All right, all right," Max said sharply. "Get that light out of there. No need to advertise we're on the way."

"Seems weird the comm cut out," Angel persisted. "Maybe we should wait until it's back on." He looked nervously into the hole.

Max twisted his neck to get the kinks out. "C'mon, get ready. This isn't a vote. It'll be back on soon enough," he growled.

Angel slung his rifle and went to the edge. "OK, Max. I'm going," he said as Tran sent Vic over and then hooked him up. "Just don't know why we lost the comm, that's all."

"Drop it," Max said. "You worry too much. Ain't so easy sending radio underground, you know. It's something with the antenna trucks, most likely. It's all very complicated. They're full of bugs."

Cap rotated the turret, sliding the light over the empty sands and back to the nest entrance. He looked at the time again and then at the huge hole. Tactical vehicles ringed the opening as surface transmission points to facilitate subterranean communication.

The truck lights were on, the motors were running, and weapons systems were active, some manned by sentries silhouetted atop the trucks, others with empty platforms, their outboard weapons controlled from within the vehicle.

The monotonous throb of the diesel engines was accompanied by an ant call oscillating from the darkness. The volume grew to a screech and then broke into repetitive shrill chirps. Cap moved his light across the desert again. The call was not far away. The beams began swinging from the other trucks. Another call answered. Lights swept the narrow trail between the dunes and glided up and down the sand slopes. There was a third call and then a fourth. Then, it was a chorus all around them.

"This is Lion One," Cap said into his comm as his eyes followed his light over the empty sand. "Sounds like they're..." he faltered as he peered down his beam along the ant path.

The tank captain licked his dry lips to curse. "Button up!" he shouted into the comm as his fingers pulled the triggers back on his fifty. The gun hammered in bursts, and tracers flew over the trail, slamming into the wall of giant insects stampeding into their position. They were ten abreast and double that many deep running down the path and along the sides of the dunes. Their long legs pumped up and down, propelling them out of the blackness at the wall of steel.

"You got them, Gun?" Cap grunted into his mic between pounding bursts of the .50 caliber. "Let them have it! Fire! Fire!" He hunched behind the shield, waiting for the blast.

The main gun of the Abrams blew. Thunder and flame jetted across the sand. The shell screamed over the trail and exploded in an airburst above the first line of ants, obliterating the monsters beneath and riddling dozens with deadly fragmentation spheres.

Unless they were killed, the giants didn't stop. The maimed mutants charged with gaping wounds in their exoskeletons, and if they left legs behind, they dragged themselves to their enemy, snapping their savage jaws for their flesh.

Cap popped up, swiveling his machine gun to a monster ant running down the dune at his tank. He pulled the trigger, ripping lines into the beast and dropping it only yards away.

The tank commander spun his turret to the battlefield just in time to see Lion Two fire and get smacked in the concussion of their cannon and instantaneous blast of the shell downrange. The blowback from their 120mm gun disoriented the ants and allowed the trucks to reform into a defensive line.

The ants had regrouped, too, and didn't give the invaders a moment to breathe. The mutant insects attacked again.

This time, the truck crews were ready; their weapons systems kicked into action, shredding the darkness with white-hot flashes from their guns and throwing ropes of fire over the desert, chopping the charging swarms of giant ants to pieces.

442

The monstrous insects fell, climbing over the ones in front of them as they advanced. Huge scouts were smashed and split by the sheer kinetics of the savage firepower dished out by the mechanized troops hosing hell into them from a wall of armor. Dozens of the giant ants went down, and dozens more were blown to bits, then trampled by the scores of bugs behind them, crushing their dead and dying nestmates to destroy the enemy.

In such close quarters, the shattering detonations stunned humans and insects alike. Sheets of fire shot from the gun barrels and strobed nightmare vignettes of monstrous ants pouring across the sand in their counterassault against the invaders.

Cap wheeled his machine gun from the front line to his eight o'clock, where the mutants had gained the flank in force. He shot an arc of death into three ants charging from the dune, and hot brass jingled across the steel skin of the tank as the bugs exploded.

His main gun pounded, and the blast knocked Cap back. He shook his head. "Let me know when you're gonna blow!" he barked into his headset. Lion Two fired right after them. The muzzle flash freeze-framed a hundred giant ants swarming into the field. Their main gun dropped to fire point-blank into the mass of insects.

The monsters had broken the defensive line; their position was overrun. The vehicles lost sight of each other as the ants swarmed the battlefield and wildly attacked the trucks. Their mandibles gnashed against the armor, they pushed, instinctively trying to flip the 15-ton units to expose the vulnerable underbelly of the enemy. The trucks were lost, unable to move in the crush of monsters, tumbled and buffeted so violently that all the crews could do was try to hang on.

The comm channel was chaos. The guns were firing wild as the monsters rocked and mauled the trucks. A spray of fifty caliber rounds from a besieged truck ran up the side of the tank. Cap reflexively ducked down into his hole. When he looked out, he saw the truck flip over, overwhelmed by a dozen ants, the top-mounted machine gun still firing.

443

Cap swung his gun around and joined in to pulverize two ants attacking the JLTV, but they were replaced by ten more.

The front end of a JLTV rose from the mass of insects; its headlights bounced in every direction as the vehicle was lifted by dozens of bugs levitating the armored truck, floating it in the hideous stew of monsters trying to tear it open.

The tank commander swung his gun around as the truck bobbed toward his tank, carried by dozens of monsters, turned and tumbled by uncountable grasping claws, probing and testing the steel skin.

Just as his grip tightened on the triggers, Cap saw the telltale spark in the weapons array atop the JLTV.

The funny thing about those mini-missile clusters is that a little electric coil glows and sputters right before they go off like a fuse on a toy bottle rocket. That's what Cap had heard; he had never seen it happen in person. He remembered a mechanic told him about the glowing tell.

Everything in his field of view was moving, shooting, screaming, a giant bug, or in some way trying to kill him, and yet, that infinitesimal fragment in his field of view, that orange scintilla glowing in a fraction of a second, hidden in a box of wires on top of a 40,000-pound truck tumbling through a boiling sea of mutant monster insects stood out.

In a flash of lower brain function, Cap realized the small sparks were a big deal. He remembered how that mechanic wouldn't shut up.

When he saw red-hot wires on the truck carried by the ants, the missile cluster pointed at the ground.

It was a holiday, but Cap couldn't remember which one. He was sitting on top of his tank, on the turret, and that wrench jockey just went on and on. It was hot, too. The guy just couldn't believe the weapons would give a visual before launch. "It is real firepower," the technician said. "They're small, about the size of a sixteen-ounce tallboy, and they pack a punch. But if they're going to show a fuse," he continued, "why don't they just blow a horn, take cover!"

The mechanic's 'take cover' was Cap's synapses' abbreviated message. He dropped, pulling the lid over his steel hole.

Two six-packs of tallboys fired into the ground under the truck, instantly atomizing a dozen ants and knocking down every bug on the battlefield. The blast launched the truck twenty feet into the air on a pillar of fire, crashing back to the ground upside down and smoking.

The hatch opened, and one of the crew dragged a teammate out of the burning JLTV.

The ants returned, flooding the field again and covering the trucks.

Cap was dazed, hard of hearing, and couldn't see straight as he got to his feet in the turret and popped the top. He shook his head to clear it and looked at the two soldiers in front of the smoking wreck. The soldier helping the other looked up at the tank commander and started to raise his hand, then was startled, ducking, looking to the side, and raising both arms against the wave of ants as they stampeded over the field. Cap watched with the sound off as the soldiers were trampled under the giants.

In seconds, the world was back to a sea of ants.

All Cap could hear in his headphones was the ringing in his ears. The main gun fired again, and the concussion swatted him back. He kept a grip on the .50 cal with one hand and grabbed something to steady himself. He shook the blur from his vision and stood up. The battlefield was coming back into focus.

Fewer trucks were firing. The bugs learned how to overcome the JLTVs. The ants were everywhere.

Two trucks at the end of the line managed to escape the fray. They ran between the dunes for almost a thousand yards before they were engulfed by a swarm of monsters that had traveled down the highway, flanking the armored invaders to attack them from the rear. The trucks were quickly turned over, lifted in the giant ants' jaws, and carried back to the party.

Between the tanks was a seething field of huge ants, black and shining as their giant eyes flashed and their jaws snapped, lifting the trucks in the air and turning them, searching for the seam.

A large scout with an injured eye climbed to the top of Drake's vehicle in front of the machine gun. The giant bug inadvertently concentrated its massive weight on the roof of the JLTV, on the seam with the front window. Right on the weak spot.

The roof buckled, and the windshields popped out of their frames. That was it. Within seconds, the top of the vehicle was peeled back like a sardine can, and the sardines inside were pulled out screaming.

Cap turned to get a gun on the bugs. He fired several bursts to clear the ants from the overturned vehicle, but it was too late. The fifty-cal kept firing anyway, blowing the bugs apart.

As he was blasting, that same leaky-eyed scout climbed onto the tank behind Cap, looming over the gunner as it searched for the man in the steel. The tank commander had just let off a burst when the hairy antennae patted him on the back.

He twisted under the ant, trying to bring the gun to bear, but the bug's leg jammed the turret, and he couldn't swing it. The monster's huge head hung over him, then lunged, snapping its jaws around the captain, but the turret's armor thwarted it.

Cap dropped into the hatchway, pulling his sidearm from his shoulder holster and firing straight up as he went down.

"Shotgun!" he yelled. The gunner thrust it at him, and Cap squirmed upwards, pumped, fired, pumped again, fired again, and again. And again. The ant relented and slid off of the top of the tank. Cap reached up, pulled the hatch closed, and dropped back into the steel shell.

"Move out and get us into a firing position. I want to see the field. We're going to blow up these stinking bugs," he said, plugging in a new headset. "Lion Two. What's your status?"

446

The radio squelched, and then the driver of the second tank answered. "It's me, Cap. It's Sal. Captain Stanley's hurt pretty bad. One of them got him, almost pulled him out." Sal's voice lowered. "He's really torn up. Oh wait, he wants to talk."

Cap's counterpart in Lion Two got on. His voice was weak and pained. "Cap, it's Stan. This turned into a mess in record time," he gasped.

"Show's not over yet," Cap answered, then said, "but yeah, record time." He knew the guy in the other tank was in bad shape to sound like he did. "Listen, Stan, we've got to move out. I don't know if these bugs can open us up, but they figured out how to get into the trucks. I saw them open one."

"I saw them open more than one," Stanley responded. "Not a good night for trucks," he said, taking deep, controlled breaths. "And there's nothing on the line from them. Dead quiet."

Cap felt his tank rocking as the ants strained against the steel behemoth, trying to find his weak point. "All right, Stan, time to go. Keep trying to raise anyone. We'll do the same," he said. "Let's see if we can make our way out of this mess and get back to our people in the tunnel."

"You think there's anyone left down there?" Stanley asked.

"We're going on that assumption," Cap answered.

"Yeah, but even if they are," Stanley coughed a few times. He got his breath back. "Even if they are, they're going to get one hell of a welcome when they come up."

"That's why we have to back off. I'm going to clear the field," Cap said. "We want to be two miles away and hope they don't follow us," he added.

"All right. Let's move out," the wounded tank captain replied. "See you back there. Let's take it slow. Maybe they'll lose interest. They've been knocking on my door all along."

"Roger that, Stan," Cap responded. "Take it easy. See you down the road."

"Affirmative," Stanley replied. "Hey, Cap, before we go, what are you calling for?" he asked.

"I want to fry these damn bugs," Cap answered.

"I read you, buddy," the radio squelched. "See you back there. Light these freaks up."

"Later, Stan. Roll out," Cap said and cut his comm. "See if you can get us out of here, bring us back to where we came from," he said to the driver. "Ahead slow."

The Abrams began moving. The lights came on, and the driver lurched the armor onward, retreating from the entrance and crushing dead ants. The big bugs scurried around the tank as it pushed them back, rumbling and belching exhaust.

The tanks took it slow, and as they became less of a threat, the ants fell back to the battlefield. Cap called HQ as the two surviving vehicles rumbled down the trail, retracing their tread marks.

"Lion One to home," he said into the headset.

"This is home, Lion One. Go ahead. We've been monitoring," the remote radio operator said.

Cap licked his dried lips. "Home, we need lightning on target one. Assets cleared. Strike on your clock."

There was a pause on the base side, and the voice replied. "Are you requesting a full strike?"

"Roger," Cap replied. "Full strike. Clear the field."

"Read you, Lion One. What is mission status?" the operator asked. "Sounds like it all went south up top."

"You're right about that, base." He paused. "Inside mission status unknown. We've lost comm," Cap responded. "Support done. We've pulled back. Only Lion One and Two are coming home. The rest are down."

There were muffled voices, and then the transmission went quiet. After a silence, the operator's voice returned. "Unexpected, Lion One. Support and strike are on the way. Sit tight, Cap."

The bruised and beaten tank commander signed off, saying only, "Roger that."

The two tanks came to a halt between the tall dunes. The turrets rotated to point their guns in opposite directions, and they put their lights out, waiting for the lightning to strike.

Drake looked at the rope hanging in the hole and pushed transmit. "Max, come in," he said quietly as the troop caught up and assembled at the brink. He waited for a reply, then repeated his unanswered transmission.

After a moment of silence, Drake turned to the group and pointed to Cho and Emoji. "Over the side," he said to them. The pair hooked up, dropped an additional line, and shouldered their weapons to go over the rim. Their lights became smaller, swinging side to side as they descended the shaft.

Emoji reported to Drake from the bottom. "We're down," he said. "Thirty meters, mostly vertical." The soldier ran his gun light along the floor and into the tunnel as he spoke. He took a few steps forward, shining the beam from one wall to another. "As far as I can see, the tunnel goes down on a steady slope." He squinted along the beam. "Doesn't look like anything but tunnel ahead. All quiet."

"No signs of life?" Drake asked.

"Negative," Cho answered. He moved the beam along the floor and stopped at Max's discarded plastic container. "Check that. There's an empty water bottle here."

Drake paused, then said, "All right. Keep your eyes peeled for Max and his team. We're coming down," Drake said and cut the comm. He turned to the group and singled out the two guys hauling the yellow drum. "Marco, Libby, get that thing ready to lower," he said to them.

Drake looked past them to three soldiers in blue and waved the colonel over.

"Oberst Nygard, I didn't get a chance to welcome you aboard." She nodded and looked into the hole as Drake continued, "The Agency doesn't usually take in outside help, but I've been a fan since I heard you cleaned up that mess on Kamchatka."

The woman smiled. "And I am surprised you have heard of the incident, Commander Drake," she attempted succinct English, pushed around by a strong Norwegian accent. "But then," she added, "the Agency has the…" she hesitated for a split second while she sought the correct phrase, "…the long reach," the colonel concluded.

"It does," Drake smiled back. "And, when this mission is over, I want to convince you to join us and extend that reach," he replied.

"I will be interested, Commander, when the mission is over," she replied, resting her forearm on the stock of the submachine gun hanging from her shoulder.

"Call me Drake," he answered. "I don't want to confuse anyone."

"But you are the commander," she said. "You do not observe rank?" Oberst Nygard asked.

"We're not so formal," Drake acknowledged. "Like a family business. Just one big family," he said. "I understand you brought two of your people."

"Yes, Nun and Renko. They are very experienced but do not speak English too much," she replied, motioning her commandos forward.

Drake nodded an acknowledgment to the pair as they stepped up. "I'd like you to take the lead on this next hole," he said to the Oberst. "There's two down there now behind the advance team with Max. You know him, I think."

"I know of Max Grunewald, yes," she said. Her soldiers nodded at the name.

Drake's voice lowered, and he leaned toward the warrior. "We've lost contact with his group," he said.

She nodded and analyzed Drake's expression. The woman nodded again, then turned to her command and spoke Norwegian.

Whatever she said, she didn't have to repeat it. The two men went to the edge and got hooked up. Nygard stood behind them and watched them drop. The Oberst stepped to the brink, hooked up, and turned to follow them over the side. She started to salute Drake but paused, changing to a casual wave. She smiled and dropped into the shaft.

The ropes creaked against the anchors as the soldiers descended.

Drake glanced at the technicians and said, "Run your checks here and get the pump primed. Maybe you won't have to make the climb." He turned and added over his shoulder, "But stand by in case we need you down there." They nodded, opened a panel on the yellow canister, unrolled a tool pack, and began working while the big drum handlers attached the ropes.

"Now for the rest of you." Drake scanned the group and picked out the three soldiers with machine guns. He pointed and said, "Burner and Udd, position here. Provide cover for both ends of the tunnel and this hole. The ropers and the techs will be here, too, so keep everyone in sight. Case is running the show."

Case was wiping the sweat from his neck, and Drake said to him, "I'm leaving you four guns to keep you safe, and you make five. The two techs, too. The other three guns are going back to the chamber, rear guard, but in shouting distance, so you should be set," he said to Case.

Case nodded. "Sounds good," he replied as he mopped his forehead. "I guess we're set."

Drake turned to the remaining soldiers awaiting instructions and motioned to the other holding a machine gun, saying, "You're Pez, right?"

The soldier smiled in reply, pushed his top bridgework out, then sucked his prosthetic teeth back into his mouth. "Yep," he said.

Drake stared for a moment, then said, "Got it." He selected two others so they wouldn't have to volunteer. "You and you. The three of you move back to keep our exit secure. Go back to that big cave where the bugs are sleeping and keep an eye on them."

"Is that all, boss?" one of the conscripts asked.

"That's all there is to it," Drake answered. "Once we're done, we'll pick you up on the way out."

He walked to the edge of the drop and saw the lines were ready. "All right," Drake said to the can handlers, "You guys get that down there." He motioned to the riggers by the brink. "Once it's down, you follow, got it?"

The moving men confirmed comprehension, and Drake reached up to clap one of them on the bicep as he turned away. "Good. See you down there," he said as he went to the hole.

The securing party was positioned at the top of the drop, and the three sentries were returning to watch over the sleeping giants.

Drake found Dr. Dhawan peering into the hole, watching the small lights land far below.

"Looks like the toughest climb yet, Doc," he said to the entomologist. "But I want you to go. We have to get deeper, and we'll need your expertise." Drake checked his sidearm and reached over his shoulder to feel the pump-action stock holstered in his backpack. He indicated to the ropers he was ready to be hooked up and looked the scientist up and down. "Good to go, Doc?" he asked.

Dhawan pushed his glasses along his nose and smiled confidently at the commander. "Very ready. I don't think there will be another opportunity to investigate this nest again."

Drake studied the doctor as the ropes were attached to his harness and checked. "I don't want you to get into trouble on the ropes. We don't have the time," he said to the doctor.

"That won't happen, I assure you," Dhawan responded. "I am a quite experienced climber."

Drake nodded slowly, pursing his lips, and then said, "Of course. And you're right about your opportunity," he said to the scientist. "At least, I hope you are. One trip through an ant nest should be enough for anybody."

Drake stepped to the edge and braced himself. "See you downstairs, Doc. As soon as you're ready," he said and bounced over the drop.

It was a quick trip down. Drake spoke into his comm set at the bottom of the shaft as he unhooked. "Is that can ready to go?" he asked. He looked up at the beams of light moving around the perimeter of the shaft high above him.

"Just about," one of the technicians answered in his earpiece. "A few more minutes."

"All right," Drake said. "Send Doctor Dhawan down and then the package when he's clear." He looked up and could see the rim defined by the moving beams of the flashlights. One of the lights dropped over the edge and began making its way down. Drake stepped back, away from the base of the drop, and heard a crunch. He brought his light down to shine on his foot and saw he had stepped on the water bottle. He kicked it to the side of the tunnel.

"The package is ready to lower," one of the tech's voices said in his headset.

"Roger. When Dhawan's clear," Drake replied tersely. "Case, what are you hearing up there? The signal's breaking up," he added.

Case's voice came back. "Same here," he crackled. "Seems like…" then the word "gone," then his full and clearer voice in Drake's set said, "Can you hear me now? I'm at the edge of the drop. Seems like we just have line-of-sight now. Don't know what happened. We're checking our base here, but I think the booster is out up top," he said.

"All right," Drake replied. He didn't like his immediate conclusion about surface communications support being out. "Keep me posted if you can." He waved his light upwards and added, "Catch you on the way back, Case."

The white walls of the caverns multiplied the flashlight's brightness, and Drake could see one of Nygard's soldiers positioned against the wall, pointing his gun into the empty tunnel ahead.

"Where's your Oberst?" Drake called to the commando.

"Oberst?" the soldier replied, motioning with his rifle down the tunnel. Drake nodded, then looked back to see small lights moving at the top of the hole, which was Dr. Dhawan in his descent.

He turned his beam down the shaft and then onto the man by the wall. "You don't have to stay here," he told him. He motioned with his light into the tunnel in front of the sentry. "Go. Join your comrades," he said.

The soldier got the gist, pointed to his watch, and flashed five fingers twice at Drake.

"Ten minutes," Drake said. "Oh, your Oberst told you to wait ten minutes."

Drake didn't care. Sand sifted down from the shaft above. He looked up to see Dr. Dhawan rappelling out of the darkness.

The scientist landed on his feet and smiled into Drake's flashlight. "That was quite a climb. And in the dark, too. Very exhilarating!" he said breathlessly.

"Well, the adventure continues, so keep your eyes open," Drake said, waiting for the drum to materialize.

He motioned the doctor away from the shaft, pointing upward. "They're lowering that drum over your head, Doc. Move out of there, in case it slips."

"Oh!" Dhawan exclaimed and hurriedly unhooked his tether. "Thank you, Mr. Drake, that is good advice," the entomologist said, scrambling from the base of the shaft and into the tunnel.

Drake took a few steps after the scientist. "Where are you heading, Doc?"

Dhawan stopped and turned to Drake. He moved his flashlight around the tunnel. "Amazing, isn't it?" His beam found the Norwegian soldier. The young commando looked at the light and then at his watch. He stood and began a quick march into the tunnel.

"Where's he going?" Dhawan asked.

Drake shrugged. "Guess he had an appointment," he replied. "We're staying put until that can gets down here. "Remember, that's the main mission, Doc."

Dhawan affirmed half-heartedly as he peered into the cave ahead of them.

A minute ground by in silence until there was a burst of static in the headphones, followed by the voice of one of the scouts. "Drake? You read me? It's Cho."

"Got you, Cho. Go ahead," Drake answered.

"Half a klick downstream from the base of the drop. There's a big hole in the floor with a rope in it. Max must have gone down there," Cho said.

"Roger..." Drake began.

Cho's voice sizzled in the static. "Hold on...hold on," he said.

Drake waited. Cho came back. "I can hear them," he whispered into the headset.

"Hear who?" Drake questioned. "Max? Our people?"

Cho's voice hissed back in a whisper over the comm. "No, no. I hear them." He cursed. "Down the hole. THEM!" he said urgently. Another expletive came through the headset, and the transmission ended abruptly.

Drake returned to the base and looked impatiently up the shaft, expecting the drum to be lowered into view. Drake saw Dr. Dhawan had taken off when he turned, and his light was far down the tunnel.

"Dhawan, Dhawan!" the commander shouted after him, covering his microphone. He looked up again and saw the bright yellow of the heavy drum lurching into the dim light at the bottom of the drop. It bounced off the walls of the shaft as it was lowered.

The drum landed in the loose scree at the base, and Drake began to untie it. He looked up to the rim and spoke into his mic. "Case, do you read?"

The voice came down from the top garbled, then clear enough to exchange a few words. "Can's untied, take your rope back, and send down the moving men," he said.

The answer crackled through his headset, "Already on their way."

Steady streams of sand showered through his beam as the large can handlers lowered themselves down the shaft. Drake impatiently walked off the sand pile at the base of the drop and into the tunnel ahead. He stopped and spoke into his microphone. "Cho? Is Dhawan there?" he asked.

"This is Nygard," the Oberst's voice answered. "Your two advance men are here awaiting directive," she said crisply. "I'm afraid our arrival startled your men, but all is okay," she added.

"Any sign of Max and his team?" Drake asked.

Cho's voice answered. "Like I said, boss, there's a couple of anchors and ropes going down this drop. But a lot of bug sounds are coming up. They seem closer here," the scout answered. "Wait, there's something else in the tun...oh, it's OK. Another one of that lady's men just got here."

"All right, Cho. And that's no lady; that's a colonel, Oberst Nygard," Drake said. "And by the way, Dhawan will be coming up on you any minute, too. Don't shoot him."

"Sorry, boss. Guess I'm jumpy," Cho said in a low voice.

"Take a breath, Cho, and keep your muzzle down," Drake answered. He turned to watch the large men unhooking at the bottom of the drop. "We'll be there in about ten minutes," he said into his mic.

Nygard came back. "I and my men will go into the hole ahead and scout forward," she said.

"Good idea, Nygard," Drake replied. "We'll catch up with you ASAP," he said and signed off.

"Let's move this thing down the road, guys." Drake started into the tunnel as the moving men slid the poles through the brackets and hoisted the drum to ferry it into the cave, following their commander.

They moved fast and soon joined the lights, waiting at the next drop. The can handlers put their load down and leaned against the tunnel wall to catch their breath.

Drake sat on the yellow drum, and Cho walked over. "The doc got here a few minutes after those Swedes jumped in the hole," the young soldier said.

"Norwegians," Drake replied, stepping to the brink. He waved the beam of his flashlight, stirring the darkness and flashing it over the walls of the descent. Dr. Dhawan stood next to him and said softly, "Your friend is close by."

Drake looked at the scientist. "What did you say?" he asked.

Dhawan turned his head to Drake. "I heard his voice a few moments before you arrived." Drake listened to the darkness. The distant buzz of bugs carried the sound of a summer night on the warm updraft. He brought his hand to his headset and spoke quietly into the microphone. "Max, Max, can you read me?"

High-pitched trills of giant ants echoed from the depths. Static flared in his headset. As he strained to listen, Drake's stare stayed on Dr. Dhawan.

"I didn't hear him on the earphone," the bug man said. "His voice came from the tunnel."

The scientist wasn't wearing his headset; it was draped around his neck. Drake spoke into his mic again, "Nygard. Nygard, come in." The only response was static.

Ammonia stink wafted from the hole, expelled from the caverns' humid breath and accompanied by the far-off chatter of the nest.

Drake crouched over the brink, listening intently. He leaned over the void. "Max! Max!" he called in a loud whisper into the black hole. One of the musclemen stepped up and held his climbing harness as he listened to the darkness. Only the insects answered.

The large soldier pulled him back, securely planting his feet on the rim of the hole.

Drake suddenly yelled into the shaft at the top of his lungs, "Max!" he bellowed.

His call bounced through the tunnels and echoed through the chambers. The ant calls from the deep paused. The soldiers looked surprised, and Dhawan opened his mouth to speak when an answer to Drake's call floated up from the hole.

"Drake…" a weak whisper twisted up from the cave. The men looked at each other to confirm all had heard the voice.

The call came again, rising on the foul-smelling breeze. "Drake!"

"Max! We're on our way!" Drake shouted in reply. He picked up a loose rope, looped it into a coil, and pushed it to Cho. "Hook me up," he said.

Emoji pulled up the other lines, and Drake knelt while Cho tied him in.

"How come we didn't hear anything from that woman, you know, Colonel Nygard?" Cho asked.

"We'll find out when we get down there," Drake replied. He cinched up and pulled his gloves tight. "Don't waste time. Tie up and get down there. You two next," he said to the scouts. "Then you, Doc. You guys drop the can and follow. Got it?" he asked.

They nodded. Cho and Emoji were already tying up as Drake took his rope and dropped over the side.

He jumped feet first into a controlled fall, quickly getting his drop and bounce rhythm, feeding the rope through his leather gloves. His light jumped wildly on the walls as his rappel brought him to the bottom fast. He unhooked and slid down the sandpile into the passage. Foot scrapes and lines slapping the wall told him soldiers were on their way to join him.

The incline leveled out, and he walked a dozen yards into the tunnel. He swept the floor with his light, then stopped and brought his fingertips to his headset, listening to the static mixed with Max's voice. He couldn't make out what he said, but it was him.

"Max, Max…" he snapped into the mic, but it got away, and the signal phased into static. Drake cursed the comm system and moved his light methodically along the walls going down the tunnel. He snapped it off and listened. There was tapping in the darkness, and whatever that was, it wasn't Max.

The noise kept his attention as Cho and Emoji came down for a landing on the steep pile of sand and ant-crete at the base of the shaft.

"Cut your lights," he whispered to them over his shoulder. He turned his flashlight on and stood it on the floor, pointing down to form a small pool of illumination in the white sand. He called them over, cautioning quiet. "Something's ahead," he warned.

The scouts went dark and unshouldered their weapons, quietly climbing off the debris pile to assume sentry positions, crouched against the walls, watching the dark.

The hanging ropes twitched, and small showers of sand fell in the dark as Dhawan descended. When he reached the bottom, the scientist was warned to silence before he could say a word. He joined the group by the light, listening to the disquieting clicks and taps, the smacks and chewing sounds from the pitch black. Each noise found a new nerve to pick.

Dhawan whispered, "They're not far away."

Emoji shifted and lifted his weapon higher.

"Stay loose," Drake said. "They've been doing that since I got down here. They're not interested in us."

"Still haven't heard from those Swedes," Cho said softly. "They could be in trouble."

"We would have heard more from them if things went bad. They might be staying low. Let's not stir things up," Drake said. "We have to wait for…"

He stopped mid-sentence when ant shrieks shot through the tunnel loud enough to make them duck and cover their ears until the sudden silence. They loosened the squeeze on their ears, listening suspiciously to the dark while their eyes made shapes in the void.

When the yellow can knocked softly against the chalky wall of the shaft, it made them jump and then laugh when Drake picked up his light and pointed it at the drum settling into the sand.

Drake took the two scouts, untied the canister, and rolled it down the slope to the flat floor as the can handlers made their way down the ropes.

Dhawan spoke over his shoulder, his attention forward, rooted in the darkness. "I haven't heard anything else," he said.

"We'll stay lights out for now," Drake said. He watched the two big men bounce off the wall and lower themselves onto the sandpile. They unhooked and slid down to the floor. Sensing the covert attitude, they clicked off their lights as they climbed off the drift. Drake filled them in as they hooked the handles into the can.

The lone light was bright enough for Drake to read the faces of the group. He looked at Dhawan and said, "I'll take the lead with the doctor." Drake turned to the rest of the group. "We'll go first, thirty yards ahead." Cho was breathing fast, and his eyes darted past Drake to the tunnel. His buddy was watching him.

"You guys next," he said to Cho and Emoji. "In front of our moving men. One light and keep it low." He looked up at Marco and Libby. The two big guys were all right. In addition to shouldering the load, they both carried plenty of ammunition. They'll be the last ones standing.

"Just remember," he continued, "any trouble, we'll run into it first, so you'll get the message. The main thing is getting the package as deep as possible, and we're just about there."

Drake picked up his light and motioned down the tunnel. "Let's go," he said to Dhawan.

Emoji snapped on his light.

"I'll signal you when to move out," Drake said as they walked away. He reached over his shoulder, pulled his compact shotgun out of its holster, and checked it as they descended the tunnel. He turned off his flashlight, set the light under his gun low, and pointed it at the floor.

Straining to hear any sound ahead, Drake touched his microphone and said quietly, "All right, come on up. All quiet so far."

Emoji looked at Cho; Cho stared into the darkness ahead and turned to the two large drum handlers. "Guess we're up," he said to them. "Moving out," he confirmed with Drake.

The four walked down the congealed sand incline. Emoji and Cho went first, holding their guns level, pointing the way.

Drake's voice crackled in their headsets. "Keep that light down. I can see it up here."

Cho lowered the light, aiming it at the floor in front of them.

The air was warm. They sweated and listened as they advanced.

The moving men hauled the yellow drum stretcher style with pipe handles through rings welded to the can. They followed the low light, carrying the weight with little effort over the smooth floor of the cavern.

"It stinks in here. You smell that?" Libby whispered hoarsely. He wrinkled his puss in revulsion at the odor rising from the darkness.

Ahead, they could see the glimmer of Drake's light.

"Lightning inbound." The voice in Cap's headset startled him from his view of the distant melee of monsters through his binoculars. The tank commander watched from his turret as the moon rode over the crest of the dune and brightened the bubbling mass of insects two miles down the trail. They mobbed their victorious field, dismembering their innumerable dead and countless injured to ferry their parts into the underground larders. Victory or defeat for the mutants, there was always something to eat.

Cap noticed the ants had no interest in the nearby opening into the nest. Well-organized lines of smaller monster ants, the workers carried their grisly packages along miles of worn trail back to the main entrances.

The large warrior insects were still in the field and easy to pick out. They stood motionless while the workers frantically completed their tasks in a chaotic swarm. Though he could not discern order in the mob, Cap conceded a collaboration in these monsters effective enough to beat a convoy of heavily armed trucks and two Abrams battle tanks. But they wouldn't beat what was coming.

A recon helicopter flew over the trail. It hovered over the swarming ants, pivoted in the air, and banked away from the battlefield.

Cap turned his head, scanning the night sky with his naked eye. All the ants were west of his position. The insects were logjammed in the notch between the dunes or headed downstream to bring the spoils of their victory home. Cap watched the undulating mass of monsters slithering in the moonlight through the oversized field glasses.

From behind, a sudden rumble exploded into a roar. An F-35 Lightning streaked in low over the tanks, low enough to throw a sand tail up and loud enough that when Cap yelled, his oath was lost in the thunder. Everything rattled as the fighter flashed past, dropping two firebombs down the trail into the mass of insects.

Each bomb carried a hundred gallons of gelled fuel and ignited in the air before impact. Cap raised his hand to his face as the heat from the tumbling eruptions of orange flames seared through the channel. The high-speed drop formed a wave of fire rolling over the monsters, breaking against them in a 1000-degree ocean of immolation.

Another jet followed, screaming 600 feet over the deck, pulling a 500-mile-an-hour wake and plowing two more burners into the ants. The first jet circled for another run with another pair of bombs. The rift between the dunes was a valley of flame.

The heat from the battlefield was stinging. Cap kept his gloved hand up against the glare. The second jet roared over for its last run and dropped more lava.

Nothing moved except fire. Everything burned and kept burning. The blast of the jets rang in his ears as a voice crackled in his headphones.

"That was Lightning, Lion One," command's voice said.

"I'll say," Cap replied.

"You all secure there?" headquarters asked the tankman. "Need assistance or evac?"

Cap looked down the trail to the pyre. "Affirmative, Base. Need a medical evac for one, our position." He looked over at the dark profile of the other M1. Lion Two returning to base after pickup. Lion One will let things cool off and wait for our party to resurface."

"Roger, Lion One," Base answered. "They'll be glad to see you. Signal when ready. We'll arrange rides for all. There's another delivery on the way to resume communications with your loved ones."

The commander smiled. "Got you, Base. We'll be waiting," Cap said. "Out." He disconnected. Orange light flickered across his face as he watched the giant ants burn.

Drake slowed his pace, then stopped. He snapped his shotgun light off, and pitch black filled the cave, holding them motionless.

"What?" Dhawan asked so faintly Drake barely heard him.

He gripped the doctor's arm to keep him quiet and in place.

"Ahead," Drake finally answered. "A light," he breathed.

Dhawan pushed his glasses up his nose and discerned the small spark moving far down the tunnel.

Drake pulled his flashlight from his pocket and pointed it forward, moving it from side to side. The distant light answered in kind.

"That's Nygard. Let's go," he said, tugging the scientist forward.

Dhawan and Drake quietly hurried down the tunnel. As they neared the light, it lifted and pointed at them.

Nygard spoke from the darkness. "There are three of us here," she said in a low monotone.

"Glad to hear it," Drake said. His short-barreled shotgun hung in his right hand, and his left waved off their light.

"We saw the broken trap, so we did not fall in. It is there." Her light went to the floor several yards ahead. "That place," she said, "is the covering of the trap. In that trap is Max and his soldiers."

Drake started forward, but the Oberst stopped him. "They are for now safe," she said.

"We heard ant noises from down here," Drake told the woman.

"Ja," the colonel responded, "They were the ant noises. We were here and watched two of the ants cover the trap. They made the noises."

Dhawan turned his head to the Norwegian officer. "You were close to them?" he asked.

"Ja. Close." She turned to her soldiers and spoke to them quickly in their mother tongue. The three laughed. "Very close, I would say, Doctor," she said to him.

"Tell me what happened, please," the doctor asked.

465

She used her flashlight to illuminate her summary of the events, showing the soldiers' path along the tunnel to the point where they came upon the ants laboring at the pit in the middle of the cave floor.

"This is where we first see the monsters," she said matter-of-factly. "We stop. They do not care that we have come. We go back to there," the colonel flashed her light against the tunnel wall. "We watch, and they work, two of them, filling the top on the hole. Spreading the, what is it? The clay, yes? They spread the clay from their mouth and cover the trap to break when we walk over it."

She lifted her light to shine on Cho and Emoji coming in as they caught up with the lumpers lugging the canary can. The big men rested their load, breathing a bit after the workout. The two scouts stood behind Drake without a word, all ears.

"These ants, I assume, were the smaller type?" Dhawan questioned the colonel. She turned again to her soldiers and spoke Norwegian to them. They laughed again.

"Yes, Doctor. The small ones." She smiled.

"They did not detect you – did not notice you?" The doctor continued.

The woman nodded, looking at Dhawan. "Ja, ja. They notice us, Doctor." She pointed the light back on the wall. "That is where we stand. Very quiet, so the big, I mean the small, ants do not see us. But one stops working the clay and walks with his...what is it?" She pantomimed with her left hand at her head, wiggling two fingers in the air.

"The antennae, the feelers?" Dhawan suggested.

"Ja, ja," she replied. "That is that. The feelers. It walks with the feelers going everywhere and then smells us, yes?" The Oberst dropped the beam to the ground. "The monster turns his head very slow with the feelers and comes to Nun and stands before him, touching him all over with the feeler, the antennae, you said." She spoke a few quick words to her soldiers over her shoulder, and Nun replied tersely.

466

"Then the ant did the same to me and the same to Renko. Smelled us all over with the filthy feelers," The woman smiled again. "Then, it went back to work."

"Wow," Cho said. "Why didn't you blast it?"

"I thought it best not to fire," the veteran commander replied. She looked at Drake.

"That is some mettle, ma'am, if I may say so," one of the can handlers declared from the shadows. "Ja," his other half added.

A soldier behind his Oberst spoke, and she turned her head to listen. "Ja," she replied, then said to the others, "Nun said it was like being rubbed with a brush, and the monster smelled of dung." Nygard leaned forward, adding, "The jaws were big enough to take us all in one snap, even if these were the little ants."

Cho shuddered.

Drake gave a slight nod to Nygard. "Outstanding, Colonel," he said. "Now, what about Max and his crew?"

"One moment, if you don't mind, Mr. Drake," Dr. Dhawan interrupted. "May I ask, Ms. Nygard, when the insects began making their noises?"

She pointed the light up to shine under the doctor's chin. "The one made the calls after smelling us. Then, both made the calls after finishing their work. Then the little ants walk into the mine." She gestured with the light into the dark tunnel beyond the trap.

"And Max?" Drake asked impatiently.

"He and his squadron are under the hole door." Nygard brought the light back to the middle of the tunnel floor. "As the monster ants work, I talked with Max Grunewald. All are OK."

"You spoke to them?" Drake reiterated.

"Ja," the woman replied. She turned her face, illuminated by her flashlight, to Drake. "That lid was broken away. The monsters were busy

467

fixing. We stood at the walls. I saw the light and heard Max Grunewald. He said a few oaths against the ants. So, I called back." She laughed slightly. "He was surprised."

Drake looked at the floor ahead. "Now, they are sealed in," he observed as he lifted the shotgun over his shoulder and pushed it back until it clicked into its short holster.

"Max said it will break if you walk on it," Nygard related. "That's how they got into the hole. The floor broke down."

"Then let's crack it open and get them out of there," Emoji said.

Drake had motioned to the can men to come forward and to run a rope through his harness. While he was being hooked up, he asked Dhawan, "Is it normal for ants to make traps? Not just barriers like the muck we came across, but concealed, complex traps like these?"

"Some do, yes," the doctor replied. "Some species, the Brazilian Pheidole oxyops for one, construct pitfalls covered with small feathers to trap prey..."

"Prey," Drake interrupted as he took the coiled rope from Marco, slung it over his shoulder, and fed an end into his harness. He motioned forward, and the group walked to the re-covered pitfall. "Watch the floor, watch your footing," he warned the others. They moved their lights over the false floor and stepped cautiously to the trap, picketing half of the circular deception. It was distinguishable by its smoother texture and higher gloss than the surrounding tunnel floor.

It was quiet in the nest. The distant bug noises were faint. Drake knelt and ran his hand over the smooth floor. He stood and tossed the coiled rope to the can handlers. "Don't let me fall too far," he told them, turning to the trap. He stepped onto the cover as Libby and Marco held the line tight, waiting for him to drop. Drake stepped into the circle, testing his footing and pulling against the tight rope.

Two more steps, and he was in the middle of the trap. He stamped his right foot twice. "It feels solid," he said, pounding his boot against the smooth white concretion. "Maybe we should try…"

Breaks radiated from his feet across the slab, and it shattered into fist-sized blocks, raining into the pit along with Drake.

The two big guys dug their heels into the chalk and felt Drake hit the end of the line, confirmed by his loud exclamation. He dangled in the pit, swinging on the rope over his compatriots.

Light from below lit the pendulant man, and Max's voice followed. "I was wondering when you were going to get here," he called to his boss as he brushed off the dust of the collapse.

Drake swung over their heads, parallel to the ground. "So, there you are," he said as he slowed. Drake moved his light around the pear-shaped pit. It was a 25-foot drop to the bottom. Max stood in the center of a wide circle of white sand, ringmaster to the other performers behind him.

"What made you decide to fall into this hole?" Drake asked.

Max did not reply. His flashlight moved with the man, back and forth in rhythm with his swing.

Drake gave a low whistle. "No wonder you couldn't get out of here," he said. "There's nothing to climb."

"Is that right?" Max asked. "Then how about throwing us a rope?"

"Everybody in one piece?" Drake asked the group. They affirmed.

"Pretty much," Max answered. "Surprising."

Oberst Nygard called past Drake from the rim of the trap. "Max Grunewald. You are ready to get out of the hole now?" she asked like an officer.

"Ah," Max called back. "I mean 'Ja.' I'm so glad the bugs didn't eat you. It was quiet up there."

"And down there, too," she chided.

Drake reached back to his harness and righted himself on the rope. "Max, let me introduce Oberst Nygard if you haven't already met."

"Didn't get the chance," Max replied. He called to the top, "Nice to meet you, Colonel. Pardon my predicament," he added with a laugh.

"Oh, you have a reputation that goes in front of this, Herr Grunewald," she replied.

One thing Max could do was take a compliment. "Well, thank you, Oberst Nygard," calling to the officer past his boss.

She looked into the pit and brought her light to his face. "Oh, I meant I have heard of you in even worse circumstances than even this, ex-Sergeant Grunewald."

A faraway insect call quivered through the caverns, then faded away, leaving it quieter.

Dr. Dhawan's voice came from the broken rim of the trap. "Hello, Mr. Grunewald," he said loudly into the pit, over-articulating each word for clarity. "I am glad you and your companions are well, considering your unfortunate circumstance."

"Uh-huh. Guess it's just not my day," Max replied from the bottom of the sand trap.

"I take it that you had no real interaction with the insects?" the doctor questioned.

Max exhaled sharply, then answered in his moderated voice. "No, I'd suppose not, Doctor Dhawan. After we fell, we all took a seat and watched a couple of them seal us in. That was about it."

"But not the very large type," the doctor interjected.

"No, not the real big ones," Max replied. "But big enough. I guess they weren't interested."

"Good thing," Drake said.

"Good thing for them," Vic threw in and slid the bolt on her machine gun for dramatic effect.

"You got that right," Santa added as he mimicked her actions with the smaller bolt on his lighter weapon.

"You're sweet," Vic stage-whispered.

"Everyone's OK down there?" Emoji called down to his compatriots.

Angel pointed his flashlight up. "Moj? Is that you? Hey Moj! All good. Ready to go, man!" He called to his bud.

Dr. Dhawan broke in on the camaraderie. "I am sorry to interrupt your reunion. I feel I should point out that your plans for dispatching the ants may be secondary to their plans for dispatching you," the doctor said. He carefully leaned over the rim of the pit, held his glasses to his nose, and looked down at the captives, shining his light on them.

"And what do you think their plans are, Doc?" Drake asked Dhawan from the halfway point.

The entomologist moved his light over the walls of the pit. "This chamber is unusually configured. This must be new," he whispered to himself as he played his light over the walls of the concavity. "The tapered bulb shape would make it difficult for any creature that fell in to get out," the scientist observed in a louder voice.

"Do say," Max opined.

"Shaped like a pear," Dhawan added, "or a pitcher." His light skipped off Vic, then moved to Santa and Angel, standing at the end of the knotted rope.

"Quite peculiar," the scientist said as he returned his light to Max.

"It is," Max said, looking past Drake. He didn't have to see the smirk on his boss's face.

"Very deep, too," Dr. Dhawan continued. "The trap is fashioned, of course, to catch what would constitute a threat by their sense. Something sizable. Unfortunately, even a human fits the requirements. This depth is at least twice the length of the largest ants. I'd say it would be impossible for one of them to get out of this. Odd, though. I wonder how they retrieve the catch?" he mused aloud. "If there were two or more, they might be able to climb on each other," he supposed.

"Too bad we're not as big as the bugs," Max said, walking off the limp from the fall. He looked up at the scientist. "I'd have to agree with you, Doc," he said in a flat voice. Drake knew that tone and smiled as he swayed back and forth. It was good Dhawan was out of Max's reach.

"There's one thing that might give you a better perspective on our situation, Doc," the ex-sergeant said. "That would be if the ground gave out, you fall two stories, and before you can get your wind back, watch a pair of giant bugs buzzin' over your head sealing you in, all the time wondering if they were ready to crawl down for a snack."

Dr. Dhawan's beam caught Max's face looking up; the soldier shielded the light with his hand.

"I'm sorry if my questions irritate you, Mr. Grunewald, but I am sure you would agree that, in the final analysis, results count, and the fact is I am up here while you, well, you are not up here."

Drake could see his friend open his mouth to reply, then close it. That wasn't good.

"Before continuing the debate about your relative positions, how about all of us getting out of here? And you can start with me!" Drake called to the top. His rope went up a few feet, stopped, and lifted again as the team above tugged. Another pull, and his soldiers lifted him out of the hole and to his feet.

As Drake untethered, he called Dhawan from the edge and asked him, "What were you going to say about their plans, Doc?"

The scientist took off his hat and mopped his brow. When he put it back on, he nudged his glasses and wagged his finger at the pit. "This is a trap, Mr. Drake. And the trap tenders have checked it," he said, waiting for Drake to nod before he continued, "The ants that were here, the ones that resealed the trap, have communicated their discovery to the nest."

The soldiers nearby listened to the doctor's presumptions.

"They will come to claim their prize." He looked into the pit and shook his head. "If there is one thing I can impart about this family of creatures, it is that they are efficient. Ruthlessly so. They do not procrastinate. They will be here soon."

Drake believed him. He looked from the doctor to Nygard.

Oberst Nygard walked off with her men and spoke to them in low tones. They left, skirting the trap and moving down the tunnel. She went back to Drake at the edge. "I think I have told my soldiers to guard no more than half a kilometer down the hall, so we are not surprised."

"Good idea," Drake agreed. He sent Cho and Emoji back to stand sentry in the other direction.

Drake tapped the top of the yellow drum twice and said to the moving men, "We're doing good, guys. As soon as we get those people out of the hole, you can roll this thing over the edge."

Marco countered the commander's suggestion, "No, we'll just lower it on ropes. We don't want to blow it in the last inning," the big man advised, nodding sagely.

Drake nodded in return. "Or that, either way, as long as it goes down the hole," he said. "But first, let's get them out of there," he added, gesturing to the hole.

The two big can handlers chopped footholds in the floor and retrieved the climbing essentials from the group in the trap. Tran had ropes and anchors, and after a few tosses, he got the gear to the team above.

While everyone was occupied, Drake opened the panel on the yellow drum, inserted the key from his neck, and turned it. A yellow underline flashed in the narrow black display, awaiting the code. He entered it on the keypad and confirmed. Five letters appeared in the panel, illuminating one character at a time to read A R M E D. The word blinked three times, and then each character was replaced by frowny faces. A time appeared to the right, counting down from 08:17:53. The seconds decayed, puzzling Drake. He twisted the key again, and the panel responded with an incompliant buzz.

That was a surprise. The can shouldn't be counting down because he hadn't set a timer. He ran his trigger finger over the smooth LED panel as he thought. The techs must have flipped the switch. Drake lightly tapped the panel twice. They had fail-safe orders. He had wondered why they had been added to the team.

Drake turned his key in the opposite direction, pulled it out, and snapped the door shut. He stood next to the can and lightly touched its top with his fingertips, tapping the metal twice.

The noise of Tran clambering out of the trap turned his attention to the edge. The two strongmen held the line as Oberst Nygard and Dr. Dhawan helped him over the top.

Drake walked to the edge of the hole and looked into the pit. Angel was at the other end of the knotted climbing rope, waiting for his cue to follow Tran out of the hole. Santa stood with him.

Vic sat in the sand across the chamber, her back to the wall and the machine gun across her legs.

Max brooded away from the rest.

"Max," Drake called down. The big man looked up, and Drake held out four fingers twice. "We're lit," he said in a monotone.

Max shook his head. "Of course," he said to himself. "Giant ants, giant ant traps, everybody's in a rush. Just typical," he complained. He exhaled loudly and stood, shouldering his rifle and concluding in a louder voice

474

for the benefit of the others, "Let's get this show back on the road! It's time to leave!"

Drake smiled and played his light across his crew and the sandy floor of the pit. The mission felt near to completion. They were deep enough; the package was armed and on the doorstep. All they had to do was drop it off and make an exit.

He watched the people in the pit, then closed his eyes for a second. Not a regular second, but it was one of those extra long ones that cram thirty seconds of what the hell into the blink of an eye because when he blinked, he was looking at a different world.

The floor went down the drain, emptying the chamber like an overclocked hourglass, sweeping Max and Angel away in the falling tide of white sand.

Santa grabbed the rope and hung on as the ground fell away, leaving him kicking the air and screaming for help.

Drake glimpsed Max and Angel floundering in the sandslide as the torrent engulfed them. He stared, stunned by the calamity and the impossibility of rescuing his men as they sank into the sand.

When the sand fell, Vic slid a few yards down until her boot heels stranded her on a seam in the wall to human fly her high above the falling floor. She caught on a few inches of ledge, couldn't move, and there was no good way down, but it was her only choice.

She looked for her teammates; Santa was bellyaching on the rope, but no Angel or Max.

The soldier cautiously leaned forward to look past her gear and gun and see where they went. The floor was a white pond fifty feet below, brightly illuminated by sweeping flashlights from above, but no Angel or Max.

Vic gasped at the distance and moved her head to see more, throwing her off balance and nearly her perch, but forced herself against the ant-crete, throwing her head back to regain her footing. She kept still for a minute or two, restricting her movement to heavy breathing.

With the sand drained, the cavernous funnel that formed the base of the trap was revealed. It was twenty meters of sheer wall down to that blank disc of white sand, a seven-floor drop from the roof to the sidewalk.

Santa wrapped himself around the rope. He didn't have the strength to climb, so he just hung. Drake's eyes darted from him to the empty trap. "Haul that man up and get another rope going," he ordered over his shoulder.

Tran was rigging another before the echo died, and the two can handlers got back to work and heaved. Santa lurched upward a few feet, and they hefted the rope again. He held that line in a death grip.

Dhawan and Nygard stood at the edge and added their lights to Drake's, shining from Santa to Vic or brightening the white pond at the bottom of the steep cone.

Seven stories below, a ripple ran through the sand. Concentric rings flashed across the floor like a rock had been dropped into the pond. The rings subsided, and a bass buzz became discernable. They listened, and the scientist moved his beam from above to locate the source. "That noise, do you hear it?" he asked, "What is it?"

The sand answered with the eruption of a powerful sand geyser, blasting a screaming Angel out of the powder in a brief trajectory that ended against the wall with an audible impact. The battered man slid down the funnel and tumbled onto the gypsum.

Vic shouted to her compatriot, "Hang on, Angel! We're coming for you!"

"Stay where you are, soldier," Drake shouted across the chamber to Vic. She was trying to find a way down the sheer wall of the trap. "You'll break your leg," he concluded.

The big men heaved again, and Santa went up a few feet. His strength was failing, and he slipped down the rope. "C'mon, c'mon," he rasped, his voice raised. "Let's go!" he screamed. They heaved him up another few feet. Santa was heavy. And he was unlucky.

"I can't hold on, man," he groaned loudly in the echo chamber. Santa's strength was gone, and he was on the verge of falling. His bloody hands lubricated the plastic rope, making it harder to hold, and the harder he tried to hold, the more lubricant squeezed out.

He slipped down a knot. His feet kicked, looking for the line to wrap around, but it wasn't there. Santa had reached the end of his rope. He wailed without a note of hope, then shrieked with finality, "I'm done! Come on, hurry up! Come and get me! Come and get me!"

A great white bug exploded from the surface of the sandy pond, stabbing its double-long legs into the funnel walls and bounding upwards in springing vaults to Santa.

The monster's maw opened, exposing an ample gullet ringed with enormous sharp and grinding teeth rippling down the peristaltic passageway. Santa's mask of terror petrified, and his scream cracked into short, small noises. He lifted his dangling legs, cringing into a bite-sized treat on a string.

The creature swayed on its radiating legs and lifted, surrounding Santa with its enormous jaws. Santa pulled in his last breath and blew it out as a piercing scream cut short when the gigantic beak shut with a snap.

The mutant shook its fat head in blurringly fast bursts, then opened its beak a crack to spit out the frayed, wet end of the rope.

This creature was singular by more than one measure. It was the largest the nest produced, twice the size of a soldier ant and wormier looking, barely ant-like in appearance. It was more of a translucent larva with long, spindly pincer legs and holes for eyes. It didn't have the big jaws of the other ants; they had fused into a sideways parrot beak, serrated with shark tooth barbs pointing inward.

The denizen of the trap attacked so fast that Santa was going down the hatch before anyone could react. In the few seconds it took to collect their lights on this trap-ant, he was gone; an empty rope hung over the inflated grub bobbing on its springy legs.

From Vic's viewpoint on the other side of the bug, the flashlights lit up the inner workings of the monster. She could see every inch of food processor Santa making his trip down the see-through insect. She looked away, turning her head and almost losing her footing again.

This monstrosity among the mutants was normally dormant, sleeping buried in the powdery gypsum. Whatever biological purpose it served, the sheer enormity of the bug served another. This denizen of the trap existed as a plug in the drain; its bulk stoppered the sand, keeping it from spilling into the cavern below. It had moved in the past, and several times, for the sand piled in the chamber below was high, almost to the opening in the ceiling. Almost.

Angel was still stunned and shaking off his collision with the wall when the monster from the trap went on the attack. First, an underground buzz started and got so loud everything vibrated like a bass speaker. The soldier was on his knees, covering his ears and sinking into the agitation when the earth moved, and the sand could no longer support him.

The entire floor lifted as the great white grub breached the vibrating gypsum and launched itself from the surface, vaulting up the shaft and climbing the wall in great bounds.

As the bug drove upward, Angel headed in the other direction, going down the drain, tumbling, smothering, and rubbed raw in torrents of white gypsum pouring through the hole like a one-second egg timer.

He rode the wall down in the sandy deluge and was swept into the drainpipe to be squashed, nearly suffocated, scraped raw against the wall, and then spit into nothingness.

After a quick shot through a short vertical shaft, the drain emptied into a vast chamber, a canyon-sized natural formation the ants encountered in their excavations and incorporated into the waste management system for their colony.

It was the city dump for the ants, where things of no use were thrown.

Angel was being squeezed beyond endurance. With no time left before his body burst open or he choked on dust, he was shot out of the cannon into the void, weightless and wondering if he had died. He got his answer by slamming into the sandpile on his back, knocking his wind out, and resetting his mental process to being painfully alive.

He huffed, and he puffed, and he got his wind back, staring up at the changing glow of the oblong drainpipe as the flashlights far above searched and reflected into the shaft. He wiped his face and breathed, watching the faint light filtering from the hole.

It looked like an oblong moon in a starless sky.

Angel laughed out loud. Then he did the primal scream. Then he shouted. "Why did this happen!? Just tell me why this happened!" he bellowed into the blackness.

"It happened because you're a greedy man, Angel," a deep voice from the darkness said.

Angel jumped in the dark, switched his rifle light on, and frantically pointed the beam in all directions.

"It's me! Put that down," the voice ordered.

A light on the business end of a Zastava came on, shining in Angel's face. He held his hand up against the glare. "Max! Wow. You kind of scared me. I thought you were the devil or something. I'm impressed. It's true, you never die, do you?" He took a breath.

The light moved to a spot on the sand. Max sat down and put the light out. "Die? That's the last thing I'm going to do," he scoffed.

Angel prattled on for a few minutes while Max didn't listen. When the soldier took a breath, the large man said quietly, "You know, Angel, life's a funny thing. Of all people to be stuck with, I don't know why it had to be nonstop you."

"Who's stuck with anyone?" Angel asked sullenly. "You could keep going down the hill," he added.

"We have to wait for them," he replied, pointing up, though Angel couldn't see him gesturing. "I just wanted to wait quietly," Max whispered.

Angel started a reply, but Max shushed him. "Quietly," he reminded the soldier.

They laid back on the snow-white peak in the dark and looked straight up at the hollow moon.

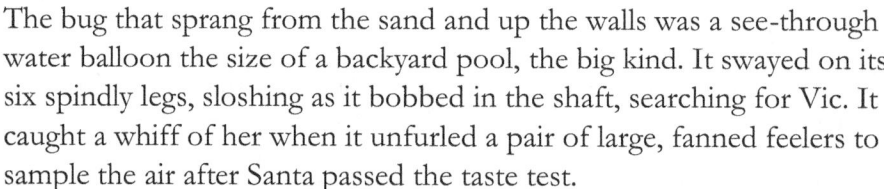

The bug that sprang from the sand and up the walls was a see-through water balloon the size of a backyard pool, the big kind. It swayed on its six spindly legs, sloshing as it bobbed in the shaft, searching for Vic. It caught a whiff of her when it unfurled a pair of large, fanned feelers to sample the air after Santa passed the taste test.

Vic couldn't move and had nowhere to go. She snagged her boot heels on a seam about as wide as a thumb and balanced over the drop by leaning back and keeping her arms glued to the wall. And now the giant grub with the food-processor teeth was looking in her direction.

The flashlights from above put on a light show inside the translucent creature, illuminating beating organs, a spectacularly reflective vascular system, and a long red swirl of digestion previously known as Santa.

The bulbosity pulled back from Vic, opened its giant beak of teeth, and coiled to strike.

Only a few seconds had elapsed from the monster's leap, Santa's demise, and the trap emptying, but you can't stay stunned forever. Drake was the first to shake it off. "Shoot that thing!" he shouted as he pulled his .45 and put five holes into the nearest leg of the monster. The limb shuddered from the wounds and retracted from the wall.

The big moving guys unslung their ARs and fired into the beast, causing it to recoil and counterattack. It twisted to the attackers above, turning its featureless face to the threat and emitting a wet hiss.

The beast rocked, swinging its blobby body and using the momentum to throw itself upward, stepping fast on its gangly legs and charging to the top of the hole.

Dhawan shrieked and leaped back; his retreat was stopped by smacking into the tunnel wall.

Nygard stood at the edge, swapping the magazine in her gun for one with a red stripe of tape.

The monster bounded upward through a hail of lead and hooked a clawed leg over the top, hissing spit as it lifted its great white bulk and pointed its pushed-in little eyes at the Oberst.

The maggot monster opened its beak rowed with teeth, and pulled back, tensing to spring.

The Oberst lifted her compact submachine gun and fired a single round into the giant grub's head.

For a moment, everything paused; even the bug seemed surprised. It wrinkled its brow in response to the glowing ember between its eyes.

Then, the luminous point in the giant's head exploded. Fireworks went off inside the bug, the lights went out, and it fell, dead as a two-ton doornail.

The big bag of bug goo fell and hit the drain hard enough to push most of its bulk through, but not all. It jammed into the hole with its legs bunched together, pointing up. On the other side of the pipe, the giant sack of bug bulged from the ceiling of an immense cavern, pendulously sloshing above a hill of white sand big enough to ski.

The Oberst watched the miscreant fall. She removed the striped magazine from her weapon and replaced it with the unmarked one. She looked up at Drake and smiled, answering his unasked question, "Bomb bullets. What you call the exploding rounds, I believe."

Drake cocked his head then stated, "There's no such thing."

Oberst Nygard nodded. "That is true," she added, "but these are much too new."

The translucent carcass was stuck in the drain. The fall wasn't sufficient to push it through the hole, which was lucky for Max and Angel.

They were lying at the top of the sand hill, looking up at the hole, maybe fifty feet above, when the grub went down the drain.

There had been flashes, and they had heard shots. Max jumped to his feet, straining to see and hear more. He was staring at the moon-shaped hole when the huge caterpillar, or whatever the bug was, burst through the hole and hung there, bulging like a balloon squeezed from the other side.

Max reflexively ducked when the thing popped out. It was gigantic. It had to be the size of a beach blimp. Big, bulging, and like it was about to pop.

Angel flattened into the sand and screamed. After a second, Max realized they hadn't been crushed to death and brought his gun to bear, turning on the light.

"Ugh," the big man said. "That is one huge sack of goo." He made a face as he looked at the bloated herniation hanging over them. It bulged pendulously, distended with its newly liquified organs. Viscous ooze collected at the nadir of the sac, preparing to drip.

"I think we ought to get out of here, Sarge," Angel said without taking his eyes off the bladder of Damocles.

"You said it," Max replied. "Are you good?"

"All downhill. No problem." Angel clicked his light on and made haste down the slope, with Max hurrying right behind him to get out from under.

Drake stood at the brink, looking down.

"Tran, we need more rope. It's a lot further to the bottom now," he said over his shoulder. "Do you have enough line?" he asked as an afterthought.

"No sweat," Tran answered. "Enough for a couple."

"But get Vic first," Drake said. He eyed Dr. Dhawan in the shadows, curled up against the wall.

"Natch," Tran replied as he cut the frayed rope clean. "I'm setting up to get her now."

Oberst Nygard stood next to Drake, squinting at the jumble of dead bug at the bottom. "That monster," she said, "was too fast."

Drake turned, looking past her to watch Tran instructing the two big guys, pointing into the pit and explaining their role in his plan with arcing gestures. "I want you to take command and get everyone out," he said to the Oberst.

"Yes," she replied. "And you will go down to there and search for your men."

"Ja," he agreed.

"Too bad," she said and smiled. "I wanted to join with you and Herr Grunewald in work."

Drake responded absently, "You never can tell, Nygard." Tran sent the two big guys to the other side of the hole and watched them pick up a line and brace themselves.

The Oberst shrugged. "Commander Drake, you are the optimist. I am the realist. How do you hope when you are so puny in the giant insect nest?"

Drake answered her, distracted by Tran, standing at the edge of the trap, signaling to the moving men with his light, "I don't know about hope. I just do," he said. "After all, what else are we here for? You have to keep doing whatever you do," he added, glancing at the colonel.

Nygard turned to watch Tran step off the edge and the glow from his light going down in the pit. She looked at the two big men across the hole when they made noise straining against the rope. One of them tied the rope to an anchor driven into the cave floor; then both ran around the brink to the spot where Tran took the leap. They took the line going over the edge, heaved it up, and tied it off. One of the big guys laid down, reached over the rim, and handed Vic's LMG up over his head. Then he got Vic off Tran's back and lifted her to the top with one arm. The other big guy pulled Tran up by his line.

484

Tran unhooked and nodded as he hurried past Drake and Nygard to collect his rope. On his way back, Drake stopped him.

"Do you need those ropes?" he asked the linesman.

Tran shook his head. "No. Got extra, and we're rigged all the way back," he responded.

"OK. Leave those two going over and leave me that one loose," Drake said, indicating the coil Tran was wrapping up.

The rope master looked into the pit and then at Drake. "Where are we going?" he asked.

"Just me," Drake answered. Tran began to volunteer. "Just me," Drake repeated, adding, "Thanks."

He stepped past the young man and called over to the moving men, "Marco, Libby, bring the can up." He pointed to a place on the precipice.

They lifted the bright yellow drum by the poles and carried it over. "Right there," he said, gesturing to the spot. "You can just lay it down." They did.

"Now take out the handles and push it over the edge," Drake ordered.

The two big guys looked at each other. Libby pulled the pipe handles from the welded hoops and tossed them into the sand. They both leaned over to look into the pit.

"That is way down there," one of them said. The other agreed.

"Guys, push the can over so you can get out of here," Drake told them again.

They made thoughtful, then disagreeable faces at the thought of shoving the drum over the edge of the cliff. "Yes, sir," Marco said. "But one thing," he said and held up the index link of his sausage mitt. "Can I ask a question?"

"Sure, go ahead," Drake consented, "what is it?"

"Well, is it OK to drop this thing that far?" he asked, pushing his oppositional thumb at the pit. He leaned toward Drake and lowered his voice, saying, "I mean that could be dangerous, couldn't it?" Marco leaned over even closer and lowered his voice to what he thought was a whisper. "After all, you don't just throw an A-bomb off a cliff, do you? It could go off."

Libby snorted at his friend. "An A-bomb? Markey, that would be an atomic bomb." He emphasized the last two words, then repeated one of them for his buddy's benefit, "Atomic." He shook his head at Marco and snorted again.

It was quiet for a moment, then Marco asked, "What do you think we've been carrying?"

His friend eyed him suspiciously, then smirked knowingly. "It's some kind of bug bomb, I guess. I don't know. But I know it's no atomic bomb," Libby said.

"Uh-huh," his counterpart responded. "What do you think those are?" he asked, pointing to the trefoils on the yellow can.

"Those? Decoration or something." He peered intently at the can. "I know. They're, you know, symbols." Libby looked harder until he got it. "Oh yeah. It shows it sprays in three directions." He nodded assuredly.

"So, you think we've been carrying a big can of bug spray down here?" Marco asked his friend. He knew his partner's knowing smile was his answer. "You are an alarming person," he concluded.

"Guys, push the can over," Drake said again.

Libby put his hands on the drum, ready to push, until Marco stopped him. "You're sure this won't blow up?" Libby asked, looking over the edge at Drake. "That's a big drop."

"It's going over," Drake said. "Want a soft landing? Aim for the bug," he advised.

The two big guys gave each other the whatever look and pushed. The yellow drum rolled off the edge and, in a few beats, impacted with a distinctly organic sound. Libby counted to three and then relaxed, confident he had not been atomized.

The new moon wasn't looking so good. Max and Angel sat with their backs against the wall a hundred yards from the base of the big sandy hill that went almost all the way up to the big dead bug stuck in the drain. They waited to see what was going to happen.

"Do you think they know where we are?" Angel asked anxiously.

Max thought for a moment. "What do you mean 'we?' Why would they even think you were still alive?" he asked.

"Me? Why do you have to…"

Max interrupted Angel's protest. "Shh!" he said, dropping his voice in the darkness. "Look up there," he whispered. "See the light up there? The light glowing through that caterpillar? That's light from the top from our guys. As long as that light's there, we wait here," Max pronounced.

"What if it goes out, then what?" Angel asked.

"That's when I trade you to the bugs for a ride out of here," Max said, snapping his flashlight on under his chin for special effects lighting.

Angel started to laugh, then stopped to listen. "Did you hear that? What was that sound?" the soldier clicked his light on and moved the beam up the mountain of sand, ending at the top and shining through the gigantic globe of bug goo hanging over it. Even at their considerable distance, they could see a tidal effect in the fluid, sloshing back and forth in the huge sac as if a stone dropped into a limpid lake hanging in the night sky.

"That is revolting," Max said and made a face as he looked away. "I'm going to take a nap," he said, closing his eyes and laying his head on his hands.

Angel didn't let him sleep. "I don't think you are, Max. Take a look," he said.

The big man groaned, opened one eye, and turned his head to look up the mountain. He opened his other eye and sat up. Max cursed in the dark as the moon flickered and went out.

Drake was about to tell the group to head back when Nygard brought her hand to her earpiece.

She tensed. "Satan," she said under her breath.

Shots echoed from the Norwegian sentries down the tunnel. Flashes preceded the next volley.

"Shots are closer," Drake said, pulling his automatic shotgun. Dr. Dhawan jumped to his feet and backed up to the wall. Libby and Marco brought their weapons up.

Nygard slid her hand into her jacket to be sure her unopened pack of cigarettes was still there and started in the direction of her guard, but Drake called her back. "Wait! Stop!" he yelled. She crouched in the go position, coiled around her submachine gun.

"Wait. Watch," Drake ordered. Her attention was riveted downstream on her soldiers. She spoke into her mic. Drake pointed his light down the tunnel and then snapped it off.

"There!" he shouted. "There's a light! They're coming back," he said. "Wait for them. Nobody's splitting up. They're on their way back, Nygard."

"Ja, ja. It's OK," she said, squinting at the approaching pinpoint of light.

"Did you try raising your men?" he asked the Norwegian commander, indicating his headset.

She nodded. "I did. There was no answer," she said.

Drake shook his head, saying, "No surprise. These sets aren't reliable." He brought his hand to his earpiece and paged the two men he sent back. "Cho, Moj, come in."

The reply was immediate. "We're here, boss. This is Cho. Nothing new. Was that shooting?" the rear guard asked.

"Everything's under control," Drake replied. "Just checking in. Stay on your toes. Out." He looked down the tunnel and saw the light from Nygard's men closing fast. "They are really moving," he said. The Oberst stood next to him, scrutinizing the approaching light.

"That light," she said out loud to herself. "It moves erratically."

One by one, soldiers turned their attention to the light. Flashlights clicked on and pointed down the tunnel. Oberst Nygard moved against the wall forward of the hole. She raised her weapon to the oncoming light and challenged in Norwegian.

Tran was against the wall on the opposite side of the tunnel. Drake stepped back from the rim of the pit and pointed his short shotgun into the tunnel, over the hole.

The light bounced wildly as it closed the distance, flashing in all directions, lighting up a giant ant eye for a split second, then bug legs in motion, and then it jostled into their beams, the flashlight dancing on the lanyard attached to the belt around the torso in a blue uniform skewered on the jaws of the ant.

The huge mutant charged in, stopping on a dime at the edge of the pit. It extended its head and dropped the Norwegian trunk into the hole. Its antennae swept the air rising from the trap.

The ant stepped from the edge of the hole. Its legs began drumming the cave floor, vibrating so fast they blurred in the soldiers' lights. The bug's back lowered, and the arched body emitted a pulsating screech to accompany the drum. Dhawan, his hands over his ears against the din, ran up to Drake and shouted in his face, "Stop it! Kill it! Kill it!"

The doctor made a wild grab for Drake's shotgun, but the soldier pushed him back, and the scientist tumbled to the floor. Drake raised his 12-gauge and moved forward on the bug, pulling the trigger as he went.

Nygard ran around the far perimeter of the pit, and her submachine gun chattered, chopping into the left eye of the nightmare. The faceted disc exploded, gushing bright syrup from the gaping injury.

Tran opened up from the other side of the hole, aiming for the gleaming black jaws dripping with Norwegian blood and shredded them to pulp.

The ant's call stopped; the monster was done for. With the last of its life, it rushed the attackers. Tran plastered himself to the wall, narrowly avoiding the bug's powerful charge. He fired as it tore past, opening wounds in the creature's thorax and destroying two leg joints, effectively severing the appendages.

Nygard had to dive under the bug to avoid being crushed against the wall. She rolled beneath its abdomen as the monster stepped around the trap, trying to keep its footing on the narrow ledges on each side of the hole.

Drake led the firing squad with his 12-gauge as Libby and Marco opened up with their ARs. The monster's wounds were so damaging that the creature finally collapsed, clawing at the sandy ledges and scraping out deep troughs in the edge as it slid into the abyss.

A two-ton insect falling seven stories onto a dangerously distended giant bladder of bug goo hit with the sound of a slap so loud they could feel it. It also provided a wallop big enough to push the remains of the humongous grub down the shaft and follow it through, A-bomb and all.

Drake's light joined the others circling the now unclogged drain. "Well, that was handy," he said.

"Did you hear something?" Angel asked. "I thought I heard something."

"Quiet," Max suggested.

They held their lights on the giant cyst suspended from the chamber's roof, hanging in space above the sandy hill. The family-sized pool of fluid in a huge water balloon distended through the hole at the top of the cave, refracting the light and filtering the glow of the flashlight beams through the milky glop.

Max listened. "Shots," he said.

The reports were muffled, very faint compared to the next volley. That was closer, and different weapons were firing in the trap above them. It was hard to judge the sound in the caverns and with the giant bug plug stoppering the drain.

Max cocked his head in the dark to listen better. A volley ended the firefight, and in the fusillade were a few distinctive big bore blasts; it was Drake's shotgun.

While the big man formulated his next observation, the dead ant plummeted. Dispatched at the top of the trap and sent into the abyss, it fell 70 feet to an explosive splashdown with the big dead grub at the bottom.

The effect of a two-ton insect falling seven stories and impacting a 4000-gallon bag of bug juice half squeezed through a hole was eventful.

Below the drain, Max and Angel were listening to the gunfire and had their lights trained on the hanging grub when the ant hit. A tidal shock wave shot through the bloated bug and ripped open the end of the sac, blowing liquified maggot goo all over the hill.

"What…" Angel began, interrupted by the drained skin of the great white ant popping out of the pipe, crashing onto the peak, and sliding down the hill.

"…the…," he tried to continue but stopped speaking to watch the head of the ant break loose from the impact and roll down their side of the sugary hill.

"Fudge," Max interjected, completing the soldier's thought. "What the fudge," Max reiterated. He kept his light on the bouncing ant head as it tumbled down the slope.

Angel started to stand, but Max restrained him. "Relax, it's not going to hit us, you'll see," the big man assured him. "Just take it easy."

The giant bug part picked up speed and shot from the base of the hill, spinning across the cavern floor, skidding to a stop a few feet away and looking straight at them.

"See?" Max asked. "There's no need for profanity. Just think it through; analyze the situation and stay calm," Max instructed. "That's what comes from experience," he added, motioning to the ant's head as it rocked to a stop. "No threat, no sweat. I assessed, and now it doesn't even get a second glance from me."

On cue, the postmortem autonomics kicked in, and the remains of the huge jaws gnashed together several times, making a sharp smacking sound and bouncing the broken and oozing head up and down.

Max jumped to his feet, cursing with everything he had, pulling the trigger on the Halloween head, letting loose a lot of lead and pent-up tension. He stopped shooting and slid back to his seat in the sand against the wall. Thick smoke wafted from the barrel of his Zastava; the ant head leaked into the sand.

Angel sat quietly.

Max's voice was a low monotone, and he spoke without looking at Angel. "Say not one word. Simply obliterate the last two minutes from your memory."

"Do you mind if I make it the last five minutes?" Angel asked. "I'd like to forget that lecture, too."

———————————— 🛸 ————————————

Drake leaned over the edge with his light, peering at the dark hole at the bottom of the funnel. It looked like that last bug pushed everything through. He heard Dhawan's footfall behind him.

"You know the entire colony has been alerted by that call to her nestmates," the scientist whispered, hoarse with fear.

Drake turned and brought his light up to the man's face. "No longer academic, is it, Doc?"

"Suddenly not," the doctor admitted. "And I must apologize for my actions. It was that sound," he said, shaking his head. "Quite unsettling."

"Don't sweat it, Doc. Everyone hits a rough patch now and then," Drake said. The scientist's expression was more than fearful. It was desperate.

Drake had seen people lose their nerve before. "Well, Doc," Drake said calmly, "it's time to head back, anyway. We're all done here."

"Oh, yes? Good. Time to go. Yes, I think our mission is complete," Dhawan excitedly replied. "I will await your instruction, Commander Drake," he said. The doctor stepped back slowly, sinking into the shadows.

Drake raised his eyebrows as he watched the doctor retreat into the darkness, then turned to the rest of the group, ready to give them the news that it was time to go and that he would stay to find Max and Angel.

"Everybody!" he called to the group. They turned, and Drake said, "It's time we…hang on," he raised his hand to his headset. "Where are you?" he asked.

Cho's voice crackled in his ear. "We're at the base of the last drop. Wait. More shots! Hear them?" the soldier reported excitedly.

Gunshots, faint and far away, echoed through the cave.

Dhawan eyed everyone listening to their headsets and pulled his on.

Cho's voice crackled with static and gunfire. "Drake, did you hear that? That wasn't us. That was way back by Case," he said hurriedly.

Right after he spoke, small arms fire shot through the tunnels. "Can you get anything from them on comm?" Drake asked the soldiers.

"Negative," Emoji came back, "nothing."

"All right, Moj, back up the drop. See if you can get anything. Relay through Cho," he ordered.

The Oberst was next to him. She turned on her gunlight and checked her weapon. She was heading into the tunnel. "That was Nun," she said, nodding to the red streak on the brink of the pit. "I must be sure of Renko," she said matter-of-factly.

Drake knew she had to do that. He nodded and said, "Be quick, Colonel." She took off down the tunnel, double-timing it into the dark.

He turned to the group again. "When Oberst Nygard returns, she will…"

Cho broke in on the headset. "More shooting. Lots more. It sounds closer now. I think…"

"Where's Moj?" Drake broke in.

"He's at the top. I can see his light," Cho answered.

"I can't hear him. What's he saying?" he asked Cho.

There was a pause, and then Cho came back. "Moj said he saw lights way up the cave at the other drop. Lights and shooting. He thinks our guys are coming down."

Drake cursed as his earpiece rushed with static. "Lights coming down the tunnel, lots of shooting, that's what he's saying," Cho relayed excitedly.

"All right. Tell Moj to get down, and you guys get back here. Don't wait!" Drake snapped into the mic. It all just went sideways. If Case and his crew beat it deeper into the tunnel, then the way back was not the way out anymore.

More shots came from the shaft. Nonstop. Emoji came into the comm. "All hell's breaking loose up there, Drake! Sounds like they're close to the top of this drop." If Moj sounded scared, Cho must be a wreck.

The gunfire sounded in bursts of rapid-fire ARs. There was no more hammer of machine guns.

Emoji and Cho both squawked in his earpiece. "At the top! At the top! There they are! IT'S THEM!" one of them yelled. The shots played in the comm set for the small group before they replayed through the tunnels. "… down the ropes! …pushed one of those techs over, coming down fast! No-no-no!" Cho shouted. "One of them fell! Grab him! Oh, man! This is bad! Run, man, run!"

There was an explosion. The sound bounced through the caverns, followed by another roar.

"Grenades! Keep...," Emoji shouted into the comm. The gunfire didn't stop. "Go! Go!" one of them crackled through the radio.

The small group by the trap listened intently to the firefight, staring into the tunnel, watching for their teammates. Tran would have bolted down the tunnel if Drake hadn't stopped him. "You can't help them run any faster," Drake told him.

Other voices broke into their earpieces, and the cross talk bubbled with warnings and headcounts. "Where's Burner? Got the bombs!" someone shouted, garbled through the static. "Going over?" Gunshots. "Auto, auto, auto!" Static. "Now! Now! Let it go!" Explosion. No gunfire. "That's all!" a clipped voice said, and a final shot rang through the chorus of ant calls.

Emoji shouted over the comm, "We're coming in!"

Drake trotted around the pitfall to peer into the darkness, looking for Nygard and a new way out. Far into the tunnel, there was a light, another spark bouncing their way; he thought of Renko's arrival and raised his shotgun.

A hundred yards down the tunnel, Nygard's submachine gun chopped, each flash projected the shadow of her firing stance on the cave wall. The firing stopped, and it was dark, almost quiet.

Oberst Nygard trotted in behind the light and leaned against the wall sucking in air. Her tunic was torn, and blood ran from her hair down the side of her face.

"Did you find your man?" Drake asked. She nodded grimly. He looked past her into the dark tunnel and asked, "Anything following you?"

"Not now. There was one. But many more down the cave," the Oberst said between breaths. She bent over and put her hands on her knees to get her wind back.

"The others didn't follow?" Drake asked.

496

"No. But I think they will. Right now, they are eating their wounded." She straightened up and wiped her sleeve through the blood on her face.

Drake nodded. "Ants are coming from the other direction, too. We can't go back. We have to find another way out." He gestured to the trap. "And that looks like it," he said.

"Deeper into Hell," she murmured, staring into the pit. Oberst Nygard looked at Drake. "Ja. Why not?" she concluded, wiped more blood, and checked her weapon. "We go to Hell."

"You may not be far off, Colonel," Drake said as he walked around the trap, heading for Dhawan, sitting by the wall and staring at nothing. "They are going to come. All of them," he said as Drake walked up. "All of THEM," he repeated. "They stopped calling. Have you noticed? They've gone quiet, but the messages are flying." He waved his right hand back and forth. "In the air," he said, "You can smell them talking."

Drake exhaled and got him to his feet. "C'mon Doc, snap out of it," he said to the scientist, lifting him by his arm. He walked him out of the shadows. "We're getting out of here, and you have to do some climbing," he said to him.

"Climbing?" The doctor blinked his eyes. "Oh, good." He looked at the pit and then back to Drake. "We're climbing up, right?"

Drake pursed his lips and replied, "Yes, but first, we must climb down." He signaled Tran over.

"Are those lines good to take us down?" Drake asked the climbing expert.

"No. They have to be secured at the bottom, so I'm going down to do that. Then send them down using this," he said, holding up a new piece of climbing gear with a flourish.

"Connect your harness to this tractor mechanism. It clicks right in. I'll show you." Tran demonstrated the hookup, twisting around to snap the hardware on the rope to his climbing harness.

"It's that easy," Tran said, "And when I get down there, I'll disengage and let the unit return. It will climb up the line."

"Really?" Drake asked.

"Yep," Tran said, "but the main thing is it governs your descent, slowing your fall down the rope."

"Wow," Drake said, impressed. "I never heard of these things."

"I have two of the prototypes," the inventor replied. "I haven't put them on the market yet. Anyway, they probably need more testing." Tran stepped to the brink and said, "I'm going to send them both up from the bottom so they learn the drop, then I'll fire one shot for go." He thought for a moment, then added, "Any more shots than that would probably mean no-go."

"Right," Drake acknowledged. The young climber slung rope over both shoulders, clicked on a light, and dropped off the cliff. A steady whir came from the shaft, and Drake leaned over to watch the light fall steadily to the bottom.

Drake turned around and stepped back from the edge as Dr. Dhawan walked up.

"We should climb up, climb out," Dhawan was muttering. "Not down. Not deeper."

"No choice, Doc," Drake clapped him on the shoulder encouragingly and turned him from the pit. "You know the ants are in the tunnel back there. We can't go that way now," he explained to the scientist.

Dhawan pointed in the other direction. Drake shook his head at the suggestion. "The Norwegian soldiers were killed down there by the ants. We can't go that way either," Drake said.

Dhawan considered, looking in both directions of the tunnel. He nodded and gazed into the pit.

Drake's pep talk was interrupted by shouts coming from the cave. Their heads turned as Cho and Emoji ran out of the tunnel and into their lights.

Cho won. He ran out of the tunnel first and fastest, colliding with Libby. The big man caught the returning sentry by the jacket and laughed. "Whoa, guy, don't worry, you found us." He brushed cave dust from Cho's shoulders and kept him on his feet.

Cho pushed away from the large man as Emoji ran out of the dark.

"Tell them," Cho panted, dropping to his knees, spent for breath.

Emoji was gulping air, too, but warned them in gasped syllables, "They're coming. All of them." He wavered and bent, leaning on his gun. "No one's left," he gasped. "The bugs in the chamber woke up. Hundreds. Hundreds. Got the guard before they could…" He had to breathe.

"… get out," Cho picked it up. "Rushed Case. Got him. Pez and Burner let them have it. Tried saving the techs. One fell, maybe jumped. Dead. The other never made it down." He dropped, sitting on the floor, breathing deeply. "Didn't matter. Didn't matter," he repeated.

Emoji spoke. "They were trying to make it down the ropes. I don't know who. Burner was one of the last, but the bugs ran them over the edge; a flood of bugs." He shook his head. "There were so many of them."

"Moj is right. It was a flood," Cho said. "They kept coming over the top like a waterfall. And people. The ants kept coming. Kept falling. Piling up." His speech slowed as he remembered. "It really didn't matter. Even piled up, they kept snapping. The whole heap was giant ants, all squirming around with those big mouths sticking out, chomping." Vic handed him a water bottle.

"A lot of people fell, got pushed over the top, fell on the bug pile," Emoji brought his hand to his eyes. "I didn't see anyone make it down, no one…" His voice trailed off.

Cho took another drink and passed the water bottle to Moj. "You could hear the snaps, their mouths snapping, they were so hard. When they bit someone, it was like they exploded." He took the bottle back and drank. "Even running, I heard that snapping, really hard." He stopped talking, becoming aware he had been miming the pinching ant mouths with his hands.

A sudden noise from the hole startled everyone and made them turn to the twitching ropes hanging over the edge. The lines were pulling as if there were climbers over the side. Guns pointed at the brink to cover Tran's climbing machine, pulling itself over the edge. A single shot chased by echoes came from the pit.

Tran's voice was garbled in the headsets. Drake leaned over the edge and could see the pinpoint of light swinging a microscopic arc. The comm became clearer.

"…over the top," Tran was saying.

Drake broke in, "Tran, I can hear you now. One of your robots came back up. It climbed right over the, wait, here's the second," he told the rope boss as he watched the contraption come over the edge of the pit and travel along the rope to bang into the anchor.

"OK, hook up your climbers like I showed you," Tran said into the comm. "Everything's set. Snap the bracket to their harness and send them down."

Drake's response paused in the static. "Just like that?" he asked. "Over the side?"

"Throw them over," Tran responded, then laughed. "Don't worry, Drake. I'll catch them."

"Roger, Tran." Drake scanned the group, settling on the scientist curled beside the wall. His headphones were hanging around his neck. "I'll send Dhawan first," he said.

The rest of the group had their headphones on. All of them turned their attention to Dr. Dhawan. He looked from face to face. "What?" he asked.

Tran laughed in the comm and said, "Fire away."

Dhawan slowly stood against the cave wall and wondered again, "What's happening?"

"You're happening, Doc," Drake answered as he stepped to the scientist and put a comradely hand on his shoulder. "We are moving our valuable assets to safety, and that means you."

"But," the doctor rejoined as Drake walked him to the ropes by the edge of the trap.

"There's nothing to it," Drake assured the entomologist. "All we have to do is turn you around," the commander narrated as he turned Dhawan and lifted his jacket to expose the attachment points of the doctor's climbing harness.

"And then we take this and click it on," Drake said as he lifted the bracket and rope to position it over Dhawan's harness and snapped it home. The connection was complete. "And that's all there is to it," Drake said, turning the doctor back to face him, putting the scientist's boot heels at the brink of the precipice.

"Now, what was that you attached?" the doctor asked with a hint of apprehension.

Drake shrugged. "The rope guy told me to do it."

"What's it for exactly? It's heavy," the doctor persisted, twisting to look over his shoulder.

"Like an elevator, Doc," Drake replied. "It's going to take you down there." He jabbed his trigger finger twice at the pit.

"Down there?" the scientist echoed.

"Down there," Drake repeated. "You're riding a prototype. Like an experiment." He put two fingers on Dhawan's chest and pressed.

It was just the push he needed. The scientist fell into the air filling a seven-story hole, and the mechanical governor engaged, slowing his descent to a dizzying but safe rate.

Dr. Dhawan bounced to a stop at the bottom of the rope, his feet just out of Tran's reach.

"You're one of the lighter guys," Tran said to him. "Reach back to your left and pull the big knob up," he instructed.

The doctor pulled, the bracket released, and he slid down the steep wall into Tran, who stopped the scientist from going down the drain.

When Dhawan disconnected, Tran sent the elevator mechanism riding the rope back to the top.

Tran held onto the scientist's arm as he pointed to the perimeters of the ledge, telling him, "Watch your step, Doc. There isn't a lot of room." Dhawan acknowledged and relaxed, leaning back against the steep wall. Tran patted him on the shoulder and said, "Stay put while I finish the next line."

With that, Tran secured the line to the anchor at the rim of the round shaft and left the coil next to the edge, ready to go. Tran estimated there were 100 meters of climbing line left, most of it in the coil for this drop. The flashlight stretched into the darkness, showing ten meters straight down.

"I can't tell how far this goes. It's just round and deep." Tran peered into the deep shaft, stirring the gloom with the flashlight beam. "It could go on forever. There's probably nothing down there."

"Is that a light?" Angel asked.

Max yawned. "What? Where, up there where the blob was?" He stretched, leaning from the wall in the darkness to squint at the hole over the hill. "Yeah, that looks like a light." The big guy got to his feet and pulled Angel up. "They're figuring out the drainpipe. Won't be long before they're coming down. We'll go and give them a hand," Max said, turning on his light.

"Why are they coming down? Shouldn't we be going up?" Angel asked, following Max's light as they walked across the floor of the great chamber to the base of the hill.

"All about who?" the big man replied. "They are not here looking for us. Now they're looking for a way out. Things went wrong up there. I'll bet it was all those sleeping bugs. I had a bad feeling about them," he added.

Trudging up the sandy slope, they sidestepped chunks of exploded bug and muddied rivulets of grub juice trenched in the snowy white gypsum.

"Ugh!" Max complained as they ascended. "Hold on. I'd say we're about halfway up this stinking pile. Let's shine our lights up there," he said, pointing his gunlight up. Angel did the same, and as they got their beams on the opening in the roof, a rope dropped out of the overhead hole and dangled just over the big dead ant on top of the heap.

A climber slid down the rope out of the ceiling, pausing in their descent to spin a light in the vast chamber. They pointed their light down, and Max and Angel pointed theirs up. The climber shouted, but the distance put them out of earshot.

The soldiers stood high on the underground mountain of gypsum in the mammoth cave, watching the light on the rope making its way down. The beam stopped for a breather and pointed at them, and a faint call again tried for recognition in the subterranean amphitheater, but still too far away.

The distant climber continued their descent, and the big man looked down at Angel. "That sounded like they called my name,'" Max said.

———————— 🛸 ————————

"There's no one left behind you?" Drake asked the returning rear guards.

Cho buried his face in his hands, and Emoji looked up and shook his head. "Nobody. No way," he said. "No one got off that pile."

"There were ten people back there," Marco whispered loudly and involuntarily. The big man looked at his partner and added, "That's bad."

Nygard was staring into the pit. "It will only get badder from doubt," she said in a calming tone and turned to the group. "Now is when we are allowed to do our best," she said, looking up at Marco's hangdog head as she walked to Drake. "And that is when we work together."

"Yes, ma'am," Marco said contritely, "I will do my best and work together."

The Oberst nodded once to the man. "I saw many ants in the cave," she continued. "They can be attacking from both directions. We should not tarry."

Drake smiled. "Not a lot of people say 'tarry,' Oberst." He raised his voice to address the group, "Time to go down the hole." The elevator returned, riding up the rope and over the edge to park itself at the anchor stake.

"Vic, Libby, you're next. Hook up and get down there," Drake ordered.

Libby exchanged glances with his partner as Vic snapped his plate in place. He turned and did the same for her. Drake oversaw the hookup and encouraged them to jump.

Libby balked and sat at the cliff's edge to lower himself hand over hand so he could test the connection to his harness.

Vic stood on the edge, looking at the big man worrying about knots. She put her light on him and called down, "Hey, Lib. It's easy, just do this." She cradled her machine gun across her midriff, stepped into the air, and gravity did the rest. The gunner shot down the rope past Libby, slowing as the governor kicked in, and they watched her light glide to the bottom.

Drake pointed his light over the edge on Libby and said, "Everyone's waiting on you, big guy. Let go, and you'll ride down to the bottom. Easy."

"I don't like it." The strong man swung on the rope and shook his head. "I could be too big, and maybe it can't handle me," Lib said.

"Tran wouldn't let that happen," Drake reminded him.

The big man held to the rope. "You're right. Tran wouldn't do that." The rope creaked. "I'm blaming others. That's my bad pattern," Libby confessed.

Marco was at the edge of the trap. "Go on, Lib. It's safe," he called down to his friend.

Libby was quiet. Marco whispered to the commander, "Sometimes heights bother Lib, and he doesn't want to face the problem. He feels…"

"Can you get him down the rope, Marco?" Drake interrupted.

The big man nodded. "He would probably go if I went at the same time," he answered.

Vic's elevator came over the top of the pit and clicked along the rope, past their feet on its way to the end of the line.

"All right, hook up," Drake said, lifting the contraption. Marco turned, and Drake snapped it to his harness. "You're good to go," he said to the large man, reaching up to slap his back. "So, go."

Marco lowered himself by hand like Libby had, and they hung on the ropes talking.

Drake stood on the edge and shook his head before returning to the group. As he was about to speak, Marco's effect was proven immediate as Libby's wail filled the chamber, Dopplering down the hole as the pair took the plunge.

There was a moment of silence, and Drake leaned back to look into the pit. Small lights moved in a cluster at the bottom, and everything seemed OK.

He looked back to Cho and Emoji and pointed at them. "When those ropebots get back, you two go next," he said. They acknowledged and took spots by the edge, waiting for their turns.

"Maybe I should go to keep the watch," Nygard said to Drake.

"No," he replied. "Stay here. They'll be done in a few minutes, then we'll go down." He looked into the tunnels. "It won't be long," he added.

"Ja," the commando replied. "Not long."

"We're next," Drake said.

"Ja," the Oberst replied and nodded grimly. "We are all next."

Drake shook his head and started a reply when one of the ropebots climbed over the top, riding back up the line. By the time Emoji finished hooking it onto Cho, the next little creeper came over the top, and Cho hooked his buddy up.

The soldiers looked over the edge, at each other, then back at Drake and Nygard.

"Go ahead. It'll be fun," Drake said with extra enthusiasm.

Cho said something to Moj, one of them waved over their shoulder, and they jumped off the cliff.

The two fell at almost the same rate. Cho came in for a landing only a second before Emoji, and each of them rode into the waiting arms of the big moving guys, there to keep the new arrivals on the ledge, the stopover on the way down the drain.

Drake was about to remark about the quiet when an eruption of insect screeches and gunfire fractured the silence.

The Oberst crouched, dropping her line and bringing her weapon up. The noise of more shots rolled down the cave. Nygard bounded toward the sound.

"No! Don't!" Drake shouted and grabbed her arm. "Listen! It's coming this way — wait for it!"

Drake turned back to the dark tunnel as the sounds of more shots rolled down the tube, followed by a light swinging wildly back and forth and running in their direction.

"Remember the light of my Nun," Nygard cautioned. She looked back, marking the edge of the pit, and planted her feet wide.

Drake heard her safety click. "Keep cool, Oberst," he said to her as he pulled his short pipe 12-gauge and pointed it into the tunnel.

The far-off light closed on them, careening forward on the beat of running boots. Drake shouted down the cave, but there was no reply. Nygard's weapon lowered, and Burner and Pez flew out of the blackness and into their circle of light, skidding into the officers' arms.

They had no weapons. Both men were bloodied, and their clothes were torn and powdered with the white sand of the caverns.

"They're back there!" Burner gasped. His chest was heaving from the run through the cave. "Hundreds, maybe. All over. Coming down the drop."

"I need a gun," Pez said. "Lost mine in the pile. Empty anyway," he panted and dropped to all fours, gulping air. His left side was covered in blood, his face gashed, and it looked like he was missing his ear.

"All right, take a second," Drake said to them, "but just one," he added. "Then we have to go. We have a way out," he sort of lied.

Pez twisted around to a sitting position as he got his wind. "Where is everyone?" he asked.

Drake didn't take his eyes from the darkness but motioned behind. "Down the hole. That's the way out," he said tersely.

"What?" Burner exclaimed. "You gotta be kidding. We're going deeper?"

Drake turned his head and looked down at the man. "You want to go back the way you came?" he asked.

Burner cursed in response. Then he cursed again to make his position clear.

"You're sure everyone is done back there?" Nygard asked them.

"Not a doubt," Burner answered.

"That's what they said about you two," Drake reminded him.

"He made sure," Pez attested, looking up at Drake. "Burner came in and got me out. Everyone else was in pieces. They was all besides themselves."

Their heavy breathing subsided. Drake pointed his light to the pit. "Time to go," he said.

An ant call shot through the cave. Everyone jumped to their feet before the screech faded, and a shrill answer erupted from the opposite direction. Pez covered his ears. As the calls died, he held his bloody fingers in front of his face and back to his new ear-hole. "What the…" he blurted. "My ear, where's my damn ear?"

Nygard was beside him and lifted her light to the side of his head. She made a face like there was a bad smell. "Ja, ja," she clucked, "That ear is gone."

Even with one ear, Pez heard the chirps and scrabbling sounds getting louder as the ants got closer.

The soldiers looked into the dark openings and then at each other.

Drake motioned Nygard to the drop. The ropes were twitching as the ant calls filled more of the cavern.

"What are we waiting for?" Burner asked.

"A couple of…" Drake began a reply but stopped when the bot ground over the edge, tractoring itself along the line. Burner and Pez followed the Oberst to the ropes and stopped, watching the hardware wriggle along the rope.

"What is that?" Burner asked.

"This," Drake said as he lifted the whirring bot, "is the way down." Nygard turned, and he snapped it to her straps. The second bot clambered over the top, and the Oberst caught it as it pulled by, holding it ready for Drake.

The volume on the ant chatter was up on both sides.

"Really time to go," Drake said, looking in both directions and over the edge into the drop. He turned his back to Nygard, and she hooked him up with an audible mechanical connection, clicking as it snapped in place.

He looked at Burner and Pez and shouted, "Sorry guys, but we only have two of these." Their eyes widened as the ant screeches roared out of the tunnels at top volume. The darkness took shape, and giant ants poured in from both sides.

Drake spread his arms and laughed like a maniac. "Give me a hug!" he shouted and grabbed Burner, pulling him tight and pushing them off the edge and into the void. Burner screamed.

Ants squeezed out of the tunnel, frenzied with the pursuit and craving to kill on a chemical level.

As the monsters burst from the tunnel and into their light, Pez reeled in panic, throwing himself backward into Oberst Nygard.

The leader of the pack was one of the smaller bugs, hardly bigger than a car. It ran in on its back four legs, keeping the front two up, stabbing and jabbing with the appendages at blurring speeds.

As the panicked Pez stumbled backward, a barbed foreleg swept over him, cutting the air an inch from his nose. He collided with Nygard and sent them both over the edge of the cliff.

As they tumbled into space, Pez fell into the Oberst's bear hug, and the ant made an extra effort to reach them but lost its balance at the cliff. The giant insect teetered, threatening to fall until the ants running behind piled on and kept her on the ledge.

The rope-bot kicked in, and the governor pardoned them from the law of gravity, easing their fall into a steady dive.

"What?" Pez exhaled. "Thought we was dead," he gulped out.

Nygard locked her arms around him as they descended the funnel.

Tran entered the shaft first, setting up the ropes along the way. The rest of the drop-ins followed, leaving only the two big guys on the ledge to catch Drake and Nygard.

When Drake and his surprise passenger came flying in, it took both linebackers to stop them from going too far. Burner bounced free, but Libby snagged him just in time to keep him from going down the hole. The battered man lifted his face from the concreted sand to peer over the edge, inches in front of his nose. He looked into the abyss, rolled his eyes, and dropped his face back into the sand.

He felt Libby's big hand clamped around his ankle, pulling him back from the drop.

"Thank you," Burner said into the sand.

Marco lifted Drake and got him to his feet. "All right," he said, shaking his head to clear the collision. He looked up at the large man, "Marco," he patted his blocker's forearm and pushed back, steadied. "OK, where do we go from here?"

"Right over there," Marco replied, gesturing to the rope down the hole. "We have to climb down on our own. Are you up for it?" he asked Drake.

Drake took a breath, but Libby answered, shouting, "Heads up! Incoming!" He jumped past Drake as Nygard and Pez came down the rope, crashing into the big guys, knocking them into Burner as he was getting to his feet and sending all of them rolling into a cursing ball of legs and arms.

Drake stood over the scrum and gave them a few seconds as he looked at the rope going over the side into the shaft. "You said that's the way down?" he asked.

As Libby got up, he asked, "And you know who's down there? Max! Tran told us before. He was up and down a couple of times and said Max and Angel are both OK."

Drake walked to the edge and looked into the darkness as the group untangled themselves. "Glad to hear about Angel," he said. "I knew Max would be all right. I knew he'd be down there waiting for us. That's Max."

Marco got up and was standing next to his partner. "Last job we were on with him, they had a nickname for him: 'Max is back.' More than once, you think 'nobody'd get out of that,' and the next thing you hear? 'Max is back.'"

Drake smiled. "Never heard that one," he said.

Then Burner chimed in. "I know one team that called him 'V2', as in version two, like he was always version two," he added.

"Yeah, I've heard him called that," Libby said, nodding. "I think that name's been around longer than he has."

Marco sighed. Drake looked at the big man and said nothing as the others assembled at the brink.

There were no rop-bots for this climb. This was a tough drop, hand over hand, and bring your own belay. Drake went first and lurched down the line into the drainpipe, leaving the lights above. His flashlight lit a monotonous vertical shaft, smooth-walled, smeared with bug juice, but with enough holds to help his way down.

After negotiating the splice to a new rope, Drake descended a few dozen yards until the wall ran out. He was out of the drainpipe, swinging in an immense darkness, and everything seemed upside down. Above, his light spread across the cavern's roof; below, a spiral constellation glowed in the black space, the lights of people moving on a hill.

Drake continued his downward slide until Max grabbed him at the end of the line and told him to let go. He dropped onto something soft with a decidedly organic sound.

"You're standing on an ant's ass," Max said, holding him steady until he had his footing.

"Good to see you, too," Drake said.

Max laughed and clapped Drake on the shoulder. "One of us is always waiting on the other." He smiled broadly, then stopped smiling and asked, "I heard some fireworks up there – what else did I miss?"

"Nothing good." Drake flashed a smile back but didn't keep it. "There's five more behind me, and that's it," he said grimly.

"Oh, that's too bad," Max responded, shaking his head and frowning. "That's really too bad," he repeated. "It's always so hard on the extras," he added.

Drake leaned over and looked at the flashlights dotting the slope between pieces of bug. "Quite a sand pile," he said.

"Just the thing for a soft landing," Max answered, motioning upward to the drainpipe, then squinting. "Looks like the next party is coming down," he said.

Drake watched the slow-falling star sliding down the line to them.

"I don't like this place," Max said. "Let's keep moving, especially with that sitting there." The big man pointed his light to the canary yellow can embedded in the slope of gooey sand twenty yards away.

"I told you there was eight and change left to go. That had to be an hour ago," Drake said.

Max made a surprised face. "Wow. Seven hours to kablooey." He brought the light back to them. "We better pick up the pace," he concluded.

Drake agreed and added impetus. "I noticed those ants up top left pretty quick once we went over the edge – like they knew a shortcut." He looked down at the remains of the troop from the 10-foot climb off the dead ant and then past them to the trek down sand mountain to the cave floor.

Max nodded. "We'll double-time them. I'll get these stragglers going and meet you down there." He pointed to the bramble of bug legs sticking out of the giant ant they were standing on and said, "That way off of the bug."

"See you down there," Drake called back as he climbed the bug leg ladder to the sand.

Max called after Drake, "Will the Oberst be joining us?"

Drake nodded. "Probably last of the five, but yes, she made it."

Max nodded in agreement. "I knew she would," he replied.

Over an hour later, Drake was standing with the company at the base of the sand pile watching the last couple of lights coming round the mountain. It was Max and Oberst Nygard double-timing it down the steep sand to the flat floor of the cave and trotting over to the group.

"Ready?" Drake asked them.

"Let's keep it moving," Max answered, still catching his breath. "You know there's only one way out, over there?" he asked, pointing with his Zastava.

"Yep," Drake replied. "No decision required. Let's move out," he ordered.

The troops fell into order and made for the opening in the cave wall across the chamber, well away from the base of the sand mountain.

"It is in the right direction," Drake said as the group moved out. "We're heading for the closest hole in the six-pack," he added for everyone to hear.

"What do you think, Doc? Three klicks at the most?" He turned and reached into his shirt to check his countdown clock. "We've got plenty of time," he lied. "All we have to do is keep moving, and when we get to the exit, call for a ride."

"I'm for that," Emoji interjected as the team approached the tunnel entrance with Drake and Max at the front.

"Piece of cake," Max agreed as they approached the truck-sized opening in the cave wall. He walked in a few paces and stopped to listen. "You can hear them. A lot of them. But far away." He turned back to the squad. "There's a breeze in there, too. Blowing out. That's good; let's follow the air."

"Sounds right," Drake said. Everyone clustered at the entrance, agreeing to more or lesser degrees. They wanted to move and were willing to go wherever the light up front pointed.

Drake leaned toward Dr. Dhawan. "How about you, Doc? Going to help us get out of here?"

The entomologist started, smiled in the light, pushed his glasses up, and gave a quick nod. "Of course," he answered softly. As Drake turned away from him, the doctor spoke up. "Do you think I could have a gun?" he asked.

Drake looked back and let his light down. He answered the scientist quietly. "Probably not, Doc." He shook his head. "Very dangerous. Not being trained and in these circumstances."

"Maybe just a small one," Dhawan persisted. "You know," he said, hesitating, "for personal use."

"Now, now, that's no way to talk," Max interjected. "We're all here to make sure it doesn't come to that. You just stick with us. We'll be out of this hole in no time." The doctor seemed unconvinced.

Drake shook his head and turned to ask the group, "Everyone ready to move out?" They affirmed as he walked past Pez. "How's the ear?" he asked in a low whisper. Pez looked around, wondering if he had heard something.

Drake pulled his shotgun. "Let's go," he said. He stood by as the troops filed down the tunnel, moving quickly and quietly over the even grade of the compacted chalk. The tunnel went on, neither rising nor falling, and they covered distance, bringing them closer to the ant calls, louder by the minute.

"I hear them, but I don't see them. Why no ants?" Max asked out loud as they double-timed it over the ant-crete.

Drake, in the lead, stopped and held up his hand. "Take a breather," he said. "If you have water, drink and pass it along." He intercepted the water bottle Max was lifting to his mouth, took a few long swallows, and then passed it back to his friend with a shake of his head.

"That's a good question, Doc." Drake looked at the scientist, bringing his light around. "Why aren't there any ants in this stretch?"

Dr. Dhawan accepted a water bottle politely from one of the soldiers and drank. He shrugged. "Who knows?" he replied. "But as you have noticed, there are no entrances to other tunnels so far. Maybe it is simply not a highly trafficked area of the nest. It is quite a large complex, after all."

"So, we're out in the sticks," Vic said from behind the scientist. "What happens when we get to ant town?" she asked.

The scientist took another drink of water and nodded as he chugged. He passed the bottle and said, "Yes. The array of holes, the 'six-pack,' as we have termed it, is the principal convergence of the nest's juncture with the surface. And I should add that our traffic studies show each entrance generally active." He pushed his glasses back, looked at his watch, and then took out a pocket compass wrapped in a sheet of paper. "Based on my estimations, we should try to use entrance number four, which has shown less activity at the time we are likely to arrive."

"Then that's the plan, Doc," Drake replied. "Do you think you can navigate the tunnels to number four?" he asked the entomologist.

Dhawan considered the problem momentarily, opening a folded paper from his shirt pocket and checking a small compass. "Yes, I believe I can," he answered. "If we can continue a route west, it will connect with the surface entrances." The doctor folded the compass back in the paper and pushed it into his shirt pocket.

Drake nodded, looking down the tunnel. "West it is," he said. "Let's get going." Those leaning against the cave wall pushed off, and the line moved out.

The troop moved fast and quietly, sticking close to the walls and crouching as they ran. The ant calls got louder. They were racing, trying to catch up with their flashlight beams.

The tunnel widened, opening to an intersection of passageways. Their lights flashed over a portal on the right, another on the left, two others in the cave floor ahead, and one in the roof above them. It was a Swiss cheese with giant ants.

A black shape, darker than the gloom in the passage, scuttled past the doorway twenty feet away.

Stench oozed from the entrances on either side, soaking the dank air with ammonia and mold.

"Welcome to ant central," Max whispered as he ran his light around the openings.

"Both of these tunnels look like they run west. Which way do you think, Doc?" Drake asked as he brought his beam to the scientist.

Dr. Dhawan took the creased paper from his pocket again, peered at it over his glasses, and held it close. He put the map back and indicated the passageway on the right. As Drake held the beam on him, the scientist answered the commander's unasked question. "It's my 'best guess' map," he said. "Based on the location of the entrances to the surface, my familiarity with typical nest constructions, ground penetrating radar, and thermal imaging, that can sometimes indicate subterranean structures."

Drake nodded. "Works for me, Doc," he said, moving the light to his second-in-command.

"I guess somebody should take a look," Max said. He went to the tunnel entrance, holding his hand down and the troops back. He inched along the wall to the hole and put his head around the corner, listening and peering into the blackness.

Max reached up and clicked the flashlight off. He lifted his left foot and put it down in the tunnel. It was quiet, except for the distant calls of the monsters. He stepped into the darkness, feeling his way along the wall and carefully setting his foot before shifting his weight. He repeated this process a few times until he was further than he thought from the entrance.

The wall ran out, and the wet breath of the nest blew over his hand as he waved it in the ink. His senses strained, reaching into the nothingness for any shape or sound. He couldn't see, he didn't hear, and he wasn't alone.

Max ran his hand along his rifle toward the flashlight and stopped mid-barrel. A low percussive roll drummed from the dark. It was on his left and close. The drumming slowed until each beat was distinct, then stopped.

Max crouched in the darkness, all ears and keeping his gun up. He wrapped his hand around the gun light and kept his finger on the switch, ready to expel the cleansing breath and snap it on. He inhaled smoothly, held it, and then let it out slowly. Mid-cleanse, something tapped his shoulder, like somebody next to him in a crowd. Twice. Max froze, moving only his mouth in the dark to form a silent curse, not daring a sound.

Bristles brushed his face. Max ran the movie of Nygard's experience in his head. The rattle started again, rising in volume, and the tempo quickened. The sound was above him and to his left. He carefully angled the muzzle of his Zastava in the dark.

The rattle died. He heard clicks and movements in the dark. He let the last half of his breath out. A drop of sweat ran down the side of his head, and warm salt spread into his eye. Gripping the gun and light, his index finger found the switch; he took a breath and turned on the light.

A giant insect eye filled the beam three feet in front of him. There was no time for either of them to blink, and both species reacted at synaptic speeds. In the same split-second Max fired, the two-ton ant charged. Max was the lucky one. He rose, pushed up against the cave wall by the recoil of his heavy gun. A dozen rounds of the AR's steel specials blew off the bottom of the monster's head, dropping the contents to the cave floor like a bucket being emptied.

The bug collapsed, instantly killed by the catastrophic assault. Max slid back down the wall. His legs stretched out to the dead bug's head.

Beams of lights scrambled into the tunnel accompanied by the tinkling of heavy weapons. Max's heart was beating like a billy club in a dive bar, and his shots were ringing in his ears. Drake stepped in front of Max and pushed the barrel of his Zastava to the side.

Everyone was in the tunnel now, and flashlight beams were swinging in all directions. Ant noises poured in from both sides of the passage, far away, at least for now.

Lights pointed both ways in response.

Vic went one way, and Burner and Pez went the other, pointing their guns into the darkness to take on any new arrivals. "Nothing moving!" and "We're good down here!" they shouted.

"It's not going to stay this way for long," Dr. Dhawan said. The strain was evident in his voice as he stared at the large pile of dead ant. "We have to go now. Please."

"This is the way, ja?" Nygard remarked, shining her beam along the rising grade. Drake and the others turned to look at the colonel as she walked after Vic.

"If it's heading west, and it's going up, it's the way out," Drake said. "Let's go," he ordered the group, pointing after the Oberst. "Let's move out!"

The troops fell in and advanced.

Vic had moved ahead to check the way forward and waited for them to catch up. "It stinks in here," she said as they marched past. "But no bugs," she added, lowering her machine gun as she fell in next to Max.

She saw the scientist and reached over to nudge him.

"Hey, Doc, how much further to the top?" she asked.

The scientist turned to the sweaty woman; rivulets of perspiration streaked her gypsum-powdered face. His hand went to his face, wiping the thickened sand from his cheeks. "I estimate we are less than two kilometers from the exit," he answered. "It shouldn't be long. Not too much longer," he answered quietly, lifting his light to shine over the shoulders of the two men in front.

Drake and Max stopped at a hole nearly spanning the entire width of the tunnel floor, leaving only narrow ledges on both sides of the opening as footholds for the ants. The line bunched behind them, and the group's lights pointed into the dark space. Their flashlights showed a black mass of bug bodies squirming through the narrow channel, stirring up an eye-watering stench.

"Get those lights out of there!" Max barked.

"C'mon!" Drake urged them along. "Don't attract attention. Keep moving!" he ordered, shepherding the scientist and soldiers past the hole along the narrow footpaths.

Though there was nothing to see without the broadside of lights pouring into the shaft, they all looked into the black hole as they filed past, except Dhawan. The scientist looked away, watching his feet as he hurried by the opening.

As they moved by the void, Burner spoke up. "I wouldn't mind dropping one or two of these pineapples down there," he offered.

"Leave them alone," Max said as the bomber passed him. "They'll be getting theirs pretty soon."

As the last soldier passed, Drake slid his timer out for a look, then stuffed it back in his shirt. "Let's pick up the pace," he called after the group. He paused, shining his light onto the Stygian procession, shuddering at the antihuman life forms, and hurried to catch up with his troop.

Drake went to the front of the line and got in step with Max and the scientist. Someone in the group called out, "They saw the lights. Why didn't they go for us?"

The commander asked the entomologist, "Why not, Doc? They ignored the lights. They didn't attack."

"Hmm?" Dr. Dhawan looked up and found Drake. "Oh, they will. It's all about job assignments with them. With THEM," he chuckled. "I suppose their soldiers are heading for us right now." He wiped his forehead and didn't chuckle. "In any event, they do not see light very well, especially not the deep nest ants. They don't need to. And, at this point, we are not considered much of a threat. I suppose we're more of a maintenance problem." He pushed his glasses up over the chalk on his nose. "Appropriateness of response is fundamental to their efficiency, after all," he concluded.

There was a muted response to the doctor's remarks before Nygard spoke from the rear of the group. "There is a noise behind us," she called out. "It is a big noise. It is a sound of many monsters."

The troop picked up speed in unison, double-timing it down the tunnel. Nygard followed as rear guard. She stopped and cupped her ear to listen to the scrabbling sounds coming after them. As the noise of the troop faded in the distance, the foot scrapes and chirps of the creatures quickly grew louder. They were gaining. She took off, running full speed to catch up with the rank and get to the front.

"They move faster. We will not outrace them," she said breathlessly as she rushed up to Drake. She grabbed his shoulder to stop him. "They will be on us in minutes, and we will fail."

The two stopped in the cave as the soldiers went by. Burner looked up and met the commander's eyes as he went by. Drake raised his hand and said, "We need a wire."

Max stopped and looked back. He saw Drake and the Oberst pulling the bomb guy and his buddy with one ear out of line. He stopped Vic, and they pressed the others to keep moving ahead. "Hundred yards up the pipe. Wait there," Max repeated as the troops hustled past.

Max watched Pez and Burner point their lights at the cave walls and then peel off to head the wrong way down the tunnel. Drake and Nygard went to each side of the cave and stood with weapons at the ready. He tugged on Vic's sleeve and pointed to them. "We do the same here to cover them," he said to her, and they each went to opposite walls to wait for whatever was coming.

Burner and Pez ran back into the tunnel just far enough. "This looks good. Three-second delay!" he shouted to his compatriot.

"What?" Pez answered loudly, bringing his hand up to the stumpy root of his missing ear.

Burner laughed, but Pez didn't hear him. The bomb man twisted his buddy's head around to his good ear and shouted his instructions. He thumped him on the chest, pointed across the cave, and pushed a metal stake into his hand. Pez bounded across to the wall and stuck the spike into the cementitious wall, stomping it in with his boot. Burner was doing the same thing on his side.

The bomb man pushed a sandwich-sized pack onto his embedded stake, pulled out six inches of wire, and depressed the button for five seconds. The ham and cheese was prearmed and ready to pair.

He ran across the cave to the opposite stake, pulling the trip wire with him. He knelt to attach the wire to the eyelet and added another sandwich to the picnic, depressing the button. Red lights blinked in unison on both packs.

Burner looked into the dark of the tunnel as the sounds scurried closer. The ant chatter was so loud even Pez could hear it. He pulled Burner to his feet, and they ran, pushing each other through the shaft back to their compatriots. Drake and Nygard raised their weapons as the two men ran by. They didn't stop; <li>they flew past the officers. Burner yelled something to Drake, and as his head turned to catch the </li>words, Nygard's machine gun erupted in quick bursts.

Drake's world turned to slow motion. He twisted, swinging his shotgun up. His head continued turning as his torso arched, aiming the 12-gauge at the heads of the giant ants rushing out of the dark and into their lights. They would be on them in seconds. Nygard's offensive stances were freeze-framed in the strobe of her muzzle flashes.

Along the way, Drake's eyes skipped from Nygard to the blinking red lights the bomb guys stuck on the walls, flashing before the rushing mutants.

He had to jump out of the way of the oncoming bug and lifted his shotgun to slow it down.

Three seconds can be a very long time.

The huge soldier ant's six legs worked in blurring efficiency to propel the monster several feet through the line, pulling the wire and closing the switches in both sandwich packs. The red lights stopped blinking and went solid.

Drake pumped, jumped, and fired on his way across the cave to the Oberst.

The first second ticked away in the synchronized timers buried in the bricks of putty as more ants crowded behind the lead monster, with dozens more following after them.

The second second ticked, and the stampeding ants bulldozed each other for the lead, filling the tunnel wall-to-wall as Nygard let her last volley blaze.

The third second clicked as the colossal charging bugs snapped their jaws and pounded their piston legs to trample anything in front of them. Drake's flying body block smashed into Nygard, bowling her over as they crashed into the floor. The lead ant lifted its head and snapped open its jaws, sensing the close-quarter change in chemistry and signatures from the enemy that must be exterminated.

The fourth second didn't come. It was split between the detonation of the first bomb and the instantaneous explosion of the second.

Both shape charges blew out from the walls, disintegrating the leading bugs and fracturing the ant-crete into a molten kinetic slurry, which explosively sandblasted the mutants behind them. A score of the huge insects was instantly killed, and dozens more maimed.

Drake and Nygard were lying flat, protected from the blowback but not the concussive force that hit like a hammer, bouncing them a foot into the air and dropping them stunned to the cave floor.

Max and Vic were next in line for the shock wave and were thrown to the ground as the salvo ripped by them on its way to Burner and Pez. They got hit and fell forward onto their faces as the blast ran down the cavernous cannon barrel to the rest of the troop, knocking them over and ironing them into the sand.

Max sat up and shook his head like that cartoon coyote. He got onto his feet and pulled Vic with him, sitting her against the wall to collect her consciousness. He trotted back, shaking the explosion off as he went. He saw Drake's limp form rolling off Nygard as she struggled to get up on an elbow.

Max stepped over the Oberst and turned Drake over. He leaned over, close to the unconscious man's face, and pulled back an eyelid. The big man let out an exasperated breath and slapped Drake in the face a few times.

"Are you OK?" he asked loudly and looked over to Nygard. She stared through the fog, shrugged her shoulders, and shook her head.

He looked impatiently at the woman, slapped Drake again, and poured water over his face. His boss stirred. Drake's eyes opened, tried to focus, then closed. Max took his jaw in his hand and shook his head back and forth. "Come on, c'mon. Quit wasting time. Get up!" he shouted. He stood and put his boss on his feet. Drake faltered and went loose.

Max's light showed the remains of ants through the smoke and a substantial amount of collapsed cave clogging the tunnel. It looked like a lot of them were dead or done for. That could keep the others busy for a while, clearing the way and chewing up their brothers or sisters or whatever. He could hear activity behind the pile.

The big man stood, cinching his belt and packs. He looked down at the Oberst and asked, "Can you get up? I can't carry both of you."

The ant noise from the other side of the cave-in was louder.

"No time for this," Max said, lifting Drake and heaving him over his shoulder. He signaled the colonel to get to her feet. She stood, steadied herself against the cave wall, then nodded she was ready to go. Max grunted under Drake's weight, and they slogged down the tunnel as fast as they could.

They caught up to Vic as she was shaking it off and took her in tow. Drake began making noises. They pushed on, picking up the bombers along the way. They could make out the troops' lights ahead and moved with all the speed they could muster as the sounds of the ants behind the rubble and carcasses of their nestmates got loud enough to penetrate the ringing in their ears.

As they trotted, their lights bounced over the walls and ceiling and mingled with the beams from the group. Max shouted as they broke into the small crowd waiting for them. "Incoming!" he croaked and staggered in, dropping Drake as carefully as he could and collapsing next to him. He was spent. "That pile of ant should buy us a couple of minutes at least," he gasped as he leaned back against the wall to catch his breath.

Nygard dropped to her knees and shook her head, still trying to clear it. Vic sat against the opposite wall with her weapon pointing down the trail they had just covered. "Always a bridesmaid," she said under her breath as she cradled her machine gun.

Drake groaned and moved, then pushed himself up on one arm. He lifted his hand to cover his eyes for a moment. When he dropped it, he looked from face to face. "Still here, huh?" he asked out of curiosity.

"Who do you mean? You or us?" Max laughed and reached over to pat his boss's shoulder. "You're still here, at least for now," he answered, handing him half a water bottle. Nygard held out his shotgun. As he took it from her, she thanked him.

Drake smiled and sat up to drink the water, looking at the woman. He watched her mouth forming words. He smiled again and shook his head, pointing to the tuning fork in his ears. She smiled and did the same, and both shrugged their shoulders.

Max stood and looked back into the tunnel. Drake didn't need to hear anything to get the idea. He saw the bomber across the cave, leaning against the wall. "Hey, Burner," he said too loud. "How about here?" Drake pointed back and forth with his index finger between the walls of the passage.

Burner nodded and handed a spike to Pez, and they pounded them into opposite walls to affix the charges and run the tripwire.

Drake struggled to his feet and swayed in place with his gun. Max wagged a finger at his boss, took the gun from him, and stuck it in the man's backpack holster.

The troop started down the tunnel, leaving the pyrotechnical pair to finish up with the explosives.

They tread quietly over the packed sand. Dhawan fell in next to Drake and tried speaking to him. Realizing his inability to hear, the scientist pulled the folded map from his pocket and put his light on it as they walked. He indicated a spot along a line and then pointed to the ground beneath at their feet. He ran his finger on the line to circles about an inch away and pointed to the tunnel in front of them. The scientist held up his index finger and mouthed the word 'one.'

Drake nodded, indicating comprehension, but he had no clue. He wondered if the entomologist meant one hour or one kilometer or one chance in a million. Didn't matter. There was just one way to go.

They moved along at a good clip for a few minutes. Drake's head began to clear, and his hearing started to kick in again. He looked ahead and saw Tran, Cho, and Emoji were up front – Tran because he knew a mission succeeded on teamwork; Emoji because he knew it took initiative; and Cho because he wanted to get out of here. Drake agreed with all three of them.

The constant tone in his ears decayed to an intermittent ring; Drake began to catch a few words and sounds breaking through. He tried to shake the bells out of his head and turned back to see Max and Vic walking close behind, and Nygard was rearguard. Burner and Pez, the mines set and their task complete, ran out of the darkness past the Norwegian to rejoin the band.

Dhawan tapped him on the shoulder, and Drake turned to the scientist, who was pointing to the right. "Hold up," Drake ordered and lifted his hand. He could hear his voice, muffled and far away. The troop clustered before him.

He brought his shotgun light around and pointed it to an opening in the wall just ahead of them. Other lights followed his, illuminating a large round hole and ruts in the floor leading inside. The passage through the wall opened into a tunnel sloping upward on the left and downward to the right. The floor was deeply fissured with ant tracks.

Warm air moved over the group and into the entrance. Drake held his fingers in the air, palm facing the opening; the updraft cooled the back of his hand. "It's sucking air in like a chimney," he said.

Dr. Dhawan leaned close to Drake's ear to say loudly, "That's what I was saying before – this is our way out." He pointed and tried to pull

Drake into the opening. "That tunnel is the passage to hole number four, to the way out." Drake heard that, and so did everyone else.

The scientist let go of Drake's sleeve and turned to hurry into the passageway. The three guys from the front followed him, Cho leading the way.

At the entrance to the new tunnel, Dhawan stopped, but Cho pushed past, eagerly bounding into the shaft, shining his light up the incline. He turned his head to call back, urging the others to follow him. "Let's go – let's go!" he yelled. "It's a straight shot from here. The air's a lot better!" He took another step up the rising shaft and turned to the three soldiers coming through the passageway.

"C'mon," Cho cajoled as he turned his head up the slope. "You don't think there are –" Cho's sentence was cut short as a giant ant rushed into his flashlight beam. It charged down the slope and past the entrance, snapping Cho into its jaws without slowing.

There was little sound of the ant's rush and none from Cho except when his weapon clattered over the floor as he disappeared down the tunnel in the beast's maw.

Dhawan cried out and fell back against the wall. Emoji and Tran jumped into the passageway, skidding onto the furrowed tunnel floor, their weapons brought to bear, pointing downward at the escaping insect. Tran fired. Then Emoji let loose. Cho was gone no matter how you sliced it.

Drake and the others didn't know what happened in the entryway, but they heard the screams and shots. They rushed to the opening with their lights pointing past Dhawan to illuminate Tran and Emoji in the tube, firing down the slope.

Before they could reach the tunnel, a seething slurry of armored ants charged down the passage, crashing into the two soldiers and grinding them under the melee.

Tran tried to jump clear, but two bugs in front caught him in midair; one chomped down on his leg, and the other snapped its jaws around his chest.

Max knocked Dhawan out of the way to get a clear shot and fired into the stream of mutant insects with no effect.

The monsters shared the prize only briefly, then pulled away from each other. Tran's leg ripped from the hip socket without resistance. He screamed, and the sound of it shot ice water into his comrades. Dhawan covered his ears and wailed to drown the soldier's shrieks.

Max fired, killing Tran instantly.

The monstrous wave continued as Emoji rose from the parading ants, lifted high and upside down in the jagged-tooth mandibles clamped around his pelvis. A curtain of blood poured over him as the beast chewed, drawing poor Moj into the meat grinder.

Max lifted his weapon, but Emoji shot first. Alive or dead, purposefully or autonomically, the soldier's gun fired wildly, sending everyone diving for cover while the ant disappeared with its victim into the odious horde.

The squad in the passage quieted as the mutants disappeared down the sloping shaft. The onslaught of the ants and the butchery of the three soldiers happened fast and was over. They were gone. The tunnel was empty. Nothing could have saved them.

Whether by deficiency or higher purpose, the ants in the tunnel had taken no notice of the interlopers in the connecting passageway. The shrinking group held their weapons in small, defensive postures as the insects scurried away. The troop sat silent, listening to the receding chirrups and rattles as the monsters trickled away into their dark labyrinth.

The local bug noises dissipated, melting into the remote chorus of calls. Drake's ears didn't ring anymore; all he could hear were the echoes of Emoji's screams. He moved his shotgun light slowly along the entrance until it settled upon the sweat and dust of Dr. Dhawan, flattened against the wall of the short passage to the tunnel. He was wild-eyed and breathing heavily. The scientist stared into the beam and buried his face in his arms against the ant-crete.

Drake turned his light on the group, briefly illuminating every face before he pointed the beam downward, lighting a spot at the center of the floor. "That tunnel is still our way out of here," he told them. "And the clock keeps ticking," he added as he walked to Dhawan. He reached down to lift the scientist by his vest, helping him regain his feet.

"Doc, we're on the last leg," he said calmly. "We go up this shaft, and we get to hole four, right?" he asked, dusting the scientist's shoulders. A particularly loud ant call pulsed from the tunnel opening. Dhawan's eyes widened, looking all around. "Hey, Doc – this way. Look at me and answer the question. What do you know about the climb out?" Drake persisted.

Dhawan stared at the man, and he blinked. "The climb out?" he repeated. "You are very optimistic, Mr. Drake," he said quietly. "It's a twenty-four-meter drop. A hard climb when the ants are eating you." The scientist avoided eye contact and smiled way too much.

Drake patted him on the padded shoulder of his jungle jacket. "OK, Doc, you wait here." He turned to the troop and waved them to their feet.

Everyone was standing, congregating around their leader.

"So far, it seems the traffic was heading down from up there." He pointed with his thumb going up. Drake turned his light on Burner. "How many charges do you have left?" he asked him.

"Two packs of putty and two firebombs," Burner answered.

"You went through a lot of them," Drake replied.

"Case was standing by most of them," Pez interjected. "He, uh…" His voice trailed away.

530

Drake nodded. "All right. We'll save that for later. Right now, we check the tunnel heading up. If it's clear, we go. You guys keep to the end of the line, and if anything comes up behind us, bomb them," Drake outlined. "Your choice – blow them up or burn them down. That way, we're protected in the back. Anything in front of us, we handle with guns. I'm hoping the only thing we run into in this direction are ants coming back into the nest and, with five other entrances, maybe they won't be using this one. After all, Dhawan said this wasn't the most popular way in for them." Drake looked at the small crowd. "So, that's the plan," he concluded.

Everyone stood, quietly looking at one another, listening to the insect chorus in the tunnels.

One of the big guys cleared his throat, then shifted his weight and said encouragingly, "Well, there's no rule it's got to be a good plan, right?"

Drake looked at him, then at Max, who began laughing. "That's true, Marco," Max said. He laughed again and wiped his eye. "You are right. Nothing says it has to be a good plan."

Max finished laughing and said to Drake, "And it's a good thing this ain't a democracy – and besides, there's no other choice." He racked his Zastava. "Who's on first, boss?"

Max was at his best when he knew everyone was going to die. He became more machine than man. Drake had seen him like this before, and he wanted him like that now. He looked at the group. Nine and Dhawan. There was a chance. Maybe. Maybe not.

He checked his gun, and there was a reply of slides and bolts from the rest of the group.

"Still nothing, right? Nobody's been getting anything from the top, right?" Angel asked, fingering his comm set.

"Keep them on," Drake said as he pushed his earpiece in for a moment, listened, and let it drop out to dangle. "We might get a signal when we get up there."

He looked at Max and said, "And to answer your question, we go first." He pointed to each of the others as he spoke. "After us, it's Marco, Libby, and Angel. Then Dhawan with Vic. Keep an eye on him."

The woman complained in one syllable. Drake smiled at her.

"After them, Burner, Pez, and Oberst Nygard. Each group keeps a distance – ten yards between. That way, we're not bunched up. Keep every eye you got open." He smacked Max on the back. "Let's see who's home," he said, and they went into the cave.

They stood against the wall of the passageway. It was quiet. They moved into the tunnel, Drake pointing upstream and Max looking down. The pair kept low and listened. Drake played his light along the rising floor and into the darkness of the empty tunnel.

"Looks good this way," he whispered over his shoulder to Max.

"Nothing down here," the ex-sergeant replied.

Drake paused, then stood. "Give me ten yards. Wait here," he said. He took a few steps over the furrowed floor. He stumbled, and his light flashed over the walls.

"What is it?" Max hissed in the dim light.

"I slipped, that's all," Drake replied. He cursed and looked down, shining his shotgun at his feet. "Watch your step," he said softly, staring at the red puddle formerly known as Emoji. Drake lifted his head and covered a few more yards. He stopped, listened again, and then called back to Max. "OK, bring them in, and let's get moving," he ordered in a hoarse whisper.

Max gave a low whistle, and Drake looked back to watch the lights file into the cave and form a luminescent caterpillar following him up the slope. It probably wasn't good to be a caterpillar in an ant nest.

Drake kept climbing, following the same path as the breeze from below. The ascent, which had remained at a constant angle, flattened out and ran straight as far as his shotgun could see. He walked onto the even grade and turned to watch the trailing lights moving up the ramp behind him as Max came over the rise.

"Long, straight tunnel-like Dhawan said," Drake whispered to Max as he walked a few steps over the level lane to join him. "He knows his ant nests. It's like he's been here before."

His large friend eyed him and said, "Sounds like you're doing that executive thinking. Leave me out of it. Want something done? You point, I shoot."

Drake twisted up a smile. "OK, I forgot. Don't shoot anyone yet," he replied, then moved his light along the floor in front of them. "Have them wait, and we'll take a look downstream," Drake said to his second. "At least they'll have the high ground while we're gone," he said as the first of the caterpillar crawled over the summit.

Max instructed them to wait at the top as he and Drake went ahead to check their path. "Make sure you keep your eyes open in both directions," he said as they walked into the darkness. "And when we come back, don't shoot us," he added.

The air was cooler as they walked further into the passage, and the ant noises were faint, deep in the nest and far away. It was like 4 a.m. in the big city – it may be quiet, but something was always happening just around the corner.

Drake signaled Max to stop, touched his ear, and pointed ahead.

Max leaned from the wall and stared into the gloom but couldn't see anything. He kept his light down, ran diagonally across the rutted floor, and put his back to the wall. He leaned out and pointed the light forward. Drake did the same, and they watched a parade of ants crossing the tunnel ahead.

He lowered his light and moved up. Max followed suit. They leapfrogged each other until they were way too close to the steady stream of giant insects. The bugs moved from the opening on the right, across the tunnel floor, and disappeared into the opposite entrance. The two men watched; the bugs kept moving.

Max whispered across the shaft. "How long can this go on?"

"I don't know," Drake answered. "But they don't seem to know we're here. I don't think we're too far from the way out." He paused and brought his light to Max. "Go back and get them. I'll wait here."

Max grunted, watching the line of mutants. He called across the cave to Drake. "OK, I'll get them," he said, but didn't like it. He pushed off the wall and glanced at Drake as he turned to trot back to the troop. "Stay loose," Max called over his shoulder.

Max's footfalls faded, and Drake turned back to study the repetitious rank of lumbering bugs. Their jointed legs lifted and dropped, pushing them along the invisible trail sensed by their swaying antennae as they followed in elemental obedience, incomprehensible to reasoning creatures. One after another, they filed from the right to march across the tunnel into the hole on the left until a final ant disappeared into the entrance.

Drake craned his neck, expecting another issue. He moved a few quiet steps forward and stopped. Still no ants. He made his way along the wall, holding his light low until he was an arm's length from the entrance to the side tunnel. He slid his hand along the barrel of his 12-gauge to the flashlight and covered it with his hand, letting only a blade of light stab through his fingers.

He listened at the edge of the opening. There were no concerning sounds, just the very distant murmurs of monsters. He brought the gun to the upright position and realized how tightly he was gripping the weapon. Fear was exhausting. He turned his head and leaned against the wall to look down the long tunnel for any sign of Max.

Alone, Drake listened again at the entrance. He took a deep breath and stepped away from the wall to stand before the breach, pulling his hand from the lens to shine his flashlight full-strength into the dark passage.

It was empty. He let his breath out, and his heart restart. He peered into the tunnel for his troops, then turned back to the darkness and followed the breeze on its way out. Without a glance back, he ran for hole number four.

He jogged, following the bouncing beam of his light through the tunnel, until there was no more tunnel. It simply ended. Drake staggered back with a gasp of disappointment. He turned, looking for the opening, the way out, but it was a dead-end.

He leaned against the cool wall with a curse, clicked his light off, and let it drop to the sand. He shook his head and cursed again beneath his breath in the darkness. The breeze blew over his face, and he thought of the bright yellow drum ticking to oblivion. He started for the timer under his shirt but pulled it back. He didn't want to know how long there was. His strength leaked away, and despair seeped in to take its place.

Max would be back with the doomed survivors of this doomed mission, and there was nowhere for them to go. He exhaled slowly and closed his eyes.

Drake had no thoughts, and there was no Plan C. He opened his eyes to the dark, but the dark was not as deep now. A hole appeared in the black above as the clouds blew across the clearing sky. Stars sparkled in the desert night above hole number four. Drake's eyes opened wider as he looked out of the nest.

He sat in the utter dark below the softly illuminating disk of night, glad he was alone.

He stood and squinted for any sign of lights, then turned on his flashlight to inspect the base of the climb. Unlike the other drops in the nest's less-used areas, these walls were grooved and had pronounced ledges and footholds. He looked back, scanning the darkness for the others, then took another quick look at the sky above.

Drake peeled off his vest and dropped unnecessary equipment, holstering his shotgun over his back. He grabbed a ridge and pulled himself up, climbing out of hole number four as fast as he could.

As Max approached the group, Nygard stepped from the wall into his light. She looked through the beam at him and then into the darkness for Drake. She stared at Max.

"He's waiting for us up there," he answered, motioning over his shoulder. "I'm here to get everyone."

She nodded. "They have been not quiet in back of us," she said, gesturing with her machine gun to the path sloping back into the darkness. Right on cue, a loud trill came from the tunnel, and flashlights swung into the void, followed by gun clicks.

Max strode to the incline and stood in front of the soldiers. "Sounds close," he said and spit into the darkness. He played his gun light back and forth. "Let's get out of here," he said. The ex-sergeant turned and walked from the edge, followed by the troops.

Max stopped several yards from the ramp, and the group assembled. He lowered his light, looking at the small party in the glow. "It's pretty easy going ahead. Just keep to the sides, out of the tracks in the middle." He paused before delivering the bad news. "We did find a couple of bugs, so stay on your toes." He watched their reaction. They looked good, except for Dhawan. The scientist was apart from the others, leaning against the cave wall. He looked worn thin enough to see through.

The air pressure dropped, and Max felt a bead of sweat roll down the wrong side of his face. That gave him about a second and a half. He grabbed Vic so hard that the air squeezed out of her with an exclamation. He sprang with her under one arm, jumping six yards away from the ramp. He calculated that, with the chaos that was to ensue, the survivors would not remember his impossible leap.

A lone ant, the size of a pickup truck, drove out of the dark and crashed into the group before they could react. Burner was knocked aside and thrown into the cave wall. Pez turned to run but was trampled by the stampeding creature, falling under its pounding legs. One of the hammers punched into the man's shoulder blade, separating his arm from his body.

The monster rampaged blindly ahead, snapping its jaws in the air inches from a diving Angel, then sending Marco flying with a glancing blow from her leg. Dhawan screamed in terror and flattened against the ground.

The giant snapped viciously when Libby put a few rounds through the insect armor. The enormous bug jabbed with a foreleg, caught the large man in the chest and sent him flying into Vic and Max, bowling them over the rough floor. At the same time, the ant struck with a bristled leg on the opposite side, sweeping Nygard forward as she lifted her weapon to fire, bouncing her off the wall of the cave.

The monster turned and rose on its rearmost legs, lifting the front ones high into the air, ready to stab.

Pez was on his stomach under the giant ant and clawed at the sandy floor, trying to pull himself away with one arm as he turned his red, fear-masked face to the monster and howled in terror.

The mutant bug foot shot down, stabbing through the man's back and punching into the floor under him. The bug lifted the limp body, holding it up momentarily and touching it with its antennae. He moaned, hanging helplessly like a bug on a pin. The big jaws opened and gripped poor Pez, savagely pulling him from the barbed leg, leaving large pieces behind. It was remarkable he stayed alive to the point the ant bent him heels to head, cracking his spine with the sound of a homerun as the bug folded him up.

Max had seen plenty, but that stopped him for a couple of seconds. He felt the heat as he regained his feet. His head was hot. He was enraged. He had to kill that bug and came up firing his Zastava at the monster.

The ant spun in the tunnel, threatening the soldier with a long stinger and deadly legs. Max ducked as an ant leg smashed into the wall just over his head. He vaulted over another jab, rolling on the cave floor and springing to his feet. The soldier bobbed and weaved through a gauntlet of insect strikes to jam the barrel of his gun into one of the joints in the armored body like a blunt sword and pull the trigger.

The rounds penetrated deeply, and the monstrous insect reacted so violently even Max couldn't duck. The spasming leg catapulted the big man into the cave ceiling, and he dropped to the floor in a shower of white sand and pain.

The giant ant made for the ramp, leaking plenty along the way.

Max sat upright with a roar and shook his head with disturbing speed. He had lost his gun, so he unsheathed his combat blade and jumped up to chase the bug and kill it by hand.

Vic got in the way. She opened up with her machine gun as the insect reached the ramp and dove into the darkness. She followed it to the brink, splitting the dark as she fired after the escaping killer. She ran down the ramp after it, but Max caught up and grabbed her arm.

"Done. Return," he ordered, pulling her up the ramp by her gun arm.

A few steps from the top, they stopped and looked back. Vic started to say something, but Max held up his hand. They listened. The darkness below stirred with more ants, plenty more.

He pushed her to run in front of him, over the top, and back to the group. Along the way, Max pulled Burner to his feet without stopping, and Vic grabbed Marco, helping the mountainous man up as best she could.

"Pick it up!" Max shouted. "They're coming!" He looked back to the edge and kept everyone moving past but held Burner's collar. "Faster! Faster!" he yelled after them. Vic and Nygard were helping the big can handlers, looking back at the rear guard.

Max saw Dhawan cowering against the wall. He put his light onto the scientist and shouted, "Move it, Doc! Go!"

The entomologist didn't react. He stared at the ramp, waiting for the monsters to bubble over the top of the dark cauldron.

"Doc! If you don't move, I'll shoot you dead," Max shouted across the passageway to the scientist. He let go of Burner's shirt and brought his light to the bomber's face. Burner looked back without expression. "You all there, Burner?" Max asked. He hooked his hand around the back of the man's neck and tried shaking him back to life.

"That bug really got Pez," Burner said. His eyes watered.

Max nodded. "It did. Now let's get a couple for him," he said, roughly clapping the man's shoulder. "Kill the bugs," he ordered.

Burner agreed to the logic of revenge and shook it off. "Kill the bugs," he echoed.

"Can you set one of those firebombs to go off after you throw it?" Max asked him.

Burner nodded in the affirmative. "Yeah, that's how they work," he answered. "Navy bombs. These are extra hot," he said as he pulled a large grenade from his satchel. "Seven-thousand degrees. We have to be far away, especially in a confined space," he whispered. "Says so on the instructions," he added.

"How many do you have?" Max asked.

"Two," Burner replied.

"Give me one. I'll go across the cave – wait a minute – I forgot." Max turned his light to the opposite wall and got it on Dhawan, still a statue in the dark. He shouted across to the scientist. "I told you to move out, or I will shoot you. But now, I won't kill you. Make your choice; run for it or get shot and get eaten."

The scientist turned to face Max's beam, but he didn't move.

Max lifted his gun and pulled the trigger. A round smashed into the wall inches from Dhawan's head, blowing sand and chunks of the ant-crete over the scientist.

Dhawan jumped up wide-eyed and ran down the tunnel after the group.

Max turned back to Burner and extended his hand. "OK. Give me one of those firebombs. If a bunch of bugs come up, we give them a hotfoot. If it's just one or two..." The big man pantomimed a shooting gun with his free hand. "Got it?" he concluded.

Burner nodded, and Max ran to the other side, waiting as the rattling mob of monsters scraped up the ramp, snapping and gnashing their jaws.

"Here they come!" Max yelled as the bugs bubbled up from the dark pit and into their lights.

The living wall of giant insects, blacker than the darkness, crested the rim of the ramp, twitching antennas and scuttling toward the men in a tidal wave of coordinated chaos. Their jointed legs pumped, pushing them forward as their big bug heads swayed and jaws snapped, hungry to be filled. The squirming mass was as monstrous as any nightmare could conjure – and they were many. The only impediment to the speed of the ants was their numbers. The surge of creatures swelled to fill the tunnel's width as they strained forward to squeeze past each other.

Max shot just to feel his gun working. The bullets tore into the tide of armored bugs and stopped nothing. The chorus of rattles and shrieks of the advancing rank pounded louder and pushed a hot stink ahead of them that burned the men's nostrils.

The two fell back several steps, firing as they went. Max concentrated on the most prominent crawling creature and stopped to plant his feet wide as he emptied most of a magazine into the monster's face. The beast collapsed, and the ones behind it simply crawled on, trampling their flattened nestmate into pudding.

Max stopped firing and ran across to Burner, shouting into his ear to be heard over the blare, pointed down the tunnel, and nodded.

They pulled the pins on the incendiary grenades and lobbed them, wheeling to run from the horde and the bombs.

They covered a good distance of the cave in the few seconds head start the delayed fuse gave them.

The grenades erupted, spewing an exothermic white-hot sauce that rocketed the nearby ants' temperature way above boiling. The first two lines of ants blew apart; monster shells popped like corn. The roaring heat flashed across the cave floor, contained by the low ceiling of the tightly packed creatures, and seared their legs to ash. The living blast furnace focused the inferno and caused dozens of the animals to spontaneously combust and form a wall of fire, blockading the advance.

Simultaneously, the flash shot down the sugar-white tunnel, turning everything in front of the running men to a blinding overexposure chased by an open oven. The heatwave propelled the shrieks of wounded and enraged ants from behind the fire fueled by their nestmates.

The two men caught up to the squad, winded but ready to go.

Max leaned against one of the big can guys and pointed forward, catching his breath. "Have to keep moving," he gasped and motioned ahead again. "Bought a little time, that's all." He looked through the shapes in the dim light and spotted Dhawan along the periphery.

"Got to go," he said and pushed off Libby to move forward.

541

The ant sounds grew behind them. The group moved faster. All ran, knowing to fall behind was to die. At the limit of their endurance, they quickened the pace, driven by the last and deepest well of human resolve as much as the rising drum of the monsters. They stumbled over the rutted floor but kept moving, forward and faster, past exhaustion and endurance, hunted by ants.

Max ran harder to get ahead. They neared the crossroad of the tunnels. He stopped. The runners behind stumbled into the one in front until they had bunched into a tight pack, wheezing and heaving when they were only halfway down the course, and the race wasn't nearly over.

"What?" Nygard asked as she gulped in air.

Max pushed himself up and away from the wall to the middle of the passage. He put his light on the wall and found the openings on the sides of the cave several meters forward.

"Where we saw the ants," he breathed. "Where I left Drake." His light showed an empty cave and Drake's footprints in the sand ahead.

Drake paused in his climb when the din of the ants reached him. He listened. They must be attacking. The sound of gunfire mixed with the next wave of ant calls. He groped over his head to find another handhold to pull himself up and climb faster.

The muffled sound of a distant explosion rushed by him, followed by a warmer breeze blowing from the nest. He pulled himself to the next ledge.

He was close to the top, standing on a narrow ledge, maybe five minutes to go. He leaned against the wall, breathing hard. The fresh air of the desert night washed over the edge, mixing with the dank exhalation of the nest. Drake drank in a few quarts of clean air and eyed his next handhold. One last push to the top. He looked up at the predawn sky and reached for a grip when a dark shape moved over the opening and grew, blotting away the stars.

The huge head of the ant hung over the hole, draping its antennae to taste the updraft before crawling into the shaft.

The big ant planted its legs on the ledges as it scraped down the walls. Its hooked claw grabbed onto Drake's perch as the massive body lowered. Another leg glided by him, then another. There were legs everywhere, each quickly finding a hold as the monster entered the pit.

The enormous body of the monster squeezed into the passage, twisting as it descended. The black carapace slithered past Drake as he pressed deeper into a concavity in the chalky cement wall.

Only his eyes moved as the bug squirmed past, and it was close enough to touch. He let his breath out as the monstrous stinger disappeared into the shadows. Drake leaned into the shaft, looking down into the black, then up at the brightening sky filling the hole at the top.

He had just found a grab on the next ledge when the sounds down the hole stopped him. They were getting louder. Now, the ant was climbing up, not down.

The extra dose of adrenaline supercharged Drake. He gripped the handhold, pulled up, found a place for his foot, and got both feet to the next ledge. He stretched for the next hold.

The shelf under his feet failed, dropping like gallows and leaving him hanging by a hand.

His feet kicked, and one of them found a toehold. His hand grabbed another point, and he pulled himself back into the climb. Another couple of ledges got him to the top of the ant hole. He threw one arm over the brink and then the other. His dangling feet looked for anything as he pulled his chin to the surface of the outside world.

Drake's foot found something to stand on, and he strained to push himself up.

Then he got a boost.

The giant ant had turned in the shaft and crawled up beneath the climber. The antennae rose on both sides of the man, and the jaws came up under him.

He didn't know it, but his boot had found the tip of the monstrous mandible as a foothold. He tested, stamping to make sure it would hold. It felt solid. As he readied to push off, the creature's antennae dragged across his back, getting a taste of the escaping intruder.

Drake felt electricity from the unexpected touch of the ant, and, realizing what it was, he clawed at the loose material around the top, pulling gypsum into the hole as he slipped backward.

The ant had a realization, too, and its chemical switches flipped on. The monster shot upward to attack, throwing Drake over the top of the hole in a somersault that landed him on the white mound of sand with only a vague idea of what happened. He knew that, though he was out of the nest, it wasn't all good. The blanks filled in as the giant ant raised its head out of the nest and planted its front legs on the rim to climb out after him.

Drake was lying on his back with his head pointing to the hole. He arched up to look at the bug from an upside-down viewpoint. The ant's feelers twitched in the air. Drake heard another ant call from the night. Other facts jumped into his thoughts. Like if he had just exited hole number four, he was in the middle of the six-pack at ant central.

He rolled to his stomach, onto his knees, and pulled out his shotgun. Drake pushed himself up into a sprinter's position and gulped air. He sprang at the ant, running up the mound to the rim of the entrance, three feet from the face of the giant bug. The antennae flicked back and forth. Its head rotated slowly to a steep angle like a curious puppy. Its two tire-sized eyes reflected the setting moon in their black facets. The bug's body arched forward, and the dripping jaws opened as it leaned down at the mouthful of a man.

Drake fed the gaping maw his 12-gauge automatic. Three blasts tore into the roots of the mandibles, blowing them apart with steel-jacketed slugs. He raised his cannon and rapid-fired four more into the face of the recoiling monster. The stunned bug fell back against the far side of the opening, steadying itself on splayed legs.

Drake walked the rim of the hole, blasting each leg as he passed, putting the barrel of the shotgun into a joint and pulling the trigger. The ant's weight shifted, slipping further into the hole, supported only by two legs below. Drake was behind the ant's head. He pointed the gun forward, blew off both antennae, and then put more rounds into the middle of the mutant insect's head.

The last slugs found a home. The bug went limp, shifted down, and its head lolled to the side. The massive horror slipped lifelessly into the shaft, and the sounds of bug versus cave ricocheted out of the hole.

Drake dropped to his knees on the sand, breathing hard and fast. The pale light of the night seemed to emanate from the sands more than the sky. He could make out the other five holes dotting the far faces of the dunes across the plain.

There was traffic at the other holes. Ants were busy at the openings. A long line was leaving, snaking over the sandy waves, heading east. After all, Dhawan might have served his purpose in picking this point of exit. He would never have gotten out if they had made for the other holes.

Drake picked one of his spent shotgun shells from the sand. He stared into the black hole, tossed the casing into it, and then looked up at the fading stars in the sky. Reaching into his shirt, he pulled the timer on a chain out and checked it, holding the face to the moonlight. He pushed it back into his shirt and ran down the trail away from the nest to the convoy.

Max turned from the tunnel and moved his light across the soldiers. "Let's go," he said, motioning into the main tunnel. An ant call seesawed out of the darkness. Other insect voices answered. Max shouted, "C'mon, you're not waiting for them! Let's go!"

The troop was slow to turn from the mesmerizing bug calls. The ex-sergeant stood behind them and waited for the perfect point in the recital to add a vocal. "Now!" he roared.

The soldiers snapped out of it and started down-tunnel, picking up steam as they went. More ant screeches followed, and they moved faster. Other insects added their voices, and the pace of the chase through the dark caverns quickened.

Max slowed and dropped to the side, letting the group pass him, and when it was quieter, he listened to the ant sounds. They were still regrouping from the explosion but would be back on the trail soon enough.

He trotted after the others, giving himself time to think. Max's first thought was fighting giant ants while free-soloing a 100-foot wall is not a winning strategy. He felt a good idea coming on when he saw the group's lights clustered ahead.

The big guy saw their backs and pushed his way to the center of the circle. "What's the holdup? What's going on?" he demanded as he barged through the front ranks.

Their lights were focused on a giant dead ant crumpled against the wall. Max stopped and added his light to the huge insect, shining it on the enormous head, illuminating a line of circular wounds punched through the thick insect armor. Quarts of sludge slowly dripped from the ant's skull. "That is one dead bug," Max said succinctly.

The big man brought his light closer to the monster and examined the wall to see if the body covered a passageway. "Nothing back here," he said. As he turned, his beam found the sleeve of Drake's jacket sticking out from under the ant.

Max bent down and looked for any parts of his boss under the bug. He pulled the jacket out and lifted it into his light. Nygard and the others crowded closer.

"That's not good," Dr. Dhawan said.

Max looked up and saw the small stars pinpointing a circle of night sky. The others had not seen the opening above.

"It's not torn," he said as he examined the condition and contents of the tactical jacket. "And the good stuff is gone," he added. The big man moved his light to the wall, slowly playing the beam higher and higher, studying the ridges, ledges, and scrapes.

The shrieks that followed them had quieted, and the silence brought their attention back to the tunnel. The group turned, peering into the deep dark with their guns. A chorus of low rattles from the darkness made them step back, leaving Max and Nygard in the front row. The calls began to rise in volume.

The Oberst stepped to the side to widen their angle of fire.

"Burner, you have those bombs?" Max asked over his shoulder.

"Yeah, two," the man replied. "But they're trip charges with a ten-second delay," he said, looking closely at the packs as he handed them over in the dim light. "At least, I'm pretty sure," he added.

Max sighed. "Great. All right, give," he ordered without taking his eyes from the tunnel of bug sounds. Burner held out the sandwich packs and spikes.

Vic came out of nowhere and took the charges and anchors, pushing Burner back. She stepped next to Max and handed him one of the sets. He looked at the woman and smiled.

"I knew you would make me do something stupid," she said.

Max nodded. "Pretty dumb," he agreed and turned back to the bristle of lights. He called to the group. "The way out is right above you. Start climbing. You'll come out at the east end of the six-pack, but at least you won't be down here."

Dhawan was at the wall before Max finished talking, staring up and squinting, looking for his first handhold.

The bomb guy hesitated and looked back to Max.

"You're done, Burner," Max said to him. "Go." The ex- sergeant's head half-turned and said in a low voice, "Really, go. You've done plenty." Burner turned and headed to the base of the wall.

"Colonel Nygard, if you would see my soldiers to the top," Max said to the Oberst, "I would appreciate it."

The Norwegian woman studied the big man and then nodded. "Ja," she said. "I will do what you order, Mr. Grunewald." She gave him a casual salute and started to turn. "Grunewald. Maybe you are Norsk?"

"Who knows?" he replied.

"I think you must be," Nygard said as she turned and went to the wall, pulling the big can guys along.

Marco brushed the woman's hand from his arm. "Hey, Max, we're staying with you," he said, standing his ground.

"We are?" Libby asked his partner.

Max turned and looked at the big guys. He smiled at them and said, "They'll need you guys up there. Thanks, though. We'll be right behind you. That's an order."

Marco stalled, then replied somberly, "OK, whatever you say." As they walked away, Libby called back, "Stay loose, Max."

Max put his light on Angel as he opened his mouth to say something. "Don't!" Max cut him off. "You've been pretty quiet. Don't ruin it. Time to move out, soldier," he ordered. Angel closed his mouth, saluted, and left Max's light for the climb to the top.

Max turned around and looked down at Vic. "Ready?" he asked. She nodded, lifted her weapon, and together they went into the darkness, keeping their lights low on the floor in front of them.

"At least a hundred yards, if we can," Max whispered as they moved through the cave. The insects grew louder – a high-volume shriek shot through the tunnel and froze them in place.

Max silently counted to ten, then moved. "More ground," he said cautiously, creeping ahead with Vic right behind him.

The aroma of charred ant grew stronger in the warm air of the cave. Max looked back at the small lights at the base of the climb. "We need more distance," he said, heading for the ant noises.

After another 50 yards, they stopped. The bugs sounded like they were right on top of them.

"Here," Max panted. "This is good. We can stick them here." Max already set his in, pushing the spike into the ant-crete with one hand while pointing across the cave to the opposite wall. "Set yours over there and pull the wire back to this one. They're already synced," he said, pointing to the red lights. "I'm going down the tunnel to reconnoiter. Back in a tick." The big man turned and jogged into the tunnel.

Vic hurried across the cave and pounded the spike into the wall using the haft of her tactical knife. It was plenty big enough to use as a hammer. Her knife went back into the sheath, and she pulled the wire to stretch it across the tunnel. The spike dislodged, falling out of the wall. She swore and stepped back to pick up the unanchored charge.

With her machine gun hanging from her shoulder, she put the spike to the grainy cement, twisting and pushing it into the wall. The wall pushed back. She pushed again. The wall bulged outward.

Pieces of ant-crete popped from the wall. The surface swelled, cracks appeared, and sand ran from the gaps. Pieces became chunks, the cracks became fissures, and the surface ballooned to bursting.

The face of the wall expanded in her light as if it were taking a breath. She turned to run.

Vic's first steps tangled her in the bomb wire, and she tripped. She got back on her feet and ran, hobbled by the wire attached to the bomb pack.

She didn't run far. At about ten yards, the wall collapsed. Undermined by giant ants, hundreds of tons of ant-crete and sand fell, opening a new entrance. The debris avalanched, spilling into the tunnel after Vic.

She outran most of the crashing cement blocks, but a couple caught up to her, knocking her down and sending her for a swim with the cement.

Vic was thrown hard, lost her weapon, and badly injured her left side. Moving her knee made her see lights. It probably wasn't broken, but she didn't want to look. She knew her leg was bad, but her left arm was worse. A jagged boulder had rolled over it, and she was sure it was gone. The soldier gulped, lifting her arm along with the most pain she had ever felt. She was surprised her arm was still there. She turned her hand to count her fingers a couple of times but only got to three. It looked like the outside two were missing.

Her whole arm was red and dripping, trussed up like those long pieces of holiday meat. The tripwire had been twisted and fouled so tightly around her mangled arm that it cut deeply into her flesh.

The dust from the collapse was thick, enveloping, and disorientating.

The monsters swarmed into the tunnel through the gap, scuttling over fallen slabs of the tunnel wall, waving their antennae and chirping loudly.

Vic pulled at the tight wire wound around her mangled arm but couldn't loosen it. She pulled and pushed herself through the debris, away from the sound in the dust cloud. She heard Max calling her. She rasped in reply, spitting dry powder, gagged, and spit out more, and then managed to cough a reply. "Here, I'm here." She coughed again. "I'm OK!" There was noise, and things were moving, but it was all going on in a white cloud.

Max yelled her name again, and his gun flashed like lightning in the clouds. Vic flattened until he stopped shooting, and then she moved.

She heard the Zastava bursts, a couple of rounds each. An ant hidden in the cloud blasted back with a bone-bending screech.

Max fired again, and it stopped.

The fine white dust hung in the air and dried every breath. Vic thought of making a mask from a piece of fabric, then laughed at the thought. She was past any long-term health consequences.

Feeling her way through the dust cloud, her hand fell on something familiar. It was the stock of her machine gun in the rubble, waiting to be found. She checked the ammo, racked the bolt, and lifted it, painfully supporting the weight on her damaged left arm. Her vision blurred and went in and out like it was on a switch.

Across the cave, Max fired again, and she didn't even duck.

She swung her weapon up, forcing her dead arm to turn and using her bird claw around the forward grip of her gun.

Max fired two bursts, and giant ants squealed in the hot tunnel close to his flashes.

Vic emitted a guttural exhalation as she squeezed the trigger. Fire arced from her muzzle as tracers flashed across the slagheap, illuminating three monsters charging Max's position. The kick pounded through her shattered arm, and she tightened her grip against the recoil.

More ants came into the strobing light of her merciless gun; she stopped firing to let them move in. They did, and she let them have it. Vic opened up her showstopper again, sweeping it over the line of mutants.

Interval tracers shot frozen lines of light as the bullets streaked through the dark and ripped into the insects. She raked the row from the front back to the entrance, dropping bug after bug in the line, dead or good as.

Her gun ran empty. She cradled it in her bad arm, dropped the bullet box, and pulled another belt out to replace it. As she agonizingly labored, she watched a new monster make its way into the tunnel. This one didn't follow the path but instead crept over the debris piles with twitching antennae in her direction.

Max's gun fired again and again. He stopped and called to her, but she couldn't make out the words over the incessant insect sounds and the ring of the machine gun in her ears.

Vic fumbled with the belt box. It would be easier with two working hands. Her bad one was a real mess, but at least it wasn't bleeding too much. The wire had so tightly tangled around her arm it cut off the blood flow.

She struggled to engage the belt and had to roll onto her weapon and use her weight to snap it in. She hoisted the gun onto her good leg, bracing herself and ready to fire.

The cloud from the cave-in was dissipating. She heard something move and could just make out a large, dark shape in the dust.

Vic let go of her machine gun, snapped her flashlight on, and threw it into the cloud past the shape. It landed clattering and bouncing light beams in the cloud. In a moment, rays of light and shadow strobed as the ant moved by the light until it was a silhouette against the glow, turning its huge bug head and flicking its feelers, throwing them in smaller arcs as it mapped Vic's location. Then they stopped, marking two points in a triangle. She was the third.

The giant ant shadow made a rattling noise. Vic dragged the gun around with her good mitt and painfully maneuvered the end with the hole to point at the monster. It stopped rattling and rushed at her.

Vic pushed back against the rubble and lifted her gun to fire as the bug charged over the debris piles, shaking its head side to side and snapping its jaws as it zeroed in on her with those shaggy feelers whipping around, sniffing everything. The mutant knew right where Vic was, and it pounced.

Its legs stabbed into the rocks one by one around the soldier, fencing her in. The monstrous insect loomed over her, twisting its head slowly and opening its jaws while, as a testament to the transcendence of evolutionary adaptation, the aberration of an insect absorbed the injured human's condition, nutritional value, and location out of thin air.

Vic overlooked the majesty of the moment and filled it full of holes.

The feelers twitched in the air as the giant ant head came down, guiding the gaping jaws to their mark. Vic sent a spray of steel rounds into the bug's face. Cool liquid jetted from the wounds, spraying the woman in a salty ooze.

The bug's head recoiled, shaking off the shots several times. It took a step to realign with its target, leaned to one side, and raised its right leg high. Vic pulled the trigger again, steadying and aiming the gun with her three-fingered claw. Blood from her wound sizzled to steam as it ran down the burning steel barrel.

The gun blazed, and the ant's leg shot down, punching a hole through Vic's ribcage.

Everything seized from the massive trauma. t-shirt design "Paranoia is a Super-Power!" She fired again as blood shot in a stream from her mouth. A tracer went through the ant's head, and Vic saw fireworks on the roof of the cave.

The monster bent its head down and pushed gently against her with its curved jaws. She heard shots as the giant head filled her fading view. The ant pulled its leg out of Vic, holding her in place with its mandibles. The jaws closed and lifted her from the blocks of sand. Her gun fell. Her left arm didn't hurt anymore. Holding her loosely, the ant carried her over the rubble.

Vic's head flopped from side to side as the ant moved over the debris to the new entrance. Others of the creatures were there, already dismembering their dead and dying; another swarm of the beasts moved in and labored at the long buffet Vic had prepared for them.

The ant carried her a few more steps to the line of the insect soldiers. Her resistance was gone, and the light was leaving her eyes. From behind the veil, she watched as a figure stole through the shadows to her aid.

Max and his light came closer. He had stealthily crept within their midst and hid behind a dead ant only a few yards from the monster holding Vic.

She could see him. They were close. Her hand weakly tried to push the huge insect's head away. It was smooth and hard. Blood was dripping from everywhere. Vic did not react as another ant moved closer and swabbed her broken body with its feelers.

Slumped over the serrated sickles of her captor's jaws, her arms and head swayed in unison with the bug motions. She could see her friend in the white mist beyond the monsters. The facets of its giant eyes glinted as its bristled antennae brushed over her. She groaned, trying to form a single word for Max. She tried, but her eyes closed to a darkness deeper than the cave. With a sudden inhalation, they opened to see Max raising his gun behind the giant black ant's head.

With only one lung to force the air through her throat, Vic breathlessly exclaimed, "Run!" She lifted her broken left arm. The ant shook its head, wagging the woman back and forth. After the shake, she held her arm up again.

A red light slowly blinked on her arm. He raised his flashlight without regard for the monsters. The beam illuminated the mangled machine gunner hanging from the mutant's mouth, and the explosive charge held tight to her arm by the tangled wire.

"Run," she hissed with her final breaths. "Please..." Vic gasped as the ant's constriction forced the last ounces of air from her chest. Blood leaked from the hole in her chest in a steady stream. Her good arm came up and clumsily found the charge. Her fingers twisted the wire coming out of the explosive pack. She pulled, and the wire popped out of the bottom of the bomb. The blinking red light went solid.

Max felt that icy flush of do-or-die shoot into his veins. He turned and ran.

The big ant with Vic's body in its jaws made its way through the throng of creatures.

Max ran like hell and covered a lot of ground.

The ant got to take one more step with each of its six legs before Vic's sandwich pack went up, taking Max's bomb on the opposite wall, too.

The explosion shot into the main tunnel and the new entrance, disintegrating the giant ants, living and dead. The force of the blast blew the structural ant-crete from the weakened tunnel walls, causing a cave-in that buried the new intersection the ants had formed.

Max ran as fast as he could, but the shock wave was faster. It blew him off his feet, throwing him through the air to crash into the cave floor, tumbling over the ruts and finishing on his back, staring into the darkness.

He lifted his head. There were no ant noises. He tasted blood and thought about standing, struggling to his knees, and raising his arms as if he were beseeching God.

His gun lay nearby, pointing upward and illuminating a bright circle in the darkness above. Max watched the lights grow and move, multiplying into a swirling river of colors as his vision faltered and his unspoken prayers went unanswered. The light show abruptly ended, and he fell forward, planting his face in the cave floor.

It was a tough climb for the exhausted invaders without any gear, but the prospect of fresh air, sunshine, and remaining uneaten was a persuasive motivation.

The shaft was ringed from bottom to top with erratic steps to accommodate the insects, and those served the climbers well. Dr. Dhawan had developed a new life force and was ahead of the others, pulling himself from ledge to ledge and going up the wall like a fly. He was going to the top and wasn't looking back.

Below the scientist, Angel was gaining. He had overtaken and passed the two big guys, assuring them he'd be waiting for them up top.

The large moving men were making pretty good time up the wall, with Marco leading the way and Libby shadowing every step.

Burner was no climber but was giving it an enthusiastic try and was slowly following the duo, pushing up the face grimly to leave this hell behind. Nygard was right behind him, lending a hand, deftly scaling the gritty face with her machine gun slung over her back. She paused regularly, listening to the tunnel below and waiting for Burner to move up the wall.

The Oberst had pulled herself up to the next ledge well past the halfway point when the blast hit.

Everyone flattened to the cement as the shock blew by, except Angel. He lost his hold and fell. In a miracle save, Libby, who was in good position, snagged the man as he slid down the face, rescuing him from a catastrophic fall.

The muscleman lifted, grunted, swung Angel to a foothold, and let him go when he was in place. Angel hugged the cliff and breathed open-mouthed. He looked at Libby and could only shake his head.

The big guy laughed and said, "Next beer's on you, right?"

Dhawan had just put his arm over the top as the noise and wind rushed from the shaft. He pulled himself onto the sand and rolled a few yards down the embankment. The scientist sat up, wiped his face, and looked across the wide basin spread between the dunes.

It was all so familiar.

He squinted across the plain, brightened by the big moon, orange and planetary, as it set over the distant mountains of the dreamlike desertscape.

The entomologist sat back on the cone of the giant anthill, resting on his elbows in the cool gypsum sugar. He watched the ants moving at the other holes, far enough away that he could enjoy the grand scale of his spectacle without fear.

Miniaturized by the distance, the giant ants worked the colossal ant farm in a model of collaboration, moving in lines, combining efforts, orderly and equal, an enactment of the doctor's assumptions and wishful conclusions of collective consciousness, of the triumphal expansiveness of being not a part, but being the whole.

Absentmindedly pushing his fingers through the sand, he plucked an expended shotgun shell from the sand as he noticed a litter of casings glinting in the moonlight.

Dhawan got up and followed the spent shells around the rim of the hole. He stopped to examine a section of ant leg – undoubtedly from the specimen at the bottom of the shaft.

He continued circling the hole to a point where he marked Drake's footprints running down the cone, leaving a long trail down and into the rift between the dunes. His path led back to the expedition.

Dhawan stood on the anthill, facing the trail to the west and the other five holes of the nest. They were crawling with bugs.

The scientist turned to see the two large men climbing from the opening. Another climber crawled over the top just a few feet away. The scientist waited until they were up, then circled the rim to bring news of their leader to the three soldiers.

They nodded as the doctor walked up. He smiled and nodded in return, then stood quietly, looking across the valley to the busy ant holes.

"Whoa, look over there," one of the big men said, pointing across the basin at a line of ants leaving the nest area. The other men tensed. Angel pushed against the loose sand and got himself to his feet.

"There's no need for immediate concern," Dr. Dhawan told them. "They are far away, and, more importantly, they are upwind of us, if you notice." He wet the end of his index finger and held it up in the gentle breeze. "They don't know we're here."

"That's all right for now," Angel said, "but the wind can change, you know."

"It can," Dhawan replied with a smile. "Which is why we should depart as soon as possible. To save ourselves." He paused. "We could follow Mr. Drake's trail." He paused again. "Hopefully, he has found safety by now."

The soldiers turned their heads to look at the scientist.

An arm came over the rim of the entrance. Burner's other arm and then his head followed. He stared and panted with his chin on the edge of the wide hole. He took a breath and pulled himself up and onto the sand, sliding a few feet down through the granular scree. "Don't bother," he gasped. "I don't need any help."

Burner lay in the sand, watching the quartet and enjoying the fresh desert air.

Oberst Nygard was right behind him. She pulled herself over the top and glanced at the small group as she got to her feet, unshouldered her machine gun, and stood at the peak of the mound to survey the desert. Her gaze dwelled on the distant ants and then went to the group.

"That's where we first entered the nest and left the surface forces," Dhawan continued. Pointing down the rift trail away from the setting moon, Dr. Dhawan added in a louder voice. "And his tracks lead that way."

"Tracks? What are the tracks?" Nygard asked.

"Mr. Drake's tracks, ma'am. His footprints lead away from here," Dhawan responded. "I would say rather hastily, too. If you look at the ground, you will see evidence of his conflict with the single ant we found at the base of the shaft. Such a confrontation would certainly be enough to encourage almost anyone's retreat," he added.

Nygard toed one of the spent shells in the sand, and her eyes followed the tracks. "Yes, Doctor, almost anyone."

"Well, as I was saying, we should follow our leader's example and withdraw," Dr. Dhawan went on. "While this is not one of the most trafficked entrances, it is only a matter of time until we are discovered. As was Mr. Drake."

"You are certain his footprints lead away from here, Doctor?" Nygard questioned. "There are sure signs of his escape?"

"Yes," the doctor replied. "His tracks go down the bank on the opposite side. They lead away, that way." He pointed again. "You can see them for quite a distance."

"Ja. Yes," Nygard said in thought, then turned to the men. "Now, you will follow him again. You will go by his trail and get back to the rendezvous point. All of you," she ordered.

Burner got to his feet. "And you're staying here, I suppose?"

"I will wait for Max and the woman soldier for a time," she answered.

"It's not very likely they survived that blast," Burner said in a low voice.

"No, it is not, bomb man," Nygard answered sharply. "But I will wait, and you will go."

The Oberst turned to the other men to start them moving as the big guys were getting to their feet. She looked at Dhawan and then walked across the slope to watch the ants on the wide, white plain.

Nygard cupped her hand around her eyes.

"Time for you to go now," she said firmly to the group. They heard what that meant. The men looked over the basin and saw lines of ants issuing from the cluster of holes.

The insects spilled down the mounds in streams, pooling on the flat floor between the dunes in an undulating black carpet, seething as it reformed into three weaving columns, twenty giants across, marching in their direction.

Oberst Nygard walked back to the top of the anthill. "Or maybe stay." She sighed and reached into her flak jacket to take out a sealed pack of cigarettes. She opened them, took one out, and stuck it between her lips. "I do not think you could outrun them, anyway," she concluded, sitting in the sand to light her smoke.

The soldiers watched the gigantic insects slither across the basin in long lines. Burner whispered aloud to himself, "Ten minutes. Maybe fifteen." He cursed and counted his magazines a few times.

Angel looked to each of the survivors, desperate for an answer. His voice cracked. "What's the plan?"

The soldier's question hung unanswered until the response of the monster ants drifted across the basin. Hundreds of soft chirps and cheeps rose from the crawling chains, sounding like a million crickets on a warm summer night. Really big crickets.

The ants marched to a drumbeat of their thousands of footfalls as the colossal column pressed forward, each following the one in front, irrevocably obedient to their instinct.

Oberst Nygard watched, repelled by her innate rejection of the insect form. They were the basest of biologies with no greater aspiration than consumption. Nothing mattered to them, and nothing would stop them except death. And they were many. The huge bug bodies became more discernible as they closed the distance. The light welled in the eastern sky before dawn.

"Plan?" Nygard asked as she let a long, satisfying stream of smoke adrift in the air. "The plan is to kill many monsters. When confronted by overwhelming forces and no hope of survival, we die well. That is the best plan we can have." The Oberst pushed herself to her feet, took another drag, and let the smoke float lazily from her nose and mouth. She held the remains of the cigarette between her thumb and first finger, then flicked it over her shoulder and down the ant hole.

"We cannot run through the sand," she said, unslinging her weapon, taking four magazines from her canvas pouch, and putting two into her side pockets. She discarded the empty ammo bag. "We would be exhausted in no time. Then we cannot fight so good." She racked her machine gun and unsnapped the holster cover. "So, this is the only plan we can have," she concluded.

The chorus of chirps grew, adding rattles and shrieks to the driving, almost mechanical wall of sound that rode in front of the bugs, flooding the desert with the relentless oscillations of the marching monsters.

Behind the soldiers, Dr. Dhawan quietly crept away. No one took note as the scientist got to his feet and scurried noiselessly over the soft sand, around the perimeter of the ant hole, following Drake's trail, stumbling and falling as he ran down the far slope of the cone.

One of the big men stared across the sands at the advancing mutants and said quietly to his friend, "This don't look too good for us."

"I guess not," his buddy replied. The large man lifted and racked the bolt of his AR, which looked small in his grip. Satisfied the weapon was ready to use, he stood close and leaned his head toward his compatriot. "Do you want me to, you know, do it, when things get bad?"

Marco turned a puzzled expression to Libby and asked him, "What? Do what?"

"You know," Libby answered, looking down meaningfully at his assault rifle.

"Do I want you to use your gun?" Marco asked, "Is that what you mean? Of course. Why the hell are you asking a thing like that?" He shook his head in disbelief.

"Well, I just wanted to make sure," Libby replied quietly. He eyeballed Angel, who was standing close by, and lowered his voice. "I just wanted to make sure you wanted me to shoot."

Marco looked away from the columns of the hundreds of advancing monster ants to scrutinize his partner's face. "Well, what else did you plan on doing with that?" He turned back to the ants, shaking his head. "I swear, Lib, sometimes you are very alarming."

"OK. OK. I just wanted to get it straight," Libby said.

Marco double-checked his weapon.

The two stood side by side, their rifles pointed ahead as the sky brightened, waiting for the sun.

Angel moved his position closer to the big guys. He cursed and held his head as he watched the ranks of ants blanketing the desert. "I thought we made it, you know?" he moaned. "I thought we were the ones that got out. I thought that when we climbed out of that hole."

Libby looked at the man he had snatched from the air and said, "At least we're out here, Angel." He smiled broadly at the man and gave him the thumbs-up.

Marco looked at him out of the corner of his eye and shook his head, bewildered by his partner's attitude. Exasperated, he asked, "You do know those ants are going to eat us, right?"

"That's very negative thinking, Marco," Libby replied, turning his smile upside down. "I think you are transmitting unnecessary pessimism," he added, looking in his pockets for another magazine.

Marco opened his mouth, but he didn't know what to say.

Libby shrugged at his partner, squinted at the bugs, then nodded and said, "Don't worry, Marco. I got you covered."

Concerned by his friend's mental state and their impending doom, Marco looked at his partner. "You know, Lib, we've worked together for what, ten years?" he asked.

"Fifteen," Libby replied.

"Fought against the odds – even won. Plenty of times, we thought it was the end, but we always got out somehow," he said, shaking his head. "Working for the Agency has been one heck of a ride."

"That's for sure, Marky. A heck of a ride," Libby agreed.

The ants were close. A couple of minutes away, close. The chorus was getting very loud.

"Well," Marco continued, "in all those times, I've never seen you lose it like this."

The leading ants reached the mountainous anthill and massed around the bottom. More crowded in, ringing the cone in a seething moat of giant black bugs, their hideous features becoming apparent as the morning light arrived.

"Like I said, buddy, I got you covered," Libby repeated.

Nygard stepped to the front of the quartet, pulling Angel to his feet along the way. The shrill insect chatter percolated up the hill, scratching at the raw fear of the soldiers.

The two big guys looked at each other and then back down at the tide of black-armored insects rising around their island. Suddenly, Marco turned to Libby. "Were you talking about shooting me?"

His friend glanced away from the insects, "Well, yeah, but not until things get bad. What did you think? That's what you want me to do, right?"

Marco's mouth opened wide as the waves of monsters swarmed the steep slopes of the sandy cone.

Nygard opened fire. Her explosive ammunition was instantly effective, dropping the first of the monsters she fired on. It fell and was buried as more huge bugs charged over the carcass.

The five heavily armed soldiers laid down a line of lead that took its toll on the advancing bugs. But they kept coming. The ants were slowed by the rising wall of insect bodies and the clumsiness of their uphill drive through the loose sand, but they kept coming.

The soldiers fell back as they shot. They gave ground in short steps, retreating behind their muzzle flashes and flying brass.

Burner and Angel were the first ones pushed back to the top, to the edge of the shaft, with nowhere else to go. The sky was brightening with the dawn, and Angel spotted an ant across the hole, running around the lip and heading their way.

Angel stood on the edge of the abyss and raised his weapon, taking steady aim at the incoming monster. It rounded the last curve of its track and headed straight for the soldiers of fortune.

Angel fired, and his bullets tore into the miscreant beast. The bug lost control of its legs and stumbled, nearly going over the edge. He lowered his rifle to watch the monster slip – then it caught itself on the brink, pulled back to the top, and continued crawling toward them.

It dragged some legs, but the others were enough to keep it on the attack. Angel fired again, putting more slugs into the monster.

The creature stopped. It lifted itself on its functioning legs and curled its body to pull the stinger under itself and point it forward. The abdomen bulged, and the thick barb bent upward. Angel aimed, and so did the bug. The monster lifted itself on its back legs and leveled the swollen tip of its body at the rifleman. Angel looked past his weapon at the peculiarly posed mutant.

In the human's hesitant half-second, the bug's bladder burst, shooting a viscous rope of acid swinging through the air to Angel. The corrosive bolo found its mark, wrapping him and pinning his arms to his sides as the thick goo smeared and stuck, melting his skin.

Angel stumbled back, screaming, and fell into the sand, rolling to stop the burning, but only succeeded in spreading it.

Burner sprang to help his comrade, ignoring the coiled creature. He jerked his hand back from the searing pain when it contacted only a drop of the blistering goo spreading over Angel and realized the fate of the boiling man. Burner raised his gun.

The rogue ant Burner assumed was incapacitated had enough life left to kill. The wounded worker ant ran at Burner and was on him before he could turn. The monster snapped its drooling jaws around his hips and jerked the shrieking man into the air, crushing his pelvis. He dropped his weapon and pushed against the heavy obsidian jaws as they chewed, opening and closing cruelly, dropping the man inch by inch through the grinder, chewing in murderous repetition, faster and faster. Finally, what remained of Burner oozed through the mandibles to the sand, thoroughly macerated and unrecognizable as human.

Angel's boiling agony had powered him to his feet as he strained against the constricting glue. He tried to stretch his arms outward against the mucoid mass and saw the bones of his forearm burst through his melting flesh as steam roiled from the liquifying muscle.

Through his scorching anguish, Angel willed his leg to move, his foot to step forward toward the hole so he could throw himself to his death and end his hell. The soldier forced his other leg to lift, and he teetered, losing his balance. He fell backward, rolling down the steep slope faster and faster, tumbling wildly, slapping the sand, and smearing the corrosive paste over his dissolving body. Like a screaming dumpling floured by the bleached White Sands, he careened into the trampling mass of insects charging up the hill.

Nygard saw his twirling legs sticking out from the whirling white ball as he went by. She leaped forward to help, but the man was too far down the hill.

Through the hammering of their weapons and over the din of the insects closing through the lead and sand, Libby heard a noise behind them. He turned and saw the car-sized ant driving at them. He swung his AR around and planted a fistful of rounds into the bug's head.

His turn caught Marco's eye, and he brought his weapon to bear on the lone bug as it got ready to squirt again. The monster braced against the downward slope with its working legs, and its pointed abdomen slid out, dragging through the sand, aimed at the soldiers. The end of the organ puckered, squeezing the orifice closed as the bulb behind it fattened, ready to shoot the burning glop.

Marco and Libby raised their weapons together and simultaneously blasted the swelling monster. The volley of high-caliber rounds split open the straining acid gland, and the caustic goo blew all over the monster's underbelly, spilling the mordant mix into the wounds.

The creature recoiled and spasmed violently, falling backward, jetting steam from the sizzling holes and distended viscera. Its legs flailed wildly, providing enough momentum to rock the beast back over the precipice to fall into the shaft.

Libby raised his eyebrows, and Marco sent it off with a curse as the bug disappeared over the edge. They turned their guns back to the shrieking line of giant ants climbing the loose sand behind the wall of dead bugs. The ants were gaining ground and closing quarters. The soldiers had only a few yards of higher ground behind them – any further offered only the pit.

They stood next to Oberst Nygard as she raised her weapon at the wall of dead ants and the bobbing giant heads and waving antennae behind them. She pulled the trigger. Her gun clicked, emptied of ammunition. The Norwegian colonel smiled, looked at the two men, and reached into her jacket. She pulled out her smokes and dropped the useless weapon, pushing a cigarette into her mouth and lighting it. "That is all," she said to the men.

Libby and Marco looked at each other. Libby beamed a broad smile. Marco countered with a sad shake of his head for his friend's mental state.

The woman rested her hand on her holstered sidearm. "You will tell me if you want an easy death," she said to the men.

"What is with you two?" Marco asked. "Why do you want to shoot me?" He stepped in front of them. "All right, you know what. For all I care, you can..." They looked over his head, and he turned to see what they were looking at.

A particularly large ant climbed onto the wall of carcasses. It pulled itself to the top of the gruesome barrier and lifted its body high to emit a pulsing siren with a bone-buzzing bass. The call stopped, and the swarm behind the barricade was silent. This new monster stood on the heap, framed against the morning sky, rotating its barrel head as if it could see, prodding the air with its antennae. It arched its back and emitted a deep vibratory rattle as it snapped its jaws together, raising its front legs higher until they pointed straight up. Its rumble became a shriek, growing louder as the monster clawed the sky.

The beast's head pivoted, hanging the air-tasting antennae in their direction. Her dripping jaws opened to advance, but the creature stopped, attentive to the new squeaks and clanks from the desert, answering her call.

"Great, like they needed reinforcements," Libby moaned.

Nygard held her pistol at her side, watching the waving antennae of the giant ant on the wall against the red rising sun. "Perhaps not," she said quietly.

The new sounds stopped. Ants on the other side of the wall began rapidly chirping, and the large ant stretched upward even higher, waving its feelers in the air, receiving messages from the multitudes behind the wall.

Libby's attention jumped from the monster ant on the mound of dead bugs to his friend, thinking how great it would be if he came up with a way out. That would show everyone. Then he thought of the long drop into the hole behind them and looked down at the Norwegian's pistol hanging from her hand. The big guy's belief in the power of positive thinking was being tested.

Marco glanced at his friend and shook his head, about to say something, when a winding scream ripped through the morning sky. Before the three of them hit the dirt, a shell from the Abrams exploded with perfect precision behind the ant bodies. It blew off the back two-thirds of the big bug and flung the head with its still-snapping jaws in front of the soldiers lying in the sand.

A shell exploded further downhill past the remains of the wall, which protected the soldiers from the shrapnel that pulverized the ants behind it. The .50 caliber machine gun followed, hammering the anthill. The three soldiers kept their faces buried as Libby cheered into the hill and got a mouthful of sand.

The ringing chop of the .50 caliber was outgunned again and again by the thunder of the tank's main weapon. One after another, the shells blew across the face of the slope, spreading the swarm of ants into a field of smoking bug parts.

The barrage lessened, the interval between blasts lengthened, and the chop of the machine gun eased. The soldiers got to their feet. Nygard holstered her sidearm and picked her empty weapon from the sand, and they made their way past the big bug head to look over the wall.

There was no more white sand hill, just broken and burning ants. Some fragments were recognizable as legs and heads, midsections, and abdomens, but few connected the way they did minutes before. Smoke columned from the slope, and the stench was thick.

Lion One roared up the steep sandy hill, smashing through ant carcasses and grinding their parts. There was no obstacle to the armored leviathan as it rolled over the remains of the enemy to the rescue.

The figure in the turret was waving to them. A voice crackled from the tank's loudspeaker. It was Drake.

The three soldiers at the top of the anthill got out of the way as the 70-ton tank came crashing through the barrier of dead bugs. It drove past them to the top, and Drake held on one-handed, throwing them a quick salute as the vehicle slowed, pivoted, and spun to a stop to face downhill. The dust and the exhaust bloomed into the air over the open cone, turning it into a volcano in a primeval landscape.

Drake pulled himself from the turret and jumped onto the steel body. He looked at the trio, from face to face to face. "You're it?" he asked pointedly.

Nygard answered, "We are all, Mr. Drake. I do not think there are more."

Drake nodded. He looked at the entrance to the nest, then turned back to them. "Onboard," he said and waved them up. "There are plenty more of them out there."

The soldiers clambered onto the tank as the hatches opened.

"Everyone inside," Drake said. "You'll want something between you and the bugs."

Oberst Nygard and Drake waited as Libby and Marco squeezed through the openings.

"You knew we were here?" Nygard asked Drake.

Drake nodded. "Once I got out of the hole, communications kicked in. I hooked up with Cap, and we got a drone overhead. Showed us where you were, real time. We knew just where to put that first shell. It wasn't luck," he answered, smiling. "Anyway, it wasn't all luck."

They watched more ants coming out of the holes far across the flat.

He gestured to the entrance to the nest. "You're sure?" he asked the colonel.

"Yes, and perhaps no," she answered. "Your Mr. Grunwald ordered me out with his soldiers. I obeyed," she continued. "It was a long fight up here, with many monsters." She held up her machine gun. "I ran out of ammunition." She passed her weapon down the hatch and leaned on the edge of the turret, looking at the determined officer. "I did not see him die, Drake, but also, he has not come out. There is a large explosion. It would be a miracle, I think."

Max's friend exhaled thoughtfully. "A miracle? That would be Max," he said as he jumped off the side of the tank onto the sand. "I'm going to wait for him."

Nygard started to climb down from the tank, but Drake stopped her. "You're going in this," he said, slapping the hot metal twice. "I appreciate the offer, but you can't help," he said. "You're out of exploding bullets, remember?"

"I am," she replied. "It could be…" She was cut short by Cap popping up from the front driver's hatch.

"Time to go," he said, then looked at Drake with surprise. "What are you doing down there?" he asked him.

"Staying," Drake replied.

"You're not," Cap responded.

"Am," Drake disagreed.

The tank commander paused, opened his mouth to reply, then shut it. He smiled, nodded, and slipped back into the metal, pulling the cover over him as he shouted, "You're the boss!" The hatch clanged shut, the Abram's engines gunned, and the vehicle started rolling away.

Drake looked up at the Oberst and gave her a quick fan of his hand. "Don't worry," he called after her, "I always have a plan." He looked at his watch. As the tank rolled down the hill, he reached into his shirt and pulled the timer out, and Drake made his unhappy face.

He trotted to the rim of the hole and shouted down, "Max!" He waited in silence. "I know you're down there," he called. "One way or the other," he added in a less forceful voice.

Drake spoke into the comm. "Cap, you better pick up the pace. You have to get on that road and gun it," he said.

The static crackled and came to life. "You know it," Cap replied through the hiss. "As soon as we're flat, we'll open her up."

The tank rode off the hill and turned onto the trail they had taken in. Drake watched the tank get smaller as it traveled between the dunes. They'd have to make the Air Force base before the timer ran out.

Drake moved counterclockwise around the rim of the cone, watching the tank's progress between the dunes. He opened the comm again. "You're going to run into a swarm of them, moving in on your right…" There was a tacit confirmation from the tank commander, then static. Drake cut the comm and watched a dark mass of a dozen insects scrambling down the dune to intercept the tank and converge on the fast-moving dot trailing a plume of desert.

Small sparks flashed from the armored fortress. Probably Nygard with the .50 caliber. The distant chatter of the gun reached his ears a few seconds later. The small dot tore through the line of ants, pulling its dusty tail as it vanished behind the bend in the trail.

"Go, man, go," Drake said aloud as he watched Cap disappear. He turned back to the hole and looked down into the darkness. It got blacker down there as the sun rose.

"Max!" he shouted into the void. Drake crouched by the brink of the deep drop to listen. The sounds of ants echoed from the nest in answer. He peered into the hole, trying to force a light or a sound from V2. He looked at his watch and knew there was not enough time to climb down, search, and climb out. He lifted a handful of sand and let it pour through his fingers as he thought, staring over the plain to the cluster of ant holes. More of the monsters were coming out, massing around the distant openings. The news of their losses at Hole Four would make them act. Drake made some calls to command and outlined a plan. They will get back to him.

He couldn't leave Max. He was probably alive. It just wasn't like him to die.

Drake lifted a hand to his headset, pressing the earpiece and listening. "Affirmative, base, eighteen minutes," he replied.

The commando jumped as a voice behind him caught him off guard.

"Heroic, that's what Mr. Grunewald was. Quite heroic," the remains of Dr. Dhawan said.

Drake looked at the scientist with surprise. The doctor edged along the precipice, speaking softly as he followed the hole, coming closer. His hair hung in all directions. He was wet with sweat, dried with sand, and stained with fear. His jacket was gone, and his pants and shirt were tattered. Drake's expression flashed through disgust and turned to cautiousness as he observed the pistol in the scientist's right hand.

"A very brave man, Max was. Do you think it's all right if I refer to him as Max?" the scientist asked as he gazed down into the entrance. Holding the gun, he pushed his glasses up his nose with the back of his hand. "I mean no disrespect. Never speak ill of the dead," he said. He laughed just a little. "And they are all dead now, you know." The doctor gestured with his gun, waving it over the hole and pointing across the depth to the horizon. "All dead down there, all of them back there, in fact, all over the world, most likely." He circled the weapon over his head and repeated, "All over."

Drake listened and waited for the man to finish his thoughts, then answered in a steady voice. "Well, we're not, Doc," he said. "I'm glad to see you made it OK," he added in a friendly tone.

Dhawan stopped brandishing the gun, brought it down, and pointed it unintentionally at Drake. He smiled and used the back of his gun hand to wipe his brow and then push his glasses up again. "Oh, I'm OK," he said. "I made sure I'm OK." He dropped his hands and lowered himself to the sand, twisting to sit with his legs over the edge of the drop. The scientist looked down and shook his head. "I'm OK," he said again.

He turned to face Drake. "On the other hand, I learned what a motivating force fear could be, Mr. Drake." He stared at the soldier briefly, then looked back into the pit. "I don't know how men like you and Mr. Grunewald do it, how it is that you are so brave. How you push yourselves forward instead of running away." The doctor turned back to Drake. "Just how do you overcome your fears?" he asked.

Drake shook his head with a shrug. "I don't know if I overcome anything, Doc," he answered. "There are always scary things. No matter what you're up against now, there's always something worse coming along tomorrow."

The scientist shuddered. "Nothing could be more frightening than those monsters in the dark," Dhawan said quietly into the hole. "I think I have had enough of ants," he added.

"I think we all have, Doc," Drake said sympathetically. The man had passed his breaking point and cracked under stress.

"I'm glad I have this," Dr. Dhawan said, lifting the gun in his lap. "It doesn't seem very likely we will get out of here." He looked over the desert between their position and the cluster of holes. The ants had pooled again at the far end of the six-pack.

"I ran away from here before," the doctor went on. "I found your trail and then told the others that you had run away and left us, that you had run and left us to die." He looked at the soldier from the corners of his eyes and brought his free hand to his forehead. "I told them you ran."

"Well, I guess I did, Doc," Drake said.

"Yes," Dhawan sighed and shook his head. "You ran to save us. I saw you go, you know. Then I saw you coming back, riding on the top of the tank like a hero, charging to the rescue. I was hiding, curled in a crevice like a coward. Because I am."

He shifted as he spoke, elevating the pistol, thrusting it forward when he condemned himself. The soldier hung his right hand, ready to unsnap the clasp on his holster, out of Dhawan's line of sight.

"I realized you must have contacted the tank, that the communications must be working. But with the remains of the immolated ants I found along the trail, I knew things had gone bad on the surface while we were below," he related.

Dhawan was retelling the story that he had already gone over too many times in his head.

"But I had to hide, you know," the doctor continued. "When I left the group at the top to go for help, there were ants down there already." He pointed across the hole and motioned with his weapon. "Years of training. I made it through. By the time you were coming back, there was nothing I could do. You had the tank, after all. You are the professional,' he said, pointing the gun toward Drake. "It was enough of an effort to make it back here, to get up the hill, and at any point, one of them could jump out, and all I have is this, not a tank!" He waved the pistol.

Drake unsnapped his sidearm in the holster, still showing rapt attention to Dhawan's diatribe.

"And what happens when I get back?" Dhawan asked accusingly. "There's no tank. It's driving away. I'm up the hill, and it's down there with everyone in it." His voice strained, and he looked at Drake menacingly. "But you're here. Why are you here? Why didn't you go off in the tank?" he demanded, jabbing the air with his gun to accentuate his questions. "Why didn't you go? Tell me! I would have gone – I would have gone in the tank. You know I would have gone."

He stopped ranting suddenly and froze with the pistol pointing at Drake. "You stayed behind for your friend, didn't you?" he asked. "Not me. There was no wondering what happened to Doctor Dhawan, no 'I wonder if he's alive or dead?' No. Who cares anyway?"

The scientist sat on the edge. His glasses slowly slid to the end of his nose, but he didn't push them back. He stared over the top of the grimy lenses at the soldier.

Drake deliberated with his hidden right hand around the pistol grip and the gun halfway out of the rigid holster.

"You came back to find your friend," Dhawan complained. He turned to look down the shaft as the bug noises sounded from the depths. The voices of giant ants rose and fell from the darkness. Dhawan pushed away from the opening, pulling his legs up and losing focus on his gun.

Drake lifted his pistol from the holster, keeping his finger on the outside of the trigger guard.

There were shots in the nest. Multiple bursts echoed from below, reverbing on their way out. Dr. Dhawan got to his knees and brought his gun forward to point excitedly into the shaft while moving back from the brink.

"Shooting! Shooting down there!" he cackled.

Drake dropped his gun back into the leather holster, snugging it in for the ride. He sprang at the doctor, connecting with a roundhouse kick to the chest, knocking the scientist out of his eyeglasses and leaving his gun hanging in midair for half a second before they dropped to the sand.

Drake picked up the doctor's pistol and went to the edge of the drop. There were small flashes far below and more shots.

"Max!" he shouted into the darkness. As he listened to the hole, he watched Dhawan on his hands and knees, feeling through the sand for his lost spectacles.

Drake stepped back from the drop and picked the doctor's glasses out of the sand. He threw them a few feet ahead of the scientist.

"They're right in front of you, Doc," he told the myopic man. "On your left."

Dr. Dhawan found the eyeglasses, and carefully lifted them to the light to clean them before putting them on.

Drake was back at the edge of the drop, listening and searching the bright morning sky, shading his eyes.

"I don't know why you felt the need to do that, Mr. Drake," Dhawan said as he regained his breath. "I don't think that my…"

"Quiet, Doctor," Drake interrupted. He looked away from the sky for a moment at the scientist who was scanning the sand. "And you don't have to look for your gun, either. I have it, so just sit there and be quiet, and you'll be OK," Drake ordered. His attention turned back to the clear blue morning above.

The scientist sat on the sand. He faced the plain, watching the ants swarming from the other holes. "I just think that, due to our circumstances, a weapon is not an unreasonable request."

Drake listened to the ant calls from below, looked at his watch, then answered the doctor, "You will be quiet. You will be quiet sitting there in the sand, or you will be quiet at the bottom of this hole."

Dr. Dhawan sat quietly in the sand.

Drake stood on the edge looking into the drop and saw a light tracing a short path at the bottom of the shaft. He shouted into the hole and listened for a reply. The light moved again. Ant shriek rose from the tunnel, and muzzle flashes sparked at the bottom, followed by shots echoing up the shaft. The light disappeared.

Sand twisted from the rim of the ant hole, blowing in thin ropes. Someone threw the big wind switch, and the wisps of sand turned to swirling sheets, whipped by the deafening roar of a helicopter hovering a hundred feet over hill number four and whirlpooling white dust from the cone into a localized sandstorm.

Drake covered both ears as he shouted into the comm, squeezing his eyes closed. The helicopter continued its climb over the anthill, centering itself over the opening. As it got higher, the windstorm lessened.

Dhawan watched Drake shouting into his microphone, standing braced against the wind on the edge of the ant hole and waving a signal in the turbulent wash to the chopper. A thick cable dropped into view, within Drake's reach. He grabbed it, put his foot into the sling, and, without hesitation, stepped off the brink to swing over the shaft.

As he floated on the end of the line, Drake shouted something to Dr. Dhawan, but the scientist couldn't make it out in the helicopter's noise. The soldier pulled Dhawan's commandeered pistol from his belt and threw it into the sand by the entomologist, followed by a curt wave.

The cable continued its rapid descent into the dark, taking Drake along. As he lowered, Dhawan saw him pull the shotgun over his shoulder with one hand while hanging on with his other.

The scientist looked away, shielding his face against the blowing sand. He retrieved his pistol and looked up to the hovering whirlybird. Soldiers like Drake were at the large door running the cable. And they were behind the glinting windows, piloting the giant flying bug. And at a gun protruding from the open door. They were everywhere.

Dhawan cupped his hands and shouted up to them through the clamor and whirling white sand. They didn't hear, didn't see, didn't care. They were wrapped in armor, oversized helmets, and utilitarian flight suits, connected by tethers and buzzing in each other's ears. The eminent Dr. Dhawan realized that he had unknowingly studied their kind for a lifetime. They were insects in a war for dominance with other insects.

Max tasted the salty ocean on his lips. He twisted to get comfortable in the warm sand of the beach and kept his eyes squeezed tight against the bright sun as he listened to the waves washing against the shore. He smiled and turned again, pushing his fingers through the loose sand.

He could almost go to sleep, except someone was blowing a horn down the beach. It was not a musical horn; it blared and got louder than the surf roaring in his ears. It must be getting closer. Max stopped smiling. If they kept it up, he would have a word with them. He didn't want to be disturbed when he was on the beach and didn't appreciate someone blowing horns while he was trying to relax.

He tightened his eyes even more to keep the noise out. The sun was extra bright in one of them, and he moved again to get the light out of his eyes. He felt warm metal against his face and smelled gun oil.

The horn started to sound more like a calliope, which was far worse. His head began to hurt, which was another vote for keeping his eyes closed, but reality kept trying to open them.

He was sure he was lying in the sand, but maybe he wasn't on the beach. He clumsily moved his hand to grab the metal and found it was his Zastava. He smiled and squeezed his gun close, moving the light from his eyes and sighing contentedly. That gun was one of his favorite things.

He unstuck his lids and blinked at the darkness.

That circus music kept blaring, maybe even louder, and that was enough for Max. He sat up even if important areas of his body objected to the movement.

The whole thing about being in a giant ant nest came back to him. The screeching hurdy-gurdy reorganized into ant calls heading his way. He twisted his head to grind out the kinks, took a deep breath, and stared past the reach of his flashlight into the dark veil of monsters.

Beach Max got back to being Max in a tunnel with a gun. He checked his weapon, felt through his jacket, and found five magazines. He stood on the rutted floor, off-balance for a moment, then moved to the center of the cave where it was smoother going. The big man turned from the ant sounds and limped toward the climb out.

As he went, the noises followed and were catching up. He pushed harder, loping after his bouncing flashlight beam.

A bug shrieked with such volume that he fell against the wall and turned his light back, half expecting to see one of those big ugly ant faces pop out of the dark right on top of him.

There were three, and they were right on top of him.

Max was so surprised he recoiled and lifted his arms in a shocked response. He yelled, "Wow!" and tripped over his own feet, falling to the cave floor, all the while firing his Zastava with remarkable accuracy into the faces of the bugs.

At times like these, he was glad to have a light on the barrel. Anywhere he lit up, he lit up. The closest ant's antennae were chopped off at the roots, and her face got half a dozen new nose holes. Max didn't know if the shots stopped the bug, but it slowed because the next one pushed past and came on strong.

The mutant scrambled over its injured companion, trampling the wounded bug with its pounding legs and larger body. Max put his light on the gaping jaws, and three rounds spit from his Zastava, emptying the weapon. The huge beast must have felt a twinge from the impact as it stopped and lifted a front leg to inspect the injury. Max turned and ran, dropping the empty mag and snapping in a fresh one.

He spun to fire but misjudged how closely the insect followed; it was just a giant ant step away. The insect attacked with a grazing foreleg jab that knocked him tumbling over the rutted floor. He rolled into one of the ruts, and the insect lunged, stabbing at him, breaking the ridge of ant-crete next to his head. Another leg shot in from a different direction and caught the slack in his jacket, pinning him to the concrete.

He was stuck and could hardly move. His gun light lit up another bug leg lifting to strike, and behind that, the feelers twitched to find him in the darkness.

Max laid his rifle across his chest with the muzzle jammed against the leg that pinned him down. He let off a burst and blew the goo-filled leg wide open, disconnecting the foot from the bug.

The creature pulled back the dripping stump, and Max rolled over the ridge into the next ditch. He lifted his Zastava to fire into the giant head. The shots chopped a wide fissure in the armored exoskeleton, and gallons of vital slush dropped from the bug's bucket and splashed across the cave floor.

Mortally wounded and leaking the last of its life, the monster attacked the man. The mutant ant came in punching – the first blow blasted the cement next to his head; the second knocked a hole in the wall under his arm. Max twisted out of the way and fired point-blank into the ant's face.

His close-up volley shattered the bug's exo-armor, and its head opened like a suitcase, dropping the internals to the floor. The monster collapsed and snapped its jaws a few more times before it went lights out, a fighter to the end.

Lucky for Max, he was on the right side of the ant because its carcass jammed the passageway. If he ended up on the other side of the dead bug, it would have been tough to get around. But it was just the thing to slow down the trailing bugs.

Max loudly combined a curse and a prayer of thanks as he got to his feet and shook it off. He started down the tunnel to the way out, maneuvering as best he could with a bad leg over the rutted floor. He could hear an ant at the blockade, buzzing like a 20-foot hornet.

The big soldier ran, hopped, and fell, and got up and repeated the process until he finally got to the chamber at the base of the shaft. He stumbled into dead bug number one and slid down to rest on the floor, breathing heavily. Max looked up to the circle of daylight. It was round and blue and far away, and the sky never looked better.

The soldier propped himself up and surveyed his path upward, starting with the dead ant. His heavy breathing stopped when he heard gunfire from above. He strained his senses, listening to the reports, and stared into the far circle of bright sky.

There was lots of shooting, but as long he kept hearing it, Max thought that could be a good sign. He also thought they could use another hand up there and got himself to his feet. He shouldered his rifle and started picking his way up the ant to begin his climb. Standing on the head of the beast slumped against the base, he got a hand and foot on a ledge and kept going. He looked up to the sky hole at the top. It was bright, blue, and round – until the eclipse.

Blackness slid over the blue, filling the circle and covering the sky.

Max shouted, jumped down the stinking ant mound, and scrambled to the floor through the tangle of legs. He rolled under the bug for cover, cramming inside a revolting crevice formed by the broken body of the fallen ant, squeezing in as tight as he could.

An acid-spewing ant, bullet-riddled and melted by its own corrosive brew, plummeted down the shaft and smashed into the cave floor right next to Max's sheltering monster, but away from him, on the other side of the big bug. That was good because, between the bullets and the acid bath, there wasn't much holding the thing together, so when it hit, it blew apart, showering pieces big and small around the chamber.

After the splash, Max stuck his face out of his hiding hole and looked around. He put his light on a two-foot piece of ant, fizzing as it melted. He crawled from under the insect, looked up at the bright circle of sky again, and took a big gulp of air.

He climbed the dead ant again, carefully picking his way to be sure he didn't grab any steaming acid-goo. When he got to the top of the bug, he inspected the wall for any spatter and saw the path was clear. He started climbing, grabbing anything that felt like a rock and would give him a way up.

As he went, the gunfire became intermittent and then stopped altogether. He tried to climb faster, though he was exhausted. He was already 40 feet up when that third ant caught up with him and scuttled into the chamber at the bottom of the shaft.

Max was past running out of steam and was holding as tight as he could to the ledge when he heard the snapping jaws and the menacing rattle of the bug scraping across the floor. He pushed his face to the cement wall and sighed. The big man closed his eyes and got ready for another of those do-or-die times. At this point, even the dumb money was on die.

He got angry. Max clenched his fist and held it as he bellowed in rage, pulled back his arm, and smashed the cement. Max was caught off guard by the force of his blow. A thunderous tremor shook the shaft. Sand dislodged from the concussion sprinkled him in the darkness.

It made more sense when another jarring concussion and another boom of artillery cracked down the shaft. A barrage was falling above, pounding the anthill. Maybe that was good news for the people up there. Or maybe not.

He reached for the next overhang and pulled himself up. As he moved, the ant rattles from below quieted. Max gained the next wider ledge. He had room to turn and shine his light down at the bug. It was coming after him, beginning its climb on the carcass against the wall.

The giant ant was atop the body of its nestmate and let out a loud trill. A smell filled the shaft that made Max think of a new set of tires. His gunlight shined on the bug.

The monster finished the pulsating call, and Max's trigger finger slowly squeezed. The center of his beam was on the center of the monster's upraised head – right between her big round eyes. The creature stood still as a statue; not even the feelers moved. Max hesitated.

In the shadows behind the mutant, there was movement. There was something else in the dark. He moved his light off the beast to the head of another ant poking into the chamber. Then another, and another – everywhere his light moved, ants filled the shaft – crawling out of the shadows and flocking around the motionless giant that had summoned them.

One after another, the crawling beasts packed the bottom of the pit. There was no cave floor to be seen; the hole seethed with bugs, chattering and rattling, their antennae swaying as they writhed together in a bubbling black stew of snapping jaws, all pointing up at Max.

More monsters crammed into the hole. They clambered onto the others' backs and took footholds on the walls, climbing higher as the ones below pushed them up. The pot boiled over.

The large ant stopped being a statue and began climbing after Max. It stood on its back legs and found the footholds on the vertical wall. The monster covered the height quickly, leading with its waving feelers, following the rich scent trail the sweating soldier shed.

The giant warrior ant quietly climbed closer to the man, spreading its legs across the hole's diameter to support its huge body floating in space, buoyed on the thick spokes radiating to the walls. One leg, then another, grappled upward in quick unison to find the next support, and the curved claw feet latched on to raise the beast higher, closing on the soldier as he climbed.

Max stretched to get a hold of the next ledge and pulled himself onto a wide concrete shelf. He stood and took a breath, looking into a deep vertical recess, a crevice just about his width. The soldier snapped off his light and rested in the narrow cranny. He could just make out the opposite wall in the meager illumination from the oculus above.

He heard soft scrapes against the shaft wall as a black shape rose in the gloom. Max unslung his Zastava and pushed back into the narrow fissure, holding the assault weapon tight to his chest.

583

The reflections of the sky high above flashed across the faceted eyes of the ant as its head turned, searching for the man.

Max breathed heavily. His heart pounded as the monster slowly opened and closed its vicious jaws, warming up for their meeting.

The head lowered. The massive body twisted to orient itself toward Max. He moved his eyes down to the wall-to-wall ants, smaller than this one, flooding the chamber and rising. He could hear them scratching toward him in the dark.

The soldier lifted his eyes to the monster before him as one antenna entered the cranny and touched Max. He shuddered and shrank back, pressing tighter into the wall as the bristles traced his face. The ant, hanging in the shaft, pivoted forward and softly hissed. The beast's face came closer, and the curved mandibles opened wide as the jet-black arcs glinted in the dim light.

The enormous head hung only a few feet away. Its mouthparts slowly closed, and the head turned in the air. Max pushed back into the cleft in the cliff wall and kept his weapon up to guard his front.

The ant struck, exploding in a furious attack. Its jaws flashed open and drove down, striking directly at Max. The pincers were too wide for the narrow crevice, and Max was at the back. They bit into the cement wall, and pieces of concreted sand exploded everywhere. As the ant's head pulled back to strike again, Max brought his gun up and fired. His rounds ripped into the huge insect, punching holes in its head and the underside of its thorax, but the force of bullets did nothing to stop the monster's momentum.

The jaws snapped at the folds of the fissured wall surrounding the man. Cement chunks flew from the monstrosity's ringing attack. Max squeezed into the gash in the rockface, burying himself from the ferocious battering of the frenzied mutant gnawing away his defense.

Again and again, the ant savaged the barrier, tearing the wall apart. Max turned his head in the narrow space, shutting his eyes to the flying shards and the liquids spraying from the mutant's wounds and frothing

584

mouth. Every time the monster pounded the rock, its gnashing jaws got closer to the man's face. He was covered in ant spit and sand, and the bug was getting closer inch by inch.

The mutant pulled back and switched the air with its feelers. Max raised his gun and fired, emptying every slug into the bug. This time, the amount of lead forced it back. The mammoth ant pulled away from the assault, pushing its front legs to move to the other side of the shaft. Max popped out of his crevice, snapped his light on, dropped his empty mag, and smacked a new one in place.

He fired decisively, raking the eyes and antennae, then obliterating the joint on the nearest leg. The ant was seriously wounded and twisted to redistribute its mass across its functional legs. Max put his light on the monster's mouth, carefully aiming to administer the coup de grâce.

The ant and Max were on the same wavelength. It lunged across the shaft, taking a suicidal leap at Max, smashing into the wall and the soldier. It hit the face of the cement and stuck for a second before tipping backward. Legs flailing, the ant tried to find a grip to arrest its fall, scratching and clawing against the walls. One of the hooked feet caught Max's jacket and ripped through, opening a wound across his chest and entangling the tough tactical fabric.

He might as well be tied to a car driving off a bridge. The enormous mass of the bug fell into the shadows, snatching the soldier along like an afterthought.

The fall was quick. The ant hit on her back with Max on top. He landed in the stiff bristles of her lower half inside a cage of curled legs and was face down in the stinking nether regions of the bug, still gripping his rifle. The glow from his light was enough to show that, outside the bars, there was a roiling sea of insects. The bug he rode down was shot, broken, and dead, added to the pile of dead bugs already at the bottom of the pit.

He rolled over and listened to the squishing noises and chirps of the ants crawling in the dark. Max lifted his gun and moved it around. The smaller ants were everywhere he shined his light.

He sat up, moved the light through the grisly bars of the dead bug's legs, and saw the faces making all the noise. Their big helmet heads looked up from everywhere, swishing their air-tasting antennae through their dark world. The collective buzz of an interloper grew. The first of the creatures climbed up the front of the bug. The rest would follow.

Max stood on the hard-shell underside of the dead monster and stomped around, testing his footing. He pushed a couple of the limp legs out of his way and reached into the back pocket of his vest for another magazine, but there was no back pocket. It had been torn away along with the remainder of his ammunition. He reached to his hip and found his sidearm was gone, too. His knife was still on his leg.

He hated fair fights.

He kept his light pointing forward of the dead bug, watching the new arrival feel its way up and investigate the body. He looked down at his chest. He was covered in blood, which normally wouldn't be noteworthy, except this time, the blood was his own.

Max evaluated his situation. He cursed, spit, and then cursed again. The noise in the chamber had eased off. It was at a tolerable pitch now. It reminded him of the insect sounds of a summer night. The low, regular murmur would have been soothing if he wasn't going to be torn apart and eaten. He cursed again but didn't have any spit left.

One of the ants climbed up and turned its attention from the carcass to the intruder. It stopped feeling the corpse and raised its sensory probes into the air, flicking them around, defining the space around the soldier like it was trying to read his aura.

Max decided to get the show on the road and shot the bug in the head a few times, carefully letting off one round at a time, counting bullets.

The ant retreated. Max followed it with his light as it scuttled into the crowd. The other ants sensed something off and pulled away from the wounded insect. It spun in a slow circle as if only one side of the oars were pulling. It stopped and made a clicking sound. Its nestmates closed in again and tore it apart. Max could see the pieces carried away in a crawling parade of bugs.

He turned his light around the chamber to look out on all of the happy faces. This would be the perfect audience if he were a headliner in Hell. He walked out of the legs toward the bug's back end and looked down at the fearsome stinger on his dead ant. It was mean-looking, curved, thick as a bull's horn, and sharp. His light moved into the seething crowd, murmuring, swaying, tasting the air, and licking their chops. They all knew where he was.

The dead ant he was standing on suddenly bucked. The jolt threw him, and he fell back, grabbing one of the upright legs to catch himself. He brought the light forward and saw several of these compact giant ants tearing pieces off the body he stood on. The corpse bounced again as the bugs swarmed to their task.

Max understood why they hadn't charged up and over the remains to get him. It wasn't the job of these half-giants. They were the clean-up crew. The bigger one he shot down was security. But the outcome would be the same. When they got to the man, they'd take him apart as well. Living or dead, it didn't matter to them. Everything on the pile went into the pot, and he was on the pile.

He thought how much he would like a flamethrower: nothing fancy, just your basic hotfoot at a hundred feet.

The diminishing body jolted again, and its position shifted significantly as the worker ants detached the head. The corpse turned, nearly spilling Max into the crowd, but he held onto one of the legs and logrolled as it turned. It stabilized, and the man regained his footing on his shrinking death raft, the SS Diminishing Odds.

At its closest, the wall was three ants away and covered with the condensed giants. He raised his gun and fired at one of them. It took three rounds until the insect lost its perch and fell into the swarm. Max thought he could shoot them off and jump across their bodies to the wall.

The ant fell, not dead but mortally wounded, into the crowd. The others quickly evaluated her status and went to work on the damaged bug, tearing it apart by the joints, gone in less than a minute.

That did not look like the path to freedom.

His raft bounced violently again, and three ants climbed up what was left of the front of Max's big dead bug boat, rocking in the troubled waters. He looked up to the light falling from above.

Drake hung on with one arm hooked around the cable and one foot in the sling as the winch spooled him down the ant hole. He dropped fast, which was good because there wasn't much time left. As he descended, he pointed the headlight on his shotgun around him, alternating between the walls and the bottom of the hole.

He'd seen muzzle flashes from the top of the hole, and on the way down, he saw more. The sound of the ants rose from the shaft, getting louder as he got deeper. He shouted into his comm set, but his connection cut out as he got further into the drop. The helicopter was hovering directly over the opening, and he had hoped there would be a better signal, but it was only static.

The pilots were doing a great job keeping the chopper in position, but the longer the cable got, the more sway was in play. He was using his free leg to kick back from the walls as the tether swung back and forth, banging him into the sides of the tunnel. His rate of descent slowed as the line spooled; the crew on the winch knew what they were doing, too. Drake wanted to get to the bottom and get Max – if it was him doing

588

the shooting. He couldn't imagine anyone else staying alive this long down there and still shooting – nobody but Max. Max didn't die.

He was about halfway down when there were more flashes below, and the sounds of shots ricocheted up the shaft. The thick steel cable swung as he lowered, and Drake twisted around to kick himself back from the wall.

His pendulating descent made it seem like he was circling the tunnel as much as dropping into it. Drake bounced off the walls more often and with more force as the length of his line increased. The ride was getting rougher, but it couldn't be helped. More flashes and shots came from below.

He was out of sync with the swing and couldn't get a leg up for the wall in time. His shoulder smacked into the concreted sand, and he was dragged across the rough surface and into an ant, which was a surprise.

He had braced for the collision with the rock-hard cave face – that was not a surprise. The abrasive scrub across the sandpaper, he expected. The face-full of ant stink and the energetic response of stabbing barbed legs caught him off-guard.

Drake kicked back and pushed off with his shotgun, clubbing at the bug, parrying its jabs. The rebound of his cable pulled him from the wall as the big ant reached with an outstretched front leg grabbling in the air. A chitinous foot slashed through the beam of his light and ripped the shotgun from Drake's grip. His weapon spun away, cartwheeling into the darkness as the cable swung him out of the monster's reach.

The force of the ant attack disrupted the regular pitch of his swinging descent into the shaft. Drake dangled from the spinning line as it found a new orbit. His arc balanced, and his eyes further adjusted to the gloom. Each time he swung, he could see the dark walls were made of ants anchoring themselves to the ledges and footholds. Their bodies arched backward, so their upside-down heads and twitching jaws hung into the shaft as their antennae monitored the environment for intruders.

Drake slowly swung to the waiting jaws of the ant on the side of the shaft. As he came closer, her shiny jaws strained wide, her feelers switched excitedly, and her body tensed to receive him. The neighboring bugs leaned in their direction, anxious to get in on it.

Drake reached for the .45 on his leg. He thought if the ant was going to eat him, he might as well irritate it first. He tightened his hold on the cable and held the handgun close to his hip, pointing it at the slavering creature as the wire swung him in.

Its black jaws dripped with yearning as he was delivered to the wall. A fast heartbeat away, and three slow shots hit the bug from below. Not his.

"Max!" Drake blurted involuntarily.

The bug lost its hold on the ledge and fell. Drake hit the sandy wall and pushed back as the clacking jaws surrounding the empty spot grabbed at him. The cable took him away as their mouths and reaching legs stretched after him.

Drake leaned back against the steel rope to look down and could see Max's light pointing up. There were more flashes as he fired.

The cable lowered, and Drake could see him battling below in the pit.

Max's light had dislodged from the gun. It was at the big man's feet, shining up, streaming beams of light through the churning mortal combat, illuminating the indomitable figure atop a dark mound of writhing monsters, clubbing them with his empty Zastava in one hand and splitting their hard candy shells with the short sword he called a knife in the other.

Drake knew Max would fight his way out of Hell, and it looked like he was doing it, but he could only watch as the pool of crawling nightmares congealed around his friend.

The cable lowered too slowly.

An ant rose behind the sergeant, lifting its forelegs, poised to strike.

590

Drake jumped onto the back of the coiling insect, aiming to straddle the bug like a rodeo star, but his aim was way off. He crashed onto the beast and bounced off, sliding into the stew of dead bugs.

Drake's impact caused the big ant to recoil and strike Max with one of its legs as it whipped around. The big guy was knocked unconscious into the gooey pile of dead bugs, with the fluids of the vanquished monsters running over him.

It was a hot, wet mess.

Drake was in the same muck beneath the giant ant playing king of the hill. Sliding under the monster, he crawled toward her head between a moving tangle of legs. Drake could see the light from Max's gun shining through a dark thicket of bug parts.

The ant leaned forward, dropping its head into the light. From Drake's view, the ant's head and twitching antennae were silhouetted in front of the glow. The jaws, slowly opening and poised to strike, waited only for the feelers to find the sweetest spot of her prey.

Drake slipped over dead ants and fell into a pool of runoff from all the holes Max put in the bugs. He climbed through the slick yolk that oozed from the shells, using wounds in the exoskeletons for handholds. Fully dredged in the dead bug goo, he glided smoothly, pushing with his feet over the armored bodies until he was under the head of the monster.

He unholstered his .45, lifted it straight up, and stuck it into the bug's mouthparts. On the way in, it brushed a group of thick bristles protruding from the base of the ant's jaws. The creature jerked away and stepped back, dropping its feelers to Drake.

He instinctually flattened into the pile of dead ants as the hairy antennae swept the air over the slime-covered heap.

Satisfied it was all goo-covered nestmates in the pile, the big ant raised its head and stepped forward. Drake lifted the .45 again and jammed the heavy pistol into the monster's mouth, emptying the magazine into the bug's head.

A few more quarts of ant vitals spilled over Drake, gushing out of the creature as it began to lean. The deluge stopped, and the monster fell off the mound into the dismembering swarm of ants.

Drake spit and wiped his face, then slid down the incline of dead ants, slipping through the muck to his friend. He worked Max out of the insect entanglement, pulling him by what was left of his jacket. Everything was covered with leaking bug juice, which helped to slide the big man out of the slick shells and down the pile, his Zastava clutched in his hand.

Max's eyelids bounced from open to closed and back to open. He squinted at Drake and dropped his knife to grasp his arm.

"You'll be OK," Drake said to him as he watched another ant climbing up the mound. It would find them soon enough. He looked at his empty gun, dropped it onto the pile of useless parts, and wiped goo from his face, freezing mid-swipe as something tapped his back.

Drake turned slowly, twisting around and lifting his arms as the last line of a hopeless defense. The steel cable bobbed in the air, stopped in its swing by the pile of bugs.

"Max! Max!" He rousted his friend as he pulled the sling over to get him in the loop and slung the Zastava over his head. If it were left behind, Max would go back for it.

Max opened his eyes. "What the…" he asked. He shook his head, trying to clear the fog.

"Time to go," Drake replied. He found room for his foot in the sling with Max and held onto the cable. He reached up to his comm set and turned it off, the prearranged signal to pull the line back. The steel cable went taut, and they were lifted through the hole like termites on a monkey stick.

The bugs followed them, spiraling around the walls of the tube in pursuit. The ride up was slow, and the ants covering the sides of the shaft were running ahead as the cable started swinging from side to side in wider arcs.

Drake leaned down and took the empty Zastava from around Max's neck. The slow swing brought them closer and closer to the climbing ants. Drake used the gun to push back from the crawling wall, pushing off the back of one of the creeping insects. Drake saw one of the ants below snapping at the unconscious Max, dangling from the sling. The drooling jaws bit the air inches from his feet as Drake put extra effort into shoving off.

Max floated back to consciousness, making noises as they swung off from the bugs. "What the hell?" he garbled, almost coming to. In the light from above, Drake could see he was pulling at the sling under his arms. "Get me out of here," the big man said hazily.

"Stay put," Drake answered, pushing his friend's head with the toe of his boot. "You don't know how good you've got it," he added. The big guy's head lolled to one side, and he looked up at Drake.

"Should have known it was you," Max mumbled as his eyes fluttered and closed.

Drake laughed as the swing to the other side of the shaft headed them for more ants. He looked up to see the hole was much closer than he expected. He clicked his comm set on. "Drake to Sky One, come in," he said into the mic.

Sky One crackled back through the static, "Go ahead."

Drake tightened his grip on the cable as they swung towards the crawling wall of ants. The bugs carpeted the tunnel, writhing and chirping to the top. The tether trolled them past the mat of insects, and big heads would pop out of the crowd, twitching antennae and snapping jaws as they dangled by. "Step on it," Drake said into the mic. "Reel us in now. Fast as you can. Never mind the bumps," he ordered.

The pilot cut in on his comm set. "Drake, it'll be my pleasure. I just lost a bundle on you," he said. "Hang on. We'll have you out of there in nothing flat."

There was a jolt as they swung closer to the ants, and the cable pulled them up, up, and away — and fast. The ride quadrupled in speed as the winch went into high gear, and the helicopter gained altitude above the ant nest.

The tunnel walls sped by as they flew up the shaft. In a few seconds, they were clear of the climbing insects and heading for the opening. Drake looked up, watching the hole of daylight grow larger. The sling bounced them off the walls hard, but only a few times and Max took most of the bumps anyway.

The daylight rushed at them, and Drake squinted at the brightness as the pair shot from the dark and spun into the light of the desert morning, pulled aloft for a twirling bird's eye view of the six-pack of ant holes.

The cable reeled them up through the cold air to the chopper's door. As helping hands grabbed the men and pulled them in, Drake could see the bugs across the plain, fuming out of the cluster of entrances. Whether in response to their invasion or as part of another plan, the colony emptied, and the nest's population spilled onto the desert.

The rescue crew pulled them through the hatch, and Drake gave them the thumbs-down and shouted into an airman's helmet that another pickup was waiting for them at the top of the anthill.

The message was relayed to the pilot. He looked back from the cockpit and waved an affirmative to Drake, and the bird went down to get Dr. Dhawan.

Mostly out of it, Max was dragged to the middle of the copter. He took a weak swing at an airman attempting to check his vitals. Drake leaned forward and pushed the Zastava into his arms, assuring the crewman it was empty. Max cradled it in his arms and quieted, smiling unconsciously.

Drake stood in the door frame and grabbed the cable. He stepped into the sling and signaled to be lowered, but one of the crew stopped him. Drake overrode him, pushing his hand away, and gestured to the anthill. He shouted over the roar and wind of the open hatchway, "Not right." The soldier corkscrewed his finger at his temple. "Knows me," he yelled, cupping his hand around his mic.

The pilot looked back and gave him the thumbs-up. Drake grabbed the arm of the winch and leaned out of the helicopter into the windstorm. The wash turned the wind into a sandstorm as the chopper descended and hovered. Through the twisting sheets of white, Drake caught a glimpse of Dhawan sitting curled up near the top of the hole with his back to the copter.

Drake slapped the crew chief's arm and shouted into his ear. "He's right there!" The soldier pointed to a spot in the whirlwind.

The chief nodded and leaned close to Drake and held up most of the fingers on one hand. "Three minutes on the ground, that's it," he shouted. He pushed a pistol into Drake's holster and a helmet over his head, clicking the visor down. He smacked it twice on the side and gave him the go-ahead.

Drake swung out of the helicopter, and the cable traveled him down. It brought him to earth quickly, and he stepped out of the sling, first looking back to the rim of the ant hole and then turning to jog over the white sand and through the strong winds to Dr. Dhawan, sitting in a ball.

He reached out and put his hand on the scientist's shoulder, pulling on his jacket to get him on his feet. "C'mon, Doc, we have to go!" Drake yelled over the chopper's weather.

Dr. Dhawan lifted his head and looked up at Drake. His face was caked with the snowy powder of the desert, and his eyes were wide and red-rimmed. The chalky mask rolled its big eyes under the eyeglasses, and his toothy red slash widened to an unsettling smile.

Drake stepped back from the doctor's expression as much as from the pistol the entomologist was pointing at him. He looked at the gun, then past the scientist's face to the rim of the ant hole, as the blowing sand allowed. "C'mon, Doc," he repeated. "No time to waste. Ants are on their way right now!" he said urgently, throwing back his visor.

The pistol came up higher, standing like a snake in front of Drake's face, slowly swaying. Dhawan followed the gun and got to his feet, keeping the Glock aimed at the soldier.

The wind carried the ant calls out of the nest. Static and a voice crackled in Drake's earpiece. "No time, Doc," Drake repeated as he stepped toward the man.

The scientist stumbled back, falling into the sand, and held his pistol at arm's length, pointed at Drake's chest. "What am I supposed to do now?" he shrieked over the swirling winds, shaking his gun at the soldier. "You tell me. What am I supposed to do now?"

Drake held his arms out from his sides and took half a step back. He smiled at the doctor. "You've got the gun, Doc," he shouted back. "So, it's your picnic. I just came back to get you. I just came to help you."

"To get me," Dr. Dhawan reiterated. "To kill me, you mean," he screamed, making his point more meaningful by shoving the handgun at Drake.

Drake raised his empty hands higher. "Doc, if I wanted you to die, I wouldn't have come back. I'd have left you for the ants or the bomb." He looked at his watch, turned, and waved across the plain, pointing to the swarms growing on the white sands. "But the ants are going to be here first." The soldier turned back and pointed to the hole behind the scientist. "And there, they'll be coming out of there, too. Any minute now."

Dhawan twisted his face and got to his feet, walking through the sand and wind to get closer to Drake. "Oh, yes. They'll be coming out of there, over there, and everywhere." He threw his arms up and wide to encompass the world. "That was the plan, wasn't it?" He screamed over the chop of the copter. "Well, the plan's working, and now it's time to tie up loose ends. They won't let any of us live. Not with what we know." He looked at Drake and pointed at him with the gun. "Just ask her what really happened to Professor Carrington. You'd think she wouldn't be like that now that she's so old, but she's even worse." His intensity drained. His arms dropped to his sides. He was unconscious of the pistol in his hand.

"You think you're a loose end, Doc?" Drake asked.

"That's why you're here. I know," Dhawan answered. "I did what you wanted. It all went the way it was supposed to, the way you had it planned. I did everything. Years without question." The scientist stood dejectedly in the sand.

Drake circled the doctor and grabbed the dangling lifeline to the helicopter. He touched his mic to transmit and told them to let thirty feet of slack loose. The soldier dragged the cable as he circled back to the doctor, giving him a wide berth.

He walked in front of Dhawan and came closer, pulling the wire. "I don't want to hurt you, Doc," he said loudly over the wind. "But we have to get out of here."

The entomologist looked over his glasses as the soldier stepped closer. He began to sob. "I didn't think it through," he choked. "I didn't think it through. I just wanted to do it to see if it could be done, to see if I could do it." The scientist lifted his empty hand, pushed his glasses back, and leveled the pistol at Drake. "And I did it," he said in a suddenly sinister tone.

Dhawan stopped sobbing and looked across the plain to the swarm. "THEM," he pointed to the mass of insects. "I brought them back. I thought it was for science. But it was for the Agency."

Drake stood with the cable tugging his left hand. His right was an inch away from his holstered sidearm.

"You need some rest, Dhawan," he said authoritatively to the unhinged man.

The doctor stood staring across the remains of the dead ants at the army of insects. His head was down, and his eyes were at the top of their sockets, watching the black columns coming their way. "Not just for the Agency, for her. For the queen," he muttered to himself.

Drake stood beside him, holding the sling and deciding the scientist's fate. "Let's put this around you. Then we can get out of here," he said as he offered the harness to the doctor. "You won't have to worry about the queen much longer. She'll be taken care of pretty soon," he added.

Dhawan suddenly spun around and pushed back from the soldier and the strop. He snapped out of his trance and aimed the gun at Drake again. "That's not it. Not the bug. Are you that stupid?" He shook the handgun at the soldier. "I'm talking about your queen, you insect!" He wiped his mouth with his empty hand and pushed his glasses back in place.

Drake stood, eyeing the lunatic and holding the swaying cable. His other hand hung near his holster. The wind roared, whipping the sheets of white sand into small vortexes that danced across the cone-top of the anthill.

"Whoa, Doc. Hold it!" Drake lifted his right hand and faced it palm out to the scientist. "Stop! You're too close to the edge. You have to be careful!" he shouted over the wind.

"Years!" Dhawan screamed. "For years, I went into those tunnels, through them all, all the way down, to bring THEM back to life. And I did it!" he howled into the winds, thumping his chest with the handgun. "Me!" he screamed into the storm. "Quiet-guy, do-what-he's-told Theodore Dhawan! I brought THEM back! I let THEM loose on the world! No matter what they want to do with THEM, I was the only one that could bring them back!" He stretched his arms into the swirling air, standing at the top of the hill, overlooking the plain swarming with his efforts.

A horn blasted from the churning maelstrom above, and Drake's earpiece crackled. "Get on board now," came the curt command.

The soldier lifted the harness and stepped toward the scientist. Dhawan lifted the Glock in response, and when Drake was just a few steps away, he pulled the trigger. The soldier stopped and looked at Dhawan with surprise. "Really, Doc?" He shook his head. "I don't know what's worse," he shouted over the wind, "that you tried to kill me, or you thought I was dumb enough to give you a loaded gun."

He took another step to the doctor, but Dhawan fell back. He pulled the trigger on the empty weapon a few more times and crawled through the sand to the brink of the ant hole.

"Dhawan!" Drake yelled at the cringing scientist. The man threw the pistol at him and turned on all fours to a kneeling position facing the hole as the first giant ant climbed out directly in front of him.

Dr. Dhawan screamed and thrashed, trying to push away from the monster towering over him. The ant's antennae zoomed in on the man squirming through the sand. Drake ran forward, lifting his sidearm and shooting with little effect. The enormous creature struck without hesitation, pecking down at the sand and deftly clamping its jaws around the doctor's chest to lift him into the air.

His screams of fear turned to agony. Other ants followed in the first one's footsteps to excitedly inspect Dhawan as he writhed, hopelessly struggling against the steel jaws of the huge insect. A new ant clamped onto the scientist's left arm and pulled, popping it from its socket. The bug ran to the edge of the hole with Dhawan's arm waving goodbye to him.

The next nightmare in line got its jaws around the scientist's legs and crushed them, squeezing so hard his femurs exploded, shooting bone fragments out of his leg.

The unfortunate doctor was not dead. Dhawan was roaring in torment.

Drake was in the sling and radioed to lift. As the cable pulled him from the hill, he aimed his pistol downward but decided not to shoot. He holstered his weapon and watched as the monsters ripped the doctor apart.

More ants boiled over around the rim of the entrance, covering the white sands as Drake was hauled into the chopper and the hatch pulled shut. The helicopter angled nose down to make speed, and they left the area behind, flying over the Bunker on their way to the small town of White Sands.

Drake pulled off his helmet and looked at Max, resting comfortably with an IV and his Zastava. The pilot got his attention from the cockpit, motioning to his headset. "You've got a call, Drake," he shouted back to the soldier.

Drake nodded and pulled on a headset. "A very difficult mission, Mr. Drake," Mrs. Messenger said. It was quiet, and there was no static.

"Yes," Drake replied.

"I have spoken with the tank commander. It seems as though you met unanticipated resistance. I am sorry for your losses," she said.

"Yes, ma'am," Drake said. "The losses were very nearly complete." He listened.

"Unfortunate," Mrs. Messenger said softly. "But I am so glad you survived. You are a valuable man, Mr. Drake." She paused, then asked, "And your friend, Mr. Grunewald?"

"He made it, too," Drake answered.

"That is wonderful," the old woman cooed. "I am so glad." She paused again. Drake could hear her breathe. "I am afraid to ask about Doctor Dhawan, however. I suspect he did not have the sand you and Mr. Grunewald so often exhibited." There were a few seconds of silence. "What is Doctor Dhawan's fate?" she persisted.

Drake let it linger, then answered. "The ants, ma'am. The ants tore him apart."

"Such a pity," she said quietly. "Such a shame." Drake listened to her steady breaths. "Such an educated person. He was a man from which we could have all learned. Do you feel that way, Mr. Drake? Do you feel you could have learned much from the doctor?"

"I suppose," he answered. "But not anymore."

"No, I suppose not," the old woman said into his ear. "The dead have so little to say," she added. "You will be back in a few minutes and safely ensconced before the event. We have everything you need standing by. Thank you for such an important mission so bravely accomplished, and I look forward to seeing you after you have rested. Goodbye for now, Mr. Drake."

The headset went dead silent, and Drake pulled it off and handed it back to a crewman. Everything began to hurt as he laid back, but as Max said to him more than once, "It only hurts if you're alive."

Drake closed his eyes to the rhythm of the helicopter heading for White Sands.

CHAPTER SEVENTEEN

THE LIGHT

Mrs. Messenger sat with Henry in the unlit office on the second floor. A large window framed the morning sky.

"We're safe at this distance?" Henry asked. "I've never seen one before," he added, anxiously looking at the disc-shaped timer in his hand and then through the window.

"Quite safe, Nephew," the wrinkled woman answered. Her small form was sunk into the high back chair behind the desk. "I have seen quite a few. I was here at the start," she said, her voice fading into recollection. "Such a long time ago."

They sat in the dim room, listening to Henry's hiccups.

"Remember," she cautioned, "when the alarm goes off, avert your eyes. He once said, 'Do not look on God's countenance." She smiled and put on her dark glasses. "It will be magnificent," she promised.

Far away, under the sand, the red numbers on the panel of the yellow drum counted down to all zeros. LED smiley faces replaced them, blinked, and became frowny faces with X's for eyes.

Then, the device in Henry's hand beeped. The woman inhaled in anticipation. Henry held his breath and squeezed his eyes tight.

The world flashed through the window, and light saturated the room, filling every shadow. Henry dropped to the floor, covering his face. The old woman in the chair raised her arms, steeped in luminance as the building shook and the earth trembled.

"Magnificence," she rasped.

CHAPTER EIGHTEEN

THE FIRE

W alt's eyes opened to a blurred snapshot of his barroom taken from a rat's-eye view. A voice floated around to find him under the table, narrating an invasion of giant ants. The incidents were widespread, said the voice. They were in buildings and tunnels, in the cities, and across the countryside. The ants were everywhere.

Old Walt had never been so cold.

"...now eleven locations reporting the appearance or attacks of giant insects. The president has declared a national state of emergency. All private and commercial air travel has been suspended. Cities and states throughout the nation have declared martial law. Military branches are on high alert and are mobilizing throughout the country, particularly in the southwest and southern states hardest hit by the infestation." The speaker paused. "This is a national emergency," the voice gravely intoned.

Walt coughed out more blood. A spark of consciousness lit a glimmer of comprehension, and the barkeep's brain fired. He remembered crawling across the barroom floor. He recalled the giant ants, the young woman, Syl shooting him, the door.

His eyes closed. The voice persisted even into his darkness.

"...have come in from New Mexico to Florida, over the border in Mexico City, as far north as Kentucky, the huge insects have been reported. These are not hoaxes. The giant insects, giant ants, exist and have been seen on many videos from many sources. Social media is flooded with eyewitness accounts, videos, and photos of these monsters. Some call them mutants or evolutionary anomalies, but they are very real and very dangerous, whatever you call them. By the most authoritative estimations, these mutant insects have caused the death of more than one hundred people and have injured countless others. One of the most devastating accounts is the unbelievable incursion of a giant insect into the tunnel in northwestern Arkansas. It is believed that the creature entered one of the twin tunnels and caused a cave-in, trapping, by some estimates, as many as two hundred motorists; the fate of most is still unknown at this time."

Walt coughed himself awake. His chest gurgled as he breathed. He was able to sit up with some effort and leaned against the wall.

"Damn it," the old man said, looking along the wall to the door. It was about a mile away, but he had to get there. He fell back into a crawling position and inched his way forward. The hole to his lung bubbled and squirted with every push.

Walt crawled forever until he reached the corner with the swinging doors, then he passed out.

His eyes opened, and light coalesced into a scene with objects he should recognize. He lifted his hand to the wall and left red stripes on it. They pointed to the box high on the wall. That was the control box for the door, he remembered.

Walt inched up the wall until he got his arm on the chair rail and steadied himself. The pain in his side bit at him, but he held on, huffing air through pale lips. In and gurgle, out and bubble. Colorful geometric shapes raced through his view. His fingers were sticky with his dried blood, helping him grip the molding.

Walt's face pushed against the wall, leaving a bloody mask on the wood. His knees straightened, and he leaned into the corner, bracing himself with the walls of the Bunker.

Walt lifted his red hand to the switch box and pushed the green button. He leaned against the corner, too spent to fall, and watched.

The slab lifted.

As the cement gate opened on the inferno, hellfire shot through the growing opening, and the glow of perdition bloomed, consuming any souls caught in its searing light.

At the end of his strength, the old man twisted in the corner and turned his back on the fire. His knees buckled, and he slid to the floor as the door opened wide and the light of the conflagration flickered across his blood-soaked body propped in the corner.

His head turned to face the inferno, and the fire sparkled in his dimming eyes. "Hell," Walt murmured, looking into the doorway to fire, "I'll be damned."

The old man was paused at that final boundary by a soft hand taking his. A kind voice called his name. The old man looked up through clouding eyes at the graceful face, filled with concern for him.

She called his name again. He smiled at his redemption, and his eyes closed as he fell slowly to the side. His face felt the cool floor, and he stopped breathing.

Nikki tried to keep him from falling but couldn't. He was soaked in blood. She stroked his face and tried to wake him. "Walt, Walt." She broke down and cried.

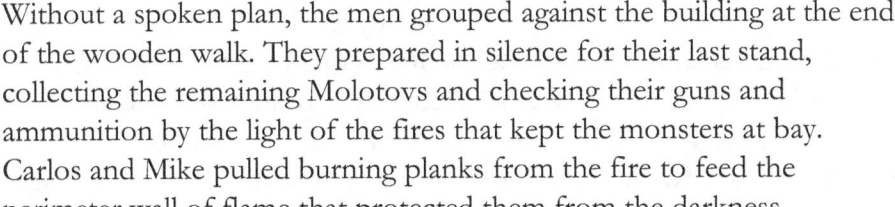

Without a spoken plan, the men grouped against the building at the end of the wooden walk. They prepared in silence for their last stand, collecting the remaining Molotovs and checking their guns and ammunition by the light of the fires that kept the monsters at bay. Carlos and Mike pulled burning planks from the fire to feed the perimeter wall of flame that protected them from the darkness.

A shriek from the parking lot froze the men in their sweat. They stared over the flames into the darkness, waiting for what would come.

"That sounded close," Tom Honey said quietly. "Sounded like it was just past the fire." The trucker stepped to the edge of the walk and reached down to the deck to retrieve his big pistol without taking his eyes from the fire line. It hung by his side in his right hand. He looked at the flickering men. They were also breathing hard and straining to see into the gloom.

Another shrill scream tore out of the darkness and was answered from a different corner of the night.

Carlos and Mike dropped wood into the fire and then sat on the edge of the walkway, facing the flaming barrier. Brandon was in a ball at the end, curled against the building, squeezing himself tight from the sounds of the giant ants.

Ray was motionless. He held one of the gasoline-filled bottles, sitting a few feet from the others on the edge of the walk, staring into the blackness over the fire.

Tom Honey thought the man seemed calm in the face of his horrible fate, courageously palming a bomb, waiting for one last shot against his unconquerable enemy. Tom thought he was brave until he looked at his eyes.

The fire lit Ray's eyes. They were open too wide, staring at nothing as they conjured the inevitable. Ray was a man awaiting execution. That wasn't courage on his face; it was a death mask.

Tom Honey studied the condemned man by firelight. He saw him as just another small creature caught at a brutal end that mattered only to the victim. The sun would rise without recollection of his existence and shine on the monsters that consumed him to fuel another hour's activity. His total was about to be collected, and it added up to nothing. He was no more than the monsters coming for him. He was just another meal in the food chain, and he knew it.

Tom Honey felt the same way.

Another shriek from the field turned the driver's attention to the lot. His Desert Eagle was heavy. He wondered if he could lift the barrel to his mouth when the time came. Tom Honey raked his cracked bottom lip with his teeth.

Another shrill call spun out of the night as the moon broke out of the clouds, weakly illuminating the rising smoke and the large dark forms closing in on them. Tom stood with the men in front of the walk and behind the fire line. It was hot and there was nowhere to go. He gripped the fifty-caliber handgun as the fear dripped off his face and into the dirt. The giant ants grouped beyond the fires.

The moon slid behind the clouds, and the monsters' silhouettes melted into the darkness.

"How many are out there?" Mike's dried voice asked.

"More than enough," Carlos answered. He leaned his rifle against the walk, picked a bottle bomb from the pile, and tossed it to Mike. "I don't know why we're waiting for them," he said. He pulled another bottle of Molotov's cocktail from the bar. He turned the bottle in his hand, feeling the gasoline inside slop back and forth.

Carlos looked down at the bomb in the flickering orange light and smiled when he read the 'Fireball' whiskey label. He pulled a short piece of wood from the fire and pointed the burning end at Mike.

"Just the nearest ones," he said to the lineman. "Maybe we can move them back some." The lineman nodded and touched the wick to the flame to ignite it. Carlos did likewise.

He turned to Ray and Tom Honey and said, "Hold onto yours in case we stir anything up." Then he looked at Mike. "Let's light 'em up."

Carlos stretched back and lobbed his bomb over the flaming perimeter. Mike followed suit, sending his to the right. The cocktail Carlos threw broke on top of an ant, fully engulfing the creature. The monster ran, dripping burning fuel and crashing into the wreckage and other mutants before its legs failed and the giant fell to the ground.

Mike's bomb hit the pavement. The flaming gas splashed on one of the ants, sending it running through the horde, across the lot, and over the highway, where the injured giant fell to the ground, unable to lift itself. Two of the insect's nestmates examined the fallen creature, running their antennae over the injuries and the rest of the huge body as the ant tried to right itself. In response to chemical signals, others joined the triage, ripping it apart, and carrying the pieces back to their nest.

As the smaller ants busied themselves with their compatriot's premortem, one large ant made its way through the swarm to the fires. It swabbed three attendant castes in the front line, running its feelers across their heads and antennae. They awaited command.

The large warrior ant bent over each, bringing its head close until their mouthparts contacted. The smaller insects stood anesthetized, having imbibed the chemical directives of the collective. The large ant arranged the workers into a line facing the fire.

The other ants cleared the area around the chosen. The swarm quieted and stood waiting, some rotating their heads and lifting their antennae into the floating messages.

The large ant tapped her front legs over the backs of the three and released an unseen chemistry that commanded action.

They obeyed instantly, charging past their instinctual fear of fire and into the flames without hesitation, plowing through the burning wood and opening a path for the others to follow.

The men with their backs to the Bunker awaited the next attack. They had firebombs ready to throw, and they hit the three monsters simultaneously as they crashed through the firewall.

Tom Honey's bottle bounced off and exploded behind his target. He lifted his Deagle with both hands, fired a single round from the heavy handgun, and dropped the worker ant. The trucker was surprised at his lucky shot.

The other two ants crashed through, wrapped in flames, scattering blazing shards and burning wood chunks in all directions. Curtains of red smoke, alive with sparks, opened wide as the monsters crashed out of the scorching oven, savagely snapping their jaws, even as the fire consumed them.

Carlos stumbled and fell but was back on his feet again with Mike's help. The pair rushed past Tom Honey, heading for the few firebombs left on the deck.

Ray retreated, dropping his unlit Molotov and scrambling up on the walk. The bottle rolled in the dust to Tom Honey's feet.

The trucker was looking over the fire, transfixed as he watched a dark, segmented form rise behind the flames to a towering monstrosity of thick, clawed legs topped by gnashing jaws, snapping hungrily at the group of men. The leviathan of horror was too much to bear. The existence of such a thing framed in fire and aiming to destroy, to kill them, to kill him, overwhelmed him.

In his nightmare of fire and monsters scored by sirens and screams, Tom Honey looked down at the heavy pistol in his outstretched arm. That pistol was the shining key to end it.

Honey lifted his gun higher and watched the fire-lit monster towering over the flames rub its front legs against the exposed underside of its body to generate the ear-splitting screech of the ants. Its head pitched back, and the protruding antennae and sickle-shaped mandibles were framed against the moon, and outlined by the naked flames as the creature played itself like a hideous fiddle, summoning more monsters to attack and feed.

"Well, if that don't beat all," Tom Honey said, drawing smoky air over his dry lips. His gaze fell from the monster and onto the barrel of his gun as he lifted it level to his head.

The truck driver narrowed his eyes on the nightmare behind the fire. He thought of the scorpion and said softly, "I'm getting a new story to tell. I am going to tell everybody about you." He leveled the pistol at the gargantuan ant.

His other hand steadied his shooting arm, and he walked forward to the blaze and the monstrous mutant. In five steps, Tom Honey let off six rounds. The report of the heavy gun exploded in his ears and hit his arms like a sledgehammer. The bullets entered, punching thumb-sized holes in the thorax, and exited the opposite side, kicking out fist-sized chunks. The ant stopped singing and twisted in the air to fall back, legs up in a dead and crumpled heap.

Fires blazed all around. Ant calls rang in the air, and there was gunfire. Mike and Carlos had thrown more cocktails to light up two ants that charged from the right and another couple of bottles to beef up the wall. One of the ants lay burning, and another ran by, enveloped in fire, crashing through the outer wall of flame and back into the lot. Once past the perimeter, the flaming insect continued running, illuminating the other giants making their way to the men. Tom Honey's eyes widened as he saw the wave of car-sized insects coming through the lot toward them, and he knew there was no way out now. He looked over and could see Carlos looking back at him. The slight man he thought was just another barfly put his fist in the air, yelled something, and gestured to the trucker. But, between the roaring fire and his ringing ears, Tom Honey couldn't hear him.

He bent over to pick up the gas bottle Ray had let loose. As he stood with the bomb in one hand and the big gun in the other, he could hear the muffled reports of gunfire in rapid succession. The trucker saw Carlos charging at him with his assault rifle leveled in his direction. The muzzle flashed. It seemed like Carlos was shooting at something behind him.

The truck driver twisted to look over his shoulder. This new monster had run through the fire and appeared out of the smoke only a few feet behind him. That's what Carlos had been yelling about.

Tom Honey turned to the ant. He brought his Eagle up and instinctively raised the bottle like a club. He froze, looking up at the foreleg of the ant, poised in the air like a snake. He knew that the creature's raised appendage would strike before he could pull the trigger, before the bottle would hit the ground, before he could blink his eyes. His face contorted, and he held his last breath.

But it didn't strike.

Instead, intensely bright light arced out of the sky, overexposing and silhouetting the giant ant and blinding the trucker as he dropped the bottle bomb and stumbled back into jumping coals and whirling dust, covering his eyes against the brilliant glare.

The huge insect convulsed as chunks of its exoskeleton blew apart in accompaniment to the mechanical hammer of a heavy machine gun.

A firestorm tore into the lot and whipped the flames, smoke, and embers into the air against the building, driven by the deep mechanical beat of an attack helicopter on top of the incandescent pillar, spitting fifty-caliber bursts and chopping the ants into pieces.

The wash of the gunship scattered the smaller fires and fanned the flames of the inferno in front of the door to the Bunker like a bellows, pushing the blaze higher and driving geysers of sparks into the night.

The chopper's brilliant white beam picked out scores of giant insects hidden in the darkness. Their senses were confused by the swirling smoke and fiery debris in the mechanized maelstrom as the helicopter hung in the sky a hundred feet over the chaos of fire and smoke, wreckage and mutants, pivoting in place as it fed hundreds of rounds of hot death to the attacking monsters.

Tom Honey scrambled up, regaining his feet and clutching his Desert Eagle. He ran with the others back to the wall of the building, all of them covering their heads and swatting away the burning briquets thrown by the wind of the helicopter as it showered extermination on the bugs.

Even Brandon was back on his feet and back to life as he screamed, raising his fists to the chopper and the bursts of the machine guns.

Carlos, Ray, Tom Honey, and Mike joined the young man at the end of the walkway, cheering the chopper on as it saved them from certain death and the gnashing jaws of the mutant insects.

Brandon jumped up on the end of the boardwalk and continued his hoarse shouts as the deadly bursts of the heavy machine guns slowed. He stopped, mid-cheer and looked across the lot as the helicopter's spotlight ran over the broken and split carcasses of the monster ants.

"Look!" he shouted to the others. "They're coming in! Here they come!" he yelled. "Look!"

The others climbed onto the walk and stared into the lot as the gunship's spotlight locked onto a moving vehicle. A truck threaded its way through the corpse field, racing along a path guided by the light from above.

The single-door pickup careened through the remnants of the firewall and skidded to a stop in front of the group. The sheriff pushed open the driver's door and got out with his rifle, swiping live sparks off his clothes with his hat and fanning them away as he surveyed the stunned and exhausted men and the walkway burning in front of the sealed entryway into the bar.

"What in the hell is going on here? Why are you outside?" he shouted over the helicopter's noise. "Where's the deputy?" He looked up and turned his shirt pocket out to look at the timer clipped inside. He held his hand up to the chopper. His fingers spread wide, signaling five.

He turned to the men who had jumped off the walk and gathered around him. The gunship loudspeaker blared through the noise and fire. "Sheriff! Going or staying? We can give you your five minutes, but no more! Use them to get aboard!" the voice called down and echoed over the landscape.

Cal turned back to the group and back to the fire burning in front of the closed door to the Bunker. "Where's Luis?" he repeated to the men.

The men clustered around the lawman and his truck and exchanged glances.

"Your deputy's dead, Sheriff," Mike said to him. He motioned with the barrel of his rifle at the fire in front of the building. "One of them got him in the first attack." He lowered his gun and his head. "Saved my life, too."

The sheriff grimaced and looked at the pyre dancing before the concrete slab. "Alright. Why in hell is the door shut? Where's Walt?" he asked them. "And, where's the girl? Where's Nikki?"

Carlos said, "We don't know why they shut us out. Luis, the old man, the teacher, and his wife, they all got it one way or another. Billy, too. One of the bugs got him," his voice faltered. "The others, they are inside. We don't know why," he said, clearing the dust and smoke from his throat.

The hovering helicopter suddenly banked and lifted higher into the air. The spotlight shot over the lot and fell on several more ants, making their way toward the Bunker. The gunship optimized its attack position over the advancing insects and opened fire. The steel rounds punched the bugs apart, cutting them to pieces.

The chopper hung over the lot higher than before, lighting up the highway and surrounding desert to detect new attackers on the way.

The voice from above crackled, "Time's up, Sheriff! Flying or frying?" Cal looked from the men's smeared faces up at the gunship lights hanging over them, holding his hat against the wash. His other hand went back to his shirt pocket. He turned to the group. "Fellows, there's no time to explain, but we've got to…" The sheriff stopped talking and stared at the fire in front of the door.

A new sound scraped through the roar of the blaze, a clanking, mechanical sound. The men's faces turned to the doorway as the huge slab began to lift, dragged up by the heavy chains buried in the walls. Looking from the anxious faces and over the fire, the sheriff could see the blast door to the Bunker rising behind the bonfire, opening the entrance to the fortress within.

"Walt's got it working!" Tom Honey shouted out. "Walt's got it going again!"

The men ran to the front of the fire and peered into the inferno, shielding their faces from the heat. Cal glimpsed Nikki, looking back at him through the fire. She shouted his name across the blaze, but the sound crackled into the rising flames, fanned by the chopper.

The helicopter loudspeaker sounded again. "Incoming! You've got incoming! Hundreds of them heading over the highway! We're coming down to pick you up now! No time left!" the voice barked.

Cal looked from the fire to the chopper, then his truck. He suddenly ran forward a few steps and wildly flagged the helicopter away. "No, no!" his shouts drowned in the noise. He shot his rifle into the air, pointed to the Bunker, and then ran back to the men in front of the fire.

"We've got to move fast, and I mean fast," he shouted to the group. "We need to get through this fire and inside. Now!"

Carlos opened his mouth to say something, and Cal shut it by snapping back, "No time. Be ready to move!"

Tossing his rifle to Tom Honey, the sheriff shouted to Carlos and Mike, "Get those guys out of the way! Get them off the walk! Clear the front! All of you get down to the end! Get out of the way and be ready to move!" he ordered.

The sheriff ran from the men to his truck. As he jumped in, the helicopter dipped down low enough that he could see Oz hanging out of the hatch, glued to the .50 cal, framed against the interior lights. His colonel was behind him and gave a thumbs-up to the lawman. The sheriff waved his white hat to the copter as the searchlight swept over his truck. The chopper rose and swung around to illuminate the ants moving from the highway into the parking lot. The heartwarming chatter of the heavy machine gun started again. The sheriff knew they could only buy them a few minutes.

Cal jumped behind the wheel, pulled his hat down, cinched his seatbelt tight, and turned the ignition. He gunned the truck and dropped it into gear. The tires spun in the dust and caught, shooting the big pickup into a tight turn, kicking up clouds as he spun around to face the fire.

The sheriff floored it, and the pickup shot past the five guys, ran up the collapsed ramp of burning boards and plunged into the fire, plowing over the roasting planks, ant parts, and whoever else was in the red-hot bed. It smashed into the corner of the concrete doorway. Cal bounced off the airbags, and the truck bounced off the building, dropping into the fire like a new log. The truck's nose was a foot from the entrance, and the body straddled the conflagration, laying a bridge over the fire.

The view from the cab looked like Cal had driven into a volcano. The flames knocked down by the crash jumped back, chasing sparks high into the air. The inferno poured heat into the truck. The sheriff shut the engine down, scrambled over the seat, and snaked out of the missing door as the flames licked at him.

Cal threw himself back, over the side of the pickup, and into the bed hard enough to pop his hat off, but he caught it before it went overboard into the flames. He pushed himself down the incline of the pickup to the back, reached over to open the tailgate, and kicked it open to the guys standing in front of the blaze.

"Move it!" he shouted as he got to his feet and stretched his arm out to take the nearest man's hand. He pulled Brandon into the back of the truck and pushed him forward, saying, "Go! Climb over the cab and jump inside! Go!"

Everyone else got the idea all at once and piled in. They made their way to the front as the truck burned, and they moved fast, with the sheriff urging them on. "Move! Faster! Faster!" he yelled after each of them.

One after another, they climbed over the cab onto the hood of the truck and jumped into the doorway into the Bunker.

Mike was climbing in when the passenger side tires blew and pitched the truck violently starboard, threatening to dump him into the flames. The fire grew all around the pickup, and black, choking smoke whirled from underneath, rising from all sides.

"Gas tank's gonna blow!" Mike yelled as he went to the front, pushing Ray in front of him. "Go, man, go! Go! Go!" he shouted behind the man as they scrambled for the door.

The pickup bed was scorching hot as Tom Honey clambered in, surprisingly agile for a man of his size. Carlos was behind him and gave him extra motivation, pushing the big man up and into the truck.

The sheriff stood, bracing himself against the steep incline, and stuck out his arm to pull Carlos, the last man out, into the truck. They clasped hands; Carlos held his rifle in the other and got his foot on the gate as thick smoke spewed from below and enveloped the vehicle, dropping the drapes on everything.

As he pulled him in, Carlos's face came out of the smoke smeared with fear. His arm pulled away violently as the thermals swirled and parted the smoke to show the giant ant behind the man. Another more violent jolt rocked the pickup.

The lawman tried to hold on but staggered and fell against the wall of the pickup, almost slipping off the raft and into the flaming sea. Carlos was dragged down the bed, flailing his arms and screaming curses. The ant lifted the man by his leg above the truck. His rifle flew out of his hand and clattered along the pickup bed, bouncing from wall to wall.

The sheriff fell on his back and slid down the hot metal to collide with the monster's leg as it slammed down onto the end of the truck, jolting the pickup and bouncing the lawman into the air. He hit the deck and grabbed the hairy appendage to keep himself from sliding into the fire. Carlos's rifle dislodged from somewhere and skittered down the bed, and the sheriff grabbed at it as it slid by, snagging the weapon by the barrel.

Cal pulled the weapon across the baking bed as he pushed himself back from the giant ant. The insect noticed the disturbance at its foot and spun its huge head, flopping the dangling man from side to side. There was a sharp crack as the thigh bone snapped. Carlos screamed.

The sheriff sat under the huge bug and braced himself with his boots, one against the sidewall of the pickup and the other pushed against the monster's leg. He jammed the AR upward and pulled the trigger, firing point-blank into the creature's hard exoskeleton. He let three rounds off, blowing a hole into the underside of the scout's carapace. Viscous goo bloomed from the wound and dripped in the fire's orange light, sizzling on the hot truck. Cal shoved the rifle and his forearm into the hole, inside the beast, and pulled the trigger again and again, holding the stock with both hands as the weapon discharged seven more times inside the monster.

The ant's head reared back and twisted, and it pushed itself further away from the pickup and abandoned its catch, dropping Carlos onto the lawman. Carlos screamed and cursed as he fell into a knotted heap with his leg pointing in an unusual direction.

The wounded ant slipped back from the fire and disappeared into the rising smoke, bouncing the men in the truck like they were on a trampoline. Carlos yelled in pain again, and the sheriff pushed him off and got out from under the mangled man.

The lawman got to his knees and grabbed Carlos by his collar and belt to get him up on his good leg.

"Sorry, no time to waste. We gotta go!" Cal gasped as he helped broken Carlos up the hot ramp to the front of the truck.

The cab was filled with white smoke, and just as Cal put his hand on the roof, the interior burst into flames.

Cal looked at Carlos. "Over the top!" he yelled, throwing him onto the roof and then pushing the injured man forward. Carlos rolled down the windshield and onto the hood. The sheriff turned to the back of the truck, hot-footed it a few steps to scoop up his hat, then took a running leap onto the roof. He bounced off the hot griddle and down the glass into his compatriot, holding his Cattleman out like he was working the rodeo.

Carlos clung to the front of the truck, leaning forward, balancing on his good leg. "Gotta jump, man," the sheriff shouted. Carlos groaned and gripped his broken leg. Cal looked down at his broken pin. It looked like he had two knees in one leg. "Whew," he whistled at Carlos. "This is going to hurt," he said as he lifted the injured man. Then he pushed off, diving from the front of the pickup, propelling them both through the rising flames and into the doorway of the Bunker.

The injured man yelled as they went flying off the truck, and they both grunted as they hit the cement hard enough to knock the air out of them. Carlos screamed murder as he landed on his broken bone and the pain turned into a shower of lights. He didn't pass out but came close as he tumbled over the cool cement floor.

Cal landed in the middle of the concrete with a thud. He looked at the crumpled lump of Carlos and reached over to knock some small coals off him. Both of them were breathing hard, but breathing was what counted.

Cal turned back to the entrance, the roaring fire in the gate to Hell.

"That's it, right? We're all in?" he sputtered.

"All in," Tom Honey groaned. "Everyone's in," he repeated breathlessly. The sheriff looked at the big driver, sitting on the floor against the wall. Wisps of smoke curled into the air from the bottom of his boots.

Cal saw Nikki at the inside doorway. Her hands were over her mouth; her eyes were wide. He pushed himself up, put his hat back on, and went to her, steadying himself against the wall. He put his hand on her shoulder and straightened up, smiling through the sweat and grime as he pulled her close with one arm. He turned his head and shouted into the hallway, "Everyone, clear of the door!" He saw they were, stretched his free arm around the corner, and pushed the blast door button.

The thick slab dropped tight into the frame with a deep boom and sealed the Bunker. A cool silence shut off the fire, the monsters, and the impending destruction.

He looked down at Nikki, licked his dry lips, and said, "Nice to see you, Nik." She buried her head in his shoulder and held onto the lawman. He lifted her chin and smiled. "Been a hell of a day. I could use a drink." She laughed, brushed a tear off her cheek, and led him across the barroom. "Will you guys give Carlos a hand into the bar?" the sheriff called over his shoulder. "He's pretty banged up." He limped after Nikki across the barroom.

It wasn't the same old bar. The sheriff felt glass crunch as he followed the trail smeared across the planks. Walt wasn't in place, and there was a bullet hole in the table.

Cal put his foot on the rail and removed his singed Cattleman, dropping it on the bar. He wiped his hand across his face to wipe away some of the grime and smoke.

His eyes adjusted to the dark. Ray was at the end of the bar by himself.

The two utility workers came into the barroom carrying Carlos. His arms were over their shoulders as they took him across the room. Tom Honey went past them to set up a couple of chairs at a table near the bar. One of the chairs was for Carlos, and the other was for his busted leg.

The sheriff watched the linemen and the trucker put Carlos carefully into the chair and help him get his leg comfortable, placing a couple of towels underneath his mangled limb. The injured man turned his head to the lawman, smiled through his pain, gave the sheriff a thumbs-up, and mimed a drink.

"Good idea," Cal said. He looked up and down the bar for Walt and then back at Nikki. Her eyes were filled with tears, and she looked away from him. He didn't like where this was going.

The sheriff heard footsteps and turned to see the two linemen taking a place at the bar a few stools down. The trucker was still with Carlos at the table. Cal looked back at Nikki and moved his hand over hers. She turned to face him. Tears rolled out of her eyes.

"He's gone, Cal," she said. "I'm so sorry."

The lawman looked down at her shirt and saw it was soaked with blood across the middle.

"You OK?" he asked her quietly.

Nikki broke down, wiping tears from her eyes, trying to keep it together. "Yes, yes. I'm OK," she sobbed, "But Walt's dead. I'm so sorry." Her voice faltered, and she took deep breaths. He put a hand on her shoulder and turned his shirt pocket out to check the timer with the other.

All the guys in the bar heard her soft voice in the deep quiet of the Bunker. Carlos was the only one who uttered a sound. "Oh, no!" he gasped. He brought his hand to his eyes.

Walt's sawed-off was on top of the bar, and wrecked shelves were where the bottles used to be.

"Where is he?" the sheriff asked Nikki.

She pointed across the dim barroom to the alcove with the old sofa under the big Remington painting.

"He's over there, on the couch," She sniffled through her words, regaining control. "I put a blanket over him." She broke down.

Cal patted her hand and walked across the room to bend over his friend. He lifted the blanket to look at the old man's face, clean and very still. He raised the shroud and looked at the hole in his chest. His face tightened with sadness. He took a breath, lowered the cover, and then returned to the bar.

The sheriff got onto his stool next to Nikki. "As bad as it looks," he spoke quietly, "I think Walt would have said there are worse ways to go. Always said he didn't want to die in bed," he said to her.

She nodded, choking back her tears. The sheriff looked at the guys sitting at the bar. "A lot different than it was this morning," he said.

The young lineman held his head, burying his face in his hands. He exhaled loudly, then looked at the sheriff. "Different?" he repeated. "Yes, kind of different," he said in a louder voice. "What I want to know is what the hell happened in here? Why were we locked out? Do you know how bad it was out there?" Brandon was white-knuckling the edge of the bar. "It was...I mean, that old guy, the professor, he was in the fire, he was..." Mike stopped his partner from going on with a hand on his arm. Brandon looked down at the bar.

"It was rough out there," Mike said to the sheriff and Nikki, "But I don't think it was any better in here or out in the desert." The utility worker's eyes wandered to the dark ceiling. "The professor and his wife, the deputy and that fellow from the end, Billy, they didn't make it," the lineman said quietly. "It was pretty bad," he said.

The sheriff got off his stool and stepped to the end of the bar, lifting the barkeep's gate. That was probably the first time he had seen it closed.

Broken glass ground beneath his boots as he walked behind the bar. His eyes followed the trail sparkling in the low light of the barroom to the doorway. He looked back to the bar top and lifted the shortened shotgun. He broke it open, took out the unexpended shells, and stood them on the bar. He looked down at the floor, bent to lift the uncorked standing bottle of Old Rocking Chair, and put it next to the shells. There was a full bloody palm print around the label.

The sheriff took a tumbler from under the bar, lifted the whiskey bottle, and poured three fingers. He set the bottle on the worn bar, raised the glass to the man on the couch, and knocked it back.

Cal got out more glasses, poured a double leg warmer of Rocking Chair into two, and pushed them over to Nikki. "Give this to Carlos," he said. "He needs it. And here's one for Tom."

She slipped off her stool and carried the glasses over to the table while the sheriff walked whiskey down the bar, putting two in front of the linemen and taking the third to Ray. Cal returned to the head of the bar and pushed a glassful across the wood to Nikki.

"I knew something happened to Walt," Tom Honey called from the table. "I knew he'd never leave us out there. What went on in here?"

Nikki took a deep breath. The sheriff reached over the bar and put his hand on her forearm. "Drink," the sheriff said. He felt the warmth in his stomach blooming from the first one he poured down his throat, and it was going to his head, making him feel better. She lifted her glass and sipped the fiery whiskey.

Everyone was quiet until Tom Honey spoke again. "Say, by the way, where's Syl, that nurse?" he asked.

"That's what I was wondering, too," the sheriff said. "To Walt," he said as he brought the glass to his lips. The warming whiskey ran down his throat to meet up with his inner glow. He looked at Nikki over the rim. Everyone took a drink.

"Syl shot him?" he asked the young woman.

She nodded quickly. Nikki's eyes filled with tears. "Walt tried to save me, and she shot him." Tears ran from her eyes.

"And she's dead?" the sheriff asked her.

She nodded again.

"Good," the sheriff replied without missing a beat. "Sort of surprised she got the drop on old Walt. I had a feeling she was on his watch list," Cal said.

He took the bloodied bottle and set it alone on the ledge in front of the mirror. He reached up to his shirt pocket with his back to Nikki and pulled it open to check his timer. He turned to her, took a small towel from under the bar, and headed for the beer.

"Well," she began, "there's more to it." She had something to tell him.

A question crossed his face as the lawman walked to the taps and filled mugs, lining them up on the bar. He pushed one across to each of the linemen sitting in front of the handles.

"I'd really like some water," Brandon said in a weak voice. "That's all I could think of out there. Just a glass of cold water."

The new bartender looked across the wood at the young man and smiled at him. "Coming up, Brandon," he said, limping a few steps up the bar to get a large glass and fill it with ice from the box and water from the tap. He walked back to him, crunching through the broken bottles, and put the tall ice water in front of the junior lineman.

"You know, Sheriff, Brandon was the one who thought up making the gas bombs out there and using the gas from the cars in the lot. I'd say he's the reason any of us are here," Mike said. He turned to his partner and put his hand on the young man's back.

The lawman looked at the young man and nodded approvingly. "Is that right? Well, in that case, this one's on the house," he said as he pushed the glass of water closer to Brandon's hanging head.

There were a few forced chuckles. Ray was crying at the end of the bar as the others sipped their beers.

Then, Carlos broke the quiet, lifting his Rocking Chair tumbler and toasting, "Here's to Billy," and drained the glass. He called across to his other friend, "C'mon Ray, have a drink to Billy, c'mon. You know he'd want you to. And to Walt. Everyone'd want you to have a drink, all of them." The injured man suddenly threw his empty glass across the barroom. It smashed to bits against the wall. Carlos buried his head into his arms.

"Another one coming up," the sheriff said. He filled a pair of mugs and pushed them to the front of the bar. "Hey, Tom," he called to the trucker and nodded at the beers. "Come and get 'em while they're cold."

Tom Honey was already on his way. "You know, I just about forgot how parched I was," he said with a raspy voice to prove his point. He lifted the mugs and took them to the table.

Cal pulled another draft and eyed the wooden runway. He gave the mug a shove and sent it gliding straight down the middle of the alley to Ray. The beer slopped out along the way, and at the end of the run, the mug hit the curb, flipped over, and crashed to the floor. Cal shook his head and said, "I guess there is a knack to it." He laughed, pulled another mug, and limped it down the bar. As he walked, the sheriff checked the timer in his shirt pocket. He set the beer down and patted the man on the shoulder. "Friends, past or present, are always with you, compadre," he said quietly to Ray and walked back to the end of the bar by Nikki. He reached down and righted Walt's stool and sat on it. He leaned forward, arms on the bar, looking at Nikki for the story.

"She did something to his gun," Nikki said. "So, it wouldn't work."

"I guess that was a specialty of hers," the sheriff said. "At least he got her." The barroom was silent.

"Well, not exactly," Nikki said. She took a drink of her whiskey and followed it with a swallow of beer. "Um, I killed her."

Brandon held his ice water in midair and stared at the young woman. Mike looked at her along with everyone else, but he added a low whistle.

The sheriff's eyes widened slightly in surprise. Just slightly. "You killed her?' he half-asked.

She nodded. "Yes. Sort of."

Cal stared at her for a moment, then repeated her words, "You sort of killed her?"

"Wait a minute. Why did the nurse kill Walt?" Brandon asked.

The sheriff lifted his hand slightly from the bar. "Hold on a second," he said to the young man.

"Why don't you fill us in on what happened in here?" he asked Nikki.

"Well, it's kind of complicated," she began.

"Make it simple," Cal said to her. "Stick to the verbs." He looked at her to continue.

"Syl shot Walt," she swallowed. "Then she took me in the back." She looked down at her hands on the bar. "She was going to kill me." Her eyes lifted to the sheriff.

"I got away," Niki said hesitatingly. "And, when I came in here, I didn't see him. I ran and looked behind the bar where she left him, but he was gone. Then I saw the marks and heard the fire and the door going up. Walt had dragged himself across the floor to open the door. He was lying over there," she motioned to the doorway.

"So, who shut the door on us?" Mike asked. "The nurse?"

Nikki turned to the lineman and nodded. "Yes, she wanted to kill us all. She thought those monsters outside would do it." She turned the whiskey glass on the bar between her fingers.

"But why? Why did she want to kill us?" Brandon shook his head. "I don't get it."

"Some people snap when things are going bad," Mike replied. "You just never know about some people."

Tom Honey piped up from his table. "No. Not her," he said, rubbing his tender nose. "She was after something. I'd bet on it."

625

"She was," Nikki nodded. She looked back at the sheriff. "She was after something. Some things I got from my aunt's estate. I just got them yesterday." She reached over to her bag and pulled out the three small journals. "These are my great-uncle's notes. He was a scientist who worked on all the things Walt talked about. All the things that are on the walls." She swept her hand around the barroom at the movie posters, atomic souvenirs, and oddities from the desert hanging around them.

"It's everything Walt said. I guess everything he's been saying for a long time. All of this, and this," she held the books up, "all of this is real. Monsters, spacemen, cover-ups, everything. And right now, we're sitting in the middle of it."

Mike said, "Yesterday, you'd be crazy. Today, it's a different story." He lifted his mug and took a few long swallows.

"Spacemen?" Brandon asked. "I mean, I've had enough with the giant bugs. So, spacemen?"

"That's why she tried to kill everybody," Nikki said. "She wanted…"

Brandon interrupted. "The nurse was a spaceman?" he asked.

"No, no," Nikki answered. "Well, maybe by now," she corrected herself, then said, "Wait, and just listen for a minute."

Cal blinked his eyes and then turned in his seat to sneak a look at the timer in his pocket.

Nikki watched him as she went on. "Syl was part of the cover-up, and all of us were a threat to that," she explained in a measured voice. "Plus, she wanted the spaceman seeds and my uncle's notes."

"Spaceman seeds," Mike repeated as he put his mug on the bar. He began to laugh. "Spaceman seeds." He laughed harder and tried to catch his breath but kept laughing and gasping, "Spaceman seeds," he said as he cried with laughter.

Brandon looked at his partner, and he started to laugh, too. Tentatively at first, but more and more as Tom Honey joined in with Carlos. Even Ray started to laugh and cry at the end of the bar.

Niki looked indignant. "This is how they get away with covering everything up!" She raised her voice and looked at Cal, who was doing his best not to laugh. "You know it's right here in these books…all these things they made movies about. All the secrets we got from space – they are all…" She stopped protesting and started laughing with them. "Oh, my gosh!" she squeaked between breaths, "I've turned into Walt."

They had a good time, and the laughter died down. Everyone felt a little better for their catharsis.

"At least we're in here, and those bugs are out there," Tom Honey said. "Like Walt would always say, 'The Bunker is the safest place to be at the end of the world.' I guess we're out of it now. Nothing to do but sit in here and wait."

"Oh, man," Mike said, getting his breath back and wiping his eyes. "One hell of a day, huh?" A few residual chuckles popped out here and there.

The sheriff reached into his shirt pocket and took out the LED timer to take a close look at it. His eyebrows raised, and he placed it on the bar.

"Day's not over yet," the sheriff said at the same time Nikki said, "There is one more thing I should tell all of you about."

The small disc on the bar began beeping urgently.

She looked at the timer and then at the sheriff. "You first," she said.

He lifted the LED disc, holding it between his finger and thumb. "Considering the time, I guess you're right. I'll go first." The sheriff took the bottle of Rocking Chair and pushed it into the ice chest underneath the bar. He put down the device, picked up his whiskey glass to drain the remainder, and set it on the bar. He looked again at the timer and announced to the room in a loud voice: "Everyone hold onto your hats."

Nikki leaned down to look closely at the disc in the dim light of the barroom. "You've been looking at this ever since you got in here. What is it?" she asked as she picked it up. "Looks like a watch," she brought it close to her face, "but it's counting down – three, two –" she looked up at him with wide eyes. "What?" was all she managed to say before the shock wave hit the Bunker.

The radiating blast blossomed across the desert and slammed into the building, instantly followed by the firestorm sweeping the land clean. The fireball incinerated all of the giant ants caught in the open, and the device's cataclysmic detonation penetrated the nest's deepest levels, obliterating the mutant insects and their eggs.

The burst of the medium-yield bomb not only destroyed the creature's nest, but the shock and heat eradicated any life the ants did not consume, plant and animal, and wiped away the evidence of their destruction. Buildings and homes, the sheriff's station, the car wrecks – everything within the mutant's perimeter was vaporized and beyond investigation.

Except for the Bunker. The old building performed as advertised. The bulky, featureless profile withstood the roaring force of the blast, even as tons of burning automotive debris were swept from the lot and hurled against the concrete façade by the atomic winds.

The thick bulwarks stood against the category ten hurricane inferno, which dashed away all of the wooden architecture, combusting mid-air to windblown ash in the blast furnace of the atom bomb. The flaming charcoal chunks mingled with the glowing embers of the giant ants and scattered across the desert.

The concussive punch hit the monolithic structure with a knockout blow and rang that building like a bell. Everything that wasn't nailed down jumped into the air. The shock wave blew the lights, swept the bar and shelves clean of anything that remained, and knocked everyone down. Carlos screamed in the dark as he toppled from his chairs to the floor, butter-side down.

The big mirror behind the bar hopped from its hangers and crashed to the floor, taking shelves of bottles, glasses, and souvenirs of years with it in a roaring clatter of exploding glass.

Silence returned after the mirror fell. Not complete silence. Carlos groaned, and somebody cussed in the dark.

They were all waiting for the next big bang to get their universe moving again, and it came at the count of three when the basement generators kicked in and the lights flickered back to life. The barroom looked different without the big mirror. The black and white photo of the Trinity explosion hung unevenly by one thumbtack.

The lamps were swinging, strobing shadows in the barroom. Wisps of dust drifted from the ceiling into the lights.

Tom Honey got up from the floor with a hand from Mike, and they helped anesthetized Carlos back onto his chairs.

"Glad that's over with," the lawman said, smiling across the bar at Nikki. He stretched one hand over and helped her upright across the bar, then winked and took a drink from the glass in his free hand.

"What happened?" Nikki asked. She looked around, assuring herself the fortress was still standing.

Cal let go of her arm. "That's something for the books, I guess. Not everyone can say they lived through an A-bomb," the sheriff said.

"An A-bomb?" she gasped. "An atom bomb? An atomic bomb?" she said, her voice rising. "They set off an atomic bomb, and we're right here. I can't believe it; I just cannot believe it!" she exclaimed. Nikki stretched her arms out to steady herself against the bar.

"Well, if it makes you feel better, think of it as a bug bomb," the lawman smiled at her and took another swallow. He walked a few steps through the broken glass, collected new mugs from under the bar, and filled them at the tap. He left two in front for the linemen. He turned to the far end and put the third beer next to Mike's mug. He beckoned Ray, waving him to join them. "C'mon up here, guy. You've got a new chair at the table. We're all in the A-Bomb Club now."

Ray climbed off his stool and walked around the bar to join the group. He smiled as he picked up his beer and sat at the bar next to Mike. He turned on his stool to face Carlos, too. Everyone raised their drink and welcomed him.

The sheriff pushed two beers to the edge. "Tom," he nodded at the trucker and turned to bring two mugs back to the near end of the bar, his end. He set them down in front of Nikki and lifted one for himself as he climbed on Walt's stool.

"An atom bomb…" Nikki repeated as she took the handle of the beer mug.

"At least they didn't drop it right on top of us," Mike said, lifting his new beer.

"Walt was right," Carlos said, slurring his words. "He was right about all of the cover-ups and lies. It's just like he told us about the fake movies being real and the weirdness in the Sands." He shook his head, then drank Walt's cool beer. "I thought he was a little crazy," his voice quivered, and he wiped his eyes with the hand holding the mug. "But I guess the world is even crazier. He was right."

"Yeah," Mike replied, "and I'll bet he will be right all over again. They'll cover this up, too."

"Going to take an awful lot of covering-up this time," the sheriff said.

That's for sure," the trucker agreed. "After all, on the news, on the TV, we saw them everywhere."

"THEM!" Carlos lifted his mug in a toast and finished it off, slapping the empty on the table just before Ray did the same at the bar.

The sheriff leaned over from Walt's stool. "The good news is, I think we're alright. Only three military fellows knew about us, and I think they're OK. They're not going to talk. We'll be alright." He took another drink of his beer. "I guess all we have to do is lay low for a few days here and then get lost. And by that, I mean don't make any noise about what we saw. No sense in attracting attention to ourselves. Those bugs are out now. There'll be all kinds of wild stories flying around. Whatever we say isn't going to add anything, even if it's the truth."

The others listened and drank their beers quietly.

"That's probably right. One thing you learn from life is that the truth doesn't count for much," Mike said.

"And we've seen what the other side is willing to do. That nurse was one of them. She shot Walt and shut the door on all of you. She left you out there for ant food. Shows you what kind of people they are," the sheriff added in a low voice.

"If it wasn't for her...Walt," Carlos's voice faltered. He was slumped in his chair, and his crooked leg was propped across a pillow on a wooden chair. His finger played along an old scar on his chin.

"If it wasn't for them, you mean," Tom Honey said. "They're all the same. The sheriff is right. You can't win against people like that."

"Sometimes you can win a little," the sheriff said, looking at Nikki. "At least she got taken care of," he said after a sip.

She looked at his eyes in the low light of the bar. "I should probably explain what happened with her," she said quietly to him.

"You don't have to, Nik," he answered. "Just put her out of your head."

"No, no. I mean about how she died, what happened, and what will happen," she persisted.

"Nothing's going to happen. You don't have anything to worry about. Nobody will care; nobody will know," he said reassuringly. "You did the right thing," he said quietly. "Try to forget about it for now."

Nikki took a deep breath that sounded loud and more than a little exasperated in the quiet of the barroom. Suddenly, three deep bangs came from the kitchen as if someone were pounding to get in – or out. Everyone turned, looking at the kitchen door.

Cal's eyes skipped from one to another. Everyone was accounted for. He turned back to her.

Nikki let her breath out and sat up straight on her stool. "Back in the freezer. That's where Syl is. Was. You should know there's more. It's not that simple. I mean the way I killed her," Nikki said. She took another deep breath.

More pounding; three hard, heavy bangs came from the back room.

The six men turned their attention from the kitchen door to Nikki when she spoke.

"Back in the freezer," she whispered, "there's this, this Thing…"

THE END

of the first book in the series, *Stories of White Sands*.

Visit www.pauldolanbooks.com